Worlds Apart

D0108254

A Novel Set in Roman Times

By

William V. Crockett

This is a work of historical fiction. All the characters and events portrayed in this book are fictitious, and any resemblence to real people or events is purely coincidental.

WORLDS APART

Cover Art and Maps by Cortney Wisbauer
Photography by Renato Seixas

WorldsApartNovel.com

ISBN: 0984860207
ISBN-13: 978-0-9848602-0-3

I dedicate this book to my son Brian,
gone so suddenly, but always in my thoughts.
Jan 4, 1983 – Mar 27, 2009

A MAP OF ROMAN BRITANNIA

CORNAVII
LVGI
CARNONACAE
GREAT GLEN
Caledonia
ANTONINUS' WALL
NOVANTAE
SELGOVAE
VOTADINI
HADRIAN'S WALL
Brigantes
Iceni
DOBUNNI
SILURES
Londinium
DUMNONII

N

MILES 25 50 75 100

FAUSTHA
STRAGEHIA
ALAUNA
TVNAMIS
SOLOANA
ANTONINUS' WALL

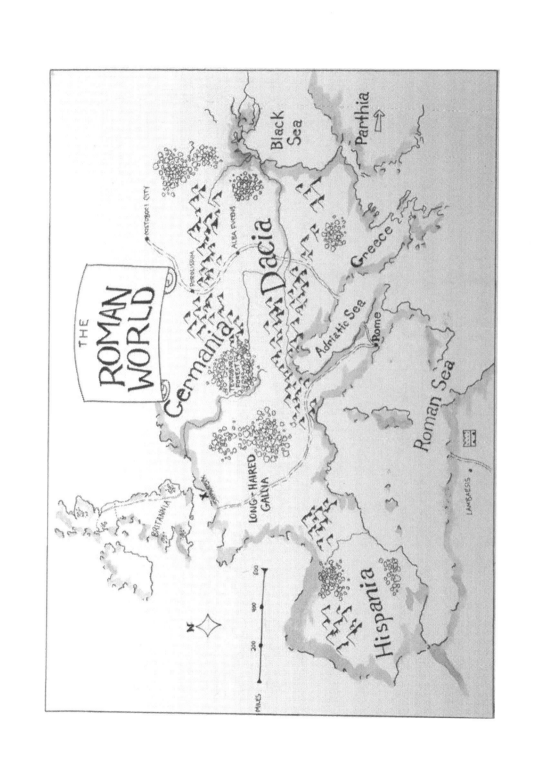

THE
ROMAN
WORLD

Germania

LONG-HAIRED
GALLIA

TEUTOBURG
FOREST

BRITANNIA

Hispania

Dacia

ALBA FUCENS

HISTORIAN'S CITY

DUROSTORUM

Black
Sea

Parthia

Greece

Adriatic Sea

Rome

Roman Sea

LAMBAESIS

N

MILES   200   400   600

TABLE OF CONTENTS

THE BEGINNING

1

She could see them against the night sky, wading through the rain-soaked heather, their swords wheeling and flashing in the moonlight as they slogged steadily toward her. "The gods are with me," the girl mumbled, but her heart was filled with terror. She dropped to a crouch, her face sweating with fear, her head whipping around as she searched for a place to hide. Never before in her eight years had she been alone, and never had she felt that she was about to die.

The grass swayed in the wind. Clouds churned across the crescent moon. In the distance an owl screeched and fell silent. How she wanted to run, to fly like a shade skimming over the heath. But that's what they wanted. That's why they were beating the grass with their swords. She would never make it to the woods—not even to the tangle of broom that grew wildly at the forest's edge.

She was trapped on an open field.

Neeve bit her lip. She didn't want to die. Not here on the lonely heath. She was on her stomach now, twisting, pushing herself into the ground, her breath coming in irregular gulps, her hands raw and bleeding as she clawed at the grass trying to conceal her thin body. She had to be part of the land, like an animal. How many times had she passed within a few feet of a hare and missed it? Then it panicked, darted into the open, racing for life. But Neeve knew she couldn't race fully-grown men. She lowered her head. Any movement would surely warn the soldiers who were even now fanning out across the moor.

They drew closer.

Neeve could see the sheen of their armor and the shape of their swords as they tramped across the darkened landscape. A silent flash of lightning bathed the moor in a ghostly blue, and one soldier paused. He turned toward the shallow lap of earth where she was lying. Fear swept over her as she flattened her body and pressed her cheek to the ground. She began to shake. Mosquitoes hovered above her head, several finding the damp skin of her neck, and a broken heather root dug painfully into her ribs. Neeve closed her eyes, wanting to shut out the world.

The soldier was near, so very near. Neeve shivered. The rain had begun to fall again, cold hard drops, but she didn't mind. The wetness made her feel safe, as if it were a cloak hiding her. She turned her eyes a fraction, afraid that even this slight movement might alert the dark warrior hovering above. But she saw nothing. She shifted her eyes again, wondering where the soldier had gone. Suddenly a dirty leather boot shattered the heather branches and came to rest inches from her trembling lips. Neeve froze. She could see the tooling on the man's bootstraps, and hear his raspy breathing through the sounds of the wind and falling rain.

Any second a sword would skewer her shivering body, impale her to the ground like a snake wriggling on a stick. It wouldn't matter that she was a child or that she was alone or that she meant the Empire no harm. These were the soldiers of Rome. They were efficient, ruthless. They never questioned orders. Within three miles of their lines, their mission was always the same: find and kill. Patrols regularly cleared the area of intruders, and to them, Neeve was just another intruder.

The brute was almost on top of her—surely he must see. How long before he looked down? One glance would do it, even in this gloom. Her back felt exposed, like the bottom of an overturned boat.

"Aaaiaii!" the soldier screeched. He twisted down toward Neeve and swept a wolf spider off his calf, then muttered something before turning and disappearing into the night, as he joined the others across the moor.

For a full ten minutes Neeve lay like a fallen branch, not daring to move or look around. The rain had stopped and the air was thick with the perfume of heather, a pungent smell that reminded Neeve of early morning walks with her father. She rose warily, inspecting the field for Romans. Nothing. She listened. Still nothing. Then something moved at the northern edge, shadowy figures poking their heads around the trunk of an ivy-covered tree. Neeve dropped to the ground again and flattened out on the wet sod. Then slowly she lifted her head. Romans did not hide behind trees, and the thought encouraged her as she squinted into the darkness. Her heart jumped. Her brothers! She could see them picking their way through the heather at the far end of the moor, their heads jerking at the slightest noise.

"Taranis! Eston!" Neeve cried, her words frightening a dozen sparrows out of their ground hideaways. She wanted so desperately to be with her brothers, to feel their arms surrounding her, protecting her, so desperately that she waved frantically and hollered their names again, like a lost child suddenly found.

They turned.

"Here!" Neeve yelled. "I'm over here!"

Her brothers were hurrying toward her now, signaling her to stay where she was and to be quiet. Neeve couldn't wait. She gathered her ridiculously oversized tunic in her hands and started toward them, but with every step the baggy material drooped lower, making it feel as if she were dragging a blanket. Then she stepped on the hem of her tunic, shrieked, and fell. She struggled to her feet and began calling out to her brothers again, but Taranis was already there, covering her mouth with his hand.

Neeve wrenched her head away. "I've been looking for you," she said in a frenzied whisper.

"Shhh …." Taranis slowly removed his fingers from her lips, his eyes holding hers, warning her to be quiet, and then with fingers still raised in front of her face, he glanced around anxiously for signs of movement. "We can talk over there," he whispered, pointing toward the tree line where the broom and gorse grew most densely.

With Neeve and Eston in tow, Taranis moved quickly across the moor and into the trees. He stopped in the shadow of a giant oak and turned toward his sister.

"I was so scared," she said, throwing her arms around him.

He pushed her back roughly, eyes blazing. "Why are you here?" he demanded. "I told you to stay home."

She frowned, not knowing what to say.

"I told you to stay home!" he repeated.

Anger surged through Neeve's chilled body and she shot back, "I know what you *told* me."

"Then go home," he said.

"No! I'm coming with you."

"Oh, no you're not."

"Oh, yes I am."

"You are not."

"I am too!" she yelled.

Taranis flinched.

Neeve gritted her teeth and gave him her most defiant look. She ignored the rain dribbling off her chin and kept her eyes fixed on him, daring him to say something. She knew he could order her home, tell her she was going, and that was that. He was the first-born son and now twelve years, almost a man. She would have to obey him. Even his name called for respect, Taranis, the ancient Celtic god of the heavens, but she knew he would give no orders today. She had seen him flinch.

"You don't realize the danger," he said, pushing her stringy blond hair out of her eyes, and she knew she had won. She just needed to hold her ground. "These are Romans," he said, as if that explained everything.

"Rot those dirty Romans!" she shouted.

Taranis took a breath but didn't respond.

"I am going with you and Eston," Neeve said, jutting out her chin.

Taranis stared at her, then shifted his eyes to the distant ridge before returning to hers. "You have to leave," he said gently. "You should be home with your sister."

"I'm not leaving," she said firmly. "And you have no right to send me home. I want to be there when it happens."

"That's not a good idea," Taranis said, shaking his head. "Do you know how angry Father would be if he knew—"

"He wouldn't be angry," she said. "He would want me there, I know he would." She looked straight at her brother, but couldn't hold his eyes, and instead found herself plucking at her hair and twirling the ends with anxious fingers. "Please, Taranis ... please let me go with you. I will be so quiet. I promise."

"There are rats," he said. "Near the top ... big, long-tailed rats. They will bite your bare feet. Isn't that so, Eston?"

Eston nodded.

Neeve swallowed. She rubbed her toes against each other, as if checking for bites. "Well ... I'll stay close to you," she said.

"We don't want you here," Taranis said, curling his lip to make the point.

"Please let me go with you," she repeated quietly, and she shifted her eyes back and forth between her brothers, pleading.

Taranis glanced at Eston.

"She has a right," the other said. "As much as we do." Eston was ten, two years younger than Taranis. He rarely disagreed with his older brother, so Neeve kept silent, hoping his words would have an effect.

Taranis sighed and took several steps toward the edge of the forest, then scanned the distant hills where the Romans had gone. "We need to get to the ridge," is all he said. "It'll be light soon."

The three started across the broad expanse that led to the rolling hills. Beyond lay the ridge, a chain of rocky hills, black against the somber skies. For over an hour they followed the same route as the Romans, the grass still bent from their boots, and they were closing in on the ridge when the first rays of light began streaking the night skies. On the tips of trees sentry crows squawked at their passing, alerting every living thing that intruders were nigh. Overhead, feathery clouds hardened with the harsh light of the emerging sun.

As they ascended the ridge, for the most part a steady upward hike, but marred by several abrupt rises and jutting ledges, Neeve heard Taranis mumble something to Eston, and she knew he was worried about her falling on the steeper slopes. Constantly, he reached down to help, and more than once Eston pushed on her backside when he thought she was in difficulty. The whole thing was silly. She had climbed bigger hills than this on family outings.

In the morning light the ridge top grew closer. Not far to go.

Thud!

"What was that?" Neeve's eyes widened.

All three heard it: a heavy sound, and then dull pounding that reverberated, as if someone were driving posts into the ground. Neeve froze, holding her breath, afraid even to turn her head. The sounds were coming from over the ridge.

Taranis stared up the hill, and then paused. "No talking," he said, pointing a finger at Neeve.

She nodded.

The two boys hiked upwards, lunging from one bush to another, forgetting about Neeve entirely so that she had to follow as best she could. Bundling her tunic at the waist, she took a deep breath, and started up the final slope, trying to follow the exact route her brothers had taken. She paused only once to catch her breath, behind a stunted green oak that the northern winds had savaged and bent like a sewing awl. When she finally reached the top, Taranis and Eston were lying on their stomachs, peering over the edge. She followed their eyes, and gasped. Before her stretched the whole of the southern countryside, and directly across the ravine at the bottom of the ridge lay a Roman fort. A big, square turf fort. But more frightening was the Wall. As far as she could see in either direction, the Wall twisted and curved like an evil, dark snake.

She had heard about it, of course; everyone had. The Romans were building a barrier across Britannia Island, Antoninus' Wall, they called it, named after their emperor. The soldiers were trying to shut out the northern Celtic tribes from the occupied southern lands. Her father said the Romans were mindless servants of order and conformity. Everywhere they went the old ways died. They all marched the same way, dressed the same way; they all lived in the same barren cities filled with cubed buildings and archways of stone.

For as long as anyone could remember the people in the south lived a quiet life, farming the lowlands—and then the legions came. Villagers had no choice but to gather in the fields outside their towns to meet the armies from Rome, but they were no match for the endless rows of steel, and many were killed, and many more were shipped as slaves to the far side of the Empire. Soldiers dragged mothers and daughters from their villages to the camps. The troops needed entertainment, and even at her age, Neeve knew what that meant. Those who survived on the island were put to work in the fields, or the mines, bending their backs in servitude to bring tax offerings to Roman masters. That is why we fight, her father had said, that is why we die. Neeve ran her eyes over the length of the Wall, stopping at the fort, her eyes lingering on the Roman soldiers she could see below. The Roman fort occupied about four acres and was built into the Wall at the highest point of a broad hillock, its timber walkways rising high above the Wall. Armed legionaries in the corner towers scanned the northern countryside for enemies, and others patrolled the fort's walkways. Much work still needed doing on the Wall, and in some places the rampart base of sandstone boulders showed through.

Roman engineers had marked the grassy hillsides with stakes, and scores of cutters carved turf bricks from the thick grass. Soldiers carried the grass cubes on their backs, holding them in place with short ropes, then stacking them on top of each other, forming a massive turf Wall. Everywhere, men stood in the dirt scars, shoveling loose earth and stone into wicker baskets and low-bed carts, which others hauled to the Wall. On some sections men pounded heavy support timber into place; in other areas they built their military roadway, which would eventually stretch along the whole length of the barrier. Thirty feet or so in front of the Wall, soldiers dug a trench in the sloping grade and heaped the fill on the north side to provide an additional deterrent to the Caledonians.

"Should we wait here?" Neeve asked.

Taranis ignored her.

"Are there rats in these rocks?" Her eyes inspected the crevices.

"There are no rats."

"You said there were."

"I made it up. Now, be quiet."

She tugged at his arm. "Do you know what I think?"

"Quiet!"

"I think it's dangerous—"

"Neeve!"

"It's-dangerous-to-stay-on-this-hilltop,   that's-all-I-wanted-to-say." She spoke so quickly her words tumbled together.

"You suppose I don't know that? One more word and you go home."

Neeve pressed her lips together and stared at him.

"I mean it," he said. "One more word."

"You have to be quiet," Eston said in a kindly tone.

Neeve dropped her eyes to the ground. "Sorry," she whispered.

Taranis and Eston resumed talking, saying that the guards seemed more interested in observing the surrounding hills than the slope below. Maybe they could slip down unnoticed. They searched for hiding places, settling on a grove of beech trees—or what had been beech trees weeks earlier—covering a wedge of land along the creek bank. The Romans had hacked down most of the trees to build their fort, but piles of branches lay in jumbled heaps, making the area ideal for observing the fort. They studied the spot, then discarded the idea. Too close. The heather would have to do. It was everywhere, and partway down the hill, it grew thickly in the dark, red soil.

Taranis descended first, slowly, causing as little disturbance as possible, one hand stretched out for balance, the other touching the hillside as he moved. Midway he crawled between two grayish red shrubs, invisible to anyone who might glance his way. He signaled Eston who descended with such skill he surprised Taranis when he emerged from the nearby heather. Neeve was less stealthy, slipping once or twice, but pleased with her performance as she wiggled her body between her brothers to feed off their warmth. She was still wet, and very cold.

Across the ravine the turf cutting, scraping and dumping continued, an endless line of soldiers shouldering endless turf cubes to the Wall. Carts came from every direction. The raw earth flowed like muddy red blood toward an open cesspit. They were close enough to see the sweat glistening on the legionaries' faces as they worked, and smell the rich soil, so newly ripped from its resting place.

"Will they see us?" Neeve asked. She whispered her words directly into Taranis's ear, trying to show him she could be quiet.

Taranis patted her back. "Don't worry," he said. "They won't see anything. Too much heather."

Neeve swept her eyes over the lookout towers, hoping he was right. She squeezed under his arm, her tunic stained with mud, her lips moving in prayer: "The gods are with us," she murmured repeatedly.

As the hours passed, the ground grew colder, and the three huddled under Taranis's coarse woolen cloak, pressed together like a litter of rabbits on a winter's day. All afternoon they waited. Neeve wondered if they had the right day, or even the right fort, but Taranis assured her there was no mistake. Everything they expected—and dreaded—would happen here today. She stared across the ravine, her eyes heavy with sleep.

Neeve woke with a start, Taranis shaking her arm. A night without sleep had been too much. She pushed herself up onto her elbows, feeling stiff and confused, shivers running through her body, and try as she might, she couldn't focus on what was happening. Roman trumpets rocked her focus, snapping her to attention, and suddenly she could hear centurions hollering and horses neighing. The camp looked different, its huge log gates gaping open, and a wooden platform measuring about twelve feet in either direction had been built beside the fort. A soldier carrying a large iron hammer inspected the rough planks, stopping here and there to bang a log into square.

Then, suddenly, scores of armed soldiers marched out of the gates and formed lines on both sides of the roadway that led to the platform. With deliberate pageantry, a procession of officers made their way through the gates, led by what Taranis said was a Roman tribune, riding on a horse. The tribune was followed by four mounted officers, two abreast. Behind the officers walked three men, hands bound, bare from the waist up. One of the men had a leather strap around his neck that fell in two strips to his knees. Two guards walked beside each prisoner.

Next came the centurions and standard-bearers carrying long poles with disks and images of Roman gods. At the top of the first standard perched a golden eagle with extended wings, a golden thunderbolt grasped in its talons, the symbol of all Roman legions. Then came three special standards that Taranis said were from Legion II: one was topped with a goat, another with a flying horse, and the last with a bearded warrior god and fierce wolf at his right hand.

"Don't look at his face," Taranis said. "He's their god of war, Mars the Avenger, very powerful. He will sense your presence."

Neeve lowered her eyes to the crossbars decorated with leather strips and wreaths. Taranis knew these things. There were other standards—a hand outstretched to the gods, fingers and thumb pointing upward; a colorful banner flying in the wind. Finally, a long column of foot soldiers followed the standards, marching uniformly, six across.

The troops lining the roadway joined the foot soldiers and formed square detachments at intervals around the platform. They stood motionless, like sculpted figures of stone.

Two prisoners were pulled onto the platform. The officers dismounted, and one read loudly from what appeared to be a parchment declaration. When he finished, the soldiers gave a shout, extending their right arms into the air. The tribune signaled the guards. One stepped behind each victim and forced his head back. The front guard raised his sword slowly, and plunged down hard into the exposed chest.

Another roar from the ranks.

Neeve felt numb. They were doing it, actually doing it. The Romans never shrank from taking Caledonian lives.

She watched as her father mounted the red-stained platform, the straps still dangling at his knees. As leader of an attack against the Empire, he would die a special death. The effort had been doomed from the beginning, and her father had known it. The Romans sent out Legion II to punish the Celts for assaulting a supply train, and for twelve long, brutal days, they burned every village and crop in a two-mile swath through Caledonia. Her father had tried to divert them with a few hundred volunteers, striking suddenly from the hills, then retreating to the swamps or wooded areas where protective spirits dwell. Eventually the Romans headed for home, but not before scores of Caledonian warriors were killed or captured. Now her father would bear the ultimate penalty for defying the Empire.

The scene across the ravine proceeded with lifeless efficiency, gray figures moving in straight lines. They exchanged tributes of, "Hail Caesar," removed the bodies, and led Neeve's father to the center of the platform. He stood calmly, gazing over the heads of the soldiers.

"Taranis, do something!" Neeve wailed, her voice raw with terror.

"Shush!"

"Ohhhh," she moaned, biting her lip.

Taranis rubbed his face helplessly.

"Please ... no ... noooo," she groaned.

"There's *nothing* we can do," he said.

Neeve jumped to her feet, her eyes darting between her brothers. "We could trick them. Make them chase us and—"

She never finished her sentence. Taranis yanked her to the ground, taking the breath from her. He turned back to the garrison, looking for signs of alarm. But all eyes were on the rebel leader.

Across the ravine, her father's expression had changed. The studied calm was gone. He leaned forward, and squinted his eyes.

"I think he sees us," Eston said. "He is looking straight at us."

The two executioners were now on either side of him, their hands wrapped around the leather strap. They checked their footing, bent their knees, and drew the straps taut. The strangle-cord was ready. They turned toward the tribune and waited.

The children watched, as if in a dream. Their father stared in their direction. Then slightly, ever so slightly, he nodded his head. His eyes stopped squinting and a faint smile appeared on his face.

The tribune's hand dropped. The executioners leaned back, straining at the cords. Cheers erupted from the ranks.

Neeve stared in horror, her mouth opening in pain and her body shaking convulsively. Her head fell forward and she pressed her face into the dirt, looking for comfort in the cold earth. Moving instinctively, and seeming not to care if anyone saw, Taranis twisted to a sitting position and slipped his hand under her thin form. Neeve resisted for a moment, then scrambled from the ground, flying into his arms so forcefully it hurt him. She clung to him as if she were drowning, her breath coming in large, irregular gulps, and as her tears splashed down her face onto his neck, he rocked back and forth, humming a shepherd's tune from happier times.

Neeve just groaned.

Hours passed before Neeve could look toward the Roman camp. The soldiers had resumed their hauling and dumping, and she saw her father and the other two heaped in a rough-hewn cart, twisted in impossible positions. It seemed like forever before the soldiers moved the cart. Her eyes followed the slab box up the hill, as it lurched and wobbled on its two enormous wheels. At the top of the dumping ramp, the soldiers rotated the cart, exposed its open back to the Wall, and stepped away. The front poles of the cart shot up, the back crashed to the ramp, dumping its limp cargo over the edge.

Neeve felt tired. And cold. She could see the Roman faces now as they stood by the empty cart, talking, looking down occasionally. One smiled. One of the Romans on the ramp smiled. Only for a moment, but he had smiled.

Taranis ordered Neeve and Eston to rest. They had a long walk ahead of them, he had said. Neeve tried desperately to sleep, longing for the night birds to come, to carry her mind away to the dark forests where sorrow and pain would be no more, but all she felt was a deadness at her core. She shifted her eyes to Eston who had curled himself into a ball, the heather partly obscuring him, and Taranis who lay huddled on the ground, his back to her, and she wondered if they really were asleep. How things had changed, she thought, in just hours. Her father's last flicker of a smile passed through her mind; she felt her eyes burning, a deep sadness gripping her soul, and overwhelmed, she buried her face in Taranis's cloak, and shut her eyes.

2

The man was enormous and had a big, stupid face. He had the eyes of a fanatic and swung his sword wildly, smiling all the while. Everyone watching knew he was a northern Celt because he wore a blond, spiked wig, and except where covered by a loincloth, was painted blue from head to foot. He dropped to a crouch and crept slowly toward two Empire soldiers who were eating lunch on the ground, their backs to him.

Vectis Trebellius Quadratus sat rigidly on his stone seat, hardly breathing, like the thousand other children in the theater. They sat wide-eyed and absolutely silent.

The Celt, now within striking distance, raised his sword. He took one more step toward the Romans ... and then crashed through a trap door in the stage, his sword banging uselessly on the empty tiles. The soldiers continued eating, undisturbed. One yawned and tossed a half-eaten goose leg into the hole. The theater exploded in laughter. Vectis laughed too, so hard he almost cried. Almost. He reminded himself that he was Roman, and now twelve years old. To be seen crying like a girl wouldn't do, like his older sister, Sabina, who was now giggling deliriously beside him, tears streaming down her face. But it was a good story, perhaps worth a few tears. Even his father was smiling.

His father enjoyed the broad humor of the theater—especially the mimes, with their irreverent stories about everyday life. They were different from the elegant pantomimes where actors told stories in a silent dance; his father hated them. Too sophisticated, he said. Often the old man would throw his head back and roar at the lewd bedroom farces and silly murder stories that concluded with imitation blood flooding the stage. But his favorites were mimes about common soldiers, glamorous highwaymen, and fools who ran the government. He also liked the children's mimes. Today, children had come from all over the capital to see the weekly presentation.

On stage now was an actor dressed like a Parthian from the eastern end of Rome's vast Empire. He was much smaller and darker and quicker than the Celt, darting this way and that, screaming and whooping, daggers flashing in his hands as he lunged at imaginary opponents and jumped, with the help of a hoist, eight feet into the air. It didn't take long for the two Roman soldiers to loop small bags of sand around his ankles to slow him down. Bag after bag was added until he could barely drag himself around the stage, until finally, exhausted, he collapsed on the tiles near another trap door. Groaning, he rolled over, and disappeared into the hole. The soldiers resumed eating to warm applause.

With the mimes over, the curtain rose from a depression in the floor and stayed up while the actors prepared for the final full-scale play.

"Can you imagine life without the theater?" Sabina asked, grasping Vectis's hand tightly and searching his eyes for an answer as if the fate of the Empire were in the balance.

Vectis smiled, knowing it was a ridiculous question.

"Oh, you're trying to act like a soldier again," she giggled. "So unimpressed with everything. Well, you don't fool me."

Vectis flushed. There was no doubt that he and everyone else loved the theater, but he could imagine life without it. It was permissible for Sabina to gush about things—she was a girl. She might be a year older, but he would be a soldier, a leader in the Imperial Roman army.

"Oh, love you, love you, love you," she cooed, striking a pose so that everyone within twenty feet would turn and notice her uncanny beauty. She sighed, her eyes caressing the far corners of the theater.

"It sure has everything," Vectis said.

"Oh, yes, everything ... trap doors and ropes and hoists." She paused, allowing her eyes to drift upward. "And that awning, did you ever see such an awning?"

The canvas awning, Vectis had to admit, was impressive. The massive scarlet canopy stretched over the entire audience, protecting them from the sun and rain. It also had a magical quality as it fluttered in the wind, increasing the theatrical illusion and casting an artificial blush that danced eerily across the great hollow below.

Music signaled that the actors were ready. The curtain dropped and the play began, a favorite in Rome: *The Rope* by Plautus. Vectis knew the play by heart. A young Roman noble named Plesidippus falls in love with Palaestra, a slave girl. They are forbidden to marry because she is a slave. But the story ends happily because it turns out that Palaestra is freeborn after all, daughter of a rich patrician.

As the play ended, Vectis wondered what might have happened, had Palaestra really been a slave. He let the thought pass. It was just a story.

Vectis bid Sabina and her maids goodbye. "I wish you a pleasant journey home," he said, knowing that she was not heading home.

"Pelopidas, the Greek vocalist, is singing at the Gardens of Lucullus," she said with a tease in her voice.

"You're meeting Atilius Titianus again! If Father finds out—"

"You shush! I appreciate the singing of Greek lyric poetry, that's all."

"You are playing a foolish game, Sabina. One of your attendants is sure to let it slip."

Her face hardened. "Not if they fear the whip." Then with a toss of her head, she laughed. "I intend to have a lovely day." Her kiss turned into a playful bite on his cheek. "Not a word," she said in warning, and she was gone.

Vectis shook his head slowly as he stared after her. Sabina's beauty turned the heads of even the wealthiest noblemen, and Vectis wished she were less rebellious. Associating with the likes of Atilius

Titianus would only bring trouble. He turned and hurried after his father, already striding down the street.

The afternoon crowds filled the cobbleways but in less than five minutes Vectis and his father arrived at the narrow side streets that led to the great slave bazaar near the heart of the city. Vectis often noticed that his father walked in a straight line while others stepped to the side. Many on the streets recognized him and nodded deferentially. He was older now and only a centurion, but he had commanded legions for the Emperor throughout the world. When trouble arose, they always called his father.

Today his father had business to attend to. The thought made Vectis tremble with excitement. *Business to attend to.* And his father had included him. For the first time, he would ride with the Praetorians—the finest soldiers in the world! He might even get to pick a slave at the market.

"How many slaves are we buying?" Vectis called to his father, who was two steps ahead.

"Forty or fifty, but Pudens will have chosen them by now," he replied without breaking stride.

Vectis found it hard to conceal his disappointment. Often he had seen men buying slaves, examining them, squabbling over the price, and he longed for the day when he could buy one himself. But that was what Pudens was for, to ease the burden on his father. Pudens was a freedman. His father had given him his freedom the day Vectis was born, as a gift to the gods. Pudens had been purchased in the Egyptian slave market, and over the years he and Vectis's father had established a close relationship. It was only natural that once free, Pudens should choose to stay.

Along with Pudens, his father had six slaves to run his affairs, four really, because two were maids that constantly fluttered around Sabina. On special days like today, her father hired additional male servants to attend Sabina on her outing, but she never appreciated it, and always complained about having so few slaves. Anyone with proper breeding, she said, should own at least ten. She hated it when her father talked to Pudens as he would an equal. He was a freedman, but still under orders. Good breeding dictated that her father speak as little as possible to those under him—especially in public. A curt order would suffice. But he cared little for social graces, and sometimes even talked to his slaves in the presence of important people! Would a farmer waste breath talking to an ox in the field? Sabina would ask in disgust. Then why should anyone bother with the opinions of human bipeds that, after all, were nothing more than talking tools?

The boy and his father passed by a small temple to Juno, the goddess of marriage, crossed a drainage channel, and entered the *Via Lata*. The noise hit Vectis like a hot blast from a furnace. Buyers and sellers shouted and pointed as they haggled over prices and traded insults. Spectators elbowed their way into the porticoes bunched along the street, craning their heads and crowding toward the more interesting auctions, oblivious to the cheerless countenances of those on sale. Everywhere frenzied slave dealers waved red-lettered boards that highlighted the special attributes of their slaves. Beggars lined the walls, some hobbling on crutches, some lying on pallets or mats. "Give!" they cried. "The gods are watching!" Between the porticoes, narrow pens bulged with human flesh, like cattle at a market. The air reeked of sweating bodies and urine, making the whole place smell like a poorly maintained stable.

Vectis threaded his way through the swarming mobs, pushing the foul beggars away, and trying to keep in sight his father's broad back. A hawker from one of the stalls tried to interest his father in the breeds he had for sale. He waved his arms animatedly and shouted in his prospect's ear, pointing to a pen filled with Greek and Thracian slaves, or so the red chalk over his enclosure claimed. Slave dealers always claimed their wares had Greek lineage, if they thought they could get away with it. Any slave speaking a modicum of Greek might be used as a tutor, especially if he had knowledge of philosophy and mathematics. Romans of modest means often purchased these alleged Greeks, knowing that even a veneer of Greek education would enhance their children's place in society.

Vectis's father was not interested in effeminate Greeks, as he called them, with their music and mathematics; he wanted bipeds with strong backs that could do a day's work. Celts and Teutons, and more recently, Africans from beyond the Atlas Mountains—these breeds held up in the fields when the sun grew hot and the plowing rough. Soft-handed city slaves were good for nothing but gratifying their owners' trivial indulgences.

Pudens waited beside a squat building at the corner of an open square. Forty slaves sat in rows with their hands bound, and behind them stood the elite Praetorian Guard. Vectis stared at the tall, well-cut legionaries with their scarlet tunics and dazzling strip-metal armor. He hardly dared believe it, but today he would ride with the emperor's personal soldiers. Vectis counted ten Praetorians, not many, but ten was all his father required for the overnight trip. Living on a centurion's pay was difficult in an expensive area like Rome, and often his father delivered slaves to the work camps outside the city to supplement his earnings. He had many friends in the Praetorians who readily furnished him with detachments of the Guard when needed, and the overseers on the farms were glad to have a man of his father's stature purchase the laborers. The slave dealers knew better than to cheat someone with access to the Guard.

"A fine assembly, Pudens," his father said as he surveyed the slaves. They were mostly large males, with a few women and younger ones thrown in to give a proper mix. "I think we need three more workers and a serving girl. It's time young Vectis here learned how to choose a sound worker."

Vectis's face exploded in joy. His father wanted him to buy slaves!

Pudens smiled and placed his hand on Vectis's shoulder. "I will teach him everything," he said. "We won't be long."

Vectis and Pudens hurried down the slope as the centurion strolled over to talk to the officer of the Guard. They passed the first stall with its whitewashed boards and iron pens filled with women, and the second, which catered to the city slave trade. His father needed bulls for the field, not serving boys or tailors.

Vectis stopped at the third stall. "How about this one, Pudens?"

"You're the buyer, Vectis. What do you think?"

Vectis beamed, appreciating Pudens's method of instruction. "Well," he said, straining to read the placards, "they seem to be from the islands of the Roman Sea—Crete and Cyprus."

"So?"

"So they won't do. Too accustomed to leisure to make able farm workers."

"Very good."

The next two stalls were screened off with signs saying, "Private Sales Only." Inside would be dealers in fine slaves: Attic speaking schoolmasters, exotic dancers, gifted artists or musicians, and, of course, beautiful men and women trained to gratify a master's every craving. For the price of one special slave, Vectis knew, he could purchase a hundred field workers in the open stalls.

Across the street a crier was announcing a recent shipment of Gauls, brute mules built for the fields, he claimed. Vectis pushed his way into the stall and toward the less crowded area at the side of the pen. The smell was overpowering. He studied the fifty-odd bodies packed into the iron stockade. Sores covered their bodies—they had been roughly treated.

"How many? How many?" called a stumpy-legged slave seller as he scurried forward, smiling artificially, and acting as if Vectis were a favorite nephew. Before Vectis could reply, the man had thrust into his hand a stick blobbed at the end with lime-green paint. "Please! Please!" he motioned toward the pen. "Pick out a handful. You don't need to buy them. Just inspect, that's all, just inspect." He signaled the slaves, who shuffled clockwise in their pen.

Vectis felt rushed, but he had noticed three well-muscled bodies that seemed blemish-free. He would make no commitment, just look. He took the stick and reached into the pen, splotching their backs as they passed.

"Ah! You've a fine eye. Three of my best!" A smile spread across his leathery face and his eyes glistened in anticipation of a sale. He swung open the gate, swept his dirty hair out of his eyes, and beckoned to the three slaves who towered over him. "Here, stand here," he ordered as he arranged them in a line outside the pen for Vectis to inspect. The slaves were huge by Roman standards, and they looked even bigger when the slaver herded them onto the raised auction stones for visibility.

More spectators pressed into the stall.

The three slaves stood mutely on their stones, moving compliantly when pushed or pulled by the slave trader. He lifted their arms and pinched the undersides to show their excellent skin tone. "These are not fragile Parthians," he cried. "These are thick-muscled Celts from Gallia. Like mules! You can work them all day!" He slapped their stomachs and shook their shoulders to emphasize his point, then stripped away the loincloth of one, exposing his genitals. "Good breeders, these Celts!" At length he returned the man's cloth, commenting that gelding was unnecessary for such fine specimens, a situation bound to please both master and slave. Laughter rippled through the attentive crowd.

For an instant, but only for an instant, Vectis pitied the pointless existence of the slaves. How forlorn they looked as they stared vacantly over the heads of the curious milling about them, perhaps thinking of different times, different places. But fate had placed them here, had it not? This was, after all, their lot in life, to serve the Empire.

Vectis stepped forward to examine the bodies. All three were bare from the waist up—two wearing loincloths, the third with leather trousers belted at the top and tied at the ankles. As Vectis checked their gums for sores, the seller chattered on about their powerful bodies, their strong teeth and bones, their keen eyesight. He promised a written guarantee that they were free from fits and depression.

Vectis glanced at Pudens for guidance and saw him frown in the direction of the trouser-clad slave to indicate his reservations. Vectis pushed his face closer to the slave and noticed a telltale mark on the lower back just above the trousers. "Strip him," he said.

The slave dealer protested, but pulled the man's trousers to his knees, revealing a recent whipping on his buttocks and legs. Vectis looked the dealer in the eyes.

"A harmless whipping." He shrugged, wiping the sweat from his lips. "He filched an extra portion of soup. He is no thief, I guarantee."

"You covered him with trousers to deceive me."

"No, no, before the gods, I tell the truth, he is a good buy." The man seemed hurt by the accusation. "I covered him because I knew it was a harmless whipping."

Pudens inspected the slave's back. He traced his finger along tiny white lines to show Vectis that there had been earlier whippings.

"My freedman thinks your slave is a troublemaker," Vectis said.

"With apologies to your freedman," the man said deferentially, "but those lash marks are from debtor prison before he sold himself into slavery. He sold his whole family—his wife and daughters are in back. You can go and see." He pointed to a smaller pen packed with women along the edge of his stall. "He will be no trouble, I promise you. Look!" He slapped the man across the face. "See, as docile as a sheep." He slapped him again and again until blood flowed from the corner of his mouth. "Eh? A sheep cowering before a wolf—he knows who is master." Then, smiling broadly: "I will give you my written guarantee. He will be as gentle as a suckling rabbit."

"We require no written guarantee," Pudens said. "We are purchasing these slaves for First Centurion Gaius Trebellius."

The slave trader blanched. "Of course! I should have recognized you …." He hesitated. "About this slave," he said, clapping the man on his back and gesturing for him to pull up his trousers (no sense in parading whip marks unnecessarily), "my information has come, how shall I say, from many mouths. But they say he is trouble free. If he causes a problem, bring him back and I will replace him." Getting a stony look from Pudens, he continued, "I will give you *two* in his place, yes, I will give you two. I guarantee it."

The trader's smile returned.

Vectis did his best during the haggling session. He kept his eye on Pudens for subtle movements of approval or disapproval, and finally they settled on 4000 sesterces for the three. It was a good price and Vectis felt elated. His father would be proud.

The slave seller was still talking as they turned to go. "These are not sows in the field," he said, pointing toward the women caged at the rear. "They have been trained properly." The corners of his lips turned upwards, more in a leer than a smile. "I myself can testify to their ... extraordinary abilities—"

Pudens spoke up. "We are looking for a serving girl. We have no need for—"

"Serving girl? Come! You come! Please," he called over his shoulder as he moved rapidly toward the rear pen. "Look! I have many girls among the women. Eight, ten of the best you will find anywhere." He ordered the younger ones separated from the women. "Eh? What do you think?" He laughed excitedly and nodded his head to indicate that they all agreed he indeed had a fine crop. "And at a good price too. For a fourth slave," he shrugged, "half price!"

Vectis glanced into the pen at the freshly dunked girls, their hair dripping wet. For men it didn't matter, but no one wanted a filthy servant girl. The dealer was shoving into his hand the stick blobbed with lime-green paint. Vectis brushed his arm aside. Something had caught his attention. Never in his life had he seen such peculiar eyes, not dark like a Roman's, but crystal blue, so it seemed as if he could peer into her soul.

"Let me see that one," he said, pointing to the girl.

"Ah, yes. The best I have." He wagged his head, giving the impression that Vectis was a shrewd slave buyer.

At the sight of the girl, Vectis felt an odd tingle run down his back. She was dressed like the others in the pen, in a drab tunic and open-strap shoes, but her manner was entirely different. She stood erect, not in the least cowed like the rest. And her eyes, she never averted her eyes the way most wretches did when a Roman turned his face toward them. She just stood there in the center of the pen, arms at her sides, staring at him. She had no expression in her face, none in her eyes, but something about her demeanor made her seem more than a talking tool at the market.

Vectis moved toward the raised stones as the girl clambered onto one of them. He sensed Pudens's disapproval. The freedman had positioned himself off Vectis's right arm and slightly behind so as not to appear to be directing his superior, but his intent was plain. He thought it unwise to choose a girl from the same stall, a girl that might be from the same family as one of the male slaves. Choosing both sexes from the same coffle of slaves was nothing but trouble.

Vectis knew Pudens was right, but he ignored the heavy breathing of the freedman. For some reason that wasn't clear even to himself, he felt drawn to this slave. He needed to see her up close, to look into her eyes, or maybe even feel the warmth of her skin.

The girl watched him as he approached the buying area. Water still dribbled from her hair and onto the back of her neck, darkening the edges of her tunic. She was his own age, had flaxen hair and a body that looked underfed. Vectis couldn't help noticing the course wool in her tunic, with its traces of green, homemade dye that long ago had faded to a blotchy yellow. It hung limply to her knees, exposing legs that were scratched and not quite cleared of dirt. She wore badly stitched sandals and stood perfectly still, except for her toes that wiggled constantly.

"She's a fine one," the slave seller said, interrupting Vectis's thoughts. "A little wiry, but she has a sound body." He reached for the bottom of her tunic, intending to pull it over her head for a body inspection. Vectis had seen slaves stand as long as five minutes with their tunics draped over their heads, and buyers poking the merchandise.

Without thinking, he held up his hand to stop the eager trader. He didn't know why, but he wanted to avoid humiliating the girl. She looked at him curiously, and for the first time seemed to sense her station in life; she averted her eyes.

Vectis tried to cover his motivations for stopping a natural move by the slave seller, saying in an exasperated tone, "I can see she's healthy. Does she have Latin or Greek?" She didn't. Had she ever worked as a serving girl, or been trained to identify fruits and vegetables? She hadn't. But she was a quick learner, the trader said, and had a face that would rouse jealousy in sweet Helen of Troy.

The bargaining was tough. The trader handled himself carefully, knowing he would answer to the Praetorians for any misconduct, but he understood his customer's desire for the slave. They settled on 1500 sesterces, not an excessive price for a serving girl, but not the half price he had promised either. Vectis knew it was ridiculous to pay a good rate for a girl he would never see again. His father would deposit her on a work farm, and that would be that. But maybe he could persuade his father to keep her. She might be useful to Sabina, he thought, knowing he was thinking of himself. The story of Palaestra, the slave girl, passed through his mind. Could this slave be the daughter of a rich patrician? She really was different. He knew, of course, she was no patrician's daughter. Even the thought made him feel foolish.

The procession of soldiers and slaves moved steadily along the flood plain of an ankle-deep stream that wound through the treed hills outside Rome. For the first while, Vectis and his father accompanied the Praetorian commander—a necessary courtesy, his father had said, and one that Vectis didn't mind in the least. But now they had dropped to the rear of the procession. His father wanted to talk.

"I have been killing men for as long as I can remember," the older man said abruptly. "It's nothing like what we saw this morning at the theater."

Vectis wrenched his head around, shocked by the comment. "What's it like to kill someone?" he asked.

His father pulled his horse to a slow walk, patting him on the neck. "War is different," he said, "not like murder ... stabbing someone in the street the way politicians do. You're all lined up. You have weapons, they have weapons—"

"Are you ever scared ... you know ... about having your arm cut off or something?"

The older man paused. "Fear's a strange thing. Even if you want to fight, even if you are brave enough to volunteer for the front lines ... when you look across at the enemy, your stomach feels like water. Your jaw locks shut, you can't breathe. But that's all right—everyone feels that way. You tell yourself you have a job to do, and you do it."

"I guess it helps to know that we always win."

"I suppose, but even the best plans fail. The enemy often surprises you. They aren't witless, and they don't fall into holes."

"But we always win."

His father nodded curtly but said nothing.

"Atilius Titianus says that—"

"Atilius! Has he come calling again?" Then, without waiting for a reply, "I intend to end his calls on your sister. The man is trouble. I've told you before that wealth without work breeds arrogance, and arrogance is the whirlwind of life."

Vectis grimaced at his stupidity for mentioning Atilius. His father detested him, so much so he would confine Sabina within the villa walls until she was wrinkled brown if he discovered how often she had been meeting Atilius secretly. Everything they owned, his father had worked and scraped for. Atilius came from a rich patrician family, broke bread with the great, and aggressively pursued Rome's elusive power. More significantly, he wanted to marry Sabina.

The sarcasm was barely disguised in his father's voice when he said, "Tell me, what did Atilius Titianus have to say?"

Vectis swallowed. "Atilius says that nothing can stop the legions of Rome." Getting no reply, he continued. "He says that Rome's enemies are like beggars at the door."

"Atilius has as much understanding of Rome's enemies as I have of weaving a woman's shawl." He stopped his horse. "Vectis, I want you to understand something. Our Empire is a fragile thing, an island in a sea of chaos." He leaned forward in his saddle and pointed to the light-haired slaves near the center of the slave column. "You see those Celts? They come from Gallia, which has been pacified for two hundred years. But there are still pockets that resist the government, won't pay taxes, won't fight in the auxiliary army, and won't abide by the laws. So now they find themselves slaves. The Celts are a stubborn people. At this very moment—while we speak—wild bands of their cousins are roaming the moors of northern Britannia. They are killing legionaries by the bag-full and about the only thing we can do is build a Wall across the island to keep them out."

"I thought we already had a Wall."

"We do," he said, nudging his horse forward. "Emperor Hadrian's Wall. But we're building another one seventy miles farther north because of the pressure on the Hadrianic frontier."

"We will have two Walls?"

"That's right.   After Hadrian died and Antoninus became Emperor, he decided to drive the most warlike Celtic tribes north into the highlands. Now they're trapped above the Forth-Clyde line and they don't like it. That's why we are building a new Wall—to keep them out. The forts along Antoninus' Wall, and a few even farther north, will be Rome's most distant outposts."

"Why don't we take over the whole island?" Vectis asked.

His father shot him a look. "You don't know ...." He swallowed his impatience and said, "Fifty years ago General Agricola took four legions, decimated every army the Celts managed to gather, but rebellion erupted on the continent and he was recalled."

Vectis made a sound of dismay.

"Rome had the whole island in the palm of its hand, and let it go."

"Why don't we take it back?"

"We tried," his father said, "several years ago. Lollius Urbicus followed Agricola's route north. He rebuilt the old forts and readied his legions to meet the highland Celts of Caledonia. But he couldn't repeat Agricola's conquest of the north. The Celts were too strong. He was defeated at Alauna—lucky to get his legions back to the Forth-Clyde line." Vectis could hear the anger in his father's voice as he talked about the Celts and the Roman generals defeated by them "Anyway," his father said, "that's where Urbicus is now, building the Wall."

Vectis tried to picture the Wall, and what the wild warriors of the north must be like. He gazed at the Celts from Gallia and imagined the others in Britannia—blue-eyed giants with long, flowing blond hair, but not roped together, not stumbling bare-footed with low-slung heads, but riding free on their chariots, whooping and screaming. They would be wearing colorful tunics with leather trousers and shoes, and their faces would be painted blue, or at least be mysterious looking, like the girl he bought in the market.

The thought of the girl shot a surge of heat through his body. He had caught only glimpses of her, a smudge of faded green tunic marching behind the scarlet clad Praetorians, head high like some captured princess. With the day far spent, he wondered how he should approach his father on the subject of keeping her. The right moment, that's what he needed. But it never came. Even during the rest stop, when he might have broached the subject, instead he annoyed his father by straying too close to the slaves, a juvenile attempt to look at the girl.

Fortunately, his father hadn't noticed his special interest. But someone had. The slave with the lash marks had glanced at the girl and then given him a knowing smile.

The sun was burnt orange, settling above the tops of the poplar trees when they stopped for the evening. On a plateau overlooking a bend in the stream, the soldiers set up camp, constructing a pen of poplar poles for the slaves, and a perimeter fence for the entire camp. Even this close to Rome, it was good discipline to erect night barriers, though they elected not to dig the usual trench around the camp.

Vectis sat with his father at the stream's edge, watching the soldiers water their horses, the animals burying their noses in the cold water bubbling over the rocks, drinking with obvious satisfaction.

His father splashed water on his face and rubbed his neck. Shaking the excess from his hands, he began telling Vectis about the great eastern campaign, when Emperor Trajan attacked the Parthians. "I was young and eager to prove myself in battle," he said, "but war is never as glorious as civilians make it out to be. It's time you understood that. You're twelve years old now, and I'm speaking to you as a man."

Vectis sat quietly. His father rarely talked about war, but when he did, it was frightening. He spoke without emotion, and sounded nothing like the men at the baths, who nibbled pickled fish and sweet cakes and droned on about their exploits on the frontiers of the Empire.

The older man looked at his son as if uncertain whether to continue, then shrugged. "At first we swept through the east like Alexander's great army. We marched all the way to the Persian Gulf. Some said that Trajan wanted to invade India—and it seemed we could. City after city fell. We felt like gods." A dark look crossed his face. "But behind us the Parthian armies were gathering. Every day the vast wastelands were filled with numberless hoofprints ... then came the rumble of the Parthian kettle drums ... like thunder shaking the earth."

"But you won."

"Yes, we won." He paused. "But not before I saw things I still see today. You asked about killing ... it's not hard to kill when you see a Roman head jammed on the end of a barbarian pike."

Vectis grimaced. "That's what the Parthians did during the uprising?" He stared at his father, unsure whether to ask anything more.

His father seemed to understand. "Not much more to tell," he said. "One morning after a hard battle, we looked across at the Parthian line, and there they were, screaming and howling—bobbing their spears up and down—Roman heads stuck on the ends. Some were friends." Vectis saw his jaw flinch.

They left their spot by the stream and headed up to their tent, where someone had built a fire. Vectis stared at his father's silhouette against the fire. He looked like the soldier he was. Gaius Trebellius Quadratus, senior Centurion of the First Cohort. One became a centurion after long, hard experience. And his father, Vectis knew, was not an ordinary centurion; he was "First" Centurion, the most respected soldier in the almost six thousand-man legion. Over him were three men: a camp prefect, a military tribune and a legate who commanded the entire legion. But once the battle began, his father made all the decisions.

Sometimes Vectis forgot his father was a premier centurion in the Roman army. He seemed like every other father. But now and then he heard, mostly in whispers, about the awards his father had received—carved discs, silver spear-shafts, several gold crowns—and he knew they had been awarded for unusual acts of bravery. And there was an odd-looking one he often wore, the *corona muralis*, for being the first man to scale the wall of an enemy city. Vectis had never seen one like it.

After dinner, still nibbling a hefty slice of fig cake, Vectis wandered along the tent line toward the corral. The sun had dropped behind the trees, blackening them against the purple sky, creating shadows that crept across the land until they smeared everything soot-dark. When Vectis reached the log pen he paused, straining to catch sight of the slave girl.

"Sst!" came a voice from inside the enclosure.

The slave with the lash marks beckoned to Vectis with his bound hands. Vectis stayed where he was. With no guard on this side of the pen, he was not about to move closer. The man motioned again, and pointed behind him. In the dim light Vectis made out the face of the girl. She wore the same expressionless look she had earlier at the market. He watched her move toward the log barrier, almost, it seemed, with a touch of sadness. Her slender arms slipped through the spaces in the logs, and Vectis was glad to see that the soldiers had left her hands unbound. She smiled at him, a tiny smile that warmed him to the core of his being. He smiled back, and moved closer.

"You ... good Roman," she said in almost unrecognizable Latin.

Vectis smiled again, and said something about trying to buy her. She didn't seem to understand, but looked deep into his eyes. After a long moment, she reached out and gently touched his hand, her fingers cool in the night air.

Suddenly, two bound hands darted out from the pen and yanked him forward. His head slammed into the poplar fence post, and his mind reeled in confusion. Someone ripped at his tunic, unbuckled his belt, and snatched away his purse. As his mind cleared, Vectis could see the girl standing well back of the fence, with the male slave who had been lashed. She had the fig loaf in her hands and what appeared to be the coins from his purse. The man bobbed his head respectfully, gesturing toward her, as if to say that he had taken the coins and bread for her benefit. He opened his palms to show he had kept nothing for himself, and from the solicitous look on his face, it was evident he wanted Vectis to hold his tongue about the theft. "Daughter," he kept saying. "This ... my daughter."

"What is going on?" The soldier's booming voice brought Vectis to his senses. For the first time he noticed that his tunic was hanging free to his ankles, his belt on the ground, his empty purse gaping open in the dirt. He bent over and collected his belt and purse, fixed his tunic to hang correctly at his knees, and glanced around at the three Praetorians encircling him, torches blazing, eyes raking the caged slaves.

"What happened, son?" His father had arrived.

Vectis glanced into the pen at the girl who stood in frozen terror. "Nothing," he said, "I ... I just ...." He stopped, aware of the tremor in his voice.

His father touched his finger to Vectis's forehead and showed him the blood. "What happened?"

"The slave I bought, he—"

"The one with the lash marks?" It was Pudens's voice.

Vectis nodded.

Within seconds, the soldiers had the slave out of the pen, face down in the dirt. One dragged the girl by her arm, and Vectis saw the pain in her face as she tried to keep her ribs from scraping the stony ground.

Pudens talked with Vectis's father, motioning toward the girl and the male slave.

His father turned to a soldier and said, "Find a tree and put him on it."

"What about her?" the soldier asked. "The whip?"

"No!" Vectis said, too abruptly. He looked at his father. "She did nothing wrong."

Vectis felt his father's eyes studying him. Then the older man spoke. "Put her in the pen. And give her back the bread."

Screams shattered the star-filled night. Somewhere in the valley below, the soldiers had completed their grisly task. The slave had been nailed to a tree.

As they sat by the tiny fire beside their tent, listening to the distant moans, Vectis told his father how he had been lured to the pen. He felt ashamed, and foolish for trusting the girl, but he could not believe she was a willing participant in the deception.

His father stirred the glowing coals, ignoring the swirling sparks, and with his eyes still on the fire he said, "Vectis, do you remember where I got your name?"

It seemed a curious question. "From the Isle of Vectis off the coast of Britannia," he answered.

"Yes, the Isle of Vectis," he mused, and his mind seemed far away. "And do you remember why I named you after that island?"

"You said it was the first time you ever fought the enemy and you never wanted to forget what it was like."

"That's right. But I didn't tell you what happened out there." He resumed stirring the coals. "Our patrol responded to the cries of two Celtic children drowning in a river. No one thought they would use children. I remember rushing down that riverbank, trying to save them, and then hearing their whoops of delight when scores of warriors emerged from the shrubbery by the river. Every Roman in that patrol—fifteen soldiers—was killed."

Vectis stared at his father.

"But they weren't just killed. They were mutilated. Those who lay wounded watched the Celts' crazed holy men going from body to body cutting off heads. They shoved them into bags and chanted softly to themselves, as if they were gathering flowers. And then they started on the wounded. Men screamed. Some pled for mercy. I was last in line. The Druids huddled in front of me, talking. Finally, one leaned down and said in broken Latin, 'Evil one, tell your commanders we do not like Romans on our land.' And then the priests left."

They sat in silence for long minutes. Vectis thought about the Celts and their bloodthirsty holy men, and their lying ways. His face flushed as he reflected on his naive behavior, sauntering up to a cage full of savages because he trusted a winsome face.

"Vectis, you made a mistake today. We all do from time to time. But mistakes can be good, especially when you're young. Today you learned an important lesson: never trust the enemy. A soldier cannot afford to be like Atilius Titianus, who talks a good battle. You have to assess your enemy with brutal honesty. If you don't, the consequences could be far worse than today. You could end up like Quinctilius Varus."

The name jolted him. Vectis knew all about Quinctilius Varus. Every schoolboy knew about Varus and his Rhineland disaster. Two hundred years earlier Augustus Caesar had sent Varus into Germania with three legions. But Varus underestimated the German leader, Arminius, who, at only twenty-five, proved a resourceful commander and a crafty imitator of Roman war methods. His attacks were swift and devastating.

One stormy day he fell upon Varus, his three legions, and their auxiliaries in the Teutoburg forest. It never occurred to Varus that the enemy might strike in the middle of a storm, or that a forest could provide excellent cover for an ambush. The centurions tried to organize into battle units, but it was no use. Their lines were stretched too thin and the weather grew worse. Winds whipped through the forest, uprooting trees and blocking the narrow paths. High overhead, lightning flashed in the dark clouds, and treetops snapped like twigs and crashed to the ground. Then the rains came, in a downpour so heavy that soldiers lost sight of the men in front. For three days panic-stricken Romans bolted through the mud-soaked forest. The enemy was everywhere. Quinctilius Varus and his commanders fell on their swords. Over twenty thousand soldiers surrendered, throwing themselves on the mercy of Arminius and his northern savages. The German leader divided them into groups and took them off into the forest. Some he tortured; the rest he hacked to pieces.

"Never underestimate your enemy," his father told him, "and *never* trust them. The Celts and the Germans are born liars. Their word means nothing." He reached into the tent for his sword. "The gladius!" he said, rubbing the blade and arcing it through the air. "It's the only thing that speaks to them." The short sword looked dark and deadly, moving like a shadow in the night.

A sudden wind rustled the trees and gave life to the perishing fire, bringing with it, it seemed, fresh moans from the lower valley. His father shook his head and motioned toward the sounds. "The darkness of the barbarian mind is unimaginable. Even trussed up like a gaming bird, that Celt thought he could steal from a Roman. Now he is food for the dogs."

"But I've cost you a slave," Vectis said.

His father winked. "Don't worry. I am sure the slave trader will be happy to contribute two or three others as a goodwill gesture. His slave obviously had a mind deformity."

Vectis asked, "Why are barbarians so opposed to anything civilized?"

"Well, this one was untrainable, probably flawed from the beginning. But if you are talking about real barbarians from beyond the Empire, you have to understand where they come from. Some places I've been, the people lived like animals before our legions arrived. No roads, no sewers, no baths, no water supplies except the river—nothing but dirt and starvation." He shook his head in amazement. "You go a mile beyond our frontiers and you've got people wearing animal skins and living in smoke-filled, windowless shacks. They have no idea of government or discipline. Laws are nonexistent. All they want to do is make weapons and kill Romans, destroy everything we have built. The first thing a barbarian horde does when it breaks through our lines is set fire to anything representing civilization—buildings, statues, books, paintings—and if we're not careful, they will destroy us."

"Why are they like that? Why are they so destructive?"

"I don't know," he said slowly, "I really don't know."

"Maybe they don't know either. I mean, maybe they don't know enough about us—what it's like to be part of the Empire. They see our aqueducts and baths and theaters, and can't understand them."

"It's more than that," his father said. "Beyond our borders are barbarians bred to kill. The Celts and the Germans are the worst. They love war. They race into battle, blowing horns and shrieking in weird voices. They are gigantic, bigger than these Gallic Celts we have here. Only Roman discipline stops them. I've seen them run from the battlefield, back to their villages, and burn their homes, slaughter their own wives and children. And for what?"

"Can you imagine if barbarians controlled the world?"

"Darkness would swallow everything," his father replied. "There would be chaos and utter darkness."

Vectis shuddered.

"Fortunately, there has never been an army like Rome's. We have the discipline, the equipment, and the will to rule the world. Thank the gods we do, because without Rome the world as you know it would be gone like mist in the morning sun." He laughed. "You should see these Celts. They wear baggy coats slit down the front that reach to the knees, and under that they have their sheepskin trousers tied at the ankles. They can't read a book or build a road, but they keep themselves as clean as Roman senators. And how do they do it? They scrub themselves in the rivers—winter and summer!" He roared. "The north is a frozen wasteland in the winter, but do they build bathhouses? No. They smash holes in the ice, and drag buckets back to their huts so they can scrub themselves." He looked at Vectis. "That's why their skin is the color of fish flesh."

Vectis smiled.

Sudden shrieks rose from the valley. They grew louder and more frenzied. The dogs had come.

As Vectis crawled into his bedding, he thought about the girl, and wondered if she could be the daughter of the man screaming in the valley. Or was she a liar and deceiver like the rest of Rome's enemies? Somewhere inside he knew the truth: she was his daughter, and down in the pen she was listening to the same pitiful cries. Vectis pulled his head under the blankets to smother the sound.

Early the next morning they passed through the valley where packs of snarling dogs were circling the crucified man's partially eaten body, now hanging tantalizingly out of reach. Above, the ravens fluttered, tugging at the glistening meat. Vectis turned his face away, feeling as if he had caused all this shame.

Vectis's father glanced at him and said, "Roman discipline is harsh, but it is effective. Brutality ensures peace for everyone."

They rode together most of the day, and Vectis saw the slave girl only once. Her hands were bound and her shoulders seemed more stooped than they had been the day before.

Vectis immersed himself in conversation with his father, fearing to be alone with his thoughts. It was as if the older man knew he needed the distraction as he described in great detail the barbarians all over the world. In the east, he said, beyond the Parthians lay India, a place of great rivers, exotic perfumes and rich jewels. The inhabitants were strange, thin-boned people who rode elephants in the city streets and drank the blood of panthers to enhance their strength. Beyond the southern borders of Egypt and Africa, he said, was snake country. It was full of spotted cats, terrifying beasts and tiny black men the size of five-year-old boys. They ran naked through the forest with wooden pipes, blowing poison darts with deadly accuracy at antelope hundreds of feet away. The Games in Rome got most of their animals from there. And finally, to the west stretched an endless ocean where only the gods could go.

It was almost dark before Vectis saw the flickering line of torches in the rolling hills below. They were spaced evenly along the stone fence surrounding a vast tract of farmland. In a world of aliens, the glow of torches looked warm and inviting, and as Vectis entered the gates, he shivered at the thought of Britannia, the Wall, and those strange, savage creatures roaming the moors.

PART ONE:
Fear and Desperation

Four Years Later

3

Taranis splashed his hands in the run-off stream for the third time, and for the third time pulled them out sticky with sap. The cedar was gummy this year. Even a scrubbing with fuller's soap had little effect. It was his least favorite work, stripping bark, but someone had to do it, and whether by chance or design (Taranis suspected by design), his brother never developed the subtle knife movements required to strip bark.

So here he was with fingers pasted together and hundreds of saplings heaped around him that had yet to be skinned, cut, and notched for arrows. And no Eston. He was in the woods somewhere, probably savoring the last breezes of summer as he searched for suitable wood to make the bow's central frame. Taranis massaged his shoulders, a grimace on his face as his fingers stuck repeatedly to his aching back. He shifted his eyes to his sister who was practicing with her bow.

"Neeve, what did I tell you?" His voice sounded strained but he didn't care. His back ached and his sister was still doing everything wrong, reason enough to set her straight. "You grip the bow like a plow handle," he said, pushing himself off the ground and approaching her. "Hold it lightly." She was standing about sixty paces from an embankment, shooting arrows at a chunk of bearskin; over the years, floodwaters had sheered a vertical wall in the dense clay, making it ideal for target practice.

"Lower. Position your bow lower," Taranis said, exasperated. "You'll never hit anything unless you listen to me."

Neeve's eyes squinted in the morning sun. "I am listening to you."

"No, you're not."

Neeve glared at him.

"Why won't you follow my instructions?"

"I am following your instructions," she said sharply.

Taranis mumbled his disagreement.

"Look," she said, her voice rising. "My arrow is below the nocking bead. I have one finger above the shaft and two below. I am concentrating on the target. I am pausing before I release the string. Just-what-you-said."

Taranis found himself staring into Neeve's frosty blue eyes, eyes that told him he was not up to the challenge. He looked away, knowing he had transferred his own frustration to Neeve. Mastering a weapon was not easy and he could see she was doing her best. She was a serious girl who worked hard at everything she did, and Taranis could never remember a time when Neeve had failed to complete a single chore, whether sewing or hauling water or caring for their few farm animals. When her work was done she would devote herself to her drawings, meticulously correcting slight imperfections in her pictures of lakes or ragged, wooden shacks. Taranis could never get over her ability to draw the places she saw, nor the coin that she often received for her work at the market. But shooting a bow had proved difficult for her.

"Try again," he said, forcing a civil tone.

She glanced at him, licked her lips, and focused on the target. Taranis hoped for a good shot; she needed the encouragement. Arrows were scattered everywhere—on the ground, in the embankment—everywhere but in the bearskin.

She aimed carefully, and missed. "Wait!" She threw up her hands to forestall any comment Taranis might have. "That was not good." She drew another arrow, aimed, and struck the ground in front of the embankment. "Wait! Wait! That slipped. I was unready."

"Neeve—"

"No, wait ...." She shot again, and hit close to the target, a wide grin spreading across her face as she turned toward him.

"Finally!" he said, and wished he hadn't when her smile faded at the corners of her mouth. He tousled her hair. "Don't be discouraged. If you keep practicing, it will come." She had the poorest bow skills he had ever seen.

He sat down and resumed his work, glancing occasionally at his sister who was staring at her bow, and twisting the fringes of her hair, something she did when upset. Taranis was concerned. These were difficult times and Neeve, already twelve, had no bow skills. She naively believed that her brothers could always protect her. But he knew different. She needed a weapon, not so much for the battlefield, but for safety.

Before the Romans, Caledonia had been a collection of rural farms and untroubled woodlands. It wasn't unusual to see girls playing games on the moors or women traveling unescorted from one place to another. But now the north country was war-ruined. Even if the Romans stayed behind their Wall, which they had of late, Caledonia would never be the same. Strangers wandered the hills, drifters and rootless warriors going no place in particular. The bow was quick and deadly, and easy for a woman to handle.

Taranis was about Neeve's age when he first witnessed the power of the bow. With his father gone, he found himself in a venomous world where only the hardy survived. He had expected his father would always be there to teach him, but like other boys who had lost their fathers, he was reduced to petty thievery, shuffling through the marketplace crowds, stealing what he could. His mother was a strong woman who worked tirelessly at their homestead and whenever possible in the neighboring fields, picking rocks. But as the months passed it became obvious even to her that more permanent arrangements would have to be made.

One day as Taranis rounded the detached kitchen behind their cottage, he found his mother under the huge willow tree, crying. "Mother ...?" he inquired, not knowing what else to say. He had never seen his mother cry.

She dried her eyes on the fringe of her tunic.   "Fetch the children," she said.

When the four had gathered under the willow, she clasped each child by the face and murmured a prayer. Then she told them about her dream—tall, bony spirits clad in rags that ventured out from the shadowy forests to collect the weak and frail.

"We have nothing to fear," Taranis protested.

"The tall spirits are coming," his mother said. "They will come with the wind and winter snows, and they will find us. If you cannot provide for yourself, you become food for the spirits." She sighed. The family would have to separate; it was the only way. Several relatives had offered to take in the women—herself, Neeve, and younger sister, Nes. The boys would fend for themselves.

Taranis picked up his bow and shook it in her face. "Why do we need to separate? I can hunt game."

"There is more to providing for a family than hunting game," his mother said sadly. "You are simply not old enough."

"I think I am," Taranis said, jutting out his chin. "Give me a chance."

"Your age is of no consequence."

"Then what?"

"If you must know … your attitude … you have no responsibility. You think you can steal from the market stalls—"

"I will never steal again."

"Phfft!" his mother said in disbelief.

"I promise before the gods."

"You always promise! You promised not to fight with the village boys."

"I can change. For the sake of the family, I can change."

"He can do it," Neeve pleaded.

"I can help," Eston chimed in.

"We'll all help," Neeve cried. "I have a drawing that might fetch something at the market."

That day the children sifted through their father's tool shed collecting everything they could: wooden boxes, cedar oil, worn out sheep skins, pig-hide window coverings, iron saw blades, a shovel, two bundles of pine-wood fence posts and a dozen sheaves of straw. Early the next morning Taranis and Eston headed for the village of Celynedd pulling a broken vegetable cart filled with their homegrown rubbish.

"Here's my drawing," Neeve said, encasing the papyrus roll in a faded tartan.

Taranis cushioned the tartan wrap with two sheaves of straw and with Eston set off down the road. Three hours later the two boys reached the hilltop overlooking the sheep pens at the edge of town. The night rains had turned the holding pens into muck-yards, a soupy mess that coated the haunches of normally brown sheep a light gray color. Several men were herding a half dozen sheep into the butcher's shed and even with a crosswind, Taranis could smell the tangy scent of fresh blood. Beyond the pens, smoke from the smelting kilns belched skyward, naked children chased each other through the grimy streets, and the buzz of activity sounded like the roar of a waterfall in the valley below. It was marvelous. The whole town throbbed with energy and prosperity, and at the center of it all lay Celynedd's enormous town square with its hundreds of merchants butting their carts end to end in anticipation of the day's bartering.

"Oh, no, look!" Eston said, pointing toward the black oxen turning the huge stones at the grinding mill. A half-dozen boys were doing sword exercises in the field adjacent to the mill. "We have to go back. Geir is with them."

Taranis groaned. Geir was tall and thick and dull-witted as a mule pulling a log. His arms were too long, his ears too small, and his face often broke into a humorless smile that did nothing to mask his rage. Lately the big oaf had begun to demand a coin, any bronze coin would do, for traveling on his toll road. It wasn't a toll road, of course, and it wasn't Geir's road in any event. Only the Romans claimed the right to extract payment for the use of their roads. When Taranis refused to pay Geir his coin weeks earlier, Geir's thugs thrashed him soundly. He could still see the anger in his mother's face when he hobbled home in tatters. He couldn't afford trouble with Geir, not with his mother ready to disband the family.

"Keep your eyes forward," Taranis said.

"I think we should go back."

"I know what you think. Keep your eyes forward. And don't touch your bow," he said, adding, "they have swords."

They continued down the rutted road, Taranis pulling the two-wheeled cart, Eston pushing from behind. As they neared the field, the boys stopped their sword practice and shuffled toward the road. One, a boy with a narrow head and a shock of red hair, pitched a stone at Taranis, and cried, "Look at the donkey pulling the cart!"

Taranis took his own advice and kept his eyes forward. No more fighting, he told himself. He had the family to think about. They depended on him now. Somehow he must avoid the village boys, get to the market and trade his goods, such as they were. Besides, he was hardly a match for boys who had fought with the Caledonian army, especially with Geir in the pack.

"Donkey!" the boy shouted as he drew closer.

Taranis kept moving.

"I am talking to you, donkey!"

The others snickered and crowded in front of the cart to block the way. Taranis steered the cart along the road's edge but a wheel caught in the rocks.

"Looks like the donkey's stuck!" a boy said, laughing.

"Help him!" Geir shouted, shoving the boy headlong into the cart. "All of you, get the cart back on the road." The boys hauled the cart out of the rocks.

Geir moved closer to Taranis with an overly concerned expression on his face. "Hope your wheels aren't damaged. Those rocks can be treacherous."

"The wheels are fine," Taranis replied.

"Good ... good," he said, rubbing his chin thoughtfully. Geir was only three years older than Taranis but already he had the heavy bone structure of a man. "By the way," he said, smiling, "what are you doing on my road?"

Taranis said nothing.

He continued in the same polite tone, "Because those who don't pay use the bush trails. I thought I told you that."

"We want no trouble. Just let us pass."

"How would that look, mountain boy, letting you pass? You're on my road and I want my toll."

Taranis could imagine his hands around Geir's neck, but he swallowed his pride. Only the family counted now. From under his trouser belt he produced a bronze coin.

Geir plucked the coin from Taranis's fingers and smiled again. "Now, that's better. Much better than last time, eh?" His face changed. "When you broke my tooth!" He pointed to a black hole in the bottom front of his jaw. "It wouldn't be right for me to forget that, would it?" He punched Taranis hard in the stomach, doubling him over, and then kicked him as he lay on the ground.

Taranis stood and dusted himself off, avoiding eye contact with Geir. He reached for the cart, but Geir's hand clamped over his shoulder. "Where do you think you're going, mountain boy?" he asked in the polite tone again.

"You got your coin."

"True. You did give me a coin. But you also caused me trouble," Geir said to the amusement of the other boys, "so today I will need two coins."

Taranis felt trapped; he had no other coins.

"He doesn't have the toll," Geir said with feigned dismay. "What shall we do?"

"Maybe there's something in this junk?" one of the boys said as he pulled out Neeve's drawing.

"Leave that alone!" Taranis shouted too late. The boy had already passed it to Geir.

A big grin spread across Geir's face. "What do we have here? Looks like Four Meadows near Blanid."

"It is Four Meadows," the redheaded boy said, "you can see Medb's mountain in the background."

Taranis reached for the drawing. "Give it back," he said.

"You got another coin?" Geir stared at him.

"Give me the drawing!"

"Give me the drawing," Geir mimicked. "Oh, I am shivering in the wind."

Taranis choked down his rage. He held out his hand. "Now! I want it now!"

Geir ripped Neeve's drawing in half. "Which piece do you want first?"

Before the rest of the pack even moved, Taranis had struck Geir three times.

Hours later Taranis and Eston returned home, their cart in a jumble, Neeve's drawing ripped in pieces, and their faces caked with blood.

"We had problems with the village boys," Taranis volunteered before his mother could say anything.

"Is that Neeve's drawing?" she demanded, her eyes on the tangle of tartan wedged between a wooden box and a shovel.

"They ripped it," Taranis said with the words catching in his throat. "It wasn't my fault."

"Did you trade anything?"

"We never made it to town."

"So now you are dragging Eston into your fights," she said, glancing at the younger boy.

Taranis shifted awkwardly. "I ... I tried—"

"Whose child are you?"

Taranis swallowed. The words cut him cruelly.

"Not your father's," she said. "You are nothing like your father. Nothing. He was dependable."

Taranis dropped his eyes.

"If your father could see you now ... I am so utterly ashamed of you, Taranis."

"I didn't mean to fight—"

"For a fleeting moment I thought that possibly, just possibly, you might take your place in this family. But I see now that I was wrong. You care nothing about what happens to your sisters or anybody—"

"I do, but ... but ...."

Her eyes filled with tears but she rubbed them away with a clenched fist, angry at her loss of control. "What am I to do? You answer me. Let the tall spirits harvest the souls of your sisters? Winter is coming! Don't you understand?" She turned her head but couldn't hide her agony.

Taranis moved closer to his mother, trying to comfort her.

"Leave me," she said, giving him her back. "You have brought shame to this family and to your father's name. When people ask why my son cannot provide, I will tell them the truth."

The next morning when their mother left to make arrangements, the four children sat in silence listening to the horse cart squeak down the dirt road and out of sight. Taranis remembered Nes crying and Eston mumbling that it wasn't their fault. But most vivid in his mind was Neeve, jumping up from the ground as if a bee had stung her, and running to the hearth to scoop out a glowing coal.

She herded it across the grass with a stick until it lay in front of the others. Then, standing barefooted on the fiery ember, she declared in a loud voice, "We will never separate! To the gods, this I pledge." The smell of burnt flesh filled the air, but without so much as a tear in her eye, she looked at him and said, "Pledge to me."

How could he fulfill such a pledge? His mother would never listen to him now. But then and there he determined never to allow anything to threaten the family. He and Eston, and even Nes, stood on the coal and pledged that they would never separate. They would always protect each other.

That afternoon when his mother returned, Taranis confessed he had done wrong in not taking responsibility. A great fear had entered his heart, he said, when the meaning of her dream became clear. He was a poor son in so many ways. He knew little about farming, could barely mend a fence or patch a bucket, never mind provide for a family during the long winter months. She had a right to doubt his ability, he said, when days earlier he couldn't find a leak in their mud-plastered roof.

But, and he looked her in the eyes, if she could be at peace with her dreams, he knew that he and Eston could provide if given a chance.

Something about his confession, or the way he talked to her, changed her mind. A month is what she gave him; a month to prove himself.

The next day Taranis and his brother set off again for town, hauling their cart, but this time hidden in the straw was a three foot oak stave. The plan was simple: Taranis would engage the village boys while Eston hurried the cart down the road and into town. It was a good plan but when they rounded the hilltop overlooking the sheep pens, Taranis couldn't help thinking about all the things that could go wrong, and instantly he felt his entire body grow rigid. Fistfights were one thing, but wielding an oak stave was quite another. The village boys had swords and might be tempted to use them. Already they were looking his way.

"Get this cart down to the village," Taranis said as he ripped the stave from the straw. "Don't worry about me." He fixed his eyes on the boys and started across the field.

Taranis knew he was in trouble the moment he saw Geir. The huge bully hardly looked like himself, hair plastered across his forehead, dripping with sweat, eyes two glazed orbs as if transformed by a wood demon. He blundered up the hill, chopping the air mindlessly with his sword, and repeating the words: "Goin' to cut him! Goin' to cut him real bad!" The other boys goaded him on with grunts and war shrieks. They picked up rocks and circled Taranis like winter-hungry wolves.

Taranis raised his oak stave and tried to concentrate on the pulsing movements of Geir's sword, but with rocks whizzing by his head, he was finding it difficult. How much time before he could turn and run? he wondered. He no longer cared what the village boys might think of him. His mother was desperate; he could see that now. The family needed him and he must never fail them again.

Suddenly Geir twisted his mouth like a frenzied dog and let out the most awful scream. He plunged to his knees, dropped his sword, and grasped his buttocks. Taranis gaped at the arrow protruding from his leather trousers.

"Leave my brother alone!" Eston's thin voice shrieked. He had left the cart and was thirty feet away, his second arrow aimed at Geir's chest. "Leave him alone," he repeated. "I'm a good shot."

Taranis knew how easily he might have lost his life that day outside the village. He remembered running to Eston, and the two of them fleeing across the field like the wind. But they had learned an important lesson about the bow. It was a powerful weapon. Even a ten-year-old boy could paralyze a gang of boys bent on savagery. If Neeve could master the bow, thought Taranis, she too could protect herself.

The village boys never bothered Taranis and Eston again. For the next several weeks, he and Eston scoured old battlegrounds for arrow tips, axes, knives and anything else they could find. These they traded for meat, blankets, water bags, pots and other household goods. Neeve and her sister helped their mother work neighboring farms, milking goats, shearing sheep, and weaving on large upright looms. Afternoons were spent collecting berries and working the vegetable garden, and the whole time, Neeve never ceased chattering about how wonderful it was to keep the family together. Their mother said not a word.

When the month expired, they all gathered again under the willow to hear their mother's announcement: "The autumn rains are coming," she said, "and we have yet to fill the root cellars. Lazy families starve during the winter, and from what I have seen, we are not a lazy family." Then she smiled that warm way she often did before their father had died, and touched Taranis's cheek. "I had no doubts," she said, "not about any of my children."

It had been a proud moment in Taranis's life. His mother was pleased, and Neeve beamed at him the whole day.

As the years tumbled by, Taranis and Eston grew more practiced with the bow, and brought home small game and even elk at times. Neeve became an excellent fisher, a skilled quilt maker, and a hard bargainer at the market. The days were long and exhausting but the family rarely wanted for food, and they remained together.

Taranis glanced up from the saplings he had been stripping to see Neeve's face glowing with triumph. Her last few arrows had struck less than a foot from the fur square. "I think I'm getting a feel for the bow," she said.

"You do?" Taranis smiled. He scrubbed his hands again and walked over to her.

Her brow furrowed. "I mean, I think I'm on the verge of something—"

He laughed.

"What's so funny?" she demanded, poking him with her fist.

"I'm sorry, Neeve. You are doing well, but in truth you don't have a great feel for the bow yet."

She grimaced. "Not so good, I know." She pulled another arrow from the basket, her face serious. "I'll get better, I promise."

"It takes time," he said, squeezing her arm as an encouragement. "You're doing better than I did at your age."

"Really?" She looked doubtful.

One thing about Neeve, she wasn't stupid. And with arrows littering the ground, it would be hard to fool her even if she were.

"Listen, after that day at the Wall when Father …." Taranis paused. He couldn't bring himself to mention the incident. "I practiced with an old village bow. Never hit where I was aiming. Then I learned about the Scythian composite bow." He took the weapon from her. "It's lighter, and more powerful, and it shoots effortlessly, a great weapon, so keep working at it."

Lately, he and Eston had begun drills with the Celtic long sword. Taranis had grown rapidly and at sixteen was bigger than most men. His brother, Eston, though only fourteen, stood as tall as Taranis and looked almost as strong. Hefting the sword proved no problem for either.

"Let me show you what you're doing wrong," Taranis said, pleased with his newfound patience. "You hold your bow too high. Don't look down the arrow at the target." He shifted into a shooting position. "See," he said, drawing the arrow back to the corner of his mouth. "Concentrate on the target, and anchor the arrow to the same spot on your face." He released the string. The arrow whooshed through the air and struck the fur to the side of the splotched yellow center.

"Hah!" Neeve hooted. "You missed!"

"That is one dead Roman," he said, handing the bow back to her.

Taranis resumed stripping bark. He usually dried the saplings in the wind for a day before rubbing them with grease. Any longer and the shafts would warp. An arrow needed to be smooth and straight for its flight to be true.

Making Scythian-style bows was more than a passing interest to Taranis and Eston. It was their livelihood. The Scythians were part of the faraway Parthian nation and were the best archers in the world. Rome used mercenaries in their armies and most of their Wall garrisons had a contingent of Scythian archers. Taranis had never seen them but he knew everything about the workings of their bow.

"What's that?" Neeve asked.

Taranis's head jerked up, his eyes on the woods where twigs had suddenly begun to pop and crackle, as if a bear were foraging for food. He relaxed when he saw Eston and their old workhorse, its back piled high with stout maple stalks, plowing through the trees.

Eston loosed the ropes, dumping the poles. They hit the grass with an earthy thud. "Hard, straight maple wood," he said. "Over fifty."

Taranis ran his eyes across the tangled mass of poles that they would soon cut into flat staves for the bows' central frames. They would glue three of the staves together, then bind the laminated wood into a circle, opposite the eventual strung shape of the bow, and finally overlay the inner side with split horn and the outer with animal tendons. After letting it cure for eight to ten months, they would untie the curved wood, bend it against itself, and string it for the first time. An impressive weapon, the composite bow; with an iron tip it could penetrate armor at a hundred yards.

"You were away a long time," Taranis said. "Any trouble?" He allowed a smile to cross his lips, hinting that his brother might have rested in the sun.

Eston didn't take the bait. "No trouble finding the maple," he said. "The hills are covered with it. But I think we have a problem."

He pointed over his shoulder. "A storm is brewing ... maybe a windstorm. I hiked over to the next ridge ... sky is darkening on the horizon."

"Looks fine here. How big is the storm?"

"It's strange ... brown in one spot out there."

Taranis looked alarmed. "What do you mean, brown? Are there clouds? Is it raining?"

"No rain. Maybe dust—"

"Where?" Taranis shouted.

"In the ... south," Eston said, realizing what he was saying.

"What's wrong?" Neeve asked in a whisper.

The boys exchanged glances. "It could be the Romans," Eston said.

"The Romans," Neeve mouthed, and her face froze in terror.

"Be calm," Taranis said. "We have dust on the horizon ... it could be a herd of sheep, maybe even the wind. None of the tribes has attacked the Wall ... so there's no reason for the Romans to be out this far. Probably a dust storm." He looked around. "Straighten up camp and we shall see about this dust."

It took them over an hour to arrive at the ridge. On the way they talked about the Romans and whether they could be marching on Caledonia again. It seemed impossible. It had been years since the Romans had invaded Caledonia. The last major battle was at Alauna, when the combined forces of the Celtic tribes beat back Rome's armies. Since then they had attacked sparingly, and everyone said that the Romans had learned their lesson and would stay behind their Wall.

"They'll never leave us alone," Neeve said.

"The Romans," Eston spat, "always pushing, always trying to grab more land for their Emperor."

Somehow the depressing conversation lifted their spirits as they trudged over the rolling grasslands and through dense stretches of trees. Eston cheered everyone, saying the Romans would be fools to attack Caledonia. Neeve and her archery skills would have them fleeing in nightmare terror.

"You think that's funny?" Neeve gave her brother a withering look. "In a year I'll shoot better than both of you."

"Neeve the Scythian," Eston said with a smile.

She made a face. "You wait."

They crested the last hill before the ridge. "We'll know soon," Taranis said.

They found themselves running across the valley floor and rushing breathlessly toward the top of the ridge. Taranis headed straight for the first chute that would give him a view of the valley. It was a clear day, not a trace of fog as they stared at the vast expanse that greeted them.

"There!" Eston pointed to a distant, shadowy line moving against a background of billowing dust. He need not have said anything. Three hours earlier, all he had seen was a dark spot on the horizon. Now the spot had taken shape. The tiny line quivering in the distance could be nothing other than a column of soldiers.

For a moment no one spoke. All their hopes of dust storms or sheep herds had faded. The armies of Rome were actually coming.

Taranis led the workhorse to Neeve. "When you get to the village, tell them what you saw. Tell them that the Romans are marching on Caledonia." He glanced back at the wavy line. "Could be a raiding party ... could be a legion or more. They'll set up camp and probably attack in the morning."

Eston spoke up: "Waste no time, Neeve. After you deliver the message, do as we agreed. Leave with Nes and Mother for the hunting cabin at Celywic. Taranis and I will come after the Romans leave."

She nodded.

"Be careful," Eston added.

"*You* be careful," she said, kissing him. "And do nothing foolish." She looked at Taranis. "Especially you. I need both my brothers."

Taranis kissed her, holding her little form close for a moment. Her arms hung by her sides, her eyes staring straight ahead. He lifted her chin. "Are you all right?" he asked.

Again, she nodded.

He placed her cheek on his chest and stroked her hair. "We will be fine, Neeve. Nothing will happen to us. We'll always be together."

She squeezed him hard, straightened her shoulders and stepped back. "Well," she said, wiping her nose, "I had better go. Help me up."

Taranis grasped her by the waist and, as if she were a willow shoot, tossed her up on the back of the horse.

"Get this elderly beast moving," he said.

She smiled weakly and dug her heels into the horse.

4

Darkness had fallen by the time Taranis and Eston reached the village. A forest of torches bobbed wildly in streets that normally boasted only an occasional lamp glowing in a window. Men screamed orders, shouted greetings, and rushed chaotically in every direction. Throngs had gathered round huge bonfires that shot sparks hundreds of feet into the night sky. Now and then Taranis recognized men from other villages as they hurried by.

"Mountain boy!" someone shouted from behind.

Taranis turned to see the grinning face of Geir. He looked every inch a warrior, his hair spiked yellow with clay and lime, his body bare from the waist up, painted blue.

"They need me for the battle," he said, "as a swordsman!" He thrust his long sword toward the black sky, threw back his head, and howled.

Taranis grabbed his arm. "Who said you could fight?"

"They have no need of you," he sneered.

"Who?" Taranis demanded.

"Bronix," he said. "Bronix himself. But he has no need for cowards ... or babies like your brother there." He looked at Eston as one would a worm.

"I am still a good shot," Eston said with a defiant face.

"You hold your mouth!" Geir shouted.

Taranis stepped in front of Geir. "Where is Bronix?" he asked calmly.

Geir shrugged. "By the second fire, I think. He told the village organizer to bring every warrior—including me—to the sword units for assignment."

"So they made you a swordsman," Taranis said.

Geir swelled his body to its full stature. "They still have room for water carriers. You had better hurry."

Taranis smiled. It seemed childish to bicker on the eve of a battle. Who could know what evils lay in wait for them? "The gods go with you," Taranis said in a serious tone.

Geir studied Taranis before mumbling a return prayer.

Taranis watched him trot excitedly toward the men gathered by the fires. How he longed to take up arms against the soldiers from Rome. Hard resolve filled his mind. "The time has come," he said to Eston. "Finally we get our chance at the Romans."

Taranis started toward the fire where he could see the huge outline of Bronix moving against the ragged flames. His body looked like a slab of wood and his arms stretched out like tree limbs as he directed people this way and that. From his bronze helmet rose two massive horns, making him appear even taller than he was, and he was already a head taller than anyone near him. Bronix terrified the enemy, his father had said. With one sweep of the sword, he often killed two or three Romans.

"Bronix," Taranis said respectfully, "I am ready for battle."

Bronix swung around and surveyed Taranis and his brother. He had sharp, piercing eyes, a golden torc round his neck, and the longest mustache Taranis had ever seen. It was red and hung well below his jutting chin. "So, what have we here?" His smile showed big, square, even teeth. "The son of Carados wants to fight the Romans," he boomed. "Well, you are too young. Go home."

"You said Geir from Celynedd could fight, and he's only a year older." He was more than three years older but Taranis stood as tall, so he supposed it was more an exaggeration than a lie.

"So I did." His heavy brow furrowed. "Let me tell you something, Taranis. Your father and I fought side by side for many years—the gods never made a better man. I owe him much, probably my life. I am not about to repay him by building a pyre for his boy." He paused. "I cannot let you fight, Taranis. You are too young."

"I must avenge my father's death," Taranis said firmly.

"Vengeance is a noble thing, but you are not ready."

Taranis stood his ground. "I am bigger than most, and practiced with the sword." He pushed the hilt of his sword toward Bronix.

"Ah, that you are. But I have spoken."

"You *must* let me fight," Taranis said with a raised voice. "The gods have called me. It is my time. You fought at the same age. My father told me so."

Bronix stared at him.

"I am practiced with the sword," Taranis repeated for effect.

"And with the bow too, I have heard." The big warrior sighed. "I grant you a place with the archers. It's safer and will give you a taste of war."

"What about me?" Eston asked. "I'm as good a shot as Taranis."

"You might be, son, but there will be another day for you." He leaned his great head down toward Eston. "Remember your father, boy, and respect what I say." He turned to Taranis. "Report to Uryen." He pointed toward a group of archers Taranis could barely make out. "Tell him I said to place you in the fourth tier. May the gods preserve you." He placed his hand on Taranis's shoulder. "You have your father's fire. Don't make this your last battle."

Bronix turned and started bellowing orders again.

Taranis could not contain a smile of triumph. Archers were like sideline guests in Celtic-style fighting, but at least he was involved. Besides, the greatest warrior of all, Bronix, was about to lead them into battle against the Empire.

He surveyed the archers gathered around Uryen. Many he recognized from the archery contests at feast days. Uryen he had never seen, though he remembered his father saying that he had heard tales about him when he was a boy. Uryen was that old. Taranis could see him emerging now from the knot of archers, his body tall and sinewy, his hair long and gray, falling loosely to his shoulders. He had a weathered, axe-shaped face with eyes that seemed tired, as if they had seen everything to see in life. He moved in a slow, drooping walk, making Taranis wonder how he could lead anyone into battle, never mind shoot with power. But everyone in the northland had heard stories about Uryen and his prowess with the bow. No one could shoot like Uryen.

Just then a rider came in at a gallop, his horse lathered and skittish in the light of the fire. The Romans had been spotted building a temporary garrison for the night.

All along the line, officers began barking orders, pacing back and forth in front of the men, waving their arms and shouting. They wore bright tunics, armor, and helmets tied under the chin. In contrast, most of the common warriors were stripped to the waist, their hair spiked yellow, their bodies painted blue to symbolize the wrath of the gods. There were also a few women here and there, mostly in the archery ranks, though some of the larger ones stood with the swordsmen.

When the officers had positioned the warriors to their satisfaction, Bronix and three commanders walked the length of the line inspecting the hastily assembled army. Often they paused to greet an old soldier or to give a word of encouragement to a new recruit.

It was time to move out. The roaring fires that had been shooting angry sparks heavenward had calmed to flickering tongues licking the rocks at their base. The night sky was clear, black and dotted with light, with occasional wisps of clouds drifting across a three-quarter moon. The chariots on the left wing led the procession, followed by the archers, swordsmen, more archers and chariots. The idea was to maintain battle readiness as much as possible. This meant that marching troops retained their prearranged battle order, with the single difference being that the baggage and supply carts were positioned in the center for protection. "This your first battle?"

Taranis turned to see a boy about eighteen with fleshy cheeks and wavy brown hair. He had intense eyes that blinked a lot. His trousers and embroidered tunic looked as if a tailor had made them; except for a bow slung over his back, he might have been heading to a town meeting.

"My first too," he continued, introducing himself as Lon. "Any word on how many Romans?"

"About two thousand," Taranis said.

"I heard that too. We have more. Maybe twice as many."

Taranis said nothing, though he doubted they had raised four thousand warriors. Maybe three thousand.

Lon jabbered on about the Romans and their methods of war. They had marched too far from the Wall, he said, with too few troops. "The Romans never fight unless they're certain of victory," he said. "I heard they might not fight at all. They are very careful ... when they see our numbers they'll probably run." He laughed self-consciously. "Too bad, because I really want to fight."

"The Romans don't run."

"What?"

"I said, the Romans never run. We'll have to fight."

Lon shuffled in silence. "How do you know they will fight? Maybe they wish not to engage such a large force. Maybe they'll see how outnumbered they are and leave." He licked his lips and mopped his brow, his eyes blinking rapidly.

"Bronix said they were legionaries, and legionaries never come this far north unless they intend to fight."

"Legionaries? I heard they were Roman auxiliaries from the Wall."

"Legionaries."

"So ... they will fight ... legionaries here in Caledonia." The boy grew quiet. He coughed as if he couldn't get air. A few more steps, his eyes closed, and his head rolled back.

Taranis grabbed his arm. "Are you all right?"

He opened his eyes. "Yes, I'm ... ah ... feeling sick. I have been like this for several days," he added hastily.

Taranis felt sorry for him. Inside, a finger of fear probed his heart too. "We probably will get no closer than a hundred yards to the Romans," he said. "We'll shoot off our arrows and move to the rear of the battle."

"True," Lon said as he concentrated on the ground in front of him. Several minutes elapsed before he looked at Taranis. "Thank you," he said.

Taranis gave him a smile of encouragement.

They moved silently over the rolling fields and rocky crests until they reached a hill bordered on one side by jagged rocks, and on the other by a forest. Taranis had often hunted in this area. In the moonlit valley below, he could see a grassy expanse dotted with heather and gorse bushes—ideal for their chariots and, in this case, a morning battle. When the sun rose, its brilliance would be in the eyes of their enemies. Bronix had chosen wisely.

The officers repositioned the army and had them sit. A stream of scouts flowed in and out of camp, reporting Roman movements to Bronix and his commanders. Rumors swept the camp that Roman scouts had been sighted as soon as the Celts had left the village fires. Apparently, the scouts had been observing the Celts the entire evening, and now the main body of Romans had begun to move. They were about five miles away.

Taranis tied a red sash around his forehead to honor his father, who had worn a bright red battle shirt. Easy for his men to see, he had said. Taranis glanced at the baggage carts where Eston was sitting. His rejection as a warrior had embarrassed him and Taranis could only imagine how he felt when, like a child banished from a hunting trip because of the danger, he was told to leave. His brother had never expected Bronix to grant him a sword position, but in view of his size and shooting skills, he had hoped for a place in the archery wing. Fortunately, he managed to secure a baggage handling position at the rear of the army, a duty Geir would have mocked, but one that cheered Eston a little.

Still, being a carrier was an important responsibility. Without storage carts battles would be short-lived. The auxiliary warriors depended on the baggage handlers to bring them baskets of arrows, so in turn, they could replenish the front. In the event of retreat, the fate of the army depended on handlers cool enough to move the carts to their fallback positions.

"Sleep!" Bronix thundered, "I want everyone to sleep." Officers all over shouted the same message.

"I can't sleep," Lon whispered. "I have trouble sleeping on my feathered cot at home. How can I sleep on the ground?"

Taranis wondered whether Lon might be joking, but one glance at his earnest face told him he was not. Lon was the son of a privileged family. "You've never slept on the ground?" Taranis asked.

"Only when I hunt with my father. But then we have tents and blankets."

"This is not much different."

"It's hard to sleep knowing the Romans are on that ridge over there."

Taranis looked toward the ridge shrouded in darkness. He could barely trace the contour of the hills against the sky, yet it seemed as if every shape were moving with malignant intent, threatening his very existence. He, too, felt beyond sleep, but as the older men one-by-one found comfortable places to rest, he followed suit.

It was still dark two hours later when the officers roused the troops. Across the valley on the next ridge, shadows had begun to move. The Romans were massing.

"The gods are with us!" the officers cried, and everyone stumbled into his pre-assigned position. Up and down the line, warriors whooped and yelled. Soon the whole camp was shouting and calling to the gods of the Celtic realm. The ensuing pandemonium made Taranis feel powerful. Invincible. He screamed the name of every god he could remember, crying out for power.

Then, from the dark woods at the edge of camp, deep voices began to chant, rising and falling in a bizarre, undulating tone, as if the heavens had opened and the gods were speaking. The Caledonian warriors fell silent as the chanting grew louder, and more insistent. Unearthly soprano voices joined the dirge and seemed to wrap around the deep monotonous chant. Then, as suddenly as it had begun, the chanting ceased, and one by one in the hush that followed, the magicians appeared from the woods, seeming to glide across the soil, the tops of their heads perfectly level. They were dressed in dark robes that fell to their feet, and hoods that shadowed their faces so no one could tell whether the Druid was a woman or man.

The warriors watched in reverent fear as the Druids circled smoothly, floating above the ground in eerie silence. It was said that Druid priests possessed magical powers and could call the winds to carry them from one place to another. They could beckon powerful storms, or lightning to strike their enemies. They could even change into animal forms and often could foretell the future.

The first shafts of light shimmered on the horizon as the Druids circled and raised their hands to the gods, some twenty yards in front of the Celtic ranks. They began moaning and swaying as the circle closed in on itself, their sighs growing louder and louder, almost to a wail. Then suddenly the tips of their fingers burst into flame.

The warriors gaped at the out-stretched flaming hands, as they flickered and smoked and died. Then the warriors began to smile. "The gods are with us," someone cried. Madness swept the ranks. "Fill us with power!" they screamed as again they invoked the names of the gods. Some leaped in the air, calling upon the gods of the Druids to open the ground and destroy the enemy. Others were spinning, first one way and then the other, whooping and hollering.

By now the sun had risen and each army stood in plain view of the other. The Roman forces waited in silence, despite the frenzied scene that greeted them. They had no idea of Druid power, Taranis thought. The holy priests were gathered in a tight circle before their army, hands raised to the sky. They uttered fearful curses and screeched the names of gods.

One of the Druids, overcome by the spirits, bolted from the circle toward the Roman lines. Partway out he stopped, his body knotting into strange, contorted positions, as if seized by unseen beings. He jumped high into the air and threw himself on the ground, foaming at the mouth and hurling invectives at the confused onlookers. Druid women lit torches, pulled back their hoods and ran shrieking through the ranks of howling warriors, their yellow hair flowing behind, their painted faces making them look like gods from hell.

Another Druid stepped out from the circle and limped slowly toward a flat outcropping of rock. When he mounted the ledge, the

Druids below ceased their movements and grew quiet. He threw back his hood and clasped his hands in front as though in prayer, his face oddly jackal-like in appearance. Power radiated from him as he stood in silence, the wind beating on the bottom of his robe.

"I am Divicos, the Druid," he said, lifting his chin, "giver of life ... and death."

His voice was scratchy and shrill. "Today, one of you will stand in the presence of Toutorix as a god." He paused, allowing his words to have their effect. His colorless eyes swept the ranks; his mouth twisted.

The warriors held their collective breath.

"Last night I heard voices calling to me from the forest. I journeyed deep into the woods, deeper than I have ever gone before. Whether I was in my body or out of my body, I do not know, but as I stood by a thick copse of twisted trees, I encountered an apparition that made me think I was going mad. The ground burst into flame; the dirt, the sand, even the lakes burned with raging fury. The torrent of fire engulfed everything except an oak tree which I climbed until I reached the top, and I found a doorway ... a moss-covered doorway to the heavenly realm."

He paused again. "Brothers, I walked with the gods. And the things I saw—the rich forests, torrents of water cascading off mountainsides—you cannot conceive. But I will tell you this: As I stood in the eternal forest, I was so overwhelmed by its beauty that I begged to stay. They sent me back. I am an old man but they sent me back. I, Divicos, leader of the Druids, am not yet worthy to tread the hills and vales of the gods." He shook his head. "When I climbed down that oak, grief overwhelmed me, but to my joy, the forest around me suddenly came alive with blissful spirits—beyond anything I had ever experienced. The night air was cool and sweet, and the lakes glistened like ice in the moonlight."

The warriors stood motionless, eyes fixed on the Druid leader.

"Do you understand?" he shrieked. "Today, this very day, some here will lie in the cool of the eternal forest! Your eyes will open in wonder and you will gaze in disbelief, as did I, at the mysteries of the gods. And when your deepest yearnings have been filled, the gods will fuse your indestructible soul into another earthly body and you will rise anew. Imagine! Restored to a life beyond dreams if ..." he raised his hands, "if you prove faithful in battle."

He groaned. "Ohhh, that I could be with you ...." His voice trailed off and he mumbled the name of Toutorix. "And one of you," he said, pointing a trembling finger, "is not a warrior of the Caledonian army. You are ... you are ...." He hid his face. "I cannot say it. My mouth is wax. But I must!" He turned back; his vacant eyes narrowed as he surveyed the solemn, upturned faces of the warriors. "You are the son of Toutorix! A god in our midst!"

The soldiers stirred and looked at each other. Divicos threw back his head and closed his eyes. *"Sunabubaluk ansenek deidi alongsung amini,"* he chanted in some long-forgotten language. Other Druids joined their voices with his, their bodies swaying, their hands in the air. "The gods are with us," Divicos said, his voice rising above the sacred chant. "I feel the presence of Toutorix ... he yearns for his son. Step forward, god among men. Reveal yourself to us. Close your eyes to the darkness of this world and rise anew in celestial light. Listen to the voice of Toutorix calling you. Step forward and tell us your name. We will wait."

The silence weighed as the warriors stood awkwardly in their ranks. No one moved or looked around.

"Speak to us, son of Toutorix," the old priest intoned. "Reveal yourself. We will wait."

The wind sighed in the far reaches of the trees.

"This is your hour, son of Toutorix," Divicos said in the stillness. "For this moment you were born."

"I am Uerix," a voice cried from the back ranks. A young warrior wearing nothing but a loincloth strode through the men, who parted immediately. His face was strong and proud looking as he mounted the rock.

Divicos bowed low before him. "You will die to this life and rise a god," he said loudly for all to hear. "These unworthy men and women who stand before you are your servants ... as am I." He bowed again. "We do not fear battle because your father, Toutorix, has come to our rescue. Your blood will atone for our weaknesses."

"I always knew deep within me that I was a god," the boy said. "I lay aside my life willingly for these comrades I once embraced as brothers."

The magician's tight little mouth smiled as he offered him a small cake of sacred mushrooms, and wine to wash it down, a sacramental meal that would blur his senses to this world, and prepare him for the glory of the next. Beside him, Druids were busy wedging poles into crevices in the rock, binding the wrists of the god, and hoisting his hands up with a long rope. With this completed, they bowed to him and joined the nearby circle of Druids.

Divicos produced a thin, bone-handled knife from under his robe. He held it high and chanted, the other Druids joining him, though his voice soared in a high-pitched wail above them all: "Majesty and splendor and victory and power are yours Toutorix, good of the forest, most ancient of gods, lord of all." He turned to the youth who was half grinning and gazing at the sky, his senses now completely dulled, as if he were already participating in the next life. "I return you to your father," Divicos said. "May Toutorix be pleased." He thrust the knife into the boy's stomach, jerked it upwards, and stepped back.

With bowed head the old man waited as the sacrifice shuddered and groaned, until finally it breathed out its spirit. He approached the youth's body, still twisting slowly on the rope, and extracted his knife. He wiped it on a ceremonial cloth and shouted, "The gods are with us." A murmur of approval swept the ranks.

On the right wing, standing with the bowmen, Taranis wondered about what he had seen. It wasn't so much his father's caution, "Trust the gods, but watch the magicians," that troubled him. It was the boy from the valley who claimed to be a god. Taranis had played and hunted with him. Was he really the son of Toutorix? It hardly seemed possible. He was no different from anyone else—actually duller than most. Maybe he got carried away and thought he was a god. But wouldn't a magician know the spirit of truth and falsehood?

Taranis glanced at Bronix for a clue. He was standing in front of the warriors, hands leaning on the hilt of his great sword, which was planted in the ground. One of the commanders whispered something to him and Bronix nodded. His face was expressionless. If he had an opinion on the Druids, he kept it to himself.

The magician was still talking. Other Druids had cut the boy down and out of respect, severed his head from his body and placed it in a golden bowl. Later it would be given a station of honor in a Druid sacred grove.

"I am your true leader," the Druid was saying. "I do not lead you into battle in the manner of Bronix, but my power goes before you like a flaming sword." He closed his eyes again and raised his hands. "My power is an ancient power—"

Divicos jerked in shock. Trumpets rocked the hills. The Romans had completed their troop movements and were prepared for battle. "The evil ones must die!" Divicos screamed, raising a trembling fist in the air. "They shall melt like wax in the hot sun. Their blood shall flow like a river and their flesh shall rot on their bones." He clawed the air. "May all our enemies burn in pain. Prepare yourselves! Hurry! Bring the chariots—"

Like a cat, Bronix bounded onto the rock. "Thank you, thank you, great leader of the Druids," he boomed. "We are truly ready to meet our enemies." He raised his sword above his head. "The gods are with us." The warriors roared their approval. Bronix motioned to one of his commanders, who escorted Divicos back to the Druids.

"Fellow Caledonians, do not fear. The enemy will not attack yet. Look at them. They are weak ... like children. Each of you has the strength of two of their soldiers. They think they are ready to do battle, but-I-know-these-Romans." The men howled and shrieked in high-pitched voices. "One Caledonian can change the plans of the whole Roman army. One Caledonian," he thundered above the cheers of his recruits, "can strike fear in the hearts of every man standing over there. Prepare for battle. We will see how disciplined they are."

Bronix stepped from the rock, spoke to his commanders, and started down the hill toward the Romans. Immediately, the commanders signaled the charioteers to form a single line in front of the warriors, and for Uryen to move both wings of his archers out at forty-five degrees from the line to protect the flanks.

Bronix was still striding down the hill toward the Roman lines. He was now well beyond where the Druid priest had dared to go, more than a third of the way toward the legionaries on the other ridge, and showing no signs of stopping. With Bronix so far from Caledonian lines, many warriors had grown decidedly uncomfortable, glancing at each other, mumbling prayers, and calling out encouragement.

Taranis inspected the enemy soldiers across the valley. Less than two thousand, he guessed. Fewer than expected. They probably had another five hundred protecting their temporary fort. A separate army of German mercenaries stood in front of the legionary ranks, auxiliary soldiers, who looked much like his own Celtic kinsmen—blond, bare from the waist up and grouped in no particular order. They carried spears, swords and oval shields.

Behind the mass of Germans, the Roman legionaries stood in well-defined rows, rows that were composed of scores of tight little boxes. Taranis had seen them march in rows before and had heard they fought in these formations, but it was surprising, nonetheless. It seemed so constricting. The soldiers themselves dressed in red woolen tunics with breeches extending to mid-calf. Heavy armor protected their bodies, gleaming iron strips that encircled their torsos, and cascaded off their shoulders. They wore smooth, iron helmets with a knob on top and a sloping neckpiece at the back. Hinged cheek-plates, tied under the chin, shielded the sides of their faces. All except the cavalry carried huge, oblong shields. Each soldier was armed with a short sword, a dagger and two spears. At the rear of each box sat mounted officers with tall, horsehair command crests rising from their helmets. They had no chariots, but instead used cavalry to protect their wings, the same horse soldiers Uryen had warned about.

Bronix was now more than halfway to the Romans, and still striding briskly. The lone figure had obviously captured their attention: the Germans were turning and whispering to each other, and even the Romans craned their heads for a better view.

Bronix stopped. He planted his sword in the dirt and rested his shield. He was closer to the Roman lines than his own.

"I am Bronix of Alauna." His voice reverberated through the valley. "Do you remember Alauna, Romans? I have a hundred legionary heads tied on the fence around my farm. They are only skulls now—the ravens like Roman brains."

He paused to repeat his phrases in halting Latin, but there was no need. The Germans were already translating his words, and by the slight movements of the legionary helmets, it was clear the Romans themselves understood what Bronix was saying.

"Where is Urbicus, your leader at Alauna? I saw only the back of him—running south to build his Wall." The Caledonian warriors hooted and whooped. "You made a mistake coming here. We are the barbarians behind the Wall. And today you will find out how barbaric we can be." His voice sounded deep and menacing.

"But why should you die? Send out a man—I will fight him here on the moor. If I lose, we will lay down our arms and become servants of the Empire. If you lose, you must withdraw your soldiers and leave us in peace. Who will come down to fight me?"

He paused.

The wind breathed softly in the stillness. "There must be one Roman without fear."

Another pause.

"No one? All cowards? Surely there is someone. Send down two—no, three men. Three centurions! I will fight three centurions! That's fair. Who will come?"

Taranis felt proud to be a Celtic warrior of Caledonia. He cheered and hooted as loudly as anyone on the hill. Even Lon had perked up. The Romans looked troubled as Bronix strutted back and forth, shouting his challenges. If the situation weren't so serious, it would have been comic. Bronix was right; he could stop a whole army in its tracks. The Romans had been poised to attack and now they stood there listening, and growing anxious.

"Am I too big? Does that frighten you—my size? We are all this big," he shouted, gesturing toward the Caledonians who began leaping and screaming in voices designed to chill the hearts of the bravest adversaries.

"Is it my sword?" He ripped his immense blade from the ground and held it up for all the Romans to see. "I will not use my sword," he said, and he threw it dramatically behind him. "I will use my knife ... it is about the size of your puny swords." He folded his arms across his massive chest. "Maybe a woman ... maybe some brave Roman will fight a Celtic woman. Muguin! Step out and let them see you." Muguin stepped out. She was a sturdy woman, as tall as any man around her.

"Yes, she's big too." Laughter and scorn filled the valley as the Caledonian tribesmen mocked the Romans. "Sorry we have no children today," Bronix hollered, "just big, nasty warriors."

He walked over to a jagged protrusion of rock and sat down in the otherwise empty valley. "Well, I intend to stay right here, and the first man who gets here dies."

Taranis saw the movement out of the corner of his eye, Roman cavalry bolting across the grass toward Bronix, and his breath caught in his throat. Everywhere Caledonian commanders were flashing signals to their chariots that abruptly lurched forward and thundered down the hill. Taranis drew an arrow. He bit his lip. It had begun.

5

Taranis's heart pounded. Gone was the wind soughing in the valley, and the lone voice of Bronix calling out his challenges. Now the earth erupted with the rumble of chariots and the screams of desperate men.

Taranis had a sinking feeling in his stomach. His arms and legs felt like bloated flesh. Somewhere in the ranks, a warrior lost control and the air filled with the odor of human excrement. Taranis prayed for courage. It's fear, just fear, he kept saying to himself. Must contain it. In a distant part of his mind, it struck him as odd that he could so want war, and yet be saturated with fear. Four years he had waited to avenge his father, and now his palms were sweating, his knees weak. He felt ashamed. His father had been a strong man, courageous on the battlefield, and at the end when they pushed him onto that wooden platform, he refused to bend before the Roman enemy. He even managed a last smile for his children. Taranis gritted his teeth. He was now a Caledonian warrior, like his father, and no longer would he play the soft-eyed cow.

"Ohhh!" Lon groaned, his hands clasping around his middle. "Ohhh, I feel sick, I can't move ...."

He looked sick. His face was ashen, his body hunched and trembling. Taranis tried to tell Lon that everyone was afraid. He clapped him on his back; he shook him, but nothing could dislodge his stupor of fear.

"Warriors! Get back into position!" Uryen's voice was clear and threatening, his spent look suddenly gone.

"He's sick," Taranis said.

"Get back into position!"

Taranis moved back.

"Sick, is it?" Uryen drew an arrow. He slipped it in his bow and leveled it at Lon. "Now you listen to me, boy. We have no time for nonsense. Either stand up and fight, or die right here."

Lon straightened instantly.

The chariots bounced down the hill, stirring up billows of dust. Crowds of Celtic warriors pushed forward into the dirty swirls, but were stopped abruptly by the commanders at the brow of the hill. Uryen beckoned his archers to follow him as he descended along the edge of the trees, until they could see the valley yawning below. On the other side, the front wall of German mercenaries erupted in war cries. They sprinted down their side of the valley, shouting as they came. Behind them the gray-clad soldiers of Rome remained tightly grouped in their little boxes, as still as death. Only the leather straps hanging from their standards flapped in the breeze.

Alone on the valley floor, Bronix waited as the Scythian archers rushed toward him. Midway they let go a rainstorm of arrows, never breaking stride. Ten yards farther and arrows again burst forward. And again. Taranis tensed on seeing their fluid movements. They could ride and shoot as well as any stationary archer he had ever seen. As fast as they loosed an arrow, another appeared in hand, aimed and ready to go.

On each volley, Bronix yanked his large shield in front of his equally large body and waited for the arrows to strike. A dozen bounced off his shield; the rest smacked into the nearby ground. The horsemen were now two thirds of the way to the Celt. Abruptly they turned at a right angle to their lines and fired another volley of arrows over their shoulders as they sped away. Again, Bronix scrunched up to protect himself but this time a missile caught him in the left shoulder armor joint. Taranis saw him reach for the rock as he lost his balance. A hush fell on the Caledonians as collectively they held their breath.

The Scythians saw him stumble as well. Two broke formation, turned, and lashed their horses toward the wounded Celt. Bronix jerked to his feet, the arrow still protruding from his shoulder. He slid his shield to the ground, resting it between his leg and the rock. Reaching across his tunic he grasped the arrow, grimaced, and ripped it from his body.

The Caledonians began to breathe again. Some were smiling, some laughing in admiration. Bronix was indestructible. Nobody would ever kill him.

The two archers were again releasing arrows. Bronix hit the ground as the missiles tore through the spot 'where he had been standing. He rose slowly and rested his shield on the rock. Behind him on the grass lay his sword, but he made no attempt to retrieve it, or even to draw his dagger. He stood quietly, studying the riders as they thundered toward him, their bows bent with arrows. They approached on either side of the rock. Seeing no weapon, they slowed and came in close, watching the big Celt warily. Bronix held his shield high for protection but exposed his left side to the more distant horseman. The Scythian smiled; he loosed his arrow. Bronix swung the shield into the path of the missile, whirled back and drove the shield's edge into the other archer's neck. The man dropped from his horse like a sack of dirt, his arrow spinning into the air. Then Bronix lunged at the stunned remaining archer, who by now had passed the rock. He caught him by the back of his tunic and flung him to the ground, slamming his head into the jagged base of the stone. Neither man moved. They lay crumpled, like jointless dolls.

Bronix swept his eyes around, seeing the German mercenaries pouring onto the flat bottom of the valley. He bolted toward his lines, scooping up his sword as he went, his giant horns bobbing and rolling as he pounded heavily across the thick grass. The enraged Germans bounded after him. Everyone wanted the glory of striking down the arrogant Celt, as Bronix had perceived they would.

The great Caledonian soon grew tired; his huge body was not made for sprinting. He had accomplished his task—he had drawn the enemy to the center, out of position. The Germans were so intent on the strutting warrior that their wings had become dangerously thin.

And they lacked support. The left wing Scythian horsemen were in disarray and the Roman officers refused to use their right wing cavalry until the left had regrouped. The Germans were on their own. Charging down on Bronix had been a mistake.

Taranis watched the big man struggling to keep ahead of the pursuing Germans. He had slowed considerably. His mouth hung open, gulping air, and his red mustache swayed across his face as he strained forward. It was hard to measure how important Bronix was to the Caledonian Celts. He alone had the courage to stand before the entire Roman army. If he were to die .... Taranis put it out of his mind ... Bronix would not die. The gods would prevent it.

The Germans had closed to less than thirty yards by the time the chariots swept by. Bronix had gone too far, been too bold. But the chariots were magnificent. They smashed through the clusters of German warriors and scattered them like birds in a field. The pounding hooves and erratic movements of the chariots unnerved the enemy, who leaped sideways to avoid being trampled. The effect was impressive. The German advance was halted immediately, and Bronix completed the remaining distance at a trot. With their leader safe, the chariot drivers whipped their carts around and headed for the wings.

The Germans regrouped, howling in wounded rage. Bronix had made them look like fools. Their prey had taunted them, and he had escaped. Like bees from a torn hive they gathered, driving straight toward the Caledonian center, where Bronix now stood. A mighty roar filled the valley as the two lines clashed. The Germans unleashed their spears and clubbed wildly with their swords. So violent was their attack, and so concentrated was their force at the center, that the Celts immediately fell back. Bronix made no attempt to hold the Celtic middle but kept retreating in the face of enemy pressure.

On the wings, the Celts were doing better. With fewer Germans, the chariots dominated both extremes of the line. Their grinding wheels ripped through the dry grass, whipping up clouds of dust, making it impossible to see. Back and forth they raced through the scattered enemy lines, spewing out rocks and blowing horns. The dark shape of a chariot looming out of the dust sent the Germans into panic. They had no defense against the blue-painted warriors perched high on the wooden tongues between the horses. The Caledonian warriors hurled rocks with their slings and jabbed rapidly with their spears as the chariots spun around in tight circles.

At the center, Bronix and his warriors were still falling back. The Germans seized the moment and plunged forward to crack the Celtic middle. Sporadic cheering broke out in the Roman ranks. The Germans were doing more than expected—perhaps they would cut the Celtic army in half. The Roman forces advanced slowly to keep pace with the charging Germans, but as the distance between them grew, they stopped. Their mercenaries were moving too fast.

"Now! Now! Now!" Bronix hollered, his voice all but lost in the clamor. Others took up the refrain as the signal spread throughout the Caledonian army.

At both ends of the line, chariots halted their twisting patterns and swept around the main body of German soldiers now hopelessly clumped in the center. The Celtic warriors followed on foot, pausing only to cut down the few remaining confused Germans. When the chariots from either wing completed their encirclement, the warriors leapt from their vehicles, hurling spears and drawing swords. The wild-haired drivers swung around sharply, almost overturning their carts as they lashed their horses toward safety at the side, and waited for a signal to return.

The Romans had hoped to jolt the Celts by sending down their German mercenaries—big men who fought with the same reckless, charging style as the Celts. They had expected a brief, sharp confrontation between the Germans and Celts, and then a quick withdrawal of their lightly armed mercenaries. They were jubilant when the Celtic middle continually dropped back in face of the German assault. But then the chariots began their sweep and the cheering stopped. Now the Germans were surrounded, and the Celts were hacking them mercilessly with their heavy swords.

Bronix had tricked them.

Taranis watched the churning middle of the battle, and the dust drifting toward him. He could still see the giant form of Bronix swinging his sword as if he were clearing brush. Taranis's archery wing had been involved minimally. They fired on the Germans, but with so rapid an assault, the archers had little to shoot at. Now targets were everywhere, squirting out from the center, fleeing in all directions. Taranis rubbed the grit from his eyes and leveled his bow at the terrified forms emerging from the dust. He didn't shoot at anyone in particular, didn't even see where his arrow went as it blended with the scores of others that smacked into the hapless Germans. They tumbled to the ground screaming and reaching out to their comrades, who mostly stumbled on by, switching directions in the hope of finding sanctuary. Some made it to the Roman lines, expecting protection, but the legionaries leveled their spears and drove them to the edges of the field. The Roman officers refused to allow defeated soldiers to mix with fresh troops.

The field cleared. The Germans who escaped grouped at the ends of the Roman line. Now the centurions began calling out orders, and it looked as if the Roman heavy infantry would strike. Everywhere the Celtic commanders were scurrying, trying to restore order to the crowds of howling warriors who had tasted blood.

"Caledonians!" Bronix shouted. He was standing in front of the milling warriors with his hands cupped to project his voice. "The battle has hardly begun. Get back into position. Listen to your commanders."

The swordsmen were finding it hard to listen to anyone. They clanged their swords on their shields and leapt into the air. Victory was sweet, and proving disruptive. The chariot drivers were more restrained. They collected their warriors and headed for the wings near the archers, who had maintained strict group discipline.

Troubled by the continued disarray, the commanders pushed the swordsmen into position, slapping them briskly with the flats of their swords and jamming them with the ends of their shields. Finally, the Caledonians spread out sufficiently to face the Romans.

They need not have rushed. The Romans seemed to have changed their minds about attacking. Positioned slightly below the rim of the valley, they stood there—three horizontal lines, one behind the other, each several men deep. The lines were spaced fifty yards from each other. Behind the first stood two units of reserve soldiers to plug holes that might develop, or to attack should a weakness appear. Behind the second line, Taranis could see eight or ten Scorpions, the mobile, ballistic machines whose foot-long arrows killed at three hundred yards. The lines themselves had gaps at regular intervals, giving the impression of many armies within an army. As Taranis watched, litter carriers emerged from the gaps. They collected the wounded Germans and stacked the dead on a dozen hand-pulled carts. The Celts waited. They always allowed their enemies to gather their dead.

Lon was overjoyed at the turn of events. The archers had hardly been involved, and now the battle was over. "I knew it!" he shouted above the persistent banging of shields. "They've had enough! They are taking their dead and running!"

Taranis squinted in disbelief as the Romans padded across the field, retrieving their fallen allies. The shield banging subsided and the Celts grew quiet. The entire Celtic army had come to the same conclusion—the Romans were withdrawing. Taranis felt pulled in opposite directions, both robbed and relieved at the same time. He had wanted a full-scale battle, but he was glad. He couldn't deny it— down deep he was glad they were leaving—he wasn't as brave as he had hoped. Yet, somehow he still couldn't believe they would leave.

When the carts had completed their grisly task, they turned and rolled quietly up the hill toward Roman lines, disappearing in the gaps between the blocks of soldiers. Again, the two armies stared at each other across an empty valley.

A deep stillness fell upon the Celts as the Roman bugles began calling to each other. Then silence. For over a minute the Celts gazed at the cold, gray, box-like formations. It was as if the Romans didn't know how to leave. Their bugles resumed, this time followed by a single, piercing trumpet sounding the advance. Abruptly they moved forward, marching lock step with others in their boxes. Even the Scythian horsemen on the wings maintained a rigid formation.

The Romans were coming.

6

Lon looked at Taranis, his face strained with fear.

"The battle is ours," Taranis said. "We have Bronix."

Their attention was drawn by the sound of iron-plated men treading down toward the valley floor. In the back of the Roman ranks Taranis could hear the rhythmical tapping of a horn, and then a blast of bugles. The gray boxes stopped a hundred paces out. More bugles. The gaps in the front ranks slammed shut, leaving a wall of soldiers, spaced six feet apart. They stood there, motionless. Only the mounted officers at the back shifted positions, pointing, shouting orders. They seemed intent on giving the Celts a long, sobering view of the army that ruled the world.

How strange they were, these short, olive-skinned men with their huge shields and needle-topped spears. Some had beards, some clean-shaven, but yet they all looked alike. They seemed unusually calm, as though bred for war. No cries rose from the ranks—no howling—only the occasional centurion's shout, and the eerie sounds of bugle calls.

The soldiers stood erect, legs astride, their spears tilted away from their bodies and their shields resting on the ground. It seemed unnatural for soldiers to be so lifeless, with no movements, save for the slight turning of their burnished helmets, which gleamed like a thousand flashing suns.

"They look like gods," Lon whispered.

"They are not gods," Taranis said emphatically—as much for his benefit as for Lon's. "They're no different from us. See the

Germans?" He gestured with his bow toward the tattered remains of
blond mercenaries huddled at the edge of the field. "They are as big
as we are, and look at them now."

Taranis turned away from Lon and eyed the mass of gray. They
were different from the Germans, he had to admit. Soldiers of the
Empire—and he forced a breath into his lungs to calm himself.

"Listen to me!" Bronix shouted. "These Roman grasshoppers
want to fight." He motioned toward the enemy. "Remember why
we're here. We are Caledonians. This is Caledonian land. We do not
allow Romans, or their paid mercenaries, or anyone else, to trample
our land. So steady your minds. The gods are with us."

A great cheer rose from the Celtic warriors and the shield banging
started again. Commanders everywhere whipped their sectors into a
frenzy. War cries intensified until even Taranis felt a blood lust
gripping his soul. The more impulsive pushed forward but their
leaders held them back; the chariots needed to clear the enemy
cavalry.

Then they came, from both wings, the Scythian cavalry pounding
across the turf. A few archers readied their bows, but at such a great
distance, Uryen waved them off. This was a job for the chariots.
Taranis watched the warriors, standing tall in their carts, rumble out
to meet the enemy cavalry. How glorious to be among them! They
weaved their patterns and hurled their spears; they balanced from the
tongues between the chariots and the horses, slashing at the Scythians.

But the speed and courage of the charioteers were no match for
quick-turning horsemen. Through the dust-filled air, Taranis could
see the Scythians darting in and out of the slower horse-drawn
vehicles. Dozens of drivers hung lifeless over the railings of their
chariots—victims of Scythian arrows and quick thrusts from lancers
who thundered by. Runaway chariots and riderless horses added to
the confusion as they wheeled about in terror and crashed, foam-
mouthed, into each other. The remaining chariot drivers saw the
futility of continuing and fled the field with the Scythians racing after
them.

Silence descended again on the valley, as the sounds of hooves
and chariot wheels grew more distant. Taranis watched the dust drift

to the ground and the rows of Roman soldiers come into focus. His father was right, the day of the chariot was over.

Then, like shadows flying over the grass, reserve Scythian horsemen streaked through the dust toward the Caledonians. The Romans had held back a third of their cavalry, while the Celtic chariots had been expended.

"Get ready!" Uryen shouted. "Hit the front horsemen—shoot before they turn—before they move out of range."

The horsemen drove their mounts straight toward the swordsmen, releasing arrows as they came. When Celtic arrows struck several riders, they abruptly turned right and sped along the Celtic front, all the while shooting arrows. Then, anticipating the other wing of archers, they pulled their mounts around and headed for the safety of the Roman lines.

Along the edges, the Roman cavalry were trying to herd the Celts together. "Take out the lancers!" Uryen yelled. He brought his bow around smoothly and let an arrow soar, never pausing to aim. Sixty yards distant, a lancer slumped in his saddle. Clouds of arrows followed, darkening the sky, and lancers at less ambitious ranges began dropping from their horses. But the missiles also struck friendly warriors and many waved their swords to draw attention. Uryen ignored them, and hollered at his archers to keep shooting. Only when the Scythians retreated to their usual defensive role on the wings did he wave signal an end.

Trumpets sounded.

Taranis shot a glance at the main body of the Roman army, who were already in motion. They moved rapidly toward the Celts at double march time. Bronix and scores of commanders stood in front of their frenzied swordsmen, holding them back, waiting for the opportune moment to attack. With the morning sun in Roman eyes, the Caledonians had a sizable advantage; they didn't want to squander it by charging uphill.

The legionaries were now in range, and Taranis and the other archers loosed their arrows at the advancing gray mass. The front line of Romans turned their shields forty-five degrees to protect their faces, making it look as if a wall of steel had rotated into position.

Those in the back ranks lifted their shields over their heads. Nothing remained exposed except the bottoms of their legs. The whole formation looked like a bizarre giant tortoise, lumbering across the field toward them.

The commanders could no longer control the tribesmen. Like a heave of water, they burst across the field toward the oncoming wall of Romans.

"Move! Move!" Uryen called, his thin face fierce and hard. "Stay with me, and keep shooting." He continued screaming instructions over his shoulder as he bounded forward, but his voice was lost in the roar of charging armies. Taranis was amazed at how quickly he could move and he imagined what a young Uryen must have been like. "Shoot faster!" Taranis heard him shouting. "Do not aim, shoot!"

The storm of arrows was forcing the Romans to maintain their tortoise shell formation, which meant blind marching. But they kept coming, at the same double-time pace. Here and there Taranis saw arrows strike unprotected legs, or bounce and slip sideways through the shields. Yet the barrage of missiles did nothing to disrupt the fast march. Their tortoise shell protected them.

Now Scythian arrows fell in the Caledonian ranks, and Scorpion bolts. Without an organized shield protection and heavy armor covering their bodies, swordsmen throughout the ranks were being struck by incoming arrows. In front of him, Taranis saw an archer topple like a man fainting from too much sun.

Uryen had slowed. He was yelling something again, something about shields. Taranis scrutinized the enemy ranks, hoping to discover what he was supposed to do. He could see that the second line of legionaries had increased their speed and were narrowing the gap between them and the first. Now both Roman lines broke into a run as they neared the Celts. The screams and shouts of men were so loud it was impossible to hear Uryen, though he was less than thirty paces away. Then Taranis understood. The Romans were about to lower their shields to throw their spears. He felt foolish. This, he remembered, was a crucial moment for the archers. He halted with the others and took aim.

A piercing trumpet call ripped the air. The legionaries stopped abruptly, their shields swinging open. Thousands of heavy, black javelins flooded the sky as the soldiers in the two lines released both their spears in rapid succession. It was over in an instant, and the second line dropped back again, but during that moment, Taranis loosed five arrows at the vulnerable Romans. All along the line, particularly near the archery wings, legionaries lay dead or wounded. Yet, for every slain soldier, another stepped forward to maintain the tidy appearance of the front wall.

With so many spears falling from the sky, the Caledonian front looked anything but tidy; it looked ragged and chaotic. The charging tribesmen lifted their shields to deflect the deadly missiles. But the Imperial army had designed their needle-topped javelins to pierce shields, and the soft iron shafts to bend on contact. This proved disastrous for the Caledonians. They were left holding heavy, unmanageable shields weighted with bent shafts that dragged in the dirt. Many cast their shields to the ground, preferring to fight with no protection than to fight with such a burdensome load.

The legionaries were moving again. They surged forward, drew their swords and shouted in thunderous voices the single word, "Rome!" Their expressionless faces sprang to life as they bolted toward the Celts and crashed into them with a noise that shook the valley.

Uryen directed his archers away from the conflict and toward the back of the Caledonian ranks. They hiked two thirds of the way up the hill and listened to Uryen's instructions. "The gods are with us," he breathed, as the archers gathered around him. "They guided our arrows, steadied our hands." He paused and looked in Lon's direction. "Every one of you has reason to be proud. Now it is up to the gods—and our swordsmen."

Taranis was content; he had fought well. Lon had never left Taranis's side, and was obviously pleased with himself. His chest swelled with pride on hearing Uryen's compliment. After Uryen had humiliated Lon in front of the other archers, he deserved some mention. Taranis glanced over Uryen's shoulder at the baggage carts near the top of the hill. They hadn't moved, and he could see the silhouette of Eston busily filling baskets with arrows.

When Uryen had finished talking, Lon followed Taranis to a small plateau near the trees, a spot that provided a clear view of the confrontation below. The Caledonian warriors outnumbered the Romans by almost a thousand, and were fighting with great zeal. Despite the loss of so many shields, and the powerful attack of the enemy, Caledonia was doing well.

Bronix ignored his earlier wound and cleared a huge hole in the Roman center. The centurions continually filled the breach with fresh troops from the reserves, but the quick-lunging Romans were no match for Bronix. With one sweep of his oversized sword, he blasted Roman shields from their hands. No one could approach the giant for fear of his wheeling sword, and the strewn bodies of Bronix's enemies were proof of his speed and power.

Elsewhere the Caledonians fought valiantly, throwing themselves at the Romans and beating them back with fearless determination.

Taranis refused to believe that the Roman method of war had anything to commend it. Their armored bodies protected them from glancing blows, necessary for soldiers who always seemed to be diving for the dirt and jabbing their swords upward. The larger Celts attacked straight on, never cringing before the enemy. Their well-muscled bodies were clearly superior to the short, squat Romans, who continually ducked and dodged like frightened sheep. But the pig-like lunges across the ground had a measure of success. They were able to drive their swords upward, under the defenses of the tribesmen.

Twenty minutes of hard fighting passed.

"What are they doing?" Lon asked.

"I don't know," Taranis said as he watched the Roman second line marching briskly toward the first. "Maybe they are doubling their power at the front ... they have not been able to move us an inch."

"And Bronix has crushed their middle by himself." Lon wore a smile of satisfaction.

The second line continued toward the back ranks of the first, threading its way forward until it reached the front. Then the whole first line turned, it seemed, all at once, and filed back to reform the second line.

Now Taranis understood. The Romans had brought fresh troops to the front.

The new legionaries appeared to have been given a plan of assault. Behind their right wing, troops were massing for some kind of push. But any plan would have to contend with Bronix and his control of the center. The Romans seemed to have no way of solving their problem, as the center grew more dangerous for them by the moment. Bronix was charging the reinforcements with abandon, bellowing and whirling his sword, crushing anyone within reach. "Welcome to the battle!" he seemed to be saying, and already his new adversaries were scrambling to keep their distance.

Those who didn't, died.

Taranis surveyed the line. It looked different. On the Roman left, the enemy fought defensively, refusing to give ground, but also refusing to attack. Those on the other wing selected weak spots and drove hard, thrusting small groups, like tiny peninsulas, deep into the Celtic lines. Into these, the Romans funneled more and more troops who pushed and shoved with their shields until the peninsulas expanded to large wedges. The Celts now found themselves jammed together between the wedges, making their long swords useless against short, quick thrusts—and many no longer had shields. The Roman right wing looked like jagged teeth chewing into the heart of the Celtic army.

Above the roar of battle, Taranis heard the trumpets again. Three blasts. He watched as the ends of the wedges pushed toward each other, surrounding and annihilating the trapped Caledonians. Taranis stared in shock. The traps closed rapidly and seemed to eat the fifteen to twenty men they encircled. Now the second line was moving forward, and this time it stayed in support of the first, leaving only the third as reserve.   The Romans wanted added strength for their maneuver.

Repeatedly, the jagged teeth of the Roman right wing thrust forward, like a mouth grinding into the Caledonian warriors, devouring them as it went.

At the center, Bronix had halted his drive through the Roman middle.   He shouted instructions to nearby commanders, pointing with his sword.   They relayed his messages, and warriors shifted to shore up the danger zones and offset the Roman strategy.

Satisfied, Bronix turned to resume his assault on the Roman center.   But the legionaries suddenly stepped aside, as if performing a parade movement.   In front of Bronix they had opened a corridor leading to the bare field where the third and final line stood.   To break through!   That was what he had wanted.   He glanced to both sides, started forward, and then froze.   On the flat grass, not fifty yards beyond the end of the corridor, sat three field guns.

"Scorpions!" Lon shouted in Taranis's ear.

"I know," Taranis said, horrified.

Bronix jerked sideways.   His shield flashed across his body as he dove for the ground, but too late.   The Romans had sited their weapons, and the darts were hurtling through the air.   Two narrowly missed, shadows ripping over his shoulder into the ranks behind; the third sliced through his shield, slamming into his chest.   Taranis saw Bronix jolt backwards and then flop to the ground, the Scorpion bolt sticking out his back.

"Ohh!" a strangled sound escaped from Taranis's lips.   He turned away.   Bronix was down, slain by one of the Empire's cowardly weapons.   For thirty years his giant figure and massive sword had struck terror in the hearts of the enemy.   Hardly anyone could remember a time when Bronix had not led the Caledonians into battle. And now they were alone.

Clouds of dust appeared on the horizon; the Scythians had returned.   The ground shook as they approached full gallop, cutting around the rear of the Roman forces and along the Roman right wing. They concentrated on the Caledonians already battered by the wedge formation. Hundreds of arrows fell on the back ranks, creating confusion and fear.

"Bronix is dead!" a Roman shouted in the Celtic tongue. Then from everywhere the Romans began to shout, "Bronix is dead! The Celts are fleeing!"

Soon the tribesmen themselves began crying out, "Bronix! Where is Bronix?"

A great fear engulfed the Caledonians. Those in the rear broke first. They didn't run--not in the beginning. They dropped back, moving away like dogs slinking from their masters. More joined them. Then whole groups turned and ran. Those at the heart of the battle saw the movement and the folly of standing their ground. Desperately they looked for ways to retreat.

The commanders tried to forestall chaos. "Fall-back positions!" they screamed as horns acknowledged the retreat.

The Romans moved quickly. The third line surged forward, hurling their javelins and cutting through the defenses weakened by the confused retreat.

All along the Celtic front, the commanders stayed visible, trying to hearten their warriors while conducting an orderly withdrawal. But their high visibility proved disastrous. Many were trapped and killed in the first moments of the assault by the Roman third line. Panic gripped the Caledonians. The Romans were everywhere, thrusting savagely with their short swords. With few commanders left, withdrawal was impossible, and the once magnificent warriors turned and fled across the moor, pulling and clawing at each other in their escape from the pursuing legionaries. Many were trampled in the frenzied uphill flight toward the woods. With swords drawn, the cavalry plunged through the sea of fleeing Celts, butchering them from behind as they crowded and tripped over themselves.

Taranis was stunned. The whole field was in flight.

"Get out of here!" Uryen shouted. "It's over!"

Over! The words struck Taranis like a Scorpion bolt. How could it be over? How could their glorious army be so easily crushed? Bronix gone, commanders lying dead, warriors fleeing the enemy .... Had some hideous insanity escaped from the bowels of the earth and bewitched the minds of free men? Sweet victory had been in their hands, and then slipped through their fingers like sand. Now they must run like frightened rabbits.

7

"Go!" Uryen hollered at the few remaining archers still mesmerized by the spectacle below. "Go and don't stop! Keep your wits about you and the gods will preserve you!"

The desperate cries of dying men, and the smell of blood and sweat and dust, rose like vapors from hell, gripping Taranis like a vise. He tore himself away and looked up toward the baggage carts. Most of the men had grabbed the horses and fled. Three or four were struggling at the field's edge over a single, unclaimed mount.

"What's happening?" Taranis lamented. "We are fighting among ourselves."

He looked back at Lon, who still stared at the tribesmen scrambling to escape. Legionaries were hacking at their victims and thrusting short swords into their exposed backs.

"Time to leave," Taranis said.

"Yes," Lon said, his eyes huge. "The Romans will be up here soon."

"First, I have to find my brother. We still have time."

Lon swept his eyes over the baggage carts. "No one's there."

Taranis didn't respond. He sprinted up the hill.

"Wait. I'm coming with you." Lon ran after him.

"Head for the woods now. I can meet you later."

"I'm staying with you," he said, glancing over his shoulder at the chaos below.

Taranis continued up the hill with Lon close behind. His eyes scanned the carts where Eston had been stacking arrows, and then raked the line of abandoned vehicles. No one. Everyone had gone.

"He must have left with the others," Lon cried behind him, breathless.

Taranis inspected the line of carts. Not a sign of life.

"No one's here," Lon said, catching up to Taranis. "We need to go."

"Eston would not leave when he could see me standing down the hill."

"He might have been ordered to leave—"

"I'm going to look at that group of carts," Taranis said, ignoring Lon.

"If he were there, we would see him," Lon shouted after Taranis.

As Taranis neared, he could see piles of arrows in the wagons. Water still dripped from a cart whose barrels had been overturned in the haste to get away. But Eston was nowhere.

"They are halfway up the hill already!" Lon screamed. "Don't you understand? We have to go!"

"You go! I intend to check these carts first."

"There's no one here," Lon wailed, running down the line of carts, looking under and around each. Then he stopped.

"What is it?"

"Someone ... young ... he's dead."

Taranis stepped over the tongue of a wagon and raced along the grass to where the youth lay. It couldn't be Eston, not Eston. He rounded the side of the cart, and there twenty feet away in the grass lay his brother, face down and twisted to one side. As Lon turned him over, Eston's his arm flung outward, slapping heavily into the grass. His body rocked for a moment and then lay still.

Taranis gazed at the white face, the slack jaw. Down the front of his tunic were dark bloodstains. A smeared trail of red along the grass indicated he had crawled several yards before his world went dark. The wind picked up, swirling the grass around Eston's head, making it look as though invisible threads were tugging at the strips of green, pulling them this way, then that.

But Eston never moved.

Taranis drew closer. He dropped to his knees and moaned. A picture of his mother and sisters flashed through his mind. How could he tell them? Especially Neeve. He reached down to feel his brother's cheek. It was cold. Along the side of his head, an ugly wound opened to the skull. Someone must have hit him with a rock or sword to get the horses. Taranis wiped dirt from the wound. Blood oozed out into his hair. Taranis frowned. Odd, it was still bleeding. How could it be bleeding if he was dead? Taranis looked more closely at his brother. Was it his imagination, or did he have breath? He put his ear to Eston's chest. Life! Life in his breast! A weak but steady beat.

"He's not dead!" Taranis shouted. He tried to check the excitement welling up in him, lest some spirit find his joy presumptuous, and take Eston from him. He looked at Lon and said, "Help me get him up. I can carry him."

"Carry him!" Lon's face showed alarm. "We can't take him. We have to leave him here. The Romans won't hurt him ... not if they find him unconscious."

"The Romans kill everything," Taranis snarled. "Help me get him up."

Lon grudgingly did as he was told. Taranis switched his arrow pouch and bow to one side as they hefted Eston over his shoulder. He was much heavier than Taranis had expected, and it was impossible to move beyond a trot.

When they reached the trees, Taranis rested. They were near the place where the Druids had filed out chanting songs. The woods stretched for miles along the ridge and down to the valley, where it opened in a grassy expanse. Most of the warriors had fled into the lower portions of the forest. This meant the Romans would remain in the lower woods. Their idea of a successful battle, Taranis remembered his father saying, was to kill as many enemy warriors as they could. The legionaries were not interested in combing the forest merely to unearth a few stragglers. Taranis reasoned that if he moved quickly through the upper elevations, just below the ridge, he might with luck avoid all Roman contact.

They started through the forest, following the natural paths along the ridge. Often they heard screams from the lower woods, and the thrashing of panicked men; several times they even caught glimpses of distant warriors plunging through the forest, but always in the lower woods.

As they pressed on, the trees grew thicker and changed from white birch to dark spruce and pines. Ahead the trail opened up into a large clearing, a meadow that looked cool and inviting with its rich textures and shades of green, and Taranis longed to lie in the grass and rest

Lon eyed him nervously, "We've got to move faster," he said. "I can carry your brother ... at least for a time."

Taranis nodded. His back ached under the load. It was during the exchange that Taranis saw them—three legionaries pushing through the bush below the ridgeline at the other end of the meadow.

Taranis grabbed Lon's arm and motioned toward the soldiers.

"They haven't seen us," Taranis whispered. "Move to those bushes ... carefully."

Lon licked his lips. He spun around, forgetting Eston draped over his shoulder, and the sudden movement spilled them both on the ground.

The sound of twigs snapping echoed through the forest. Taranis dropped to the ground, craning his head to see the reaction of the Romans. Nothing. They seemed oblivious to the noise, and now Taranis could see why. At the side of the meadow lay a giant overhang, where Taranis might have hidden, had he come across it earlier. One soldier was approaching the rocky cliff while the other two concealed themselves behind trees at the sides.

Suddenly, two bare-chested Celts burst from their hiding place. They darted through the trees toward the lower slope of the forest, and then halted. A Roman, sword drawn, stepped from behind a large cedar. Taranis could see the tribesmen lacked swords, probably lost in their flight. They faced the Roman with knives only. Their heads jerked in terror as they looked for a place to run. They started toward the cave, but the legionary shifted to block the path. They turned in the opposite direction, but by now the other soldiers had joined the first.

One Caledonian looked familiar. Taranis gasped. It was Geir of Celynedd. A surge of heat flooded Taranis's body. What should he do? What could he do?

The Romans encircled the Celts. They made a game of it, shrieking in mock Celtic war cries and making fake charges. They dove forward, jabbing Geir and his friend with the points of their swords, just enough to make blood trickle from the wounds. The boys' terror seemed to fascinate the Romans and put a glow on their faces.

Taranis burned with fury. He could not hide in the bushes, or sit idly while Geir died. He drew an arrow and pictured the iron-tipped missile piercing the chest of one of those jackals.

"What are you doing?" Lon grabbed at Taranis's bow.

Taranis pushed him back.

"You can't hit them from here, they're too far. You'd just give us away."

"What do you want me to do, watch them die? I know one of them."

Lon fell silent.

The soldiers continued whooping and feinting thrusts at their victims. Taranis concentrated on one of the Romans, where the strips of armor fastened together. Even at this distance, his composite bow could pierce the man's armor, if it struck squarely. He took careful aim, held his breath, and then sighed. He lowered his bow and closed his eyes. The soldier's constant movements made accuracy impossible. Lon was right. Short of charging foolishly through the trees, he could do nothing.

The game was soon over. The Romans assumed a crouched position, moving deliberately. One dropped low as if to charge, then stopped. The soldier to his right burst forward, thrusting his sword through Geir's stomach. At the same time the Roman at the rear charged, driving his weapon into the back of his victim. Both fell to the ground. Geir writhed in pain, clutching his middle. Even from his distant hiding place, Taranis could hear the gurgling sounds. One of the soldiers scowled, and chopped his sword downward on Geir's face. He said something to the others and they all laughed.

Under cover of the brush, Taranis watched as they stalked away. He felt like a coward. How could he have hid in the bush and let Geir die? He should have done something other than hide. He glanced back at Lon, whose eyes were wide open, and staring in the direction of the departing Romans.

A movement caught Taranis's attention. Eston groaned and rolled his head. His eyes fluttered and his arms pawed the air. He grew louder, his voice rising in a babble. Taranis slid beside him and placed a hand over his mouth.

The Romans stopped. They eyed the end of the clearing.

Taranis pressed down on Eston's mouth. The soldiers began talking and pointing with their swords.

"Keep him quiet!" Lon whispered. "They'll hear."

"I'm trying," Taranis said through his teeth.

The seconds dragged as the Romans conferred. Then they turned and continued their search beyond the meadow.

Taranis kept his hand over Eston's mouth, whispering in his ear, trying to reassure him. But in the dream world where Eston existed, sound and silence were one. His muffled cries rose and fell, sometimes punctuated with shouts.

Lon crawled beside Eston, knife in hand. "We have to do it," he said, "you know we do."

Taranis looked up, speechless.

"They'll come back," Lon whimpered, "sooner or later, they'll come back."

Taranis ripped out his knife and thrust it under one of Lon's rapidly blinking eyes. "And they will find you dead," he hissed. "Nobody is touching my brother—not you, not the Romans, not anybody. Do you understand?"

Lon shrunk away.

"Now, listen to me," he said, sheathing his knife and again covering Eston's mouth with his hand. "Those Romans are patrolling the ridge. And you are right, sooner or later they will find us—with or without Eston. But we can take them, if we attack first."

"We can't kill three Romans. You saw what happened to the others."

"They had no weapons. We do."

Lon looked doubtful.

"Listen. They won't be expecting an attack. They think we'll run like everyone else. Surprise is a powerful ally." He looked down at Eston, who moaned. "Anyway, we have no choice. Each of us will take a side. You go behind those bushes," he pointed to a clump of eight-foot yew trees laden with berries, "and I'll hide behind that rock. The Romans will circle back and hear Eston. But before they get to him, we'll have excellent shots. Take the Roman nearest you and I'll take the one nearest me. We can both attack the remaining soldier with our swords."

"If our arrows miss—"

"We won't miss. They expect us to run. So we wait ... until they are within thirty feet ...." Taranis rose and met Lon's eyes. "We have no choice. You know that, don't you?"

"Yes. No choice." Lon's eyes began to blink again and he looked intently at the ground, as if he were rehearsing the whole confrontation.

"Once it begins," Taranis said, "I'll need your help. You won't leave me out there, would you?"

"I won't run," Lon said with conviction. "I'm frightened, I admit that." He swallowed hard. "I'm frightened to die, frightened of the gods ... and what will happen." He looked away. "I don't know why ... no one else has these fears."

"Everyone has them."

"Not you. Your hatred of the Empire binds your fear. When we were looking for your brother, you didn't care how close the Romans came. And minutes ago ... you would have killed me."

"You wanted to kill my brother."

"To keep him quiet, is all. I couldn't have killed him, not really."

"It doesn't matter. Right now we need to deal with those Romans."

Taranis stared at his brother and wished he would wake. The sun streamed through the leaves, sprinkling his face with shifting patterns of light, making it seem as if he were moving. Eston's groaning continued, but softly now. Taranis tried to focus his fragmented thoughts. Fear gripped his mind. His plan ... something about it was not right. His stomach knotted. He realized his blunder. He had expected his brother to continue babbling, but now he was drifting into a quiet slumber. There would be no reason for the Romans to enter the meadow if Eston grew silent. The trap would fail. Then Taranis or Lon would surely be exposed in the Romans' sweep of the ridge.

He scanned the clearing.

"Quick," he said, "help me carry Eston to that tree."

They propped Eston against the smooth bark of a single beech fifty feet inside the meadow. Now it mattered little whether Eston babbled, Taranis thought. The Romans would see him when they approached the area.

"I think we're ready," Taranis said. He looked into Lon's eyes and said, "Remember, we have no option. It's either ambush them and fight at our choosing, or hide and fight all three when they discover us."

Lon nodded.

"Let us do our worst," Taranis said, gritting his teeth.

"No matter what happens," Lon said as if he were pronouncing an oath over the body of Eston, "I will not run."

Taranis grasped Lon's arm, "I know your heart." And then he added, "Don't worry, we can do it."

Taranis glanced at Eston and headed for the rock. Using his brother as bait worried him, but it was the only way. If these were the last Romans on the ridge, to get by them meant freedom. He hunched up against the rock, drew an arrow, and waited.

Less than ten minutes later the Romans returned, strutting through the forest. Entering the clearing, they stopped. They had seen Eston.

Taranis begged silently for courage. His eyes followed the Romans as they started down the grassy corridor. Good, he thought, they assume Eston is wounded and has collapsed under the tree. They continued a third of the way into the meadow, and then paused.

Taranis tensed. They sensed a trap. One moved cautiously down the meadow toward Eston. The other two spread out and hung back a few hundred feet. Taranis's mind raced. Should he allow the first Roman to pass? What if he hacked Eston with his sword the way they had done to Geir? He had to take the chance. How could they fight two Roman soldiers? As much as he had tried to encourage Lon, fighting two fully armed Romans would almost certainly mean death. He signaled Lon, but the boy's eyes were fastened on the point man, his bow bent and ready to release.

The Roman was within striking distance, an easy shot. Taranis drew his arrow back, but hoped Lon would wait for the other two before shooting. He didn't. The arrow whooshed through the air, struck the shoulder armor of the point man, and bounced to one side. Taranis released his arrow. It caught the Roman under the armpit, dropping him to the ground. He thrashed about, arched his back, and slumped over.

Behind him, the other Romans shouted in alarm. They raised their shields, covering everything from their knees to their eyes. Then they moved forward.

Taranis jumped from behind the rock, bow in hand. At the last moment he decided against using his sword—a plan was growing in his mind. He moved into the open. Lon hesitated, but then, true to his word, emerged with his sword drawn.

As if it were planned, Taranis and Lon found themselves paired with the enemy across the field. Taranis approached the shield-covered Roman opposite him, keeping his bow taut and level with his enemy's eyes. As they drew nearer, the soldier slowed to a cautious shuffle.

The Roman opposite Lon was tall and moved quickly toward the boy, taunting him with snarls and mock grunts. A shieldless youth made inviting prey. The tall soldier closed the distance to Lon rapidly, and was now twenty feet to Taranis's side. Taranis kept his eyes on his own opponent, his arrow aimed straight ahead. On the periphery, he noticed the tall Roman glance his way as he passed. Taranis paid him no mind, but stared straight ahead. The soldier returned to his task, and moved toward Lon.

Taranis swung around and loosed his arrow, hoping for a hit, any hit, on the tall man's unprotected side. The arrow smashed through his wrist and his sword fell to the ground. Taranis whirled back as the soldier screamed. Off balance, Taranis pulled his sword, bracing for an attack from the thickset Roman in front of him.

It never came. The legionary had missed his opportunity. Taranis had exposed his back when he looked away to shoot his bow, but the legionary did nothing. Now he was banging his sword on his shield as if he were trying to regain his focus. He moved closer, circling.

Taranis held his long sword in front of him, remembering how Bronix had never let a Roman in close. He looked into the angry eyes of a stumpy, thick-legged legionary, sweat streaking down his face from under his helmet, the black stubble on his chin glistening wet. He slowed, studying Taranis for weaknesses. He held his flat sword underhand, quite different from a Caledonian, and Taranis recalled the Romans' diving technique in battle.

Suddenly, the man dropped his shoulder and drove forward with his shield. He jabbed his sword repeatedly, arcing it upwards. But his shield and heavy armor slowed his attack. On the battlefield Taranis might have been wounded, but here in the open, he quickly sidestepped the lunge, and swung his sword. It caught the back of the man's helmet, creasing it. The Roman tottered, dropped his sword, and fell to the ground.

Taranis rammed his blade at the fallen soldier, missed, and thrust again. This time the blade struck the Roman's shield and the impact jarred his own sword out of his hand. For an instant they stared at each other, realizing that neither had a weapon. Then the soldier rolled sideways, grasping for his short sword. Taranis dove at him, pulling his knife as he did and driving it through the other's cheek. The soldier screamed and twisted to one side, then swung back, hammering his elbow into Taranis's chest.

Taranis gasped. He couldn't breathe. A hot pain told him his ribs had broken. The man jammed his hands upward into Taranis's face, his fingers probing for the eyes. Taranis struck again at the man's head. A thick forearm blocked the thrust, and Taranis struggled to pull his head back from the fingers that tore at his face. Suddenly, the man punched him sharply in the neck and tried to flip him over. Taranis brought his knife around in a wide arc, stabbing the blade through the side of the Roman's helmet.

As Taranis tugged at his knife, he turned toward Lon at the other end of the clearing. Still in combat, Lon was moving backwards, almost running, swinging his sword as he moved. Taranis could see that his arrow had wounded the Roman. His right arm hung limply at his side, the blood soaking his twitching hand. He had no shield, but clutched a ten-inch dagger in his left hand.

Taranis picked his sword from the pine needles at the edge of the clearing, and started toward the soldier. The Roman glanced at Taranis, tensed, and sprang at Lon. It was a desperate act; he had no desire to fight two Celts at one time. Lon's sweeping sword struck the man's iron-plated shoulder and bounced to his neck, splattering blood in the air. But the soldier's momentum could not be stopped. He knocked Lon from his feet and fell heavily on him. His dagger hand rose and slammed into the boy's chest.

Taranis blanched.

The man pushed himself off Lon and rose to meet Taranis. The gash on his neck looked deep. He held his head to one side, bending into the wound, then moved forward. Taranis stepped back to keep his sword between him and the soldier. He circled the Roman to the right, making it difficult for him to use his knife. The man turned, in pain. Then he paused, and his body relaxed. He gestured toward Lon with a half smile, as if to say that Taranis would soon join him on the ground. In spite of himself, Taranis felt his eyes move toward his fallen friend.

In that second the soldier jerked forward, wheeling his dagger and grasping at Taranis's tunic with his bloodied hand. The speed of his attack stunned Taranis. Instinctively, he propelled his arms forward in defense, and pain jolted through his ribs. The butt of Taranis's sword caught the soldier's injured wrist. He cursed, but kept coming. He shifted to the right and stepped inside Taranis's guard. Taranis jumped back as the point of the Roman knife passed over his shoulder and down into his forearm, carving a long, thin crescent. Taranis spun to the side, bringing his sword around and slicing a chunk out of the man's leg. It was not a heavy blow, but it was enough. The Roman shuddered and sank to his knees.

Taranis stepped forward and looked into the eyes of his enemy; they were filled with hate. Blood poured from his neck and leg, making him weaker by the moment. Taranis smiled triumphantly. "This is Caledonia!" he shouted into the Roman's face. "And I am a Caledonian warrior!" He knocked him over with a thrust of his foot and left him to die at the meadow's edge. "A Roman should suffer as long as possible," he murmured.

8

Four weeks had passed since Taranis emerged from the woods carrying Eston. They had spent the month at the cabin of an elderly woman who tended Eston with motherly care. Taranis worked hard filling her woodsheds and clearing stones from her fields to show his appreciation. His ribs still ached when he breathed, but he never let on he was in pain, afraid the gentle woman would insist he do nothing, and that, Taranis knew, would be wrong. Under her constant care his brother recovered slowly, sometimes sleeping whole days at a time. But now he was ready to journey to their hunting cabin at Celywic. He looked fit; even his wound hardly showed through his dark hair.

Lon had died almost immediately. Taranis had knelt beside him and watched him die. Lon never moved; he never even whispered a word. Once, a frail smile touched his lips when Taranis mentioned the neck blow that had disabled the Roman. But mostly he lay still, gazing up into Taranis's eyes, blinking slowly. Then, with a slight turn of his head, still staring at Taranis, he closed his eyes forever.

Lon deserved a funeral pyre, where the gods could savor the sweet smell of ash drifting in the winds, but the living take precedence over the dead. So Taranis had covered his body with leaves, and then hurried to his brother under the beech.

It took three days of walking to reach Celywic. Taranis and Eston followed an ancient roadway worn smooth by countless feet. It wound around steep rock faces and through valleys green from constant rains. Crisp northerly winds chilled their faces and filled the land with the pungent scent of mountain pine and fermenting meadow grass. They crossed over the last set of hills and reached a broad valley, bordered on three sides by low-lying mountains. Below, a swift-running stream called the Ordvgi River snaked its way toward the southern end of the valley, where a wall of unmortared stone ringed the tiny village of Celywic. In the outer regions, individual farms dotted the valley and rock fences enclosed herds of bony, brown sheep. Hidden away in the pines beyond the stream, below the gray-faced mountain, was the cabin where his mother and sisters were waiting.

"Why do you think the Romans are attacking Caledonia?" Eston asked.

"I don't know," Taranis said as he picked his way down a steep slope, bare except for a few hardy trees that had survived the constant rockslides. "I suppose they could be retaliating for our raids along the Wall, but raids are nothing out of the ordinary."

"Maybe they're preparing an offensive like the one years ago against Calgacus at Mons Graupius."

For fifty years the bards had sung about Calgacus's thirty thousand, and their tragic encounter with the legions of the bloody Agricola. Calgacus had refused to run, or to endure injustice. He planted his sword at Mons Graupius and called on the valiant of the north to stand with him against the tyranny of the Empire. Choosing to die rather than to serve foreign masters, his thirty thousand flung their bodies against the hordes of Rome, but as the day wore on, the legions steadily encircled the Caledonians, and with vast numbers of cavalry and superior weapons, the Romans won the day.

"The Romans plan their attacks in detail," Taranis said. "If they were intending to enslave Caledonia, we would have seen them massing legions."

"Could they be testing the strength of our people?"

Taranis shrugged. "More likely, they are trying to frighten the tribes into submission—or drive us into higher elevations where we'll be less a problem to them."

They crossed the rock-filled river and trekked along its stony bank until it veered east and dropped off in white, churning eddies.

A feeling of elation swept over Taranis as he listened to the roar of the rapids and felt the spray on his face. They had lost the battle, but the spirits were upon him—he could feel them. They had given him strength to face the enemy, and courage when his heart grew faint. His father would have been proud. He glanced back at the water surging around yellow-stained rocks, bubbling its way through the bend and downstream. The wind now came in gusts, and the air smelled like rain. Tiny conifers, stunted by winter winds, grew along the water, some so near their roots protruded through the bank like withered fingers.

Five minutes from the turn in the river, they found the cabin. Taranis's father had built it with raw logs and mud plastered in the cracks to keep out the cold.

Taranis glanced around the cleared area in front of the cabin, no more than a rough patch of ground cluttered with rocks and stumps, and badger furrows that criss-crossed in every direction. Near the cabin a twenty-foot section had recently been purged of weeds and saplings, and the little rock oven on the outside wall indicated the cabin was occupied, with piles of dry wood heaped on its holding basin.

"Well, someone's been here," Taranis said. He poked at the ash pit and found live embers at the bottom of the black soot.

"It's Neeve," Eston announced, emerging from the door. "I found a sheaf of our arrows, and there's fresh grass on the cot. She also has some kind of a doll here ...."

Taranis took the cloth doll from Eston's hand, an odd thing made from what looked like one of his mother's tunics. It rolled out into six attached dolls, a father and mother and four smaller children. "I guess this is me with the light hair, and you with the dark," Taranis said, pointing to the two larger children dolls. "I think I look more handsome."

Eston's smile faded as he glanced back toward the door. "Only one bed's been used," he said. "I think she's alone."

"Alone? How could she be alone?"

"Taranis! Eston!" a voice shrieked from the woods.

Neeve's skinny body darted through the trees and down a rock bank until she reached the open ground at the side of the cabin. She threw her arms around Taranis's neck and squeezed him hard. Then, squirming out of his arms, she bounded over to Eston, almost tackling him by the doorway.

"I thought you had been killed," she said as she kissed and hugged him, and kissed him again. She turned to Taranis. "I heard what happened, and when you didn't come ...." She swallowed a breath. "Well ... I thought maybe the Romans got you."

"We're fine," Taranis said. He managed a smile even as the memory of screaming men running for the woods echoed in his ears. Neeve smiled back, but he thought he detected something in her eyes. "We'll tell you all about it later," he said, motioning for them to sit on the split-log benches along the cabin front. "Where are Mother and Nes?"

Neeve swallowed and tugged on her hair.

"What happened?"

"They ..." her voice sounded choked, "the Romans captured them. They got everybody at Vercellic—all the women, I mean, that went there."

Neeve looked at her brothers, first one, then the other, as she described the events following her ride to the village. When she had arrived to warn of the Romans, warriors were already gathering from the nearby farms. They knew about the raiding party and had sent the women and children out on carts—over thirty wagons—for the eastern towns. Neeve had stopped at the nearer villages and was told that her mother had gone to Vercellic.

"They burned the whole town," she said, looking at Taranis. "There was nothing left of Vercellic. Not even the surrounding farms."

"All the women at Vercellic taken," Taranis said, thinking out loud.

"And at Auxois and Navan," Neeve said bitterly. "That's what people said."

"They took them to the camps," Eston said.

Taranis nodded, his mind filled with despair. "On their way to the slave markets," he said.

The three sat quietly. Some things were better left unsaid. "What is this?" Taranis asked finally, picking up the doll he had laid by his foot.

Neeve reached for the doll and said, "I made it from one of Mother's tunics."

Taranis shot her a look. "When? Not after you left Vercellic?"

She nodded.

He raised an eyebrow. "You went back to the roundhouse ... didn't you know the Romans were sweeping that area?"

"I knew. I saw them."

"And still you went back?" There was anger in his voice.

She made no reply.

"What is the matter with you? We told you to come straight here."

She cast her eyes down.

Taranis glanced at Eston and shook his head. "She is sure to get herself killed doing these reckless things."

Eston agreed. "You need to grow up, Neeve. Why would you go back to the roundhouse when we told you to come here?"

"I don't know."

Her brothers made sounds of frustration.

Silence fell for another moment, and Taranis saw Neeve straining to maintain her composure. "I had to go back," she choked out, "I just had to. I knew I would never see Mother and Nes again, and I was afraid the Romans would burn down the homestead."

"All the more reason to head straight north to Celywic," Taranis said leaning forward and pointing his finger to make her feel the gravity of the situation.

Tears now filled the bottom of Neeve's eyes, but she forced them back. "I can't remember what Father looks like anymore," she said in barely a whisper. "His face is a shadow. I remember his hands rubbing my cheeks—big hands—but his face is gone." She drew a breath and released it shakily. "I just wanted to snuggle into Mother's bed once more, and feel the straw all around me, hugging me the way she used to. Is that so wrong?"

"No," Taranis said, shifting his eyes from hers to the trees at the side of the cabin, "it's not wrong at all." Her lips had begun to tremble, and he could no longer bear her pain.

She pushed her fists into her eyes and continued. "Do you know what I did when I walked through the door of our roundhouse?"

Taranis waited.

"I collected everyone's extra tunic and sat for hours pressing them into my face, smelling them, making sure I'd always remember. I was afraid I was alone, afraid that even you and Eston were never coming back." She gestured limply at the doll. "I stuffed the dolls with shredded cloth from each of our tunics—every tunic except Father's, of course. His are all gone now."

Taranis stared at the odd-looking doll. Neeve was still talking quietly about stitching a sliver moon into the mother, father and sister dolls. Their mother had always taught them that the new moon symbolized death, and hope in the afterlife. He wished he and Eston had scolded her less severely. Now he could think of nothing comforting to say. He reached over and laid his hand on her leg. It was the best he could do.

As she finished her story, Eston's stomach growled. Neeve jumped to her feet and almost shouted when she said, "I have nets in the river." She obviously wanted to sound helpful after bringing such horrible news. "They'll have fish by now."

"Good girl," Eston said. "You check them and we'll build a fire."

Neeve fetched a thatched basket from the cabin and scuttled down the overgrown path that led to the stream. When she was out of sight, Taranis said to Eston, "I know … I know, send her away, right? That's what you're thinking."

"You're the one who said we can't look after her, that she'll get hurt."

"I remember," Taranis said quietly. He propped his head back against the cabin wall and thought about his pledge to keep the family together. His fingers probed the weariness in his face. "Neeve likes

Celywic," he said with uncertainty in his voice, "but I don't think we can leave her here."

"No, not here," Eston replied. "Celywic has good people, but within months the scum of the area—there are always some—will stumble across her. She's not safe alone. If we could find an older woman—"

"We can't knock on village doors ... we need kin, not strangers."

"We have kin," Eston said in a low tone.

Taranis looked at him in disbelief.

"We might not like the choices," Eston said, "but sometimes there are only bad options."

"Are you talking about Dumnori at Aidan?" Taranis asked sharply. "I am not sending her to Dumnori. Never! I don't trust him. Neeve would be better off fending for herself than having Dumnori as a guardian."

"I was thinking about Pablius and Matidia."

Pablius! He hadn't even thought of him. No one ever spoke his name, except his mother.

"I know he's Roman," Eston continued, "but what else can we do? We have nobody. Matidia is Mother's sister. Maybe she married a Roman, but she will do right by Neeve."

Allowing a Roman to instruct Neeve sickened Taranis, but he feared Eston was right. Matidia was a Caledonian; she knew their ways and would be a loving mother. But she was far away, in the southern regions of Britannia Island.

They found Neeve draped over a large rock near the center of the river. She had rolled her trousers above her knees and was tugging at her nets. She glanced over her shoulder. "No luck on the first net," she called, "but I think I have something here." She twisted the net and pulled it from the water. "Perch!" she hollered. "Two perch!"

Neeve leapt to her feet and bounded across the rocks, landing with a splash at the shallow edge of the stream. Water showered her and again she shrieked with delight, waving the fish over her head. Taranis reached down and caught hold of her slender wrist, lifting her onto the grassy bank. She stood before her two brothers, clothes soaked, but face beaming as she held up her prize.

Taranis smiled and reached for the net. "Beautiful fish, Neeve. You've done well."

She looked pleased. And then she saw something. She glanced from Taranis to Eston and back again. Like the last rays of day fading in the hills, the light drained from her eyes. She wiped the water from her cheeks and shifted uneasily. "What's wrong?" she asked.

"War's coming," Taranis began. "We cannot look after you."

"I'm twelve years old. I can look after myself. I have been here two weeks. I have set traps, caught fish." She pointed at the nets still moving with the occasional shudder of fish.

"Neeve, we've already talked about this—"

"You pledged to me!" she yelled. "You pledged! You stood on the coal and said we would never separate, that's what you said."

"I know but—"

"It's because I tried to do something on my own, isn't it? You told me not to go to the homestead, and I went, so now you'll punish me."

"Neeve, listen—"

"I'm not a child anymore!" She plopped down on the grass, pulled her knees to her chest, and looked up at Taranis.

"Neeve—"

"Please let me stay. I admit I was careless. Let me stay and I will never take chances like that again. Never." Her face held the desperation of one trapped in a pit, and it tore Taranis's heart.

"You don't understand," Eston said. "Mother's gone now and we would dishonor her and Father if we let anything happen to you. We're responsible for you now." He knelt beside her and spoke gently. "With war in the air, who knows what might happen? We can't leave you on your own." He paused. "You would do the same in our place."

"No, I would not," she shouted. And then, to herself, "I would never send you away."

Eston didn't reply. A family of squirrels chased each other over a fallen log and into the brush.

"Where will you send me?" she asked, still staring at the ground.

"To Matidia," Eston said.

"Matidia! That's beyond the Wall ... beyond the second Wall ... hundreds of miles!" she said in astonishment. "She married a Roman. You can't send me there."

"There's no other place," Eston said.

Neeve turned to Taranis, pleading.

Taranis gave her a look of regret. "It won't be long—maybe a year or two, till things settle."

"It's so far," she said, her voice growing smaller.

"You'll be safe there," Taranis said.

"I'll never see you again."

"Yes, you will."

"No, I won't. And you know it."

Taranis knelt in the grass and put an arm around her.

She stared deep into his eyes and said, "I don't want to go."

Taranis looked away. The stream sounded so loud bubbling over the rocks. Somewhere downstream he could hear the haunting call of a loon, and a voice whispering that Neeve might be right. He might never see his sister again.

9

The years had been kind to the family of Trebellius. When Vectis's father retired from the army, he managed to scrape enough money together to purchase a villa outside of Rome. Vectis stayed mostly at their family home in the city, continuing his morning schooling and afternoon training in war games. He cared little for his lessons in Greek and Latin, and hated the endless copying from Herodotus and Virgil. But well-bred Romans must understand history, mathematics and rhetoric. Rhetorical skills he did enjoy, for he well knew the importance of a persuasive argument. How could one lead without the ability to persuade?

Most of all, he took pleasure in the country and often journeyed to the villa to sit and talk with his father, who took pleasure in their conversations. They went on extended hunts together, looking for deer or wild boar, and on the rare occasion when they found nothing, the servants selected from the herds a well-fed lamb to grace the dinner table. Life was good.

But it was about to change.

On the storage trunk in his room were papers that registered him as a recruit at Legion III in North Africa. Soon he would be a full-fledged legionary in the Roman Imperial Army. He knew the dangers, but he was impatient to see the world and to take his place alongside others in the Trebellius family—particularly his father— who had served in the military. At night when he lay in bed, he sometimes imagined the warriors in other lands, like the huge Celts that roamed Britannia's snow-capped mountains and honed their swords in the dark forests. He could almost hear the thundering hoofs of Parthian ponies racing across oceans of glistening sand, and see the wind-filled rectangular sails of Egyptian warships as they glided down the mighty Nile.

On many occasions Vectis found himself in the cellar where his father had stored military gear from his excursions to the outer provinces of the Empire. One morning as Vectis was examining the sizeable collection of bows, he heard his sister, Sabina, call out, "Ahh, there you are! I've been looking all over the villa for you."

"I'm busy," Vectis said, without taking his eyes off the Sarmatian and Indian bows he was comparing.

"I should have known I'd find you here ... yeech, what awful stuff," she said, curling her lip in disgust at the room lined with weapons and equipment.

"These are treasures from lands at the edge of the world."

"Gruesome junk is more like it." She poked her finger at the horsehair top of an old Greek hoplite helmet. Dust floated upwards.

"Have you ever seen something like this?" Vectis asked, gesturing with the Indian bow. "It's bamboo, and over five feet long. The same kind Alexander faced in his Eastern campaigns. And look at this Balearic Island sling. It can kill a man at a hundred yards. And this Greek pike—"

"Oh, Vectis, you can be so dreary sometimes," she said, pushing her way through the crowded aisles. "The room stinks!" She spun on her heel and started toward the courtyard, shouting behind her as she went, "Come out here. We need to talk."

He followed her out and sat on the stone bench facing the fountain. Water spewed from the beak of a giant eagle, sparkling in the morning sun before falling to the surface with a slap. Rows of violets, hyacinths and lilies decorated the paths and, in the distance, newly trimmed vines twisted their way up the stuccoed inner wall.

"Now isn't this better than that depressing little room?"

Vectis smiled. "Much better. But you want to talk about Atilius Titianus, don't you?"

A mischievous smile spread across her face.

"I thought so. Well, I can't help you. Maybe Mother can do something."

"She says nothing can be done ... Daddy doesn't like Atilius and he won't allow me to marry him."

"What do you think I can do?"

"Ohhhh, Vectis," she caressed his arm. "Talk to him. Tell him that marrying Atilius is paramount in my life. Tell him to think of *me* and what I want." Her face puckered in a tiny pout. "Tell him his little girl loves Atilius and wants to marry him."

Vectis hated this talk. He wished she would just say what she meant without all the cutesy prattle. "All right, I'll speak to him," he said. "But it'll do no good. The last time Atilius came calling, Father refused to open the villa gates."

"That was years ago. I was so young then and promised to Marcus Clodius."

Vectis wondered how sincere she was when she dropped her eyes in seeming respect for Marcus, who had been taken by a fever the winter before. Her grief passed quickly as she chattered on about Atilius and his properties on the fashionable Esquiline Hill, and his position in the Senate. Soon he would be very important, she was saying, opening her eyes wide at the prospect.

"You had better stop dreaming," Vectis said. "Atilius is not a proper suitor—you won't be allowed to marry him."

"I will marry him. I will." She stopped to fix a fold on her beautifully draped stola. "Oh!" she shrieked, "a stain! I've a stain from that dirty little room of yours. Rust or blood or something. It will never come out!" She stared at it a moment, and then, resigned to her fate, continued. "You know, Atilius isn't worried at all. He says Daddy will agree to the marriage. You can't deny a senator, he says."

Vectis let his face show his pessimism.

"Besides, Atilius says he has a tiny surprise that might help Daddy make up his mind."

"What surprise?"

"He didn't say, but I pray he's right."

"Not much surprises Father, and not much changes his mind."

"Oh, Vectis, I'm afraid ... Daddy can be so stubborn."

Her words tumbled out as she pictured a miserable life of poverty without Atilius. Vectis wondered how much he should say. It bothered him that his father never talked politics with Sabina. How was she to learn about the real world? He was certain his sister knew something of Atilius's scheming ways, but how much he couldn't say. Well, he at least owed her the truth. "I am sorry you find the situation so upsetting," he said. "I said I would talk to Father, and I will, but you should know that I think he's right. Atilius is no good for you."

Sabina rolled her eyes.

"Atilius is not what you think—"

"This is silly! Atilius is perfectly wonderful. I don't know why Father dislikes him so."

"You know why. Atilius's family was involved in the army purge when Hadrian was emperor. Father said a lot of good men died for no other reason than political egos."

"But that wasn't Atilius's father who killed those people—it was Emperor Hadrian. Atilius told me his father tried to stop Hadrian's insanity."

"Atilius's father," Vectis said sharply, "was knee-deep in the killing—he even tried to seize the Empire. It was only after his own name appeared on Hadrian's enemy list that he began to preach peace."

"I don't believe it. Anyway, Atilius had nothing to do with what happened. That was his father and uncle ... and they are both dead."

"Oh, Sabina, everyone knows Atilius was involved as well."

"No, he was not ... he told me everything. He hasn't done anything wrong. Just because his family may have erred a long time ago ...."

Vectis looked away.

"It's not fair," she said, "Daddy will ruin my life. I could marry a senator if he wasn't so stubborn. A senator! But now ...."

"You need to face the truth."

"The truth is," she said, tilting her head so that the ringlets in her hair framed her face, "Atilius is one of the most intelligent men in Rome."

"He's shrewd, I'll give him that, like a snake in the rocks, poised to strike."

"That's Daddy talking. You hardly know Atilius. He's kind and gentle."

"It's not just Father, Sabina. I've heard other people—"

"They're jealous of him."

Vectis breathed deeply.

"They are! Anyway, he has many good qualities."

"Not to mention he's rich."

"Outrageously rich," she giggled. "In the slaves' quarters alone he has Greek crafted frescos and polished Laconian marble worth an Equestrian's fortune."

"Is that why you want to marry him, because he's rich?"

"Of course not." She dropped her eyes. "I only meant it would be beneficial to have someone of his stature in the family. He knows just about everybody in Rome there is to know. Besides, I am already seventeen. Most girls are married by now. People are talking."

"Nonsense. Everyone knows that Marcus was your intended. It's not your fault a fever took him. I know a dozen men in Rome who would draw the sword to marry you."

"Yes, that is true," she acknowledged with a touch to her exquisitely plaited hair, "but how many have the potential of Atilius Titianus?"

"How can you want to marry someone like him? He's selfish ... and arrogant, and he looks like a vulture the way his head droops over. Do you really want to marry someone twenty-five years your senior?"

"If he's a rich senator," she said firmly.

And an egotistical ass, Vectis thought.

The conversation with his father lasted five minutes. Against his better judgment, Vectis tried to advocate for Sabina, describing how she felt about marriage with Atilius. His father listened quietly and then said he respected Sabina's wishes but thought marrying Atilius was a bad idea. In fact, he thought it was a very bad idea. He would allow Atilius to visit that afternoon out of deference to his office as a senator, but in the end, he would deny his marriage proposal. Plenty of other men could satisfy Sabina's thirst for the Esquiline Hill. She would surmount her present disappointment. It was a difficult decision but would work out for the best.

Vectis turned to go. His father's mind was set.

The older man said, "I want to ask you a question."

Vectis steeled himself, knowing the question.

"Do you think Sabina should marry him?"

"That is her stated desire."

"But do you think she should marry him?"

"It's her life," Vectis said, avoiding the question.

"Yes, and I will not let her throw it away."

Senator Atilius Titianus woke that morning to the sound of flutes playing softly in the corner of his room. Ten minutes he lay with eyes closed, visualizing every event that would unfold on this most important day. The stream of his life was about to alter. He opened his eyes. Two servants raised him gently to a sitting position while others bathed his feet in warm water. He sipped a cup of heated apricot nectar and allowed his face to be washed in wild asses's milk to rejuvenate his skin. "I'm ready," he said, and stepped down from his bed. The servants removed his sleeping tunic. One knelt before him proffering an elongated silver bowl wherein he relieved himself. A second washing, this time in lavender water, more apricot nectar, a taste of cheese on fine wheat bread, and he was ready to don his breakfast tunic.

The servants swung open the bronze latticed windows at the side of the room, inviting in the crisp morning air. Atilius loved the feel of the morning breeze on his face and the sound of birds serenading each other. A thin mist drifted across the distant fields of his vast estate, but soon it would vaporize with the rising sun, the way opposition did in the face of a well-devised plan. A good day, he thought; yes, this will be a good day.

An hour later found Atilius in the courtyard, humming to himself, something he liked to do when he was alone, especially when it was time to feed his pet fish. These morning periods were the only time of the day he could relax, be himself. "I can see you," he said, leaning over the stone barrier that encircled a shallow pond. "Time for breakfast." Scores of colorful, six-inch fish hung motionless in the water—a pleasant scene that delighted him. He circled his net until he felt weight straining the mesh.

"Let me look at you," he said as he jerked the net out of the water. "Oh, my, my, four little fish, and what pretty colors ... red and yellow ... and ... ohhh ... one even has spots. You are lovely, aren't you? Fat little rascals, too."

He trudged over to a matching pond that was considerably deeper.

"And how are my big fish doing? Hungry? I have friends who want to visit you. But don't worry, they cannot stay long—they have an engagement with destiny." He chuckled to himself. He loved his own witticisms.

"Well, time for breakfast." He flipped the net over and the little fish splashed into the water. His eyes followed the drama eagerly. The surface foamed white as the shadows darted toward the colorful forms. Atilius delighted in feeding his fish, watching the little ones thrash about trying to avoid the jaws of the bigger ones. Today, one had escaped, concealing itself behind a jutting rock at the side of the pond where twists of ivy grew. It amused him. He picked up a stick and tapped the rock to draw attention to its hiding place.

"Oh, oh, I think they see you," he said as the shapes approached. Another splash and the water regained its calm veneer. "Ahh, how sad," he murmured, "the big fish always eat the little fish. But, that's fate, isn't it?"

It was early afternoon when Atilius stepped out of his carriage at the Trebellius estate. His confidence surged as he swept the grounds with his eyes. Rather tiny, he thought, and not well kept. A fountain, a bathhouse, a few flowers, some bushes scattered around the

perimeter, farmlands, a stockade—little to brag about. Where were
the slaves? Less than ten in the whole villa, Atilius mused, nothing
like his own estates. He had more than two hundred in his Rome
lodgings alone. Only a handful had accompanied him, of course.
Sabina had warned him that her father disliked pampered Romans
with their fawning slaves. No point in irritating the old man.

He scanned the property again, pleased by what he saw. Yes, this
little villa needed a patrician's touch. He could do a lot to improve the
seedy plot of ground, starting with an expansion to a more acceptable
size. Still, it wasn't bad for a plebeian, not bad at all. Old Trebellius
must have found a bag of money. He breathed deeply in anticipation.

A freedman introduced himself as Pudens and led him to the
door of the main house. The elder Trebellius stood alone in the
entrance corridor near a poorly sculpted bust of the goddess Minerva.
Instead of a toga, he wore a soldier's tunic, dagger and all. Sabina and
Vectis were nowhere in sight, as Atilius had expected. The old man
wanted to give him a quick thrust to the heart and send him on his
way. Well, this wasn't the battlefield, and if there were thrusts to the
heart, he would administer them.

"Gaius Trebellius," Atilius said in his most cordial manner, "how
good to see you."

"Yes, good to see you too, Senator."

"What a splendid estate. I had no idea you lived so luxuriously.
The arrangement of flowers in the courtyard is charming—not
ostentatious like some I've seen—tastefully done."

"Thank you. I suggest we talk in the library."

Atilius followed him into a tiny room stuffed with books and
scrolls, and accepted a cup of wine. The pathetic yellow and brown
mosaic, cracked at one end, spoke volumes, as did the faded, floral
cushions deposited on the wicker couches. He chose a fur-covered
seat by the window and sat down. They chatted about villas, about
Rome's growing sprawl, and the current situation in the Empire.
Atilius knew it was his place to introduce the subject of marriage. For
a father to presume an offer of matrimony would be improper. He
took another cup to relax himself, fixed the broad purple stripe on his
toga, and plunged in.

"You know why I'm here ... I wish permission to marry Sabina. You are a great man and everybody in Rome respects you for your exploits as First Centurion in the legions you have commanded. I come from a noble family. I am a senator and a wealthy man. Sabina would lack for nothing and I would treat her well. It is customary for a woman to bring a dowry and I will accept gratefully whatever you deem reasonable. But, as a gift to seal our friendship, I offer one million sesterces for you to use as you please. Naturally, I would say nothing of this to anyone, and from time to time, you may have needs that I, as a family member, would be happy to provide. If you consent to this arrangement I will inform my steward to prepare a magnificent banquet to honor the house of Trebellius."

With the speech over Atilius leaned back, and reached for his cup. His words pleased him; they respected the house of Trebellius while at the same time brought home the realities of the situation. This was not a marriage among equals. Atilius sipped his wine and allowed his eyes to wander the rows of books and parchments lining the shelves. It seemed an appropriate gesture, as if he had an interest in the shabby collection of the elder man. After a brief silence Atilius returned his eyes to Trebellius who was sitting, stone-faced, staring at him. "Amazing parchments," Atilius volunteered. "From you vast travels, I take it."

Trebellius said nothing.

In the uncomfortable silence Atilius swallowed some wine and glanced once more at the books. The old man looked angry, but he was probably embarrassed at having someone with Atilius's wealth and status flattering him amid such obviously scruffy surroundings. Atilius wondered if a little patrician pressure was in order. He straightened his back, leveled his eyes at the man, and waited.

"A generous offer," Trebellius said finally, "but I cannot accept."

Atilius gaped at him in disbelief, and then recovered, realizing that this was not a genuine rejection. Trebellius was undoubtedly ill at ease with his station, felt embarrassed, and wanted to be asked again. The man had pride, which was perfectly reasonable. Atilius nodded and said gently, "I understand, Gaius Trebellius. With respect I must tell you that I very much desire this union, and of course, your daughter feels the same. Give me leave to prepare a festive meal like none Rome has ever seen."

Trebellius rose. "Thank you for coming, Senator Atilius Titianus; we are not worthy of your noble patrician family. I will call my servant to show you out."

Atilius felt his face flush. He stood out of habit—when your host stands, you stand—but he wished he hadn't. Atilius boiled with rage. He should have sat there calmly instead of popping up like a frightened schoolboy. This unrefined trench digger was a man of enormous pride, and appeared not to understand what Fortune had laid at his door. He seemed to take pleasure in watching a patrician beg favor of his inferior. Atilius had to seize control of the situation. "If I might," he said, keeping his composure, "I desire a few more minutes of your time."

"Of course," Trebellius said, without having the grace to seat himself.

Atilius ignored the slight and continued, "As I said, both Sabina and I desire this union. We had hoped—*I* had hoped—that you would allow me to shower your daughter with enormous bounty, and of course, equally, give me the honor of situating your entire family in a more acceptable manner."

"Our situation is fine," Trebellius said, "and I have given you my answer. I cannot sanction this marriage. I'm sorry."

Atilius rubbed his face, as if it would help him grasp the situation. "Gaius Trebellius," he said, "this is a comfortable villa of which you should be proud. Few centurions attain such things. But— and I say this with admiration and respect—it hardly qualifies as the envy of Rome. I am offering you one million sesterces. I cannot believe you would pass up such a proposal."

"There are other considerations."

"Intriguing. Other considerations, you say. I wonder what they could be." He furrowed his brow as if in thought. He was beginning to think the man might be dull-witted. His whole villa would fit into the stables of Atilius's poorest estate. And he had the temerity to spout off about other considerations. "I might be missing something,"

Atilius said politely, "but from what I see, this villa cannot sustain itself. Shouldn't this be a factor when a father plans for his family?"

"How we manage is none of your business."

The centurion spoke quietly, but Atilius saw the flash of anger in his eyes. He scolded himself—*you've got to do better*. "I am truly sorry," he said, "my question was rude and unforgivable. I did not mean to imply—"

"Apologies are unnecessary. I think we've concluded our business."

"Yes, you are right ... I should not have come." *Got to take the pressure off.* "I should have known my father's involvement in that army purge ... well, I am deeply embarrassed. I promised Sabina I would try. It's better this way. May I have your permission to tell her that events have not worked out as we had hoped?"

"I have no objection."

"Again, I apologize. I have gone beyond the bounds of decency. You have been most gracious." The old man looked uncomfortable. He wasn't sure how to handle the conversation—good, Atilius thought. "It's just that I love Sabina." He smiled wanly. "She has uncommon beauty. I would have been the envy of Rome. But it is hard, I know, to put the past behind us. At first I thought my family was right to follow Emperor Hadrian's orders in the purge, but now I know they were wrong. Hadrian was insane at the end ... I have made a fool of myself in coming here ... it was irresponsible ... what was I thinking ...?" He let his voice ramble, as if he were thinking aloud rather than speaking.

Neither man said a word. The silence weighed like a leaded cloak. Atilius stood quietly, as if lost in the corridors of past events. Patience, he thought. Let the silence crush him.

Atilius knew the power of silence better than most. It was his ally. The weaker man always cracked under its pressure. He couldn't stand the tension and would begin talking, making concessions. Atilius maintained his silence. Wait ... wait, he said to himself. The seconds passed slowly, awkwardly. But old Trebellius was tougher than expected. He wasn't easily maneuvered and seemed to have his mind made up. Better to try something else before he suspects manipulation. A dose of truth is effective, he thought, especially if I appear vulnerable.

"I should perhaps tell you," he began, "there are other reasons why I wanted to marry your daughter besides her evident beauty."

The centurion looked interested.

"I might as well speak candidly. The truth is I am not universally liked in the Senate. Some, like Senator Titus Severus, take a special delight in ridiculing me behind my back." He paused to take a breath before continuing. "It's not entirely the fault of Severus, I must admit. I do have a substantial number of weaknesses. One will be obvious to you—I have never held a battle command. You have. In fact, without flattering you, there is no one in Rome your equal. You have fought all over the world and your heroism in battle is undisputed."

"Well, I hardly think—"

Atilius lifted his hand. "Please, let me finish. This is by no means easy for me. I know ... I know Severus and others laugh when I comment on frontier policy and issues of war. I suppose they have a right. I do not have firsthand experience. But you do. More than anyone."

The old man looked away and muttered, "My day has passed."

Atilius waved him off. "You recognize what can or cannot be done on the battlefield." *Don't overblow things. He knows you're ambitious. Keep it believable.* "This marriage, I admit, would help me politically. Senators would naturally come to me for advice, knowing that I would draw from your vast experience. And, indeed, I would benefit by having someone like you to consult. From time to time you could address the Senate—"

The old man's eyes narrowed. "And I suppose you'd trot me out to support one of your causes—"

"No, no," Atilius said. "That was the furthest thing from my mind." *I said too much. I'm losing him.* "I just meant that once in a while you might like to come to the Senate to present *your* ideas."

"It doesn't matter because, as I said, Sabina will not be marrying you."

Stupid, stupid, stupid. I had him and I lost him. Atilius covered his displeasure well. He tried to smile. Grasping the old man's hands, he thanked him again. His mind raced. He had tried everything but nothing worked. The man was incredibly stubborn.

Now he had but one option, and it was risky. Make a mistake, and he could end up on the library floor with a dagger in his neck. The soldier was not someone to trifle with. But what else could he do? He was telling the truth about his image needing a boost in the Senate. For some reason people regarded him as weak and untutored in military strategy. That irritated him because he believed he understood military matters quite well. Marrying the daughter of First Centurion Gaius Trebellius would silence many tongues. It was brilliant. He would gain instant respect. Best of all, as time passed, he could force the centurion to support him on the Senate floor. But first he would have to gamble. This was no time for timid actions.

"I want you to know," Atilius said, "that I still respect you and will continue to defend you whether or not we are linked by marriage."

"What? Why should I need a defense, Senator?"

The centurion was plainly angry, but Atilius pressed on. "I am sure you have heard the rumors," he said. "So far I've managed to suppress them."

"What rumors?" Trebellius demanded.

"They are not worth repeating. Malicious lies."

The soldier lowered his lids and looked straight at Atilius. His eyes were cold and unmoving. He was not a man easily bluffed. "Let's not play games," he said. "I don't like you, never have. I wouldn't trust you more than I would a lying Celt. You are an ambitious muck gatherer. You'd accuse your mother of treason if you thought it might improve your reputation in the Senate. And knowing some of them, it might." He moved closer to Atilius, as if he wanted to be within striking distance. "Now, I will ask you this once. What rumors?"

Atilius felt the sweat on the back of his neck, and his hands grew thick and clammy. He swallowed hard and stepped back, trying not to give the appearance of a man cowering in the face of danger. There were no rumors; just informants who had whispered stories in his ear.

"It involves Spurius Fabius of Syria."

"Go on."

Atilius thought he detected a change in his expression. "Some have wondered where you got the money to buy this villa. Even with your slave delivering activities and the extras as First Centurion, they say you could not possibly have raised the necessary funds."

"There's no Eleusinian mystery here," Trebellius said, "I won the money gambling. Nothing else to do in the army."

"Exactly what I said. But some insist that you lost a great deal of money to Spurius Fabius. They say you killed him along with three others in his tent and then took everything they had."

The old man said nothing.

"Personally," Atilius said, "I do not believe a word of it. But the problem is that one of those men in the tent was nephew to Antoninus who is now the Emperor."

Atilius could see his speech was having its desired effect. Trebellius was thinking, perhaps wondering what to do next. Too late. Time for the big fish to eat the little fish.

"I know you care nothing for the whisperings of idle tongues," Atilius said, "but I am truly worried about Vectis. He has shown a remarkable ability in military studies and war games. I've seen him in action." He laughed in admiration. "Incredible courage. Strong and quick. Handles opponents twice his size with ease. I can tell you that a number of people have their eye on that boy. And now he's entering the army. Well ... well ...." He shook his head and assumed an expression of concern. "I am afraid his career could be destroyed if the Emperor hears the rumor. Even if the Emperor does nothing—for he is a good and kindly man—some lunatic is bound to kill the boy to please his superiors."

The old man sat down, his shoulders slumped. He breathed heavily and studied the mosaic on the floor for a long minute. Atilius hardly dared believe his eyes. When he had told Sabina he had a tiny surprise, he had no idea ... the pride of Rome's legions looked like a whipped slave. Maybe he did kill those men in the tent. He caved so quickly. Excitement tingled the senator's mind; he felt giddy. His informants assured him the information was solid, but they always swore on the gods that every word they said was true. This was better than he had expected.

"What are you saying," Trebellius said finally, "that if you don't get your way you'll spread this ridiculous story and destroy my son?"

Atilius looked hurt. "Absolutely not! I will stamp out these lies whether or not you allow me to marry—"

"If I do grant my permission, can you guarantee that these stories will end?" He really did look defeated.

"I can guarantee it," Atilius said in a level voice.

Vectis sat in silence as his father gave his reasons for allowing Sabina to marry Atilius. He had never known him to look or talk this way, as though he were resigned to a fate written in the heavens. Sabina should be allowed to find her own way in life, he said. Perhaps he was wrong to try to legislate Sabina's happiness; she was old enough to make her own decisions. It was all very unconvincing.

"I don't understand," Vectis said. "Why did you change your mind?"

"If I were choosing, I would not choose Atilius. But I should have given Sabina some freedom of choice. I forgot that ... for a time."

It was an awkward moment. He could see pain in the corners of his father's eyes. Vectis had never known his father to lie to him, but he suspected he was lying today. Both men looked at each other and silently agreed to pretend for the other's sake. And then it was over.

"Well," his father said, "you must be excited about entering the army. When will you leave?"

"Later in the week. I asked to train as a regular. I want to learn from the bottom up."

"A regular?" His father looked shocked. "I thought—"

"Next year I will be posted as a tribune, but right now I want to test myself."

"Test yourself, sure, but the regulars ... it's not like war games at the baths."

"I know."

"No, you don't know. It's the real thing ... wartime discipline. Men die—"

"I know that, and I intend to be careful."

"See that you are. The Roman army has changed over the years. Half of the recruits come from the dregs of society—barbarians with no education or training. A centurion can't be everywhere ... a code of silence prevents soldiers from talking." He paused and said, "Don't get on the wrong side of the officers. Sometimes they have to administer harsh justice. Do what they tell you and keep your mouth shut."

"I'll try to be like my father—First Centurion of the legion," Vectis said.

"You can do better than your father, son, a lot better." There was sadness in his voice.

10

"Smile, Balbinus," Atilius said as the Senate procession left the Imperial palace in Rome. "Fortune favors its children. My fate cannot be denied."

Atilius's aide smiled obediently—as if this day presented no danger for him or the senator. They moved slowly past the Temple of Apollo toward the Sacred Road leading to the Old Forum. On the right the colossal, ninety-nine foot statue of the Sun god soared skyward, and beyond that stood the massive Flavian Amphitheater, home of the Games.

Atilius acknowledged the cheering crowds, thousands of citizens packed behind a wall of soldiers lining the streets. He and the other senators walked deliberately, feeding on the accolades of the people, basking in the jubilation of the onlookers who waved their scarves and craned their necks to glimpse this or that dignitary as he passed in procession. Shouts and plaudits for individual senators rose above the clamor, and once or twice Atilius heard his own name called out.

Weaving their way through the procession of senators were scores of minstrels, dancing and playing their flutes merrily. Atilius patted one on his back as he passed, then waved at the crush of citizens thronging the streets. Over four hundred senators had assembled for the Emperor's speech. Some were aged, white-haired men who for years had been absent from Rome; they whiled away their days in the provinces, preferring the amenities of country villas to the intrigues of Rome. Others were young, and eager to win favor with the people and the Emperor. Scattered throughout, senatorial aides walked with their ubiquitous wax tablets and styluses, ready to scribble down the musings of their senators along the way. With togas bleached a brilliant white and tunics conspicuously positioned to show the broad purple stripes of their ranks, the senators were easily identified. Brooches of fine sapphire, ruby and amethyst fastened their garments. Their distinctive red sandals glistened with pearls, and when they waved, their fingers flashed costly rings of every sort.

"Look around you, Balbinus. Only in Rome"—he gestured expansively—"would you see anything like this."

They were passing the Temple of Venus and Rome, its gleaming roof held aloft by four hundred columns each forty feet high. The processional turned left and funneled through the Arch of Titus with its bas-reliefs showing the destruction of Jerusalem over seventy years earlier. Depicted on the Arch were scenes of glory: victorious Roman ancestors carried overhead the seven-branched candlestick and silver trumpets from Yahweh's Temple, proving again that no god could stand before the might of Rome. Atilius sneered at the stupidity of nations that dared to challenge the destiny of the Empire. When would they learn?

He glanced back at the processional, stretching as far as the eye could see, and ahead to the heights of the Palatine Hill where the Imperial palace rose in tiers of balconies, domes and pinnacles. Special detachments of the scarlet-clad Praetorian Guard, trained to protect the Emperor, were now joining the procession. Soon the Emperor himself would enter his chariot for the ride to the forum.

"The Praetorians march like no other soldiers in the world," Atilius said.

"They shall march for you, one day," Balbinus said in a low voice, his cherubic face beaming.

"Let us hope this is not the day," Atilius said darkly.

"Do you suppose the Emperor knows?"

"Our dear Emperor Antoninus may be a blind lover of peace, but he is no fool."

"He knows?" Balbinus looked alarmed. He had been away for several days conducting the senator's business in northern Italia and was not privy to the latest news.

"You can relax, Balbinus. He knows ... some things, but not all. He will not move against me, you can be sure of that. I have my enemies ...." He glanced ahead to see the hated outline of Senator Titus Severus waving at the people, "But too many senators agree with my position. I doubt Antoninus will even ask me about the situation."

Directly ahead the gilded roofs of the capital shimmered in the morning sun, and with every step, the crowd grew thicker, and louder. At the entrance to the Old Forum the senators saluted the Virgins at the Temple Vesta, keepers of the eternal fires of Rome. The senators raised their palms in respect to the Temple of Divine Julius Caesar and toward the Triumphal Arch of Emperor Augustus.

And then they entered the Old Forum, the soul of the Eternal City.

The roar was deafening. Atilius swept his eyes over the great plaza filled with people, and he couldn't resist rubbing his palms together like a man stumbling upon a cache of gold. Something about the crowd, or the occasion, or the magnificent structures—he didn't know—but something filled him with a thirst for power. He could feel it surging through his body like a hundred beating hearts, a craving that could never be satisfied until the accolades fell on him and him alone.

Here he was in the ancient forum of the Republic, nothing more than a flat, open area at the base of five of the Seven Hills of Rome, but here the business conducted shaped the lives of people in far-off kingdoms. Here the will of Rome shook the world.

Atilius paused to savor the moment. He had walked the paved tiles of the forum often, but never had he felt its power as he did today. Surrounding the celebrated plaza, breathtaking stone buildings and marble pillars rose majestically. Walls painted in brilliant blues, greens, and reds glowed with vitality. Gold-tiled roofs and winged goddesses mounted on solitary columns glinted against the sky. Every niche, every roof and gable, sparkled with statues of the gods. Some were carved in marble, others in plain gray stone; many were covered with flesh-toned plaster, their heads adorned with skillfully cut hair. Here Jupiter conversed with Mercury, Ceres and Mars; there, another cluster, this time mortals appealing to the Greek god of healing, Asclepios.

And the great ones of Rome's glorious past stood in marbled splendor, now statues with hands outstretched as if embracing their children.

"They are all here," Atilius said, making his voice heard above the continuous applause. "Scipio, Marius, Pompey ...." His eyes roamed the rooftops. "Think of it, Balbinus—Caesar stood where you are standing, and Augustus, and Trajan. Conquerors all." He gestured expansively and drew a deep breath, as if tapping a source of energy from days gone by.

"There's room for another statue," Balbinus whispered discretely into Atilius's ear.

"Yes," the senator mused, "yes, there is. It will take a steady hand, but there is room indeed."

The processional continued through a corridor of shifting white togas, their wearers restrained by urban troops and the vigilant soldiers of the Praetorian Guard. To the right loomed the huge Basilica Aemilia, used for business transactions and social gatherings. Now they were passing the even larger Basilica of Julius Caesar on the left, the law courts of Rome. Crowds of well-wishers cheered from its upper balconies, tossing flowers and sprinkling crocus saffron that drifted onto the passing senators.

They neared the Rostra. More temples and public buildings. Off to the right hundreds of people had gathered on the steps of the Senate house, under its lavish porticoes, and in front of its enormous bronze doors.

Atilius ascended the steps of the Rostra with its prows of captured warships, memorials to naval battles of bygone days. He glanced up at the Golden Milestone, a lofty stone pillar covered in bronze and overshadowing the Rostra. A hundred and fifty years earlier Augustus had engraved it with the names of the main roads leading out of Rome. All roads, from the Euphrates to Britannia's

Walls, led to this spot. Again, Atilius felt a stirring as he contemplated the extent of Rome's empire, and the access he had to its power.

Atilius and Balbinus stood with the senatorial gathering at the top of the Rostra, waiting for the Emperor to arrive. The air was thick with the smells of burning incense from scores of altars set up along the edges of the ancient platform. It was not long before the Praetorians strode through the masses of people and formed square detachments across the front of the forum. At the center of the last cohort, standing in a ceremonial chariot, came the Emperor, Titus Aurelius Fulvus Boionius Antoninus, the Pius.

"Well," Atilius said in low tones, "we will soon know what Antoninus intends to do about his Wall in Britannia."

"I've heard rumors that the Emperor is upset over our part in the attacks." Balbinus's voice dropped to an almost inaudible tone. "Do you think he knows about our bribes of the centurions and tribune at the Wall?"

"Your bribes, Balbinus, not mine."

"Of course, Senator," Balbinus said. "I did not intend—"

"He knows," Atilius interrupted, "as everyone knows, that in the Emperor's absence I instructed several of our garrisons to attack the Celts. He might suspect more, but he has no assurance of his suspicions."

"He won't abandon his Wall?"

"No reason to abandon it, at least not yet. Since our legionaries burned the Celts' fields and shelters, they have retaliated all along the Wall. Antoninus must either strengthen the Wall-forts or declare full-scale war. He won't abandon the Wall—he cannot do that, can he? After all, he built the Wall. It would be a supreme embarrassment to leave." Atilius chuckled to himself. "Those northern Celts may lack intelligence, but they are tough, restless barbarians. Should be interesting, what happens in the next few years."

"And what the Emperor does."

"Yes, indeed," Atilius said, his smile broadening.

Two snow-white horses drawing the Emperor's chariot stopped at the foot of the Rostra. Antoninus had replaced the ostentatious chariot of his predecessor, Hadrian, but there was no denying the splendor of the Pontifex Maximus, Imperator of Rome. Around his chariot stood his Praetorians, their gilded armor flashing in the sun, the scarlet plumes of their crests fluttering in a sudden breeze.

Antoninus raised his arms to the crowd. The Old Forum exploded with cheers as he turned slowly, acknowledging their homage. He hung his head, as if he felt unworthy of their continued applause, and then, in a sign of respect, he opened his palms to the crowd.

As Atilius watched the bearded Antoninus garnering all the praise, he felt his blood rise. He could not deny that things had gone well under his reign, but Rome's well-being was due more to fortune than good administration. It galled Atilius that Antoninus should have risen to such heights, a common man by anyone's judgment, a man with few talents and, in truth, a man who had ascended the throne by mistaken fate. Bare months before Hadrian's death, his handpicked successor, Lucius Aelius, had died, and Hadrian was desperate. He hastily adopted Antoninus as his son and heir, a man with little to commend him. In the years since, of course, Antoninus had done nothing to advance the glory of Rome, but sat timidly in his palace, praying that the nice barbarians would remain in their territories. As far as Atilius was concerned, both Emperors Hadrian and Antoninus were fainthearted caretakers who merely preserved the borders of the Empire, never expanded them.

Antoninus ascended the steps; his gold-embroidered, purple robes swayed back and forth, brushing the marble. Behind him walked his adopted son, Marcus Aurelius, chosen to follow Antoninus as the next Caesar. Atilius burned within. He saw himself wearing the purple, waving at the people, expanding the Empire. He sensed his calling, a fearful lord before whom great armies were destined to tremble. He would conquer Britannia once and for all, retake Mesopotamia, humble the Parthians, and go where even Alexander had faltered—India. Rome would be rich beyond reason.

Atilius shook his head. With Antoninus steering the ship, Rome would be lucky to maintain its borders. Kingdoms that didn't expand soon shrank. Barbarians not taught the fear of Rome eventually grew courageous and pillaged the frontiers. The problem with Antoninus was his mistaken impression that peace was the supreme goal of the Empire. It was not. Conquest was.

Antoninus entered the central Rostrum, placed one hand on the marble balustrade, and raised the other for quiet. He was greeted with a tumultuous cheer. Atilius cheered as loudly as anyone and beamed in garish admiration. For five minutes the crowd hailed the Emperor and the glorious Sun god; they pressed closer to hear the words of their Caesar.

"Roman citizens," he began, "seven years ago I accepted your petition and the entreaty of the divine Hadrian to be your emperor. Seven years ago our frontiers were weak and unstable; now they are strong and secure." The crowd cheered. "Seven years ago corrupt circuit judges conducted vendettas against loyal senators; these I have removed." The senators responded with genuine applause.

"Seven years ago," he paused for effect, "bands of rebellious Celts flouted the laws of Rome. They rampaged through Britannia province and killed many Romans. These criminals I captured and sold into slavery." Another cheer. "Some escaped our legions and fled north. I consulted with the Senate and built a second Wall to hold the murderous Celts in their place. This has worked well and allowed me to concentrate on improving conditions at home."

Antoninus described the harbors, bridges, baths and amphitheaters he had built, the orphanages and charities he had established throughout the Italian peninsula.

"I have done my best to give Romans the life they deserve." Cheering shook the forum. "But now," he said with hesitation in his voice, "we have another challenge."

Balbinus glanced nervously at the senator but Atilius's eyes remained fixed on Antoninus.

"The northern tribes in Britannia are again on the move; they have attacked our outposts along the Wall and have in some areas inflicted serious damage." He took a full breath and said loudly, "This-will-stop!" A deep growl of agreement rose from the people. "I am now opening the doors to the Temple of Janus. Who can withstand his wrath?"

Silence fell on the crowd as behind them the doors of the vaulted temple slowly opened. Inside, incense burned, drifting upwards and curling around the face of the two-headed Janus, protector and sustainer of Rome's armies in time of war. Several priests stood beside the altar, preparing a sacrifice to the god.

Antoninus resumed his speech: "I have instructed parts of Legions II and VI, and several auxiliaries, to reinforce those already at the Wall."

"You were right, Senator," Balbinus whispered.

"As many of you know," Antoninus continued, "I was at my villa in Lanuvium when the crisis arose. Word of the difficulties came to the Senate before it came to me."

Atilius flinched. A vein in his eye throbbed as Antoninus talked about the Senate's role in government policy.

"I am told that while the Senate debated what to do, one senator took it upon himself to order—in my name—an attack on the Celts in the north."

"Senator ..." Balbinus gasped, white with fear.

Atilius shot his corpulent aide a warning glance. Balbinus resumed his stiff stance and said nothing. As Atilius returned his eyes to the Emperor, he caught sight of Senator Titus Severus, who must have guessed the nature of the Emperor's concern, for his face had twisted into the smirk Atilius had come to hate. Atilius shifted his feet, and waited.

"Atilius Titianus," Antoninus said, "step out from the senators."

Atilius's heart pounded as he heard his name. He stepped forward awkwardly, obeying the Emperor's command. He felt naked standing alone at the podium edge, feeling the eyes of thousands searching him, scrutinizing him. Lined up across the forum, the stern-faced Praetorians waited, eager-eyed, as if they were inspecting a bird in a cage. Courage! Have courage, Atilius told himself. The infant Hercules strangled a pair of vipers in his cradle. Surely I can stand here without shaking. Fortune favors its children.

He turned toward the Emperor.

"Atilius Titianus, you have rendered the Empire a great service, and I thank you."

The sudden noise of the crowd numbed Atilius's mind. He heard the cheering, his name shouted in admiration, but mostly he felt as if he were observing the event from some distant pinnacle of the forum. He hardly remembered stepping back or receiving commendations from other senators. Antoninus continued his speech, but Atilius's mind was far away. When it was over, he received word that the Emperor wished to speak with him in the Senate chambers. Overjoyed, he set off for the Senate, pushing his way through the crowds.

"Atilius!" Sabina cried. "Here! Over here!" She waved a scarf frantically in the air, trying to catch his attention. Atilius could see her now, standing on the steps of the Basilica of Julius Caesar, and surrounded by a score of senators' wives. The women stared at him in open admiration. And why not? After such praise from the Emperor, others would naturally want to rub shoulders with him. He was a man on the way up. He smiled and lifted his hand in recognition, and then on a whim threaded his way through the crowd toward Sabina.

Balbinus hastened behind, calling out, "Senator, the Emperor ...."

Atilius paused. "Yes, yes, my audience with Antoninus, I have not forgotten. Stay here, I shall return momentarily."

Atilius could see that Sabina wished to bask in his glory—show him off to the other women. They had been married only months, and although her station was significantly lower, he had done well. Already other senators were asking his opinion on matters of frontier policy. Having a father-in-law like old Trebellius gave him the respect he deserved, as he knew it would. Soon he would have him speak to the Senate ... maybe some words in support of his new son. The thought pleased him. But he had to tread lightly with Trebellius—he was a hard man. Wouldn't accept even a single sesterce after the wedding. "I have no need of your money," he had said. "Sabina has chosen to enter your household, and that is her right. You have my blessings." Atilius wanted more than his blessings—he wanted his influence. He would have to move carefully, but in the end, he knew,

Trebellius would give him what he wanted. The old man would do anything to protect that precious son of his.

"Oh, Atilius," Sabina cried, "I am so proud of you." She threw her arms around him and covered his face with kisses.

"My! My! Quite a reception," he said, smiling at the surrounding women. "Would that I could stay longer, but unfortunately I have a meeting with Caesar Antoninus."

"The Emperor! You have a meeting with the Emperor," she bubbled, looking around at the other wives.

"I am certain it is a small matter of state he wants to consult—"

"A small matter! First he praises you in front of the city, and now he wants to consult with you. What will be next? The trouble with you, Atilius," she said, squeezing her cheek to his shoulder, "is that you don't give yourself enough credit. Soon you will be a consul, like your father." She rubbed his arm enthusiastically and kissed him again.

"Well, I hardly think the occasional word with the Emperor puts me in line for a consulship," Atilius said modestly. "I am just happy to serve Rome."

Sabina clung to his arm. "Maybe someday you could even be Emperor—I can't think of anyone better ...."

A jolt shot through Atilius's body. "Sabina, you dishonor the gods who have in their wisdom appointed others to rule over us. I have no desire to be Emperor. Besides, the Senate is filled with men more qualified than I, and most of their wives are standing right here." He smiled, trying to look relaxed. "Now, if the celebrated women of the Senate will excuse us ...."

Atilius led Sabina up the steps into the basilica. He signaled an attendant, who scurried about to find an empty room. With the door closed and Sabina's maids outside, Atilius turned to face his wife. She looked inquiringly at him to ask whether something was wrong. He slapped her hard across the face, and then again. She fell on the floor, sobbing. The utter foolishness of the woman astounded him. He grabbed her by the arm, yanking her to her feet.

"No, no, please, Atilius ...." She raised her hands as if that could protect her. He banged her arms aside and slapped her again. It felt good. How could old Trebellius have raised such a politically naive daughter? Perhaps now she would think before she talked. He pulled her to her feet again, gently this time, wiping her tears and lifting her chin.

He looked into her bruised, rapidly swelling face. "Sabina, I want you to listen to me. Never again will you say that I desire to be Emperor."

She stared at him, her eyes wide and unmoving.

At the Senate building, a contingent of Praetorians stood in front of the bronze door. One of Antoninus' aides led Atilius and Balbinus to the room chosen for the meeting. Throughout the building—at every doorway, in the upper balconies, in every hall—the scarlet warriors kept watch.

The door closed behind Atilius; he and Balbinus found themselves standing on an exquisite mosaic floor depicting the campaigns of Julius Caesar against the Celts in Gallia. The reception area was richly furnished with broad couches and marble tables, and although Atilius had often been in the room, today everything seemed different. The Emperor had honored him publicly, and now he had requested a private audience. This had to reflect favorably on him in the eyes of the other senators.

Atilius waited by the door as Antoninus finished talking to his adopted son, Marcus Aurelius, and to the Centurion of the Guard. The centurion left the room without a word, or even a nod, making Atilius feel vaguely uncomfortable.

"Ah, Atilius Titianus," Antoninus said, looking up, "come, come, have some grapes." He motioned with his hand to a table filled with grapes, wine, cheeses and breads. "Two years ago I casually remarked that I liked grapes, and now everywhere I go ... well ... you can see ... grapes. I don't dare say I like desert mushrooms—some poor fellow would be sent to the African deserts looking for them."

"I am sure he would count it a privilege to serve the Emperor," Atilius said.

Antoninus' face showed his disagreement. He flopped on a couch, expelling his breath wearily. Marcus Aurelius sat on a couch opposite the Emperor, leaving Atilius and Balbinus conspicuously standing alone.

"You know," the Emperor began, "I never wanted this position. For three weeks Hadrian implored me to take it—on his deathbed. What could I say?" He ate a grape, grunted his approval, and took two more. "Now that I'm here, I intend to avoid the adventuresome paths of my predecessors that buried us in debt. The Empire is large enough—in its present state it takes a year to travel from one end to the other. Further growth invites chaos."

The Emperor sighed. "Even my small expansion in Britannia has mired me in problems. I thought if we drove the troublemakers north, built another Wall, peace would follow. But that isn't happening, is it? Now that I've built my Wall, I suppose I will have to defend it. It would be embarrassing to spend all that money on defenses, have everyone in the Empire calling my turf barrier Antoninus' Wall, and then, at the first sign of rebellion, run south to the protection of Hadrian's Wall. Besides—" he laughed out loud, "I was vain enough to name Britannia's most distant outpost after my departed wife, Faustina. I would rather explain to a hostile Senate how I lost the whole Wall than to have Faustina's apparition come to me in the night when her fort has been reduced to an ash heap."

Antoninus' expression hardened as he looked at Atilius. "Can you imagine how some opportunist in the Senate might treat such a debacle? Someone always wants to be Emperor. I would have to break my promise about not beheading members of that august body." He took another grape and gazed out the open window. "Hadrian might have lost his sense at the end, but he had wisdom. From now on, I intend to follow his policy of increasing discipline in the army and strengthening the borders. I will stamp out injustice, if that's possible, and lead the people to a new era of prosperity."

"Well spoken," Marcus Aurelius said.

"Yes," Antoninus mused, "I should have included that in my speech." He moved his eyes to Atilius. "How long have you been in the Senate?"

"Four years."

"That makes you a junior senator, does it not?"

"Yes, I suppose it does," Atilius said, surprised at the abruptness of the question.

"Then you have done well in such a brief time. Of course, you have enormous wealth. That in itself is power, isn't it?"

Atilius swallowed.

The Emperor continued. "Your father, Rufus, was a senator, wasn't he? A consul, as I remember. Yes, and there was that nasty business when he tried to overthrow the divine Emperor Hadrian." He chortled. "I sincerely hope certain traits don't run in the family."

Atilius shifted awkwardly and tried to say something.

"Oh, I am sorry," Antoninus said, "I did not mean to embarrass you. It was my little attempt at a joke." He waved his hand, indicating his desire to change the subject. "I am told you have considerable influence in certain circles of the Senate."

"There are some who agree with my positions."

"You sent a message to Britannia's legions in my name." Antoninus' voice carried no emphasis, but his intent was clear.

"I would never presume such a thing," Atilius said. "The truth is, I knew a decision had to be made ... you were in Lanuvium—"

"And you sent a message in my name."

"With respect, I merely pointed out to a senior officer in Britannia what you might want done ... but no, I issued no orders in your name."

"And you had no fear of Senate criticism? Apparently, they were still debating the issue."

"Yes, that is true," Atilius said. "The senators were far from consensus, but my courier message was little more than a reminder of standard orders: legionaries are obliged to protect frontier installations from attack."

"Why did you not send a message informing me of this dilemma?"

"But I did," Atilius said, flustered. "Gaius Balbinus sent a messenger ... we waited two days before sending even my simple reminder." He looked at Balbinus, who nodded immediately. "And let me add that I saw this situation as an emergency. I cannot imagine ever needing to—"

"Yes," Antoninus said, leaning back on his couch, "I should hope not."

Atilius felt his face flush.

Antoninus rubbed his short-cropped beard. "Tell me, what exactly was this emergency that came to the Senate?"

"We were told the Celts had attacked the outposts along the Wall."

"Interesting," Antoninus said, "because I've had word that the uprising came *after* our legions went north of the Wall."

"After!" Atilius looked shocked. "I do not think your information can be accurate. The Senate received three separate messages from different garrisons along the Wall—two centurions and a tribune—they reported massive attacks under way."

"We seem to have a difference of opinion among observers. What do you make of that?"

"Well … that's a good question," Atilius said, hoping to sound thoughtful. "I suppose the point to keep in mind is that whatever the reports, for years these Celts have attacked our Wall-forts. It was time we replied in kind."

"Yes, you may be right. Conflicting reports are troublesome ...." He slapped his thighs. "Well, we shouldn't worry about it. Truth has a way of getting out, don't you agree?"

Atilius promptly agreed. His discussion with Antoninus was different from what he had expected. With the Emperor sitting, and him standing, it felt more like an investigation than an audience.

The afternoon sun was warm and inviting after the cool of the Senate building. The enormous crowds had dispersed by the time Atilius and Balbinus made their way to the baths.

"I'm glad our audience with the Emperor is over," Balbinus said. "My innards burn like a kiln. Couldn't even eat!" He rubbed his stomach, visible even in his loose-fitting toga. "Could you make out what he was saying? I was not altogether sure."

"He was warning us, dear Balbinus, not to interfere in Britannia. For all his talk about driving the warlike tribes north, that was not his real motive for expanding beyond Hadrian's Wall."

"I've heard the rumors ... when he ascended the throne, he wanted to appease the old marshals from Trajan's time."

"Nothing of the sort. The marshals were of no consequence. Antoninus is no different from anyone else. He cares about two things: money and power. He assured the Senate that creating a second Wall would enhance the Imperial treasury, and the opposite has happened. He also needed to gain the army's trust, so what better way to look like a Caesar than to expand the province that the first Caesar brought into the Empire?"

Atilius exhaled. "It was a master stroke, I must admit. The people danced in the streets for days. The army embraced Antoninus as a conquering hero, even though his Imperial backside was flattening cushions in Rome during the whole campaign. After twenty years of static borders, everyone was ready for some kind of conquest—and oh, how the army fell into line when Antoninus gave them something to cheer about. But not the Senate. Antoninus' Wall has become a financial nightmare. It soaks up any benefit we might derive from Britannia. And now with these renewed attacks, we must spend even more on security. I can tell you, the Senate is not happy."

"But the army supports him."

"For now. But the army is tired of skirmishes. Send in the troops and finish it, they say. Cautious thinking is an irritant to them. And I agree."

"But why would he honor you in public?"

"That was no honor, Balbinus. I foolishly thought it was—damn my pride. Antoninus is making a statement. He is telling the Senate and the army that he fears no one. By honoring me he appears magnanimous and strong at the same time."

"But he still has problems in Britannia."

"Yes, he has problems. He knows a growing number of senators share my view, that if we pacified the whole island, inevitably the Celts would become model subjects." Atilius frowned. "Antoninus forgets what Julius Caesar proved two hundred years ago. The Celts need a firm hand. Remember Gallia? Even when Julius Caesar defeated Gallia's Celts, still they refused to obey. It was only after he massacred their women and children and cut the hands off their soldiers, that they learned proper behavior. That is what we need now—someone with firm resolve. In one year we could have the Britannic Celts as passive as those in Gallia."

"The Emperor is against expanding our territories."

"Such foolishness could cost Antoninus his crown." Atilius felt his cheeks heat with rage. "The Celts will continue their attacks because they know the Wall signifies weakness. We have no stomach to fight them, so we build a Wall—an absurd policy."

"And when they overrun the Wall, the Senate will see that you were right all along."

"Yes, but meanwhile we must keep the pot boiling. Burn their towns, capture their women—we must do everything short of destroying them."

Balbinus smiled. "Our centurions at the Wall need little encouragement to retaliate. Just a promise of a transfer out of that place does it."

"Don't become careless—"

"Be assured, Senator, nothing can be traced to you. I have a cousin here in Rome who handles the details that need doing at the Wall."

"A cousin? I am not sure I like that."

"A distant cousin," Balbinus said hastily. "He has a Greek name ... comes from the Greek settlement area around Cumae, south of Rome. No one could connect him with me."

"Just the same, send him away for awhile, somewhere safe, perhaps the army. It should not be difficult to get him in and out of the army—a few letters will do it. Who would suspect a recruit? Mind you, pay him well—we might have use for him later."

"I'll send him immediately. Maybe North Africa—"

"Yes, yes," Atilius said impatiently, "and the tribune, what about the tribune and centurions who sent messages to the Senate? Antoninus is sure to search them out."

"They will say nothing. They are absolutely loyal."

"How loyal can they be if they are willing to lie to their Emperor? Silence them. Many brave Romans die in Celtic raids, do they not?"

"I will attend to it."

"Of course you will," Atilius said. "Now to the baths. It has been an exhausting day."

11

It was the worst spring anyone could remember. No one ventured out as icy winds lashed the countryside and torrents of rain beat on the open steppes. For over a hundred miles, Vectis had pressed through the storm, traveling the Roman road from Rusicade to Timgad in the province of Numidia, North Africa. He was thankful for his two extra mounts that enabled him to continue his journey with a minimum of delay, but the going was tough. Streams of dirty water filled the gutters along the roadsides, overflowing the curbstones with sludge in the low-lying areas. The wind came in gusts and at odd angles as it whipped across the empty grasslands, lifting his oilskins, and soaking his garments underneath. By the third week, Vectis was exhausted; his hands gripped the reins like claws, protruding awkwardly in front, and he was wondering if his journey would ever end.

Late one morning, a dark outline appeared against the gray skies. He shielded his eyes and peered through the rain. Mountains! Finally, in the distance he could see mountains. Hidden in the hills, he knew, was the legionary town of Timgad with its lively inns and soothing bathhouses. He drew in his cloak, wiped the water from his face and pictured himself floating in a hot pool, drinking warmed cups of spiced wine. A chill ran down his back at the thought, and he quickened his pace.

For hours Vectis followed the road as it rose steadily and flattened out in a vast plateau of rolling grasslands. The city of

Timgad stood starkly against the naked sky, a warm haven beckoning him to come in from the biting winds.

"This is it," the innkeeper said, pushing open the door of a depressing little room.

Vectis saw something scurry under a pile of straw in the corner.

"There's a cot," the innkeeper continued, "blankets on the table and lots of straw. Good and dry too." His front teeth were brown and rotting. "I dug a trench around the buildings, so even in this weather, you don't need to worry."

Vectis stared at the room in disbelief. Was this what the provinces were like?

The innkeeper picked up his disappointment. "It's not much," he said, "but there's nothing better round here. We never get rain like this. Most places are flooded. They've got an inch of water covering their floors because they were too lazy to dig run-off trenches." His rough laugh ended in a prolonged cough that sounded as if he were about to bring up his insides. He stepped away from the door, turned his head, and spewed a stream of slime onto a clump of centaurea thistles growing by the door. "You want it, or not?" he asked, wiping phlegm from his mouth and rubbing it into the sleeve of his already stained tunic.

Vectis took the room and asked for directions to the main bathhouse. A few hours in the hot pools, some steam and a rubdown—that's what he needed.

"Can't use the bathhouse," the innkeeper said, "they're replacing the boilers. They had to stop work because of the rain. Some small ones, but you won't get in—filled with locals."

Vectis spent the night on a mattress stuffed with lumpy straw. He pulled the blankets around his neck and listened to the sound of the wind whining outside, banging the shutters. The continual rumble of thunder grew more distant in his mind as sleep crept over him. Tomorrow would be another day, but tonight, at least, he was warm and dry—he barely noticed the rustling movements beneath his cot.

At dawn, Vectis pulled himself stiffly from his bed and gathered his things. The wind had calmed, coming in occasional bursts through the streetside colonnades, but the heavy rains continued as he started out, beating on his hood and cascading down his front. The horses snorted and tossed their heads, trying to escape the rain buffeting their faces.

Vectis found himself staring at the blue limestone pavement, and the large drops splashing in puddles at the edge of the road. He passed the city limit markers, and the dark tombs lining the roadsides—some tall and thin, some like peak-roofed houses, low and somber. In the gray light, he could see carved images of the inhabitants peering out at him, their faces throbbing with vitality forever gone. One was young, much like himself. Vectis shuddered. Was he so different? Had he ridden this same road, laughing and talking about joys yet to come? And now he gazed inertly at travelers, a silent testimony to the mercurial power of the fates. Or was he a harbinger of death? In the training camps men die, his father had said.

Vectis hunched over, pulled his hood across his face, and headed down the road. It was noon before he arrived at the huge legionary camp of Lambaesis, home of Legion III, the guardian of Africa.

Vectis passed by an assembly of shacks, tents, and stone huts that stretched for miles across the flat terrain. Every Roman base had its colony of followers, as they were called, even if the colony had permanent structures, as this one had. The outside colony was populated with local people—merchants, tradesmen, their wives and children, day laborers for the fort, and, of course, plenty of prostitutes to service the soldiers. Legionary camps like Lambaesis required a large colony of followers to function properly.

A thousand feet from the fort, the wooden ramps and walkways began. Vectis tied his horses and followed the six-foot wide walkways that led to the fort. Surrounding the entire complex, the legionaries had strewn grass and reeds, giving a smooth, pleasant appearance to the land. It was an illusion. Underneath, Vectis knew, traps and pits, impaling stakes and knifelike slivers of metal awaited the unwary. After the pits came a belt of closely packed stakes, easily

seen, and bristling with barbed iron hooks. Anyone trying to cross—
especially at night—would be torn to shreds.

Finally, two broad trenches encircled the fortress to prevent
enemies from mounting an attack near the walls. The trenches were
half filled with run-off from the stubborn rains, and mud oozed over
the edges and down into the water, making it certain that when the
grounds dried, the legionaries would again be dredging with their
baskets and shovels. The fortress wall itself was a vast earth palisade,
twelve feet high and topped with a twelve-foot wooden wall. High
overhead Vectis could see the ramparts and fighting parapets, and
soldiers on lookout duty. No enemy would surprise Legion III.

In times of danger, Vectis knew, the legionaries could remove
their walkways and seal their gates, but now the entrance gaped open
and four soldiers, two on either side, stood guard in the pouring rain.

"Recruit?" one asked with a smirk.

Vectis said he was.

"Straight up to the praetorium." He pointed to a massive stone
building dominating the center of camp. With its impressive four-
way arch and brilliant yellow-stuccoed roof, the praetorium rivaled
anything Vectis had seen in Rome. "Don't get lost," one of the guards
said. The soldiers exchanged glances that only the initiated could
share.

Vectis marched as professionally as he could along the wide road
leading to the stone building. He intended to look like a soldier, even
if he was not one yet. On the way he was amazed at how dry the
grounds were, considering all the rain that had fallen. The legionaries
must have dug scores of run-off trenches. Near the arch two guards
directed him to a paved courtyard. Someone would be out to see him,
he was told.

The courtyard was empty and enclosed on three sides by
porticoes with workshops and rooms opening off them. It looked like
the business section of town with shops for carpenters, ropemakers,
tanners, ironworkers, bronzesmiths, saddlers, and brickmakers. On
one side stood a basilica with broad steps and colossal statues.

A door in the stone building cracked open.

"Recruit?" The centurion squinted his eyes, clearly displeased to have rain spraying in his face.

Vectis started to say something, but his words created a pained look on the centurion's face.

"Two miles west," he snapped. "Give me your papers." His hand poked out the narrow opening.

Vectis reached into his oilskins and produced his papers and a letter of recommendation written by his father. The man yanked them out of his hand and as an afterthought asked, "How old are you?"

"Sixteen."

"Sixteen!" The centurion shook his head in irritation. "You need to be seventeen."

"In Rome they said I could—"

"Rome? You're from Rome? Then, maybe I had better read your papers carefully," he said with mock respect, and slammed the door.

Vectis buried his arms under his oilskins and waited.

Again the door opened, this time so wide Vectis could see the entire room. "Come in!" a smiling tribune shouted.

Vectis glanced around the room as he entered. It was bare, except for two big, brass lamps, several chests, and a broad shelf stacked with books. On one wall was a poorly painted fresco of nymphs frolicking in a garden. Someone had heaped maps on a low wooden table. Nearby, three officers warmed themselves around a portable charcoal brazier. They looked up now and then, obviously curious about their visitor. The tribune invited him to share the warmth of their fire, and apologized for the absence of the legate, the legion commander. He shrugged away the problem of Vectis's age, saying that a year one way or the other made no difference. Off to one side the centurion sat watching, saying nothing.

Vectis saw a letter in the tribune's hand, not from his father, but from someone else. His heart sank.

"Not often we get a recommendation from a senator," he said. "You should be posted as a tribune."

Vectis explained about his father, his years as a legionary and centurion, and how he wanted to test himself in the same way. They didn't understand, as Vectis expected, but they gave him a document certifying he'd had been approved and placed his letters in a chest with a pile of others.

Two miles down the road, Vectis found the training grounds—a small circular camp protected by a seven-foot ditch, traps, and a makeshift fence. In contrast to the main camp, the only permanent structure was a wooden centurion's hut near the center of camp. The place was depressing. Puddles of water lay everywhere. In the worst section, sleeping tents rose like sails from a lake. It was as if the officers had chosen the worst location for the legionary tents to make their occupants work harder draining off the water.

The recruits were digging trenches and hauling mud to the camp's edge. Others pulled rock-filled carts and dumped them in the trenches. They looked different from the soldiers in Rome—they had a Mediterranean, raw-boned appearance. And sprinkled among them were black-skinned recruits from beyond the southern mountains.

Vectis found the centurion—a thin man named Vatinius— standing on a raised wooden platform, shielded from the rain by rough canvas stretched overhead. Behind him stood two subordinate officers, one muscular and short, the other thin-hipped, with skin as black as coal. Vatinius hollered at somebody across the compound. His balding head flared red, and the veins in his neck bulged.

"Imbecile!" Don't you know which way is north?" He slammed his heavy centurion's cane onto the platform, his eyes riveted on an engineer in the distance. Then turning and stabbing his finger in his officers' faces, he screamed, "Get out there and straighten up that mess! If you don't, find a shovel because you'll be up to your knees in mud, digging."

The two nodded and hurried off to do the centurion's bidding. Vatinius stared after them, his jaw set, veins still swollen. He glanced down at Vectis standing in the rain, ignored him, and glowered at his officers, who were arguing with the engineer.

The centurion paced back and forth, his erect body moving like a caged animal. He kept the three-foot vine stalk in constant motion, turning it, rubbing it, smacking it against the palm of his hand. He paused beside a shelf lined with scores of helmets; even in the drizzling rain they seemed to sparkle.

"Enough!" he shrieked. "Bring him here! I want him now!" He kicked a half-dozen helmets off the platform into the mud. "Bend him over the edge," he shouted as the officers hurried the unfortunate engineer toward the platform. They pulled off the man's body armor and tunic and bent him over the corner of the platform, exposing his back. The shorter officer looped a rope around his wrists.

"Get away from him," Vatinius said. "I don't want him held or tied." He dropped to one knee, yanked the man's head back by the hair, and hissed in his ear, "You will learn Roman discipline. I will cane you six times. If you move or make a sound, my officers will cut off your head, and stuff it into the trench you wouldn't dig. Is that clear?"

The engineer tried to nod.

"Good. Then we understand each other. When we're finished here, if you can walk, you will go back and do as my officers say."

With that, Vatinius rose and brought his vine stalk around, crashing down on the man's exposed white flesh. The engineer arched up, but uttered no sound. Six times Vatinius crashed his cane down, ignoring the blood splattered on his victim's back. The last few blows forced groans from the engineer's lips, but Vatinius said nothing about the sounds. He motioned for several recruits to place the broken man in a cart, and instructed one to wash him in the river and have him taken to the surgery.

Vectis watched silently as they hauled the engineer across the compound and out the gates.

The centurion cleaned his hands and face in a basin of water, then toweled himself. He paused, remembering Vectis still standing in front of the platform. He beckoned with his fingers. "Let me see it," he said.

Vectis put his approval certificate in the centurion's outstretched hand.

"Vectis Trebellius Quadratus," he said, reading the certificate. "Your *Praenomen* is Vectis? What kind of name is that?"

Vectis had heard the question before. "My father named me after an island," he said.

Vatinius turned to the remaining officer. "Get Vectis," he underscored the name, "outfitted and ready to go. By the next trumpet call I expect to see him wielding the most important weapon in the Roman army."

Ten minutes later Vectis stood fully dressed in the supply tent. He looked every bit a Roman soldier, from his hobnail sandals to his gleaming helmet. He had no weapons—he would receive them later, he was told. Recruits were not yet worthy to bear such sacred objects of Imperial trust. Right now, he would learn Roman discipline, marching, and how to care for his equipment. Soldiers usually wore yellow tunics and leather helmets during work details, but Vatinius insisted on full gear. No matter how dirty their armor became during the day, the next morning it must shine like the sun. The supply clerk marked his equipment for identification, handed him three gold pieces for joining the army, and informed him that a month's advance pay had been recorded beside his name in the ledger. Then he was marched out into the rain toward the platform where the centurion stood.

This time when Vatinius saw Vectis he walked immediately to the front of the platform, scroll in hand. "Do you swear," he began without so much as a glance at words, "to perform with enthusiasm whatever the Emperor commands, to follow your generals wherever they lead, to obey your officers in all circumstances, never to desert, nor to shrink from battle on pain of death?"

Vectis answered with the words he had been given: "I so swear, on pain of death."

"You are now a soldier of the Empire," Vatinius said. "May the gods preserve you."

With the oath completed, Vatinius turned back to his work. The officer handed Vectis a numbered chit, telling him he could rest when they called his number. Vectis then deposited his helmet on the platform and marched to a trench. In his hands the officer placed the most important weapon in the Roman army—a shovel.

Vectis drove his shovel into the soaked turf, wrenched the sod loose, and dumped it into a waiting cart. Steadily, along with two other soldiers, he scooped out a drainage ditch, three feet wide, three feet deep, that sloped toward the trench circling the camp. Behind them, others filled the ditch with rock and sand, smoothed and packed it.

The two recruits with him in the trench were as different from each other as it was possible to be. Julian Quintillius was a white-skinned, North African recruit from Cyrene, about twenty-one, with a ready smile, and a distinct joy for living. He seemed to find perverse pleasure in the most mundane things. He talked constantly about the leisurely life he had left behind in Cyrene—the afternoon baths, the women who sought his companionship. Now, he said, he was a mud specialist; in his four days as a soldier, he had examined thousands of chunks of mud and not one had failed to excite him.

"Take this lump of mud," he said, holding it up as if inspecting a rare jewel. "We are the first ones in the history of the world to see it. Not Caesar, not Alexander—just you and me. Have you ever thought of that?"

"Put your nose on the trench bottom and you'll see even more," Vectis said.

Julian's face showed his dissatisfaction. "You have as much imagination as our thick-necked friend," he said, gesturing toward the sullen-looking soldier scraping dirt at the end of the trench.

Vectis had already greeted the soldier, or at least had tried to, and received no reply. Unlike Julian, the man never said a word. He was older, distant, and the kind best left to himself. He had thick fingers, powerful arms, and a broad chest that combined well with his brutish face.

On the platform, Vatinius banged his vine stalk against the struts. "These trenches," he hollered, "will be finished this afternoon."

Vectis stopped digging and watched the centurion repeating his words, slowly, loudly, from each side of the platform.

"Better keep working," Julian said. "If Vinestalk sees you resting—"

"Vinestalk? They call him Vinestalk?"

"Vinestalk Vatinius," he said. "He carries it wherever he goes, canes someone every hour."

"I saw what he did to that engineer."

"That'll be you if you stop working."

Vectis started digging with renewed vigor. The rains had stopped and Vatinius prowled the maze of trenches looking for slow-moving workers. He issued a stream of orders, always in his loudest voice, and always punctuated with a brisk blow to the back of anyone he considered a slacker.

A horn sounded. An officer called out a number, and a quarter of the men left their trenches for a twenty-minute rest. Others emerged from the few dry tents, trudging toward the carts and trenches where they had earlier been. Julian looked at his number and smiled. He turned, said something to Vectis, and started out of the trench. Without warning, the big man was beside him, grabbing him roughly by the arm.

"Give me your chit," he said, holding out his hand.

Julian glanced down at the big man's shovel, held low, and poised. He sighed. "Sure, we can trade chits. In fact, I would like that." He reached into his tunic for the chit and said, "Mud-digging is my favorite activity."

The man said nothing, handed Julian his own chit and left.

"Why did you do that?" Vectis asked, annoyed. "You should have given him a face-full of mud."

"Yeah, maybe."

"I wouldn't have given him my chit."

Julian stopped shoveling. "Look, I'm not here to fight that half-barbarian. Chances are, in a few months I'll never see him again. You should think about that too. Last week he stabbed a recruit in the leg."

"He's not supposed to have a knife," Vectis said, immediately thinking how naive his comment must have sounded.

Julian just shrugged.

"Didn't one of the officers see—"

"Nobody saw or reported anything," Julian said.

Vectis stared at Julian.

"There is definitely something wrong with him. When he arrived a week ago he ate a live frog, in front of everyone—just chewed it up."

"Why ... why would he do that?"

"I have no idea," Julian said. "To show us his power, I suppose—who knows? I'm just telling you he's strange. Have you noticed his age? He can't be a new recruit. Maybe he's a runaway slave or a discipline problem from the regular army—I don't know. I heard he killed someone, and that's why he's here—for discipline."

"Well, he shouldn't get away with—"

"I agree, but a rest period is not that important."

"It won't stop there. He'll be back. His kind always comes back."

"If he wants something else, he can have it," Julian said. "My ambition is to survive training and get out of here."

Vectis turned back to his work and pondered his father's warning to mind his business. He had said he would, yet he knew he would not have given up his chit.

Late that afternoon, when they had finished the drainage trenches, and the compound was finally dry, Vatinius marched his company, a century of eighty men, down to the river. In the Roman army the smallest division of men was called a century and a full century was never a hundred men, always eighty or less.

"Get that mud off you," Vatinius shouted. "A Roman soldier is a clean soldier. And a clean soldier is a healthy soldier." They scrubbed their clothes and bodies as Vatinius stood at the river's edge and harangued them on cleanliness.

"More barbarians die every year from dirty water and filthy clothes than from the combined swords of the Roman Empire," he declared. "Do you know why?"

"Fumes!" the men shouted from the water.

"Fumes from dirt and sweat and stagnant water can kill you. The Roman army has never suffered a plague, and never will. Do you know why?"

"We keep clean," the men replied in unison.

With the lesson over the men rinsed their equipment and headed back to see what delight the cook had fixed for dinner.

The morning sun had partially risen as the recruits assembled for inspection. Vatinius strode the line looking each man in the eyes, examining armor for tarnish, and smacking his vine stalk across the back of any whose armor showed spots of discoloration.

"Today," he roared, "you will learn to march. You will march until the nails on your boots are gone. You will march until you are the best marching century in the Roman army. Do you believe that?"

"Yes, Centurion," they shouted.

"You will run, and swim, and carry logs, and climb ropes until your bodies glisten like Corinthian granite. You will push yourselves to the limit, and then you will go some more. And when you meet some poor, dumb barbarian army, you won't need swords to defeat them—you will rip out their hearts with your hands. That's how mean you'll be. Do you believe that?"

"Yes, Centurion."

"Some of you fat-bodies are a disgrace." He whacked his cane across the stomach of one of the recruits. "You ride around in daddy's carriage stuffing pork sausages and honey cakes in your mouths. The only exercise you get is chasing slave girls into the bush. Those days are over! You are now a legionary in the Roman army. You will march all day and fight all night, and you'll never get tired because Roman soldiers don't get tired."

Vatinius stopped in front of Vectis, looked him over from the knob topping his iron helmet to the nails on his boots.

"Vectis, isn't it?"

"Yes, Centurion."

"Glad you're in the army, boy?"

"Yes, Centurion."

"Not afraid you'll bruise your elbow or blister your little feet?"

"No, Centurion."

Vatinius reached for Vectis's hand, inspected the blisters covering it, and then shook his head. "Haven't done much digging, have you Vectis?"

"No, Centurion."

"But you like digging, don't you? Toughens those powder-white hands."

"Yes, Centurion."

Vatinius then gave his standard speech on trench digging, a lecture Julian said he had already heard three times.

"Trench digging builds the body," Vatinius intoned, "and it feeds the soul. When a legionary beds down at night, sleep comes easily. Why?" His eyes swept the men. "Because he surrounds himself with a trench, a stockade and traps. That's why! No barbarian tiptoes around a Roman camp in the dark, unless he wants a broken leg."

Vectis glanced at Julian, who mouthed in unison, "unless he wants a broken leg."

"Before battle," Vatinius continued, "the Roman army always builds a camp and leaves a third of its forces to defend the walls of that camp. That's why we destroy our enemies! When things go poorly for us in battle—which is seldom—we simply retreat to the safety of our fortified camp. When things go poorly for a barbarian army, they've nothing to do but run." He nodded his head, and gave the men a knowing look.

"So that shovel," Vatinius shouted, "not the spear or the short sword, as you've probably heard—but the shovel strapped to your backs is the real reason for the success of the Roman army." He smiled to himself, pleased with his speech. Then he continued down the line.

He stopped at the next man, pushed his face to within an inch, and spat out the words, "You look like a coward. You'll run first chance you get, won't you, boy?"

"No, Centurion," he said sincerely.

"I intend to watch you," Vatinius shouted, shaking his cane in the recruit's face. "You understand?"

"Yes, Centurion."

"And you, what's your story?" Vatinius said, stopping in front of the soldier with the thick neck. "You're as old as I am. A discipline problem, aren't you?"

"No, Centurion," he said with a noted lack of enthusiasm.

Vatinius paused, and smiled. "You don't seem to be soldier material. My guess is that you don't like taking orders. Now, if you don't like taking orders, we could have a problem, because I like giving orders." He rubbed his vine stalk slowly, as if thinking. "Well, I really don't care what your problem is ... I know your type ... and I will break you, as I've broken so many others ...." Vatinius turned to leave, and then asked, "What's your name?"

"Kallias."

"Kallias! That's a Greek name. Do you sing?"

"No."

Vatinius jabbed his cane into Kallias's chest and hollered, "No, what?"

"No, Centurion," Kallias said with anger visible on his face.

Vatinius continued as if he hadn't noticed the anger. "I once heard about a Greek priest from Thrace who sipped wine from a big, glass phallus. I'm told he wore a chiffon gown and a golden hair net, and at sunset he could be seen combing the hills for young acolytes to train in the ... ah ... secret arts of Greece." He smiled. "You ever heard of that?"

"No, Centurion."

"Perfumed his bristly neck every day, decked himself out in ribboned mitres, and read Aeolic poetry from the island of Lesbos. You must have heard of him—or someone like him." He stared at Kallias. "Well?"

"No, Centurion."

"But Greek soldiers like young boys, don't they?"

Kallias seemed to be searching for words.

"And you like boys too. That's why you enlisted in the army, isn't it?"

"No, Centurion."

"Vectis is a young boy." He motioned toward Vectis. "You can't wait for some dark night to get your hands under his tunic. Isn't that right, Greek?"

"No, Centurion."

"I think you're lying to me."

Kallias said nothing.

"I demand a response."

"Centurion, I joined the army to—"

Vatinius whirled around, bringing his cane heavily across Kallias's face. His helmet flew from his head, and bounced off the next soldier onto the ground. Kallias staggered to one side, but didn't fall. He wiped the blood from above his left eye, looked briefly at it, and then straight into the eyes of Vatinius.

"Don't you egg-eye me, Greek!" Vatinius screamed. "And stand up straight! Around here you will learn the meaning of the word discipline. When I talk to you, you will say either, 'Yes, Centurion,' or 'No, Centurion.' Do you understand?"

"Yes, Centurion."

Vatinius lowered his vine stalk and moved on to the next man, then, turning back, he said, "You don't like me, do you Greek?"

"Yes, Centurion," Kallias said with hate burning in his eyes.

Vatinius smiled at the ambiguity in the answer.

The succeeding days were filled with marching: slow march, quick march, accelerated march at a run. At one point Vatinius became so enraged that he tied in rows the feet of the entire century to keep them in step. His vine stalk continually encouraged the troops, and once even Vectis felt its sting.

Every afternoon the exercises began promptly at the sixth hour, with the sun high overhead. They always began with a ten-mile run—to liberate the spirits in them, Vatinius said—then the long and high jump, followed by log lifting. Lying on their backs, they lifted logs with their arms, sat up with logs on their chests, and ran with logs on their shoulders. Then they climbed ropes and concluded the exercises with swimming training in the river.

Vatinius never spared the vine stalk, especially on the back of Kallias. In private the Greek talked obsessively about killing the overbearing centurion, but to his face he held his tongue.

Before long, Kallias's continual tirade against Vatinius found a few listening ears. His grumbling appealed to the scum in the camp—soldiers who had no respect for Rome or her traditions, whose only motive in joining the army was the steady pay and the possibility of looting some unfortunate city. It was common to hear men discussing ways Vatinius could meet his end. Most seemed harmless fantasy—burying him alive in a trench, or staking him out on the night steppes, food for the jackals—but others sounded serious. Vectis decided to follow his father's advice; he kept his mouth shut and minded his business.

But one night his worst fears were realized.

12

It was sundown. All over the camp men were polishing their helmets and body armor, making them shine like the sun. Vectis and Julian had just sat down outside their tent, readying their equipment for the morning inspection, when between the rows of tents, they noticed the square form of Kallias coming their way. Following closely behind were the familiar shapes of his two friends, one a Kallias look-alike, only younger, the other, a cadaverous type with sunken eyes and a perpetual grin on his face. Vectis kept polishing his armor, never once looking up. The Greek stopped in front of Julian, dropping his helmet and strip armor.

"I want this done by morning," he said.

Vectis's neck grew hot. He glared at Kallias, and heard himself saying, "Clean it yourself! He's not doing anything for you."

"It's no problem," Julian said hastily, "I can finish it in a half-hour."

"No," Kallias said, "no, you won't have to do it because bucket mouth here will do it. Won't you bucket mouth?" With that he kicked his equipment over toward Vectis.

Vectis stared at the equipment, his mind searching for the right response.

Kallias's look-alike stepped toward Vectis, and shoved a knife under his ear, "If it's not done, you'll be dead in three days," he said. "As sure as you are sitting here, you will be dead."

"It'll be done," Julian interrupted, "don't worry."

"I want to hear you say it," Kallias said as his underling pressed the knife into Vectis's neck.

"It'll be done," Vectis said.

"It better be," Kallias sneered.

"Who cares about polishing a few pieces of equipment?" Julian said as they watched the three return to their tents.

"I care. I will not do it."

Julian looked up. "You don't have to. I got us into trouble. So I'll do it."

"No one will polish his equipment."

"Vectis," Julian said with alarm in his voice, "you don't know what you're saying. That Greek will kill you."

"I'll keep out of his way for the next while."

Julian shook his head. "It's not worth it. He has a growing number of friends now. You can't hide from them all. I'll shine his equipment and be done with it."

"Next week he will ask for your pay. No, I told you before ... once you start, it never stops."

"So I end up doing extra duties. So what? How much has he bothered me since he took my chit in the trench? Hardly at all. This is ridiculous. Give me his armor. I could have finished it by now."

Vectis pulled the equipment closer. "He told *me* to do it. It's my responsibility."

"Your responsibility, but he'll come after us both."

"You might be right," Vectis said, "but I think it's me he's after now."

"Your pride is that important? You would risk everything for the sake of your pride?"

Vectis thought for a moment and then looked Julian in the eyes. "I don't know what it is. Maybe pride ... but I can't do it, Julian, and I can't let you do it either. I just can't. I am sorry."

Julian nodded with a look of resignation. "I try to avoid useless confrontations," he said, "but I am no coward. If the Greek comes after you, he'll have to deal with me too."

"We'll die together," Vectis said with a smile.

"Together," Julian said.

The trumpet rang across the compound; morning had come. Vectis tied the last thong on his body armor and looked up to see Kallias striding bull-like through the rows of tents. His eyes fastened on Vectis, then darted around looking for his armor.

"Where's my equipment?"

"There," Vectis said, pointing toward the edge of the tent.

"You—" Kallias stared in disbelief. His armor lay in the dirt, grimy and unpolished. His fists clenched as he whirled around to see Vectis departing for morning inspection.

"Oh, you are dead!" he screamed after Vectis. "Dead! Do you hear me? Dead!"

Vectis kept walking. As he neared the fall-in point, he glanced back to see Kallias on his knees, scrubbing furiously at his helmet. Then, at a run, he strapped on his equipment and stepped into line bare seconds before Vatinius appeared.

Vatinius walked the line slowly, examining each recruit's equipment. He stopped and peered at the armor joints of one man. "You're not cleaning those corners. I see tarnish!" His cane crashed down on the man's back. "How many times do I have to tell you people? War is more than weapon techniques—you must control the minds of your enemy. When they see you lined up and your armor flashing like the furnace of hell, believe me, they will fill their pants and cry for their mothers."

He continued down the line, shouting and striking the recruits when it seemed appropriate. And then he reached Kallias. His eyes took in the sight, slowly.

"Step out here," he said quietly.

Kallias stepped out.

"Your armor has not been cleaned. Are you testing me?"

"No, Centurion."

"Trying to make a fool of me?"

"No, Centurion."

"Then what is it with you, Greek? You like dirt and filth? Is that it?"

Kallias closed his eyes, his jaw clenched. "No, Centurion," he said between his teeth.

Vatinius looked for a long moment into Kallias's eyes, then stepped back to address the recruits.

"The problem we have here is simple.   This man is stupid. Beatings don't work because he is like a dumb animal. I could beat him all day long, but he still wouldn't respond. So I have to think of new ways to assist him."

Vatinius instructed his officers to march everyone to the edge of the compound, to the latrines.   Then he ordered several recruits to remove the boards from one latrine, leaving an oblong hole. Vatinius walked to the edge and looked in. He turned his head at the smell.

"Why, this hole is nearly full," he exclaimed. "It would be a shame to cover it over when we could empty it and use it again. You like filth, Greek, so I intend to let you empty it."

"Strip, Kallias," the black officer said sharply.

Kallias's face reddened with anger.

"Now!" the other officer shouted.

Kallias mumbled something to the officers, glared at Vatinius, and pulled off the stained armor. Then he piled his clothing on top.

Unable to resist a bare back, Vatinius swung his vine stalk across the exposed flesh, then hollered into Kallias's ear, "You worthless Greek, you will obey every order without question. Now, get into that hole."

Kallias walked over to the edge, grimaced, and jumped in, sinking to his hips, then slowly to his chest. He stared up in blind rage, his eyes stopping at Vectis.

"You will fill your cart and dump the waste one hundred feet beyond the compound," Vatinius said. "This latrine will be cleared by swimming training-hour this afternoon. There will not be a speck of filth here, or on the trail to the dumpsite. If there is, you will eat it."

Kallias worked amazingly fast; by noon he had completed his task. He shuffled down to the river with a cloud of flies following him, cleaned himself, and then returned to scrape the paths he had trod.

During the next three nights Vectis hardly slept; he and Julian alternated watch, expecting an attack—but none came. Throughout the day, Kallias ignored him, never saying a word, not even looking his way. He seemed to have had enough. Even the haranguing about Vatinius had stopped. Every task he accepted enthusiastically, every order he obeyed with a snappy, "Yes, Centurion." Vatinius seemed pleased with his model soldier.

As the days passed into weeks, Vectis himself wondered whether Kallias could have changed. They had said three days, but it was now well over a month since the polishing incident. Maybe he had decided that vengeance was useless.

Every day the endless marching drills continued, the log lifting, the rope climbing. And the tasks grew more difficult. Today the century would march a half-day with full packs and a load of rocks; they would climb a cliff and set up camp—trench and all—before dark.

As the sun rose, Vectis knew the day would be scorching. No rain had fallen for weeks and the ground was cracked and dry. Eighty men marched briskly out of the camp with only three mules to haul the water. Everything else they carried: armor, weapons, shovels, pickaxes, rations, cooking pots, stakes to build a stockade fence and, finally, the load of rocks.

Within an hour, Vectis felt the cramping pain brought on by the enormous weight on his back. He shifted his packs to prevent the straps from cutting into his skin, but no amount of adjustment eased the burning in his shoulders, or the pressure on his back. As the hours wore on, sweat ran down his face, soaking his tunic and streaking the helmet fastened to his strip armor. The heat extracted every drop of moisture from his body until his skin felt like parched clay. He longed for water, just a dribble to cool his mouth, but Vatinius had ordered no rest-breaks until they arrived at the climbing site. A Roman soldier had to be disciplined, he said.

The sweat on the African officer's back glistened in the blazing sun. His body was lean and hard, and his dark skin looked almost purple against the chalk face of the cliff. He moved steadily upward, spider-like, his fingers and toes searching for fissures and outcroppings on the rock. He wore nothing but a loincloth, and around his waist was wrapped a long, thin cord. At the halfway point he paused in seeming relief as the cliff wall gave way to a steep chute that angled to meet the flat ground at the top. There they would make camp.

The African ascended the incline until he reached a loose rock. Carefully he unwound the cord, weighted it with the rock, and threw it out over the edge of the lower face. That done, he continued to the top with the cord tied around his wrist. At the bottom the other officer knotted the cord to a thick climbing rope, and tugged twice. Within thirty minutes, the black officer had hauled up the rope, secured it, and descended. He dressed quickly and began his second ascent, this time laden with full gear, and followed by the recruits, spaced ten feet apart, bearing rock-filled packs.

The climb went as smoothly as could be expected. Loose rocks struck one man, and he fell to his death. Another lost his nerve at the halfway mark, then regained it when he heard Vatinius screaming at him from below. But the weeks of rope-climbing, constant drills, and harsh discipline had achieved their goals. The recruits were able to march without water, climb steep grades with reasonable efficiency, and even set pulleys to haul up mules in rope baskets.

Two-thirds of the group had reached the top when Vatinius started up. He carried the same weighted packs as the others but somehow pulled himself up with ease. Below him on the rope were two recruits, then Vectis, then the rest of the men.

Vectis had climbed with packs before, but never with ones so heavy and never at such height. His arms ached as he pulled himself up, gripping the rope with his feet to lessen the strain. Loose dirt and stone continually fell from above, striking his helmet and shoulders, and filling his eyes and mouth with grit, though never once had he looked up. He concentrated on the rope, and on his hands, careful to keep them close to his body for protection from falling debris. Several times he paused to rest, but only briefly. Below, the remaining officer hollered at anyone who paused too long, and Vectis knew that at the top, special assignments awaited those who slowed the climb.

At the halfway mark, Vectis felt relieved that the most dangerous part—the straight drop—was behind him. He eased himself over the edge to the slope that extended another hundred feet upwards. Ahead he could see Vatinius moving up the rope steadily, and men working at the top, digging trenches and setting up camp. Vectis thought about the long days of training he had endured, days that seemed endless. But after this climb he would be a full-fledged soldier in the Roman army, ready to begin combat instruction.

An assortment of pebbles bounced down from the top, striking him on the shoulders and pack. Stones followed, and a few larger rocks. Something was wrong. Someone was shouting ... fighting at the top .... Vectis strained to see past the men on the rope above, but the dust kept coming. His eyes burned. He turned away, blinking rapidly. Now he could hear Vatinius screaming, almost shrieking. More sand and stones. Vectis pressed his face against the rock as the rubble struck his helmet. He tried to pull himself closer to the top, away from the sheer drop not ten feet behind him.

Above, the fighting continued, and then seemed to stop. A group of men now had hold of the black officer and threw him twisting and turning off the embankment. He bounced and rolled down the incline, clawing with his hands to slow his speed. Then he slid on his back, his arms and legs spread wide, his body pressed against the rock to maintain friction. He slowed and stopped directly across from Vectis.

The African pulled himself onto his stomach and inched his way upward. Vectis could see that his eyes were closed, his tunic in tatters. He was in pain, and moving mechanically. A large rock bounced by him and over the edge, and then another. Vectis glanced up. Kallias's look-alike, his grinning friend, and several others were pushing rocks over the edge. One caught the African on the side of the helmet, and another struck his arm. He lost his grip and slid several feet. Another hit him, this time in the shoulder and face. His body went limp, and slid over the edge.

"Get off the rope! Off! Now!"

Vatinius had already climbed to the side of the rope, was pulling off his packs, and shouting to the men below. Vectis stared up in horror. At the top of the incline, he could see Kallias sawing rapidly at the rope, his knife flashing in the sun.

Vectis ripped off his packs and moved away from the rope, clutching at the rocky incline awkwardly, his hands rigid, his heart pounding. He saw himself losing his grip and plunging to the bottom. The image unnerved him. He heard something above him, a rumbling, then the rocky handholds began to shake. He jerked his head up. Suddenly, from out of the sky, the stone-filled packs of the men above came crashing down the incline. Vectis moved instinctively to the side, flattening his body, and searching for footholds in the rock. Nothing. He began to slide. He grabbed frantically at an outcropping and steadied himself as the stone-bags shattered beside him and bounced on past. He could see the two men above scrambling up the rope, trying to gain some distance before they trusted themselves to the harsh incline. It was a mistake. The rope abruptly snapped, throwing the men outward and yanking them downward like stones plummeting toward an abyss.

"The problem we have here is simple," Kallias shouted to the men around him. "Vinestalk wants to get up this hill, but rocks keep falling on his head." He kicked some loose stones down toward the centurion. "And you down there," he called to Vectis, his face darkening, "I haven't forgotten about you."

Vatinius started up the slope toward Kallias, climbing on all fours, like a crab. Vectis followed, unsteadily, testing each protrusion of rock before trusting his weight to it. One slip would begin an inexorable slide to the cliff wall.

"That's right, Vinestalk," Kallias called, "you keep coming. I want to see your face before you die."

Vatinius worked his way up until he reached the less steep grade near the top, directly below Kallias. He straightened his body slightly, looked up, and said, "You really are a mindless Greek. Do you know what they do to soldiers who kill their officers?"

"Who's killing an officer? The rope broke. It was a tragedy, a real tragedy—"

"They beat them with rods and let their bodies rot in the sun. Sometimes they chop their heads off and jam them on spikes—like the barbarians. Every one of you up there," he screamed, pointing his finger, "will be executed if you stand by and do nothing. It's not too late—"

"It's too late for you," Kallias yelled as he stepped toward a large rock.

"Listen to me—you men—stop this now and the worst you'd get is extra duty. It's the Greek I want, he's the one—"

Kallias had the rock waist-high. "Nobody's listening, Vinestalk."

"They'll find out, you know they will. Stop this nonsense and let's get back to setting up camp."

Vectis's eyes swept the group behind Kallias as the centurion continued talking. A sizeable number of the men were there ... he wondered about the fighting ... probably some, like Julian, had objected and were overwhelmed. The rest were out of sight, not wanting to get involved. Still, Vatinius's words were having an effect. The men seemed uneasy. Killing an officer and a half-dozen recruits stranded on the rope was no light matter. Maybe there was hope yet.

Kallias positioned himself directly above Vatinius. The centurion kept moving up the embankment, never taking his eyes from his enemy. He was now yards away and finding the climbing easier on the less steep grade. Behind Kallias, the men had begun arguing, and renewed hope surged through Vectis. It was short-lived. Kallias shouted something over his shoulder, and they fell silent. Then, taking aim, he thrust the rock out with his knee and down. Vatinius dropped to the ground and twisted sideways, but not enough—the boulder landed with a crunch on his back. He screamed, clutching his ribs. Kallias hauled another, heavier rock, bracing it against his chest as he moved closer to the hunched centurion. Pushing the rock with his body, he dumped it down toward Vatinius. It landed a foot short, and to the side.

Kallias stared at the unmoving centurion, thinking. He drew his knife, ignored the cautions of those around him, and edged his way down the slope.

As Kallias neared, Vatinius lifted his head and said something to him that made the Greek roar contemptuously, "I knew you'd beg for—"

Vatinius's hand shot up and wrapped like a snake around Kallias's ankle, yanking outward. Kallias threw his arms backwards, windmilling. He lurched sideways and tumbled to the ground, rolling over Vatinius and past him down the hill. He stopped short of the steeper grade. The centurion clutched his side and moved down toward Kallias, who appeared dazed. He kicked the Greek in the face. It had no effect. He kicked him again. Kallias caught his leg and dragged him down. He swung his knife at Vatinius, but the centurion grabbed him by the wrist. They wrestled, as if they had forgotten where they were, and suddenly they pitched downward out of control, bouncing apart and sliding into the chute where the rope had been. The lighter centurion slowed himself first, but continued his downward slide. Kallias, below, flung his arms out desperately, but couldn't stop his slide. He rolled onto his stomach and jammed his knife with two hands into the rocky surface, stopping not a body length from the cliff wall.

Vectis watched from across the slope as Vatinius slid helplessly down toward the Greek. He clawed at the rock the same way the black officer had, but he couldn't stop. Kallias set himself, and waited. His knife arced through the air, down into the centurion's chest.

It might have been reflex, Vectis didn't know, but Vatinius jerked forward, grasping Kallias around the middle. He twisted the Greek to a sitting position and for an instant the centurion's eyes locked on Vectis. "Roman discipline!" he shouted, and pushed out with his legs. Kallias screamed in terror, his arms grasping air. Vatinius clamped a hand over the Greek's mouth as the two plunged over the cliff.

13

The interrogation of the recruits proved useless. At the bottom of the cliff the surviving officer had seen nothing, couldn't remember the order in which the men had climbed or anything unusual before the ascent. Everyone claimed to be in the group that tried to stop Kallias. Julian, though the conspirators had knocked him cold, fell under the same suspicion as the others. Even Vectis appeared guilty; some said he had climbed down the slope to help Kallias.

Surprisingly, Kallias survived the fall. He had landed on Vatinius. He now lay in the surgery at Lambaesis, recovering from crushed bones, and awaiting the results of his senatorial appeal.

It took three weeks for the new centurion to arrive. Three weeks of interrogation, of constant marching, of confinement. Rations were reduced from wheat to barley, and for two long, humiliating days the men were forced to stand in the parade ground at Camp Lambaesis, beltless, their tunics hanging loose at their feet, their hands holding pieces of horse dung.

When they returned to the training camp everyone was talking about the unusual centurion who would soon arrive, and what they had heard about him at Lambaesis. In his youth, it was said, he had been an enemy of Rome. His black African marauders had made a mockery of Rome's southern borders, sweeping down from the Atlas Mountains, terrorizing the defenders. The legions of the Empire were ill equipped to fight this kind of war. They preferred large battles with vast armies pitted against each other.

But the marauders were quick and crafty, never settling long in one place, never opening themselves to a mass attack. Finally, Rome sent an elite group of legionaries who tracked and eventually overwhelmed the marauders. The centurion in charge of the legion was so impressed with the courage and daring of the marauder leader that he spared his life, selling him to a gladiator school. After three years, and more than a hundred kills, he was granted freedom and citizenship on the condition that he enlist in the army as a special instructor in weapons. Lately, he had developed another specialty — disciplining rebellious soldiers.

The African sun was intense as Vectis waited in ranks for the new centurion to appear. Great drops of sweat ran down his cheeks and dripped from his chin, soaking his tunic. His head ached and his feet burned, but not once did he or his fellow recruits so much as flinch in the hot sun. Punishment was coming, and no one wanted to draw attention to himself.

Now he could see the special centurion as he moved to the wooden platform at the center of the compound. He had big hands and shoulders, and eyes that shone like the dark creatures of the night. He sat down on the railing edge and removed several sheets of paper from a leather folder stamped "Legion III." Vectis suspected it was the report from Camp Lambaesis.

A legionary called the recruits to order, then waited as a contingent of fully armed soldiers formed a line opposite the rows of men. When the troops were ready, the African centurion glanced up to acknowledge the legionary in charge, but remained seated. He was no longer reading, but staring off at some distant point on the horizon. Finally, he slipped the report inside the folder, breathed heavily, and turned toward the recruits standing at attention. He pushed himself off the platform railing and moved slowly toward them, his eyes studying each man.

Vectis watched him approach, moving like a giant black cat stalking prey. Everything about him — his dark, glowering face, the way he shifted his eyes, his powerful chest and forearms — spoke of death.

He stopped in front of the men and crossed his arms. "This training unit has killed two officers of the Roman army," he said in a deep voice, with an accent that betrayed his North African origins. "Mutinous acts cannot be tolerated, and so they sent for me. Draw a number ... every tenth man ...."

He didn't need to continue. Everyone understood the punishment he had chosen. Decimation. Every tenth man would die.

"I hate gambling," Julian whispered to Vectis, "always seem to lose."

Vectis nodded and turned his eyes reluctantly to the soldier working his way down the row. He reached into the helmet and pulled out a chit slashed three times. Instinctively, he covered it with his hand, as did the other recruits. With the chits distributed, the legionary returned to his position behind the dark centurion.

Again, the centurion surveyed the men. "If you have number three, remain standing. The rest, sit down."

The men dropped to the ground. Vectis looked down at his number again, as if he had been mistaken, or as if somehow the number might magically change.

"Vectis!" Julian whispered from his position on the ground. The color had drained from his face.

"Well ...." Vectis shrugged and half-smiled at Julian. "I guess ... I ahh ...." He couldn't finish the thought—he didn't know what to say.

The soldiers moved quickly through the men to the stunned seven still standing. They took Vectis by the arms, one on each side, and led him toward the front where the exercise logs lay. He had time only to say over his shoulder, "Write my father a letter."

They bound his arms behind him and knotted a length of rope around his neck. Almost gently, it seemed, the legionaries placed him in line with the others. Vectis found himself short of air and tried to breathe deeply. He glanced down the row. No one looked up or struggled, no one cried or pleaded for his life, and the murmuring of the fates grew louder, like the sound of distant hoofbeats. Death was fast approaching, and there was nothing anyone could do. The men had the same hopeless faces he had seen in the slave markets, eyes staring without seeing, shoulders slunk low, some trying to gather their drifting thoughts, or perhaps recall a life too soon gone by. Behind each man stood two soldiers, one with his hand over the wrist binding, the other holding the rope.

"State your name for the recording officer," the centurion said, looking at the first man.

"Marcus Velleius Martialis," he said, hardly lifting his eyes.

"Marcus Velleius Martialis, you have been judged guilty of insurrection. You are sentenced to die in the decimation." The centurion nodded to the legionaries, who led the man to the place of execution. The executioner stepped forward and took the rope. He pushed the man to his knees and drew the rope down until the victim's neck lay flat on the log. The axe crashed down.

"This is Roman justice," the centurion said in the stillness following the event.

Vectis felt his stomach react at the sight of a head lying in the dust, but he forced himself to be calm. He gazed at the trees clustered near the edge of the compound. He had never looked at trees before, not really. A shame he had never taken the time.

The second man had to repeat his name, his voice was so low. The third and fourth came and went. Each time the centurion repeated his words, "This is Roman justice."

"State your name," the centurion said to the fifth. Vectis heard the name but couldn't focus on the words. What did it matter? he thought. In a few minutes his life would be over. Death would come and his spirit would dwell on another level.

Death!

The idea frightened him.

Staggered him.

Fresh sweat broke out on his forehead as he thought of the afterlife and its terrors. He wasn't ready to die. He didn't believe in the gods. No one did. Only the untutored imagined a world filled with cold, menacing spirits. He had seen soldiers from the lower classes on their knees, soothing the spirits supposedly living in the rivers and forests and swamps. They bowed before their altars and cried out, hoping their supplications would curb malevolent influences drifting in the air. But the gods couldn't exist, could they?

And what about the mystery religions he had so often ignored? Maybe the preachers of the eastern deities were right. They sounded convincing. How could he have presumed that the glorious Mithra would accept him in the nether gloom? And what about Isis, the goddess of death? Maybe she was waiting right now, talons ready to sink into his feeble flesh. Even the loving Chrestus demanded his followers to sacrifice everything. What had he sacrificed to merit forgiveness?

Vectis prayed for mercy, for an endless void. He watched as they led the man in front of him to the dark log. Now he stood alone, first in line, his protection gone.

"This is Roman justice," came the voice, and they cleared away number five.

"State your name."

"Vectis Trebellius Quadratus," he said, trying to speak in an even voice to mask his terror.

The eyes of the centurion met his, lingered for a moment, then shifted away. "Vectis Trebellius Quadratus," he said, looking back, "you have been judged guilty of insurrection. You are sentenced to die in the decimation." He nodded to the legionary. Vectis felt himself walking toward the log. His heart thumped frantically. He felt panic rising as he looked down at the log, at the blood-splattered ground. A childhood nightmare passed through his mind ... it was always the same ... someone covering his face with smooth wax, smothering him. He forced his mind away, picturing himself lying in the cool grass, looking up at the leaves, so many shades of green.

The legionary beside him had hold of his shoulders, turning him to face the log. He saw the rope exchange hands. Gently, but firmly, a hand pushed him down. He was kneeling now. The faces of his mother and father, his sister, faded in and out, obscuring the movements around him. He saw the tombs lining the road outside Timgad, and the youthful face warning him of his impending death. Even the sorrowful countenance of the little slave girl from the *Via Lata* in Rome appeared for a moment, then disappeared behind a stockade fence. He sucked in some air; it felt so clean, so good. The rope tightened, drawing his neck forward.

Someone stepped behind him and placed a hand on his shoulder.

"This is Roman mercy," came the deep voice of the centurion as his knife slipped through the wrist-bindings.

Vectis remained on his knees, unsure what had happened. Someone pulled him up. The recruits were on their feet mumbling words of approval, as again Vectis heard the same words of mercy, and number seven was also freed.

At sunset the men heard the door of the centurion's cabin open.

No one moved his head or turned his eyes; the century remained motionless as their new centurion moved steadily around them toward the front. For nearly five hours, he had kept them standing in ranks to hear his address. After the decimation he had said simply, "Wait here," and the troops waited. The legionaries had departed for Lambaesis, and the centurion remained alone with the recruits.

During those hours, Vectis's mind swirled with images of life and death, and his own narrow escape. It seemed incredible that the fates alone had saved him. He wondered about the centurion. Had he intended to bestow mercy on the last two? But why? Merely to demonstrate that Rome believed in mercy as well as justice? Maybe he opted for mercy because Vectis looked younger than the others, or because he disbelieved the report that Vectis had climbed down to help Kallias? More likely, Vectis concluded, granting mercy was a tactic. The recruits would be more inclined to follow a man who was hard but fair. Whatever the answer, he was glad to be alive. He hardly noticed the hours passing, and the sun sinking, glowing red, like a ball of fire.

The centurion faced the recruits, his back to the rapidly dropping sun, his body dark and featureless, the edges of his armor glowing crimson, like heated metal.

"Repeat after me," he said. "I swear to perform with enthusiasm whatever the Emperor commands, to follow my generals wherever they lead, and to obey my officers in all circumstances."

The men repeated the words.

"I will never desert," the centurion continued, "nor will I shrink from battle on pain of death."

The voices chanted in unison under the darkening sky, an eerie sound, like an oath on a grave.

"In the next five weeks," the centurion said, "I will instruct you in methods of war. If you violate this pledge, you will die. There will be no investigation, no appeal. I will simply kill you." He moved closer to the men, his face still veiled by the dark, and his eyes showing only a trace of movement. "The gladiators of North Africa call me Jupiter because I am a god among men." He paused. "Is there anyone who doubts that?" Nobody spoke. Jupiter moved silently down the line until he came to the biggest man. His hand bolted out, seizing him by the throat. "You have doubts?" he asked, still looking at the troops. The man gasped and shook his head. Jupiter released him and stepped back, his face now a shadow rimmed in purple.

"You will address me as Centurion, never as Jupiter. You will never talk to me unless I talk to you first. And you will never, ever look me in the eyes. If you do, I will consider that a challenge, and you will die. You look only here," he said, pointing to his chest.

Vectis dropped his eyes, but soon found himself staring at the outline of Jupiter's face. He forced his eyes away, wondering how he would keep from glancing up.

"Tomorrow we begin training in weapons. Dismissed."

The next morning at inspection the recruits faced their centurion. He walked solemnly across the compound, his left hand resting on the hilt of his sword. Vectis kept his eyes down until the centurion had passed. He looked familiar. Something about him—his deliberate walk or the way he swung his arms—reminded Vectis of something from long ago, something long forgotten. Try as he might, all Vectis had was a vague recollection, a childhood dream perhaps. No, not a dream. He did know this centurion, from somewhere deep in his past.

Jupiter was completing his inspection near the back rows when Vectis heard him say something. Someone laughed nervously. In a dead calm voice Jupiter asked: "Why are you looking at me?"

In spite of himself, Vectis whipped his head around to see who Jupiter was confronting. The centurion was standing before Kallias's look-alike.

"Didn't I warn you about looking me in the eyes?"

The man turned away.

"It's too late now," Jupiter said.

The man stared at the ground, his mouth tight and angry.

Jupiter moved closer. "I am talking to you, soldier. You think this is a game?"

Rage spread across the man's face as he stood dumbly, refusing to speak. His defiance was total as he shifted his eyes to Jupiter. Last night he had made it clear to everyone what he thought of the new centurion's rules. Ridiculous, he had said. He thinks he's a god, so nobody can look at him. The first chance I get, he had said, I'm leaving this insane place. Now he stood glaring at the centurion, plainly angry at himself, at Jupiter, at everyone, for not having looked away. He was caught like a fly in a web. Beside him stood his friend, grinning nervously, his eyes darting around.

Jupiter spun on his heel and strode to the front. "Up here," he said, "and bring with you that smirking fool."

The centurion yanked out his sword, drew a huge circle in the sandy earth, and waited for the two soldiers to reach the front.

"These recruits have challenged my authority," he said loudly for all to hear. "You will now learn what happens when someone disobeys me."

He turned to the two men standing uncomfortably across from him. "Move into the circle!"

They hesitated, and then stepped across the line.

"I intend to kill you," Jupiter said, his voice matter-of-fact. "Here are the rules: if you step out of this circle, I will have you executed. If you refuse to fight, you'll be executed. There is only one hope—you have to kill me." He raised his voice, addressing all the men. "If either of these men cuts me down, both go free. The legate at Lambaesis knows my methods. Nothing will be held against anyone."

Vectis felt his face heating, his breathing growing irregular. The emotions of the previous day flooded his mind, and he could feel the misery the men were experiencing. Not that they didn't deserve to die; if anyone deserved death, it was these two. They were as guilty as Kallias for the men who perished during the climb. But the casual way Jupiter used terror bothered him. He enjoyed killing, almost thrived on it.

"Are you ready?" Jupiter asked. "Here, you will need these." He threw his sword at the feet of the grinning soldier and his dagger near the other. They picked up the weapons and gaped at the defenseless centurion. Jupiter wiped his hands on his leggings, crouched, and started toward them. They glanced at each other, then jerked forward, their eyes on the rapidly approaching centurion. Three feet from the men he stopped, moved laterally, and reached out tentatively with his left hand. His right hand flashed down and snatched the sword by its blade, driving it into the side of the more distant look-alike of Kallias. Then, sweeping it back, still gripping the blade, he tore a rough hole in the other's chest. Both men crumpled to the ground, dead instantly.

During the next four weeks, nobody looked into Jupiter's eyes. Vectis's fears of accidentally glancing up miraculously disappeared. He found it easy to keep his eyes fastened on the centurion's chest. And a curious thing, Jupiter wore the same medal his father treasured, the *corona muralis*, for being the first to scale an enemy's wall.

But the man was nothing like his father. His father deplored senseless killing; Jupiter loved it. He was a barbarian in Roman clothing. Barbarians never change, Vectis thought. They are born to murder and destruction, and no amount of training can change them. Only after generations can the foul behavior natural to their kind be bred out. True Romans killed, certainly, but they killed the enemy. They didn't murder their way to the top. Jupiter, it seemed, had murdered his way to authority in the Roman army.

If the officers at Lambaesis wanted to teach the recruits a lesson, Jupiter the gladiator was well chosen. He cared nothing about life or death, as long as he cleaned out the troublemakers and produced disciplined troops.   Like Vatinius, everything was discipline and obedience; but unlike Vatinius, Jupiter would stop at nothing to achieve his goals. On the third day, he crushed a man's skull with a wooden practice sword for speaking without permission.   Then he lashed his body to the camp gate as a lesson to others. When they began to use real weapons, a recruit swung his sword instead of thrusting it underhand. Jupiter forced him to stand legs apart in front of the target while the entire century ran by, thrusting their swords at an X painted under his crotch. "You were lucky this time," Jupiter said to the shaken recruit. "Next time I'll blindfold the men." No one doubted that he would, and no one swung his sword.

It was twilight again—time for Jupiter's nightly talk. Vectis and Julian had filled the camp vats with river water and were standing in front of their tents, strapping on equipment and checking for tarnish. Jupiter was not as fastidious about tarnish as Vatinius had been, but he inspected three times a day, and no one wanted to be caught with something amiss.

"Ready?" Vectis asked.

"I am," Julian said as he adjusted the shoulder belt that held his sword under his right arm. He slipped the leather case off his shield and collected his two needle-topped spears.   "Well?" he asked, standing at attention so Vectis could inspect him.

"You look fine," Vectis said. "Tilt your spears away from your body more. There. Now you're perfect."

"You are too," he said, eyeing Vectis. "You have that brutal look Jupiter admires in a soldier."

"It has been a brutal camp," Vectis said, his face serious. "Different from what I expected."

"You've changed, you know."

Vectis nodded.

"Since the decimation," Julian said.

"I expected to die," Vectis said. He never mentioned his vision— that he seemed to feel his severed head rolling in the sand, and see his headless body draped over the log. The thought made him shudder.

"Anyway, it's over, and now for some reason I don't have the same fear of death."

The bugle sounded, calling the recruits to the parade ground.

"Well, I still have a large fear of death," Julian said, "so we had better get going before Jupiter leaves his cabin."

The two made their way through the tents toward the parade ground. The armor and weapons felt natural, almost comfortable, they had worn them so much since Jupiter arrived.

"Less than a week to go," Julian said. "All we have left is a training exercise. How bad can that be?"

"Depends on the exercise."

"Jupiter told someone it was a war game."

"I wonder how realistic he will make it?"

"His favorite subject is killing," Julian said wryly. "What does that tell you?"

They lined up in their assigned spots and awaited the centurion.

As usual, Jupiter stood at the edge of the parade ground with his back to the setting sun, the fading light glinting off his armor. Seventy feet away the century of men waited in its box formation. A bugle sounded. The troops started across the parade ground toward Jupiter, keeping in step with a horn tapping out the rhythm. Another bugle, and the box stopped. The recruits stood legs astride, spears tilted away from their bodies, shields resting on the ground. They stared straight ahead, not at Jupiter, or anything in particular. Just straight ahead. For five minutes they held their positions as Jupiter silently inspected them. Then someone coughed.

"Silence!" Jupiter shouted.

Vectis expected the centurion to seek out the offender and strike him down. But he didn't. Instead, he explained the importance of suppressing all urges to talk, cough or move.

"Silence unsettles the enemy," he said. "Relax your minds. Be confident. Concentrate on the heartbeat of your adversaries. They are shrieking and howling—crying out to their gods. And they are filled with fear. Terrified! They know what the Roman army can do. Now they become desperate. They send out some hulking champion who challenges you. Who will fight me? he cries. Are the Romans cowards? Send me your best centurion! I will fight him one-handed! Now the enemy warriors run around wildly, laughing and hooting. Anything to steady their drooping knees. You don't hear them. You don't see them. They are a noise that will soon be lost in the wind."

Jupiter walked the breadth of the recruits, talking about the confidence Roman soldiers had, knowing a third of their troops were behind them, defending stockade walls in case of retreat. He reminded them they fought only twenty minutes before fresh troops took their place. He added as if an afterthought: "Even hardened barbarians grow tired ... I know."

He picked up a spear. "Absolute simplicity," he said, holding the lead-weighted spear aloft. "This is the weapon that built the Roman Empire. When you hurl this at a charging mob," he jerked the weapon toward the recruits as if he intended to throw, causing the men in the line of fire to flinch, "the battle is over." His lips curled into a smile. "They can stop it with their shields or their bodies. In either case, they're ruined. A shieldless or wounded enemy is destined for the rivers of Hades. It is only a matter of time."

It struck Vectis that he had looked up at the spear and down to Jupiter's chest without the slightest temptation to glance at his eyes. He even had seen his mouth smile, if you could call Jupiter's sneer a smile. Now, in the near dark, as he stared at the centurion's body and listened to his flow of words, he felt a strange, hypnotic sensation. It wasn't so much the content of Jupiter's words as the rolling cadence of his voice, perhaps the low tones, or the deep shadows that steadily swallowed the remainder of the day.

"Your job is to protect the Empire," Jupiter said. "You do this because you are Roman soldiers, and Roman soldiers never defile their sacred trust. I would sooner cast myself into a pit of Egyptian vipers than violate my soldier's oath." He threw his spear to the ground. "One day you will stand on the frontiers of the world—in some lonely outpost that only the mind of Mithra can find. You will look into the eyes of the barbarians and see hate mixed with awe. Then you'll know who you are—Roman soldiers! The sight of you will chill the heart of the bravest warriors. There isn't an army in this world that can stand before you—and they know it. For nearly a thousand years, soldiers of Rome have advanced steadily to the ends of the earth. They have put to death the kings of this age and have shaken the pillars of the world."

He pointed his finger at the recruits. "That is your heritage. Every one of you. You might come from a conquered nation or a family of poor means—but now you are Roman. You are as much a Roman as the men of Caesar's army. You train the way they trained, you fight the way they fought. You are the arm of Rome now—the power of the Eternal City. Don't ever forget that. Everywhere you go, you bring order and civilization. Every square foot of ground you tread upon, you claim for Rome. Once you strap on Roman equipment you become a light to the nations, a master of foreign deities. So walk like masters, act like masters. When you go into battle, remember, endless lines of soldiers fed by an Empire of endless resources stand behind you. Rome will never disappoint you. See that you remain worthy.

"Now," he said, abruptly changing subjects, "tomorrow we begin final exercises. For weeks you have been practicing weapons, battle tactics, defending and sieging forts. Now you have an opportunity to demonstrate your skills. At sunrise you will set off for old Camp Romanus, a day's march to the south. You will have two days to restore her defenses sufficient to withstand an attack from another camp's recruits. They will have two hundred and forty men, more than triple your number, because it is easier to defend a fort than attack it. Your weapons will be wooden swords, and every soldier will carry a dipper of red ocher. Strike your enemy in a vital area with the paint and you've got a kill. Five observers will accompany each group."

The harsh rays of the dying sun were now replaced by the soft light of the rising moon, and with it came a chilling breeze. "Leading your group," Jupiter continued, "will be Vectis Trebellius. If anyone disobeys his orders, it will be as if he had disobeyed me. And you will pay for your blunder." He dropped his head before uttering his parting words. "If you fail, and those other recruits overwhelm your fort, every one of you will be posted to Camp Lambaesis for the start of your permanent duty. Dismissed."

Vectis stood in silence. Why would Jupiter choose him to lead? He was the youngest soldier in the century. He felt embarrassed to command men ten years his senior. And the punishment for losing ... permanent duty at Lambaesis! Everyone knew about their insubordination, the dung holding, and the decimation. Duty at Lambaesis would be unbearable. And he'd be responsible if they lost.

"I know what you're thinking," Julian said, jolting him from his thoughts.

Vectis shook his head in disbelief. "Leading your group," he said, mimicking Jupiter, "will be Vectis Trebellius, a soldier of vast experience." He would have groaned if he weren't afraid of appearing so weak. "You know, Julian, I could have been posted a tribune—not a military tribune, not at my age—but a staff tribune, shuffling dispatches and learning how a legion works. But no, I wanted to take the route of the legionary. Now I've got to defend that fort or we'll all end up at Lambaesis eating dung for the next two years."

"You'll do fine. At least no one will disobey you."

"That's true," Vectis said, allowing a smile to cross his face. He could count on Julian to see the bright side. "They sure won't disobey me—no matter how outlandish my orders."

Vectis felt better after talking to Julian. He lay in his tent trying to remember what he had learned about defending forts. He would simply have to make the fortress impregnable—even if he had to work the men till they dropped. No matter what happened, he promised himself, no one would overrun that camp.

14

Six columns of thirteen men, three mules, and five observers left the compound the next morning. Vectis tried to look the part of a leader, raising his arm formally, and shouting "Hail Caesar" as he passed Jupiter standing by the door of his lodge, but he received only a nod in return. Hours later he found the old road that led to Camp Romanus. Long stretches lay buried in the drifting sand, but with its unswerving lines, the soldiers were able to follow it through the hills and steep canyons, and finally along the narrow gorge that issued onto the arid plain of Romanus. There, on level ground, at the edge of a long-dried riverbed, lay the ruins of the camp.

"It's nothing but a pile of rubble," Julian moaned.

Vectis squinted in the afternoon light. Julian was right. The fort had been reduced to a mound of crushed stone and broken timbers. "We'll know better when we get closer," Vectis said, striving to be positive. "It's the ditches that count. If they have some depth, we can clean out the filled sections and maybe even restore the old trap-holes."

The view from the Romanus plain did nothing to improve their spirits. The compound looked like the ruins of an ancient city, with collapsed roofs and broken walls, and drifts of sand from the western dunes. A pack of dogs crept from a cellar, cautiously observed the intruders, then scurried off. Vectis felt sick. How could he possibly fortify this rubble in two days? It looked like it had been derelict for half a century. Here and there, he could see the telltale marks of campfires—probably desert nomads using it for shelter. The garrison was definitely Roman, with traces of bathhouses and streets laid out in perfect squares. It might have been a training fort at one time, Vectis thought, but it was useless now.

He walked the perimeter, inspecting the once seven foot ditches that had safeguarded Roman lives, but now little more than elongated dips in the ground. With every step he grew more discouraged. Debris from the ancient walls, sand, and the relentless desert winds had done their work. Everything would have to be redone. Sections of the walls remained standing, which was good, but they looked unsteady, ready to topple with the slightest blow. He glanced around, giving the compound a long hard look, wondering whether it was even possible to turn the rubble into a defensible position.

The real problem was the size of the fort—too big. Seventy-five men could not defend its walls even if they managed to rebuild them. And how could they possibly dredge the trenches? That alone would take days with such a small force. Construct a tighter fort? he wondered. Choose a section with a solid wall, add a new wall to enclose the area, and then scoop out another ditch. It was possible, but with so much debris around, the enemy could easily fill the trench, heap rocks against the wall, and breach the fort. But what option did he have?

"We're wasting time!" shouted a soldier named Lepcis. "You're supposed to be our commander. What do you want us to do?"

Vectis shot a glance at Lepcis but said nothing. He ordered half the men to rebuild his scaled-down fort and half to dig trenches around it. They worked till nightfall, not even taking time to set their tents. They would sleep under the stars. As the men searched for a smooth piece of ground and unrolled their bedding, Vectis heard them griping about his plans, and he wondered whether Vatinius or Jupiter had ever heard similar complaints.

What worried him was the viability of the fort. How could they survive the allotted four days with an improvised defense? A day or two, sure, but four days? He checked on the sentries, had a swallow of warm water from a water bag, and began his own search for a sleeping spot.

He lay on his back, staring up at the blackness spattered with countless points of light. What would he do, he wondered, if this were a fight to the death, if he really were facing a hostile force? Would he try to construct a defense, or attack? Maybe surprise them along the road in one of those steep canyons.

The next morning Vectis woke stiff and cold. It always surprised him how icy the night desert could be. He gulped down some dried fruit, relieved himself, and set the men to their tasks. The work progressed slowly. He inspected the terrain facing the fort, a flat, broad plain, perfect for an army of superior force. Soon the plain would be filled with enemy recruits bent on destroying his defenses— and they would, too. They would dump rubble in his trenches the first day and pound his walls flat the next. He and the others would trudge off to Lambaesis in disgrace—

"Centurion!" came a mocking voice, "how deep you want these ditches?"

Anger flashed through Vectis. What's the matter with these men? Didn't they realize in two days the place would be crawling with soldiers? Look at them! Smirking, enjoying a cheap joke. He hadn't asked to command. He ran his eyes down the line of men leaning on their shovels—they moved like old women. This will not work, he thought, not in two days.

For a moment he froze, weighing the possibilities. He would gamble. What else could he do?

"No more digging ditches," he hollered, "I want you out of there! Now! Get boards, stone—anything—and pile it along the front of the trench. Pack it with mud. Make it look as if we have spent days dredging the old trenches. The rest of you," he felt excitement surging through his body, "forget what I said about building a new wall. I want you to make it look like we have restored the fort. Prop up the walls if you have to, but make certain the front of the fort appears intact to scouts observing it from that ravine." He smacked his hands together. "Get moving!"

Nobody moved.

Every man in the camp was staring at him. Even Julian looked stunned at his sudden outburst. Of course, he thought, how could they know my plan? I sound like an excited child. Got to be calm, more controlled, explain myself.

"This fort will not withstand a four-day siege," he began, "no matter how hard we work. Back there," he pointed toward the ravine with its canyons and narrow passageways, "is our best hope. If we can convince them we intend to defend this fort, we can surprise them from behind. These are not battle-ready legionaries—they are recruits like us. They won't expect us to do anything except follow standard procedure. If we attack first, we'll wipe out half their men before they even form up in battle lines."

"I say we follow procedure and fortify," one of the men said.

Another growled, "We were told to rebuild the fort, not to hide in the hills like barbarians." He looked at the observers for support. But there was none. One made a gesture indicating his indifference to what they decided.

"I think we're safer here than in those rocks," said another. Several murmured their approval.

"This is not a Greek plebiscite," Vectis countered, "I am telling you what we will do."

Everyone began to talk at once. Men were turning their backs and shaking their heads in disagreement. None of the words were distinct, but Vectis could hear them groaning, saying his plan was ludicrous, he was a boy, it wouldn't work.

Vectis had no idea whether his plan would work either, but he was certain of one thing: any scheme to rebuild would fail. He also knew he had to gain control, fast. Before he realized it, he had flung a fistful of rocks at the closest knot of men.

He eyed them as they grew quiet. "For the next four days—like it or not—I am your commander and you will do as I say!"

They looked at each other, hesitating.

"Julian! Start at this end," he gestured toward the men in the trench. "Take the names of those who refuse my orders."

Julian climbed over a mound of broken stone that used to be a wall and confronted the first man. "What is your name?" he asked coldly. "Jupiter will want to talk to you."

The man's face blanched. "I'm ready to obey orders," he mumbled, "not sure what to do, is all."

"Fine!" Julian shifted his eyes to the next man. "Name?"

"I'm ready," he said, raising his palms upward to show his utter willingness.

"Anyone else?" Julian demanded, looking from face to face. The entire group began nodding in agreement.

Julian turned to Vectis. "Looks like everyone is eager to obey your orders, commander."

"There! Right there," Vectis said, pointing his finger toward a brook emerging from the rocks and cutting across the valley. "That's the nearest water to our fort. They will set up camp there."

Vectis and Julian lay on an overhang of rock above the valley. For an hour, they had inspected the canyon passes, planning their attack.

"How can you be sure?" Julian asked. "Maybe they'll camp on the plain."

"I don't think so. It's too open there, too near our fort, and too vulnerable to a night attack. My father always told me to think like the enemy. Well, the enemy today are recruits. They are terrified of making a mistake. They will do everything properly. In the valley here, they have water, a rock face to protect their backs and wood to complete their siege machines." He looked toward the narrow ravine that opened onto the plain. "The ravine is their only worry. They have to pass through it to get to the plain."

"And we'll be there."

"Right. We'll leave four or five men in the fort to keep visible. Their scouts will report what they see—a fortified Camp Romanus. No reason to hide in the rocks when we have a fortress to fight from."

It took longer to build a sham fort than Vectis had expected. But he had made the right decision. If it took a whole day to erect flimsy wall-fronts and earthworks, any defense would have been doomed.

Vectis surveyed the fort from the smooth bottom of the ravine, where it opened onto the plain, the same spot where later that afternoon enemy scouts would stand. Almost certainly, they would not venture any closer onto the plain—too easy for a small group to race out and capture them. Vectis felt mildly satisfied with the fort. It looked real enough. Soldiers patrolled the ramparts, and smoke fires gave the appearance of meals being cooked. He could even hear the occasional rumble of voices—a necessary part of the deception—and the braying of mules. He had hoped to build higher walls and a better rampart for the sentries to walk. He could see other flaws, but from this distance, the scouts would no doubt count them as weaknesses to be reported.

Vectis walked down the ravine to the narrowest section—about fifty feet across—where they planned to attack. Two piles of rocks were heaped opposite each other. Farther along another two piles were ready. Vectis studied them. Perfect, he thought. The mounds blended well with the steep hillsides, invisible traps for the enemy.

He watched Julian organizing the troops, readying them for the attack. With no margin for error, Julian was repeating his instructions to ensure complete unity among the men. "Remember," he said, "they will leave a third of their men behind in their night-camp. The first rockslide will shut that group out of the battle. The second will seal the far end of the gorge to prevent the main body from escaping onto the plain. Dust will be everywhere. Hit five or six in the chest with paint, then get out of there. Head back to the rocks and wait for the observers to clear out the dead. Watch you don't get paint on yourself, or you'll be one of the dead. If we are lucky, only a remnant will be left to deal with."

"What about the ones still in the night-camp?" someone asked.

Vectis stepped forward. "We will tell them there's been an accident," Vectis said, "a rockslide. We need their help. When they come out, I will signal with a bugle, and we paint them red."

The men smiled, showing their approval. Not only would they defend themselves, they would annihilate the enemy.

"Suppose they don't trust us?" Lepcis cried. "Suppose they ask an observer to confirm that the war exercise is over. Then what do we do?"

Lepcis's voice was irritating, high-pitched and whining, but Vectis knew that others might have the same fears. He replied in a detached voice, "Then we head back to the plain and wait. Their forces will be so shaken, I doubt they can defeat us in a set battle."

"They're coming!" shouted the lookouts perched high on the rocks overlooking the inner canyon.

Vectis ordered everyone to his assigned place. They had an hour before the scouts would arrive, but the men needed time to settle into their areas. It wouldn't do to be stuck overnight in an uncomfortable spot when silence was essential.

Less than a half-hour later, a single scout made his way cautiously along the canyon floor, and a half-hour after that, three others appeared. Vectis was glad he had insisted his troops conceal themselves immediately on sighting the enemy. His lookouts had missed the lone scout, seeing only the three behind him. The other recruit leader was more cautious than he had expected, and it made him uneasy as he thought about his desperate plan.

At the mouth of the ravine the first scout stopped. He had noticed the fort and waited for the others to catch up. The three were in no hurry. They continued at their same steady speed, apparently having been instructed not to depend on the observations of the first. Vectis noted their careful scrutiny of the hills, their eyes roaming the rocky inclines for movement. They would see nothing. Only a few of his men were watching, and they were spying through the crevices of piled rocks.

The scouts studied the fort a full five minutes. Abruptly, two hurried back through the canyon, leaving the other two as lookouts at the ravine mouth.

With the first test over, Vectis sighed in relief.

Two hours passed before the main body of soldiers appeared. They had twenty to thirty pack animals pulling carts loaded with the moving parts of their siege equipment. Trees near the brook would supply the heavy logs necessary for ramps and battering rams.

As Vectis had guessed, the troops set up camp near the brook. A contingent dug a trench, another constructed a picket fence, and another organized the camp. The commander, a tall, thin-headed man, and three others walked the length of the canyon to see the fort for themselves. They glanced up occasionally in the narrow sections, but with the shadows lengthening and the winds wailing down the pass, blowing up sand, there was nothing to see.

As night fell, Vectis prepared himself for the cold. He shoveled out a shallow channel in the sand the length of his body. Then, wrapping his thin blanket around his legs and banking them tightly with sand, he covered himself with his shield. He reflected on the day. So far, things had gone well—the scouts believed the fort was occupied, and the night-camp was set up in the exact place he had hoped. But tomorrow was the real test.

At exactly sunrise the enemy army rose, ate, and left their camp. A third of the men stayed behind to maintain the camp; the rest assembled their portable machines and cut down the necessary wood. By mid-morning they had hauled a half-assembled battering ram out of their camp, along with a dozen wooden flats that would form the basis for their siege tower.

They pushed and pulled their machines slowly down the canyon, toward the narrower part, and the first rock piles. Vectis could feel the excitement rise in him as he watched the soldiers lash their mules steadily toward the trap. He relaxed his hands, suddenly realizing they were clenched tight.

The bulk of the enemy was now directly across from the rocks. Another hundred feet and Vectis could signal the slide that would shut them off from their camp. "Keep coming," he murmured.

Suddenly the enemy commander held up his hand. The soldiers stopped. Vectis peered through his rock shield, stunned. What could be wrong? He scanned the men on the hillside. They were well concealed, and many now stared up in his direction, questions in their faces. Vectis did nothing, hoping they would stay where they were and maintain silence. Back on the valley floor a half-dozen men inspected a wheel on the battering ram. Some began to dismantle the machine—removing the heavier beams from the top portions. Others propped up the damaged wheel, removed it, and rolled it to the side. A group of carpenters went to work with hammers and saws.

Five minutes passed.

Fifteen minutes.

Waiting seemed to frustrate the commander. He paced back and forth near the carpenters, periodically scanning the rocky ledges surrounding his troops. The sun was now burning the hillside and making the exposed sides of the rocks untouchable. Vectis mopped his brow as he squinted through the rocks stacked in front of him. Gnats balled above him, assaulting his face and sticking to the sweat on his neck. Below, the commander abruptly stopped pacing. Whether out of concern for his position, or to keep his recruits busy, he ordered several up the sides of the hills to inspect the crevices and scrub bush along the canyon walls. Grumbling, they dipped the blunted ends of their wooden swords into their paint-containers and started to climb.

Vectis groaned inwardly. A wheel splits and now the enemy is combing the rocks. They were bound to stumble over somebody—his men were everywhere. Vectis could see them trying to dip their swords with minimum movement. If the fight broke out now, his troops hadn't a chance. The enemy forces were too large. Surprise was the only way.

The carpenters had completed their work and were rolling the wheel back to the elevated axle. In seconds they had it on, secured, and lowered to the ground. The soldiers on the hillsides continued their sweep, moving closer to the hidden men. Someone will panic, Vectis thought. There's always a weak link. He glanced down at the battering ram. They were replacing the upper beams, but too slowly. The soldiers were now within yards of his men.

Across the ravine, a soldier called out. All eyes fastened on him as he lost his balance on a steep patch of loose rocks, and tumbled twenty feet down the incline. He lay groaning, holding a dislocated arm.

The enemy commander scowled, showing his disgust. He signaled his soldiers to return, leaving the injured man to find his way down alone.

In short order the procession was moving again, plodding onward. The mules brayed under the whip; men groaned and cursed. Vectis watched with renewed spirits. Then it happened. Someone bumped his stone shield. Rocks jarred free and bounced down the hill. Only a few stones ... hardly noticeable under normal circumstances, but enough on this day to startle wary soldiers guarding the flanks. They signaled their commander, who again called a halt.

His eyes searched every dip and crag of the gorge, then stopped. The brilliant morning sun reflecting off the rocks made it impossible to distinguish the piled rocks from the scattered ones, even though Vectis could see he was staring straight at their trap.

Sweat poured off Vectis's face. The troops needed to move a good fifty feet more before he could trigger the slide. The commander shielded his eyes, trying to see what refused to be seen. He turned his head slowly to the sunny side of the gorge, looked startled, whipped back to the shaded side, then again to Vectis's position.

He knew.

Vectis felt his breath grow shallow. What should he do? A blast of trumpets echoed through the ravine. The soldiers below dropped their ropes and ran toward their commander. Within seconds, they had grabbed their shields from the stacks lining the machines and formed a hollow square, six deep, with the commander at the center. They stood motionless, except for the few who had yet to dip their swords.

Vectis watched with a sick feeling growing in his stomach. The soldiers in the gorge stood ready, staring up at the hills. Why doesn't he move his men? Vectis wondered. He's seen the rock pilings.

"I know you're up there," the commander shouted. "I'm not blind. Some of you are too eager to see what's going on down here—I can see the sun reflecting off your armor."

"I knew it!" came Lepcis's voice from somewhere downhill. "I knew this wouldn't work!"

The commander continued. "As I see it, you have two choices: surrender or fight." His eyes roamed the hills as he spoke to his invisible adversaries, his face aglow with triumph. "I would think it better to fight. That way they will question only your intelligence for hiding up there, not your courage."

Vectis knew he was trapped. Anger burned in him. He could see the amusement on the soldiers' faces below. If this were a real war, he thought, I'd destroy that commander. The fool hadn't even seen the rocks. All I need do is signal and the nearby slide would bury them.

"Well," the thin-headed commander sang out, "what do you want to do, continue the game, or head back to the baths at Lambaesis?"

The name jolted Vectis. Lambaesis! Humiliation and ridicule! And he was the cause. I won't surrender, he thought, as he stepped from behind his rock shield.

"I will give *you* two choices," he hollered down to the commander. "Surrender or die."

Silence.

The commander smiled and began speaking in a leisurely, condescending tone, as if he were talking to an imbecile.

Vectis signaled toward the distant canyon-mouth. On both sides, men began working at the barrier rocks with wooden levers. The rocks popped free, triggering the slides. A tremendous roar filled the valley as thousands of tons of rock crashed down the canyon walls, filling the valley below. Dust burst outward, swirling up and darkening the far end of the canyon.

Vectis pointed to the rocks heaped nearby, and on the shaded side of the ravine. "You will throw your swords to the edge of the ravine and lie on your faces. If you don't, you are all dead."

The commander's face turned ashen on seeing the rock piles. "You ... you can't do that," he sputtered. "This is an exercise."

"This is war," Vectis shouted. "Throw down your swords now!"

"No!" he screamed back. "I don't believe you! You can't just—"

Vectis called across the gorge to Julian, who commanded the shaded side of the valley. Out of the corner of his eye, Vectis noticed the observers scurrying out of the line of destruction. Julian pried a three-foot boulder loose with a pole. It rolled down toward the troops, picking up speed as it dropped. The tight formation on the ravine-floor disintegrated as soldiers scattered from the path of the oncoming rock. Near the bottom, it flew from a ledge and hurtled through the air, shattering the rear support timbers of the battering ram.

"Faces on the ground, or both piles go."

"You must be insane!"

"On the ground."

"All right!" he said, casting his sword to the side and motioning his soldiers to the ground. "But these are not the rules! You'll see what happens when we get to Lambaesis!"

He put his face in the sand.

Camp Lambaesis was as intimidating as ever. The praetorium, with its massive stone arches, radiated power, and to Vectis's mind, a certain intolerance for rash behavior. He had arrived two days earlier and had relived the desert exercise a hundred times. Would he have loosed the rock? He didn't know. At training camp, he had condemned Jupiter for his brutal ways, and now his own brutal decisions were under review by the officers at Lambaesis.

He waited in the courtyard, as he had months earlier, but now the square hummed with the sound of tradespeople and merchants selling their wares. Crowds flowed in and out of the square like a rolling sea, and Vectis felt utterly alone. He had been standing at ready for three hours.

A door opened in the stone building—the same door he had entered that rainy afternoon. He passed through the outer room with its fresco of nymphs, down a hall, and into a chamber where the legate and three other officers waited. In the corner sat Jupiter.

The legate motioned for him to stand facing the officers. "Well, Vectis Trebellius Quadratus," he began stiffly, glancing at a slate in front of him, "we have been discussing your unusual experiences in the desert. The other commander complains you exceeded the stated purpose of the exercise and endangered the lives of Roman soldiers.

We have interviewed the observers and have talked to your centurion." The legate glanced over at Jupiter. "We agree with him that far from being condemned, you deserve credit for your resourcefulness in a hopeless situation. Accordingly, a commendation has been attached to your record. Do you have any questions?"

Vectis shook his head.

"Good. Then you will want to talk with your centurion." With that, the officers rose, nodded to Jupiter, and left the room.

Vectis turned toward Jupiter until he could see the medal on his tunic.

"Anyone who would ambush from the hills of a ravine," Jupiter said coldly, "ought to be selling fruit in Carthage. He has no business commanding men in the Roman army."

Vectis kept his eyes on the medal.

"Ambushes fool children and dogs," Jupiter said, "not trained soldiers." He paused. "Go ahead. Talk."

Vectis swallowed. "I was not fighting trained soldiers. I was up against recruits."

"Recruits? Even recruits should have suspected you'd be in the hills."

"I considered my enemy, and acted accordingly. The fort was not defensible."

"And if the enemy had swept the hills instead of trudging through like dull sheep?"

"There were miles of such hills. They couldn't check them all because the exercise would be over in a week ... and I reasoned they would get tired of checking suspicious-looking hills as they moved along."

"Suppose your enemy had scouted around your mock fort?"

"I thought they wouldn't."

"Suppose they had?"

"I don't know."

"What if they had taken the long way around the canyon and approached the fort from the back side?"

"I never thought of that ... I guess I figured it would take too long."

Jupiter grunted. "You've got imagination. That counts for something. The rockslides show you've got backbone. But the ways of the barbarian seldom work. Roman consistency—that works." He leaned against the wall. "I know ... because Roman ways and a smart commander put chains around my neck. Never forget, it is no accident that Rome rules the world." He rose. "Trust your instincts, but don't forget your training."

He strode out the door, leaving Vectis alone in the center of the room.

PART TWO:
Power and Glory

Ten Years Later

15

It was near dawn when they hoisted the cage above the fire. The naked man crouched inside, screaming and twisting, making the cage wobble drunkenly. His long hair was matted from sweat and his body streaked with dirt. Tongues of fire leapt to caress his feet, fell short, and leapt again. Circling the bonfire, the Druids chanted words of praise to the ancient one, Toutorix, lord of the blood tribute.

Taranis and Eston stood mutely with a dozen other commanders of the Celtic army, huddled against a wall of oaks that marked the inner boundary of the forest shrine. Stretches of melting snow still lay on the ground, remnants of a harsh winter. A single flute pierced the night air, and the chanting grew louder and more frenzied. A covey of ravens beat their wings to the sky. Taranis wondered why the ravens hadn't been startled earlier with the man's hysterical screams. A Druid trick, he guessed. More flutes joined, and soprano voices floated through the trees, blending with the screeches of the caged man. Taranis glanced up. Poor wretch. Probably stole a crust of bread and someone turned him over to the Druids. His feet were likely blistering by now, and it would be some time before they lowered him into the fire.

"This is an evil place," Taranis said.

"Don't say such things," Eston whispered. "Who knows what gods linger in the air?"

"It's not the gods I speak against."

Eston turned his eyes toward the Druids. "Say nothing more, I beg you, not until the sacrifice is complete. I sense the spirits rebuking me."

Taranis understood Eston's fear of the gods; he too shuddered in their presence. But the Druids angered him. He had long thought about the hooded magicians and their efforts to control the minds of tribesmen—especially leaders like himself. They delighted in mystery. After ten years of war, he had yet to see their faces. In the tension-filled moments before a battle he had sometimes glimpsed a priestess's face when she pulled back her hood to expose her head to the gods. But this was rare and only added to the mystery. The high priest, Divicos, was the sole Druid who showed his face, a tight-skinned skull whose eyes sank more with the passing years.

The Druids were swaying now, their bodies flowing with the chant. Some held their hands in front, clasped; others raised them as if receiving nourishment from the spirits. Now and then, a breeze caught the side of a hood and their eyes flashed with firelight. But mostly their faces remained hidden, dark and enigmatic.

Who could deny the Druids' sacred power? They understood the secrets of nature, knew the names of spirits that governed the wind and rain, and here in the woods often communed with the older gods. They could even appease the wrath of severe deities like Toutorix and Esus, and empower warriors preparing for battle. All this Taranis knew and respected. But they never seemed content with their priestly role. They desired power, and the tribal leaders to do their bidding. With Bronix and the old commanders gone, Divicos had seized the mantle of authority for himself.

Taranis nudged Eston, who was staring up at the man whimpering in the cage. "I don't speak against the gods," he repeated.

"What if some spirit tells the Druids your words? We need the priests. The warriors will not fight without their power."

Taranis spoke in measured tones. "Don't be concerned. We shall obtain the Druid blessing. Remember, we are Caledonian commanders. The priests serve us, not the other way around."

Eston grimaced. "My heart pounds in my throat."

"This is Divicos's strategy. He wants control. Events are moving too fast and he doesn't like it. When he gave his blessing to step up attacks on the Wall, he didn't expect us to be so successful."

"Do you think he knows about the River Carrac meeting?"

Taranis thought a moment. "Every commander at the River Carrac is here today. That cannot be a coincidence. He must know about the meeting and our plans for a general assault on the Wall."

"What will Divicos do?"

"Reassert his power," Taranis said.

They turned back to the caged man.

In the blackness of the grove, the commanders waited, their backs to the trees, their minds braced for the Feast of Toutorix, a ritual difficult even for hardened warriors. Away from this place, in the real world, warriors often joked about the Druids and their blood lust. But here in the sacred grove they shifted clumsily, fingering their swords, as if that could protect them from the lurking spirits.

Like the others, Taranis feared the malevolent powers of the gods. He needed the priests for protection, but he never trusted them and their secret arts. There was no way to know what they truly wanted, nor to what extremes they might go in using their mysterious powers. He had been forbidden to speak with anyone except Divicos, and in his absence, a priest named Cathbad. Once he'd overheard Cathbad arguing with Divicos. It was his first inkling of power struggles among the Druids. They had seemed so at harmony with each other, united in purpose. But Taranis now knew better—and he knew to be careful. The Druids might be rife with blemishes, but when it came to the gods, they were his only hope. With marked apprehension, he waited for Toutorix to come.

Abruptly, the wind picked up and the treetops swirled violently. Taranis felt a cold breeze on his face, and saw the fire sputter as if something were choking it. Suddenly, it flared orange, then a brilliant red. Druid tricks, he had heard people say. But it all seemed very real.

The pace of the chanting quickened as the priests moved away from the fire. All eyes turned to the far end of the grove and the closed door of the sacred temple. The huge wooden door swarmed with carvings of birds, foliage, and brightly painted fish. In the four corners, spiral designs overlaid with highly polished silver burned in the radiance of the fire. Most impressive were the enormous stone pillars of the doorframe, which were inset with skulls—enemies on the left, sacrificial victims on the right, and the great ones in the lintels overhead. Bronix was there, at the top near the center—forever enshrined as the greatest warrior ever. No one could look on the temple entrance and doubt the power of the grove.

The door opened and the chanting stopped. In the entry stood the hooded Divicos, a heavy blackthorn cane in his right hand, his body stooped, his pace deliberate as he limped slowly toward the fire. The man in the cage fell silent and pressed his face to his knees, doing his best to bow.

"Divicos, the Immortal!" he cried. "Merciful High Priest! Friend of the gods ... forgive me."

The cage swayed and tipped as he crawled along its edges, rubbing his burns and clutching the wooden bars. His eyes darted from the high priest, to the Druids, to the fire below, and back to the high priest.

"Favored of the Awesome One, I beg you—"

"Yes," Divicos's voice crackled as he limped along, "you shall meet the Awesome One soon." His eyes swept the treetops. "Yes ... yes," his voice dropped to a whisper, as in a trance:

> *Dark One, are you restless?*
> *I sense the soft waves of your groaning,*
> *The raven ravenous among the corpses of men.*
>
> *Dark One, can you hear me?*
> *I wail for the rich plains of Euphoria,*
> *The dried blossoms drifting away in the dust.*
>
> *Dark One, are you thirsty?*
> *Can you taste the thick milk of thanksgiving,*
> *The twisted ruin of the faithless packs of men?*

Divicos, his robes glowing pale orange in the firelight, looked up at the caged man. "Toutorix is standing at the door," he breathed, "waiting for you. I feel his presence."

"Oh, please! Merciful defender of the poor," the man sobbed, "I will serve you forever—"

"Yes, yes, I am sure you would," Divicos mused. He turned his back on the man, bowed his head, and chanted quietly to himself. The man's voice died to a whimper.

After a time Divicos motioned to the Druids, who unearthed a long pole, damp from the ground. With great ceremony, they carried it to the fire where they rolled it back and forth across the burning logs, leveling them. On each roll, sparks and flame shot upward, searing the man's legs. He screamed. Other Druids unearthed more poles, and placed them crosswise on the fire to make a grid for the cage to rest upon.

The victim bounded rat-like from one side of the cage to the other, his hair falling across his face. His terror-stricken eyes fastened on the warriors hidden in the shadows, seeing them for the first time. "Please! Oh please!" he cried, pulling the strings of hair off his face. "You are not like them!" He crawled on his knees, trying to protect his blistered feet. "I fought for Caledonia. I have climbed the Wall ... was wounded by a Roman sword. Look!" He pointed to a wound on his side. "Please, help me! I struck the butcher because he sold me rotten meat. I never meant to harm him. Please, believe me. It was an accident. I'll make up for it ... do anything you say ... just listen ... I'm a good warrior. Last year I fought with Commander Innel when he was killed at Cleddans in the West. And with Taranis under his red banner at Kinneil."

Taranis felt uncomfortable hearing his name. The other commanders continued staring at the fire; they had heard similar pleas before.

It grew worse.

"Wait!" he shrieked, thrusting his arm through the bars, his finger pointing at Taranis. "You are Taranis, the commander! I fought for you. Please, help me! You can save me—you are a god! I know you are!"

"How often do we have to endure this?" Eston muttered in low tones.

"Be thankful they're not stuffing animals into his cage to rip him apart as he burns."

"Finally!" Eston said, as the Druids lowered the cage.

"No! Noooo!" the man cried as he neared the fire. The sickening smell of burning flesh flooded the grove.

Divicos raised his walking stick and cried out: "Toutorix stands at the door."

"May he be satisfied," the warriors and priests intoned.

"The wrath of Toutorix falls on the disobedient," Divicos wailed.

"May our enemies burn in pain," came the unified voices.

Divicos nodded to the three priests lowering the cage, their hands wrapped tightly around the ropes as they inched it downward. The man was now five feet from the inferno, jerking and twisting away from the fire that was shooting up in squares between the logs. Suddenly the priests released the ropes, and the cage dropped, crashing onto the logs and bouncing several times before it came to a solid resting place.

Screams filled the grove.

Like flies to honey, the Druids buzzed around the shrieking man. They studied his every twist and curl, his clutching and quaking. Taranis heard Divicos laugh in delight. Toutorix was pleased. The great god of the blood tribute was speaking through the contortions of the sacrifice and telling Divicos what he needed to know.

For over a minute the man's shrieks pierced the air. When he finally collapsed, and while he was still groaning, the Druids dragged the cage from the fire, doused it with water, and swarmed the smoking crate to more closely monitor the twitches. Eagerly, they poked the charred body with sharpened willow shoots, and jabbered breathlessly if their thrusts produced a response. This done, they again hoisted the cage back into the fire, heaping dry branches and sticks against it. The wood ignited. Flames leapt high into the air to meet the rising sun, and the Druids danced and sang.

Divicos sat hunched in the center of the temple—a dark, narrow room with a high ceiling. Bowls of pine resin burned blackly in the corners, the heavy smoke seemingly intent on smothering the flame, so little light escaped. Taranis coughed up a mouthful of soot, and moved away from a cluster of bowls. Lining both walls was a single row of skulls, beginning at the entrance and feeding into a central shrine at the far end. The shrine itself sat on a raised slab of rock that extended outward for sacrificial offerings to the gods. Above this crouched a hideous beast—six feet tall and three feet wide. Its sculpted body had scales covering its forearms and back, and its taloned paws grasped two lifelike severed heads, whose eyes were closed in death. And from the gaping mouth of the beast, a human limb protruded.

The commanders crowded awkwardly into the temple, saying nothing when Divicos pulled his hood across his face and turned toward the beast, as if he wanted to commune with its powerful spirit. Bent over his gnarled walking stick, his bony fingers restless on its polished surface, the old priest seemed absorbed by the shrine, and the blackness surrounding it. The sun had risen hours ago but inside the Druid temple it was dark and cold, and saturated with the power of the dead

"The spring tribute from the evil ones is small this year," the Druid said in a raspy voice, never once turning his head. "Even with the extra portion my priests added, it is small. Let us thank the gods for their unspeakable mercy." He began praying to himself.

"I thought you asked the Romans for more," said Forgall, a big, red-haired warrior whose dislike for the Druids showed through. "After we divide this, we'll barely have enough for weapons, and nothing for food."

Taranis noted Forgall's restraint. On the way to the Druid grove, he had spoken bluntly about the priests and their greed. They continually took more than their fair share of the silver and gold tribute, he had said.

Divicos turned toward the warriors and removed his hood. His hair was long and gray, his skin pasty white and covered with brown aging spots. He fastened his eyes on Forgall and smiled thinly. "The gods have asked for you by name, Forgall. How often have I stood in the portal and satisfied them with the blood of others? And you dare interrupt my meditation ... testing me. Perhaps next time when they are near I shall whisper your name."

Forgall rubbed his hand across his mouth. "I meant simply that we need more tribute from the Romans."

Divicos's voice revealed his irritation. "I have told you, the evil ones gave us less this renewal season. Much less. The tribute is now half—"

"Half!" Taranis's eyes narrowed in disbelief.

"I need not repeat myself," Divicos said in a murmur. "They will not pay more—not unless we halt all harassment of their lines. With so many headstrong commanders, I could not very well promise them peace."

"Have you told them we will burn their forts to the ground unless they double the tribute?" Taranis asked.

"They know the dangers of impetuous youth," Divicos said pointedly.

Taranis felt the sting of the rebuke. He was not an impetuous youth. He had been a steady hand in the war against Rome for ten years. He had struck behind Roman lines so often, the enemy knew him by name. He and his warriors had saved numerous villages from certain destruction. During the long, dark winters, his men filled the granaries—even those of the Druids. To be called a wet-nosed youth in the presence of other commanders was more than he could bear.

"The high priest should know the dangers of impetuous tongues," he said, looking squarely at Divicos. Taranis felt Eston's hand on his arm as a caution, but his rage would not leave. He stood in Divicos's face, wanting to strike him down.

Divicos turned his head slightly as a concession, easing the tension. In a calm voice he explained, "The evil ones will not pay more because of our raids, and because their Emperor has become involved in another war."

"Their wars are good tidings for us," Taranis said. "They cannot send as many soldiers to Caledonia and we'll overrun their Wall and destroy their forts. Then everything will be ours."

"You listen to me," Divicos said, "all of you. I know about your plans, and I will not sanction open war with the evil ones. The signs are not right. You saw the sacrifice. Where were its hands pointing? North! The one before even faced north. The gods are not with us in the south."

Taranis's rage had subsided. He knew it was folly to overstep himself with Divicos, but he was determined to say what everyone was thinking. "We want to attack *now*. If the gods are not with us in the south, why have we been so successful in our raids at the Wall? We are the commanders of the northern tribes, and every one of us here has won victories—"

"Your *victories*," Divicos hissed, "have come at the cost of my intercession. I have many duties. I cannot send priests every time some warrior wants to attack the Wall. How much plunder do we receive? Eh? Almost nothing!" His hands shook as he gestured with his cane. "You have no understanding ... like beasts of the field." A light glimmered in his sunken eyes, like a torch at the bottom of a well. "I could easily keep my Druids in the forest. Is that what you want?"

Taranis said nothing. Without the Druid sacrifice, his warriors would shrink from battle. And Divicos knew it.

The old priest smiled with his mouth, sensing victory. "We will discuss this again at the festival of the new moon, when the earth brings forth her abundance. Perhaps the signs will change."

Taranis debated with himself whether to speak. The old priest was a man of exceptional power, and not easily quelled. But somehow Bronix had been able to control the excesses of the Druids. There had been a time—before Divicos—when it was common for tribal leaders to depose the high priest. Surely Divicos recognized the danger. Even a high priest had to be careful how he dealt with commanders of the Caledonian army.

"Taranis, do something!" A brash, young commander named Cronn whispered his urgent appeal, obviously hoping for a stronger response from his senior commander.

"No, no," Taranis said, waving off Cronn's distress. "If the high priest finds it too tiring to appoint Druids before our battles, perhaps Cathbad would be willing."

Divicos's eyes flashed and his lips twisted with rage. Taranis wondered whether he had gone too far. The old priest was capable of pronouncing a death curse on those who opposed him. But again, his face smiled coldly, exposing the black spaces between his teeth.

"Cathbad is not the high priest," he said quietly. "I am high priest. I have the power. Do any of you doubt that? Eh? Speak up!"

"None of us doubts you," Taranis said, "and none of us desires another high priest." He paused, allowing the unthinkable to sink in. No one had ever hinted at the possibility of removing Divicos from power.

Divicos turned his sallow face toward Taranis. His skin looked thin and sticky. "Oh, I know about you," he said. "A god, that is what they say you are. Taranis, god of war!" He cackled. "We even heard it this morning, before the dawn." His face changed and he screeched, "Well? Are you a god, that you should speak such things to me?"

"I'm a commander in the Caledonian army."

"Yes, well, that is good, very good." He seemed to lose his train of thought, then recovered, saying in a fatherly tone, "So far you have raided the mile forts along the Wall—and have done well. But the large forts have multitudes of soldiers. Yes, multitudes. They could simply hold off our warriors until the legions arrive, and then what would we do?"

"The legions will not come," Taranis said. "They are afraid to leave the Brigantes and Selgovae tribes unguarded in the south."

"Easy to say. Yes, very easy. Commanders always think they know the thoughts of the evil ones. I have heard it all before. Then the legions come ...." He trailed off, mumbling sacred words to the gods.

"Great high priest," Taranis said respectfully, "at the River Carrac meeting—"

Divicos broke in, his voice piercing. "The evil ones have built a road into the heart of Caledonia. Five giant fortresses! That is what they have north of the great Wall. And do you strike them? No! But now you want to attack the Wall itself."

"Those northern outposts are included in our plans—"

"No, no, no, tell me nothing of your plans. The signs are wrong ... all wrong to repel them from the Wall. We will wait a little longer, and strike together. Then our land will be free and the gods pleased. Meanwhile," his voice grew thin, "we will content ourselves with what we have been doing. Yes, we will attack them where they are weak, and sow fear in their hearts. That is what we will do."

"When we came here," Taranis said tersely, "we understood that—"

"Yes, yes," Divicos interrupted, sucking in his breath, "I know the intents of your spirit, and agree. We are all busy with our duties, but be assured that my Druids stand ready to perform the necessary rituals wherever you need them. May Toutorix go before you, and may Lug be your strong right arm. That is all. Now," he said looking around, "I must attend to the morning rites." He lifted his hood and turned his back. The meeting was over.

The commanders hesitated, unsure whether to leave or press their desire to mount a general offensive against the Wall. Earlier when they had discussed Divicos and his manipulative ways, they smugly believed themselves ready for the old wizard. They were wrong.

Everyone knew the Druids received far more Imperial tribute than they acknowledged. Since building their Wall, the Romans had used Druid mediators to distribute bribes. It was a time-tested method by the Imperial army the world over to appease warlike tribes. Keep the enemy's bellies full and you ward off unrest. But the Druids always took more than their fair share, and now, if the Romans were driven from the Wall, the tribute would leave as well. Divicos was not about to let that happen. Several of the commanders were moving toward the door when Taranis spoke.

"Great high priest, you have said we will talk after the summer harvest. We want to talk now. Our armies are ready—"

Divicos dropped to the floor and rocked back and forth, humming. His arms locked around his legs, his body hunched like the husk of a dried beetle, and his voice grew louder and deeper.

Taranis ran his fingers through his hair, unsure what to do. Something had pulled Divicos into another world—a world of spirits where only the anointed dared tread. The commanders glanced uneasily at each other, and Forgall coughed to lessen his anxiety.

Divicos snapped forward, and then whipped back, his posture suddenly erect. His shoulders squared and his head twisted oddly toward the men. "I see a dark tunnel." His voice reverberated, as if he were in the tunnel himself. "And pits where men are chained. There is no sun or moon, nor light of the stars. Only silence. And cold. A deep, aching cold. The men cry out for release, and rake the walls with ragged fingers. But no one hears. No one comes. For them, there is no sacrifice. No rebirth." His face glowed with an unholy light and his eyes stared without seeing. "These are they who mocked the gods, whose insolence knew no end. Now they writhe in misery—broken, forgotten." Divicos's body tightened and shook violently, as if something had hold of him. His mouth wrenched open and from his throat came a choking noise. He pitched forward, vomited, and flopped back, his body hanging sideways like a sacrificial victim. "Leave me!" His voice sounded hoarse and exhausted.

One by one the commanders filed out into the light, unsure of what had happened.

The commanders journeyed back to their villages in silence, an embarrassed group, their speech coming awkwardly. They had expected to force Divicos to endorse a general attack against the Romans and their Wall. Instead, the old Druid had played on their fears and uncertainties, twisting their minds to suit his purposes. Now they would have to continue—probably until the winter snows—the same harassing tactics they had always used against the Roman menace. At the River Carrac every commander agreed that the Romans no longer had the power to resist a full-scale assault on their turf barrier.

Taranis felt ashamed. As a senior commander he or Forgall should have been stronger with the cunning priest. But they had been as feeble as the others. On the second day, when he and Eston broke off from the rapidly dwindling troop to head for home, he was glad.

"I don't trust Divicos," Eston said. "The Druids have always been our negotiators, but we have no idea how much the Romans give them. The Druids have come to depend on the tribute. They are content with the Romans ravaging our land, so long as it fills the temple coffers."

"That might be," Taranis said, "but it's more than gold and silver. The Druids are terrified of war."

"How can that be? The Romans are weaker now than ever. Look how easily we've breached their Wall—dozens of times!"

"The Druids think Rome will send legions from Gallia to destroy us. And you know what will happen to the Druids if Rome controls Caledonia."

"I hadn't thought of that," Eston said.

They rested their horses and talked about the Druids' fate if Rome were to have her way. The Romans often met with Druid emissaries—out of necessity—but it never diminished their hatred for the priests. Every nation the Empire devoured had been purged of the ancient religion. Long ago, the continent had been filled with sacred groves and magicians interceding for the people. Now, few remained, and those were hidden deep in the woods.

"After our experience in the grove," Taranis said, "my respect for Bronix and the old commanders has sharply increased."

Eston smiled. "There's more to being a commander than fighting battles—is that what you mean?"

"Divicos is an old man, Eston. He walks stiffly and forgets his words. But in the grove he has a fearsome power."

"If we could lure him away from the grove ...."

"Yes," Taranis said, nodding. "Maybe at the festival of the new moon."

The two journeyed in silence again until they reached a place called the cut-off. They slipped from their horses without comment and led their mounts up the steep embankment. This close to home, they chose the shortcut up the stony incline rather than the road that wound around the hill. As the horses bolted upward, Taranis found his eyes lingering on the familiar rocks and clumped bushes. Pleasant thoughts drifted through his mind—thoughts about his childhood, when he and Eston would race up the slope, pushing and tripping each other, trying to reach the upper grasslands first. Neeve would complain about her bigger brothers leaving her behind, and as often as not, a word from their mother slowed them down. But those days were gone, and the hill was no longer fun. Just a shortcut to the plains, and home.

At the top, Eston continued the conversation interrupted by the rough climb.

"The problem is that Divicos hasn't attended a festival in three years," he said. "The high priest always speaks through representatives."

"True, but if we honor the Druids with a feast, and invite the townspeople from miles around—"

"We might force Divicos to come."

"And a rumor could sweep the villages that the high priest has an important announcement."

"That the Druids have sanctioned a full-scale assault on the Wall?"

Taranis grinned. "Yes, that could be the announcement."

"When the Druids hear the rumor, they'll be in a spot, will they not?"

"I would think so."

Eston smiled. "Either they go along, or they disappoint half of Caledonia."

"The truth is … we should have driven out the Romans long ago. The old commanders would never have tolerated these delays. We have the power *now*. I might know nothing about the spirit-world, but I believe the ancient gods are sickened by what they see. They can't be pleased with foreign armies and strange gods in our lands."

"But Divicos walks with the gods. He does their will."

"I confess, that puzzles me," Taranis said. "But I think I understand now. Divicos knows spells and incantations that call down the power of the gods. If he chooses, he can constrain the gods to help us in battle. At the feast we'll have him on our own ground. He will have no choice but to endorse the attack."

"But we must have a public agreement, not one proclaimed in a shrine."

"Yes, we don't want the Druids changing their minds."

As they neared the homestead, four small children streamed out to meet Eston, squealing and laughing and calling out to their daddy. By the door of Eston's roundhouse stood his wife, Emer, smiling and whisking the hair off her face. She was tall, redheaded, and had a plain, but not unattractive look.

Eston jumped from his horse and pitched the first child to reach him into the air. The others were at his legs, tugging on his trousers, demanding attention. His oldest boy, about seven, acted with more reserve, trying to be a man. Eston plopped him in the saddle with instructions to water, feed, and rub down the horse. The boy beamed, pressed his heels into the horse's flanks and pounded off toward the shed.

In moments like this, Taranis felt the emptiness of his life. It was his fault. Over the years there had been many women he might have married, but for one reason or another he never did. Now, as he watched Eston carrying the children and kissing his wife, he wondered how wise he had been.

"Taranis! Come here!" Emer cried, "I have wonderful news." She kissed him on the cheek and pulled out a papyrus letter. "Neeve! It's from Neeve!"

Taranis knew it was from Neeve. She was the only one who had ever sent him a letter. Couriers brought them across the Wall every six months or so, and it was the one warm spot in his life. He had intended to send for his sister, but as the years wore on, he knew she had been right. They would never see each other again. The war to drive out the Romans never came, and Caledonia grew more lawless than ever. He and Eston continually found themselves involved in some raid along the Wall, or attacking columns of soldiers that strayed too far. It never seemed to end. Then Neeve got married. That was five years ago; he hadn't received a letter since.

He took the stiff paper from Emer's hand. Neeve addressed her letters to both brothers, but Taranis kept them in a special box in his roundhouse. Often he would take them out and gaze at the strange marks she had made far away beyond the second Wall. He couldn't read, but sometimes he would trek down to the village where Domnall the weaver lived. The old man would slip the letters from their cases and read them aloud, one by one.

"What does she say?" Taranis asked, trying to keep the excitement from his voice. He noticed Eston leaning closer. No point in hiding it, he thought. They both missed little Neeve, with her large voice and demanding ways. The words "little Neeve" struck him. She was now twenty-two years old—a grown woman.

"I took the letter to Domnall," Emer said. "Neeve is coming home. She intends to live in Caledonia."

Taranis stared at the paper, as if he could understand the smooth, curving marks written on the papyrus sheet. Home, he thought. Neeve was coming home. He looked up at Emer and asked, "Is she bringing her husband? Does she have children? What does she say?"

Emer shrugged. "She just says she is coming home."

16

Atilius leaned back and smiled. Never had Rome seen such Games. The Flavian Amphitheater was filled beyond capacity—over fifty thousand people, if you counted the standing-room crowds packing the top tiers.

The noon break had come, and with it a small breeze to check the sweltering heat trapped in the arena's vast hollow, but it did little to clear away the acrid smell of blood and dust hanging in the air, stinging the nostrils. Yet nobody seemed to mind. The mobs were still buzzing about the morning's entertainment—elephants with sharpened tusks pitted against rhinoceroses, lions against bears, and six gray wolves loosed among three hundred rabbits. How Atilius had laughed as the rabbits scattered before the frenzied wolves.

And there were the novelty acts devised expressly for gamble-crazed Romans who risked life fortunes on the chance blow of a sword, or the whims of an animal. Five successive pairs of gladiators fought each other—blindfolded. Then came the loose-limbed panthers that prowled among fifty victims tied to stakes. Numbers marked near the top of the stakes helped the gamblers choose which man they believed would live the longest. They cheered as the panthers moved silk-like through their terrified quarry, springing suddenly and seizing their prey by the neck, while disemboweling them with their hind legs.

The beast keepers quickly surrounded the survivor, loosed his bonds, and brought him before the Emperor at the Imperial box. With cries of "freedom" coming from every section of the amphitheater,

Emperor Antoninus declared him a free man and ordered a pouch of silver be given him. The crowd roared its approval as a toga-clad official appeared, carrying the silver solemnly over his head. But the man couldn't move. He stood rigidly on the arena floor in front of the Emperor, dazed, staring at the pouch in his hands, until finally he was led away.

And then came the most memorable event of the morning—the clash of the titans, as it was called—a dozen club-bearing dwarfs pitted against an equal number of women armed with swords. The dwarfs won.

The sweating throngs jamming the amphitheater were sated for the moment, and the afternoon gala promised to eclipse Vespasian's loftiest dreams for his circular arena—if everything came off as planned. That was the catch. Plans, like prophesy, often failed, and Atilius was more than a little concerned about the risks he was taking. But for now, spirits soared. People laughed and called out greetings to each other. Many cradled lunches of coarse bread smeared with a mixture of fish and cheese. Some had carcasses of geese or ducks, cooked that morning, and splendid fruitcakes for dessert. Others, of more modest means, held rolls of goat meat that they dipped in honey. And there was wine. Everyone had jars and jars of wine to cool their throats and wash down the food.

Atilius signaled a hawker plowing through the crowds in the section nearest the podium. The man looked startled. Then, gathering his wits, he wiped the top of his box and pushed his way toward the senator. When he reached the cordoned area, he waited, intimidated by the occupants scattered throughout the well-cushioned marble seats, and the concentration of scarlet Praetorians around the perimeter. Inside sat the distinguished of Rome: senators, wealthy patrons, ladies of the Imperial family and, reclining above the empty Emperor's box, the Vestal Virgins, keepers of the eternal fires of Rome. Sexual intercourse with a sacred Virgin brought instant death, and the Virgin—her blood still hot in her veins—would be entombed in the earth.

Atilius rose, knowing thousands of eyes were following him, and that people would talk for days about the great Senator Atilius

Titianus, sponsor of the Games, eating the food of common folk—
while Emperor Antoninus withdrew to eat jellyfish and eggs with the
privileged.

"Well, what do you have?" Atilius shouted good-naturedly.

The hawker reached into his crate and began pulling out pork
sausages, salted meats, dried fruits, and small skins of wine and
quince juice.

"A sausage and some quince juice," he said loudly.

The hawker quickly examined his sausages and handed the
senator a fat one, along with a clean skin of quince.

Atilius accepted them, smiling. "Hail to the Emperor!" he said,
raising his hand.

The man bobbed his head in respect. "Hail to the Emperor," he
replied.

"The Emperor Antoninus is dining elsewhere," Atilius said,
gesturing toward the empty Imperial box. "How can you serve your
Emperor when you cannot see him?" He reached into his toga and
produced a gold coin. "Here, this will help you remember."

The man stared at the coin with Antoninus' image stamped in it.
It represented more than a year's work. He took it carefully,
examined it, and then thrust it in the air for all to see. Those nearby
burst into applause, calling out Atilius's name as he moved back to his
seat.

"They love you!" Balbinus gushed. "Look at them! They know a
leader."

Atilius was pleased with the remark, but ignored it. Even in front
of Balbinus, he wanted it clear that Senator Atilius Titianus was above
flattery. But Balbinus had divined the truth. The Roman people
would indeed make him Emperor if they could. As the time neared
for his move against Antoninus, he would need the support of these
very people—if only to force wavering senators to sanction his bid for
the purple. He carved a small piece off the sausage and handed the
rest to Balbinus, who took it agreeably. Below, trained monkeys were
outwitting their trainer, who was dressed in the ridiculous garb of an
Egyptian pharaoh. Some tripped him with rope while others dumped
buckets of water on his face when he fell to the sand. The crowd

hooted with laughter, enjoying the break from the morning's blood-fest.

Suddenly, a lion burst from a door at the far end of the arena. He bounded toward the monkeys. The trainer jumped up, calling his monkeys to him and looking around desperately for a place to run. A hush fell on the amphitheater as the monkeys clung tightly to the man's legs and arms, and screeched plaintively at the lion rapidly closing the distance. At fifteen paces, the cat flew into the air, landing directly in front of the hapless group. His body tensed and jaws opened, and out came a rabbit that darted around in the hot sand.

"Wonderful!" Atilius exclaimed as the crowd cheered and whistled. He turned to his aide. "Balbinus, what can I say? You have done a superb job organizing these Games."

Balbinus's ample cheeks flushed with delight. He tried to say something, but with his mouth full of sausage, he thought better of it.

"The races at the Circus Maximus last week," Atilius continued, "were hailed as the most exciting ever. And this week has been stunning. Rome has not seen Games like these in years. Innovative! That is what they are. Not the usual fare."

Balbinus dabbed his mouth with a cloth. "All because of your generosity," he said in a fawning voice.

"Yes, this has taken a major bite out of my coffers. I had no idea of the distance that proper animals must be transported. It is amazing how our Games have emptied the world of these beasts. No elephants in North Africa, no lions or panthers in Mesopotamia, and the hippopotamus gone from Nubia. It is well that people in those regions live safer because of Roman ingenuity in removing their dangerous animals, but now we have to scour India and the jungles beyond the Atlas mountains to get what we want. The Games are not cheap anymore ... not cheap at all."

"Just the expense of the trappers ...."

"Ah, yes, the trappers. With the fees they charge, I would not be surprised to see them buying up land in Rome herself." A smile crossed his face. "But, by the sacred Virgins, it is worth every coin, Balbinus, every coin."

"Oh, indeed, Senator. The people are blessing your name."

"Then you have heard them—"

"In the streets, at the baths, in the Senate—your name, on everyone's lips."

Atilius savored the thought.

"And I've heard something else too," Balbinus said. He leaned forward as if someone might overhear his words, though no one was within twenty feet, and the clamor of the crowd assured privacy. "If Atilius puts on such spectacular Games with his own money, they say, what would he do with the treasury of Rome at his disposal?"

Atilius leaned back on his cushions, and in spite of his desire to sound modest, found himself gesturing expansively and saying, "A distinct bit more than our present Emperor. *That* the people could count on."

The sun came out from behind the clouds. Atilius shielded his eyes. "I suspect the sun is here to stay. We do not want our dear citizens uncomfortable."

"I will take care of it immediately," Balbinus said. He rose with some effort and made his way to the front of the podium. At the base of an eagle-topped column, he unfurled a red banner. Within minutes the sailors tending the masts and awnings at the rim of the amphitheater's fourth story began working on the ropes. Slowly the massive awnings shuddered and vibrated their way across the arena. Under the brilliant skies, the yellows, blues and reds shimmered like the silk sails of a gigantic ship.

A sudden silence in the arena pricked Atilius's curiosity. He glanced down. The sands were empty except for a bear, a fully armed gladiator, and several oval baskets bristling with spikes. The gladiator moved cautiously toward the bear, taunting him with his outstretched sword. The beast swatted at the sword. He missed. Again, and this time the sword flew from the gladiator's hand. Stunned, the man jumped backwards and stomped his feet.

Atilius grinned. He loved the noontime with its humorous fripperies. Now the gladiator was pretending to be insanely angry. He threw off his armor and shield, and ripped at his linen underclothes until he stood there in nothing but a loincloth, his fists trembling in rage. He kicked at the equipment lying in the sand, and hurt his foot. His howl filled the air. He thrust an accusing finger at the bear and shrieked insults until his face flamed crimson. Then, without warning, he charged the beast. The bear reared up on his hind legs and swept a paw at the man's head. Fearless, the gladiator pummeled the bear's stomach with his fists, then darted for one of the baskets, the bear snapping and growling at his heels.

The crowd screamed in delight as the bear tried to dig his antagonist out of the basket. But every time he struck, he tore his paw on the spiked cylinder.

"Look!" Atilius cried. "The people love it! This is the best intermission yet."

"How gracious of you to say so," Balbinus said, directing the senator's attention to the arena, "but the best is yet to come."

The man suddenly popped up from the basket and cuffed the animal in the snout. Atilius laughed. The crowd cheered. Stunned, the bear staggered backward, seemingly confused as the gladiator hopped out of the basket and renewed his insults at the top of his lungs. Then the man swelled his chest and took several giant steps toward the bear, flexing his muscles and shadow-boxing within inches of the animal's nose. The bear roared and swiped at the man's head again, almost catching him. Almost. Like a blur the gladiator burst forward, as if he had been waiting for this moment, striking and cuffing the bear a dozen times all over the head. The bear swayed, staggered sideways, and crashed to the ground. The man turned to the crowd, boxed the air, and bowed to thunderous applause.

"Incredible! How did he do that?"

Balbinus beamed, pleased with his success. "Woven into the gladiator's leather gloves are poison-tipped, metal goads."

"Very clever," Atilius said, nodding his approval. "I am beginning to think there is no end to the talents of Rome and her people."

"Or to the noble men who by their generosity make all this possible," Balbinus said.

The senator and his aide paused to join the applause for the boxer as he left the arena. Behind him came the ring-cleaners, dragging the carcass of the bear through the death gate.

Atilius leaned back and said, "It seems you have chosen your trainers wisely."

"In truth I have used my cousin, Kallias, to organize—"

"Are you referring to that Greek miscreant who works under the arena, and does nothing to earn the stipend I give him?" Atilius didn't hide his irritation at having to talk about vulgar fellows like Kallias. The Greek worked in the chambers being dug under the arena, if one could imagine. Sometimes he cleaned the sewers and hauled off corpses. How much viler could life be? Even his appearance, head crushed as it was from the cliff-fall, reminded Atilius of a hellish underworld demon. And of course, there were the bribes that had to be sent to cover the trouble he caused in North Africa.

Balbinus dipped his head respectfully and said, "The celebrated of this world, like yourself, quite naturally have an aversion to the baser things of life. But in his own way Kallias is a gifted man, and quite useful."

Atilius frowned but motioned for Balbinus to proceed.

"If I might say, I assigned my cousin the primary responsibility for overseeing the noon entertainment."

"The bear?"

"Yes, the boxing bear, the lion with the rabbit in its mouth and, well, you can see," he said, gesturing toward the arena.

Atilius eyed the gangs of men below who were scurrying about planting fake bushes and branches in the sand, trying to give the appearance of a forest where hunters could pursue wild game. Suddenly, a collection of exotic animals scuttled through the openings at the opposite end—peacocks, piglets, anteaters, spotted ducks, ostriches, and an assortment of colorful lizards. Tiny black men with blow-darts followed the clucking mass, playing up to the crowd as they darted across the sands, dropping to a crouch and stealthily crawling on their bellies. They launched their darts only at distant moving targets, and screamed hysterically when they missed.

The senator smiled.

Encouraged, Balbinus chatted on about his cousin, and how he might be used in Britannia, but Atilius found his eyes drifting to the

Emperor's empty box. Of all the times for Antoninus to disappear, he thought, just before the afternoon Games. The day's main attraction had been designed strictly to please the stupid fellow. Atilius glanced once more at the empty box, then down to the arena where workers had roped off the center area to keep out the frenzied animals while they prepared for the big event.

"The Emperor should be here soon," Balbinus said, anticipating his senator. "I informed his aides about our surprise. They must have told him."

"Of course they told him!" Atilius snapped. "The man tries my patience." Atilius felt a burning in his stomach. He had gone out of his way to please the Emperor, and now the buffoon was dawdling somewhere ....

"Perhaps I should talk to one of his aides."

"No! I will not prostitute myself to him. He knows what I have planned. If he chooses not to come, I will accept that as the way of the fates."

"The Emperor often excuses himself from the Games," Balbinus observed.

"A weak man."

"A pious man perhaps, good and kind."

Atilius snorted. Balbinus well knew his opinion on that. Weak leaders never exerted their power for fear of opposition, and the Senate was so delighted with Antoninus' habit of consulting them before acting that they conferred on him the unusual title, *Pius*. Antoninus the Pius, they called him. Atilius was sick of hearing about the kindly deeds of their Emperor. Had any Emperor before Antoninus been called Pius? Had any Emperor been lauded for kindness or for his forgiving spirit? No, they ruled with the fist of Hercules. Anyone with eyes could see that Antoninus' so-called pious nature sprang from uncertainty and incompetence. "His fears blind him," Atilius murmured. "He simply does not understand."

"He doesn't understand the significance of the amphitheater for Rome."

"Precisely. He has no stomach for blood, and believe me, Balbinus, blood is what built Rome."

"I'm afraid feeble behavior is not limited to our Emperor," Balbinus said. "His adopted son, Marcus Aurelius, has become the fool of Rome. He is worse than the Emperor. He sits in the Imperial box—when he's here—writing letters and documents. I'm told he hates the Games. He attends only because the people expect it. It's a slap in the face to any good Roman."

"And a mockery to the Emperors who created the power he enjoys. Can you imagine Julius Caesar, Augustus, Trajan—any of them—acting the part of a timid housemaid? The Imperial attitude of today would sicken them." He shooed a fly from his face. "Well, there is no use talking about it when—"

"Forgive me, Senator," Balbinus said, his eyes darting to a passageway leading from the amphitheater. "One of my informants has signaled me. Emperor Antoninus is on his way!"

"I thought as much. Dangle a scrap of meat and the dogs come slavering every time. When Antoninus discovered what I had planned for this afternoon, the oracle at Delphi couldn't keep him away." He sneered. "How many times has Antoninus tried to introduce culture to the mobs? And he always fails. Do you know why?"

"Because the amphitheater is not the place for poets and minstrels."

"You have said it well, Balbinus. The amphitheater is a school of courage and valor. A place where the bold reap riches, and cowards, death. And that is precisely what makes Rome great. Nothing surprises us, or horrifies us. We understand the shock of combat and the consequences of defeat. From our earliest days—"

He broke off, distracted by a brawl that erupted in the upper tiers. Urban soldiers assigned to the section were already pulling the men apart. "From our earliest days we've participated in the mystery of death. Killing is as natural to us as a good meal. We learn everything here, and in hundreds of other amphitheaters we have built across the world." He sighed. "This is what Antoninus and his kind will never understand. They think the Games are entertainment, a diversion for pleasure seekers. They are wrong. Superiority! That is what it is. A demonstration of our superiority over the barbarians. A place where the Roman mind is bathed in blood."

"What you say is true, Senator. That is why I am still apprehensive about having a Greek singer—"

"Greek singer! Pelopidas is not some Aetolian peddler of tunes. I grant that he can be insufferably arrogant, but we need not marry the man, just use him for a time. To bring him to the amphitheater is a major accomplishment."

"Oh, I agree totally. Still," he wagged his head, "nothing kindles Roman passions like Greek arrogance."

"I share your fears, Balbinus, but I want to prove something to Emperor Antoninus and the few followers he still has remaining in the Senate. I, Atilius Titianus, can win the mobs of Rome—even with sophisticated fare. Do not worry about Pelopidas. He will perform admirably. I have seen to that."

Balbinus nodded unenthusiastically.

Atilius smiled. "The reason Antoninus has failed so miserably in events like this is obvious. The man is entirely unimaginative. He tries to pound culture into the common Roman's ears, and that never works. Today I will teach him and the self-appointed sages of Rome that Senator Atilius Titianus can handle our citizens on any level." He poured himself some quince juice. "I will give the people culture— and they will love it. One merely requires the appropriate setting."

"Well, Pelopidas is certainly the pinnacle of elegance and grace," Balbinus said, his spirits noticeably lifted. "They say his voice is sweeter than a canary's. And your idea of flooding the amphitheater for him—a triumph!"

Atilius nodded, acknowledging the compliment, but only he knew what it had cost him to cozy up to the egotistical ass. Money was the least of it. Never had he been so humiliated. "Senator Atilius Titianus to speak with Pelopidas," he had said to the door attendant at Theater Marcellus's central habiliments room.

"The magnificent Pelopidas is resting his voice," came the reply.

Atilius tried to be courteous: "Please inform him that a senator of Rome wishes—"

The door closed.

Atilius flushed, and instinctively glanced around to see if any in the theater crowd had noticed the slight. A few had. He tapped on the door again.

This time when the attendant tried to close the door, Atilius restrained it with his hand. "Slave," he said in whispered desperation, "I wish to speak with Pelopidas. If you deny me entry, I will spend as much as it takes to buy you, and this very evening I shall have your mouth stuffed with burning coals."

Moments later the attendant ushered Atilius into a chamber heaped with violets, roses, hyacinths, and lilies—all purchased from Rome's expensive hot houses by ardent admirers. At the far end of the ornate room sat the magnificent Pelopidas, like a monarch on his throne, lavender robes cascading down his ample body. With his cheeks and lips still painted red from his performance, and his wig removed, and a silver hairnet binding his thinning hair, he looked like a giant toad surveying his kingdom.

He waved away his circle of Egyptian slaves and said in an unusually high voice, "You have a personal message from the Emperor?"

Atilius hesitated, suddenly realizing what the door attendant must have said.

"Well, do you or do you not?" Pelopidas's thick lips rolled impatiently.

"I bring you an exciting offer—"

His head whipped around to the door attendant: "You said he carried a message from the Emperor! I will have you flogged for this."

"I am Senator Atilius Titianus—"

"Yes, yes," he said wearily, "you flatter me with your accolades, whatever they might be. If you have flowers or messages, leave them with the others. Now I really must rest my voice."

"I understand—"

"No, you do not! You Romans have never understood the artist. You think music simply flows out of me as if I were a wooden flute. Right now, this very moment as I speak, my throat aches like a bruised reed. Of course, nowhere in Rome can I find honey and clover oil, the only thing that soothes my throat."

"You are right," Atilius said solicitously, "I failed entirely to appreciate your suffering—"

"Oh, don't patronize me. I am not an imbecile." He coughed, wincing painfully.

Atilius's cheeks grew hot with embarrassment. "I apologize," he managed, "I was simply trying—"

"Yes, yes, apologies accepted. Now I must rest." He turned away.

Atilius stared at the back of Pelopidas's pompous head and swallowed hard, knowing that he had to win quickly or come away empty-handed. "Theater Marcellus is a splendid house, but rather small to showcase your talents. I should think the amphitheater would be the perfect setting."

Pelopidas turned slightly.

Atilius continued: "Of course Emperor Antoninus and the senators would attend."

He turned further.

"And since the amphitheater is three times the size of Marcellus, it seems fair that you should receive three times the remuneration of your theater performances."

The ploy worked and Pelopidas agreed to grace the amphitheater with his presence, though Atilius wondered whether the prize was worth the humiliation.

"Flooding the amphitheater," Balbinus was still babbling, "pure genius."

"It was the right decision," Atilius replied. "We had to do something. Antoninus would have brought him out with nothing but a dais to sing from. Can you imagine this mob listening quietly to Greek lyrics when they could have leopards ripping the stomachs from screaming barbarians?"

"I can imagine Venus searching for me in the night before I could imagine that," Balbinus replied.

"The truth is, I need this elaborate backdrop to keep their attention. Not only will the water quench this infernal heat," he patted his forehead with a sponge, "but it is of no small consequence that before Pelopidas even sets foot in the arena, the announcer will inform the crowd of the naval battle to follow. I do think even the Roman people can be made to enjoy an interlude of song-fest."

"They will bless your name for it," Balbinus said.

"To be safe, we might announce the names of the gladiators scheduled to fight after the naval battle."

Balbinus swelled with pride: "That has already been cared for, Senator."

By now, the hunters had eliminated the animals, and were leaving the sands to warm applause. Scores of men scoured the arena for dead or dying beasts and removed them quickly. Atilius watched absent-mindedly as workers transferred the shrubs from the arena floor to the huge portable island, already in place. The sight of the island never failed to excite the crowds. Over the years, they had witnessed glorious naval battles, and every imaginable siege of the island, including women defending against blind pirates who arrived in boats. Sometimes knife-wielding gladiators were charged with clearing the island of Egyptian crocodiles, or saving a heroine stranded among lions and bears.

The workers made a last sweep of the island, positioning a shrub here and there to conceal the trap doors leading to the walkways inside the portable island. Soon the amphitheater would flood with water, the music would begin, and Pelopidas would miraculously appear from a hidden entrance on the island.

The vein in Atilius's eye throbbed. His gamble to introduce culture could easily fail. It was pride, he knew, plain pride. He wanted to show the powerful in Rome that nothing was beyond his ability. Up till now, his Games had been enormously successful, but lyrical singing was a risk. His dreams of being Emperor rested heavily on maintaining the goodwill of the people. After expending so much time and money, he didn't want to ruin everything now.

Below, the men had finished checking the floodgates and were signaling the engineers that the arena was ready. And then the water burst forth, surging across the smooth sands of the great amphitheater. It never ceased to astonish Atilius—the wonders of Roman engineering.

A sudden roar of the crowd indicated that Emperor Antoninus had returned. He acknowledged their homage with a wave of the hand, and then nodded politely to Atilius, the benefactor of the Games. Most of Rome's notables had returned and were chatting blithely with each other. They grew silent as a powerfully voiced man announced the afternoon's events. The mention of Greek musicians drew scattered hoots, but overall the mobs seemed excited.

The arena bowl was now filled, and from the portals in the side, graceful palms that had been thatched to approximate giant leaves floating in the water, were being launched. In each of the thatched vessels, now numbering more than twenty, two scantily clad maidens sang and played their lyres. The crowd cheered, waiting expectantly for something to happen.

Suddenly, Pelopidas appeared on the island in a glistening white toga, his voice rising above those of the maidens. A hush fell across the tiers of people as Pelopidas's voice soared, and blended with the others in a melody sweeter than Rome had ever known. Atilius watched in silence; he had never seen the mobs so stilled. Every eye followed Pelopidas as he walked the island serenading the maidens, whose voices echoed across the water.

Five minutes of delight passed. Ten minutes. Pelopidas might be an insufferable Greek, Atilius thought, but his voice was a gift from the gods. Even jaded Roman senators leaned forward, straining to hear every note. Atilius rejoiced.

Then the worst thing possible happened. It started in the upper tiers. A murmur of conversation, at first. Boredom? Indifference? Atilius didn't know, but with each passing minute, the crowd grew more restless. He had made his point; he had given them culture and they reveled in it. But it was beginning to wear. He had Balbinus send someone to signal Pelopidas.

The Greek kept singing.

The murmur became a growl.

Then the hooting began.

"Do something!" Atilius shouted.

Balbinus snapped to his feet. "I'll send Kallias through one of the island trap doors to coax—

"Just get him off and start the naval show!" Atilius wiped his lips and glanced around. He saw gleeful looks on the faces of several senators, and even some in the Imperial box. How they loved to see him fail.

Titus Severus leaned back and called to Atilius. "A lovely voice," he said, smiling. "Ideal for the amphitheater."

Atilius turned away, not willing to indulge his enemies more than necessary.

The discontent grew. From every section of the amphitheater, the mob hissed and jeered. What is the matter with that Greek? Atilius thought. Surely, he must hear the hoots of the crowd. But he keeps singing. The man is so wrapped up in his voice that he hears only himself. Why hasn't Balbinus done something?

Pelopidas stood at the center of the island with one hand in his toga and the other extended toward the crowd. He was reaching for one of his high notes, eyes shut tight, when a lion peeked his head around a bush not fifteen feet from him. Another, a lioness, stepped out and shook her body violently, then stared blankly ahead. The brilliance of the afternoon light seemed to stun them after being caged in their darkened cells. The lioness yawned, then suddenly struck at the lion with a paw. He jumped back and let out an angry roar. Amazingly, Pelopidas seemed oblivious to the noise and started strolling toward the now very attentive cats.

He stopped.

The crowd burst out laughing.

Pelopidas took some large steps backwards but kept singing. His face radiated desperation as he eyed the podium and gestured toward the lions.

Atilius was shocked. That reckless cousin of Balbinus's had released lions onto the island. This wasn't some barbarian singer; this was Pelopidas—the pride of Aetolia. What would the other senators think? And the Emperor? He glanced over to the Imperial box. Antoninus' face was as hard as stone. He did not like what he saw. Yet, he did nothing.

Atilius's breath was coming hard. His eyes swept the senators and dignitaries on the podium. They were sniggering at the turn of events. One caught his eye and nodded his approval. "Brilliant!" another exclaimed. Others called out similar things and then turned back so as not to miss the island drama.

Atilius immediately realized what was happening. Rome always had a secret dislike for Greece, with its pretensions of sophistication. Rome was master of the world: from the Euphrates to Britannia's Walls, kings crawled before her. But not the Greeks. Never the Greeks! Oh, they paid their taxes, mouthed the appropriate words to Roman officials, but in their hearts they felt superior. It was written on their arrogant faces. Their philosophy, their art, their music, their mathematics—to them it was all superior. Rome was nothing more than a city bulging with soldiers. Savages, tasteless and cruel. Even this Pelopidas cared little for what Roman citizens wanted. He kept singing, expecting Greek culture to dominate.

The notables on the podium were craning their necks to see, relishing the Greek singer's predicament. They glanced back at Atilius, their faces radiating admiration for his ingenuity. They believe I planned this all along, he thought. Emperor Antoninus might not be happy, but as weak as he is, he will say nothing. The man never had the courage to oppose a consensus.

By now Pelopidas had stopped singing; he was running to the far end of the island, waving frantically at the podium. The crowd was screaming, and even the singing maidens in their thatched boats were laughing at the absurd sight of Pelopidas, toga hiked above his knees, scrambling over the bushes.

The lions moved slowly down the island, eyeing their prey. Suddenly, the female bolted, cutting through the artificial brush with incredible speed. She hit Pelopidas in the chest, knocking him flat. Her mouth clamped on his neck and shook him until his wig flew off. The other lion seized a leg, trying to snatch away the prize. They growled and tugged against each other as the crowd shrieked in near frenzy.

Atilius marveled at the power of such beasts. And he was relieved. It could have been a disaster, but the gods were with him.

"What did you think of that?" Balbinus asked as he slipped in beside his senator.

"I am not sure I like feeding Pelopidas to the lions. The Greeks in Aetolia have reason to complain."

"Accidents happen."

"Yes, they do."

Balbinus smiled. "The crowd is chanting your name again."

Atilius stood to acknowledge the cheers. It was worth a Greek singer. Then, sitting, he said, "Your cousin has a knack for arranging things. You trust him?"

"Without reservation."

"We need someone reliable at the Wall. Perhaps, as the time nears, we might send him to Britannia ... we can talk about the details later."

The crowd stirred again. Something in the water had overturned a boat, and two girls splashed about in the waist-deep water, calling for help. One shrieked, and was yanked below the surface. The other twisted around, hysterical. She thrashed and screamed as though something had hold of her legs. Her body jerked back and forth, then skimmed twenty feet across the water as if propelled by some unseen force. Then she too disappeared beneath the surface.

"What is this? Another surprise from your cousin?"

Balbinus was finding it difficult to contain himself. "Kallias said he would prove he is worth the stipend you award him." Another thatched boat upended. The large jaws of a reptile emerged, snapping shut on the body of a struggling maiden.

"Crocodiles! There are crocodiles in the water!" Atilius cried in delight.

"I knew you'd be pleased."

"Pleased? This is marvelous! Look at them trying to paddle to shore ... and the crowd! They have never seen anything like it."

Atilius followed the drama eagerly. Boats were being crushed everywhere as the reptiles tore apart the soft material and dragged their occupants to the bottom of the water. Swirls of dark red, and clumps of floating palm fronds marked the spots where they had been. A few maidens made it to the arena's edge, only to be thrown back by the howling mob.

"Oh, look," Atilius said, pointing down in front, "one has managed to climb the podium."

"She won't get past the fencing. Even a gladiator couldn't make it up here."

On a whim, Atilius rose and walked down to the podium where the girl was clinging to the fence overhanging the water. When she saw the senator approaching, she cried out for mercy. Atilius looked into her frightened eyes and smelled the fear, like succulent vapor, rising from her damp body. He examined the fencing. Balbinus was right. She would never pull herself up. Should I spare her? he wondered. The crowd might like that. Better to let them decide, he concluded. The amphitheater was about the only place they could visibly influence a senator, and that they especially enjoyed.

Being a merciful man, he held out his hand, thumb up. The mob roared to life, most thrusting their thumbs downward and hollering at each other, trying to influence the judgment.

The girl sensed the mood of the crowd and called out more urgently. Tears flowed down her cheeks as she begged the senator to spare her life. Atilius knew what the crowd wanted and turned his thumb down. The life of one girl would be well spent if it won him the approval of the masses. A mighty cheer shook the arena, and then died as the senator moved toward the fencing. He picked up a metal fastener used to secure banners to the podium and tapped the center strut near where the girl was hanging.

Nothing happened. He banged harder.

The sight of the reptile leaping from the water made Atilius jump. It was huge and its jaws ripped the girl from the fencing like meat hung out as bait.

When he caught his breath, and with the crowd shrieking his name, Atilius murmured to himself, "Sad. Big fish always eat little ones. But that's fate, isn't it?"

As the weeks passed, Atilius basked in the glory of his successful Games. The whole of Rome was talking. Senators he once considered dangerous to his ambitions praised him publicly. Even Senator Titus Severus gave him grudging approval. Most importantly, Emperor Antoninus finally understood that he must appease Atilius. The capacity of the Games to catapult a senator to power was astonishing.

For years he had been patient. His marriage to Sabina had given him a measure of respect in frontier policy matters, and there were times, though not many, he had even persuaded old Trebellius to speak for him in the Senate. Atilius's constant criticism of the expenditures to maintain Antoninus' Wall had won him many powerful friends. Everyone understood the foolishness of emptying Rome's coffers to control a few outposts on an island at the edge of the world. How often had Atilius stood in the Senate to make the point that provinces were supposed to fill Rome's coffers, not empty them?

And now the Games. He had always given generously to projects that directly affected the citizens of Rome, and to Praetorian causes to ensure their support. But the Games pulled everything together. The time was right.

"Balbinus," he said as he gazed at the distant outline of the Palatine Hill, "Sabina tells me Vectis is back in Rome. Send for him."

"Shall I arrange a dinner, something formal perhaps?"

"No, have him meet me at the Senate. Some things are best said in the halls of power."

"You want him to go to Britannia?"

"I think northern Britannia would be a fine place for my brother-in-law."

Both men smiled.

17

Neeve was coming home.

Taranis had determined to build his sister the finest cottage in Caledonia, even better than her quarters in the southern Roman regions. For months he and Eston had spent every spare hour on the cottage and its grounds. He hated everything Roman, but he knew their craftsmen could build structures far superior to anything in Caledonia. He also knew that many southern Celts had found pleasure in the Empire, an irresistible black pleasure that smothered their spirits. There was no denying that Roman ways lured the weak. It was as if their culture bewitched the Celts in the occupied lands, so that bondage seemed preferable to liberty.

Increasingly, during the last few years, Taranis found himself thinking about Neeve and her life in the Roman world. He feared she had become entangled in Roman ways, like a dove floundering in a hunter's net. He could still see her, hugging her knees on the banks of the Ordvgi River, begging to stay, but he'd ignored her pleas and sent her into the heart of Roman lands. It seemed so long ago. Yet now she had broken free. She was coming home.

And so from early morning till the last rays of the sun—on every day he and Eston could spare from their duties as Caledonian commanders—they worked on the compound. They built a roundhouse into the hillside in typical Celtic style, added a Roman bath complete with a boiler they had acquired from the village trader, and finally, a courtyard similar to the villas they had heard about in the south beyond the Wall. All that remained was to dig a few run-off trenches to clear the grounds of water. Its beauty would stun Neeve.

Neeve drove her carriage through the huge log gates of Antoninus' Wall and into Caledonian territory. Spring crocuses trembled in the winds, mimicking her anxiety, and the northern lands seemed unusually quiet and surprisingly empty. "What am I doing here?" she wondered out loud. Everything—the housing, the roads, the few people she met—all looked different from her childhood memories, so foreign and curiously unfamiliar. Her travels from Hadrian's Wall to the Antonine frontier had been a rude shock, and Neeve was afraid. What if she no longer belonged in the land of her memories? What if no such land existed? Just an assortment of dreams, pleasurable images from long ago that soothed her when the weight of life became intolerable.

What if her brothers didn't want her, finding her more Roman than Caledonian? And there was that other, awful possibility. What if her brothers had changed, had become the monsters the Wall soldiers said they were? They even mentioned Taranis by name, calling him the blood god. He wore a red tunic in battle, they said, and killed everything that breathed—soldiers, women, children, even cattle. Neeve refused to believe the tales. Taranis might wear a red tunic in battle—like their father had—but he was no blood god. She had been away a long time, but her heart told her that her brother was still the same.

A cooling wind scurried through the grasses and moaned in the hollows that pitted the rocky flats. She leaned back on her carriage seat and let the palfreys follow the rutted road. She would not listen to her doubts, but to the inner current of peace that flowed through her in this land of mountains and crystal clear lakes. She had made the right decision, and she knew it. She glanced around at the barren land and smiled to herself. Free, in Caledonian land! The soldiers at the Wall-fort would never have understood. To them Caledonia was a threat, a place of evil where hostile warriors lurked in every shadow. She remembered their blank stares when she requested to travel beyond the frontiers of the Empire. Yet they approved it. Even with the heightened tensions of past years, the gates remained open for travelers and merchants—at least, during daylight hours. The Romans still had a string of five forts beyond the Wall, but in these days soldier columns traveled to the outposts only when carrying necessary supplies, and only along the main road connecting the forts.

She drove her carriage several miles beyond the Wall, and stopped. It was good to breathe the free air of her homeland, and especially good to leave behind the repressive measures of the Roman military.

Life in the Empire was no different from life in a military camp. The Roman army held everyone accountable, and soldiers could be brutal beyond belief. How Romans loved to talk about their laws, ethics, and standards—but their laws applied to citizens, not barbarians, and Celts who voiced divergent opinions often disappeared.

Not that life had been unkind to her in the south. To the contrary. Certain aspects of it had been quite pleasant, and she, more than most, had experienced its comforts. Life in the Roman world was like drifting in a cloud: it seduced both mind and body. It caressed you with hand servants and lavish baths, with art and theater. It taught you that nothing outside the Empire had value, except as it contributed to the enjoyment of those inside. This arrogance—for that is what it was—an unwavering belief in its own superiority, was responsible for the dark side of the Roman spirit.

An evil craving.

A disease that lurked below the surface.

Oh, they hid it well. In the glitter of Roman opulence, in the fluid tongue of honeyed speech, you could almost miss it. The most noble of Romans hid it like a rotting ulcer. Death. An obsession with death. They loved to watch things die.

Neeve had tried to look beyond it, tried to immerse herself in their ways. She perfumed her body and plaited her hair, reclined on their down-filled couches and draped herself in Milesian wool. But at night in the stillness of her darkened room, she heard the screams of the amphitheater, and the laughter of the disgusting crowds.   And inside, her revulsion grew.

Her husband during those years had been an important official in the local government. At least, that is what she thought he was. Like hundreds of other nationals, the Romans allowed him to administer a provincial sector, and act as a liaison between them and their Celtic subjects. As Neeve soon discovered, he was nothing more than a tool of the Roman government, an informer used to control the people.

We must be careful, he would often say, the Romans might discover this, or might discover that. He hired elegant tutors to correct her accent and to improve her reading and writing skills in the Roman language—Empire officials admire dedication, he told her. She grew weary of hearing about Empire officials and their thoughts on every facet of her life. Empire officials expect wives of their provincial administrators to model proper behavior, he would say. They expect them to be quiet, but not silent; publicly minded, but not politically intrusive. They should care about their people, but report untoward behavior.   Naturally, they will strive for a comely countenance: coiffured hair, appropriate dress, colored cheeks and lips. Proper women never wander about the markets, plain-faced and hair blowing in the breeze. Nor do they work the loom like common peasants. Above all, they have a sacred duty to bear children and to raise them up in a manner that pleases the Empire.

In their years of marriage, she bore no children for the Empire, and it was the great disappointment of her husband's life. He never knew, but each day she drank the juice of the silphium plant to ward off pregnancy. Her worst mistake, she judged, was her decision to stop sending letters to her brothers.   Imagine what the Roman overseers would think, her husband had said, if they discovered that a wife of a liaison official had relatives among the warlike Caledonian tribes.

How wrong she had been to neglect her family.

As time passed, she could no longer bear seeing her husband bob his head in deference to the Roman master, and suggest ways the occupation force could tighten its grip on the people. He did anything to curry favor.   He even passed along names of those potentially dangerous to the Empire. The Romans were here to stay, he would say, so we might as well learn to live with them. What they did with the information was not his concern. If the people were innocent, they had nothing to fear.

His self-serving words were as transparent as they were immoral, and Neeve could live with him no longer. She wrote up a bill of divorce and served it herself. She gave no reason, so as not to humiliate him in front of the witnesses, but he knew, and accepted it quietly. Only as she was leaving did he say, "I was stupid to marry a demented Caledonian. You tribespeople," his voice had grown bitter, "are so superior to anyone who believes in Roman order."

She was right to leave him. But often as she lay in bed at night, she wondered whether she was any better. Had she not smiled agreeably at the empty-headed chatter of pampered women? Or held her tongue when she might have spoken?

She glanced back at the Wall, and then flicked the reins. The carriage lurched forward.

Neeve passed the cut-off leading to the upper grasslands and home. Memories flooded her mind as she encouraged the carriage horses along the narrow road that curled around the hill. She thought about the races up the embankment with her brothers, and the times she had scrambled down, heading for the village with its rich smells of cooked meat and freshly ground grain. And she thought about her mother and father, and little Nes, who were no more.

Within ten minutes she could see the tired old willow behind the family roundhouse, its branches sweeping the mud-plastered roof like the shabby beard of an aged man. There were three cottages now; when she had left there was one.

She stopped in front of the center cottage and peered at the two men digging trenches near the rear. They were bare from the waist up and streaked with mud. The bigger one with red hair laid his shovel aside, bounded out of the trench, and stood there wiping his hands on his breeches.

"Neeve?" he said finally.

Neeve stared at her brothers. How much they had changed! Giants, they were, with huge muscled arms and broad chests. They were bigger than the enormous gladiators that paraded through the streets on Londinium's contest days. Eston looked odd, with his thick red hair and Caledonian style mustache. She glanced beyond him to Taranis, who had pulled himself out of some kind of run-off dugout at the end of the trench. His hair was long and yellow like hers. She shifted her eyes back to Eston and smiled. "Thought you were rid of me," she said awkwardly, and climbed off the carriage.

He smiled back. "We never wanted to be rid of you, Neeve."

"I know." Her voice was quiet and her face serious. She stepped forward, uncertain, and embraced him.

"I have mud all over me," Eston said, trying to keep himself from touching her dazzling white Roman tunic.

Neeve crushed into him, wanting to feel her brother's arms around her. The years melted away and an overpowering surge of emotion swept through her. She threw her head back and cried: "I love mud, and I love you!" Then, squeezing her eyes tight, she kissed him twice. His face tasted of sweat, of salt and grit.

"Neeve," Taranis said, "you look so different."

"Do I? Well, how do you think you look to me?" She almost shouted, feeling a child-like euphoria warming her cheeks. She stepped toward Taranis.

He smiled. "It hasn't been the same since you left." His eyes examined her face.

"No little Neeve to order around?"

He nodded.

They hugged, and for the first time in years, Neeve felt peace in her spirit.

"I'm living in the old family home now," Eston said. "Taranis can't find a wife—he stays over there by himself. You will live here."

"This house has a number of surprises," Taranis said, glancing at Eston. "You'll not find another like it in all of Caledonia."

"Maybe not even in Roman lands," Eston chirped. He laughed, enjoying the intrigue. "You also get a large square of land with the house, so you'll be considered a land owner at village meetings."

Neeve stared at the windowless cottage with mud and rocks dumped haphazardly at the front and sides. Puddles of muck covered the sunken sections near the back, and flies constantly buzzed her head. Roundhouses were smaller and dirtier than she had remembered.

"Of course, we still have to level the ground," Taranis said. "When we open the trenches, the water will drain, so don't worry about that. We'll whitewash the stone walls, plant ferns and ivy along them—"

"Like a Roman palace," Eston added.

Neeve smiled weakly.

"When the trenches are finished that will be a courtyard," Taranis said, pointing to the mud piles at the side of the house. "And we still remember how you hate rats. Eston and I pledge to track down any rat that comes within fifty feet of your cottage."

"Don't suppose I'll forget that," Neeve said.

"We expect you to call on us regularly."

"We have shutters," Eston said. "Next week we'll cut window-holes and put them in."

"What's that building over there?"

Her brothers looked at each other and grinned, clearly pleased she had asked. They marched over to the little rock house built into the side of the hill and flung open the door. Taranis's voice trembled with excitement: "This, Neeve, is your own private bathhouse!" They stood there beaming, watching her expectantly.

"It's ... wonderful," she said, hoping they hadn't detected her shock on seeing the dirty, little room. They hadn't. They were too busy pointing out its special features. At the top, they said, were vents designed to let out the steam and provide light. Along one side was a cedar bench and slabs of cedar flooring, and taking up most of the area was a shallow, stone depression that they quickly explained would be her hot pool. Once they heated the boilers and opened the flow doors, hot water would pour in, filling the pool. When she finished bathing, all she need do is open the flow doors on the other side and allow the pool to drain.

Everything worked by downflow, they said, as they left the room and scrambled up freshly cut steps. Eston stood at the top of the hill and pointed at a dugout designed to collect rain. It had a rock base, he said, and with the continual run-off from the mountain, it would never stagnate and could be used as a cold-water pool.

"And it won't freeze," Taranis said, "at least during most of the winter." He seemed intent on assuring her of the system's viability. "Movement is what does it," he continued, "and a clear exposure to the sun—that's what keeps it working." They showed her the overflow canals that carried excess water to the trenches below, and again insisted they would clear her grounds of mud within days.

As they trooped down the steps, and her brothers jabbered about sizes of boilers and ways of using water flow doors, Neeve felt ashamed. They had done so much work, just for her. Look how pleased they are with themselves, she thought. They have no idea the opulence of private Roman bathhouses, with their marble swimming pools and sculpted wonders, their vaulted ceilings and silver ornamentation. They would have no way of knowing how crude their heating system was, compared to the Roman method of heating the floors and walls of buildings. But no matter. This was *her* bathhouse—a gift from her brothers.

Taranis was still talking. "All you do is open that flow door, and water will fill the boiler. Heat it, open the other side," he pointed to a door leading from the boiler to the rock house, "and the only bathhouse in Caledonia starts cooking."

Neeve hugged her brothers. "Thank you," she said. "My compound is wonderful." Then she smiled and said, "See that you keep a sharp eye out for rats."

As the weeks passed, Neeve renewed her acquaintance with the north country. Every morning she joined the women who prepared the soil for the fall planting of barley. The summer days were cooler than usual in the highlands, but with the hours she spent plowing and plucking rocks from the fields, she hardly noticed.

In the beginning, Neeve's back ached so severely that she despaired of ever walking upright again, and more than once she longed to plop herself down—just plop right down on a Roman couch and sip fruit juices. But, of course, she couldn't do that, and slowly, as her hands grew calloused and her arms strong, she actually enjoyed her work as a Caledonian land owner.

She also returned to her practice of the Scythian bow, so abruptly halted ten years before. The years had given her no advantage; she was as miserable a shot as ever. But each day, at least, she improved. In the late afternoons she would use her tiny bathhouse: her brothers had laid in a large store of wood, and so after lighting the fires, she would grit her teeth for a scrub in the freezing pool, and then scurry down to the warm waters of the bathhouse. Amazingly, the system worked.

The rumors she had heard in Londinium about the Caledonians rising again were true, and every day in the fields she listened with excitement as the women talked about Caledonian tribes as far north as the Lvgi and Carnonacae that were preparing for war. Even the powerful southern tribe, the Brigantes, whose people dwelt on both sides of Hadrian's Wall, was holding war councils. It looked as if the whole island would finally rise up against Roman oppression. The Brigantes were the key, everyone said. Just the threat of Brigantian unrest gave the Romans night sweats. If the Caledonians could convince the Brigantes to threaten Antoninus' Wall from the south, other tribes between the Walls, such as the warlike Selgovae and Novantae, might join in the southern attack. Then the Caledonians could drive down from the north, trapping and devastating the Romans on the Wall.

One day as Neeve was picking rocks from freshly turned soil, she wondered aloud whether the tribes could so easily dislodge the Romans from their forts along Antoninus' Wall.

"Their forts will be ash heaps by spring," said a big, rough-looking woman, whose task it was to haul the rocks to the edge of the field.

"Why would the Romans abandon such a well-defended Wall as the Antonine?" Neeve asked.

"Well-defended!" The woman laughed. "There are miles of undefended earthworks, and no legionaries man the forts, just poorly trained auxiliaries. The men have crossed over dozens of times."

Seeing the surprised look on Neeve's face, Eston's wife, Emer, continued. "The Wall looks formidable, but it's not difficult to cross at night, believe me. Even some of us have crossed over."

"Really?"

"I went to see my husband's parents," a woman said with a shy smile, "during a lull in the winter snows."

At the edge of the field the big woman called over her shoulder, "The Wall's not there to stop us from sneaking across." She dumped her rocks. "Not even much help in stopping a major assault from our warriors."

"Then why is it there?"

"To control our movements," Emer replied, "and to prevent the men from returning north to Caledonia with spoils after an attack."

"You mean it's there to slow us down?" Neeve said.

"Exactly," the big woman shouted. "The Romans like large battles. With the Wall, they can gather their troops and meet attackers in formal combat. It matters little whether our armies breach their defenses, we still have to reckon with the Roman soldiers on the battlefield."

Emer spoke up. "When the northern tribes send their warriors, we'll be strong enough to defeat them even in a formal conflict."

"What happens if the Romans send their legions stationed in the south?" Neeve asked.

"We worry about that," Emer said, "but the men think the Brigantes threat in the south will keep the legions where they are."

"And what do you think?" Neeve asked, looking around at the women.

Worry showed on their faces. "I think the legions will remain in the south," the shy woman said, "but I expect the Romans will kill many of the men."

"And women too," Emer said. "Those of us without dependent children are expected to take up arms."

The others nodded grimly.

That afternoon Neeve found her brothers reinforcing the fencing around the sheep pen. During the night wolves had chewed their way in and killed several sheep, and now that they had found easy prey they would be back.

"We could light torches," Neeve said.

"Anything is easier than this," Eston agreed, wringing the sweat from his tunic. "But torches won't stop them for long."

"We could wait for them," Taranis said, "put arrows in a few, but who knows when they'll return?"

Neeve sharpened a pile of heavy poles with a not too sharp axe. As she watched her brothers taking turns pounding them into the ground, she asked about the Wall and the coming war.

"Our strategy is simple," Taranis said. "We'll attack their five outposts beyond Antoninus' Wall. These are the toughest garrisons, much stronger than anything they have on the Wall. When the Romans see their outpost forts in trouble, perhaps being destroyed, they'll have to decide whether to send their legions from the south."

"We don't think they will," Eston said, "because the Brigantes will be massing in the south. They need those legions as a balance against the Brigantes."

"And the auxiliaries on Antoninus' Wall can't help the outposts," Taranis said, "because we'll have positioned five or six Caledonian clans along its length. With the Wall itself threatened, the soldiers defending it will have to stay put, and the Romans will have no choice but to abandon their outpost forts."

"Once that happens," Eston said, "the Wall defenses will crumble. When defeated soldiers from the outposts race south to the Wall, the defenders on the barrier will know they're next. "

"With Caledonians on the north and Brigantes on the south," Taranis said, "the auxiliaries manning the Wall-forts will panic. They'll flee to their other Wall in the south, or be trapped."

As the weeks flowed by, Neeve became convinced that freedom was possible; her father's talk of tearing down the Wall was no longer a dream. Every day, it seemed, messengers from various tribes rode in to consult with her brothers. In the winter, she was told, when the Romans least expected it, warriors from every tribe would mount a full-scale attack on the five outposts beyond the Wall. But much needed to be done. Weapons and armor stockpiles were inadequate, wall-scaling shields were almost nonexistent, and ramps to bridge the ditches around the forts still awaited construction.

Late one afternoon, as a group of Brigantes warriors were leaving, Neeve asked her brothers the question that had for months been tearing at her soul. "The Wall soldiers call you the blood god," she said bluntly.

Taranis nodded. "Does that bother you?"

"No, not deeply."

"I can tell it does. What did the soldiers say?"

Neeve made a noise of apology for even mentioning it.

"Neeve?" Taranis was looking at her. "What did the soldiers say?"

"They said you kill wounded soldiers, women and children."

"Roman lies," Eston scoffed. "They say anything to frighten the people. I have heard tales that we eat the innards of dying men, then swallow their eyes to blind them in the next life. It's all a fear tactic. Better ruled by Romans, they say, than bloodthirsty Caledonians."

"We do kill wounded soldiers," Taranis acknowledged, "but rarely women and never children. We also slaughter the livestock, burn granaries, weapons—anything that will frustrate the enemy."

Neeve hung her head. "I'm sorry I doubted you," she said.

Taranis shrugged. "War is a shameful affair and I take no pride in much of what I do. But the Romans will not leave and bloodshed is the only answer."

Neeve felt a cloud lift from her mind. She hadn't realized how much the soldiers' comments had disturbed her. Killing to rid Caledonia of Imperial power was one thing, but murdering innocent children—Roman or not—she could not abide.

Taranis interrupted her thoughts, "Our raids across the Wall have accomplished little beyond instilling fear in the enemy," he said. "We kill a few scouts or engineers, burn down some granaries, and, if we are lucky, destroy a patrol or supply train. But we have no real count of the soldiers in each fort or how they intend to defend against an assault. Are reinforcements being sent? How much cavalry do they have? What kinds of weapons have they stored? We know nothing of these things."

Neeve thought for a moment. "There must be a way to get work inside one of the forts, especially in Caledonia."

"The outposts have grown wary of day workers," Eston said. "But for some reason mapmakers, scouts, and engineers are in great demand." He laughed to himself.

"What Eston means," Taranis said, "is that when we find them in the hills, we slit their throats. Romans cannot fight without their scouts or engineers."

"And the mapmakers," Neeve asked, "what's so important about them?"

Taranis shrugged. "They chart the rivers and valley floors in case their army has to venture into unfamiliar regions. It seems like wasted effort. Why chart the whole territory when most maps will never be used? Scouts could tell a commander in short order what he needs to know. But the Romans are always making maps, so we kill their mapmakers."

The conversation continued. As commander of the Caledonian army, Taranis had the responsibility of destroying the enormous outpost fort, Faustina, the Romans' most northerly post and by far the best equipped. Burn it to the ground and they would know they were in trouble.

"I could make maps," Neeve said, interrupting the conversation.

Her brothers looked at her, not comprehending.

"I said, I could make maps. I have used Roman maps before and I know I could make them."

Taranis looked her straight in the eyes. "What are you saying? You want to hire on as a mapmaker?"

"Why not? The Romans often hire native people to do work. Most of their scouts come from our tribesmen."

"Traitors!" Eston said. "That's why we slit their throats."

Taranis nodded. "Don't you understand? Mapmakers get killed all the time. How long do you think you would last if you stumbled on a raiding party?"

"How many women mapmakers are there?" she asked, irritated. They were treating her like a child. In an overly patient voice she said, "You could simply instruct the Caledonian war parties not to slit my throat."

"We can't give instructions like that," Taranis retorted. "It would involve hundreds of people. The Romans would be sure to find out. Silver loosens many tongues, even among Caledonians."

"Then you instruct only the leaders of the raid," she said firmly. "They could direct the warriors away from me."

Her brothers fell silent, exasperated.

"Well?" She was not caving in.

"Listen to me, Neeve." Taranis's face showed a vulnerability that moved her. "I love you. Eston loves you. You have no idea how happy we are to have you back. For years we sat around the fire at night, talking, wondering how you were faring, worrying about you. And now you are here ... we can't lose you to such foolish ...." He paused. "It is true, if our raiders came across you, the leaders could give some reason for passing you by. But the Romans ... if they ever discovered—"

"Even if they did not," Eston interrupted, "I would hate to think of my sister wandering around a Roman camp. You don't exactly look like the old leather-faces that haul water in the village."

Neeve was not unaware of her beauty. Her former husband had attained his status largely because of it. "I understand," she said, "but I know the Romans better than you think. They are slaves to authority—trained from birth to obey those over them. I know scores of important Roman names in the south that could be used to great advantage. And I speak their language. Once in the fort, I could listen to the gossip, maybe even read their dispatches."

Eston turned to Taranis. "It is a big risk, but—"

"Too big."

"I wouldn't be there that long," Neeve volunteered.

Taranis said, "You just arrived—"

"And I want to help."

"You can help right here."

"Picking rocks?"

"If Neeve could get in," Eston said, "it would certainly be an advantage."

Neeve said, "I want to do something significant. I am a landowner, in case you've forgotten."

Taranis said nothing. Neeve could see the struggle—weighing his responsibility as a Caledonian commander with his concern for her. Finally, he spoke. "I agree. Neeve can go. As a landowner, she has a duty to fight wars, and who knows what she might learn in the fort? Her information could prove more valuable than anything we've learned to date." Then looking at Eston, he said, "But I go with her."

18

The Senate was packed with dignitaries when Vectis arrived for his meeting with Atilius. Inside the main arch, minstrels danced and sang under brilliantly painted banners announcing the birthday of a senior senator. Hanging from the balconies behind them were ornamental ribbons and streamers, laurel branches and pennants. Everywhere in the large, oval Senate room slaves wended their way through the crowds, hoisting platters of meats and sweetbreads.

From the second floor balcony, Senator Atilius Titianus watched Vectis moving swiftly through the knots of people, hardly pausing to nod even to the most celebrated of Rome's elite. Atilius followed Vectis with his eyes, observing every step, every turn of his head. Not comfortable at all in ostentatious gatherings, Atilius thought, but he carries himself well, self-assured, just like his father. And like his father, he had distinguished himself as a soldier—in Egypt and North Africa—as Atilius knew he would. It was a shame to betray him.

"Vectis, my boy!" Atilius called, flashing a smile. "Stay right there."

The two greeted each other in the center of the room. "Politicians!" Atilius said, gesturing to the commotion around them. "Not quite like the army, is it?"

"Not quite."

"You look well. Is there anything you lack? No point in having family in the Senate ...."

"Thank you, I lack nothing. But I came with a friend, a tribune ... it seems that the Praetorians—"

"Ah, yes, the Praetorians can be protective. Where is this friend of yours? On the Senate steps?"

Vectis nodded. "His name is Julian Quintillius."

Atilius signaled a guard, instructing him to bring the tribune to Balbinus, his aide. Balbinus, he said, would give him a proper tour of the Senate while they talked. "But first," he intoned loudly, "let me introduce you to Senator Alfenus Crescens, whose birthday we're celebrating."

They pushed their way through the crowd to the place where the old senator sat. He smiled amiably as he listened to Atilius's words: "Senator, this is Vectis Trebellius, son of Gaius Trebellius, whom I am sure you know." The old man squinted at Vectis and said something praiseworthy about the elder Trebellius, adding that he had known Vectis's father as a boy.

"Vectis has recently returned from the Egyptian wars," Atilius said, "and was the military tribune in charge of operations."

Alfenus Crescens was impressed. He patted Vectis on the arm. "Rome needs men like you and your father ... that is the great tragedy of today ... too many provincials directing the army. I remember a time when the army was run by blooded Romans!" He coughed weakly. "Such a tragedy—"

Afraid the old man would forget himself and give a speech, Atilius interrupted. "I agree, Senator, it is tragic when the Roman army cannot stop barbarians from plundering the Empire. Why should we tolerate the murderous Celts in Britannia, for example? Should we let them rape and pillage innocent people? I say no!" He gestured toward Vectis. "I am proud to be part of the great military family of Trebellius. Citizens like this stand between us and chaos."

The senator seemed touched by Atilius's words. He turned to Vectis. "May Rome's blessing go with you, my boy, and if you would not think me presumptuous, my blessings too."

Vectis thanked the senator, wished him a long life, and followed Atilius out of the room.

Once they were alone, Atilius said, "I know I embarrassed you in front of Senator Crescens, but I meant what I said. Your father—and now you—are the real protectors of Rome. I wish I had your military gifts, I sincerely do. The Senate does well in evaluating the dangers facing us, but few senators have the ability to do anything about it." He smiled. "We are good at talking, I suppose."

Vectis looked mildly uncomfortable, which was exactly what Atilius wanted him to be. He had learned long ago that a mixture of flattery and self-deprecating statements was the surest way to win someone over. Speak unfavorably about yourself, and your opponent will respond in the most positive manner. As Atilius expected, Vectis now paid tribute to the Senate. "The Senate has produced Rome's greatest generals," he said.

"Gracious of you to say so," Atilius replied, "but I'm afraid the days of Marius, Pompey and Caesar are over. Old Crescens might be right. Too many provincials in the army, and maybe in the Senate as well."

"You said you wanted to talk."

The boy was a bit too abrupt for Atilius's liking, but he leaned forward and spoke as one would to a friend. "Vectis, I asked you here today because Rome is in trouble."

"Trouble? In what way?"

"With the Celts in Britannia. They are stronger and more united than ever. Put bluntly, we could lose everything north of Hadrian's Wall."

"How soon do we anticipate major hostilities?"

"We think we have a year or two before the Celts gain the capability to overwhelm our Antonine defenses, but do it they will. Rome needs your help."

Atilius watched Vectis closely, trying to read him. He knew the boy was wary. Old Trebellius had infected his son with his ridiculous suspicions. Ever since Atilius's family had sided with Emperor Hadrian in his army purges, the elder Trebellius had been irrational. He misunderstood everything. He criticized Atilius's family for not opposing the purges in Hadrian's last years, and then when Atilius's father had tried to oust Hadrian to stop the killing, Trebellius accused him of disloyalty to the Emperor, and trying to seize power. There was no pleasing the old man.

Now Atilius needed to use the son. But he had to tread carefully because the father's hatred had undoubtedly tainted Vectis. The only positive element was that old Trebellius had a reputation for keeping things to himself. The boy probably knew nothing about how Atilius had secured Sabina as a wife. He likely had a general distrust for the household of Atilius Titianus, but his dedication to Rome should overcome that.

Vectis spoke: "What can I do in the province of Britannia that a hundred others cannot?"

"You can solve a crisis rapidly building here in Rome."

Vectis looked puzzled. "I don't understand."

"The truth is that the Senate is facing a delicate situation. We have spent enormous sums of money to maintain Antoninus' Wall, and now ... well ... it may have been fools' money. The Emperor has become obsessed with the problem. He wants to reconstruct the Antonine barrier with stone and mortar, like Hadrian's Wall in southern Britannia. But Rome's coffers are empty. We simply do not have the funds to rebuild his Wall."

"So you want me to ...."

"To assume command of the most powerful fort in northern Britannia. It is called Faustina, named after Emperor Antoninus' wife. The fort is situated on the north side of the Antonine barrier in the heart of Caledonia; if you notice anything unusual, you will report it to me. You will have freedom to strike anywhere you see the beginnings of rebellion."

"It has been my experience that small strikes irritate the enemy. Only massive force quells them."

"That is precisely why the Senate needs someone like you, someone we can trust. The Celts will become frustrated and eventually mass for war, and they might try to take the fort, and possibly the Wall. Then the legions in the south will come to your aid and deal with the problem at the source—they will eliminate the Caledonians. The Senate has concluded that reinforcing our legions with auxiliaries to crush the Celts would be significantly cheaper than pouring gold into a Wall."

"The Senate has concluded this?"

"Yes."

"All of them?"

"A significant number."

"Will I have an Imperial edict for my action?"

"You have the blessings of the Senate."

"But not the Emperor."

Atilius sighed. "I will not hide anything from you. That is precisely the problem. Emperor Antoninus insists on rebuilding his Wall. He refuses to take military action, even small operations. I suspect he yearns to build an eternal monument to himself."

Vectis looked him squarely in the face. "I am a soldier sworn to obey the Emperor's wishes. I dislike political maneuverings."

"I appreciate what you say. The Senate wishes it had alternatives … but your actions will save the Emperor's Wall for him. You will not breach your loyalty oath. Never would we ask that of you! You simply provide the Emperor with what he desires most—a secure Wall—even if you attain it by other means."

"If what you say is true, how do you expect me to attack the Caledonians? As I understand it, there are only about a thousand soldiers at the larger forts. Military action carries risks. We are bound to lose men."

"The Senate is not thinking of a major campaign. Small, well chosen strikes, that is what we need. After your successes in Egypt, the Senate has great confidence in you. You need have no fear about losing men, we will reinforce you as necessary. If the Caledonian tribes mount a full-scale attack, well, then the legions will come." He raised a deferential hand. "One last thing. *You* make the decisions out there. No one in the Senate is asking you to commit yourself to our strategy. If, for some reason, you conclude that attacks are unnecessary or unwise, that is your decision. Dispatch a letter to me and I will inform the Senate. Then we will reassess the situation."

Vectis placed his hand on his chin, thinking.

Inside Atilius rejoiced. The boy might have had his successes on the battlefield, but he was no match for Senator Atilius Titianus. He needed Vectis out there, that was certainly true. But whether he attacked the Caledonians was of little consequence. Once out there,

Vectis would quickly learn the futility of attacks. The Caledonian tribes controlled the whole area north of the Wall, including the northern arterial road with the five outposts. All the talk about striking the Caledonians without the Emperor's permission was a ruse—a ploy thrown in to mislead him. And it worked. Now Vectis was debating with himself whether he should obey the letter of the law, or initiate unauthorized attacks, which in the end would serve the interests of Rome.

Completely overlooked was the real reason Atilius wanted Vectis in Britannia. He needed a sacrificial goat. If his information was correct, the Caledonians were already massing for war, and having his own brother-in-law in such a dangerous situation would demonstrate to the Senate that Atilius Titianus had indeed done his utmost to support the Emperor.

Besides, if Vectis were foolish enough to strike the Caledonians, it would never succeed; it might even provoke a war, putting the entire Antonine Wall in jeopardy.

He looked at Vectis struggling to make a decision. Too much political thinking is not good for soldiers, Atilius said to himself, it confuses them. Time to conclude our session. "The Senate," he said, "realizes the sacrifice you are making and wants you to know that in the event of hostilities, the legions will be sent forthwith."

Vectis nodded. "I will give you my answer in a few days, after I consult other senators to get a broader view."

Atilius maintained his composure. He couldn't let Vectis wander around the Senate alarming people with war talk. Senators such as Titus Severus would dearly love to speak with the boy. Atilius gave Vectis a sincere look. "The senators I represent—a majority of the Senate, I might add—are anonymous and must remain so. They are taking an enormous risk in opposing Emperor Antoninus, but they do it for the good of Rome. In truth, they fear to discuss such sensitive matters with anyone outside the Senate. If they bare their souls to you, they have no guarantee you will hold your silence. I am sure you understand. That is why I volunteered to speak on their behalf."

"I see," Vectis said. "This makes it awkward, doesn't it?"

Atilius knew this was a weak point in his plan. Vectis wanted to verify what Atilius was telling him. The boy was more perceptive than he had expected; years of war had hardened him. He smiled, trying to appear unconcerned. "You need not decide today. Think about it and we can talk again."

Two days later Sabina's ornate carriage rolled up to the Trebellius villa, a dozen guards and as many body servants following alongside. Vectis had not seen his sister in over three years and he couldn't help smiling as she stepped grandly out the door of her carriage. Wealth suited her.

"Oh, my, my," Sabina cried as she swept toward him, "you look so strong and handsome in that soldier's tunic! Believe me, there are plenty of women—women of substance—aching to make your acquaintance. If you think I intend to let you seclude yourself here for your entire stay in Rome, well, you simply are mistaken." She kissed him, taking care not to wrinkle her garments.

He smiled again. "You look wonderful, Sabina. You must be the most beautiful woman in Rome."

"Oh, that is so nice." She bowed elegantly, accepting the compliment. Soon they were sitting by the fountain on the stone seats where they had discussed family matters since childhood. Their conversations usually centered on Sabina and her latest trauma, but today was different. Vectis had received a note saying she had urgent business to discuss. As he listened to her prattle on about the doings of Roman society, he wondered what could possibly be urgent in her life. Then, abruptly, her forehead wrinkled and her mouth tightened, and she began to talk about their father's failing health. Sabina was convinced that their mother's passing the winter before had greatly added to his deteriorating condition.

"He looks terribly frail," Vectis agreed. "I should perhaps remain in Rome until his strength returns."

Sabina leaned forward. "You cannot sacrifice yourself in that way. I have scores of personal servants, and we can easily care for him. You are an officer in the Imperial army now. You cannot be bound by the capricious temper of family matters." She smiled and patted him on the chest. "You must be free to respond to the needs of the Empire—and I understand that—even if it means leaving Rome."

Vectis frowned. "You know about Britannia?"

"Just that the Senate wants you there."

"Atilius told you?"

"Yes."

He took a deep breath.

"I can certainly care for Father," Sabina repeated, "and you can go to Britannia. Rome will be better served with you there. At least, that's what I think."

Vectis furrowed his brow. He might have been amused hearing his sister talk politics, so out of character it was, but he was growing uncomfortable with the conversation.

"I know you don't respect my judgments on these matters," she continued, "but I have thought deeply about this. You should go."

He stared at her.

She shrugged. "I mean, it doesn't matter to me, but I know your convictions about duty to the Empire. There's really no reason to stay. As I said, I can care for Father."

"Why do you want me to leave?"

"I don't."

"Yes, you do."

She played with the sleeve of her stola.

"Sabina." His voice chided her.

She shifted uneasily. "Well, there are things involved here—"

"What things?"

"Just ... important considerations."

"Such as?"

"Such as Atilius's promise to the other senators. He assured them you would go. Now, if you don't, he will look foolish."

"That is no concern of mine."

She sat quietly for a moment. "Maybe it's time for the truth," she said. "You never liked Atilius. You said that along with his wealth he brought pain." She looked away, her eyes brimming with tears. "You were right, Vectis. He is good at giving pain."

Vectis touched his sister's hand, but could think of nothing to say.

"I'm sorry," she said, dabbing her eyes. "I am not telling you this to gain your pity—I have learned to live with my mistakes. It's Father I'm concerned about. I am afraid that if you decide not to go, Atilius could punish him ... and you have seen his condition."

"What did you say?" Anger flashed through Vectis. "Explain to me, Sabina, how Atilius could hurt Father."

"Well, years ago, Father killed a nephew of Emperor Antoninus. Atilius knows about it and threatens to spread the story. I cannot imagine what the Emperor would do if he found out."

Vectis felt relieved. "I have known for a long time about those so-called killings. Father said I should know the truth in case stories ever surfaced. He told me he won a great deal of money from a Syrian named Spurius Fabius. The man refused to pay and tried to kill Father. When the fight was over, Spurius Fabius, the nephew of Antoninus, and two others lay dead. Father is guilty of nothing."

"Oh, Vectis, I believe that. But what would others think? What would Emperor Antoninus think? I am not saying that Atilius will use the story if you refuse to go, but I assure you, he can be cruel when he chooses. He is a proud and ambitious man, and he'll stop at nothing. Sometimes I think he wants to be Emperor."

Vectis felt his jaw tighten and his breath grow shallow. He had an overwhelming urge to kill Atilius, but knew it was a useless emotional response. A murdered senator would prove more humiliating to his father than the false stories. He tried to think. No doubt the Celts should be crushed, and he had been ready to accept the commission before Sabina came. Yes, he would suppress his emotions, and go. For the sake of Rome and his father, he would go, and for the sake of his sister, he would not confront Atilius. He would let the senator think Sabina had convinced him to go, as much as that irked him.

Besides, he thought, in Britannia he would pass through the Isle of Vectis, and that would surely please his father.

The weeks since his decision had been filled with preparations for the journey to Britannia. Julian had agreed to accompany Vectis, but only after much persuasion; the North African hated the cold. Today Vectis's father had arranged for them to meet a centurion named Aulus Pertinax, who would also join them. He was the best, his father said, absolutely the best. And a good First Centurion was worth a cohort of men.

One morning as Vectis was packing his leather travel bags in the second story room at his father's villa Julian burst through the door, pressed his back against the wall, and closed his eyes.

"What happened, Julian? A maid slap you?"

"This is no time for jokes," he said, his face ashen.

Vectis grew serious. "Are you all right? You look sick."

"I feel sick."

"Is something wrong?"

Julian rolled his head back and laughed insanely. "You will not believe it," he said.

Vectis gestured for him to go on.

"Jupiter's here!"

"What did you say?"

"I said, Jupiter's here! He's standing in the courtyard!"

Vectis stepped over to the window and peered through the shutters. It was Jupiter, all right, standing in his father's courtyard. Vectis moved away from the window. "Did you talk to him?"

"Talk to him! To Jupiter? No, I didn't talk to him. But he saw me. I was about to go outside ... and there he was. I looked right into his eyes ...."

"And?"

"And nothing. I dropped my eyes and ran up here."

Vectis moved back to the window. Jupiter was taking packs off his horse; he had just arrived. A slave stood awkwardly nearby, trying to assist him, but Jupiter would have none of it. He wanted to do the work himself. He hadn't changed, Vectis thought, not in any way. He still moved quickly, efficiently, and his powerful body looked the same—like one of those stone statues along the Nile.

Vectis studied him a moment. He really had not changed. Some gray in his curled hair, a few more lines, but about the same.

"Stay here, Julian. I intend to talk with my father."

"I can assure you," he said, "I will remain within these four walls."

"I know who he is," his father said to his startled son. "I used his full name because ... if the truth be known ... I thought you might refuse to take him with you."

"You were right about that," Vectis replied.

"But you will need a man like him."

"Father, I have spent ten years in the army, and *never*, I repeat, *never* have I met anyone like Jupiter. The man kills for sport."

"He didn't kill you."

Vectis's mind raced back to those moments when he had knelt before the log, when absolute terror had gripped him. He shook the thoughts from his mind. "Jupiter spared me only because he wanted to show his merciful side—obey him and you might get mercy. It was all a tactic."

"You are wrong, Vectis. He spared you because I spared him."

"What are you saying?"

"I am saying that I know Jupiter better than you think. Six months I tracked his marauders with the best legionaries Rome has ever produced."

"That was you? You were the centurion they sent?" Vectis was astonished.

"He never made a mistake, never wasted effort. It was only because of superior numbers that we eventually trapped and overwhelmed him. He has good instincts and the skills you will need in an untamed province like Britannia."

"Father, please don't ask me to—"

"Years ago in old Cyrenaica I was the first legionary to fight my way over the city wall. Bravest thing I ever did. They gave me the *corona muralis*." His gray eyes fastened on Vectis. "Jupiter did it three times in the space of two years. Three times!" He breathed with some effort. "You need him, son, and I'm asking you to take him."

Vectis looked into his father's face. He had grown so old, with puffy circles ringing his eyes, and stooped posture. Rarely had he called him *son*. It was a simple word, but Vectis knew his father was trying to reach him. He was appealing to him from the corridors of their collective memories, a father to a son.

Another memory flashed through Vectis's mind, prompting him to ask, "Did I ever meet Jupiter when I was young?"

"He used to play soldier with you, marching back and forth, flinging out his arms — it was the game you loved most."

Sabina wandered away from the matching fishponds, crossing the garden toward the villa. As she passed a rear lounging room that opened onto the lush garden, she heard the murmur of voices, and then someone saying her name. She hesitated, and shot her eyes up and down the corridor. Servants were not permitted in this area, but she checked nonetheless. Then she pressed against the wall and listened, her horror growing with every word.

"She deserves the credit," Atilius was saying. "When Vectis wanted to pursue the Britannia question in the Senate, I thought I had lost him. If he had discovered that no anonymous majority of senators existed ... but all that is past. He is on his way to Britannia, thanks to Sabina. Like everyone else, he has a weak point. He couldn't bear to have old Trebellius shamed in his final years."

Balbinus responded: "From the information Kallias gives us, we might not even need Vectis Trebellius to stir up trouble. He thinks the Celts will attack no matter what we do."

"I have ceased predicting what the Celts will do. For ten years I have waited for them to overwhelm Emperor Antoninus' Wall, but they keep delaying. I suppose the Druids might be the problem — they hold such tight controls on their warriors."

"But now that the Senate has forced the Emperor to cut their spring tribute —"

"Ten percent! What kind of cut is ten percent? I have repeatedly told the Senate we need to stop the tribute altogether. The Celts just use it to arm themselves and put pressure on the Antonine barrier."

"Isn't that what you want?"

"Of course that is what I want! That is what I *need* to humiliate Emperor Antoninus. But a ten percent decrease in tribute will never motivate the Celts of a full-scale attack. I must persuade the Senate to support a fifty percent reduction in the autumn tribute. Perhaps that will infuriate the Caledonian warriors and goad them into action."

"With your permission," Balbinus said tentatively, "I might suggest ...."

Atilius murmured his consent.

"There might be a way to decrease the Caledonian tribute without troubling the Senate."

"Continue."

"We could replace the Imperial emissary in charge of disbursing the Caledonian tribute."

"Worse things have been done in Rome," Atilius responded in a knowing voice. There was a long moment of silence as he contemplated the possibility, then he said, "With our own emissary, one we could trust, you are saying that it would matter little how the Senate votes."

"A humble thought, my lord. The emissary—*our* emissary—would simply inform the Druids that the tribute has been decreased to half, or nothing, if we choose. No one would know because those cursed priests always lie to their people about what we give them."

"We could use Kallias," Atilius mused.

"Kallias would be a wise choice as Imperial emissary, but he would need empowerment as the chief tax collector for the Antonine sector. Most of the tribute comes from the Caledonian people themselves. As the tax officer in charge of other gatherers, he would have freedom to move around as he pleased ... and of course he could send us reports on the tribes—"

"I have decided," Atilius said. "Decrease the tribute to a quarter, and have Kallias tell the Druids that the rest is delayed."

"A wise decision, Senator. Any problems can be blamed on an untrustworthy emissary. The funds have been delayed—the standard defense of the thief."

"There will be no problems, Balbinus. But I do believe in prudent planning."

"Indeed, Senator."

"As to the Imperial issues, I will attend to them, and you ... you will make certain that Kallias has a senatorial edict to use local troops and ... it would be better not to use my name, or his. Assign Kallias a new name, and designate Senator Alfenus Crescens as the sponsor. If it ever gets back to the old fool, he won't remember whether he sent the man or not. And every week I want a dispatch from this cousin of yours—firsthand information, that is what I need."

"When shall I inform Kallias he is to leave?" Balbinus asked.

"In ten days. It will take that long to arrange matters."

"Do we still need Vectis if Kallias—"

"Be assured, we need Vectis at the Wall. Not to provoke a war— though his strikes at the enemy might just create the crisis we want. No, we need Vectis for political reasons. Can you imagine how I will sound in the Senate when I, for the good of Rome, am forced to abandon a member of my own family? My deepest desire, I will say, is to send legions to support the troops at the Wall. But how can I vote for that when the Dacians on the continent are like a dagger pointed at the heart of Rome? The Dacian threat is the graver, I will say. And when the Wall falls, and my own brother-in-law is killed, everyone will mourn my loss, and everyone will remember Senator Atilius Titianus called the Wall *Antoninus' folly*."

"Then we strike."

"It will happen quickly. First, the Wall will be overrun, then will come the accusations against Antoninus, then his death. I will achieve what my father only dreamed of."

"At times like this," Balbinus bubbled, "I see an aura of light about your brow, azure in color, and full of promise for the future."

Atilius said nothing.

"Rome will be the better for having felt your touch, Senator. Or might I call you, *Emperor*."

Two days later Atilius sat rigidly, staring at a letter. "Has anyone seen this?" he asked.

"No one." Balbinus stood before the senator. He had just given him a brown courier's pouch. In it was Sabina's letter to Vectis.

"Are you certain she has written no other letters?"

"I monitor everything that enters or leaves your villas. I have arrangements with couriers as far as Gallia. She has written no other letter."

"Then how ...?"

Balbinus glanced toward the door. "She must have been listening outside," he said. "She even tells Vectis about the plot to remove Antoninus."

Atilius sighed. "She has not seen her father since her indiscretion?"

"She has not. But it would be prudent to monitor old Trebellius's dispatches nonetheless."

"It is sad indeed when family trust dissolves."

"Trust is a two-edged sword."

Atilius breathed out heavily. "What am I to do with Sabina? It pains me, Balbinus. But she leaves me no choice. I have given her everything, and this is how she responds."

"If she will write a letter like this, Senator—"

"How true. How terribly true."

"I could find someone to release this burden."

Atilius shook his head sadly. "I could not bear another touching my precious Sabina. In *my* arms, surrounded by *my* love, she will find Elysium."

"A nobler spirit this earth has never known."

He sighed. "Do you suppose the gods will forgive me?"

"The great, as you once said, have no need of forgiveness. Their destinies are written in the heavens, and often they must remove those with no vision. Julius Caesar took up the sword against Pompey, and Augustus had to deal with Marc Antony."

Atilius dropped his voice. "The way of the fates is hard. I remember as a boy reading about Alexander the Macedonian and his great remorse after plunging a dagger into the heart of his dearest friend, Cleitus."

Balbinus nodded his sympathies. He tilted his head forward and said, "Without upsetting you, Senator, I might say that when Nero removed his wife, Octavia, he had far less reason than you."

"In some ways she has been good for me ...."

"Like a fair wind," Balbinus said.

"She loves the gardens of this villa, the pools ...." He dabbed a tear. "She will feel only the soft warmth of the gods enfolding her, this I vow."

The next day as Sabina soothed herself in the garden, Atilius plucked her delicately from her couch, and with love in his eyes, carried her squirming to the pool. "Yes, I understand," he whispered into her terrified face as his gentle hands held her thrashing body tenderly under the perfumed waters until the surface smoothed.

19

Taranis's mind was set. He would accompany Neeve to Fort Faustina. He had no misgivings about entering a Roman garrison. The soldiers might know his name, but none had seen his face and lived. Besides, he could scarcely allow his sister to stroll into a Roman fort alone, especially when he had no idea how she might be treated. Eston could carry on until he returned—which wouldn't be long, just long enough to make it known that Neeve had a brother. The mere thought might afford her some protection. They would be mapmakers, not uncommon in a land where whole families labored at the same vocation. True, the Romans might discover that he couldn't draw maps, but the risk was minimal.

So the two packed their travel bags, mapping tools, and Neeve's dismantled loom, and set off for the district where the fort was located. There they spent several days constructing a series of maps of the surrounding region.

"Are you certain the fort commander is named Didius Rufinus?" Neeve asked for the third time. Her anxiety showed as they neared the city of followers, a tent village settled a mile or so from the fort. Even at Rome's most northerly outpost, Celts eagerly profited from the presence of the enemy.

"I am certain," Taranis replied. Then, twisting around on his horse, he said, "Neeve, we can still abandon this scheme. Turn right around and head back to the mountains. It's not too late."

"I'll be fine."

Taranis persisted. "There's no shame in abandoning a plan that does not feel right."

"I'll be fine. Really, I will."

Neeve didn't feel fine. In the distance she could see the red-tiled roofs of the main fort-buildings, and sentries walking the outer ramparts, and guards at the gates of the huge turf fortress. The site had been well chosen. It was situated at the confluence of two waterways, leaving enemies with the unenviable choice of bridging fast moving streams at the rear, or picking their way across a broad field in front that was filled with traps and barbed iron hooks. The closer they approached, the higher the walls appeared, and the deeper the trenched semicircles in front. Fort Faustina was well protected.

Her mouth went dry. She glanced at Taranis. He was concerned, she could see it in his eyes. At the homestead, she had convinced her brothers that Roman ways were familiar to her, and they were. How often had she attended Roman military functions and talked with army officers? Countless times. But this was different. This was the first time she had come as a spy. She tried pretending she was back in the south, attending another boring military reception. Her husband was beside her, laughing too heartily at their humor, ever eager to please his masters, like a dog groveling for a scrap of meat. The memory rankled her, flooding her body with a calm she desperately needed.

They nudged their horses toward the hitching rail at the beginning of a heavy, wooden rampway that led to the fort. Neeve cleared her throat and said, "I feel better now."

Taranis's eyes searched her face.

"Much better."

He reined in his horse and climbed down. "I don't want mistakes, Neeve." His voice was firm. She had heard him talk to his officers in the same tone, and it struck her that Taranis had a side she hardly knew. He was not just a brother; he was Taranis, the Caledonian commander, and he was telling her that she too had become a Caledonian warrior.

Neeve slipped from her horse and responded in kind. "I will make no mistakes. Once through the gate, I'll be fine, you'll see." She tied her mount to the rail and hooked her bow over the spare she kept on her saddle.

"Take one of your bows," Taranis said. "The Romans expect a Celt to have weapons."

They walked up the sloping ramps toward the gates. Only the gate's smaller port entrance was open, with guards on either side. "Hail Caesar!" Neeve said loudly in the Roman tongue.

The guards eyed them. "State your business," said one in reasonably clear Celtic.

Neeve continued in Latin, projecting a calm that belied her emotional state. "My business is with Camp Prefect, Didius Rufinus," she said.

The guard looked at her more closely. It was rare for a native to speak Latin. Even many of the auxiliary troops had trouble with the language. He shook his head. "All inquiries must go through the centurion of the gate. Come back tomorrow at sunrise."

Neeve motioned to the maps rolled under her arm. "We were told to come now. We are mapmakers."

He hesitated, then sauntered over to the other guard. After a brief discussion, he disappeared inside the doorway and returned with an officer.

The officer stood in the entrance, surveying his two visitors, then demanded to see their maps. Neeve unrolled a scroll. He ripped it from her hands, ran his eyes over the drawing, and then studied the two Celts again. "Mapmakers, eh?" he said, looking at them as though he had never seen such hirelings before. Then turning, he said, "Let them pass."

A soldier stepped forward. It was standard practice for visitors to deposit their knives and swords when entering a Roman fort. Neeve removed her bow and pouch, and handed the soldier the knives she carried. He dumped them on a holding shelf, and then grinned as he ran his hands leisurely over her body in his search for additional weapons. Taranis shifted sideways toward the Roman, two knives flashing in his palms, bare inches from the man's stunned face. Then, abruptly, he turned the handles toward the soldier as if he were merely offering them.

"My brother does not like people touching me," Neeve said hastily.

The soldier glanced up at Taranis. "Better calm him down," he said. "He'll get in trouble doing that." They searched Taranis none too gently before allowing him to proceed.

The officer led them through the portal to the center of camp, where they waited outside a large, square building. A group of soldiers near the parade ground glanced in their direction, and then returned to their conversation. One was describing loudly, and in great detail, his recent exploits with two prostitutes that apparently resided in the colony of followers. The door opened in the square building. The officer of the gate clumped out. "Wait here," he said and left.

An hour passed. Neeve rehearsed a hundred times the few words she intended to say. She sat on a bench and fiddled with the empty knife case strapped above her ankle. She rubbed her hands on her trousers and tugged at her hair, and stopped only when she received a stern glance from her brother. Eventually, she found herself staring at the now vacant parade ground, and wondering how many Caledonians the Romans had executed on the wooden podium there. She forced the thought from her mind. Sometimes she could think of the most awful things. She looked up at Taranis, who was studying the fort. His eyes moved slowly across the compound, as if he had never been inside a Roman fort, which, Neeve suddenly realized, he had not.

Her stomach churned. Spies! That's what they were. And Romans executed spies. She cleared her throat. It was dry again. She would do better if she could just get on with it. All this waiting was taking its toll.

"Mapmakers!"

The voice made her jump. Neeve turned to see a clerk's head poking out of the door. He had a lethargic look on his face, making it clear that calling people was not his favorite duty. They followed him through the door into a darkened hallway, only to be stopped by guards who again searched them for weapons. This time the guards checked her quickly. Someone must have mentioned the incident at the gate.

Camp Prefect Didius Rufinus was a short, bloated-looking man with stubby fingers and a round face. His purple-blotched skin seemed incapable of stretching any farther to contain the tubes of fat that rolled down his body, and he continually took large swallows of wine from an oversized bronze cup adorned with coiled snakes. He reminded Neeve of an engorged wood bug.

Rufinus was seated behind a broad table that overflowed with documents and wax tablets. Around him, filling the room, were piles of equipment and assorted items, including Celtic weapons, temple masks, and wood carvings. He glanced up, sneezed, and returned to his work. In his left hand was a piece of Celtic tartan that he used for blowing his red, bulbous nose. Evidently, he had a cold. Neeve watched him elbow a bigger space for the sheet of papyrus on which he was trying to write. He muttered something and pawed through a mound of documents at one end of the table, his dull, circular eyes lighting up when he found what he was looking for.

Turning to the three officers gathered behind him, he handed over the sheets of papyrus, grunting something about Imperial bureaucracy that Neeve couldn't quite hear. That done, he gulped more wine, wiped his nose, and then leaned forward on his chair to study the pair before him. An officer addressed them in Celtic.

Neeve stepped forward, bobbed, and smiled. "I Roman speak ... good," she said with a horrible accent. No point in letting them know her true abilities. The guards at the gate would hardly be chatting with the camp commander.

Rufinus snorted. "Yes, I'm sure you Roman speak good. Let me see your maps."

Neeve did nothing.

"Maps! Maps!" he shouted, beckoning with his doughy hand and sloshing wine over his papers. He scarcely noticed when one of his officers stooped to clean up the mess.

"Ah, maps," Neeve said, holding them up and smiling cheerfully.

"Ignorant people," he muttered, snapping the maps from her hand and laying them out on his cluttered desk. "I am so glad to be leaving here." He looked up at Neeve and pointed wearily at a map. "Where is this?"

Neeve gestured to the west, indicating that she had drawn the area between the fort and the western hills.

One of the officers peered at the map and nodded. He recognized the section. He examined it again and told the prefect it was well done, but constructed differently from most maps. Looked more like a drawing than a map, he said. She had marked the roads and pathways clearly and used tiny houses to indicate villages. Distances had been properly noted, as were mountains, valleys, and forests.

Rufinus grew impatient listening to his officer's musings. "Is it readable or not?" he asked.

"Quite readable," the officer replied. He glanced at Taranis's samples and signaled his approval.

"Map good, yes?" Neeve smiled broadly. "You hire ... brother ... me. Pay many sesterce."

On hearing the word sesterce, Taranis spoke up, repeating the prearranged words and rubbing his fingers together. "Sesterce, yes!"

Rufinus stared at Taranis. "Amazing," he said. "Sesterce is probably the only word he knows."

The officers laughed.

Taranis laughed too, making the officers laugh even more.

"You know other Roman words?" Rufinus said slowly, as if he were talking to an imbecile.

Taranis had little understanding of Latin, but promptly discerned that he was being mocked. He smiled and repeated loudly, "Sesterce, yes!"

Neeve grinned eagerly. "You hire, yes?"

"What tribe you from?"

"Tribe ... Votadini," Neeve replied, identifying themselves with the most peaceful of Celtic tribes. "I two years ... south Wall Hadrian." She opened her arms expansively. "Have many friends ... at Hadrian. Learn Roman tongue there."

Rufinus chewed on his lip. "Do you have family in Caledonia?"

"Caledonia!" she repeated, allowing fear to cross her face.

His eyes narrowed. "Caledonia, you from Caledonia, yes?"

Neeve shook her head violently. "No! We Votadini—peaceful people. Caledonia ... crazy warrior tribe." She drew her finger across her neck to indicate she knew Caledonian Celts would slit her throat if they caught her making maps.

Rufinus raised his eyebrows and looked at his officers. "Well, what do you think?"

The officers discussed the pair opposite them. Neeve heard them say they had only one mapmaker left and he was too frightened to leave the fort. They examined the map samples again and all agreed they were well drawn. Rufinus said he thought the two Celts looked reliable, then observed with a chuckle that even if they were not, the four officers would be gone before the mapmakers could cause trouble. The next commander would have to deal with it. "The point is," Rufinus said, "we need mapmakers, and they can draw maps." He grinned. "I would guess she could do a lot of things well."

The officers chuckled. With the subject opened, one felt free to comment on Celtic women and their considerable sexual appetites. Another officer, not wanting to be left out of the banter, remarked that he had noticed Neeve's eyes roaming Rufinus's body, and every time she used the word sesterce, she thrust her hips at the prefect.

Laughter again.

Rufinus fastened his eyes on Neeve and ran a big, purple tongue across his puffy lips. He sloshed more wine down his throat and onto his stained tunic. The thought of having this disgusting man touch her filled Neeve with revulsion, but she managed to keep up the pretense of not understanding what they were saying.

"Well," Rufinus mumbled, wiping a drip from his nose, "maybe we should see how badly she needs this job." He pointed at one of his officers. "Get me more wine, and then take that giant she calls a brother for a walk. Set him up with what he needs. Make him happy."

He turned to Neeve. "Good maps. I hire you. Now we talk about sesterces."

Neeve provided the appropriate excitement. She whipped around to Taranis and jabbered in Celtic. "He has hired us as mapmakers," she bubbled. "Now he will tell me about the pay." She turned back to Rufinus, looking pleased. "Prefect," she said, "you ... good man. Like Julius say."

"Julius?"

"Julius Verus."

When Rufinus heard the name, his mouth dropped. Neeve continued. "He send me. He say, no fear Didius Rufinus ... he take care you."

Rufinus blanched. To no one in particular he mouthed, "She knows Legate Julius Verus, the new governor ... of the whole province." He stared at her. "You know Legate Julius Verus?"

"Yes, yes, we friends ... good friends." Neeve smiled again to allow the significance of her words to sink in. "I go back see Julius ... when Rome wife finish visit. I tell Julius ... you good ... you treat me good."

Rufinus chewed on his lip again. His officers looked as stunned as he did. Then a dull light lit Rufinus's eyes. "The governor knows about me," he said, "in this forsaken outpost! I met him only once, but he still remembers." He cleared his throat and turned to his officers. "This bodes well for promotion—for all of us. Make sure these two are treated properly." He proceeded to talk about pay.

Good pay.

20

The first weeks of travel with Jupiter were awkward. Julian never spoke to him and rarely looked him in the eyes. Even Vectis, who pushed himself to be natural, often found his eyes on Jupiter's familiar chest. But time has a way of erasing past fears, and by the fourth week, Julian felt relaxed enough to tell the centurion a joke; Jupiter didn't smile.

Vectis had no doubt that the presence of Jupiter increased his own chances of survival in Britannia. His concern was whether he could control the man. As the prefect in charge of the five outposts, Vectis could not afford to have his orders challenged. His father had assured him the centurion posed no threat; he was a Roman soldier and would obey orders. But Vectis remained unconvinced. Jupiter was a forceful man, set in his ways. It would be folly to leave without an understanding.

Vectis remembered those long minutes he had stood in the corridor outside the library, listening to Jupiter and his father talk. There was a certain formal aspect to their speech, but it was evident that the two men shared a mutual respect. Vectis glanced at the stuccoed walls, trying to pluck up his courage. Several times he started toward the library door, then stopped. His mind swept back to a terrifying moment in his childhood, when the sleigh in which he was riding broke through the winter ice, and he almost drowned. But he would gladly return to that moment, if only he could avoid walking into his father's library. He took a deep breath to calm himself. It was ridiculous, he knew. Why should this man intimidate him? Was he some untested neophyte that he should cower before a centurion, or was he an experienced Roman soldier, an officer of significant rank?

A shadow fell across the opposite end of the corridor, startling Vectis. It was his father's freedman, Pudens, who encouraged him with a small smile. Vectis returned the smile but felt embarrassed. Even Pudens knew he was afraid of the centurion. He sucked in his breath and strode down the corridor toward the library.

His father looked up from a tray of pickled fish, strawberries, and date bread. "Ah, Vectis. You remember—"

"Yes, of course! Jupiter!" he said too loudly, trying to sound relaxed in his use of the forbidden name.

The centurion continued cutting his date bread, not even looking up.

"It is an honor to have you in our home," Vectis said, unsure what to say.

Jupiter turned slowly toward Vectis, as if he knew his former recruit had been hiding outside the library all this time. Vectis pushed the thought from his mind and looked straight at the centurion. The cold, penetrating eyes that met his unnerved him, but he held his gaze. If he expected to command this man, he had to at least look him in the eyes.

"Jupiter? You call me Jupiter?"

Vectis's face flushed. He was stunned. In his worst imaginings, he never thought things would go this badly. Trying to cover his embarrassment, he heard himself say, "It was the highest god I could think of."

An amused look spread across the centurion's face, as if he had been testing the younger man. "I think Jupiter is a fine god," he replied.

The moment weighed awkwardly as the three men stood in silence.

"Well," Vectis's father said, picking up the crock of wine, "it's nice to renew old acquaintances. What we need now is more wine. I'll fetch Pudens." With that, he left.

Alone in the library with Jupiter, Vectis cleared his throat. "This is a good time to talk," he said, "about Britannia."

Jupiter turned toward him, but did not reply.

"We need to talk about Britannia," Vectis said again, realizing how witless he must sound repeating himself.

"All right, let's talk," is all he said.

Vectis again thought he detected amusement in the centurion's face. Or was it mockery? He didn't know, but the possibility that Jupiter might be amused at his feeble attempts to appear strong irritated him. "The Senate has asked me to go to Britannia," he said abruptly, "and I understand you have asked permission to accompany me."

"That is correct."

Mentioning the Senate was pretentious, Vectis knew, but he felt more important saying it. Worse was his use of the word *permission* that underscored the centurion's need to gain Vectis's consent. But if Jupiter felt anything, his face masked his thoughts.

"It's not easy to take orders once you have given them," Vectis said.

Jupiter sidestepped the intent of his words. "Your father is an unusual man," he replied. "He asked me to accompany you to Britannia. I want to do that."

Vectis decided to be direct. "Can you take orders from me?"

"I can take orders."

"From me?"

"From you."

"Without reservation?"

Jupiter exhaled. "I understand your concern, but you need not ask the question three times. I said I can take orders, and that should be sufficient."

Vectis stared at him, uncertain what to say next.

The centurion continued: "You should know that I have followed your career since you left training camp. You have done well. But you must also know a centurion's job is to advise his superiors. Can you take advice?"

"I can."

"Then it's settled, isn't it?"

It didn't feel settled, but in the following weeks, Jupiter never once tried to usurp his authority. He was quiet, but dutiful.

The three soldiers maintained a good pace, exchanging horses at the legionary depots every fifty miles or so. With a signed letter affixed with the great Senate seal, they had no trouble procuring their needs. The senatorial letter decreed that all assistance be given them to speed their journey to northern Britannia. Minor provincial officials fawned over them, often mentioning their own names several times, hoping to be remembered. Occasionally, one would stare at Jupiter, but no one risked saying a word about his unmistakable African heritage. If the Senate had sent him, that was reason to repress their curiosity.

The channel crossing proved more hazardous than expected. Caught in a late summer storm, the light Roman galley blew off course and landed at the great chalk cliffs on the east side. They never did see the Isle of Vectis.

Once in the province of Britannia, the pace slowed. Thick fogs and heavy rains plagued the travelers, making it difficult to follow even the straight Roman roads. Julian continually complained about the weather, moaning that it had rained every day since they had set foot on the island. The three stopped at Britannia's provincial headquarters in Londinium. The governor, a hawk-faced man named Julius Verus, greeted them correctly, but with little warmth. Verus was a brilliant general recruited from the German frontier to deal with Celtic unrest. When he heard they were from Rome and heading toward Antoninus' Wall, he demanded to know what Emperor Antoninus intended to do about the Caledonians. Vectis told him what was permissible to know. A debate had arisen, he said, whether to refortify the Antonine frontier, or to supplement Legions II, VI, and XX with auxiliaries.

Verus exploded. "Fools! Don't they know that while their polite debate continues, those Caledonians up there are sharpening their swords? They take our bribes and mouth words of peace, but it means nothing. Celts never tell the truth. They are planning to fight, and soon." He stalked over to a map and jabbed his finger at

Caledonian territory. "Rome thinks the problem is restricted to the Caledonian tribes above the Antonine frontier. What they don't understand is that Caledonian unrest is causing turmoil throughout the province. The Brigantes, Selgovae, and a half-dozen other tribes," he said, pointing to their respective regions, "have stored weapons for years. We know that for a fact!" He slapped the map in disgust. "How can I maintain the peace with legions at half strength? I need more soldiers now."

"As I understand it," Vectis said, "legionaries are on their way."

"Legionaries are on their way!" he repeated angrily. "I have heard that song for two years now. All they send are replacements, and even then we are not maintaining our numbers. Do you know that if we added up every available soldier—auxiliary and legionary—we would have less than fifty thousand? Fifty thousand to control this entire island." He leveled his eyes at Vectis. "And if hostilities begin? What do they expect me to do?"

"If hostilities begin," Vectis said, "they say they will send legionaries from the German frontier."

Verus laughed derisively. "Oh, they will send them, but when? After half our northern forts are smoking hulks?"

Vectis said nothing. In the back of his mind was his conversation with Senator Atilius Titianus. Atilius had said that in case of hostilities, the southern legions would come. But apparently Verus's legions were anything but strong.

In the lull, the governor's face flushed deep red. He gestured weakly in apology, realizing that the men before him would be occupying one of those northern forts. "I am afraid I have been preoccupied with my own problems. Forgive me. I never asked which fort you would be commanding."

"Faustina," Vectis said.

"Faustina," he repeated slowly. "That's above the Wall, the most northerly fort. Then you will be the prefect in charge of the five outposts." His face showed the chagrin he felt. "I suppose you know the outpost forts are, to use senatorial language, not entirely secure."

"I understand. My orders, for good or ill, are to organize the defense of those outposts."

Verus fell silent, and then spoke in a more personal tone. "I hope you also understand if the tribes revolt at the Antonine barrier, I cannot march north with my legions unless I receive troops from the continent. As it is, I have sent all the auxiliaries up there I dare. My first priority will be to maintain Hadrian's Wall, or we could lose the entire island."

Vectis thanked him for his candor, and asked that a courier be sent to inform Faustina's present commander of his impending arrival.

The next morning they set out north, passing through flat expanses of fertile land scattered with rich forests and winding rivers. The trees lining the banks were bowed with thousands of black birds that, when startled, darkened the skies in their flight. Bands of fallow deer roamed the fields and long legged cranes idled in the quiet marshes. It looked like a hunter's paradise.

After weeks of steady riding, they reached Hadrian's Wall, a massive stone barrier that stretched majestically across the hills and farmlands, from one edge of the skyline to the other. Vectis had never seen anything like it, and his pride in the Roman people almost overwhelmed him. Who else could have built such an engineering marvel? He stared down the road toward the Wall, a road that was perfectly straight. Only a Roman could construct something like this, he thought. He had seen Roman surveyors laying out their roads countless times, moving from hilltop to hilltop in unswerving lines. Often they would light a fire on a distant mound, and then use their staffs and plummets to plot a direct course to the smoke, pounding in their marking rods as they went.

He examined the length of Wall again. What must these people think of such achievements? Not much, he concluded, since they were determined to return to living their coarse, vulgar lives. His father had been right: the darkness of the barbarian mind was unfathomable.

The trio spent less than a day at Hadrian's Wall, but long enough to see the Wall's dilapidated conditions. Verus's predecessors had done nothing to maintain the barrier. The trenches were sodden with mud from the constant rains, the ramparts had largely vanished, and trees and shrubs were growing wildly right next to the Wall. The mile forts and turrets were also worthless, rotted from years of neglect. Rome had been trying to lessen expenditures in Britannia, and for a time the arguments made sense. Why service an unnecessary Wall when the more northerly Antonine barrier had taken its place? Now, with Caledonians restless in the highlands, and Rome blind to the danger, provincial officials were hastily addressing the weaknesses of Hadrian's Wall. Governor Verus had authorized complete restoration of the Wall's defenses. Britannia must see to its own defense, he had said.

On the advice of Verus, Vectis accepted a contingent of soldiers, archers, and scouts to accompany them beyond Hadrian's Wall. The territory had been growing more unruly by the day, he had said, and the farther north one traveled, the more dangerous it became. Three officers without legionaries made inviting targets.

During the following week, their rapid pace north slowed to accommodate the escort soldiers who marched behind them. Everyone had donned thick woolen cloaks and knee-length breeches, practical outfits worn the world over by legionaries in the cooler climates. Even with the extra clothing, Julian complained about the increasingly bitter weather. Each morning he woke with a shudder and headed straight for the fire where the orderlies were serving bowls of hot porridge and heated Celtic beer, a beloved drink of legionaries stationed in Britannia. Then, alone with Vectis and Jupiter, he continued his favorite subject: Britannia's miserable weather.

"Look at this travel bag," he groused, tossing it to the ground. "The leather is frozen!"

"It's only stiff from the night air," Jupiter said.

"Frozen like a bronze cast," Julian mumbled. "How can it be cold in summer? Oh, I know, the island has suffered unseasonable winds. Hah! I've heard that for weeks. The truth is, it rains all day, and freezes all night. Even the grass is rock hard. This is the only place I know where you can break your toes running through the grass."

Jupiter grunted. He had heard it all before.

"And when did we last see the sun?" Julian continued. He glared up at the slate sky and then at the surrounding oaks as the wind flapped the shivering leaves. Julian fell silent when a legionary officer approached Vectis. He never complained in front of the soldiers, which was probably why Jupiter tolerated his comments. Yet over the long weeks of travel, Vectis could see that the centurion had actually grown to like Julian. They were such opposites: Julian with his humor and constant moaning, and Jupiter with his silence and permanent scowl.

For his own part, Vectis was thankful for the contingent of thirty soldiers. He had been loath to accept them because of the time they would add to the journey, but now as they passed through the low country, he realized Verus had been right. The people were rude and distant. Even the scenery seemed less hospitable and devoid of Roman influences, as if the populace was collectively resisting the Empire. No longer did they encounter villas or even Roman style houses. In the town squares, where one would expect to see proper Roman tunics, villagers went about their business in tribal tunics and trousers. Women's hair fell loosely to their shoulders, instead of the tight curls or braids common in Roman society. Small things, but they told Vectis much. More significantly, on the open roads he noticed that Roman officials, and even soldiers, never traveled alone; they moved in groups of ten or more.

They were passing another town with its clusters of roundhouses built neatly into the brown hills when Julian called out, "Does this look like part of the Empire to you?"

The three scanned the village market, little more than carts piled high with goods: sacks of flour, vegetables, sheep and pig skins, layers of brightly checkered cloth, and tools of every sort. The villagers stiffened as the soldiers passed. Some stopped their work to watch the column treading by, but most continued their business, glancing up occasionally with empty expressions on their faces.

Jupiter spoke: "The map says these are Votadini."

Julian laughed in derision. "Oh, then these are the peaceful Celts. Our friends! What do you suppose the Caledonians look like?"

"Maybe repulsive like you," Jupiter said.

Vectis smiled to himself. Jupiter had made a joke.

They were five miles away when they first saw Antoninus' Wall. It followed the contour of the land as though someone had stretched a thin, black cord along the horizon. From a distance it had a fragile appearance, but as they neared it grew in size until it dominated the skyline. It was immense—a thirteen foot turf wall topped with a heavy timber palisade, which extended another ten feet in the air. At regular intervals he could see huge turf forts with imposing gates and watchtowers, and red-tiled roofs on the main fort-buildings.

Vectis inspected the Wall. Except for a stone foundation and limestone culverts to carry off water, the entire Wall was built of turf blocks. It ran about fifteen feet across at the base, and tapered upward to a width of three feet. There were no fighting platforms at the top, but the legionaries had built a broad military road a hundred feet south of the Wall that stretched along its entire length. In case of attack, troops could move quickly to the problem area from the dozens of forts and fortlets along the Wall. No one feared sneak attacks on this frontier. Besides the Wall to contend with, the Caledonians would have to cross a forty-foot ditch, ten feet deep, lying directly north of the Wall. Small groups might slip in and out on a moonless night, but mass attacks would take time and be detected immediately. Overall, Vectis thought, Antoninus' Wall was a formidable barrier.

They stayed the night at a fort on the Wall, where they exchanged Verus's legionaries for a contingent of auxiliary soldiers. Years earlier the legions had built Antoninus' Wall, but now they were stationed far to the south, and the Wall was maintained solely by auxiliaries. Although equipped like legionaries, the auxiliaries were non-Roman citizens drawn from the provinces. Roman commanders ensured that they were better trained than the barbarians, but they were not of the same caliber as the legions. Rome placed these foreign soldiers on the frontiers where they could absorb the first shock of hostilities. Then, with the enemy's assault blunted, the disciplined legionaries would arrive and drive out the invaders.

The next morning the three set off north from the fort with their auxiliaries, fifty marching soldiers, a dozen mounted archers, and a handful of scouts to ensure that there would be no surprises along the way.

Beyond the Wall lay Caledonian territory.

Heavy, gray clouds lumbered across the skies, heralding the end of summer. As the massive timber gates closed behind them, soldiers lined the fort's ramparts and fighting parapets to see them go. Some shouted words of encouragement; others, a group assigned the unenviable task of maintaining the ditches along the Wall, called out "Hail Caesar" to their comrades. The escort soldiers marched briskly up the road, ignoring the attention they were receiving. It would be a serious breach of conduct, even for auxiliaries, to turn their heads as they marched. But Vectis could hardly miss the apprehension glistening on the faces of his escort. There was no denying it. They believed an ill fate had chosen them to leave the relative safety of the Wall.

"You would think we were marching off a cliff," Julian said as he glanced back at the soldiers watching them from the fort.

Jupiter snorted. "These are the most poorly disciplined troops I have ever seen. No wonder we are having problems up here."

Vectis agreed. The discipline was appalling. He wondered what he would find as he journeyed farther north.

They started up the old arterial road built first by the great Agricola in his conquests of the north country fifty years earlier. It was empty now, used only by the occasional soldier column transporting goods to and from the five outposts strung out above the Wall. Vectis glanced at the surrounding hills and dark stands of trees, places where large war parties could easily be hidden, but he maintained a relaxed posture, knowing that soldiers were taking their cues from him.

Over the last two years, Roman officials had grown reluctant to travel a road where Caledonian attacks had become commonplace. In the past, officers begged for outpost assignments where promotions came easily with the supposedly dangerous duty on their records. In truth, the forts north of the Wall were perfectly safe. They were double the size of most forts on the Wall, and eminently capable of protecting themselves. Although situated on the northern rim of the world, they were surprisingly well equipped, boasting the best bath and recreational facilities in the north. Of course, duty above the Wall could not be compared with duty in the central parts of the Empire, but it was untroubled, and in the end, could only enhance a soldier's career.

But lately things had changed. The Caledonians had grown bold, and the Roman defenders, timid.

At the first outpost, Vectis was appalled by the sloppy conditions of the camp. The outer ditches and barricades were in reasonable shape, and the turf walls were enormous—forty feet wide at the base. But inside the fort, chaos reigned. Carts piled with arrows and spears and other assorted weapons were parked haphazardly against the turf walls, supply barrels stuffed with everything from nails to flour clogged the fort's walkways, and the doors of almost every storage room had been left ajar.

"Well, I see this commander wants everything in the open where you can get at it," Julian said with a smile.

"A rat's paradise," Jupiter muttered.

As they waited near the inner gatehouse for the fort commander to arrive, Julian and Jupiter commented on the poor training being given to soldiers on the parade square, and the apparent nervousness of a patrol about to leave the fort. Vectis said nothing but realized that his task of organizing outpost defense would be more difficult than he had supposed.

Up the main roadway came the post commander, flanked by ten officers as if he were on parade.

"Impressive," Julian said.

Vectis could hear Jupiter's heavy breathing behind him and was thankful the centurion had chosen not to say what he was thinking. The company stumbled to a halt in front of the visitors and stood there swaying. Vectis could see Julian trying to catch his eye. He ignored him. The spectacle was sufficiently ridiculous without Julian helping it along.

The commander, a scrawny, cream-faced man, was undoubtedly a political appointee, dressed as he was with greaves, helmet and crest.   Greaves were designed to protect the lower leg, but the commander was so short that the greaves extended halfway up his thigh. Worse, Roman soldiers hadn't worn the antiquated protectors for a half century.   Only a political appointee would find them fashionable. Equally ludicrous was his flame-red horsetail crest that rose majestically from his helmet. Since he was wearing it in the fort, Vectis assumed he did so to appear taller than he was—which was shorter than everyone.

The commander cleared his throat, evidently a signal for one of his staff to begin the introduction formalities. An awkward silence. Someone had forgotten to assign an official greeter. Then came the eye movements and the unsettled looks on the faces of the staff. Finally, to everyone's relief, one of the officers stepped forward and intoned: "In the name of the Imperial armies of Rome, Commander Gaius Jovius Herculius Commodus welcomes you to Fort Colania, guardian of the Empire's northern rim."

Vectis acknowledged the commander and introduced Julian and Jupiter.

Commander Commodus nodded slightly through narrowed eyes. He then pointed to his officers, introducing each with a flourish, but reserving the most laudatory remarks for his own "humble personage," as he twice called himself. How he maintained even the muddled conditions at his garrison was a mystery to Vectis.

Commodus held out his hand for Vectis's senatorial letter, and then launched into an evaluation of the situation facing the outposts. He was not long into his monologue before Vectis realized that he knew less about military matters than an army cook.

"Oh, there is no doubt these Caledonian barbarians frighten many," he said, "even some outpost commanders. But the true test of power comes from in here." He pointed to his narrow chest. "How do we contain savages that think heavenly forests await them if they die murdering Romans?" He gave a knowing laugh. "We take the battle straight to them. That's what we do. I can tell you it matters little to me what the odds might be. The greater their numbers, the greater their discouragement when defeat comes. That's what I always say. It's a matter of understanding the barbarian mind. Take the Votadini, for example—"

"May I ask where you came by your keen understanding of the barbarian mind?" Jupiter's voice betrayed no contempt, but Vectis knew it was there.

"An African centurion, eh?" Commodus studied Jupiter a moment. "Can't say as I have ever met one like you before. Heard of your kind, of course, but in North Africa and Egypt, never this far north." He chortled. "There will be no hiding you from the bloody Caledonians once the snows fall."

Jupiter's eyes never moved from the little man.

"Yes ... well," Commodus chortled again, "with a bit of luck—and the beneficence of the gods, of course—we won't be here for the highland snows, eh?" He scratched his nose with surprisingly long fingers and said to Vectis, "I understand you bring withdrawal orders." They were still standing within the shadow of the gates when he spoke, and several soldiers gambling with lots near the inner gatehouse moved closer to hear the reply. Vectis glanced at them, shocked by their breach of discipline.

"Oh, don't worry about them," Commodus said with a wave of his hand, "can't keep anything secret in a garrison like this."

"That has not been my experience," Vectis said bluntly. "Send them back to their posts."

"Prefect Vectis," Commodus replied in full voice, underscoring that he cared little whether anyone overheard, "out here we handle things differently. We are more relaxed when it comes to—"

Jupiter brushed past Commodus toward the men. "Back to your posts!" His deep voice reverberated in the silence as the men scuttled away.

Commodus's head whipped around like a chicken's, from Vectis to Jupiter to Vectis again. "Your ... your centurion ordered my men! He cannot just ... just order my soldiers around at will. *I* command this post."

Vectis saw Jupiter's eyes flash and he waved the centurion silent. Turning, he said, "Commander Commodus, the post in your care is a disgrace. Fortunately, you are now under my authority, and if my First Centurion chooses to discipline disorderly soldiers in any of the five outposts—and that includes this one—he will do so. Is that understood?"

Commodus's mouth moved soundlessly.

Vectis pressed the issue. "I hear no response. Do you wish to lodge a formal complaint?"

Commodus shook his head. The flesh of his cheeks had grown red with indignation and embarrassment. He glanced at his officers behind him and tried to regain some sense of dignity. "I should like to know," he said, sucking himself up to his full height, but taking care to keep his voice low, "when the withdrawal will take place?"

Vectis frowned, knowing the incident with Commodus would be whispered through every level of the fort by noon, and if he were ever to have an effective working arrangement with the man, he would need to smooth over the humiliation.

"You seem like a commander who values straight answers," Vectis said, thinking nothing of the kind, but hoping the statement would be flattering to Commodus, "so I'll not hide anything from you. There will be no withdrawal."

Commodus's mouth twitched. He had expected another answer. "But ... I thought the outpost auxiliaries were to be redeployed along the Wall, and the commanders sent south. There must be some mistake."

"No mistake. The Senate has charged me with organizing the outpost defense and I can tell you that Rome will not surrender the northlands to the Caledonians. In fact, at this very moment," Vectis said, trying to instill a confidence he didn't have, "Rome is preparing to send legionaries, should hostilities arise."

"Hostilities? There's not a place in the Empire more hostile than the Caledonian highlands. We're hanging by a thread out here." He laughed in derision. "I cannot believe that Rome intends to do nothing about our situation." His eyes jerked back and forth as if he were trying to come to a decision. Then, taking hold of Vectis's arm, he guided him behind the gatehouse out of sight of the others. He pulled off his helmet, revealing an absolutely hairless head with neither eyebrows nor eyelashes, something that had escaped Vectis's notice. He wondered now whether Commodus wore the helmet for reasons other than enhancing his height.

Vectis felt pity for the man as he fidgeted with the crest on his helmet. He looked the picture of despair, all pretense of bravery gone. "Prefect," he said in a whisper, "you must transfer me south. Given the present conditions, I do not belong here. I am not a soldier." He gestured at his military clothing and laughed nervously. "I contributed a sizable sum to a cousin, hoping for a modest posting that would give me military experience ... and this is what I got. Fort Colania! I was told that Colania was the safest outpost because it's the first fort on the arterial road and only a mile north of the Wall. But it is a long mile to that Wall." He groaned. "Don't you understand? Unless Rome pulls us out, we will all die here. The Caledonians are coming and there is nothing we can do to stop them."

Vectis's pity instantly changed to disgust. The man was an utter coward. He wanted to play the fearless warrior in public, yet when it came to the test, he was more than willing to let someone else die in his place. "Commander Commodus," Vectis said in as civilized a tone as he could manage, "I cannot transfer you. Once we start that—"

"You *can* transfer me—"

"I can, but I won't," Vectis said. "Now, whether you like it or not, you are a commander in the Roman army. Act like one."

Commodus clamped his mouth shut, contemplating his next move.

The surest route to disaster, Vectis knew, was to start granting transfers to officers. Continuity was important. Even incompetent officers like Commodus served a purpose, if only to maintain morale among the soldiers.

"Gaius Commodus," Vectis said, trying to sound like a friend. "I need you here for the next few months, but if you improve conditions at Colania, I might be more disposed to reconsider your transfer request."

Commodus's eyes shone at the prospect. "Oh, thank you," he bubbled. "May the gods cover you with their wings—"

"Let me warn you," Vectis said as he glanced at the circle of soldiers gathering on the roadway, "a commander like you bears many burdens. You must keep your fears to yourself. This morning's talk in plain view of others does not help."

"Oh, I agree fully, Prefect Vectis, and I apologize. Never again will—"

"Just give me your appraisal of the situation out here."

"Most certainly," Commodus said in a conspiratorial tone. "I can see that you have had a great deal of military experience, and with someone of your abilities in charge of the outposts—"

"What is your appraisal?" Vectis was growing impatient.

"Yes, of course."

"And don't dress up the information. I want the raw truth." Vectis bent his head toward the man. "Is it possible for you to do that?"

"Oh, most certainly. The raw truth. Well ... let me think, I have been out here for over three years and, ah, things are definitely deteriorating."

"Go on. I need specifics."

"Prefect, this is difficult for me. As commander of Colania, I have done my best—I'm sure the other outpost commanders will say the same—we have exhausted ourselves trying to protect this northern road. The truth is ... the Caledonians have grown brazen of late, attacking everything that moves between the forts. The worst is the blood god—wears a red tunic and is named Taranis, after the Celtic god."

"Tell me about him."

"I don't know much really, except that he has instilled enormous fear in the men. His sudden attacks on the Wall and supply trains along the arterial road have devastated morale. He never leaves anyone alive. Soldiers literally tremble when I send them north to the other outposts."

"Why don't you flood the road with soldiers and the hills with scouts?"

Commodus gave Vectis a look one might give a deranged man. "The troops are completely demoralized. No one wants to travel the northern road, much less wander through the Caledonian mountains."

"I need to know more about the arterial road."

Commodus rubbed his face. "We have done our best, Prefect, but there are simply too many of them and too few of us. They own the road. Every foot of it. Only supply trains protected by scores of soldiers travel it now. And only during the daylight hours. If war begins, Caledonian warriors can cut us off from the Wall before we could even send a messenger." He shook his head to emphasize the horror of their predicament.

"What would you recommend we do?" Vectis asked.

"If I were prefect ... oh, I don't mean—"

Vectis motioned for him to continue. Commodus's obsequious mannerisms grated on his nerves.

"I ... ah, I would tell Rome that the outposts cannot survive."

"Anything more?"

"No, except to say how extremely pleased I am that Rome has placed you in charge, and if I can be of service ... anything you need ...." He glanced around and whispered, "Naturally, I will say nothing about our transfer discussion."

"Naturally," Vectis said.

He thanked Commodus and left with Julian and Jupiter. Never had he heard a Roman officer—if you could call him an officer—so cravenly solicit personal relief. In the end, the Caledonians might overwhelm the outposts, but they would pay a price. Neither the Emperor, nor the Senate, nor Vectis, had inclination to abandon the posts.

As they moved north along the deserted arterial road, they spotted the first Caledonian warriors—riding smoothly through the hills with their long hair flowing across the backs of their colorful coats. Scouts, Vectis guessed, trying to determine what goods the column of soldiers might be transporting.

At the next two forts, Julianus and Alauna, Vectis found the conditions poor, but nowhere near the chaos at Colania. He did, however, hear the same concerns he had at Colania: that the outposts were short on men, short on supplies, and in danger of being overrun by the Caledonians. Commander Lupus at Alauna was the more outspoken and his words had a desperate ring to them. There Vectis and his party stayed the night. After dinner, Lupus asked as tactfully as his fear would allow whether Rome had read the outpost dispatches. "The Caledonians are at war *now*," he said. "I grant they have not as yet massed their armies, but large bands of warriors roam at will, testing everything. We are prisoners in our forts. We cannot survive. I respectfully suggest we withdraw." Lupus had more to say, most of it negative, and all of it in polite but despairing tones. Vectis did his best to calm the commanders, but he knew his words were hollow because he had a poor understanding of the situation.

Only at Stragenia, the smallest in the string of outposts, did Vectis find a disciplined officer in command. Appius Priscianus was an experienced soldier with assignments that stretched from Mesopotamia to Hispania. He was a hard man with a penchant for speaking his mind. It was easy to see why, in the twilight of his career, he had been relegated to this tiny outpost on the edge of nowhere.

The Emperor had a good heart, Priscianus declared, his thick eyebrows bobbing up and down, but little understanding of the provinces. The Senate was filled with power seekers who cared more about themselves than they did Rome. Governor Julius Verus was a brilliant soldier, but vain, and vain commanders protect home territory at the expense of outlying garrisons. Priscianus expected that Verus would sacrifice every soldier north of Hadrian's Wall if he thought it would protect southern Britannia and his reputation. The outgoing prefect of the five outposts, Didius Rufinus, was a drunken fool, who had so little military training that a raw recruit could have managed better. And the other outpost commanders at Colania, Julianus and Alauna? Incompetents who couldn't manage a tavern on the Egnatian Way.

Despite his hostile speech, Priscianus was not a man given to excessive fears, which made his opinions on the Caledonian threat the most disheartening. In precise, unadorned language he detailed the hazards facing the outposts. The tribes were beyond restlessness, he said, and were preparing for war. They sensed that Rome was tired of defending its northern territories and would leave if pressed. Then, as if he were a soothsayer, he predicted that the promised legions would not come, and that his bones would forever lie in the frozen snows of Caledonia.

From the time he had left the Wall, Vectis saw something in the eyes of soldiers he had seen only once before. And it disturbed him. Four years earlier during the North African revolts, he had been a tribune in charge of organizing defenses in the African outposts. Tiny forts in the desert sands were directed to hold their positions until reinforcements arrived. Never would he forget the faces of young legionaries who hailed Caesar smartly as he left, but whose eyes mirrored the death they had already embraced. There the soldiers accepted fate and waited, hoping the legions would arrive before the hordes of Mauri warriors. Most never made it home.

Here the eyes of the common soldier showed a similar concern. They knew the Caledonians were coming, and they wondered whether the legions would arrive in time.

21

A warm breeze drifted across the river valley as the column of soldiers arrived at Outpost Faustina. Vectis saw the squatters first, a shantytown of tents and wooden shacks encircling Faustina and its protective earthworks, like weeds crowding a patch of garden. Blue smoke from hundreds of cooking fires hovered above the spruce and juniper trees, giving the distant scene a hazy appearance.

Within twenty minutes, the three officers had reached the fort's entrance ramps that sloped up toward the gates. The guards were doing their best to look impressive, standing as they were at full attention, arms rigid at their sides, spears resting against the inside of their wrists, and tilted outward. As the huge log gates opened, the column halted on the wooden rampway.

Vectis and his officers rode slowly up the ramp and stopped ten feet from the entrance. "Tribune Vectis Trebellius Quadratus approaches Outpost Faustina," Jupiter said formally. "He requests an audience with Camp Prefect Didius Rufinus."

The guards stared at Jupiter, shocked by his dark skin.

"Well?" Jupiter said brusquely, his eyes fixed on one of the guards.

"The Camp Prefect is …." He broke off, flustered, then regained his composure, saying in a loud voice, "Prefect Didius Rufinus left with his personal staff and escort five days ago."

Jupiter turned to Vectis. "The camp commander is not here." His voice registered his disgust.

Vectis could hardly believe the commander had left before his replacement arrived. He asked the guard, "Who has charge of the fort?"

"Officer Mamercus Nepos. Shall I inform him you are here?"

A contingent of soldiers arrives from the outside, Vectis thought, and no one informs the camp's acting commander. Not insubordination, but someone—probably the centurion of the gate— wants to embarrass him. "There is no need to inform him now," Vectis said. "I will do that."

Jupiter spoke. "Where is the centurion of the gate?"

An officer stepped forward and identified himself.

Still seated on his horse, Jupiter talked in slow, menacing tones. "I care nothing about your petty disputes with Officer Nepos. What I want to know is why these men opened the main gates."

The officer licked his lips. "We saw Roman soldiers and assumed—"

"There was no identification."

"But I—"

"Guards," Jupiter said to the soldiers at the gates. "Take this man to the parade ground. Remove his belt so that his tunic hangs loose. He will remain there until the tenth hour when he will receive five lashes. After that I will address the troops."

Five lashes was harsh, but Vectis knew better than to countermand his centurion in front of others. A First Centurion's job was to organize and discipline the men. He had asked Jupiter to set a tone as soon as possible. He should have known it would happen before they even entered the fort.

Officer Nepos was reclining on the floral pillows of a broad couch in the camp prefect's office when Vectis arrived. He jumped up, rubbed his face, and began talking incoherently about how delighted he was to have the new prefect and his officers at Faustina. His face looked anything but delighted. Imprinted on the side of his head, in white circular designs, were the floral patterns of the couch. Officer Nepos had been sleeping. He stood uncomfortably before his superiors, like a man forced to stand naked in public. His artificial smile did little to hide his humiliation at having been so ill prepared for the new prefect.

Vectis glanced around the square room that seemed more like a repository of old equipment than an office. Pushed over to one side were Celtic axes, hammers, iron-tipped missiles, and horse harnesses with ornate leather tooling. Near the front of the room stood a stout table filled with wax tablets and papyrus documents. He surveyed a heap of empty courier pouches and broken Celtic weapons that someone had dumped into a corner.

"We didn't expect you for another week or we would have removed Prefect Didius Rufinus's belongings," Nepos said hastily, sensing a rebuff. "The prefect collected items of this sort—most of it he took with him. I will have this stored and sent to the prefect on the next supply train."

"Destroy it all," Vectis said.

"Destroy it?"

"Everything, except for what is on the table."

Nepos looked at the three officers, opened his mouth as if he were about to challenge the order, and then clamped it shut.

Vectis motioned toward the reclining couches, inviting Nepos to sit. "I need to know all about this fort," he said, "its officers, its training methods, its weaknesses and strengths—whatever you think is important."

Nepos sat erect on the edge of the couch, trying to sound in command of the situation, whatever situation they happened to be discussing. For two hours, Vectis, Jupiter and Julian listened and asked questions. As the conversation continued, and glances were exchanged, all three came to the same conclusion: Outpost Faustina was headed for disaster.

When Officer Nepos had been dismissed, Julian looked incredulous. "This is Rome's most distant outpost, we are surrounded by blood-drinking Celts, and Nepos thinks everything is fine!"

"I don't think he expects to be here long," Vectis said. "He thinks we're here to dismantle Faustina."

"Like all the outpost commanders," Julian said. "Where are they getting this?"

"From the sloppy prefect who ran this place," Jupiter said. "After receiving his transfer, he had no stomach for telling his men the truth, that he was leaving them in a dangerous situation. So he hinted that they might soon be withdrawn."

"Then his escort soldiers repeated the story when they stopped at the other forts," Julian said, understanding.

"Our fate is here," Vectis said, "and we need to understand the situation we are facing. As in Egypt," he said to Julian, "make it known that silver can be had for information on the Caledonians."

"I'll have informers wearing out the gate hinges in no time," Julian said.

"Good." Vectis leaned forward and looked at Jupiter. "Our first priority is to increase battle readiness. These soldiers train like retired legionaries in the provinces. How can they be fit, drilling three times a week?"

"It's a cool climate," Jupiter said, "we could drill three times a day."

Vectis agreed, though he wondered how the men would respond to such grueling training. These were auxiliary soldiers, not legionaries. Jupiter's methods—though effective—would shock even battle-hardened legionaries. But right now, if Fort Faustina was to survive, it needed Jupiter's special abilities.

One thing disturbed Vectis about fort operations: the alarming number of non-Roman personnel with access to the garrison—the Celtic tribespeople who assisted in cleaning, cooking, transporting goods, translating, and a host of other activities that made for a smooth-running fort. Faustina was too exposed. He ordered the number cut by a third.

As tribune in charge of fort operations, Julian was responsible for organizing non-Roman personnel. "Not one Roman scout or mapmaker here. All non-Roman," he said from the couch where he sat, comparing two ledgers with the list of Celtic personnel.

"All? What happened to the Romans?" Vectis demanded.

"Killed," Julian said, showing him the ledger. "The Caledonians have killed every one of them. So now we have only non-Roman—"

"Spies," Jupiter said.

Vectis turned to Julian. "What about it? Could they be killing Romans to fill the slots with informants?"

Julian studied the ledgers. "I cannot deny it, but I don't think so. The Caledonians have killed as many non-Romans. And engineers— killed six in the last year. They could never hope to replace engineering specialists with their people. Seems like they attack exposed targets." He showed Vectis the ledger again, pointing to more than twenty names of non-Romans that had been stroked out, indicating they had been killed. Another fifteen were missing, possibly dead, but more likely deserters. "Most of our non-Romans have run off ... only two scouts and three mapmakers left."

"Then we cannot cut scouts or mapmakers," Vectis said, "but I want to see all five of them. Jupiter might be right. We could have spies wandering about."

Julian spoke. "Including the four engineers we brought with us, we have six. Not a lot, but sufficient. I'll send for more engineers and increase the number of mapmakers."

"Patrols," Jupiter said abruptly. "We need to reactivate the night patrols."

Vectis still felt awkward when Jupiter suggested something. His suggestions had a way of sounding like orders.

"We also need to clear our lines," he continued, "move the squatters back ... we don't know who these people are. Never heard of letting the enemy crawl within a foot of your camp."

As evening drew near, the three left the office, headed down the corridor and out onto the parade ground. At Jupiter's request, the first encounter with Faustina's soldiers would take place at dusk. They mounted the square, wooden platform that had been positioned with the setting sun to their backs. With the sun's rays diffused in the cloudy Britannic skies, the affect was less dramatic than North Africa's fiery red skies, but it would have to do.

Jupiter unfurled a papyrus scroll, opening it to its full length of about eighteen inches. He read the decree, sealed by Caesar Antoninus himself, appointing Vectis as prefect of the five outposts, and then read from another scroll that gave commendation from the Senate in Rome. Handing the scrolls to Julian, he talked about Vectis's accomplishments in Egypt and North Africa, and the Emperor's desire to have one of his premier officers organizing the outpost defenses of northern Britannia.

Jupiter's glowing introduction surprised and embarrassed Vectis. The auxiliary soldiers, probably none of whom had ever been to Rome, stared at him with reverence on their faces. Liberator of North Africa, brother-in-law to a senator, son of Caesar's premier centurion in Rome—and now Rome's hammer in Britannia. The speech was brief, and somehow avoided flattery, while at the same time instilling fear and respect in the men, which, as always, was Jupiter's purpose.

Vectis acknowledged Jupiter's remarks with a nod, introduced Julian, and informed the men that radical change had come to Faustina. The Emperor had named the fort after his wife, and now was shamed by its sloppy deportment. It was a lie, of course, but a lie that would prepare the soldiers for the shocking ways of their new African centurion. He turned without introducing Jupiter, and with Julian, left the platform. Jupiter, he knew, liked to introduce himself.

Moments later Vectis stood at the window slats in his office, watching Jupiter stalk around the parade ground. The troops appeared frozen in place, staring straight ahead, as Jupiter glowered in the faces of soldiers he didn't like. Finally, he signaled the gate centurion to be brought and tied to a post at the edge of the platform.

"This man," he said, pointing to the centurion, now naked from the waist up, "has breached his duty as an officer. Because this is a first offense, I have decided merely to strip him of his senior centurion rank, and administer only five lashes. I will appoint a new gate centurion tomorrow." Jupiter shifted his eyes to the soldier with the whip and nodded. The soldier raised the whip, and brought it down with a crack.

When the screams had ceased, and the disgraced centurion taken to the surgery, Jupiter moved closer to the men, keeping the fading light at his back. "In North Africa I trained gladiators to fight. They called me Jupiter because I am a god among men." He paused, surveying the troops. "Is there anyone who doubts that?"

Vectis grimaced and turned away. He did not envy the soldiers of Faustina. For years they had sipped at the fountain of Roman discipline, and now they were about to be plunged into its brutal depths. He had no concern about troop readiness; they would be fit when the time came.

Neeve returned from her mapping assignment, cold and wet.. As she approached the gates, she knew something had happened: the sentries walking the ramparts had been doubled, the gate-keepers, though they knew her, asked to see her directives before they allowed her entrance, and inside, all the storerooms had large iron locks on them, and guards posted at the end of each row. Neeve cut through the narrow buildings towards the center of camp, and stopped. Lying on their backs in the rain were scores of soldiers, lifting logs, and walking among them was a powerfully built man who seemed to glide when he moved.

He had the darkest skin she had ever seen.

She found Taranis in the stables and handed him the maps she had drawn. He slipped them from their protective leather case to examine them.

"What has happened—?"

"The maps first," he said, holding up his hand. Then he asked questions about her drawings. He always asked her questions. Not once had he been called upon to explain his maps, but her brother was careful, wary of making the *mistake*, as he called it, the mistake that would forfeit their lives. Even now, with his planned departure in a few days, he meticulously studied the drawings. He left nothing to the winds of destiny.

As she watched Taranis study the maps, she thought about how her confidence had grown. Her simple ability to draw maps had proved more valuable than anyone could have guessed, a talent that had provided Taranis with Roman credentials and access to places he otherwise could never have gone. By completing both their mapping assignments, she had given him time to meet with Brigantes leaders and to observe the operations of other forts. But the most important information came not from outside Fort Faustina, but from the Latin documents that lay piled innocently on the prefect's table. On numerous occasions, Neeve had been able to steal across from the mapmaking room to the large office of Prefect Rufinus. Among his papers, she found a document showing the distribution of Scythian archers in the forts along the Wall, a complete list of Fort Faustina's military assets, and even the schedule of the food and weapons trains that resupplied the outpost forts.

Neeve shifted on her feet, trying to distract her brother. She was growing impatient. "Well?" she asked, gesturing to indicate the changes in the camp.

Taranis looked up from the maps. "The new prefect ... is trouble. I intend to slip out of the fort tonight, after dark. You must be extremely careful—"

"Shouldn't you wait until morning?"

"Neeve, in two days this place has changed drastically. I might not get out tomorrow. This prefect checks everything, suspects everyone. No one comes or goes without authorization. I have to leave *tonight*." He squeezed her shoulder. "You'll need to play map drawer a while longer," he said. "I'm uneasy leaving you, but unless we know what changes the prefect intends, the information we have given the commanders is useless."

"We planned for me to be alone," Neeve said, trying to sound businesslike. Her lips quivered in the damp stall. Her feet were numb from the cold, and the chill crept up her legs. She hugged herself, feeling the wet clothes, and imagined herself wrapped in a warm, dry blanket. "I'm not afraid," she said, hearing her voice crack.

"Be afraid. It keeps you alert."

The wind swirled outside, spraying water through the window slits near the top of the rough, pinewood walls.

"Remember," he said, "there's no reason for them to suspect you. The only danger is that they might discover I cannot draw maps." He pinched her cheek. "Remember also what I taught you about your possessions. Never carry anything, or leave in your room anything, that you don't want them to see. Expect them to search your quarters when you are gone, your saddle bags when you tether your horse, and sometimes even the clothes on your back."

"I will remember."

"Memorize *everything*.   Never hide a written document anywhere." He thought for a moment. "You might have someone write your name on a tablet, with your scratches underneath. Leave it in your room. If they find it they will think you are learning to mark your name, and no one marking a name will be suspected of being able to read." He looked at her.   "Be careful, Neeve, especially in trying to obtain information from the prefect's office.   Be very careful."

"I will."

He embraced her. "I know you will."   Then holding her face he said, "At the first hint of trouble, you leave this fort. Agreed?"

"At the first hint," she vowed solemnly.

"Tomorrow, when they ask where I am, tell them I sometimes grow restless, you heard me talking about a village woman—"

From behind came the unmistakable crunch of a boot. Someone had entered the back stables. Taranis continued talking in the same tone, but had now switched to complaints about the rain and the difficulty of mapping in such miserable weather.

"Mapmakers!" a soldier called from two stalls away.

"Here," Taranis said in Latin. Then shifting to Celtic, "What's the matter now, the new prefect wants us to map mountains in this storm?"

Many of the soldiers had been stationed in Britannia for years and had a reasonable understanding of the Celtic tongue. Some were themselves Celts recruited from the southern end of the island, and it wasn't unusual for soldiers to pretend ignorance to glean bits of knowledge that might be useful. The soldier stopped at the entrance to the stall, looking at Neeve for a translation. Behind him were six other soldiers. The new prefect, it seemed, used detachments to deliver his messages.

"My brother he complain about rain," she said.

"I thought you Celts liked this weather." He grew serious. "The prefect wants to see you both—immediately."

"Now?" She pulled at her clothes to indicate that she needed to change.

"Now." His face was uncompromising.

They followed their escort across the compound, now empty of soldiers lifting logs. Sheets of rain slanted to the ground, splashing in puddles that had pooled in the lower areas. It was still afternoon, but clouds darkened the skies, turning the compound a muddy gray.

Neeve had grown familiar with the complex of offices in the central building, but now, as if she and Taranis might lose their way, their soldier escort ushered them to the tiny map room and stood guard over them as they removed their outer cloaks and hung them on the wall pegs. Neeve was in the process of wringing out her hair when she felt a firm hand on her upper arm. She followed the guard down the hall toward the prefect's office, her hair falling lifeless to her shoulders.

The prefect's room was broad and square, with a series of smaller rooms leading from it. When they entered, she was surprised at the change. The familiar piles of documents and heaps of Caledonian tools and weapons were gone. In their place was a stark room with several benches and couches, and a table—empty except for a few stacks of documents.

Two scouts were receiving instructions from the prefect seated behind the table. Apparently, the role of the scout was to be increased radically. Neeve stared at the uncluttered table, and the documents organized neatly at one end. He must be reviewing the entire operation of the fort, she thought. Imagine what she could learn if she had time alone to look over those documents.

She studied the prefect. He had the fine bone structure of a privileged Roman. Every hair in place. Almost pretty, she thought. He looked up, and his eyes locked on hers. He smiled. A familiar smile she had received from many men. She looked away, not wanting to appear too forward. Her hair felt sticky and wet, and she wiped the water that still dribbled down the back of her neck. I must look like a drowned rodent, she thought, but no matter; she knew what thoughts had passed through his mind. Maybe the new system will not be so threatening after all. She turned her eyes to the table, coveting it.

As the scouts trundled out, the African centurion she had seen earlier pushed in through the door. Water ran off his broad back as he strode the length of the office, and disappeared into an adjacent room. Neeve disliked him. He carried with him the reek of death.

The office was now empty except for her and her brother, two guards, a translator, and the prefect. The prefect beckoned with his hand and spoke through the translator.

Neeve approached him and said, "I Roman speak ... good." What works once should work a second time, she thought. It did. He complimented her, saying her Latin was excellent. It was a promising beginning and Neeve felt more relaxed as she returned to the side of her brother.

The dark centurion reappeared, his black eyes sweeping over Taranis, his gaze cold and unemotional as he shifted his attention to Neeve. She felt uncomfortable as he surveyed her body, especially since he showed none of the interest the prefect had shown.

"I want the guard at the door," the centurion said to the soldier in the hall.

Moments later the guard stepped inside the office. "Yes, Centurion," he said crisply. His professional manner did nothing to conceal his fear.

"Why is this Celt wearing weapons?" The centurion's voice was calm, but his whole demeanor unnerved Neeve.

"Former Prefect Rufinus allowed her—"

"No Celt will wear weapons in this building. Understood?" He then advised the man he would lose a month's pay.

The guard bobbed his head, relieved his punishment had not been more severe. He stripped Neeve of her knives and left the room, and she, not wanting to engage the centurion, kept her eyes on the floor. Then from a back room another man appeared, moving leisurely across the room as if he owned every square inch. He had a hard, athletic-looking body with weathered skin, confident eyes, and a natural reserve that said he trusted no one. Neeve realized her mistake. Here was the real prefect. The fine-boned officer at the table must be a tribune.

"These two are mapmakers," the tribune said, looking over his shoulder at the prefect.

"Where's the third?" the prefect asked, without even glancing their way.

The tribune replied that the former prefect had granted him a transfer to a fort south of the Wall, and then he quipped, "Apparently the man felt vulnerable out here—I can't understand why." For the next few minutes the two officers talked about things of no interest to Neeve and she tried to relax, but the more she listened to the new prefect, the more uncomfortable she felt. His face had a lean, perceptive look, and he always probed for information. He was not much taller than she, but tall for a Roman, and quiet in demeanor. Finally, his eyes settled on her.

He stared at her for the longest time.

She stared back, showing she had nothing to hide.

He instructed a guard to spread their maps across his table, and through the interpreter he said to her, "When I arrived, the officer in charge said you knew Legate Julius Verus at Londinium."

"Yes, yes, we friends ... good friends."

He ignored her efforts to speak the Roman tongue and again said through the interpreter, "I dispatched a courier to Legate Verus to verify your information. You have no objection, I suppose."

Shock hit her. He must be testing her, she thought. He wouldn't have sent a letter. "Very good," she said, trying to smile—anything to suppress her concern.

"Did your brother go with you to Londinium?"

She persevered in his language to make the point that her Latin was rudimentary. "No, brother stay home," she said.

"Why did you go there?"

"Relatives."

"Is that where you learned to draw maps?"

"Yes."

The prefect turned to Taranis. "Ask him where he learned to draw maps."

The interpreter asked the question.

"From my sister," came the reply.

The prefect studied Taranis a long, intimidating moment. "You don't look like a mapmaker."

Taranis said nothing.

The prefect continued. "You look like a warrior."

Neeve felt her breathing grow shallow as the translator spoke to Taranis, but her brother showed no sign of surprise or fear. He shrugged. "I have done many jobs. You know us Votadini. We have lived under Roman rule for years and never once rebelled. We practice with weapons, but we are not warriors."

The centurion spoke up. "Ask him where he got that scar on his forearm?"

Neeve did not like the way the three officers looked at her brother. Anxiety spread through her, like a growing numbness, but she could think of nothing to say or do.

Taranis looked at the crescent shaped scar, and said a friend had cut him when he was a child.

The prefect walked over to the end of the table and picked up a blank square of papyrus paper. "I want you to sketch out a map of the river and hills behind the fort."

"I find map drawing difficult to do from memory," Taranis replied.

"Then your home village," Vectis said. "Surely you can sketch the area around your home village."

Taranis opened his hands and said, "I have not been there for so long. I would have to see it." He motioned to the maps on the table. "It might be better if I explained what I drew yesterday."

The prefect rejected his suggestion. "I want you to draw something, on this paper, *now*."

"Prefect," he said, "the truth is I cannot draw maps. My sister has worked double time drawing all my maps for me. I am here only because I did not want her alone among soldiers."

The shock hit Neeve like a cold wind. Taranis had exposed himself calmly, as if it were a tiny lie that was perfectly understandable. But it was not a tiny lie. They would assume he was a spy, perhaps kill him. Even the interpreter had trouble translating what her brother had said.

Then the three officers began discussing what to do about Taranis. They were talking low and very fast, but it soon became apparent to Neeve what the centurion was suggesting. He wanted to execute Taranis.

Desperation seized her as the conversation continued. The tribune said they had over a hundred sectors yet to map, and that the woman was sure to leave if her brother was executed. The centurion agreed they needed mapmakers, but thought deception could not go unpunished. Such harsh punishment, the tribune countered, could frighten away the remaining Celts, and the fort needed them to operate efficiently.

Neeve could take it no longer, and blurted out, "No, please ... my brother ... he feared for me ... please." She looked straight into the prefect's face, pleading.

He held up his hand for silence, and in that instant as their eyes touched, she saw something she never expected in a Roman. Compassion.

They returned to their conversation, but now the prefect was speaking, issuing orders. He would banish Taranis from the fort that afternoon.

The African centurion stood rigidly, scowling.

22

Kallias stared at the familiar landscape. He knew everything about this island, its backward peoples, its continual rains, and now as autumn set in, its miserable cold. He tethered his horse to the hitching post outside a prosperous farming manor. Outbuildings filled with grain and stokeholes for heating winter rooms told him he had come to the right place. He glanced at his tax sheet and signaled the officers behind him to call the soldiers to order. For weeks he had been collecting taxes from rich landowners that thought they could escape from paying Rome what they owed.

He collected taxes personally, especially at the larger estates. With the power of the Senate behind him, he had been able to demand the tax collection records at the forts along the Wall. It had proven extremely profitable. Already he had extracted enough to pay the Druids their reduced tribute at the scheduled meeting later in the month. Everything else he collected would be his, and never again would he work for a dead man's wages under the amphitheater.

Not that it was easy to wrest taxes from these tight-fisted Celts. They had the money all right, hidden somewhere, but to find it was a supreme chore. He selected large estates like the one he was on now in hopes of uncovering a cache of gold or silver coins. He could see the Celt looking from his window. Now he was coming out the door and speaking in that gibberish of his.

"Interpreter! Get over here!" Kallias shouted. "What's he babbling about?"

"He says the unusually cold weather damaged the crops this year and begs you to wait until the next harvest."

"Bad crops!" Kallias scoffed. "That's all I ever hear." He pushed his face toward the lying Celt. "Tell him I want the Imperial tax now, all of it."

The Celt shook his head and opened his hands to show he had nothing.

Kallias removed his dagger and held it up in front of the straw-haired man's face. "Tell him if I don't get the money, I will cut his ears off and stuff them in his mouth."

When the interpreter finished, the man began shaking his head and mumbling gibberish again. Kallias watched him screw up his face in feigned agony, trying to evoke pity. This Celt is like all the rest, Kallias thought; he thinks his drama will earn my sympathy.

He gave the man a humorless smile and ordered two soldiers to hold him. He was sick of their lies. He yanked an ear forward and sliced it from the man's head. The man screamed and rolled his eyes in horror. Kallias held the ear an inch from the Celt's nose. "The money!" he yelled, "or I take the other!"

A woman came shrieking from the house, waving a pouch and shouting something Kallias didn't understand. No matter. He knew she had plenty of money. He snatched the pouch from her and opened it. One silver temple coin of Domitian, and a handful of bronze pennies. He tucked the silver *denarius* in his purse and threw the rest in the dirt.

"You have more, don't you?" He grabbed the woman roughly by the arm. "I know you do. A whole sack full ... buried somewhere."

She was staring at the side of Kallias's face, where the cliff fall had left him misshapen, then suddenly she wrenched backwards, trying to get away. He tightened his grip. She cried out something, pleading, hoping to rouse sympathy from the soldiers behind him. Kallias snorted. What fools these people are! She thinks Roman soldiers will intervene—violate an senatorial edict—to rescue Celts who won't pay their taxes. He twisted her wrist and hollered: "Gold! Where is it?"

She was shaking now; terror lit her eyes. Always the same, he thought. They look at my face, see the deformity, and think they are dealing with some witless tax gatherer too feeble-minded to use the power at his command. But they soon understand. He caught her behind the head and twisted it toward him. She wanted to look at his injury? He'd give her a good look. "Gold," he mouthed in her face.

She began to cry.

He almost laughed out loud. She'd have to do better than that if she hoped to manipulate him. Her crying turned to sobs and she gulped air uncontrollably. He looked at her closely. Something about her tears and the despairing sound of her voice stimulated him, and reminded him of the women under the amphitheater in Rome. How they begged for mercy! They would do anything to escape their fates. But this one—he rubbed his face in her hair and sniffed deeply—this one had the fresh scent of the wind and the trees. She was big, too, wide-hipped and lean. One thing about these Celtic women, he thought, they have the bones to please a man. And most were like mares in heat. They just needed a little encouragement.

He showed her the knife and pushed her toward the back of the house. "I'll be a while," he said, grinning. "I intend to collect my taxes."

The husband yanked his arms free and burst toward his wife. Kallias spun around and drove the dagger into the man's stomach. Air rushed from his mouth as he doubled over. "What is the matter with these Celts?" Kallias said, looking at the man coughing up blood on the ground. "I'm not doing anything different from what he does every night."

He turned toward the house, and stopped. Someone was hiding behind the low wall in the west portico, he was sure of it. He waited, and moments later when the wind picked up, he saw a flutter of hair at the edge of the wall. He smiled, knowing who was there. "You can come out now," he said as gently as his gruff voice would allow, "I see you."

Before the interpreter could complete his sentence, a tiny head moved slowly into view, revealing first the fine golden hair of a little girl, then a freckled cheek, and then one blue eye. He covered his mouth in pretended surprise but got no reaction. The eye continued staring at him. He pulled out the silver *denarius* and placed it in the flat of his palm, offering it to her. Children liked gifts, he knew. It worked. She edged toward the coin, but in the same instant, the woman behind him screamed some kind of warning, frightening the girl, and causing her to flee across the courtyard as if a devil were chasing her.

Kallias turned on the woman, enraged. "Do you think I would harm that little girl? Well, do you?" he shouted, not waiting for the interpretation. "I come from Greek ancestry, from Demosthenes and Aristotle. My people were civilizing the world and building great cities a thousand years before any of you on this cursed island could build a fire."

The woman stared at him, wide-eyed and unmoving. He felt his heart pumping angry blood, like black sludge, but he fought the darkness. Yes, he could be brutal, he knew that. But he had never harmed a child. Not once! Quite the opposite; he loved children. He glanced toward the courtyard; a soldier had scooped up the girl and was bringing her back. When he set her down, Kallias could see her little fingers trembling. All that woman's fault, he thought. I ought to snap her neck. Calm. He needed to calm himself. Children could tell when grown-ups were annoyed. He took the coin out again and knelt on one knee, hoping she would trust him more if he scrunched down to her size. At the orphanage in Rome the children felt better after he explained about his face, so he beckoned her closer and through the interpreter, told her the story of how he injured his face—saving children trapped in a burning temple. He had told the tale so often that he sometimes believed it himself.

Throughout the story he kept the silver coin in plain view, concluding with the words, "So don't be afraid of me, I would never hurt you." When the translator finished, Kallias took the girl's hand and placed the coin in it. "See," he said, smiling, "this is yours to keep."

The coin slipped from her rigid fingers. He picked it up and tucked it back in her little hand, wrapping her fingers around it. "You're not afraid of my face anymore, are you?"

She shook her head.

"And you know I would never hurt you."

She swallowed and spoke in a whisper, banging her bony knees together. The interpreter said, "She thinks you'll hurt her mother."

"Is this your mother?" Kallias asked, motioning to the woman.

The girl nodded.

He patted her head and stood up. Looking at the woman he said, "Everything would have been all right if your man hadn't attacked me." From his pouch he drew a golden *aureus*—two months pay for a Roman soldier—and held it up for all to see. He deposited it in the woman's hand. "Until you find a new husband, use that to look after the little girl."

As he was about to leave, the girl darted toward her mother and flung her arms around her waist, burying her face deep in the woman's tunic. Kallias could see tears in the mother's eyes, and although his bones still burned, he knew he had done right by the child.

Vectis spent the morning talking with Julian about fort organization. Julian had a knack for bringing order out of chaos, and in less than a month he had cut Faustina's non-Roman personnel by half, while increasing the efficiency of day to day operations. The fort was more organized, in better repair, and undeniably more secure than it had been in years. But the new measures required additional duties for both soldiers and non-Roman workers, something that had brought a groundswell of complaints.

"The non-Romans are petitioning you directly," Julian said, leaning forward on his couch. "They say increased work should bring increased pay."

"Deny their requests."

"Denied," Julian said, setting the document aside, "but we will lose some of them."

"Understood. What about the soldiers?"

"Not in the best of spirits. The radical changes in training—"

"Have they looked over the fort walls lately?"

"They still expect orders will come to abandon this garrison."

"I see. Well, defense preparations will continue." He took a breath, looked Julian directly in the eyes, and said, Now, what's this about Jupiter?"

"The soldiers are complaining about his methods."

"We expected that," Vectis said.

"Yes, but now with the spear throwing incident—"

"I take it they have said nothing to Jupiter."

"Not a word. The soldiers are terrified of him, especially now that he has put another one in the surgery."

"How is the soldier?"

"Should be ready for duty in two or three months. No broken bones, but he has a nasty wound in his upper thigh."

"What happened? Jupiter reported the event to me, but with few details."

Julian's face showed resignation. "The usual. A soldier protested a forced march exercise, so Jupiter had him tied to the gate, and then painted a circle around him. The soldiers were supposed to hurl their spears at the circle, strike within the paint, but avoid the man."

"And one hit him in the thigh."

"Two, actually. Almost in the same spot. Jupiter kept them throwing until everyone struck within the circle—an entire maniple of one hundred and sixty men."

"And now the troops are eager to obey Jupiter."

"They are, but they blame you as prefect for allowing Jupiter so much latitude."

"I have no doubt they do," Vectis said. ""But these soldiers have to be ready, and like it or not, Jupiter's methods work."

"No disagreement on that. Our auxiliaries are rapidly becoming disciplined soldiers, but you should know who is being blamed."

"What news do you have from the other forts along the arterial road?" Vectis asked, changing subjects.

Julian assumed an expression of mock cheerfulness. "Good news. With better reporting methods and more messengers, we now have excellent communication with the other outposts."

"And the commanders? How are they adapting to change?"

"Not such good news—they resent your intrusions in their fort operations." He glanced down at his notes. "All the commanders see a need to coordinate the defense of the five outposts, but most think you are moving too quickly in a province you know little about. They dislike having to inventory supplies and weapons, they hate the stepped up training schedules, and they especially object to the visits by Jupiter. They see no reason why their own First Centurions should not organize their defenses."

Vectis felt a weariness creep over him. Everything he had done was vital if the forts were to survive. But like carts following ruts in a road, these shortsighted commanders wanted to follow the same comfortable path—no matter where it led. "Do they all feel that way?" he asked.

"All except Priscianus at Stragenia. He's the lone exception. Commodus at Colania praises you to Olympia's heights, yet he's as bad as the others when it comes to implementing your orders. He prefers former Prefect Rufinus's model of leadership."

"Astonishing."

Julian smiled. "Apparently, except for settling minor disputes, Rufinus let each fort make its own decisions."

"That day is over."

"Your commitment to changing the present operating procedures has brought joy to old Priscianus's heart."

"And your assessment of him?"

"Overbearing but dependable. His post is well organized, and according to Jupiter, his soldiers are the best disciplined. So you can see why he applauds your efforts." Vectis nodded. "For the time being we keep the pressure on. Let them scream if they want, but make certain they boost fort efficiency."

"It will be my pleasure."

Vectis looked at Julian and felt a twinge of guilt for having prevailed upon him to give up Rome with its warmth and beauty, to come to a bleak and sodden land at the edge of the world. "No matter what we do," Vectis said, "we cannot protect ourselves out here. These outposts above the Wall are too vulnerable. Even if the legions are sent quickly, I doubt we can hold out long enough ...."

"I try not to think about it," Julian responded. "We might do better to set our minds on less weighty matters." He motioned to a pile of petitions on the table.

"Are these disputes from the outpost commanders?"

"Not the truly petty ones, those I have resolved. But at least you will see what occupies the minds of your fellow fort commanders—all except Priscianus at Stragenia, of course—he has a way of taking care of his own business." Julian reached across the table and picked up a handful of petitions. "These you need to rule on," he said. "The commanders involved have staked out their positions, and refuse to budge unless the order comes from you." He tilted the first to catch the light from the window. "Commander Commodus at Colania refuses to give Commander Lupus at Alauna a flow valve for the boiler controlling his hot baths. Commodus complains that he has only one spare, and in any event, he would never give Lupus the flow valve as long as Lupus continues to hoard the fish allotments from the autumn catch."

Vectis stared at Julian a moment before saying, "I understand your frustration in dealing with issues like this, but why bring them to me?"

"You need to rule. They will not listen to a mere staff tribune."

"How many other *urgent* rulings do I need to make?"

"About twenty-three," Julian said, sifting through the documents. "Some have to do with uneven grain or pheasant allotments. This one," he held it up, "has to do with road upkeep, this one concerns the placement of auxiliary insignia over the fort gates, this one the number of iron-workers in the forts. There is even a dispute between Commodus at Colania and Senecio at Julianus about who should have more priests. Senecio has a larger fort than Commodus, but Commodus has better facilities, buildings of stone, and more shrines and altars for the priests."

Vectis took the documents from Julian and dumped them in the waste box near the door. "I want you to send a message to the fort commanders, except Priscianus. Tell them I find their complaints petty and irresponsible. In three days I want them resolved—all of them. If they are not, I will make decisions unfavorable in the extreme to the parties involved."

"I guess that takes care of that," Julian said.

"I hope so. Other concerns?"

"Just one."

Julian told him about reports of Romans antagonizing the Brigantes south of the Wall—rapes and unprovoked murders. With the increasing restlessness of the Brigantes tribes, rumors of Roman atrocities floating about were nothing less than alarming. If the outposts were forced to fight the Caledonians, it would not do to have hostile Brigantes between the Walls. They could disrupt the flow of supplies coming north to Antoninus' Wall, and might even join with the Caledonians in a general assault on the barrier. With attacks coming from both the north and south, the Wall defenders would need a quick response from the southern legions, or everything might be lost.

They moved to positive items. The arterial road linking the five forts north of the Wall had grown more secure. Not one of their supply wagons had been seized in the last two weeks. Julian attributed it to three things: the willingness of the forts to increase patrols, more scouts, and Caledonian uncertainty about the changes.

"It won't last," Vectis said, "the Caledonians need supplies and will adjust."

"And you recommend?"

"That each fort do its training outside the garrison, somewhere along the road. Jupiter has a commitment from the other forts to train their troops four hours every day. The centurions could drill half in the morning and half in the afternoon. If we varied the times, and if we maintained contact using scouts, the arterial road would be safer than the Appian Way outside Rome."

"Have you talked to Jupiter?"

"Of course! Do you think I would make a suggestion like this without consulting the First Centurion?"

Vectis smiled.

"Actually," Julian said, "it was Jupiter's idea. My task is to coordinate the times and organize the scouts."

"What about Faustina's soldiers? They already drill three times a day—"

"And the griping in the barracks grows. But that should change. Jupiter thinks the troops have improved enough to reduce training to twice a day."

"Is that what he plans to tell them?"

"Yes, but I doubt anyone will be fooled. Jupiter is reducing training because he needs to allow for marching time along the road. Still, it should build morale."

Vectis agreed. "With a secure road, good night patrols—not only here, but at the other forts—we have begun well. What we need now is a special unit. We might even catch our friend, the blood god." He handed Julian a statement detailing his ideas for a flexible unit capable of pursuing Caledonian insurgents beyond the arterial road.

Julian looked over the statement. "Has Jupiter seen this?"

"No, why?"

"Well, a unit like this will take a large bite out of Jupiter's time."

"I suppose it will."

Julian pursed his lips.

"You have something to say?"

"No, it's just that ...." Julian shrugged and said, "Jupiter still doesn't—how shall I say this?—he isn't overly receptive to my orders yet."

"If the centurion has a problem," Vectis said sharply, "tell him the prefect's door is always open."

"I most certainly will do that." Then he added with a wry smile, "You've certainly grown into the job."

"We need this counter-insurgent unit, Julian. It's the only way to put fear in the Caledonians, and Jupiter's the only one who can handle it."

"Barbarian tactics ... we are getting desperate, aren't we."

"If we are ever to return home—and we will—we need to try everything."

"Oddly," Julian replied, "I find no comfort in that at all."

As the weeks passed, Neeve observed radical changes at Fort Faustina. The soldiers seemed forever to be drilling, and lately they had begun to train along the northern road that cut into the heart of Caledonia. And not just Faustina's soldiers. All the outposts had heavily armed troops marching the arterial road, and so many scouts in the surrounding hills that Caledonian warriors had abandoned their attacks on supply wagons.

The African centurion they called Jupiter spent his mornings instructing eighty handpicked men, along with twenty Scythian archers. Several times when Neeve was supposed to be mapping, she observed them training in the hills: daggers in their mouths, crawling on their stomachs, sometimes swimming, sometimes climbing. All this she reported to Taranis and Eston. Her brothers thought the special group might be future scouts, since the new commander had increased the scouting role dramatically.

The frustration for Neeve was the clandestine way the new commander made decisions. When Rufinus had charge of the fort, even the common soldier knew the times and schedules of everything. Now, only the Prefect Vectis, his tribune and First Centurion knew anything. They alone scheduled the night patrols, the supply wagons, the soldiers' training times. Neeve needed access to the prefect's office. She knew his type—so organized he was sure to have the bath schedules laid out neatly on his worktable. But he was also guarded. On many occasions Neeve felt his eyes on her back, watching her, perhaps suspecting her true motives for being at the fort.

Yet, after the departure of her brother, the prefect had issued orders, privately through his tribune, that no soldier was to bother her. No one had, except Officer Nepos, whose hands always seemed to brush her when they passed in the narrow halls. But even that had stopped after she cuffed him on the side of his head with a leather riding bag.

Neeve sat on the bed in her tiny sleeping quarters, thinking about her morning ride to the bend in the river, where she had washed her hair and scrubbed her body. The river was growing colder and soon a skin of ice would form, making it more difficult to bathe. She would have to find another spot, one with quick-moving waters that rarely froze. But that was a problem for another day.

She needed access to the prefect's office, but how? The handsome tribune crossed her mind. She could easily entice him; he had a weakness for women. But the commander was careful about who entered his office. When Rufinus was in charge, a steady stream of people flowed in and out, and often he left his office unattended, making it possible to slip in alone. Now it was different. Even if she won the tribune's favor, it was no guarantee she would be trusted in the central office. The tribune visited with scores of women, but never had Neeve seen one enter the office. She thought about the dark centurion, but dismissed him immediately. He held unusual power, which would give her access to the office, but he was so distant that Neeve couldn't be certain her charms would win him over. She had no choice—it was either the prefect or content herself with general information.

Neeve collected her bow from the wall rack and headed out to the practice area on the north side of the compound. As she crossed the parade ground she saw the prefect talking to his tribune and two Scythian archers. She eyed the thin-boned archers with their long black hair and sleek faces. Such marvelous bowmen, she thought. No wonder the Romans hire them to do their killing. If only she had their skills. She stopped, struck with an idea.

The tribune was the first to notice her approaching. He smiled, showing his white, even teeth, his extraordinary good looks. For a moment Neeve wondered whether he might be the simpler route to the information in the prefect's office. No, she told herself, it was nothing but her weak spirit talking, an excuse to avoid the unpleasant, yet necessary, task that lay before her. She had to be strong; she had to pluck up her courage and approach the prefect himself. He was the gateway to everything.

The tribune stepped out toward her. "How may I serve the mapmaker?" he asked with a twinkle in his eyes.

Neeve kept an intense look on her face, as if she were concentrating on his words. She would be trusted in the office only if they believed her language skills were poor. Even in the southern occupied areas, not one Celt in a thousand could speak Latin, much less read army dispatches. If she kept alert and spoke haltingly, no one would ever suspect she could read.

"I require ... prefect ... for arrows," she said.

"You require what?"

"Prefect ... for arrows," she said more loudly.

The tribune turned to the prefect, and with a smile said, "She wants to shoot you with arrows."

"Like everyone else," he mused. "I won't be long." He turned back to the Scythians.

Neeve studied the prefect, trying not to stare, as she sometimes did. He had the air of a leader with a mission. A dangerous type, she concluded, watchful and cautious. She could hear him encouraging the two Scythian officers, but she could tell he had little tolerance for failure. They nodded respectfully and left. The tribune left also, but not before giving her a warm smile, as if they were old friends. Finally, she was alone with the prefect.

He turned and his eyes explored her face. "Your maps," he said, "they are well done. But I'm not sure I understand them."

Neeve beamed. "You like maps? Very good. I thank you."

"Come by my office tomorrow," he said, enunciating the words, "about the fourth hour, to explain maps."

"The fourth hour ... yes, I tell everything, fourth hour." Neeve was elated. An invitation to enter his office! The former Prefect Rufinus was notorious for ordering non-Roman women to his office, and then demanding they lie with him or face dismissal from their duties. But this prefect was driven not by animal passions, but by an intense desire to make the outpost forts invincible. He was by far the more dangerous. She had seen it before. His kind talked gently, and smiled at the appropriate times, but all the while scrutinized every word. She must be vigilant lest her own words expose her.

A thought suddenly jarred her. Could he have received word back from Legate Julius Verus at Londinium? She had never met the legate. What if Verus responded that he had never heard of her? No! She scolded herself. She was just anxious. How could a fort prefect send a courier to ask the governor of Britannia about a supposed mistress? Of course he could not, she told herself, feeling better about it all.

The prefect was speaking. "So you have a problem—something about arrows?"

"Arrows, yes. I need arrows," she groped for words, "very bad."

"You need a supply of arrows?"

"No! No! I have much arrows. I need *straight* arrows." She emphasized her point by imitating the action of shooting a bow.

The commander looked puzzled.

She pointed toward an archer in the distance. "I need Scythian."

"A Scythian."

"Yes, Scythian."

"Ah! You want a Scythian to ..." he hesitated, "to get you straight arrows?"

"No. I need Scythian ... for ... straight help." Again, she gestured with her bow.

"A Scythian for straight help," he repeated, not comprehending.

Neeve watched his eyes for signs of frustration. He had to believe her language skills were weak, but she did not want to irritate him. If she herself felt frustrated speaking in such a stilted way, he must find it doubly so. She decided it was time to help him discover what she was asking. She pointed to a cart near the parade ground, aiming at it with her bow. "Target," she said, "straight help ... for target."

His brow furrowed. "You want a Scythian to help you hit a target?"

"Yes, target."

"Instruction, you want instruction."

"Yes, yes, instruction," she said, allowing relief to spread across her face.

"I think we need an interpreter," he said in a surprisingly gentle tone.

"No, no, I speak much Roman ... need more words, is all. Soon I learn ... you see ... learn much soon." She vowed to make a big leap forward, and soon. Talking like this was exhausting.

"An interpreter could help—"

"No, no," she said, looking as sincere as she could. "I desire to ... learn language." The last thing she wanted was an interpreter at her elbow every time she met with the prefect.

"I learn speak," she continued, gesturing to her mouth, "but never words ... for the papyrus."

"For the papyrus? You mean written words?"

"Yes, written words. Never."

"You don't think you could ever read?"

"No, no. Never. Numbers I know ... I put numbers on maps, but not words. People talk about ... papyrus words. Hah! I see no ... words, just marks, dark marks. Hear words, yes. See, no." Neeve watched him closely to make sure he understood the message. He had to believe she could not read.

As she continued talking with the prefect, she felt more secure. She had to be careful, but he might not be as shrewd as she thought. He might even be a touch overconfident, not an uncommon character defect among Roman officers. They supposed themselves superior in every way to the peoples they enslaved. Her mission was possible after all, really possible.

He asked nothing about her background, her brother, even about their deception of claiming he was a mapmaker. The prefect seemed interested only in finding ways to improve her skills as an archer. He was treating her as he would any scout or mapmaker. And why not? She *was* a mapmaker—and a good one too. Sometimes she forgot that. She was struck by the irony of it all. Anything he could do to strengthen her abilities, he had said, contributed to the security of the fort. This Roman was so arrogant, so patronizing, he assumed she posed no threat to the great Roman Empire. He could afford to play the benevolent master when he and his kind had Caledonia by the neck. Well, if she got into his office, things might change.

PART THREE:
Love and Betrayal

23

Vectis stared at the water clock by the window. It was almost the fourth hour. His morning had been crammed with meetings, first with Jupiter who stated briefly that the new counter-insurgent unit was fully operational and reasonably effective—Jupiter's way of commending his prefect for starting the unit. Vectis appreciated the comment and acknowledged it with a nod, but other things were on his mind. The mapmaker was coming that morning.

Meeting after meeting dragged on and Vectis was finding it hard to focus. Even the present one with two officers from Fort Stragenia proved a challenge to his concentration. The fort's commander, Priscianus, was organized and competent, and his officers had been suggesting innovative ways to improve outpost security, but Vectis knew the mapmaker would soon arrive. He glanced at the clock again and wondered what questions he should ask about her maps. Yesterday he had assumed he would have time to look them through, but with the morning so busy—

"Prefect?" An officer was staring at him.

Vectis realized his eyes were fixed on a tiny mole on the officer's left cheek. He glanced at the others in the room, eight in all. They were waiting. Even Julian was looking at him, waiting for a reply. Someone must have asked him a question, and now they expected a response.

"Repeat the question," Vectis said.

The man looked shocked. "I asked no question, Prefect."

Julian interjected. "Prefect, we were discussing the squatters, and you were about to make suggestions."

"Of course," Vectis said, not remembering anything. He cleared his throat. "I have a touch of the wet season." He massaged his stomach to indicate his discomfort. "We will continue our discussion after the noon meal. A bowl of hot boiled calf with smooth broth is all I need." He forced a laugh. "And maybe a cup or two of Celtic beer would help us all." They smiled politely and Vectis motioned toward Julian. "The tribune here will schedule the time."

Julian returned after he had escorted the officers from the building. "Your next appointment is outside," he said, with an overly concerned look on his face. "Shall I send her away due to your sudden illness?" He was enjoying Vectis's discomfort.

Vectis busied himself with the maps, partially because he needed time to study the sketches, but also because he had no desire to look into Julian's eyes. When he had given Julian instructions to protect the mapmaker from the soldiers, he had done so under the guise of fairness. She'll be a target, he had told Julian, make sure nobody bothers her. We cannot afford that kind of problem at the fort. Now that he had canceled a meeting for no other reason than to talk with the mapmaker, he could hardly pretend to Julian that his interest was for the good of the fort. He kept his eyes down as he spoke, "Have my aide detain her briefly before sending her in."

"She seems like a fine mapmaker," Julian said.

"Thank you, Tribune. You may leave."

"A very fine mapmaker."

Vectis looked up. "Yes, you've made your point. Now leave me in peace."

He grinned and left.

Vectis resumed studying the sketches, which numbered over thirty. They were arranged according to sectors, and dated in the right hand corner. There were two styles of maps, as if by separate mapmakers. He checked the names stamped under the dates, all by Neeve mapmaker. Then he noticed that the earlier drawings were different from the later. Interesting, he thought. Not all that important, but at least he had something to query her about. He piled the earlier ones on his left. When she first began, she had the habit of shading certain portions on the map. The rivers and mountains were drawn as an artist might sketch them, except it appeared as if you were viewing the regions from the heavens, looking down on them. The maps were also drawn in proportion, again with an artist's flair. He looked at the more recent works on his right. Not much different from regular Roman-style maps, with their heavy emphasis on travel routes, and little concern for relative distances.

The aide tapped at the door and asked Vectis if he was ready for the mapmaker. Vectis replied that he was and instructed the officer to suspend searches of non-Roman scouts, mapmakers, and couriers, both at the entrance to the building and outside his office. If they chose to wear their weapons, that would be permitted. Things were now under control, he told the aide, and it was unlikely that any would murder him in his own office. In truth, he wanted the mapmaker to feel more comfortable about entering the central building. Already he had noticed that she came as little as possible to her tiny map room, probably to avoid the unpleasantries of a search. Soldiers could be thorough when they inspected women.

He could see her approaching at the far end of the corridor, tall and firm looking. He glanced down at his table, empty, except for the maps. He had taken his documents to the back rooms; she couldn't read, but it never hurt to be cautious.

When he looked up again she was standing in the doorway, wearing the same colorful tunic and leather trousers as the day before. And, of course, her knives—Celts loved their knives, and now she would again be able to wear them in the building. Vectis marveled at the Celtic penchant for strapping weapons in the oddest places. Hers were on her hip and above her right ankle, the latter partially concealed.

"Enter," he said, with what he thought would be the right mix of business and civility. She stopped in the center of the room and waited. Vectis met her eyes, and found it hard to keep from staring. They were so clear and so blue that it seemed as if he could peer into her soul. She had no particular expression on her face, which struck him even more because she looked remarkably like someone from his forgotten past. A little girl, a slave girl. Only he never did quite forget her, and he never quite washed away the guilt. At night in his dreams she came to him, reaching out her slender arms through the rough timber of the stockade. Who was to say whether the gods were testing him, perhaps giving him another chance?

Another chance!

An odd turn of events, to be sure, but how could he deny the feelings welling up within? This mapmaker was stronger in body than the slave girl, but something in the eyes, in the way she carried herself, reminded him of that slave.

From the first moment he saw the mapmaker, hair dripping wet in his office, he couldn't help thinking of the slave girl he had purchased so long ago on the *Via Lata* in Rome. The girl had died, he had heard, after only five years on the farm, but he could still see her standing on the raised block with her head held high. In the rude world of the slave trade, with its sweat and greed, she shone like a precious stone. But she was taken from him, and never again did he meet anyone like her.

Until now.

How similar was this mapmaker, he thought, with eyes like sapphire and a face that glowed. From across the compound, or through the slats of his window, he would see her moving briskly about her business. She was never one to linger in a crowd, and even on nights when a juggling or mime troupe came to the fort, she would remain in her quarters, weaving on her loom. But mostly she made her maps. Mapmaking had become a dangerous business in the northland, and Vectis would have understood had she asked for a slowing of the schedule posted in the tiny map room. She never did. She rode out alone, and returned a day or two later, assignment completed. And now, here she stood in the center of his office, poised, yet somehow distant, as though within the inner sanctum of her soul lay guarded mysteries.

"We have two kinds of maps here," Vectis said, breaking the spell. He showed her the two stacks and asked for an explanation.

She inspected both piles and shrugged. "Clerk officer ... he say change ... give me Roman map. I study map very much ... very long time ... then I change."

"You changed from these picture maps—"

"Yes, he tell me ... change ... so I change."

"Are you saying that one of my officers asked you to change your maps, conform them more to a Roman style?"

"Yes, clerk officer."

"So you studied Roman style maps?"

"Yes, yes ... study ... much study. Now have ... best Roman map." She patted the more recent pile on his right.

Vectis spread the earlier maps across the table. "These are good too," he said, trying to encourage her. He pointed to the shaded areas and said, "I assume you have learned that darkening areas to make your maps more attractive is a waste of time."

"Yes, clerk officer tell me that." Her tone sounded defiant.

"You don't agree."

"He is officer, I am not."

"But he's wrong."

"Yes."

"You think it's better to darken certain areas?"

"Yes, yes, of course." She bent over the table and ran her finger along the shading. "Darker ... is valley ... more grass ... look darker so I draw darker. With map, Roman know where is hill, and where is valley."

Vectis looked at her. "So all these shaded areas are valleys?"

"Yes, darker is valley."

"Then the lighter portions are hills," Vectis said, stating the obvious. "And here we have mountains because you picture them as mountains."

Vectis listened, sometimes with difficulty, to her unequivocal explanations on how she thought maps should be drawn. She enjoyed talking about her picture-form style, and constantly pointed to details she wanted Vectis to see. Often her hair fell across her face when she leaned over the table, and for one passing instant, Vectis felt the urge to touch the flaxen strands that seemed so loose and clean.

"I change river too for clerk officer," she said.

"Well, I don't think changes are necessary. The rivers in your earlier sketches were done especially well."

She looked pleased.

"I do have one question ... about distances? Why not simply mark them instead of drawing the map to scale?"

"Distance?"

"Yes. Why draw a scale map like an engineer when you could simply mark the distances?"

"Your words ... like air," she said, gesturing to show they were floating beyond her.

"The distances, why not just mark the distances?"

"Mile?"

"Yes, the miles."

"I mark mile!" she said proudly, jabbing her finger on the distance markings. "Here! Here! And here!"

"I see that. So why draw a scaled map?"

Her face was blank.

Vectis tried again. "Why take so much time drawing a picture map when the distances—the miles—are marked."

"It take no time. I draw fast. I best drawer."

Vectis started to say something but she interrupted.

"And," she raised a finger in the air, "engineer mark mile, that true, but engineer give Roman ... ah, Roman flat mile. Sometimes ground not flat. So picture map better."

Vectis understood. Roman engineers recorded dead-level distances—the shortest distance between two points—which did not take into account the undulations in the land. Map miles were often shorter than actual marching miles, and to reflect the actual distances, the mapmaker drew everything to scale, shading the valleys and lightening the hills.

He could not help smiling as he collected the maps. She was certainly interesting. "Sit down," he said, motioning toward a short couch beside the table. "From now on you are to draw your maps in picture-form. You have done a fine job."

She nodded her thanks.

"Now, about your practice session," Vectis said, sitting down across from her, "it was good?" He was asking about the Scythian instructor he had sent her.

"Yes, yes," she replied, "I was ... much good. I can get better, Scythian say, but much good now. Scythian gave me ... special arrow. He say it make me better."

It was clear to Vectis that this mapmaker had no lack of confidence—even if it was misplaced. The Scythian instructor told him she was hopeless as an archer and could hit things only at close range. But according to her, she was ready to join the Scythian corps. Vectis had never met anyone with such a positive view of herself. The Scythian had supplied her with arrows from his personal stock in hopes of bolstering her confidence, never realizing how absurdly pleased she was with her own abilities. She was the best archer, the best at language, the best mapmaker. She was a good mapmaker, he had to admit, but hardly the best—she was the only one they had!

"You understand you can have a Scythian instructor anytime? I have arranged that for you."

"I thank you. Language instructor ... you make that?"

"You want language instruction too?"

"Yes, language too."

"I will send someone to your quarters after the noon meal."

"I soon speak ... much language."

"Good, then we'll be able to talk more ... easily." He took a deep breath and thought about what he was doing. How could he be so unrealistic as to strike up a relationship with a Celtic woman when he knew he could never trust her?

"I ... do much language," she said earnestly. "Work at bow and do language."

Vectis smiled. "Maybe to save time you could practice with a Scythian language teacher."

She seemed not to understand at first, and then returned his smile. "You laugh at me, that true?"

"A little."

"I maybe surprise prefect."

He would have preferred that she called him by his *Praenomen*, Vectis, but to suggest it would have been improper. He knew her name, Neeve mapmaker, and being her superior, any address he used would be in order. It might be good to start using her name right now, he thought. He reached for a map, "Your name is ...."

"Neeve."

"A pretty name," he said, feeling foolish for uttering such banalities. "What I mean is, I have never heard a name like that before. Unusual."

"No, no, very common. Every village ... much woman use Neeve. Very common. Even cow ... sometime ... Neeve."

"Cows are given proper names?"

"Yes, yes."

"No."

"Yes, sometime my mother ... she call, 'Neeve,' and five cow come ... cottage."

They laughed together. Vectis had no idea whether her story was true, but it felt good to laugh, to share something intimate. He looked at her still smiling, still watching him with those sparkling eyes, still enjoying her joke. He wondered what it would be like to touch her cheek or caress her hand.

What ridiculous thoughts streamed into his head! How could he even think such things about someone he knew nothing about? Spies were everywhere. He might excuse himself if he were an adolescent, but here he was a grown man, fawning over a Celtic woman, miles beyond the Antonine barrier. It had to be the gods, he told himself, or a Druid curse sent to distract him. A curse? Julian would laugh him to scorn. Fetch me one of those Druids, he would say, let him curse me.

The truth was obvious. A woman of haunting beauty, a bleak northern province, and a memory that would not let him go. Add that to his empty life ... it wasn't hard to see what was happening. Still, he enjoyed being with her.

"You ... far from home ... from great Rome City."

Vectis agreed, far from home.

"You ... alone for Rome City?" she asked.

"Alone?"

"Yes, alone ... sad for Rome City, sad for ... far family, sad for far friends. Alone."

Vectis pondered that and concluded she must be asking whether he got lonely in Britannia. He replied that he hadn't been away long, but he did miss his father and sister, and a few servants. He mentioned the death of his mother and the sudden aging of his father. His father had reached that time in his life when he needed his son, and to be away from home distressed him. Vectis wondered whether he should ask about her family, but since he had ejected her brother from Faustina, he let it pass. He concluded by telling her that Britannia had a special beauty, with its cold streams and snow-capped mountains. He had a deep respect for the truth, inherited from his father, but he supposed a kindly lie was sometimes better than bald truth. Only a sorcerer could find beauty in this frozen wasteland, he thought.

Neeve seemed to enjoy listening to him prattle on so he remarked on the richness of Britannia, with its grain, and deposits of iron, tin, coal and lead. He told her that hides from Britannia were among the most cherished in Rome.

"Yes, Britannia ... have much good things. But ... different, yes? Rome ... city of gods. I see picture ... here, in heart," she closed her eyes and placed the flat of her hand on her chest to indicate that she was trying to imagine what Rome must be like. "Silver towers," she said with her eyes still closed, "I see silver towers ... up to heavens, and Rome gates filled with jewels." She opened her eyes. "Rome City ... much towers. Yes?"

"Towers, obelisks, columns, all kinds of things."

She shrieked and slapped her thigh. "I knew there be towers in Rome City!"

Her sudden outburst took Vectis by surprise. He almost jumped.

"Jewels!" she shouted triumphantly. "Much jewels in Rome gate. Yes?"

"No, no jewels in Rome gate."

"No jewels?" Her face fell in defeat. "But gods walk in Rome city," she said reverently, hopefully. "You saw gods?"

"Neeve," Vectis said, conscious of using her name for the first time, "there are many temples in Rome—beautiful temples with pools of water and winged statues—but no gods walking the streets. Just people like you and me. Rome is a beautiful city, but no gods."

"No gods," she said thoughtfully, "no jewels in Rome gate."

Vectis felt bad for having spoiled her visions of Rome. It was not uncommon for provincials to fantasize about the Eternal City. It had, after all, bestridden the world like a colossus for nearly a millennium. And the soldiers didn't help. Those of Roman origin loved to astound the locals with stories of gold dusted paths winding through the city and night streets ablaze with light. They talked of trees clustered in the city intersections, laden with every kind of fruit, summer and winter. Citizens of Rome, so the story went, strolled the avenues eating their fill.

"Neeve, there are jewels in the temples," he said, not wanting to disappoint her, "and innumerable treasures in Rome's spacious palaces. There are broad forums with foods from every part of the world, fountains, triumphal arches, marble roads, marble floors, marble buildings with gilded roofs ...exquisitely sculpted statues—"

"Yes, like city of gods!" she exclaimed.

She seemed so happy to have back part of her fantasy that Vectis told her of the long senatorial processionals on festive days, of kings that came to Rome to pay homage, of exotic animals from the four corners of the world.

"Rome City ... so different," she said.

"Like no city in the world," Vectis said, allowing his natural pride to show.

"That why ... hard for you. If I go away ... leave Britannia ... I miss. Yes? I miss. But Rome City! Much ... much hard for you ... because ... so beautiful. Yes?"

"That may be," Vectis said, wanting to change the conversation. He was deeply proud of Rome and its accomplishments, but he knew there was more to the city than its outward appearance. There was the intrigue, the wrangling, and the continual clawing for power by senators who never seemed content with their station in life. In a backwater province like Britannia, the capital of the Empire might seem glamorous, but the reality could be far less agreeable.

"Some day I go Rome City," she said, "see everything ... see towers, senate people, animals, see everything!"

"It is quite different from here. You might not like it. People hurry through the streets, crowds are everywhere."

"Like Londinium," she said with a knowing smile. "I was in Londinium City. I know big, crowd city."

"Londinium?" Vectis laughed, and wished he hadn't. He sounded like the great man from Rome talking to the country maid. He had seen it before, Roman dignitaries swaggering about the provinces, complaining in overly loud voices about the primitive conditions they were forced to endure. 'Why, in Rome ...' they would say. And the common people hated it. He turned to Neeve and said as sincerely as he could, "Londinium is a wonderful city, but it is really a sleepy village compared to Rome."

"That even better," she said. "I like see big, big city. Rome people ... I know, good people."

"Even though we conquered your homeland?" Vectis was curious how she would respond to such an abrupt question.

"That long ago," she said. "Now we Empire people! Have law, have safety, have much road for travel. My father he say ... before Rome ... people no travel, tribe fight other tribe, no law. Like Caledonia! Tribe people fight, kill!" She twisted her face in revulsion. "Rome law good. Bring much safety. I like."

"Roman law is good," Vectis said, uncertain whether she was telling the truth. "We make mistakes but at least the law is fair, even for noncitizens. The Caledonians have not yet come to appreciate us, which is a mild way of saying that they hate us."

"Caledonian hate everybody."

"You are from the Votadini people south of the Wall."

"Yes, Votadini."

"Good people, the Votadini. Peaceful."

"Yes, peaceful."

Vectis kept his tone conversational. "The Votadini are north of the Brigantes, are they not?"

"Yes."

"The Brigantes are more warlike than your people, the Votadini."

"Yes, I think so."

"Brigantes tribes sympathize with the Caledonians, yes?"

"No understand."

"The Brigantes like the Caledonians, yes?"

"No, I think Brigantes people like Rome people."

"Even I don't like Rome people sometimes."

She smiled.

"It's not an important question," Vectis said, "Curious, that's all."
He stretched, hoping to convey a relaxed attitude. "The problem is
that I know too little about northern Britannia to understand the
reports I receive. This morning, for example, I received another Wall
notice about dissension among the western Brigantes tribes. I don't
know whether to take it seriously."

"I think it ... few angry people. That all."

"Then you have heard nothing about strife among the Brigantes?"

"Strife?"

"Raids, attacks ... war talk."

"Ah, war talk. Some, yes. But Brigantes ... big Celtic tribe ... from
before first Wall Hadrian, to Antonine." She spread her arms to show
the vastness of the area. "Brigantes peace people, not like war."

"And the western tribes?"

"Not many do rebellion ... some, yes ... but they bad people."

"What about you? You feel no anger toward Rome?"

"No, no. Rome people good. Give me mapmaker work. Some
worker at Rome forts ... say bad about Rome. I not do that. Rome
people good."

"Rome has its share of bad administrators, bad soldiers, but I'm
glad you find us at least somewhat agreeable."

"Yes, Rome people good ... and you good. I know you help me
when brother leave. I hear soldier say ... no hurt mapmaker. Prefect
make order. I thank you."

Vectis felt his face flush, an uncommon feeling for him. He had
no idea she knew. "A woman should feel safe in a Roman fort," he
said, as if he were giving a speech to his officers. "Fort security

depends on everyone being—" He stopped. She was looking straight into his eyes, probing him deep inside, exposing the secrets of his heart. "Well, I think ... that is, I was concerned for you," he said, telling the truth.

She touched his arm, sending warmth through his body. "What is concerned?"

"It means I ... I want no harm to come to you." The feel of her fingers was almost too much.

"You ... good Roman."

Vectis pulled his arm away—too abruptly. She looked shocked. Those words, he had heard them before. "*You good Roman,*" the slave girl had said, and then her father knocked him senseless. Celts are born liars, he reminded himself as he moved behind the table. He needed to act more like the prefect he was. What did he know about this Celt in his office? That she reminded him of the girl locked in his dreams? He couldn't deny his attraction to her, but at least he could clear away questions that bothered him. Was it likely she had been the mistress of Legate Julius Verus? If she had lied about Verus, and about her brother making maps, maybe she was lying about other things. Naturally, he couldn't ask Verus about his liaisons in Londinium, but he might be able to bluff her into telling him the truth. The question was whether he could do it and not alienate her in the process.

"I apologize for my hurried manner," he said, raising his hands to show his absentmindedness, "I have forgotten about *that.*" He pointed to the water clock by the window. "It and Julian run my life, but I have so enjoyed our conversation."

"I too, Prefect," she said, rising.

"We will talk again, perhaps about a land of mystery—Egypt."

"I like that. Egypt ... I heard about."

"One other thing," Vectis said, trying not to sound like an inquisitor. "You said you knew Legate Julius Verus?"

"Yes, in Londinium."

Vectis could see the question made her uncomfortable. "I want to show you something," he continued, "a letter from Londinium." He held a finger up to indicate that he would be only a moment, then went through the doorway of the nearest back room. He picked up the first report he saw, a report from the livery officer, detailing the improvements made on the stables. He walked back into the office and around the table. "This is from Legate Julius Verus. He has never heard of you. We even gave him your description. Why do you think he denies knowing you?" He handed her the document and studied her for any information he could glean.

She gazed at the document. Vectis could see the stress in the corners of her eyes. He felt a twinge of pity when she nervously stroked her hair. The most reasonable course for her to take, he thought, would be to suggest that Verus does not want their relationship trumpeted about. Vectis waited, knowing what her answer would be before she voiced it. There was no way to discover the truth, but her face told him much. He was sure she had lied.

"Prefect, this ... papyrus word tell truth. I not know legate." She handed him the document and fastened her eyes on the plank flooring.

Her response shocked Vectis. To stay with her story would have been easy. Who could prove her wrong? Besides, everyone knew that Celts had a weakness for lying, and as lies go, this one was trivial. She probably concocted the story to wrench more pay from the former prefect, Didius Rufinus. Julian told him she was receiving as much as a master scout. Vectis had let the allotment stand.

She was looking at him again, waiting for his response. At least he could be sure of one thing—she had told the truth about not being able to read. Anyone, even with a modest reading skill, would have known that the document had nothing to do with Verus.

Vectis asked, "Why did you lie to me?"

"I not ... lie to you. I lie to Prefect Rufinus. I afraid ... Rufinus ... even with brother. I tell him Legate Verus ... friend." She patted her chest. "I tell him we good friend. He surprise ... get afraid. Treat me good."

"So you continued the same story when we arrived in hopes of better treatment."

"Yes. But you fair. I no need legate story. Now I feel bad. You want me go ... like brother ... I go."

Vectis had no desire to see her leave the fort, and something else, he was glad she had lied about Verus. Women who won favors from officers as exalted as Verus, did so by rising through the ranks. They moved from officer to officer until finally they secured the prize they had set out to gain. Vectis found such women hard and unfeeling, not at all what he perceived in Neeve.

"You may stay," Vectis said, "but I expect you to act like a proper Roman aide, and always ..." he held her eyes, "always tell me the truth."

"Yes, truth. I tell truth ... always."

24

The morning drizzle had stopped by the time the Druids arrived for the village feast. Taranis was standing near the cooking pits that ringed the town when he heard chanting and flute-like music. Moments later the dark-robed priests emerged from a copse of trees near the high ground west of town. By now Taranis had grown accustomed to the Druid passion for mystery. Everything about them—their thick hoods and silky movements, their smooth chanting and fierce screams—blended in some odd way to create the illusion that where they stood was hallowed ground.

Taranis watched them filing out one by one as if they had magically appeared in the woods. In reality, their horse-carts were roped on the far side of the grove, but to the people it appeared as if an oak had opened and allowed them passage from one forest to another.

The village overflowed with warriors from a dozen Caledonian tribes, and everyone strained to see the processional gliding across the fields, chanting as it came. Moments before, the crowds had been savoring the rich aroma of meat roasting in open-air pits, twenty in all. The stags had been skinned and placed in the pits at sunrise, and throughout the morning, they had been roasting slowly over the coals in the earth. If the only reason for attending the festival of the new moon had been the reward of pit-roasted meat, the village would have been thronged. But a rumor had swept the Caledonian towns that the Druids were coming, and not simply to impart their blessings.

Divicos himself was coming to announce something that would change the course of the northland forever.

Multitudes filled the narrow streetways and broad marketplaces at the edge of town. On the roofs of the roundhouses and clinging to every available tree were young warriors trying to glimpse the processional. The expectant mood of the crowd pleased Taranis. He knew that finally the Druids would do what they should have done years before—call on the gods to purge the Roman menace from their land.

A stillness crept over the crowds as the Druid chant grew louder and nearer. "The old priest," Taranis could hear people whispering, "where is the old priest?" A thousand eyes searched the string of Druids for Divicos, but they saw no telltale limp to mark the ancient magician. The chanting ceased, and the magicians walked the length of the hushed village, disappearing into a large roundhouse surrounded by old trees.

Taranis made his way to the central roundhouse where Eston and the other Caledonian leaders had gathered. He was disturbed, and puzzled by the absence of Divicos. As he pushed through the crowds, warriors kept asking him about the high priest, and the announcement.

Until now, events had moved smoothly, or at least Taranis thought they had. The problem of convincing Divicos to leave his sacred grove and appear at the feast had been solved almost with ease. At first, Divicos refused to do anything but send a few priests. Taranis dispatched a messenger to Cathbad, imploring the sub-priest to stand in for the aged Divicos who, he said it was rumored, had a death sickness. A few careless words by the messenger soon fueled the rumor and set the priests' tongues wagging. It wasn't long before the commanders were informed that Divicos, high priest of the Druids, would himself bless the festival of the new moon. After that, it was simple to spread another piece of gossip, unknown to the Druids, that Divicos would make an announcement of great import.

"You've heard?" Eston said the moment Taranis entered the large meeting room. "Divicos was not in the processional. He must have stayed behind in the grove."

"Curse that old priest to hell!" Forgall shouted, pushing his way through the commanders. "I have grown weary of his tricks, his deceptions, his lies."

"What are you suggesting?" Taranis asked. "Replace Divicos with Cathbad?"

"Why not?" Forgall replied. "With Divicos back in the grove we can set Cathbad up as the new high priest."

"Easier to control Cathbad than Divicos," said the young commander, Cronn. He had a hard look about him, enhanced by a recent battle wound on his right cheek.

"But we cannot be certain that Divicos remained in the grove," Eston said.

Taranis asked, "Was Cathbad among the Druids?"

"Of course he was," Forgall said.

Taranis raised his voice. "Did anyone recognize Cathbad?"

"I thought I detected his walk," said an older commander named Eogan, "but I cannot be certain."

"Anyone else think he saw Cathbad?" Taranis asked.

Eston glanced around. "I cannot be certain either, but I think Cathbad was near the center of the processional."

"If Cathbad is here," Taranis said, "then so is Divicos."

"Divicos is *not* here!" Forgall said impatiently. "If he were, we would have seen him in the processional."

A number of commanders voiced their agreement.

"Forgall may be right," Taranis said, "but Divicos is a cauldron of deception. I, for one, cannot imagine the high priest allowing his rival, Cathbad, to attend this feast alone, especially when he knows how easy it would be for us to make a new high priest."

"So what are we to do?" Cronn asked.

"Proceed with our plans," Taranis said, "as if Divicos were here. The people expect the Druids to make an important announcement, and that is what will happen."

Eston said, "The Druids have another announcement—"

"No tribute!" Forgall roared, his voice shaking with rage. "The Romans have denied us our autumn tribute!"

"All of it?" Taranis was shocked.

"Yes," Forgall shouted, "every last coin."

Eston spoke up: "As the Druids tell it, the Romans have delayed the autumn tribute until Caledonia becomes less hostile."

"Less hostile!" Forgall spat. "With no tribute, we will teach the Romans the meaning of hostility."

Eogan glanced around. "Could the Druids be holding out on us?"

"They always grab more than their share," Forgall said.

"But they would never take it all," Eston said.

"I agree," Taranis said. "The Druids have little desire for war, and they well know what no tribute will mean to us. I suggest we go to the Druids now, and follow our plan, with or without Divicos."

Taranis and five senior commanders pushed through the crowds packed into the central square and along the Way of Victory, as the main road was called, until they arrived at the Druids' large roundhouse. Taranis knew that the lack of tribute was a serious blow, but it might not be as serious as many of the commanders thought. If preparations for war continued at the same pace, they could easily begin the campaign during the next few months, and then there would be no need for the winter tribute. The grains and stores at even one fort would more than supply their needs. The question was whether the Druids would sanction a winter campaign.

Inside the roundhouse, the priests had transformed an ordinary meeting hall into what looked remarkably like a Druid temple. They had sealed the window openings and erected an altar at the far end of the room. The plaster inner walls they encased in dyed animal skins, giving the effect of being trapped in the loose-walled stomach of a beast. Here and there slender shafts of light slipped through the barriers, only to be smothered by burned resin—a sickly sweet smoke that hung in the air. A dozen skulls lined the altar, and at the center a single lamp flickered in the darkened room, making the empty eye sockets menacing in their blackness.

Suddenly, the lamp flared blood red and hissed like a snake.

The commanders flinched, and stared at the flax wick sputtering on the altar. Now a lone priest stepped forward and spread his arms, chanting slowly, as if he were calming a raging demon. It was Cathbad; Taranis recognized his voice. He had never seen his face, but he knew the voice. Gradually, under the influence of the sub-priest's cajolery, the gods vexing the lamp were soothed and the golden light was restored.

Taranis licked his dry lips and wondered whether he and the other commanders had gained anything by wresting the Druids from their power center in the grove. The gods seemed to follow them. He glanced around the shadowy temple. At the edges he sensed the presence of spirits, powerful dark spirits, waiting to swallow up those who opposed the Druids' will. He took a deep breath and told himself that these same gods wanted the Romans out of Caledonia. Now was no time to waver. Caledonia depended on him.

"That's Cathbad, isn't it?" Eston whispered, more as a statement than a question.

Taranis nodded.

"Do you still think Divicos is here?"

Taranis squinted through the gloom to the cloaked bodies scattered facedown on the birch flooring near the altar. It seemed as though a spirit had slain the druids. "Divicos might not be in this room," Taranis replied, "but he's at the feast somewhere."

Taranis dreaded these contacts with the Druids. After all these years, their rituals still caught him by surprise, and he could never be sure what were authentic visitations of deity, and what were Druid tricks. Today the commanders had planned their own surprise, one that would force the Druids (he hoped) to bless an immediate war with the Romans.

Silence enveloped the temple. The commanders stood clumsily along the back of the hall, waiting for the kneeling Cathbad to signal that the ceremony had concluded. Minutes passed as the sub-priest communed. Then the breathing began, heavy, coarse breathing that seemed to be everywhere in the room. The commanders exchanged glances but kept their thoughts to themselves.

Cathbad rose and turned toward the commanders. The other priests awakened as well from their spirit trance and formed a semicircle around the altar. They chanted a final tribute hymn to the spirits, a low moan that sounded like a dying animal.

"You invited us to the feast," Cathbad intoned, as though he were still caught up in the spirits. "What would you say to your mediators?"

His voice sounded artificial to Taranis, a contrived sort of speech designed to frighten weak-willed men. It irritated him, almost as much as having to discuss matters in a darkened room, and that gave him strength. "We invited Divicos, high priest of the Druids," Taranis said curtly. "We have no interest in speaking to one of his sub-priests."

"There is only one sub-priest of the Druids," Cathbad replied in a normal voice. "I am he."

Taranis smiled inwardly. He had wounded Cathbad's pride by lumping him with the common priests. "Tell us about the tribute. There have been rumors—"

"Rumors!" Cathbad sneered. "Yes, ever since we arrived we have heard rumors ... rumors that the Druids have an important announcement, rumors that we are about to bless a war with the evil ones."

"You are," Taranis said. He decided it was best to take the confrontational route with Cathbad. "Now, tell us about the tribute."

Cathbad seemed uncertain how to respond. Even robed as he was from head to foot, he could not hide his discomfort. He rocked back and forth from heel to toe, rubbed his hands in a wringing motion, and then coughed nervously as if the delay would provide him with the guidance he needed. "Let me ask you," he said finally, "what have you heard about the tribute?"

Forgall spoke up: "No autumn tribute! That's what we heard." He ran his fingers through his red hair and looked around at the other commanders for reinforcement. There was a murmur of agreement.

Cathbad raised his arms to signal that he understood. "You have heard correctly. There will be no tribute this season. The evil ones have chosen a foolish path."

"They have chosen war," Taranis said with no emotion in his voice. He wanted the Druids to conclude that war was inevitable. "Preparations have already been made with the Brigantes and Selgovae for a winter campaign. All the Caledonian tribes are in support."

Again Cathbad hesitated, and seemed to be searching for the right tact to take. "The evil ones have given no tribute this season," he repeated, "but the Druids will take from the temple treasury to supply the needs of the people."

"What does that mean?" Forgall asked.

Cathbad ignored the harsh tone of Forgall's question and spoke gently. "It means that we will supply up to one quarter of the usual autumn tribute. In the spring we might find a return of the tribute."

"It's of no concern whether the Romans intend to resume the tribute," Taranis said. "War will begin this winter. All the commanders have agreed." In the dark, he stared at the faceless shadows beneath Cathbad's hood. "The Druids must call down the gods to guide the work of our hands."

"The Druids are prepared," Cathbad said to the surprise of Taranis and every commander in the temple. "The signs are right. No longer will the gods be denied the blood of the evil ones."

The commanders stood speechless. They had expected the Druids to oppose any movement toward war. Eston broke the silence. "Does the high priest agree that the signs are right?"

Cathbad replied, "Both the high priest and the sub-priest agree."

The strange reply was not lost on Taranis. Cathbad was saying he would sanction war, even if Divicos failed to do so, and he wanted the commanders to know it. He must believe, Taranis thought, that he has the power base in the Druids to replace the high priest. He just needs an excuse—and support from the commanders—to do it.

"We want the high priest's blessings now," Taranis said, "here at the feast. The warriors must know that the spirits go with them."

"You need not fear. The blessings will be given."

"By you or by Divicos?" It was a blunt question, but in the current atmosphere, it seemed appropriate.

Cathbad replied: "The high priest will give the blessings. It has always been so."

Taranis decided not to pursue the issue. It was sufficient that Cathbad would claim the high priest's mantle, were Divicos to balk at sanctioning war. Finally, Eston asked the question everyone was wondering—where was Divicos?

Abruptly, the mood changed, as if the Druids were expecting the question. They mumbled sacred prayers and raised their hands. Cathbad slipped back into his artificial voice, calling out the name of Divicos. In the background the priests chanted repeatedly, "Where the winds blow, and the trees sway."

When the chanting slowed, Taranis repeated Eston's question about Divicos. Cathbad cocked his head, listening. Then from behind the altar came a sudden beating of wings and a raven swooped around the room. It passed over the commanders' heads and flapped back to the altar, where it lighted on the shoulder of a priest.

"Make your requests," Cathbad said, motioning toward the raven.

Forgall started forward to see Divicos in raven form.

"Be warned," Cathbad said sternly, "the spirits transforming the high priest will not suffer long the scrutiny of the vulgar."

Forgall stepped back. When it came to the world of eternal shadows, his curiosity could wait.

Taranis stared at the raven, its sleek body glistening in lamplight. Could it really be Divicos? He had no doubt the gods could change Divicos if they chose—the gods could do anything—but had they done so in this place, at this time? He thought not. It wasn't that he chose to doubt; he simply could not bring himself to believe. Try as he might, he could not accept the raven jerking its head about on the priest's shoulder as Divicos in altered form. Besides, he thought, Cathbad would not have spoken so forthrightly with Divicos in the room. Divicos must be somewhere else.

"Speak!" Cathbad cried. "The gods grow impatient."

Eston leaned toward Taranis and murmured, "We can't talk like this. We need the people, and we need to follow our plan."

Eston was right. He had to convince the Druids to leave their makeshift temple.

"Great high priest," Taranis said, addressing the raven, "we have seen this mighty feat, and are astonished. The gods are truly with you." He paused. "But we are simple warriors and understand little of the spirit world. How can we go back and tell the other commanders we talked with you in the form of a raven? And the people? How will they believe us?"

Suddenly, as if in response to the question, the raven shook from its perch and swooped about the temple, screeching and beating its wings. On the altar the lampstand shuddered, then collapsed — melted, as by a great heat. The Druids let out hideous shrieks and screams, and their voices seemed to come from everywhere in the room.

Taranis squinted his eyes, trying to see in the gloom. A blinding light flashed on the altar. The commanders jumped. Some cried out.

Then silence.

Darkness.

One by one, the window coverings fell off, and light filled the temple. Only it no longer looked like a temple. No skulls. No lamp. Not even an altar. Just a roundhouse meeting room with dyed animal skins covering the walls.

The Druids were gone. Taranis heard their distant shrieks in the public square. He eyed the door to the roundhouse. Closed. How they left mystified him. He lifted the skins to see if they had cut an opening in the wall.

"It doesn't matter how they got out," Eston said, "what matters is what they might say to the people."

"It *does* matter," Taranis said in frustration. "They control the people with these ... tricks. I don't believe half of what they do is from the gods."

"Neither do I but—"

Taranis put his hand on his brother's shoulder. "Don't worry. We will follow the plan." He looked around. "Do you have our surprise?"

Eston motioned to a leather carrier beside the wall. "Safe and healthy," he replied.

"Let's get to the square before the Druids take control of everything."

A light mist dampened the afternoon air but no one noticed—everyone was fixated by the cacophony of shrieks and screams building among the Druids. The crowds were packed so tightly into the square that even the commanders had difficulty getting to the rope-enclosed center. They pushed their way through, sometimes roughly, until finally they reached the roped off circle of raised stones.

By now the Druids appeared out of control, darting crazily about the enclosure, leaping and hurling themselves to the gray stones. Their screeching ripped the air like the agonized cries of dying gods, and the ferocity of it all amazed even Taranis. He could see the people standing in awe, hardly daring to raise their eyes, lest they glimpse a hideous demon peering out from a fold in a Druid hood. When the madness finally ceased and the Druids glided into the circle of spirits, a great silence fell upon the crowd.

Smoke curled around the Druids as they continually murmured, "Where the winds blow, and the trees sway." Soon only the hoods of the Druids were visible, as if they were floating on the smoke. Cathbad stepped from the circle and called out the name of Divicos. No response. He tried again. Still nothing.

He began mumbling prayers, punctuated with savage invectives that rebuked the gods. A chill wind passed overhead, swirling the smoke in a strangling motion. The people grew still. Cathbad cried out as if buffeted by angry spirits, his body torn this way and that, his contortions like those of a helpless demoniac. High-pitched laughter erupted from him and he pointed toward a giant elm near the edge of the square. Heads rotated to see what had so abruptly changed his demeanor. His laughter trailed away. "From the land of endless trees," he sang, "from the winds beyond the mountains, Divicos has come." He switched to a booming voice. "And now from his heights, his spirit mingled with eternal being, he breathes upon you." All faces turned upwards, straining to see Divicos's spirit in the leafless elm tree.

And then they saw it.

A single raven. Glossy black against the sky. It clung to a slender branch at the top of the tree, its sharp eyes and quick-turning head following every movement in the scene below. Suddenly, the raven lighted from its perch and drifted down toward the Druids, who had resumed chanting. "Where the winds blow, and the trees sway."

"Divicos," Cathbad intoned, his arms upraised toward the descending raven. The bird settled into the shadowy smoke and disappeared.

Taranis knew what would happen next but he had no idea how it would be done. At the edge of the roped off enclosure he had watched every movement of the Druids. They could not possibly have smuggled Divicos into the circle—or could they? The smoke was now filtering away, and through the haze at the center of the circle, Taranis saw the stooped form of the chief magician, Divicos. Taranis glanced at his brother, who returned a bewildered smile. None of the commanders believed Divicos could truly change into animal or bird form, but then again ... the gods sometimes chose to do strange things. Better to restrain one's doubts, lest they tempt the spirits.

When the circle opened and Divicos stepped forth, a fervent cry rose from the people. "I am Divicos, the Druid," came his scratchy voice, "giver of life and death, peace and destruction." He slipped back his hood, exposing sunken, skull-like features and long, wispy gray hair. "On the wind of a dream, from the land of deep layers of cold fire ...."

The people listened intently to his oration about life beyond the present world. Three times he damned the evil ones, but fell short of announcing war. Taranis grew exasperated waiting.

Divicos's voice grew louder and stronger, and he built to a climax. "The evil ones trust in swords and shields," he cried, "the sons of the land call upon the hallowed groves. The evil ones wag their tongues, laughing at the sacred temples, mocking the ancient gods." He cackled. "But as surely as rains fall to the earth and streams flow to the rivers, so will corruption be washed from our land." A light rain began to fall, as if a sign from the gods. Divicos stepped back and turned his face toward the enchanted shower. It was an act of triumph.

Long moments passed as Divicos stared heavenward, savoring the moment. Cold droplets splashed down, soaking his face and hair, and still he offered himself as a shrine.

On the edge of the circle, Taranis's mind raced furiously. Divicos might never bring himself to announce war. He had seen it before. The old priest had a way of skirting uncomfortable issues, yet giving the appearance of having discussed them fully. The fate of the northlands was in the balance, and Taranis knew he must face up to the Druids. The gods wanted a free land, an unpolluted land—Divicos had said so himself. It was a matter of timing, and there was no advantage in delay.

Taranis swallowed hard and moved toward the center of the square, crying, "Let us all turn our faces to the gods, and thank them for Divicos and the power of the Druids." An explosion of praise and ecstatic utterances filled the heavens. When the prayers subsided, Taranis kept his eyes on the people, never once glancing at the high priest. Cathbad he could confront, but the old priest was another matter. He was counting on the presumed rift between Divicos and Cathbad to protect him on his next move ... and, of course, he knew the power of the surprise planned by the commanders. "The Druids have divined the times," Taranis shouted before Divicos could respond, "and the time for war is now!"

Cries of exultation followed, during which Eston handed him the leather carrier. Taranis carefully lifted out the precious contents, resting them in his palms like holy treasures, for that is what they were: five acorns and three slender cones. "These sacred sources of life—acorns of oak and cones of yew—come from the dark forests of Gallia, from the shrine where the gods first visited the Druids thousands of years ago. The evil ones of Rome have tried to stamp out Druid power in Gallia, but a flame still flickers in the forest, at the first shrine. Dimonus, high priest of Gallia, has sent us this gift, and begs our high priest to plant them in the fields between the Walls. By this act of faith, he says, the evil ones will shrivel like leaves on an autumn tree." Taranis paused before raising his voice in jubilation: "The Druids have divined the times, and the time for war is now!"

The crowd roared to life.

The old high priest's mouth twisted as he said, "If Dimonus is so sure about the power of these seeds, he should plant them throughout Gallia." He cackled to himself as Taranis handed him the carrier.

Taranis looked squarely at him. "Either you or Cathbad must call down the gods."

"I am high priest here," Divicos hissed, "I decide when to call on the gods."

"Decide, then," Taranis said. Then in a softer tone, "We have the power to destroy the Romans, high priest. We will not fail you."

Divicos waited for calm and then spoke obliquely about winter's promise issuing into the life-giving spring. He talked about trees bursting forth in life and compared the earth to a fertile maiden waiting for impregnation, but nothing about war. As he rambled on, Taranis began to understand—Divicos was calling for war in the spring, a significant concession, but not what Taranis wanted. The magician knew he was trapped and was making the best of it by delaying the inevitable until spring. In this way he would have four or five months to influence events, perhaps even delay through the summer.

To postpone until spring was a blow. The commanders had decided that the Roman forts would least expect an attack in the cold winter months. They would naturally think that siege equipment required river transportation, and would not expect the Caledonians to use sleds over fresh-fallen snow. Now they must wait until spring. Divicos had cleverly supported the commanders' war efforts and had blunted the threat from Cathbad. Who would rise up against the aging priest over the delay of a few months?

25

The rich autumnal colors had faded into the gray-blue that heralded the coming of winter, and a light mist chilled her hands and face as Neeve rode along the arterial highway five miles south of Faustina. She tucked her cloak around her legs and swept her eyes along the low hills in the distance. She knew how dangerous this empty stretch of land could be. Yet she was glad to be on the open road, free from the watchful eyes of the prefect. Neeve shuddered as she thought about how intense he could be. Oh, he tried to disguise it with idle chitchat, but his motives were transparent—he wanted to extract every piece of information he could from her. And he trusted no one.

Over the past three weeks, she had seen him four or five times. After that first day, they talked about simple, nonthreatening things such as the cooling weather, the foods in distant lands like India and Syria, and the various festivals held in Rome. She made a great show of language study—a tedious bit of chicanery, especially when it included a tutor who grilled her every waking hour. But at least now, with her improved language skills, she could talk to the prefect in less halting phrases.

Her mind drifted back to their first conversation in his office. It was her fault, she knew. She had been too eager, said too much. Her praise of Rome and feigned innocence had raised suspicion in his mind. And touching him was the wrong thing to do. How foolish she had been to think that a light touch might encourage him to place more trust in her. She could still see him recoiling like a snake sensing danger, and then pointing at the clock as if he had forgotten an appointment. He wasn't good at concealing his inner motives, she thought. All his friendliness was designed to lull her into lowering her guard, an act he probably used with everyone he interviewed.

But in spite of himself and his suspicious nature, the prefect enjoyed her company. Neeve was pleased with the way she had handled herself. At the worst moment, when he had quizzed her about Legate Julius Verus, she made the right choice. Now, almost certainly, the prefect believed she had no reading ability and he even seemed to appreciate her blunt admission of guilt.

He was different from most Romans. The ones she had known in the south loved to spin preposterous tales to impress the natives. Not the prefect. He restrained himself—no stories of fountains overflowing with milk, or giant trees with golden fruit—but true to Roman form, he did brag about Imperial palaces and kings that crawled to Rome to beg its favor.

She marveled at the insensitivity of the Roman mind. Only events that affected them and their precious Empire mattered. The prefect actually expected sympathy when he mentioned his mother's death, as if he were the only one who had experienced loss. He even displayed his mother's gold wedding ring—all he had left, he said. Was he blind to the agony his people had caused Caledonia? Were the deaths of ten thousand Celts of no concern to him? Could he be that self-centered? His mother died in bed surrounded by the comforts of home; Neeve's was dragged to the Roman camps and doubtless raped repeatedly until she died. His father was lonely in his declining years; hers was garroted for saving innocent villagers. And what about little Nes? She was as good as dead.

All this suffering because the Romans had an insatiable urge to dominate the world. His words kept coming back ... that he missed his servants. Servants! Slaves was more like it. When he talked about Britannia, he thought only of what benefited the Empire. Britannia is a wonderful place, he said, from here we get grain, hides, coal and iron. The Roman message was simple: give your masters everything of value, and peace will flow like a river.

Movement in the distance interrupted Neeve's thoughts. Someone—a horseman—was lurking at the far end of the Roman road. Instinctively, she loosed one of her bows from its strapping, and fixed her eyes on the speck drawing closer. Lone riders bothered her. Too unpredictable. She scanned the rolling land on both sides of the road. Someone else was moving along the western horizon, and although at first she could see nothing in the east, she knew another rider was there. She squinted her eyes to make certain her guess was correct. Three horsemen, no doubt about it. She relaxed. Roman scouts for sure; they always traveled in threes. One of the new methods for controlling the arterial highway. Flood the road with scouts and report all Caledonian activity to the soldiers patrolling between the forts.

Ever since the arrival of Prefect Vectis, the scouts' role had changed drastically. They had become like disciplined legionaries. They were not to stop for food or drink, not to talk to travelers, not even to help each other in case of attack. Only report. Find the nearest fort or patrol, and report.

As he neared, Neeve could see the scout was a Roman auxiliary soldier, not a non-Roman assistant like herself. Another innovation. Every scouting team included at least one auxiliary soldier to insure professionalism. She didn't recognize him and assumed he was stationed at Stragenia, a fort with a reputation for discipline, though not the bastion of discipline Faustina had become. He was studying her, Neeve knew, trying to decide whether she might be a threat. Concluding she was not, he continued along the road.

"A damp morning!" she called, knowing he would not reply.

He nodded, but said nothing. Neeve had heard that the dark centurion, Jupiter, used informants to test the scouts, and punishment for failure was severe.

"Hail Caesar!" she shouted, raising her arm.

"Hail Caesar," he replied without thinking.

She smiled.

He scowled.

On an empty road, it was the only diversion she would find.

Twenty minutes later she located the engineering markers pounded near the road edging, slim iron posts topped with red linen strips that flapped in the breeze. They ran due west through a field of heather, dropped onto a broad moor with patchy grasslands, and then fell to a river that swept off into the horizon. She surveyed the area, looking for the best vantage from which to draw her maps. As she studied the land tract, she hardly noticed the column of soldiers approaching along the road.

Through the mist, they looked like a day patrol, but as they neared she could tell their numbers were larger. Much larger. A long column of soldiers with a thick-chested officer riding a dappled-gray stallion. His shield and helmet were strapped to the side of his horse, and his hair was short and dense, like meadow grass. Neeve pushed back the hood of her cloak, moved to the side of the road, and waited.

"Hail Caesar," she called to the approaching officer. Her voice was level and serious. It was always wise to address unknown officers in the standard manner.

He twisted his head in her direction.

Neeve gaped at him, and then tried to hide her disgust. Something heavy had crushed the right side of his face, like a rock from a catapult. He had a grubby look about him, not like any Roman officer she had ever seen. Even the normal side of his face had three days of black stubble that matched his hairy arms and unkempt appearance. What kind of officer is this?

He looked her up and down the way a slave trader inspected bodies at the market. She felt like washing. "Hail Caesar," he said finally, in a tone that sounded contemptuous of everything, including the Emperor.

"I come from Faustina," Neeve said, "a mapmaker."

He ran his tongue over his teeth, spit on the ground, and kept riding.

Neeve's eyes followed the soldiers as they passed, and the thick-chested officer she hoped never to see again.

Senator Atilius Titianus floated lazily at the shallow edge of his pool. A light breeze drifted across the water, bringing with it the scent of juniper and laurel shrubs planted along the walkways. Two servants worked on his arms and legs, kneading them, banishing the day's weariness from his aching muscles. They had remarkable skill in their hands, firm but gentle. The fact that Atilius had ordered a servant flogged the day before greatly increased the efficiency of the others. He tucked that away in his mind. He had been too lenient of late, much too lenient. More floggings, that's what they needed.

He moaned in delight. They had begun to work his neck and back, skilled fingers that searched every muscle fiber for hidden tension. He closed his eyes and allowed tranquility to wash over him. It had been a hard year. A year of intense pressure. After his successful Games, he had spent his days wooing the influential of Rome, contributing to their favorite projects, supporting their Senate policies, and above all, assuring them—without ever saying it—that were the fates to catapult him to the Emperor's throne, he would remember his supporters. They would profit handsomely indeed, he hinted.

That was the key: convince the powerful that small risks could bring enormous gains. Convince them that emperors come and go, that the events of history flow like a great river, and only those who study the currents of the age are blessed by their posterity. A prudent man never chains himself to the destiny of another, lest the currents change and the waters ravage him.

Atilius knew that a small number of senators, led by Titus Severus, disliked his growing power and rejoiced over his slightest failure. They had no understanding of the numerous ways his rule would benefit Rome. With them he was extremely cautious. Knowing they would never support his bid for the purple, and knowing that they ran to the Emperor with every bit of gossip they sniffed out, he shunned even the appearance of ambition, hoping to lull them into inaction. When the time came, he wanted them to hesitate, to give him that space he needed to seize control. Then they would reap the rewards of their shortsighted behavior.

"Senator?" Balbinus stood near the edge of the pool. He patted a leather case. "I have good news from Britannia."

Atilius found it hard to wake from his dreams. He reached for his servants, who helped him from the water and wrapped him in warm towels. Others brought couches and a low table replete with assorted cheeses, breads, meats, and several varieties of wine. The servants understood well the desires of the senator's guest.

Balbinus flopped his bulk down on a couch and waited for the servants to wash and anoint his weary feet. That done, he waved them away and reached for the cheese and bread. "Another dispatch from Kallias," he said between bites. "You will find it interesting. He has talked with a certain Gaius Commodus at Colania, commander of the first outpost fort on the arterial road north of the Wall. Commander Commodus is extremely unhappy there and will do about anything to be reassigned."

"Indeed," Atilius said. "I wonder what he would do for an equestrian rank here in Rome. Establish communications with him, using Alfenus Crescens's Senate seal, of course." He looked at his aide. "What else does Kallias say?"

"He talks about the Druids."

Atilius leaned forward. "He has met with the Druids?"

"He has. Disbursed the quarter tribute ... and received a violent reaction."

"Go on."

"The Druids told Kallias that even full tribute would not satisfy the Caledonian commanders. They need more, much more."

"How did the meeting conclude?"

"They took the quarter tribute and screamed repeatedly the words ..." he glanced at his notes, "May our enemies burn in pain."

"A promising phrase. What does it mean?"

"I am told it is a Celtic ceremonial curse. The Caledonian people use it lightly, but when spoken by a Druid, it has solemn consequences. In this context we can roughly translate it as a promise that Rome will pay in blood."

"Excellent!" Atilius declared. "Excellent."

Vectis and Julian stood gazing at a set of parchment maps that detailed the area north of Faustina. More than fifteen years old, their edges were cracked and brown, and many sections were unreadable with water stains.

"Might as well be blind as use this," Julian said. "Our patrols say the maps are useless—the mileage readings often have no correspondence to the stone markers on the old roads, distances to rivers or mountains are garbled or left unmarked."

"Are you asking to send the engineers north?"

"I am. There are still scores of sectors east and west of the arterial road that need mapping, but I think the northern sectors take precedence." He picked up one of the crumbling maps. "If we ever have trouble north of Faustina—"

"Which is likely," Vectis said.

Julian nodded. "Then we'll need something more than this to guide us."

"Have you located any mapmakers?"

"It's difficult to find non-Romans who will work north of the Wall. Too risky. But I have located four auxiliary soldiers who can map—the commander at Velunia on the Wall is sending two, Commodus at Colania another two. They should arrive any day. Meanwhile, I suggest we send the engineers north to begin measuring and staking, and Neeve along with them to do her mapping."

Sending a mapmaker with engineers was unusual. Engineers took days to stake out an area; a mapmaker needed scant hours for the same tract of land. It was plain what Julian was trying to do—protect Neeve. By having her travel with the engineers, she could take advantage of their soldier escort. Months earlier, when Vectis had arrived, he assigned soldiers to escort every engineering pair that went into the field, to prevent the continued loss of these valuable officers. In time of war, the forts would need their engineers.

Mapmakers, too, were important, but he couldn't justify sending escorts to protect them. Faustina's soldiers were everywhere but in the fort—along the arterial road, patrolling the hills, guarding the engineers—and there was a real danger that Faustina would become a hollow fort, an empty bastion ripe for a surprise Caledonian attack.

"We cannot send mapmakers with engineers," Vectis said. "You know that."

"I know that mapmakers are important for us right now," Julian countered. "They should be escorted."

"How many escort soldiers? Twenty? Thirty? Five or ten will do no good. Foot soldiers can't move as fast as a mapmaker on a horse, all they do is attract attention. A mapmaker is safer alone." Although Vectis wanted to find a way to give Neeve protection in the field, he could not rearrange the fort schedule for one person. Cutting back on her mapmaking duties was the logical move, and this could be done once the other mapmakers arrived. They had almost settled the issue when a clerk brought news that a column of soldiers was approaching.

Twenty minutes later the soldiers entered the gates, headed by a big, barrel-chested man. As protocol demanded, Vectis waited in his office for official word that someone had arrived.

Vectis listened to his clerk describing the visiting officer and his request for a meeting. He was puzzled that Rome would send an emissary to such a distant place as Faustina. "Did the emissary say why he was here?"

The clerk replied, "To examine tax records of the Wall-forts and the five outposts."

"Tax records!" Vectis was still puzzled. "Outposts don't collect taxes." He turned to Julian. "Do we have any tax records here?"

"All the records from the five outposts are kept here, but we have no tax records, because as you said, we don't collect taxes."

"What about road excise taxes?"

Julian frowned. "A few land owners along the arterial road have been asked to pay for road upkeep, but the amount is insignificant. If that's what he wants, I can find the document."

Vectis motioned for Julian to get the record sheet, then waved him off. "First, let's find out what our Roman emissary wants," he said, heading for the door.

They crossed the compound to the stables where the emissary was taking off a saddlebag and giving special instructions to the stable hands on how to care for his stallion. Most of the soldiers had been taken to their sleeping quarters. They would no doubt be eager for food and the hot baths.

Vectis stopped. The emissary! Something about his shape ... the bull-like neck. He felt he should be afraid, cautious. He approached slowly, staring at the man, trying to remember. Someone long ago ... in Egypt. He licked his lips, thinking. No, not Egypt ... North Africa. His hair felt prickly on his neck as he remembered. The Greek! He was certain of it. The side of his head had been crushed, distorting his facial features, but it was the Greek all right. He tried to recall the name as his eyes took in the thick, hairy arms and broad back. Then like a flood, it hit him: Kallias! Kallias, the bull-necked Greek was here in Britannia, in Faustina, and an emissary from Rome.

Vectis walked up to him and said, "Welcome to Fort Faustina. I am Prefect Vectis Trebellius."

Kallias turned and looked at him. He held out his senatorial edict and said, "I am Helvius Marcellus, here to examine the tax records of the five outposts and to discuss your assessment of the Caledonian threat in the north." He sounded bored, expecting his authority as a Roman emissary to bring total submission from Vectis. "You will supply me with troops when I leave," he continued. "The auxiliaries from the Wall-fort at Coria have authorization only to deliver me to Faustina. They will return to the Wall in the morning. I, however, will remain for several days."

Vectis read the edict and noticed that the old senator he had met in Rome, Alfenus Crescens, had endorsed it. Had Kallias stolen the edict? It identified the emissary as Helvius Marcellus. Or had some benefactor given him a new life? Vectis remembered the stories that circulated among North Africa's legionaries when they released Kallias from the surgery at Lambaesis—after killing a centurion! How could they release him? Unless the Greek had a benefactor ... like Senator Crescens.

Vectis stared at Kallias. The fall had drastically altered his face, making the side of his head look flat, except for a confusion of scars that jutted out, like layers of rat-tails. It was odd seeing Kallias after all these years, and the man didn't even recognize him. Then another thought struck him—the rash of murders among the Brigantes.

"Have you been collecting taxes?" Vectis asked.

"I said I was."

"Where?"

"Where what?" Kallias did nothing to hide his irritation.

"Where have you been collecting taxes?"

"West of here," he said with hardly a glance at Vectis, "south of the Wall."

"There has been trouble with brutalities in those sectors."

"There's trouble everywhere."

"But more among the Brigantes in the West. I asked if you've heard of it."

"I've heard nothing. Now—"

"Centurion!" Vectis called to the officer who had been with Kallias. "Have there been any irregularities in your travels with the emissary?"

"No, Prefect."

"Brutalities, deaths, anything like that?"

"Several days ago one man was killed, but he attacked the emissary."

"Was it provoked?"

"The emissary tried to take the man's woman."

"Enough!" Kallias shouted.

"Silence!" Vectis said, "or I will have you restrained." He looked at the centurion and said, "Anything else?"

"Prefect, I have nothing useful to say about the emissary or the incident." It was obvious the centurion disliked Kallias.

Vectis turned to Kallias and said, "Emissary, you were about to say something."

Kallias fixed his eyes on Vectis. "Do you see this?" he asked, waving his edict. "This authorizes me to inspect records and collect taxes, and if someone attacks me, then he won't need to worry about taxes again. Do you understand? Now, I intend to go to the baths, and when I finish, you will give me a report—"

"I don't give reports to filthy looking Romans."

"What?"

"Look at the spots on your armor," Vectis said. "You should have that cleaned."

Kallias looked down at his armor, and back at Vectis.

"Even recruits clean their armor."

"What are you talking about?" he retorted, his face a mirror of disdain.

"I'm talking about North Africa."

Kallias opened his mouth, and licked his lips. "What about North Africa?"

"I know that you killed a centurion."

Kallias sneered. "Britannia's rain must have rusted your head."

"The centurion's name was Vatinius. You remember, Vinestalk Vatinius."

Kallias glanced around, showing uncertainty for the first time. "We're wasting time. I have never even been to North Africa, and don't know anybody named Vatinius."

"Your name is not Marcellus. It's Kallias."

Sudden recognition lit his eyes. Then his lips curled into a smile. "The kid with the bucket mouth," he said finally.

"You will get nothing here, Kallias, no records, no troops— nothing."

He waved his edict. "Oh, you'll give me what I want—"

"Leave now or I will have you flogged out of camp."

Kallias's smile faded. "Do you know what you're doing? This is a senatorial edict! You disobey this—"

"I disobey nothing. You're an impostor."

"I hold in my hand the power of the Senate!"

"You hold in your hand a stolen edict."

"The Roman Senate has authorized me—"

"Groom!" Vectis shouted, "bring his horse."

Kallias stared at Vectis in disbelief. He spat on the ground. "That's what you'll be worth—spit—when I get to Legion XX south of the Wall."

"Then I suggest you climb on your horse—"

"I demand a council with the senior officers of this outpost."

Vectis turned to the guards behind him. "This impostor seems to have a hearing difficulty. Flog him, and escort him three miles south of the fort. He wishes to reach Legion XX."

26

Neeve hunched over a mixture of hair-clippings and straw she had drawn from her saddlebags, encircling the tiny mound with her thick, woolen cloak to shield it from the wind. She had chosen a flat piece of land bordered by a series of hillocks on one side, and a river on the other. Repeatedly, her flintstarter flashed, lobbing yellow globes of fire onto straw that refused to light. Even in the saddlebags, the straw could not hide from the probing fingers of mist. She blew gently on a smoldering blotch. It died. Again. A tiny flame licked upward. She bent over the precious flickering light, drawing her protective cloak around it and crumbling twigs on top. Then, leaning back, she added larger ones until the flames flared in the wind. Within minutes a strong fire burned cheerfully, warming her bones and heating a cup of Celtic beer.

These were the times she dearly loved—alone, her mapping done, chilled, yet warmed by a delicious, open fire. Not the comforts of her Roman life south of the Walls, but not trivial either. At least in Caledonia she could contribute to the freedom of her people. She sipped the hot beer, then dropped a hard biscuit into the cup, fished it out and chewed the softened side absent-mindedly.

The afternoon sun burst through the clouds and glinted off quartz-flecked rocks in the icy waters below. It would take hours before the light trailed into darkness, time enough to ride north along the arterial road to Faustina. And time enough to rinse in the river. Neeve shuddered as the wind shook clumps of scrub willows along the banks. She set off to scavenge more wood in a nearby stand of pines, returned with an armful of twisted branches, and dumped them on the fire. Then, sitting cross-legged, she tugged at her leather boots.

It had been the worst day of Kallias's life. Whipped, humiliated, scorned. A dull-witted barbarian, that's what they had called him. Nine times they lashed him. He hadn't cried out. Bit through his lip, but not one utterance of pain. When it was over and he was being taken through the gates, he scoffed at the prefect. Said he felt nothing. That's when the prefect replied, "Get this dull-witted barbarian out of my sight."

Dull-witted barbarian?

He was descended from Greeks, aide to a senator in Rome, and now a wealthy man.

He patted the long, narrow bag hooked to his saddle that contained the equivalent of sixty thousand sesterces, more than the prefect would make in ten years. They hadn't even thought of examining his belongings. They knew he had been collecting taxes, but never thought to check his bags. Who was dull-witted?

He kept riding south on the arterial road, his entire body burning, his back flashing hot pain at the slightest movement. It would get worse, he knew. Crusts would form on the wounds, crack, bleed. He shifted in his saddle. They had even whipped his buttocks. He was eager to get to the legion base south of the Wall, where he would tell them the whole rotten story of his abuse. The smug Vectis Trebellius thought he had stolen an emissary's papers, but he would soon find out how wrong he was. Then he'd pay. They would execute him for disobeying a Roman edict. And Kallias would be there, watching. Looking into Trebellius's eyes at the moment of death.

The throbbing was intense. He pulled at his tunic to keep the fabric from sticking to the lacerations on his back, and he wondered whether he should bathe his wounds before going much farther. Dirt and sweat created fumes, he remembered, and fumes in open wounds could kill you.

Neeve waded into the ice-blue waters, taking care not to splash herself as she moved—she hated the shock of cold water hitting her before she was ready. The current felt surprisingly strong and Neeve was glad to be on the upriver side of a fallen tree that had swollen black from the flowing waters. Her breath caught in her throat as the river-bottom suddenly dropped and water surged above her waist, plowing rudely into her and sweeping on down the river. On a warmer day she might have enjoyed the little surprise, but today, well, she could do without such surprises.

The wind seemed harsher now as it whined along the river channel, bending the willows and crinkling the water's surface. Tiny goose bumps popped up on Neeve's rapidly purpling skin, and her lips quivered. With shoulders hunched, arms folded across her front and pressed firmly against her skin, she tried to shut out the cold. But the chill was deep and penetrating. She sighed, knowing the time had come. Gritting her teeth, she plunged down with a splash, holding herself under the icy flow while she rubbed and kneaded her body. She braced her back against the fallen tree, and moments later surfaced with a loud moan, still continuing to scrub her body, this time with a supple pine cone liberally smeared with fuller's soap. It was the only way to do it, she told herself, drop like a stone.

As a girl growing up in Caledonia, Neeve had never minded washing in the cold streams, but years of easy living had changed her, had made her long for hot, languid baths and slow massages with oil. She shook the thought from her mind, soaped and rubbed her hair in the water, wrung it out, and headed for the fire.

From the arterial roadway, Kallias spotted the river that wound through patchy grasslands and flowed westward. He had noticed the river earlier on his journey to Faustina, but had no reason to check the milestones for its location. Now he remembered. It had been near the engineering stakes, where the mapmaker was working.

Nine lashes. They had given him nine lashes. The searing pain made his back feel like it had been roasted in fire.

He thought about the screaming victims he had seen literally roasted in Rome's amphitheater. Smeared with pitch and tied to stakes, how they had screamed when the torches lit them up. Screamed as their hair burst into flame. Screamed until their voices choked in the swirling soot. Then, like lamps at midnight, with the pitch on their bodies consumed, they flickered, and smoked, and died.

He had no pity for them. They were enemies of Rome. But he was a Roman emissary, a senatorial aide.

His back burned.

Vectis Trebellius. A proper Roman.

The bucket of vomit. He'd watch him die.

But first, he must wash. Wash the fumes from his torn flesh. Numb the pain in a cool river. He saw the engineering stakes and nudged his horse toward the distant river.

Neeve dried herself by the heat of the fire, rubbing her bare body vigorously with the flat of her palms. Twice she looked over her shoulder at the trees, unsure why the birds had suddenly stopped chirping, and wondering whether someone might have stumbled upon her, and was watching her from the tall willows.

She paused, ran her eyes over the trees and across the grasslands, saw nothing, but began to feel uncomfortable standing as she was naked in front of the fire. Rubbing her body one last time, she pulled on her trousers and tunic, and wrapped herself in her cloak. For several minutes she sat motionless in front of the flickering fire, soaking up the heat. By now her belt, boots, and knives were in place, and her hair fluffed dry over the fire. She felt better.

Neeve eyed the sun beginning its downward arc, and decided that she had overstayed her time. If she were to reach Faustina before dark, she would have to push it. One final sip of hot beer and a quick inspection of her sketches would put her on her way. The last thing she wanted was to forget a distance marking or discover that she lacked some major detail essential to the completion of a map.

Still seated by the fire, she scanned each map for errors, and then stopped. Something didn't feel right. A sound? She cocked her head, listening. Quiet. Maybe a dead limb had dropped in the thin stand of pines, or a hare had scurried through the heather. Probably an animal, she told herself, but the awkward feeling persisted.

She suddenly felt vulnerable sitting and rose abruptly, her eyes darting around. She tried to be reasonable, but couldn't shake the feeling that something, or somebody, was watching her. She moved toward her horse and slipped the maps into their case, then loosened the thong holding her top bow. Over her saddle, her eyes scoured the clumps of scrub hazel and small hillocks where a predator could be hiding. Wolves? she wondered, grasping the bow. Couldn't be wolves during the day. Nor any other animal. Her horse wasn't skittish in the least.

An icy finger raced up her spine. Someone was behind her. She whirled. Just the fire sputtering in the wind.

She rubbed her bow with nervous hands, then expelled a long, slow breath to calm herself. It helped. The whole thing was ridiculous, she told herself. No one was here. Besides, as a Roman mapmaker under the protection of Prefect Vectis, she had nothing to fear from the conquerors. And the Caledonians were her people.

There it was again. What is that? she wondered, stringing an arrow. A soft shuddering ... coming from somewhere in the hillocks. A horse? A stranger with a horse watching her? She thought she saw eyes glinting from behind a tree, but couldn't be sure. She stared at the spot, wondering, thinking, then glanced around, feeling uncertain. Get out of here, screamed every fiber in her body. Get out of here now! Leave the cup, leave the fire, just go!

Fear controlled her now. Cold, irrational fear. Still clutching the bow, she started toward her mount, and froze. A man emerged from the bush that covered one of the hillocks, a square-bodied man standing beside a dappled-gray stallion.

Neeve breathed out in relief. A Roman. The one with the crushed head. Something about him troubled her, but at least he was Roman, trained from birth to obey superior officers.

"Hail Caesar," she called, tilting her bow downward, as if she were unconcerned.

He led his horse toward her, saying nothing.

"You're the officer I saw earlier today. Where are the soldiers?"

He snorted and continued toward her, walking in a stiff-legged fashion.

Fear morphed into near panic and Neeve spoke loudly to give the impression of authority, "I am under orders from Prefect Vectis Trebellius, chief officer of the five outposts, to map this sector."

He stopped thirty feet from her. His brutish face twisted in rage. "Prefect Trebellius is dead!"

The thunderous outburst shocked Neeve, and frightened her. She tried to maintain an outward calm as she cast her eyes around for an avenue of escape. There was none. She had waited too long. By the time she mounted her horse, he'd be on her. She looked back at him. Never had she seen such hate. His bull neck bulged in anger, and the scars on his crushed face flared purple.

"The engineers are with me in this sector," she said desperately. "We were about to leave." She looked around as if expecting them to arrive any moment.

"Take off your clothes, girl. Let's make this easy."

"The tribune at Faustina, Julian Quintillius, has given orders for my protection." She tried to sound in control. "They will whip you in the parade ground if—"

He laughed harshly. "You stinking whore. I've already been whipped."

Neeve raised her bow.

He ducked behind his horse and yanked his shield from its leather case. His legs moved awkwardly, as though in pain. Probably from the whipping, if he was telling the truth. Neeve racked her mind trying to figure out why a Roman officer would rape her when he knew she was protected by the outpost command. Even if Prefect Vectis were dead, it made no sense for this brute to molest her when she would surely report him.

Cold fear swept over her. He intended to kill her. Rape and kill her. She inched toward her mount, keeping her bow leveled in his direction. "I am leaving," she said, "and will say nothing about this incident. I will—"

He burst across the grass, crouched, shield covering almost his entire body.

A soft cry escaped her lips as she stepped backward. Her mouth went dry and panic seized her like the jaws of a reptile. She looked desperately for an opening to launch her arrow, then loosed it with no thought of its direction. It passed silently over the shield, landing somewhere in the grass. The next second he hit her, the boss of his shield crashing into her chest, knocking her to the ground.

He was on top of her, shrieking and cursing like a madman. Her head felt as if it were spinning in giant circles. She tried to sit up but fell back in a dizzying faint. As her world stopped reeling, she realized that his legs were straddling her waist and his back was arched in a curiously erect position, as if he were trying to gain control of pain.

She reached for the knife on her hip. It was gone, knocked free in her tumble. Suddenly, he pushed down onto her, his weight crushing the breath from her lungs. She felt his heavy lips and rough beard sliding back and forth across her mouth, and his hand kneading her breasts. She tried to move her head to breathe, but one of his hands gripped her hair and held her fast. He kept rubbing his mouth on hers, his cheek pressed tightly against her nose. She gasped for air, twisting and pushing against his bulk. Air, her body screamed for air! She clamped her teeth on his lower lip, and ripped savagely like an animal.

He squealed pig-like, and jerked her hair backwards until she thought her neck would break. "You want to bite? Eh?" Blood and saliva dribbled from his lips as he pressed his face into hers.

She smelled the foul odor of his breath and heard herself pleading in a tiny voice, "I'm sorry, I'm sorry, please, I'll be good. Please." As if she were outside her body and looking down on another woman, she felt humiliated by what she saw.

He leaned back and laughed. "You'd better be good. Or I'll snap your pretty neck." With that, he grabbed her tunic and ripped it down the middle, exposing her breasts.

Neeve reached up with her arms. "I'll be good," she said. "Don't hurt me."

He sucked at his torn lip and smiled, anticipating the pleasure.

He intends to kill me, she thought, as she felt his hands groping for her trouser belt. She moaned, and drew her legs up, then reached for the knife strapped above her right ankle. She felt the thick handle filling her palm, and intense power as she pulled it back and slammed all six inches of the blade into his thigh. For a moment he continued fumbling with her belt, as if nothing had happened. She ripped the knife out, intending to plunge it into his back. In that instant his voice rasped out a guttural sound, and he flung an arm outward, knocking her hand away, and sending the knife spinning. He clubbed her in the head with his fist. And again.

Neeve fought the wave of darkness that rolled over her, threatening to entomb her forever. Was this how she would die, raped and beaten by a Roman animal? No! No! No! She bolted upward and thrust her hands under his tunic, raking his back with her nails. Chunks of flesh filled her hands. He shrieked and twisted like a rat in a fire. Neeve pulled away and scrambled crab-like across the grass, whipping her head around, looking for somewhere to run. The horse! She saw her horse and started toward it.

A hand grabbed her legs, spilling her face down on the grass. She screamed and wrenched her ankles loose. Only no hand had hold of her legs; she had tripped over her trousers. Somehow the man had unhooked her belt clasp, and pulled her trousers to her knees. He was still on the opposite side of the camp, howling, and trying to keep his tunic from sticking to his back. She turned away, clutched the top band of her trousers, and hobbled toward the horse.

Hours had passed since they banished Kallias from the fort. Vectis paced the oak floor of his office, thinking about the situation he had created by his lack of control. The guards had returned from escorting Kallias, and now Vectis could proceed with his plan—if you could call it a plan. He had decided to kill the filthy Greek. Somewhere along the arterial road, he would find him and kill him.

A knock at the door.

Julian entered. And Jupiter.

"I've told him everything," Julian said, "about Kallias in North Africa, Vatinius's death ... and about this afternoon."

Vectis eyed Jupiter. "Then you know what I must do," he said. "It's a long way to the next outpost, Fort Stragenia. Kallias will stay the night—and tell Commander Priscianus that I humiliated him, that I disobeyed a senatorial edict, that I had him whipped. Priscianus will have no choice but to report it." He shook his head, amazed at his own audacity. A Roman emissary. Whipped!

"He's an impostor," Julian said.

"We don't know that," Vectis replied. "His papers might be legitimate. He called himself Kallias in North Africa, but his name could be Marcellus. He must have authority behind him or he would never have escaped execution in North Africa."

"Whatever his real name," Julian said, "we can't let him get to Stragenia. Once there, he will demand that Priscianus give him an escort to Legion XX beyond the Wall."

Vectis walked to the window slats that overlooked the stables. "I have ordered two horses. With a change of mounts I can overtake him before Stragenia—"

"That's why we're here," Julian said. "I have proposed to Jupiter that he take ten of his counter-insurgent unit—"

"Permission denied," Vectis said. "Kallias would almost certainly shout that he's a senatorial emissary."

"I will choose men who are loyal," Jupiter said.

"Whipping Kallias in front of soldiers is one thing, killing him is another. I won't place our men, loyal or not, in that position."

"Then permit me to go alone," Jupiter said.

Vectis shook his head. "I created the problem and I will solve it."

"Prefect," Jupiter said formally, "Our roads are safe during the day, but nighttime is another matter. I salute your penchant for taking risks, but alone on the road, you might never return to Faustina. You must remember that you are a prefect, not a common soldier. Even if you elude the Caledonians, you might find this Kallias fellow a formidable foe."

Vectis scowled. His pride wanted to speak about his own skill with a knife and sword. Controlling himself, he said, "After the whipping he got, I doubt he'll be at his best."

"At his best or not," Jupiter said, "when it comes to killing in the dark, I have years of experience. Besides, the outposts need your talents more than mine."

Vectis recognized the last comment as nothing more than a sop. He accepted it as gracefully as he could, knowing that the African centurion was right. From what his father had told him about Jupiter's days as a marauder, no one could match his stealth and cunning. Vectis had faith in his own abilities to prevent Kallias from reaching Fort Stragenia, but with Jupiter, he knew it was as good as done.

Neeve's horse slowed and then stopped on the crest of a small hillock. "You tired?" she asked, patting the horse on the neck. She had been riding hard, trying to reach the relative safety of the arterial road, and she knew her mount was exhausted. What she needed was one of Jupiter's patrols. She scanned the grassy slopes dotted with rocks and heather for help, and for signs of the brute Roman. He was following her, she knew, but with his heavier weight and painful injuries, he had fallen back.

"Not long now," she murmured into her horse's ear.

The gods had truly sheltered her with their wings. She whispered thanks to Nemetona, the Celtic goddess of war. Apart from bruising on her forehead where the Roman had struck her, her body seemed intact. At first she had simply headed the way the horse was pointed—anything to get away—but now she was circling in a wide arc toward the Roman road. She tightened the cloth bindings, securing her ripped tunic, and swept her eyes over the sloping grasslands again. Satisfied that she was in no immediate danger, Neeve turned the horse around, and started down the hill.

Something was wrong.

The horse refused more than a few halting steps. She tapped its flanks with her heels, but it balked again. Neeve glanced around at the empty hills. She slid from her mount and ran her hand along its front leg. Heat on the shin. A sprain, a muscle tear, she couldn't be sure. She pressed lightly and the horse shuddered, and pulled away.

"Easy," Neeve crooned, rubbing the horse's nose. "A little rest and you'll be fine." She wondered whether the same would be true for her.

Neeve coaxed the horse to the bottom of the hill where she walked him, slowly at first, and then briskly. No limp. She climbed on his back and nudged him forward. He seemed fine on the flat. She pressed her knees into his side, hoping to ease him into a gentle trot. He stopped. He could walk, but resisted any attempt to increase his gait.

Neeve guessed she was about a mile from the road, and was deciding whether to abandon her mount, when she saw him. More to the point, he saw her. Her heart pounded as she stared at the outline of his thick body slumped sideways in the saddle, and moving through the hillocks at surprising speed. She jammed her heels into the horse. He jerked forward, stumbled, and then refused to move.

"No, no, no," she kept saying to herself. She flicked the reins, moving the horse out at a walk. Too slow. He'd be on her before she got a hundred yards. She pulled up, her eyes darting around for a place of safety. Cold perspiration broke out on her forehead. A rock-field. She had to find a rock-field where his horse couldn't go. He was wounded. She could outrun him.

No rock-fields.

No rock-fields anywhere!

Trees! She squinted at a distant bluff stained orange by the falling sun. Maybe she could run to the trees and hide. She'd never make it. He'd chase her down. She imagined his thick fingers around her neck, and her mouth went dry. Useless hopes filled her mind: maybe the lameness was gone and her horse could run again. Think! she told herself; time was draining away. She had no knife. Only one bow to stop him. But what use was a bow when he had a shield?

"The gods are with me," she whispered in a trembling voice. Over and over again, she murmured her prayer. Today she would die, but she would not die easily. The gods were near. She felt their strength. She turned her horse around, loosened the thong holding her bow, and waited.

About twenty yards out, he slowed his horse to a walk. She could see his cruel eyes now. And his hog-like body, listing in the saddle. He was in pain.

"How's your back?" she asked, not caring how enraged he became. "And your leg?"

He stopped thirty feet from her. "I know you got a lame horse." He paused to let his words sink in. "Back there I would have just slit your throat, made it easy for you." He looked at the sun, muddy orange in the sky behind him. "Dark soon. That's when the wolves come out. After I finish with you, I'm roping you to a tree ... let the wolves have a taste."

The sound of his voice angered her. She would die, but he would get no pleasure. She would bite and kick and rip his back. She would pound his leg and claw his eyes. She would never give in. Never. And when the wolves came, she would endure the pain knowing that this Roman animal never got one scrap of satisfaction. She jerked her bow up and released the arrow. It smashed into the top corner of his shield that he hastily pulled across his body. She loosed another one. It sailed to the side. She could see the grimace that darkened his face each time he was forced to move. He might be hurt worse than she thought. Maybe when he dismounted she could get to his horse somehow —

He bolted forward, yelling and lashing his horse like a Scythian cavalry soldier. Neeve bit her lip, and drew her arrow back tightly to the corner of her mouth.

She groaned audibly.

No target.

He had given her no target; only his eyes peered over his shield, and it was not enough, not with her bow skills. The horse thundered toward her. Flecks of foam spattered its lips, and steam, like smoke, poured from its bulging nostrils. She stared at the powerful chest of the horse, its heavy muscles and pounding legs, and then lowered her bow.

The arrow struck above the muscle joint on the horse's left shoulder. Like a ceremonial animal, it dropped to the dirt, carrying the man with it. Kallias's head drove into the ground and the horse slammed into him, crushing his body.

Neeve's muscles tensed as she stared down at the man struggling to lift his head. She kept her bow trained on the back of his neck, uncertain what to do. Men like this were incapable of feelings. They fed on the terror they produced in others. They enjoyed watching others suffer. They deserved death. How many innocents had he brutalized? How many had pled for mercy and found none?

He was looking up now but couldn't focus his eyes. The fall had knocked out some teeth and his face was swelling rapidly. Neeve readied her bow but realized it would be foolish to leave him dead in the same sector where she had been mapping, where a scout or patrol could find his body. Her mission was to get information. She was posing as a mapmaker for one reason only—to get information—and now, if she killed a Roman officer, even one disciplined for misdeeds, she could jeopardize everything back at Fort Faustina. Better to leave him alive.

"Help me," the man moaned. "Can't move my legs, please help me."

"You deserve nothing," Neeve said, "nothing."

"Please, I ... I have gold. Help me sit up ... I'll die here. Find a scout to help me ... you can have the gold."

"I'll build you a fire, and send someone back, but you have to sit up yourself." She did not intend to get close to him ever again. She paused. Something looked wrong. His hand ... he had pushed it under his body, about where his dagger would be. He wanted to kill her! She was ready to help him, and he wanted revenge.

"You Roman pig!" she shouted, and shot an arrow into the center of his back. He shrieked and tried vainly to reach his hands around behind him to extract the arrow. Neeve could see the dagger now, lying a few feet from his body. She was taking no more chances. She shifted her weight on her mount, and put another one in him, this time at the top of his shoulder. And another, near the first. His body tightened as he gasped for air, then flattened onto the earth when he expelled his last breath.

Neeve watched him closely for signs of life. He lay face down in the dirt, not moving, not making a sound, not even opening his eyes. His arms were sprawled in front of him and his head was turned to the side. Neeve wondered if she should put another shaft in him to make certain he was dead, but the thought sickened her. If he wasn't dead now, he would be in moments. No one could survive such wounds.

She glanced at the dappled-gray, now twenty feet away. It was trying to stand. She could see it pushing with its front legs, its muscles trembling, until overcome by the strain, it wobbled and collapsed to the ground. Having no knife, she looked around for a suitable stone. One blow on the forehead would put the poor animal out of its misery, but everything was either too big or too small. She drew a handful of arrows from the quiver on her saddle, shoved them under her belt, and slid from her mount.

The gray was struggling again, as if it knew that to stay down meant death. Neeve spoke softly: "I won't let the wolves get you." She moved within arm's length and aimed carefully at the underside of its neck. The thought of killing such a beautiful animal bothered her, but she knew it had to be done. As the shaft drove in, the horse snorted and twisted, then toppled over on its side until it lay still, breathing softly. She had missed the artery, and in truth had not expected to kill the animal with a single shot, only prepare it for a sword thrust.

Neeve scanned the saddle. No sword. It must be on the underside, pinned. She walked around the horse and saw part of the blade sheath, and tried unsuccessfully to free the leather strappings. She dropped to her knees and tried pushing the horse, and then whistled, hoping to get the horse to lift up. Nothing worked. The horse was down and not about to move. Neeve pulled at the saddlebag, hoping to drag out the sword. It wouldn't budge. She tried a narrow, solitary bag, wresting one of the flaps open. She grabbed hold of it and tugged as hard as she could. It pulled free, spilling a treasure of coins.

Even in the fading light, the gold and silver shone richly, and Neeve knew she had stumbled on an incredible prize. The Roman was telling the truth! Not even for an instant had she believed him, but here it was, a king's treasure at her knees. If ever the Caledonian people needed Roman currency to buy weapons and food, it was now. The gods had brought her through this trial, and rewarded her. The picture of the Roman beast drooling over her and ripping at her clothing sickened her. No amount of money was worth the horror he had put her through. But at least some good had come from her revolting experience. Out of the putrefaction of dung sprang flowers, and from this day, many lives would be saved. The thought of handing such wealth to her brothers warmed her inside and soothed her mind. She scooped up the coins and dumped them back into the tube-shaped bag, then lugged them toward her own horse standing near the fallen Roman.

Neeve eyed him, his thick arms and fingers, his stubby ears and brutish face. She needed his dagger; it was the most humane way to end the stallion's suffering. Five or six steps would do it. Six quick steps and she could grab the dagger, and run. The Roman couldn't harm her now, not with three arrows protruding from his back. She ran her eyes over him again. It was silly, she knew, but something about his position bothered her. His arms seemed to have moved from when last she saw him. They seemed poised, like a cat ready to pounce. A sudden chill swept over her as his eyelids fluttered; or had she imagined they fluttered?

Her bow!

Near the dappled-gray. She dropped the saddlebag and backtracked, her eyes riveted on the Roman. The gray would have to wait. She snatched up her bow and fumbled with an arrow, trying to string it. It slipped from her fingers. She pulled another from her belt. It fell. Her fingers were trembling, her mind numb. He was alive! But he couldn't be alive. Not with three direct shots into his back. On her hands and knees she searched blindly for the arrows, still unable to take her eyes off her tormentor. She was losing control. Becoming witless. She ordered herself to be calm. Seconds passed as she composed herself, and then, collecting her arrows from the rocky soil, she moved softly toward the saddlebag, and the Roman.

Smudges of purple were darkening the clouds, and long shadows coiled behind every rock and bush. Neeve had made up her mind. To stay longer would be foolhardy. She would leave the stallion, leave the Roman, leave everything behind her, everything except the saddlebag. She couldn't abandon that, no matter what the danger.

The bag lay ten feet from the man's outstretched arms, which struck Neeve as frighteningly close, closer than she remembered. She licked her lips. The thought of being near the brute—even though her rational mind said he was dead—made her palms sweat. She stopped several feet from the bag, her heart racing and her imagination summoning all kinds of dreadful pictures. She raised her bow, took another step, and then paused.

The man was still, very still.

She glanced down at the bag.

Almost there.

A few more steps.

She shuffled closer, crouching, her eyes on the man. Gingerly, she took her right hand off the bow, and stretched out her fingers toward the bag.

Suddenly, his body tensed, his muscles bunched, and his head lifted up. He tried to shout something, but his voice choked off as he charged on all fours across the stretch of ground between them.

Neeve froze. She thought she had been ready, but she was not. Her bow and arrow had fallen away; she was defenseless.

The Roman looked like a broken-legged spider as he pitched and lurched toward her, the arrows in his body jerking back and forth, his huge torso scraping the ground, and his hands gripping the soil like claws. He twisted his head, and from his mouth came a repulsive gurgling sound. Neeve managed a few backward steps, but tripped and fell. She lay on her back, helpless.

He came to a shaky stop several feet from her. His left leg dragged, and with each breath, blood bubbled from his mouth. He rotated his head and looked straight at her. His breathing was coming hard now as his eyes swept over her body, and past. Then, craning his head, he listened.

He didn't see her! He had looked directly at her and he hadn't seen her. Could he be blind? Could the fall have blinded him? Neeve lay as still as death, watching his every move. He sucked in his breath and tried to cough, but a profusion of blood spilled from his lips, choking him. Pulling himself together, he stiffened, and again listened. Neeve reached for a pebble, cautiously, afraid that even the slightest movement of her arm would alert him. It didn't. She threw the stone to his far side, where it landed softly in a clump of grass.

His head whipped around and his sightless eyes stared in the direction of the sound. Then, with a sudden burst of energy, he bolted toward the place where the sound had come from.

Neeve scrambled to her feet, knowing that his movements would obscure her own. She hefted the saddlebag over her shoulder and hurried to her horse. Behind her the man had stopped his jerky assault. He was listening again, trying to fix on her position. Neeve looped the straps through the iron collar on her saddle, ran as lightly as she could to the front of her horse, and grabbed the reins.

She tugged, but he wouldn't move.

"You'll be all right," she said quietly, and nuzzled her face into his. The sound of her voice sent the man into a rage and he charged along the ground, circling, unsure where to go. Neeve forced herself to be calm and whispered soothing words into her horse's ear, all the while tugging gently on the reins. Finally, the horse moved and followed her slowly away from the river, toward the safety of the grasslands that lay in the distance beyond a series of low hills. As she rounded the first hillock, Neeve glanced back for a final look. All she saw were purple shadows. The man and the dappled-gray blended into the darkening landscape as if they were permanent features of the land.

Neeve was more than a half-mile away when darkness fell. But above the whispering of the wind, she could hear his screams; the wolves had come. Her only regret was that she had been unable to spare the stallion.

27

Neeve spent two days scouring the hills for her brothers. She purchased a fresh horse in one of the villages, and on the third morning found Taranis and Eston at a Caledonian training camp for new swordsmen. When Taranis heard about the emissary, he exploded in rage. Despite Neeve's insistence that the emissary was dead, Taranis sent warriors to the mapping sector with instructions to bring the emissary back alive so that he might exact his revenge. It was too late. What they found was a contingent of Roman soldiers poking at the half eaten-carcasses of the man and his horse.

"Scouts must have stumbled across the body and alerted a patrol," Eston said. "I'm worried that the Romans will connect Neeve to the emissary's death."

"That's not a concern if she remains with us."

"I'm close to getting the information we need," Neeve said.

"The information is good but the risks—"

"I'm willing to take the risks. Everyone takes risks."

"The Romans know where you were making maps," Taranis said. "It's too dangerous now."

Neeve saw herself back in the fields picking rocks. How could Taranis think it was too dangerous when for years he and Eston had risked their own lives? Well, she did not intend to trot dutifully back to the fields. Her work was important to Caledonia. "I'll say I was somewhere else," she said.

Taranis shook his head. "You checked off the sector in the map room before you left. Now an emissary is dead. If you lie about where you were they will think you are hiding something. Besides, those arrows of yours are specially made."

"All right! So they will know I killed the emissary. The man tried to rape me! No one would suggest that I sought him out and killed him for his money. How would I know that he carried so much gold and silver?"

"Even if she did," Eston said, taking Neeve's side, "she could hardly expect to overwhelm a trained Roman soldier."

"Only a lunatic would think I planned this," Neeve said, overstating her case.

Taranis sat quietly and then said, "You say Faustina's prefect whipped the emissary for insubordination?"

Neeve's hopes soared. "The Romans themselves are probably glad to be rid of him."

Taranis frowned. "Still, he was a Roman emissary. And there is the matter of the saddlebag he carried. Would they have any idea of the amount?"

"They would expect him to have some coin."

"But not a saddle bag full."

"Not a saddle bag," she said, agreeing. "Only armed soldiers transfer large funds."

"Yet he had the coin."

Neeve looked at her brother and said, "The prefect would never have sent him out alone if he suspected he carried such wealth."

Taranis was puzzled. "Could he have stolen it from a fort? Not likely," he said, answering his own question. "Even emissaries from Rome wouldn't have easy access to the fort treasuries. He must have overseen the tax gatherers south of the Wall."

"And stolen it there," Neeve said.

"Then no one will be missing a bag of coins," Eston said.

"More importantly," Taranis said, "no one will suspect Neeve has stolen anything."

"I could take some coinage back," Neeve said in a thoughtful tone. "I know this prefect ... he places a high value on honesty. Already he wants to trust me, I'm sure of it. He just needs a reason to restrain his natural caution in dealing with Celts. I think this is the moment. Already I've been in his office, and soon I hope to see Outpost Faustina's records."

"Don't be too eager. That's how mistakes are made."

Neeve nodded, trying to assure Taranis she would take the utmost care. In truth, she did intend to be doubly careful. The prefect was a suspicious type.

"Well," Taranis said, with a clear lack of enthusiasm, "we will put a handful of coins in a pouch. If, by chance, someone does suspect that the Roman had a saddlebag filled with gold, he will assume that the emissary became nervous and hid it somewhere, intending to retrieve it later when properly escorted. It should be obvious to everyone that, had Neeve found such a treasure, she would not be reporting for mapmaking duty."

"How likely is it that the emissary killed the prefect?" Eston asked.

"Not likely at all," Neeve said, "but it doesn't matter. The officer who would assume responsibility, a tribune named Julian Quintillius, trusts me more than the prefect does."

Her assurance had the opposite effect. Now Eston was repeating his brother's caution. The incident with the Roman emissary had shaken them, as it had her. She pledged again to be extremely careful.

"One last thing," Taranis said. "Avoid the dark centurion. He's different from other Romans ... and very dangerous."

The morning sun glinted off the gold-tiled roofs and stately columns across the forum. Already the hum of activity had begun, with charcoal cookers smoking, and vendors hawking fruit, roasted meats, and honeyed breads to the citizens rushing by. Scrubwomen, having wiped the night mist from the marble walkways and stairs, were gathering their towels in baskets, and at the base of the Rostra, rudely clad workers shoveled mortar into cracks that threatened the ancient podium. Here and there clusters of senators had gathered, some talking and laughing, some giving instructions to their fluttering aides.

Outside the bronzed Senate doors, Atilius listened to the complaints of three senior senators and a banker. A waste of time, he thought, as the banker prattled on about issues of no consequence. What did it matter whether the priests were demanding a few sesterces more for noon sacrifices, or whether an equestrian upstart, whom the senators were now denouncing, had been caught wearing the senatorial broad stripe? The Empire was in shambles! Barbarians testing the borders everywhere! He sighed inwardly. Powerful men could get exercised about the most inane things.

He was beyond them, he knew, and not because he was the overwhelming favorite for consul this year. As lofty a station as consul might be, he disdained such honors. The stars in their courses had determined something far greater for Atilius Titianus. His destiny was to rule. He would be Caesar, or gladly yield his neck to the sword. His calling was to change the face of the Empire, under the guidance and protection of the gods.

His eyes drifted to the people milling below on the ancient forum, and he wondered what had become of Balbinus. His question was soon answered. On the far side of the plaza, he caught sight of his corpulent aide, plowing through the rapidly building crowds. Atilius excused himself, and descended the glossy marble steps to the forum floor. No sense in having Balbinus collapse at the top of the stairs, and besides, privacy was better achieved in the din of the crowds, not under the prying eyes of meddling senators. He watched Balbinus navigating his way around a band of smiling financiers who were shamelessly trying to lighten the purses of overly blessed Syrian merchants. Rome always welcomed investors.

"A morning from the gods," Atilius called to his aide.

"The gods bring fair skies," Balbinus replied, breathless, "but not good news, I'm afraid." He frowned. "Old Trebellius will not be addressing the Senate again. His strength is spent and his words come in whispers. I doubt he will last the week."

Atilius grimaced. He knew the old centurion was near the end, but he had hoped to use him one more time. He contemplated the defeated posture of his aide. "All is not lost," he said. "True, I would have liked a word from Trebellius about the dangers of our weak policy in northern Britannia, but dying testimonies have their place too."

Balbinus looked puzzled, then smiled. "A testimony that we will provide. Yes, I understand. An excellent idea. With Vectis at the most distant outpost, it would be natural for Trebellius to think of his son at the last."

"And of Britannia."

"True. Perhaps a comment about the foolishness of Emperor Antoninus building his Wall?"

"Yes," Atilius mused, "but a prophetic comment. Prophecy takes wings while truth lies bound on the ground." He glanced at a ragged boy, probably a thief, darting behind the Castor Temple with three Vigiles, Rome's police, in dogged pursuit. Another sign of Rome's decline, he thought. He dragged his mind back to business. "The moment Trebellius dies I want it spread about that ... ah ... when asked about Antoninus' Wall, Trebellius's dying words were: 'To the land of shadows I must go, and my son will soon follow. A curse be on Antoninus and his Wall. Already they are melting into the earth.'"

"That will set Rome buzzing."

"See that it does. And when your aides spread the tale, have them add that I was furious with you for having allowed the servants to reveal Trebellius's dying words. You will say Senator Atilius Titianus finds it unseemly that some are using Trebellius's dying words to embarrass the Emperor over his failed policy in Britannia."

"It will be done, Senator. Throughout the discussions, I will make certain the gossip centers on the enormous waste of Rome's coffers in maintaining a doomed Wall."

"Very good."

"I will also subtly remind people of your long-standing predictions that Antoninus' capricious Wall would fail."

"Yes, my predictions," Atilius murmured to himself. He had been young then, but he had indeed predicted that a second Wall would fail. At first, it had been merely political expediency to gain him stature in the Senate, an issue on which he could plant his sword, but again the gods had smiled on his efforts. As it turned out, he had been right. Rome should have invested heavily in one massive troop expenditure, taken the island, and controlled it the way they had Gallia. Then, as the years rolled by, Roman influence would have transformed these Caledonian barbarians into model citizens, and an enduring peace would have been built. But such logic was lost on the timid Antoninus. He would rather muddle along until the Empire crumbled, or until someone grew weary of his incompetence and removed him from power.

Fortunately for Rome, Antoninus' tenure as Emperor would soon be curtailed.

Neeve averted her eyes from the slender, unmarked document lying on the Prefect Vectis Trebellius's table. She knew what it was. Yesterday she had seen Julian with it in the back room, and from his conversation with Vectis, she guessed it had to do with troop numbers at the various forts. It was a most valuable document.

Satisfaction filled her as she thought about the preceding weeks, and how she had wended her way into the prefect's confidence. She had gained his trust, and with it, pieces of information vital to the Caledonian war effort. Prefect Vectis had become careless. He was treating her like a pretty mapmaker with no higher aspiration than to curry favor with the great conquerors of Britannia. A humble, awestruck maid was what they liked. Act properly and the masters might dust a table crumb your way.

She smiled at him; he was still talking.

He obviously enjoyed her company. Almost every day when she was not out mapping, he found some reason to meet with her, and often they would talk in the central office. Oh, he tested her at first, leaving documents on his table marked "Urgent" or "Outpost Strategy" to see if she would glance at the titles, revealing her ability to read. She never did. And when he slipped out for a few minutes, she never touched the documents. She was afraid he might have marked them with a hair, or flour dust, or the tiniest fluff of goose down. She didn't know whether he did, but she was not about to nibble the bait.

After those first weeks, he seemed satisfied with her honesty, and at times even left her unattended while he trotted off to perform some duty or other. That's when she found the supply schedule for the five outposts, and days later, the shipment notice of horses to Colania, which Taranis and his warriors promptly intercepted.

She shifted on the couch, keeping the troop document out of her line of vision. The temptation to stare at the brown folder was an enormous burden. He was still talking about the troubles he was having with the other forts and querying her every so often to make certain he wasn't boring her. She nodded politely, as if she were hanging on every word, then tried to steer him into areas beneficial to her information-gathering task. She'd never realized—even after living in Londinium, a city thick with legionaries—how much dissension existed among Roman officers. It bode well for the Caledonian cause.

An orderly brought them each a cup of hot tea. She could feel the prefect's eyes on her as she stared silently into her cup, sipping the brew. She glanced up and smiled again. No doubt about it, he liked her—liked her and now trusted her. She could see it in his eyes. Of course, she couldn't take credit for everything. A large part of that newfound trust had grown out of her terrifying encounter with the Roman emissary. The prefect never explicitly said he felt responsible (having released the emissary hours before), but his efforts to make up for the mistake were noticeable, not only to her, but to everyone.

On the parade square, with scores of soldiers and officers present, he had formally honored her for her bravery and honesty in returning Imperial moneys. Her decision to bring back a handful of coins had won her great favor. Faustina's officers were astonished that a non-Roman worker would return such a prize, and Vectis instructed that a gold *aureus* be marked beside her name in the monthly wage ledger, recognition of her honorable behavior in returning the pouch of money. No one seemed to notice or care that she had given no explanation about being absent for two extra days.

Soon after, Julian informed her of other changes. He kept the conversation business-like, pointing out that Faustina's officers had noted her exemplary conduct as a Roman worker. Accordingly, she would be moved to a large guest room reserved for visiting dignitaries. She also would have exclusive use of the baths in the late afternoon when the soldiers had finished, and could order special meals from the camp kitchen. She was even offered a clerical position in the fort to ensure her safety. This last benefit she declined. With supply and patrol schedules now being changed weekly, she needed an excuse to leave the fort.

The movement of the brown folder interrupted her thoughts. Vectis had it in his hand now, squaring it to the end of the table. He liked things tidy.

"Neeve," he said, straightening a box of styluses to match the rectangular frame of the ink jar, "I intend to talk personally with the outpost commanders in the month of Ianuarius, before winter sets in. Along the way, I might need an interpreter, and your language skills have improved dramatically. Would you consider coming along?"

It was a priceless opportunity to examine the other forts. She sipped her tea and said coyly, "I would like to visit Fort Colania."

He laughed. "You mean you want to meet Commander Commodus."

"I do not believe there is a Commander Commodus, at least, not ... like you say."

"I hear he is actively seeking a wife," the prefect said, "a tall, Celtic wife."

"I am tall," Neeve said agreeably.

"Then you will come?"

"You pay me mapmaking rate?"

"Much more. Interpreters are valuable."

"Hmmm," she said as though deep in thought. "More pay, I maybe get rich Roman husband ... yes, I will come."

A clerk at the door interrupted their conversation. The supply officer needed Vectis to sort out some confusion on the other side of the post. With the Caledonians intercepting more and more of the supplies, shortages had become a daily nuisance. Neeve rose to leave, but when asked to await his return, she put up little resistance.

She watched from the window until the prefect had veered off main street, then picked up the folder and slipped out the document. Her breath caught in her throat. On just three pages, running from east to west, were the exact number and kind of soldier in every fort and fortlet along the entire length of Antoninus' Wall. She studied it briefly and replaced it. So much data. How could she memorize it? Obviously, she could not. She mulled over the problem as she wandered toward the window to check for the prefect. Taking the document was out of the question, and Taranis had warned her never to copy anything. Yet the information was critical, so critical it was worth the risk. She made a decision: she would copy it.

With her back to the door and the document half out of its case, she took a clean papyrus sheet and pulled the wax sealer from the ink jar. She stirred a few drops of water into the black, gummy mixture. Then, rapidly, she scrawled the abbreviated names of the first three forts, and across from them, the numbers of auxiliary soldiers.

Voices outside.

Neeve froze.

The prefect was coming down the hallway.

She reached for the document case.

The door opened behind her.

He stopped just inside the room.

"What are you doing?" the prefect asked. Neeve tried to think. She was caught. Taranis had warned her and she hadn't listened. Now they would execute her as a Caledonian spy.

She forced a laugh. "A secret," she replied, and pushed the bottom half of the troop document back into its case. Furiously, she scribbled across the page, trying to turn the names and numbers into pictures of faces and working tools. Around them she slashed a box cart, the kind with the big wheels that Roman work details used. She had begun to sketch a man pulling the cart when he stepped in front of the table.

"No, no," she said, trying to sound lighthearted, "not ready yet." She bent over the drawing to obscure his view, and touched up the numbers to make them appear more like men's faces in a cart.

"Neeve, let me see what you're doing."

She kept working. "Almost finished."

"Neeve, please!" He pulled the sheet away.

"Prefect is so impatient," she scolded him lightly.

He studied the picture and then asked, "What is this?"

"It is not so good," she replied, giving him an apologetic look. "The picture is you ... pulling the whole fort and people and everything. You work too much and need rest. I thought maybe we—" she dropped her eyes in modesty, "maybe we might walk along the river. I know a pretty place."

He looked back at the picture. "I would like that. Perhaps another day."

From the corner window of his office, Vectis watched Neeve as she prepared to leave on another mapping assignment. Always another mapping assignment. This time she was going north, which concerned Vectis. Already they had lost one of the new army mapmakers in a northern sector. It mattered little that he had offered her prime duties within the safety of the fort. Most non-Roman workers begged for jobs like that. But Neeve insisted on leaving the fort, saying that she thrived on drawing maps. If the recently arrived mapmakers were mapping the northern sectors, so would she.

Three weeks had passed since her unfortunate encounter with Kallias, three weeks, he must admit, of surprising joy as he grew closer to this fascinating woman of the north. But behind her smile and overt ways Vectis found a void he couldn't quite identify. At times he was tempted to tell her about the slave girl with the penetrating eyes that she so closely resembled, the girl who still called to him from the faded fringes of his mind. But always he sensed a distance, and he wondered whether he would ever truly know the real Neeve mapmaker.

She had finished talking to the gatehouse guards and was now moving back to her horse. A soldier good-naturedly flipped a pebble over her shoulder, striking her horse on the flank and making him flinch. She said something in reply that made him and the other guards laugh heartily. Everyone liked her, he thought; she was so at ease with all types of people. A remarkable woman. And a quick learner. Her progress in speaking the Roman language was astounding, and it pleased him deeply. He watched the gates open and close, and Neeve was gone.

Immediately Vectis left the office, crossed the parade square and turned down a narrow passageway that intersected with the next broad way. At the corner he entered a large, sparsely furnished room—the mapmaker's sleeping quarters.

The living space was darker than he had expected, with pine-slab walls and slit windows. To the left of the door stood an upright loom with balls of wool fastened to the top support, and thread hanging down, and clay loom weights hanging even lower. In the center she had placed her army supplied bed and wooden storage trunk. Tiny oil lamps with blackened spouts sat on iron shelves in three of the corners, and in the fourth were piled balls of yarn and the woven squares of cloth from her loom. Evidently, she was concerned about having an open flame near the combustible wool.

Vectis knew what he had to do. He headed straight for the wooden trunk at the foot of the bed and removed the lid. Meticulously, he searched through Neeve's clothing and two soft leather bags that contained her personal items, all the while taking care to fold and replace things exactly as he found them. If she were a spy, he would soon find out. A Celt had fooled him once. But never again.

He snorted to himself, realizing how foolishly he was acting. Why would a Roman prefect poke through the belongings of a non-Roman worker? He should have ordered a room inspection. But then … others would think he distrusted the mapmaker. He didn't distrust her, not really. After the incident with her brother, he naturally sent scouts to follow her on her mapping assignments from time to time. But checking on the working habits of non-Roman personnel was one thing; searching their rooms was another.

Yet it had to be done. He was the arm of Rome in Britannia, and the safety of the fort was paramount. He thought about the recent problems the outposts were having with the Caledonians. They were devastating the supply trains. Even varying the times of shipments and using decoys had little effect on the enemy's ability to intercept the carts. They seemed to know which trains carried supplies, and which did not. Vectis had been forced to shift more soldiers to escort duty, leaving other areas unprotected. Jupiter was right. The

Caledonians had been too fortunate of late; there was a spy under the table somewhere. Vectis knew his duty. He must investigate every avenue of exposure, from Roman officials to couriers to non-Roman workers. And that included *every* non-Roman with access to high-level information.

From his earliest days in school, he had learned that non-Romans were the gates through which disaster flowed. And Celts were liars from birth. Outsiders, he had been told a hundred times, must earn a Roman's trust. So here he was, rummaging through the belongings of Neeve mapmaker, hoping that his trust was not misplaced. He cast his eyes around the room, looking for suspicious objects. He examined the floor and ceiling for hiding spots. Everything was as it should be. He squeezed her feather pillow for hidden objects, then removed each woolen blanket separately, and inspected the straw mattress.

Nothing.

Under the cot he found a narrow box and a woolen wrap. He opened the wrap and discovered an odd looking doll that rolled out into six attached dolls, a father and mother and four smaller children. It was very old, and frayed, and the edging had been stitched countless times through the years. Sewn into three of the dolls, the mother, the father and one of the children, Vectis found the sliver of a new moon, indicating perhaps that three of her family had died long ago while she was a child. He returned the doll gently to its woolen wrap, not wanting to damage an obviously precious keepsake.

The box contained several reed pens, a well of lampblack ink, drawing chalk, four old Roman maps, and copies Neeve had made of them. Apparently, she had used the maps to practice Roman map-drawing techniques. She also had sketched people and scenes around the fort. They were surprisingly lifelike. One of Jupiter gave the centurion a menacing look as his thick fingers pointed toward a group of soldiers exercising in the square. She captured him just right, Vectis thought. The next one had a smiling Julian stretched out on the grassy incline of the turf walls, talking to three women. And she had sketched several drawings of Rome, complete with towers and jeweled gates, and gods floating above the city. Vectis smiled. There was no way to persuade her of the truth. She would always have these illusions about Rome.

And then he saw himself. He and Neeve were sitting on the grassy bank of a river, watching the water flow by. Vectis felt strangely warmed as he stared at the drawing. A simple scene: she with her head resting on his shoulder, he with his arm holding her close. In her hand was a single flower with several petals missing. He drank in the imaginary scene. Then, abruptly, he returned the drawing to its place. He felt like the intruder he was. These were the private thoughts of Neeve, and for him to be pawing through her things struck him as somehow vulgar, like a man spying on a woman through a chink in the wall. Hastily, he leafed through the rest of the papers, forcing himself to be professional about his mission.

He found only one item of significance, and it reinforced his trust in her. Near the bottom of the stack lay a single square of papyrus on which Neeve had been practicing her name.

28

After leaving Faustina, Neeve traveled north for over an hour before turning west to find her brothers. She had more supply train information. As a precaution she always headed straight for her designated sector, even though she had not been followed since the early days of Prefect Vectis's tenure. Suspect everyone and everything, Taranis had said; it was the key to survival.

Now, back in the northern territory, she sketched the terrain as fast as she could. With all the detours required of her, little time remained to complete her assigned task—drawing maps. The morning air was crisp and cool, and Neeve paused to watch a young stag lope across a moss-covered moor, moving from one sheltering wood to another.

She understood its desire to seek refuge in the forest; at Faustina Neeve felt equally exposed, and sometimes wished she could ride into the hills and never stop. Of course, she had reason to be proud of her accomplishments, but if her brothers knew of her recklessness ... foolishly trying to copy a document. Well, they would not know because she would not tell them, and never again would she be so careless.

It was all the more foolish given the excessive measures she had taken not to arouse suspicion, even drawing pictures of Rome to demonstrate her simple imaginings. After leaving the prefect's office, she had hurried to her quarters and sketched a number of other drawings she hoped would promote the prefect's trust in her.

As she completed her sector map and slipped it into its leather case, she thought about the drawing of her and Vectis, and wondered why she had drawn it the way she did. When she left the prefect's office, she had intended to sketch them walking by a river, not huddled together, shutting out the world. Curious, she thought, how her drawings reflected her inner needs. She sometimes felt very alone, riding the silent moors, weaving cloth in her room, scrubbing at the empty baths. Her lifestyle provided sanctuary from the unpredictable queries of others, but it extracted a price. In her heart she cherished her times with the prefect, and enjoyed seeing him laugh and tell his stories about faraway places. He was Roman, but underneath, he seemed a decent man, not at all what she had expected. Maybe that's why she added the flower with missing petals—to remind herself that some relationships are doomed from the beginning.

Neeve led her horse down a steep grade and along a trickling creek that twisted and turned every few yards. The hills were covered with pine, scrub oak and feathery larch trees, but soon, she knew, the forest would give way to woodlands and easily traveled moors. Once in the lower expanses, she could ride east to the old Roman road and south to Faustina.

As she rounded a rocky knoll, she spotted a Caledonian training camp less than a mile away. It occupied the northern side of a hill, and trees on three sides screened its location. Anyone approaching from the south would surely pass it by.

She looked around anxiously, knowing she was in unfamiliar territory. Most of the Caledonian scouts in the regions adjacent to the five outposts recognized her on sight. They were unaware of her activities at the fort, but knew she was Taranis's sister, and could be trusted. Here it was different. The commanders would know who she was, but commanders didn't scout the forest looking for intruders. She changed course, leading her horse away from the creek. Better to skirt the camp than be found by an impassioned warrior bent on killing Caledonian enemies. If she were caught with maps, she might disappear as abruptly as the army mapmaker.

Traveling across the hilltops proved easier than leading her mount down the wooded slopes. Neeve followed an animal path that circled naturally around the Caledonian camp. She was beginning to relax when she saw movement in the trees below. A head turning or a branch pulled back—she didn't know, but something was out there. For a full minute she watched, hardly daring to move. A squirrel or fox? she wondered. She rubbed her horse's nose softly, trying to quiet him while she decided what to do.

The sun popped from the clouds, sprinkling patches of polished splendor, but the forest was still. Even the birds had grown silent, a clear warning of danger. Suddenly, a shape darted from the trees, up the hill, and veered off scant feet from her. A large buck, frightened enough to take an uphill route to escape danger.

Something definitely was down there. Now she could hear movement. Not a scout's stealthy steps, but a steady treading up the hill, on a broad front, and relentlessly toward her.

Hunters! A whole party. Probably from the training camp. Others would be above her, waiting for the buck to emerge. This was not a good place to be, she realized. It looked like she had been spying on the camp, taking gold from the Romans to betray her people. And if they found her maps ... the thought made her knees go weak. She knew what they did to spies—slashed their eyes and let them wander the forests as an example to others. Recently, they had started binding them to the tops of saplings that bowed under their weight, leaving the victims to dangle just beyond the snapping jaws of the wolves. As the night wore on, the sapling bent more and more until the wolves had their meal. Rarely did a tree wretch, as they were called, survive.

She tried to focus her thoughts, to think of a good reason she would be near the training camp, but nothing seemed convincing. Even if she called out that she was Taranis's sister and a Caledonian spy at Fort Faustina, they might still strike her down. Traitors always claimed to be on a secret mission for one of the commanders.

She had made up her mind. She would get past them to the safety of the camp. The commander would be her protection. Neeve led her horse over to where she would have a clear path down through the trees. Then, edging toward a mass of rock, she waited. At the bottom of the path, she heard twigs snapping, and saw the bushes trembling, and then, emerging from the dark leaves, a hunter.

"Hello!" she sang out in a nonthreatening voice. "Is anyone there?" The woods seemed to swallow her words, leaving an eerie silence. The hunter had disappeared. "Hello!" she shouted with more determination. "I'm up here, near the rocks."

The hunter moved. She could see him behind a lavender bush. He was ill prepared to find a woman and a horse in the middle of the woods. His shock was total.

Neeve seized the moment. "I'm looking for my husband. I was told he would be at the training camp." She did her best to giggle. "We have just been married! His name is Sencha. Do you know him?"

"Wait there!" The man did not sound friendly. He signaled something to the hunters on either side of him. "Are you alone?" he asked as he moved cautiously up the path. Neeve noticed that he kept his arrow taut in his bow.

"I'm alone," she replied, "except for my horse."

He approached slowly, and Neeve could see that two other hunters were scouting the surrounding area to make certain she was alone. "I don't know anyone named Sencha," he said as he neared. "What are you doing here?"

"I need to see the commander," she said, stepping on the ledge and swinging onto the back of her horse.

The hunter lunged for the reins.

She slapped the horse's rump and drove her heels into its side. The powerful animal bolted forward, knocking the man sideways. Down the sloping trail she flew, crashing past three other hunters who had remained at the base of the hill. Something burned into her upper arm, and she knew a hunting arrow had found her. She yanked on the reins and the horse veered into the protection of a stand of widely spaced pines. For several minutes she guided her horse through the trees, and down the next section of scrub woodlands, ignoring her throbbing arm. The thought of an arrow striking her exposed back made her shudder and spurred her on. In the trees she was safe.

As the woodlands flattened out, Neeve increased the pace, and for the first time looked down at the arrow protruding from the fleshy underside of her arm. Dark red blood had begun to dry in a long stain that stretched from the wound to her elbow. She touched the shaft and pain shot through her arm, which told her to leave the arrow alone until she reached the camp.

She turned forward again, and was instantly catapulted from her saddle. A hot flash exploded in her shoulder, and she lay on the ground, groaning. The sky spun crazily and her mouth drooled, as if she were about to throw up. She stared upward. A branch. A broken limb had caught her in the shoulder. She lay still, not wanting to move. The hunters! She could hear them yelling. She twisted to a sitting position, pushed herself up with her good arm, and hobbled to her horse. Fortunately, it had stopped a few feet away.

The voices grew louder. Neeve knew she had to get to the camp. She tried and failed to hoist herself onto the back of her mount. Her head dropped against the side of her horse, and she could feel its coarse hair on her forehead. "Too much," she heard herself saying. "Too much. I can't do it." She raised her eyes and saw men running on the hill above her and pointing in her direction. Panic seized her. She clutched the left front horn of her Roman saddle and gasped as she forced herself sideways over its hard edge. Then, with a sudden twist, and a blinding, shredding pain, she righted herself. "Go," she said, squeezing her knees and closing her eyes.

The Caledonians had planted their banner in the center of the training camp, a yellow square embossed with dark birds in flight. Neeve went limp with joy when she saw it. The commander was an older man named Eogan, a friend of her brothers, and someone Neeve had met many times. Moments later two warriors carried her into his tent.

Eogan examined the arrow wound himself and told her what she already knew. The arrow was deep and would be painful to remove. Then he inspected her rapidly swelling shoulder, grimaced, and shook his head. It was bad, he said, very bad. She would have to remain at the camp until she mended. Neeve refused, telling him that Faustina was the key to the war effort and she could mend there. He understood, but warned that the three miles to the Roman road would be punishing. Once there she would be on her own.

A Caledonian medicine man interrupted their conversation. He cut the arrow out with quick movements as Neeve clenched her teeth. Then he filled the wound with soothing mud that dulled the pain. Her collarbone, he said, was broken and protruding from her skin. It needed to be pulled into line. Again, Neeve refused. She could claim to have removed a Caledonian arrow herself, but hardly that she had set her own collarbone. He protested, assuring her that no one could tell whether a bone or a tree branch had punctured her skin. Neeve wasn't so sure. Roman doctors were not easily fooled. Besides, she reasoned, what better way to ensure the enemy's continued trust than to stagger back to the fort.

Once on the road, Neeve's brave words turned to dust in her mouth. Eogan was right. In her condition three miles was a long, agonizing journey. Even riding with a warrior who held her the entire way did little to ease the suffering that flooded her body. When they reached the road, the escort warriors were reluctant to leave her, and insisted they could deliver her to the fort gates without Roman scouts detecting them. They were skilled warriors and Neeve knew they could probably do as they said. But it wasn't worth the risk. The pain was intense, but she was not delirious and could manage. If the Romans saw Caledonian warriors helping her, the whole charade at Faustina would be over, and maybe even her life.

Waves of nausea rolled through Neeve. Her head ached, her back and shoulders ached, her whole body ached. Perspiration beaded on her forehead, although she was anything but warm. She kept her horse at a walking pace, but still, she seemed to jerk and bounce as he moved, and she was finding it difficult to stay in the saddle. An hour from the fort she saw two riders approaching at high speed; it was the dark-skinned centurion and a Scythian officer.

The centurion pulled her from the horse and laid her on the coarse grass by the roadside. He knelt beside her and said, "The scouts that reported you will be at the fort by now. A cart will be here soon."

Neeve nodded that she understood.

He examined the mud-smeared wounds. "I'll do this first," he growled, stripping the mud off her arm and washing it clean with a skin of water. "Never plaster wounds with mud. It creates fumes." His face darkened as he turned to her neck. "You've got a bone where it shouldn't be," he said. "It needs fixing. Are you ready for a little pain?"

"Do you know what you are doing?" Neeve whispered, trying to smile.

"I am a centurion. Centurions can fix anything." He poured water over the wound.

"Ahhh!" Pain seared her shoulder.

"Almost done," he said, placing one hand on her shoulder, the other on her neck.

She screamed. She knew she had screamed because she felt her body arch and the breath expel from her lungs. The centurion was spreading his cloak over her now, talking in a soothing voice, reassuring her that the worst was over. "You're a good soldier," she heard him say from far away. "Braver than most."

It didn't seem long until the cart arrived. She opened her eyes as if from a deep sleep. The Prefect Vectis was there, supervising her transfer from the ground to the straw-filled cart. They gave her something to drink—a foul tasting mixture of wine and myrrh—and covered her in a warm blanket.

Vectis was talking to her now. He was thankful the fates had spared her, he said, and assured her that soon she would be resting comfortably in the fort. Then he asked, "Who attacked you? Caledonians?"

Neeve tried to clear her mind. "Hunting party," she said. "I ... got away."

"Did they come from a training camp?"

Expecting this question, she replied truthfully, "Yes, a large one on a hillside."

"Where? Can you tell me where you saw it?"

"Not sure," she said, slurring her words and hoping to sound incoherent. In truth, she *was* feeling incoherent. The wine and myrrh were having an effect.

He persisted. "Concentrate. Was it in your sector? Above it? Below? Where?"

Neeve knew she had to give an answer. She gave him an approximate location, knowing there was little danger to Eogan and the Caledonian camp. Training camps commonly shifted locations in the event of enemy intrusions, and with their system of scouts, a large Roman force would be detected five miles away.

"How many warriors were in the camp?" It was the centurion's voice.

"I do not know ... too far away. Maybe three hundred."

"We might never have a better opportunity," she heard the prefect say to Jupiter. "With one blow we could put the fear of Rome in every Caledonian from here to the northern sea."

"I agree," the centurion said.

"Is the size of the camp a problem?"

"No. If there are too many, we will withdraw."

The prefect nodded. "Are your men ready?"

"We can be there by nightfall."

Neeve realized what the Romans intended to do. With their special soldiers, they would surprise Eogan in the night. But there would be no surprise. She had not given the precise location of the camp. They would tramp around in the woods until Caledonian scouts alerted the camp ... and then Eogan would destroy them. She felt a surge of guilt. Jupiter had allowed her to see his gentle side, and she rewarded him with death. She overheard him talking to the prefect again, complimenting her, and he rarely complimented anyone.

She opened her eyes and saw the powerful centurion leaning over the wooden rails of her cart. "When I come back in two days," he said, "I expect you to be practicing your bow, not resting in the surgery."

Neeve smiled, but inside felt soiled. He would not come back.

The gardens and walkways of Atilius's villa were thronged with the notables of Rome. Scores of servants wended their way through the crowds, tempting the guests with delicacies rarely seen in Rome: tongues of flamingoes, strips of Adriatic turbot wrapped in lettuce, livers of charfish garnished with sliced cherries and pomegranates, and everywhere, shouldered in heated baskets—fine Picenian biscuits. In the center of the garden stood an eight-foot block of Egyptian marble, graced at the top with a silver urn. Inside rested the ashes of Gaius Trebellius Quadratus, First Centurion of the premier legions of Rome.

Many of the guests extended their sympathies to Atilius, who stood with his back to the polished granite railing that swept along the broad central pathway and down to the pools and sculpted hedges of the lower gardens. On his right stood the bust of his favorite emperor, Trajan, the last true Caesar in Atilius's view, the last one to expand the territories of Rome. Now and then, a guest would stop to give a word of encouragement.

"A noble farewell," said one.

"A proud gathering," said another.

"May the fates be your support," said the visiting procurator of Cilicia. "I certainly am."

Atilius understood his message. He had received many in similar fashion this day, and he was gratified. Here before him was another powerful friend who would lend support, should Atilius seize the throne. He replied in kind. "I have always admired the Greek philosophers, especially Heraclitus who said, 'Life is an ever changing stream.'"

"How appropriate to quote Heraclitus on this occasion," the procurator said. "One never knows what changes the fates may bring."

Senator Alfenus Crescens was shuffling in his direction, with Balbinus supporting his right arm. He knew what was on the old senator's mind, and was prepared to deal with it. As Crescens crept closer, Atilius shook his head and wondered how his rotting, old body still functioned. He belonged in the tomb with Trebellius.

"Most noble Senator Crescens, the gods have favored me," Atilius said in greeting.

"Ah, there you are, Senator ... the good Senator ..." Crescens said, forgetting Atilius's name. Then, recovering, "You bring great honor on the house of Trebellius."

"An impoverished courtesy," Atilius replied. "He deserves more."

"One of our finest," Crescens said. "I remember him as a boy, you know. Remember him as a boy." His voice trailed off.

"You have lived a long life," Atilius said.

"Yes, a long life."

"Balbinus tells me—"

"I am the oldest living senator," he said, not realizing his interruption. "Sergius Gallienus is gone now. Died last winter, I was told. Of course, he hasn't lived in Rome for twenty years. The Island of Rhodes—that's where they all go now. Warmer there, the Island of Rhodes. Didn't help Gallienus, though. Gone now, died last winter—"

"Truly a shame," Atilius said. And then moving ahead, "Balbinus tells me you have a problem with one of your appointees."

He looked confused.

"In Britannia," Atilius added.

He sprang to life. "Not appointed by me!"

Atilius laughed. "I cannot remember half the appointments I make."

"I never appointed this ... this Marcellus fellow. A thief, that's what he is. Stole the Wall tax, I was told. Couldn't be a blooded Roman. Probably from the provinces."

Atilius was thankful he had taken the precaution of giving Kallias the name Helvius Marcellus. He had not expected the Druids to tell the Wall commanders about the reduced tribute. Now rumors abounded. Nobody knew whether the Druids were lying, or whether the Antonine sector's chief tax gatherer was a thief.

"You have no need for concern," Atilius said, "the man is dead. Killed by a Caledonian Celt."

"A Celt?"

"Even the Celts do righteous deeds," Atilius said.

Crescens didn't answer. He seemed lost in his own world of thought.

As the old senator left, Atilius was satisfied. Crescens would be quietly blamed for poor judgment in appointing an unproved tax collector, and the issue would be closed. Kallias was silent in his grave. His continued existence would have proved embarrassing for Atilius. The moment he had heard about the Druid complaints, he instructed Balbinus to have Kallias killed. Fortunately, the deed had already been done. It had been a difficult few weeks, but the gods had a way of favoring their own. Still, as the time drew near, he would need to be more careful.

Balbinus intruded on his thoughts. "The arrangements," he said, gesturing, "you have said nothing about them. Are they satisfactory?"

Atilius swept his eyes over the tiered gardens filled with the powerful of Rome. "Half the Senate is here," he mused. "A pity our Emperor was unable to come."

"Yes," Balbinus said, suppressing a grin. "Some say he was upset with the dying words of the noble Trebellius."

"Unfortunate," Atilius replied, "but the dying have no fear of speaking the truth."

They stood for a moment longer, until Atilius judged his aide had waited long enough. He enjoyed controlling situations like these, but he also believed in lavishing praise where it was due. "Balbinus," he said, placing a hand on his shoulder, "you have done splendidly. Your idea of having a statue of Trebellius carved for his tomb was excellent, but bringing the block of marble here to symbolize his strength and power is nothing short of genius. Do you know how many comments I have received?"

Balbinus bubbled his thanks for underwriting the expense.

"Placing his tomb on the Appian Way is not a cobbler's wage," Atilius acknowledged. "Old Trebellius demands more of me in death than he did in life."

"It's his revenge," Balbinus tittered.

"These past months have tried my strength," Atilius said solemnly. "First, my beloved Sabina. And now the elder Trebellius. A heavy mantle for anyone."

"You have borne it well."

"I am pleased with both funerals," Atilius said, allowing his eyes to drift across the faces of the people congregated in the gardens. "This public gathering for Trebellius is superb, and as for Sabina, it was the right touch. A small setting appropriate to the tragic occasion. Everyone talked about my need for privacy in the hour of my grief. I won many friends when I begged their forgiveness for not including them at the ceremony. They could see my loss was too weighty to be paraded publicly."

"It was a taxing day for you."

"I miss her deeply."

"I understand, Senator."

"Well, let us not dwell on the dark side of life," he said, rubbing his hands. "There is much to rejoice over, is there not?" Without waiting for a reply, he said, "You have completed the letter to Vectis?"

"I have. It expresses your sorrow over the loss of both Sabina and the elder Trebellius. Coming so close together as they did, the deaths have left you devastated, and you implore Vectis Trebellius to forgive you for being the bearer of such dark tidings. Naturally, I make him aware—discreetly—of the great expense you went to so his father might receive due honor. But the truly remarkable achievement of your letter, if I may say, is its subtle tones of emptiness and loneliness—which I know you feel. Yet you rise above your own personal anguish, knowing you have a higher calling in your service to Rome."

Atilius remained silent for a moment.

"Have I captured your feelings, Senator?"

"You have done well. Your words are like a glass reflecting my inner being, and even now the thought of such loss brings me pain."

"Perhaps a cup of wine."

"I would like that."

Balbinus signaled a winebearer, and the two sipped slowly, greeting others as they passed.

"Ah, Trajan!" came a familiar voice behind them. Atilius turned to see the hated Senator Titus Severus strolling down the central pathway, followed by several other senators who could not think for themselves. "The greatest conqueror of them all," Severus said as he gestured to the bust of Emperor Trajan.

"He was indeed," Atilius replied.

"A shame his ambitions of conquering the Parthian Empire drained the treasuries of Rome."

"If Emperor Hadrian had not given up the eastern provinces after Trajan's death, the Parthian treasury would now be in Rome's coffers."

"Perhaps," Severus said. "But then the fates cut Trajan's life short. A pity." He smirked. "Often that is what happens, is it not, when people become too ambitious? The fates cut them off." He cast his eyes around the garden and said, "Lovely gathering."

Atilius said nothing as Severus and his tiny knot of fools continued along the pathway. A day of reckoning was coming; Atilius could afford to wait. He turned to Balbinus and said, "We were talking about the letter."

"Yes," his aide replied. "I expect you will want it sent to Britannia by rapid couriers."

"No, I think not." He dropped his voice. "I want everyone, including the clever Senator Severus, to know of my affection for Vectis. Send the letter by Imperial courier, one that can be bribed. That way the whole Senate will be secretly reading my mail."

Balbinus moved closer to Atilius and said, "You were wise to have me monitor Trebellius's dispatches. A few days before his death he tried to send a scurrilous letter to Vectis. Without any evidence, the old man suggested you might have been involved in Sabina's death."

"He was an unreasonable man," Atilius said, "filled with hate." He paused to chat with several women who strolled by. Since Sabina's death he had become the most sought after man in Rome. Yes, he said to another cluster of well-wishers, losing old Trebellius was a blow to him as well as Rome. As Atilius spoke, he thought about his role in the Trebellius family. Here he was honoring a man who all his life had steadfastly refused to honor him, who poisoned his boy against him, and who even produced a daughter capable of betraying her own husband. It took depth of character not to be bitter.

Atilius again sipped his wine. "This Commander Commodus at Colania ... you say his letter confirms what Kallias had said?"

"Yes, he desperately wants to return to Rome. Your offer of a rich equestrianship has him slavering like a dog under the table."

"As well it should." He rolled the cup in his hands. "Perhaps Commodus might probe the other outpost commanders—cautiously, mind you—about whether they too might desire a well-endowed equestrianship in Rome."

"With the proviso that they vacate their outposts when Commander Commodus does?"

"Well," Atilius said, not wishing to deal in the unsavory aspects of politics, "things are moving nicely, I would say. I trust you are having no problems sending and receiving letters under Senator Crescens's name?"

"It has been quite easy, actually."

"Good. See that Commodus destroys every dispatch we send. I have great hopes for this man."

29

Neeve slept the entire first day at the fort. Her body seemed to have shut off its normal needs to concentrate on mending itself. Vectis had placed her in the spacious quarters he enjoyed as prefect, and for three days she lay healing in the broad wooden bed, waking only occasionally. A maid stationed outside the room tended to her needs, and the camp doctor, who came by twice a day, pronounced Jupiter's work first-rate, and Neeve on the fast road to recovery.

Vectis was relieved. How easily events might have been tragically otherwise. The thought of losing Neeve, of finding her body lifeless in the hills somewhere, was more painful than he could have imagined. He was to blame, totally and absolutely. As prefect, he knew the dangers lurking in the north, and when Julian reported a second army mapmaker overdue, he wasn't surprised. He couldn't justify sending escorts with the mapmakers, but no longer would he allow Neeve to map the northern territory—notwithstanding her protests.

On the afternoon of the third day, Vectis found her awake when he came by. Her face had regained its color, though not under her eyes, where the skin held stubbornly to its sallow hue.

"The maid told me this is your room," she said, lifting her hand feebly.

"The best place to care for you," Vectis said. "Better than the surgery."

"You are very kind."

"Nothing of the sort," he said, pulling an iron stool toward her bed and sitting. "A defender of Rome deserves this and more. Of course, even if you had done nothing meritorious I would have insisted they place you here."

"I do not understand."

Vectis glanced away awkwardly. He was attempting to tell her indirectly that she meant something to him, more than the sum total of her contributions to Rome. "I simply meant that you are important to this fort ... and to me, and I wanted you to have the best care possible."

"No, no," she said, oblivious to his halting admission of devotion, "you called me a defender of Rome."

"For helping Jupiter complete his mission. He would never have succeeded without your information. For such loyalty to the state," he said formally, "the prefect of the five outposts has awarded you a silver *denarius*. It has already been posted in the ledger."

"A silver *denarius*?"

Vectis smiled. "You'll be rich if you keep this up."

"Jupiter has returned to the fort?"

"Mission completed."

She looked unsettled. "The centurion is here? At the fort?"

"Is something wrong?"

"What did the centurion ... I mean, how did he ...?"

Vectis tried to calm her, telling her about Jupiter's success in the northern sector, but avoiding the grisly details.

She struggled forward and exclaimed, "They killed all the Caledonians!"

"Neeve, what's wrong?"

She flopped back and closed her eyes. "Nothing is wrong. I was afraid ... the centurion might be trapped in the woods."

Vectis understood her concern. She was not a soldier and had never sent men to their deaths. Because of her, Jupiter had been ordered out on a dangerous mission and she fully expected him to die. Now she was relieved. Vectis assured her that things had turned out well. Jupiter was not one to get trapped in the woods; he destroyed the enemy completely, from scout to commander. Their war banner of birds in flight now hung in the temple of Mithras at the end of the broad way.

Throughout the explanation Neeve lay motionless, eyes closed. From deep inside came a shuddering sound that reminded Vectis of a dying child. He slipped beside the bed and cradled her head, trying to comfort her. "You shouldn't have moved that shoulder so abruptly," he said. "Injuries like this take time."

"I know," she said, covering her face to hide the pain.

"Is it aching badly?"

"Yes, deep inside."

He brushed his lips against her hair. "I wish I could take the pain from you."

"Thank you." From behind her hands she said, "I am so ... amazed that such a small band of soldiers could destroy a large Caledonian camp."

"Jupiter is an amazing centurion," Vectis replied.

The next day Vectis found Neeve sitting up in bed, looking well. "This is a surprise," he said. "The shadows have vanished from your face."

"And I feel good too. I had barley soup, and a hot bath." She motioned to a copper tub still steaming on the floor in the adjacent room. "The maid helped me scrub."

"It's good to see you up."

"I wandered about your living quarters—I hope you do not mind—looking at your collection of horn cups, and odd little books. Can you read them?"

"I can the Latin and Greek ones," Vectis replied, "but not the Hebrew and Syriac." He stopped. She had no idea that different languages had different script.

"And that head on the pedestal—what is it?"

"A bust of Chiron," he answered agreeably, "the Greek god of wisdom. I keep it to remind me how dull-witted I can be. I bought it from a street vender in North Africa when I was a youth. He told me artisans had carved it from a rare marble mined deep in the Atlas

Mountains." He smiled to himself. "I paid a month's salary for the privilege of owning a cheap, plaster bust."

Her smile lighted the room.

"You do look better today," he said.

"With strapping to hold my arm firm, the surgeon says I can return to my quarters tomorrow."

"I'm happy for you."

"And Prefect is also happy to have his own room again, yes?"

"Call me Vectis. It's fitting after wearing my sleeping gown for four days."

She ran her fingers over the red soldier's tunic and smiled. "Yes, I shall call you Vectis. Thank you."

Such a nice smile, he thought, as he accepted her invitation to sit on the bed.

They talked about their families—his in Rome and hers in Votadina. The conversation was effortless until she mentioned that working at a Roman fort especially pleased her because she was able to earn Roman coin. To that Vectis responded,

"You might have kept the emissary's purse," Vectis said.

She looked at him. "Not all Celts are thieves and liars."

Her words were gentle, but Vectis couldn't help feeling the sting of rebuke. It was common knowledge what Romans thought of Celts—thieves and liars all. He tried to repair the damage. "I'm sorry, I did not mean—"

"No, please," she lowered her head, "it is I who must beg your forgiveness. Even we Celts know that the guilty despise the truth. And I am guilty." Then she talked at length about her brother—an awkward subject. She was sorry for having deceived Vectis. She realized he had been merciful, and as things turned out, her brother had found work in a Wall fort soon after leaving Faustina, hauling supplies. She touched his arm in a gesture of thanks, and the cool of her fingers warmed his heart.

The conversation continued along a comfortable path, and the hours fell away. After a time he helped her change positions, and remained seated on the foot of her bed. Then she asked, "Why is it that the dark centurion commands so much authority?"

Vectis laughed. "Because he is a god."

It was the wrong response. She really wanted to know. Vectis leaned against the wooden mast of the bed frame and explained that good centurions in the Roman army had far more power than their rank would suggest. He sketched his father's history, then Jupiter's, and not once during his commentary did she interrupt or avert her eyes. In fact, her face remained like stone, as if she were memorizing every word. Only when he told her about the African marauders and Jupiter's knowledge of terror warfare, did she register a trace of anxiety, but Jupiter had that effect on people.

He concluded with his own near death experience in the decimation, which drew a change of expression—compassion, he thought. He took the occasion to stress that her image of Rome was misinformed, that alongside good people were contemptible ones— like Kallias.

She stared at him with those eyes and said, "But not you. You ... you are a decent, compassionate Roman."

Vectis thought about her earlier, more rudimentary words, "You good Roman." He winced as he thought how suspicious he could be. Through his mind flitted the flaxen-haired slave girl from the *Via Lata*, watching him through the hewn rails of the stockade fence.

He knew he ought to tell her about the slave girl, but he couldn't. He was afraid, he supposed, that his confession would drive Neeve away. "I once bought a slave girl who looked like you," he imagined himself saying, "but she betrayed me, so I had her father killed and sold her to a work farm where she died soon after." No, he would not burden her with his confession just yet. Instead, he heard himself saying, "I am happy that you find me compassionate, but compassion often springs from less praiseworthy deeds in one's past. And the longer you live, the more you wish you had acted differently."

"I cannot imagine you doing ... horrible deeds."

"Sometimes the worst deeds are the deeds we leave undone." He shifted on the bed. "But I prefer not to talk about the evils of my life, especially when I am trying to impress you with my virtues."

"You are?"

"Certainly."

"Then I am very impressed with your virtues, Prefect."

"You are impressed with my virtues, *Vectis*."

"Yes, *Vectis*," she repeated slowly, looking him in the eyes.

It seemed as if she were seeing him for the first time. He smiled and said, "If your mapping missions continue to prove dangerous, we could become good friends. I will visit you in the surgery and then have you transferred here."

"And we can have these most enjoyable talks."

"It has been ... pleasant," he said, searching for the right word, "better than tending to fort business."

She smiled. "Better than fort business? I thought Roman officers never wasted time."

"We don't," he said, returning her smile. "But you are not a waste of time. Quite the opposite," he said seriously.

She bit her lower lip and gazed at him silently.

He wished he had said nothing. "You don't need to respond," he said.

She dropped her eyes. "I want to respond," she said in a whisper, "because I too enjoyed this afternoon." And then smoothing the covers around her waist, she shook her head. "I have said too much. It is all wrong."

"What could be wrong?"

She shook her head again as if to will the conversation away. "Such foolish things that come out of my mouth."

"I did not find your words foolish."

She sighed heavily. "I know, and I am so very sorry."

Vectis searched her face, trying to find a clue to her strange behavior.

She gave him the saddest smile. "We are so different, so vastly different."

"Neeve—"

"Please," she turned away, "I have spoken too much ...."

Vectis sat quietly on the edge of the bed, unsure what to say or do. He could hear her breathing at the other end. So near, yet so distant in some curious way. He couldn't leave the conversation hanging like this. He glanced up to find her staring at the empty wall and said, "We do have one thing in common."

She turned back.

"We share the same bed."

She seemed grateful for the frivolous comment. "The whole fort must be talking."

"They are. And speaking of the fort," he said, rising, "I must be about my duties. You rest. See that you vacate my sleeping quarters by tomorrow."

She responded in a gruff legionary voice, "Before the sixth hour, I shall be gone."

Taranis and Eston had just inspected several camps dedicated to the building of siege ramps, towers and covered ladders when they heard the shocking news.

Eston stared at Taranis. "The Romans took all the heads from the bodies? What would they do with them?"

"Probably bury them somewhere. They are trying to unsettle us."

"I have never heard of Romans taking heads."

"More important," Taranis said, "is how they managed to surprise and overcome an entire training camp."

"Eogan was a good commander. I find it hard to believe that he failed to post sufficient scouts."

"I agree. Most of the warriors were killed in their tents, so either Eogan posted too few scouts and even fewer camp guards, or—"

"Or what?"

"Or the Romans have a strike force capable of finding and eliminating Caledonian observers at night."

"Do you know what you're saying? Romans don't slip through the woods like Iceni trackers. They fight set battles."

"Yes, Romans fight set battles, but somehow they ...." Taranis grimaced. "There is only one Roman who does not look or act like a Roman."

"The dark-skinned centurion," Eston said.

"Neeve said she observed the centurion training soldiers to crawl through the woods with knives in their mouths."

"They are desperate. Sneaking out at night, taking heads."

"The Romans want us to feel nervous in our own camps," Taranis said. "But this time the gods are on our side. By summer all Rome's soldiers will be gone."

Neeve squinted into the brilliant morning sun and laughed triumphantly at Vectis, who rode beside her. "And you say the sun sleeps in Britannia!" Vectis grinned but offered nothing in his defense, which told Neeve that he enjoyed her little barbs.

Six mounted officers and a century of soldiers accompanied them on their tour of the outposts. Behind them came the carts filled with weapons and trench shovels and stockade materials in case of a prolonged attack, and finally came the Scythian archers, each with an extra mount. Eight scouts also accompanied the troop, and occasionally Neeve spotted them signaling to each other in the hills. The Romans traveled prepared, even on a brief tour of the outposts. Neeve was the official interpreter, though she doubted her services would be required. Over the past few weeks, she had again made a visible show of language study, improving little things, so she would no longer need to continue her time-consuming charade of studying the Roman tongue.

Late morning brought the first glimpses of Fort Stragenia, a chunky, turf garrison, about half the size of Faustina. Neeve had passed by it a dozen times but had never been inside. A mile out, the road descended into one of the many glens that typified the north country, and Stragenia dropped from view. Neeve glanced at Vectis, who was talking with a soldier, and she thought about how different he was from what she had expected. He was far more considerate than she would have imagined a Roman officer. She had stirrings of affection for the prefect—more than stirrings, if she were truthful. She knew she had crossed a dangerous line the moment she felt guilty about deceiving him. And her foolish admission that she enjoyed his company was simply irresponsible. What was the matter with her? Surely she could have responded some other way.

So far she had managed to suppress her emotions. He was a Roman officer, she continually told herself, bent on destroying the Caledonian people. The chains of oppression he and his kind brought shadowed any spark of decency he might possess. Her job was simple: win his confidence, and gather information. That was all there was to it. There was nothing more.

But it was not that simple. After her sojourn in his quarters, and her daily contact with him, she found it increasingly difficult to deny her feelings. She liked his straightforward manner, and the way he smiled and looked at her. Sometimes in their walks by the frozen river's edge—which had turned into a daily ritual—she would press close to him to shut out the biting winds. All this pretense, she thought. It was almost like love.

Love? It couldn't be. She would not allow it.

To enjoy someone's company was different from love, she told herself. At night in her room, she would squeeze her eyes tight and remind herself that love was never born of deceit, that theirs was a doomed relationship, that she had a higher responsibility to her brothers and Caledonia. But like a blind woman delighting in the sounds of a game she could never play, Neeve treasured those times with him, and refused to believe he was like other Romans.

He was gentle and understanding, and she had plenty of evidence. She could still see him bending over the cart rails, fluffing the straw around her and covering her body with wool blankets. How worried he had looked. Even with the black centurion and a contingent of soldiers looking on, he never hid his concern for her. He was not an evil man, not even an unkind man. As prefect, he could have demanded anything of her, but he never did. She could not deny it; there was something genuine about him, something warm and inviting.

Already she had kissed him. Not really a kiss, she reasoned, more like a token of deepening friendship. One evening as she was braiding fabric pieces from the loom, he knocked at her door. He had come to see how her shoulder was mending, and their time together had been undeniably pleasant. Selecting fabrics from her basket, he arranged them in maladroit patterns that made her laugh. Then he watched her work the loom, and helped her when the pain in her shoulder made it difficult to weave. Together they slid colorful weft threads into place by hand.

Later, as he was leaving, he looked at her in that haunted way he sometimes did, as if his mind were trapped in a distant place. She leaned forward and kissed him softly on the cheek, and he responded, kissing her along her ear. It was a tender moment, until a jolt shot through her shoulder and caused her to gasp. He stepped back and apologized for having bumped her arm. Glancing down at the binding on her left arm, she said, "It's not your fault. The Caledonians have put their curse on me. I am burning in pain." They both laughed.

Stragenia's towers emerged again as the road climbed the other side of the glen. Neeve's shoulder had healed by now and she felt no pain as she stretched in the saddle. It had been a long ride. Ahead she could see the cluttered tents and shacks that dotted the riverbank near the fort. The followers were well represented everywhere, it seemed.

Inside the gates, Neeve felt the cold efficiency of a well-run Roman fort, with soldiers moving quickly from one place to another. No idlers here. The little shops on the main road were humming— carpenters, leather workers, fullers, tailors, ironworkers. A snappy tribune informed them that Commander Priscianus was drilling his elite troops on the parade square, and would arrive shortly. Meanwhile, they were invited to the dining hall for the noon meal. Vectis sent his soldiers with the tribune but ordered provisions readied for him and the officers to eat on the way to the next outpost. He then headed for the parade square with his officers and Neeve in tow.

About fifty men groaned under the weight of enormous logs strapped to their backs; round and round the square they staggered. Others lunged at bundles of twigs, ramming their shields into the twisted mass and driving their swords upward. Some threw practice spears at straw targets, some fended blows from Celtic long-swords.

At the far end men climbed ropes on makeshift walls, and others on platforms tried to push them off. In the center sat three catapults and piles of rocks. Teams alternated loading and unloading the machines. Such drills, Neeve had thought, only Jupiter could inflict on men. But a disciplined soldier managed Stragenia. Vectis was right. The Caledonians would have trouble with this fort. She must warn her brothers about Stragenia.

Prowling from group to group was a balding man with bushy eyebrows who acted as if he were a drill centurion. Nothing escaped his attention and in a crisp voice, he singled out men whose efforts were less than exemplary. He turned when he saw Vectis.

"I like to train them myself," he shouted as he strode across the compound toward Vectis. "I don't have the luxury of a centurion like yours to beat out the laziness." He stopped in front of Vectis, acknowledged Neeve and the officers, and said, "Besides, I will know what they can do when the time comes."

"The time is coming," Vectis said.

His face hardened. "A winter attack?"

"Doubtful. They are building by the rivers and we have no reports of sleds being built or mules being gathered."

"Spring, then."

"Or summer. I have conflicting reports. But they are coming."

Priscianus nodded.

Neeve listened intently. Everyone knew that the Romans had paid spies roaming the hills, but this was the first time she had heard the results. It was frightening how well informed the Romans were, even to their guesses about the time of the attack. Naturally, they could not know the exact time because the Caledonian commanders themselves were still unsure when the Druids would bless their long-awaited offensive.

Vectis continued, "The more powerful Caledonian groups have pledged to destroy the outposts, and I suspect the Brigantes and Selgovae tribes will assault the Wall from the south to pin down the Wall soldiers."

The comment surprised Neeve. The Romans had miscalculated. They had no idea how deeply rooted the rebellion was among the

Brigantes; they assumed that the bulk of the attack would come from Caledonian tribes north of the Wall. Come spring, the whole of the lowlands would be in revolt. Neeve glanced around the compound with a vacant look, trying to appear bored. Taranis valued information on Roman expectations.

"What about the distant north?" Priscianus asked.

"The Carnonacae?"

"And the Cornavii, the Smertae, the Lvgi—those beyond the great glen. I've heard unpleasant rumors from scouts." His huge eyebrows rose, punctuating the thought.

"My information is weak, but your rumors may be correct. The Caledonians will strengthen their armies with warriors from the far north, but how many, and whether whole tribes are coming, I don't know."

"I feel the snow on my bones already." There was no humor in his voice.

"Let me encourage you," Vectis said. "In my dispatches to the Senate and Londinium, I stated that I have no less than five independent reports that the Caledonians, the northern Brigantes, and a collection of fourteen other tribes are planning a full-scale uprising, and that it will come with the spring thaw."

"Five independent reports, fourteen tribes," Priscianus repeated with a wry smile. "It never hurts to be specific when you overstate the case, especially with the way Rome dithers on major decisions. Did you make a direct request for legion support?"

Neeve thought the question was rather blunt for a Roman officer to ask his superior, but Vectis took no offense. He replied, "Without the legions we will forfeit the whole northland. And I told the Senate so."

"That should do it," Priscianus said, then added, "I hope."

Later, as the escort soldiers were marching out the gates, Priscianus spoke in a lowered voice to Vectis, so low that many of his words were lost in the sound of marching feet. It was a warning about Commander Commodus at Outpost Colania. Neeve edged around the side of her horse, pretending to adjust the saddle pad, but Priscianus's words were too garbled to make out. Neeve glanced over her shoulder. The escort officers were already leading their horses through the gates and she knew she ought to be with them. She lingered a moment, decided the risk was too great, but then changed her mind when she heard Priscianus speaking again.

"I have one additional piece of information," he said. Neeve busied herself with the girth strap, loosening it a notch. "It's about the Caledonian named Taranis, the one the soldiers call the blood god. He will be leading the assault on the outposts, and specifically, Faustina. I can tell you from years of bitter experience that he has a way of instilling fear in our troops." Priscianus mumbled something else, ending with the words, "I thought you should know."

On hearing her brother's name, Neeve felt a jolt go through her body, and then another at the unmistakable sound of footsteps behind her.

"What are you doing down there?"

Neeve jerked her head around to see one of the fort's junior officers. "Nothing ... I was—"

"Is something wrong?" he persisted.

"No ... you startled me, is all."

His face scrunched into a frown, his curiosity growing. Neeve gathered her wits. "Yes, something certainly is wrong," she said, pulling on the girth strap. "The stable has—" She flopped back in what she hoped would look like frustration. "Well, you can see. Someone has not cinched this properly and I cannot seem to—"

"Neeve?" It was Vectis.

She blew her hair out of her eyes. "I thought my shoulder had healed completely—"

Without waiting to be told by his superior officers, the young soldier dropped to his knees and grabbed the girth strap, cinching it tighter. Vectis acquainted Priscianus with Neeve's shoulder injury, and the older man expressed his sympathies. She responded politely, but with the danger past, her mind was far away. To have her brother's name mentioned by the Romans, and to hear the grim tone in Vectis's voice, brought home the reality of the coming conflict as nothing else had.

They stopped for less than an hour at Fort Alauna and then moved on to Julianus, where they stayed the night. The escort soldiers were glad to cease marching and headed straight for the large bathhouse. Vectis and his officers talked with Senecio, the fort commander, and promised to talk more after the night meal. But first they would retire to the baths; the enticement of hot and cold pools proved too compelling. For her part, Neeve scrubbed off the day's dust in Senecio's ornate bathing tub, and then went to the hall adjacent the kitchen where she and the officers dined on roast pigeon and honeyed sparrows' eggs. The wine was bitter to her taste, but it was strong and warmed her inside.

Between the meal and his meeting, Vectis proposed that he and Neeve take a small tour of the garrison. To Neeve's eye the fort appeared in reasonable shape, but Vectis pointed out numerous modifications that needed to be made.

As they passed the fort's bakery, the aroma lured them closer until they were standing at the doorway talking about the taste of stone fired bread. But the grinder had already gone, and had taken his bread with him. Inside, the smells of oven bread and freshly ground grain lingered in the air, summoning memories of the village mill where Neeve had grown up. She grabbed a scoop and shoved it into one of the grain bins, and froze. Something furry bumped her hand, something with claws that scurried up her arm toward her face. Neeve screeched and jerked backwards as it flew off her shoulder and disappeared into a darkened corner of the room. She stood there trembling.

Vectis whirled around. "Neeve! What is it?"

"A rat! It was a rat! A bristly, filthy rat!" She could feel the trail of scratchings where it had clawed its way up her arm. "Ugh," she managed between gulps of air.

Vectis was beside her, holding her. "Breathe," he said, "slowly and deeply."

Neeve shuddered.

"Do you want to leave?"

"Just hold me."

He did. After a few minutes he lit the torches along the walls and some smaller oil lamps to ease her mind. "The rats will stay in their darkened holes," Vectis said.

"Thank you." She happily slipped back into the enfolding comfort of his arms. For what seemed an eternity she clung to him, pressing against his warm body, nuzzling her face into his shoulder. Gradually, the outside light faded and the room grew more dependent on the flickering torchlight.

"This is so relaxing here with you," she said in spite of herself.

"And so natural," he said. His lips brushed her cheek and neck, and she moaned. He kissed her softly around the mouth. She parted her lips and invited him to her, and for one wondrous moment, it seemed as if they were joined in soul.

It was irrational, she knew. How could she feel such things for a Roman? After her episode with the emissary, she thought she could never trust another man, especially a Roman. But here she was eagerly kissing Vectis and wanting more. With her heart on fire and her judgment gone, she clutched at him urgently, so much so that it frightened her. And then, inexplicably, he drew back. Gently, but firmly, he placed his hands on her arms and moved her away. For an instant Neeve felt hurt and a little foolish, but it soon passed. She had sensed for some time that Vectis was troubled by past deeds that had nothing to do with her.

"My meeting with Senecio and his officers," he said, acting as if he had forgotten about it.

"We had better hurry," Neeve replied. "You know how quickly the Imperial army sends out search parties." She had not even bothered to disguise her irritation.

He accepted her comment as justly deserved and they left the bakery. In a perverse way it pleased Neeve that past guilt tormented Vectis. It lessened her own. Over and over again she reminded herself that he was a Roman and she a Caledonian. He might not share in their arrogance, nor treat others as bondservants, but he represented the Empire, and must be driven from Caledonian lands. Why should she feel guilt about deceiving him? It was his Empire that crushed the spirits of free people, that whipped valiant warriors in the public squares until they wept openly at the feet of Roman masters.

She would feel no shame in doing her part to rid Caledonia of such people. She would subdue her emotions and do what was necessary. But it was a cheerless task. The very pleasure of his company anguished her soul.

30

Early the next morning they set off for the last outpost on their tour, Colania. The awkwardness from the night before had evaporated with the morning dew, and Neeve and Vectis enjoyed every minute of their journey.

"Does he really wear greaves?" Neeve asked, referring to Commander Commodus's penchant for wearing outdated armor.

"I have told you enough about the man. I cannot have you laughing in his face."

"And he struts around with a huge, red, crested plume on his helmet?" Neeve snickered. "How shall I ever control myself?"

"You had better find a way," Vectis said, sounding suddenly like a prefect. "Commodus might be more than just a buffoon."

"What do you mean?"

He shook off the question and said wryly, "May I remind you that you are a hired translator under my authority, and if I ask you to fake sincerity, you will."

"Yes, Prefect."

"Besides, crested helmets aren't all that odd."

"You said he wears them in the fort."

"So I did," Vectis said, grinning.

"I cannot remember ever seeing a crest on a Roman helmet."

"Legionaries don't wear them anymore, but centurions still put them on during battle so their men can see them. And in Rome the Praetorians wear them on parade. I think Commodus is trying to bring back the glory of the Julian Empire."

Neeve held her tongue. Glory indeed. It was moments like this that helped refocus her mission. She knew all about the Julian Empire. Since childhood she had heard songs of the bloody generals sent from Rome—Julius Caesar and Agricola—and Britannia's heroic but futile attempt to stave off slavery.

Neeve was about to get down to business and ask Vectis serious questions about Commodus that might help her discover Priscianus's concerns, when scouts flashing signals from the hills interrupted their conversation.

"Square the ranks," Vectis called to the centurion of the auxiliaries. The officer relayed the command to the trumpeter, who blew several short blasts, and instantly the soldiers moved into their hollow square formation, enclosing the officers, the carts, and the Scythians' extra mounts. The huge block spilled over the roadway but moved at the same speed, with the exception of the archers who ranged along the sides and rear.

"It's nothing critical," Vectis said to Neeve, anticipating her question. "Scouts report a group of Caledonians ahead."

"Will they attack?"

"No, it's a small band, and there are no other hostiles in the area."

Neeve was relieved. She couldn't bear to see Caledonians killed in front of her. And down deep she knew she had another concern—the safety of Vectis.

"Squared marching can be cumbersome," Vectis continued, "but the gods preserve the vigilant. Besides," he smiled at Neeve, "I have an important guest to protect."

"Guest? You mean me?"

"Of course."

"I thought I was the hired translator."

"You have no idea how important translators are to me," he said.

Ahead, a scout was making signals and pointing to a wood stretching along the western side of the road. Suddenly, Neeve understood what they would find, and it sickened her. As they neared the track of timberland the square halted. A dozen or more soldiers fanned out into the trees and surrounding hills to provide an additional scouting shield for the main body of troops.

"The Caledonians have tied someone, probably one of our spies, to a tree," Vectis said, pointing past the soldiers to a sapling bowed under the weight of its victim.

Neeve turned away. She had seen what the wolves did to tree wretches.

"Neeve?"

"I prefer not to see."

"He's not ... Neeve, the man is alive."

"Alive?"

"Yes, alive." Vectis gave her a reassuring pat on the hand. "He's been here only a short while. That's what those Caledonians were doing when the scouts spotted them earlier—tying him in full view of the arterial road. Barbaric, but it makes for an extraordinary warning. Ever since the Caledonians introduced this punishment, we have had a difficult time enticing Celts to spy." He dismounted. "Come with me, I will need you to interpret."

They made their way through the front ranks of the hollow square and across a ragged field of heather to the edge of the woodlands where the soldiers were untying the tree wretch. He was on the ground when they arrived, rubbing the rope burns on his arms and legs. Neeve felt vaguely uncomfortable when she saw him. He had a large, flat face with teeth missing in the front ... and she had seen him before. No, she corrected herself, she had talked to him. She glanced upward, trying to think, as if from the vast emptiness of the sky an answer would come. Somewhere ... in a village or among the squatters outside the fort, she definitely had met him. But where? Not knowing could be her undoing. Her heart thumped in her chest.

Vectis stood over the man, studying him. He turned to Neeve: "Ask him why the Caledonians tied him to this tree."

Neeve brushed past the soldiers and positioned herself to the side of the spy. She would be a voice, just a voice translating the questions and answers. With luck the spy might not even see her. He would find it more natural to keep his eyes on Vectis, than to twist his head around to see his translator. She asked the question.

"Look what they did to me," the man wailed in the muffled speech of the toothless. "Can't feel my hands or feet, can't swallow, my mouth's dry. Wine. Need wine."

Neeve repeated his words and Vectis called for the wine. Within seconds a soldier from the main body of troops had crossed the heather field with a filled skin and deposited it in the man's outstretched hands. He choked down several large swallows before coughing up a mouthful on his tunic. The residue still dribbled from his chin when he resumed speaking.

"My name's Morann of the Epidii, the horse people. I am ..." he sucked on his gums, "I *was* a messenger for my tribe." As Neeve translated he rose shakily to his feet, then paused and looked at her. His brow furrowed.

Neeve panicked. He knows who I am! She tried to translate but her tongue refused to move. Haltingly, she completed her task, then bounced her eyes nervously between Vectis and the spy. Her hesitation would only reinforce whatever suspicions he might have, yet she seemed unable to do anything about it. In her mind she kept seeing him with his finger pointed, accusing her. She needed to act, and quickly. Racing through her mind was one slender hope: if she couldn't remember where they had met, perhaps neither could he.

She stepped in front of the man and spoke with all the confidence of a Roman, hoping he would cower in the face of authority. "The prefect has asked you why the Caledonians tied you to that tree. Are you a thief or murderer? Because if you are—"

"No, no," the man protested.

Neeve pushed her face closer. "Then why the tree?"

She held his eyes, determined to replace his curiosity with fear. Everyone knew the Romans punished troublemakers severely.

"I ... I was put here because of my work for the Empire." As Neeve translated, she watched him for signs of recognition. Nothing. His sole objective was to convince everyone that he was a Roman loyalist. As he regained his composure, he listed his successes as a spy, and the numerous ways he had benefited the Roman occupation. Neeve was shocked that a Celt born in the free north would so casually talk about betraying his people. His main concern, it appeared, was how best he could fill his purse with Roman money.

"I was doing well," he said, "until this band of Caledonians came by. Caught me with a pouch of silver and wouldn't believe I found it stuffed in a rotted out log." He laughed roughly, exposing his toothless front. "Even witless Caledonians grow suspicious when they find a year's wage on a man."

Neeve translated his words without emotion even though she had the overwhelming urge to smash her fist into his flat face. The intensity of her anger surprised her; never had she met anyone as unprincipled. Betraying his people for money! Give him silver and he would boil children for the village feast. She wondered how many had died because of him. At least the Romans pursued their goals out of duty to their Emperor. This man cared only about himself and how he could feed his insatiable greed.

Her fear was gone. It left the moment he began describing his treacherous deeds and his manipulation of unsuspecting Celts to gain information. No longer did she care where they had met. It was enough his spying days in Caledonia were over and that he presented no additional threat to her.

As they traveled toward Fort Colania, the man continually drank from his skin, and often glanced at her, once even grinning, as though the two shared a secret. Neeve was glad when they reached Colania, for there Vectis sent the man on his way. "The Caledonians know who you are now," Vectis said. "If you don't want to become victuals for the wolves, I suggest you stay south of the Wall."

Neeve translated.

He scrunched his lips over his gums. "Silver. Need silver and a horse. They took everything."

"Rome never forgets her friends," Vectis said. He pulled two silver coins from his purse—an overly generous amount, Neeve thought—and handed them to the man, who clutched at them eagerly, rubbing them between his fingers.

He looked up at Vectis, not satisfied. "Horse! I am Epidii! Horse people do not walk—we ride."

Neeve translated: "I demand a horse. I am of the Epidii tribe and we never walk, we ride."

Vectis replied, "Today you walk. You can buy a horse with the silver I gave you once you reach the Wall."

Undaunted, the man tried again. "Prefect, Rome has much wealth and I have only these two coins. Could you spare something more from your purse?"

"Prefect," Neeve said, translating, "Rome has so much wealth, yet you give me only two coins. I want more from your purse."

When Vectis heard the translation, his eyes narrowed. "Be on your way," he said, "and be grateful for your life."

Neeve turned to the man. "The prefect wants you to leave Caledonia and never come back. He says, 'Be grateful for your life.'"

The man cursed under his breath but made no reply. An officer pointed south, saying in garbled Celtic that Antoninus' Wall was within an hour's walking distance. Neeve repeated the information to make it clear. Again, he stared at her, an uncomfortable, long, sneering stare, and then he left.

As Neeve watched him shuffling down the road, she suddenly remembered where she had seen him. He had been one of the messengers that visited Taranis in the village during those first days after her return to Caledonia. Did he remember? she wondered. Or had he only vague recollections? No matter. To return to Caledonia would undoubtedly cost him his life. She was safe, at least for the present.

Fort Colania was by far the most imposing Roman fort Neeve had ever seen. Its soaring ramparts and turrets were a third higher than those at Faustina, and its massive turf walls were easily forty feet thick at the base. With deep trenches slashed across the front, and spiked traps and rows of iron hooks, Colania looked impregnable.

"Amazing," Neeve murmured as they passed through the log gates and heavy turf walls.

"It is impressive," Vectis acknowledged, "but don't be deceived by the physical structure of a fort. They all have weaknesses."

"What could possibly be weak about this fort?" Neeve asked, more for her own curiosity than for the information she continually gathered.

"A fort's weakness is always the same—its gates. But a wise commander examines everything. Sometimes a fort has brittle walls or is susceptible to fire." His eyes drifted away. "I remember a gigantic fortress in Egypt—had been standing for centuries. Impossible to destroy, we were told. We heaped wood and tar against the mighty wall, cooked it for a day, and then doused it with river water. One tap and it shattered like fine glass." He grinned. "You should have seen their faces!"

"Before or after you killed them?" Neeve asked, striving for humor, but sounding exactly the way she felt inside—bitter about Roman conquest.

His smile evaporated. He was hurt.

"Oh, Vectis, what a miserable thing to say. I am sorry." And she was, not only for revealing her feelings, but for the pain she had caused him.

"I understand," he said, gamely trying to retrieve his smile.

"I really did not mean—"

He stopped in the entranceway, with the turf walls towering on either side. "Neeve, when we first met, you said you felt no anger toward Rome. But you do, don't you?"

Truth was always best, she reminded herself, insofar as one could tell it. She closed her eyes before speaking. "Yes, I do feel anger when I think of how powerless we are in our own land, and how destructive your vast armies can be." She looked at him. "Is that too much honesty from a Celt?"

"No," he said, "much of what you say is true. I wouldn't repeat it too often, though. We Romans find it hard to face the truth about ourselves. We can be brutal in pursuing our objectives—of that there can be no doubt. But I should tell you that I was in charge of that campaign in Egypt and we didn't kill all the inhabitants—not even one, actually. They were so stunned at the frailty of their defense that the city elders flung open the gates and offered their lives in exchange for the preservation of the people."

"And what happened to those elders?" Neeve asked, wishing she had better control of her tongue, but somehow wanting to pursue the question to the end. She scolded herself. What did it matter how the Romans treated people in Egypt? Caledonia was weighing in the balance and could ill-afford her self-righteous questions. She groaned inwardly. It was clear what was happening. She was becoming too familiar with the prefect.

"Neeve, Rome has her faults, but she does not kill wantonly. That city and those elders are still there—trusted friends of the Empire." He moved her closer to the turf walls to let the soldiers pass. "I'll not deny that sometimes I have used harsh means to subdue the enemies of Rome. I am a soldier. But always I have tempered duty with mercy, and I want you to know that. I am no butcher."

"I never thought you were," Neeve said softly. She felt wretched for having placed him in such a defensive posture. "Anyway, I had no right to say what I did. I might have misgivings about Rome, but never about you. I wish I had held my tongue."

"If you had held your tongue, there would still be a barrier between us, only I wouldn't know it."

A heaviness came over Neeve. So much he didn't know—about her, about Caledonia, about the extent of the uprising that would forever tear them apart.

"I do not want barriers either," she said truthfully, "but you must remember that I am a Celt and sometimes conquered people lash out. It is our only defense."

"But you should not feel like a conquered people. Britannia is part of the Roman Empire. I thought you understood that." He sighed. "The Empire is the greatest gathering of peoples and tribes and tongues ..." he searched for words, "it's a noble union with opportunity for all."

Neeve said nothing.

"You think I am spouting Roman platitudes. Did you know that the forefathers of the last three emperors—including our present emperor, Antoninus, came from the *conquered* provinces?"

"No, I did not."

"Yes, it's true! Don't you see?" Excitement glistened in his eyes. "Rome is not out there somewhere. It's you and me, and even these people in Caledonia. One day I expect someone from Britannia to wear the purple in Rome."

"That is hard to believe."

"No more difficult than it was in the last century — " he pulled her closer to give space for the weapons carts that rumbled into the passageway, "for people in Hispania or Gallia to believe that Rome's emperors would come from their number."

She nodded her understanding.

"I would never ask you to be a zealot for Rome," he said. "We have sufficient already. But I am a Roman, a soldier of the Empire, and in great need of your approval because," he gave her a lop-sided grin, "because I ... well, I think I love you."

A blast of dust from a cart covered them. Neeve blinked her eyes, trying to clear them of grit. "You do not love me," she said, raising her voice over the noise of the carts. She did not like the idea of deceiving someone who loved and trusted her. "You are just lonely and I happen to be here."

"Don't you think I have thought about this?" he shouted over the carts. "I do love you, and felt that way from the moment I set eyes on you." Another cart approached, spewing dirt as it came. Neeve pulled her cloak over her head for protection. Vectis muttered something and stepped in front of the cart, causing the driver to stop abruptly when he saw the stern countenance of his prefect. That settled, Vectis gestured for Neeve to join him, and together they proceeded down the corridor, no longer plagued by swirling dust.

"Not the best place for an intimate conversation," Neeve said.

"No, it is not."

Neeve could see by the tense look in his face that Vectis wished he had never broached the subject. "Thick walls," she said, glancing along the sheer side of the turf. It was an obvious attempt to ease back into their earlier, more relaxed conversation.

"Yes, very thick."

"We were talking about the weaknesses of forts," she said, persevering.

"Yes, and I boasted about my brilliance in Egypt—a ludicrous attempt to impress you that only managed to drive you away."

"Vectis, I ...."

"No, no, say nothing. I couldn't bear to hear polite disavowals." They stopped inside the walls and waited for the carts to make their way through the entranceway. "You are right," he said, deciding to go with the change of conversation, "we were talking about fort defects, and I said that one has to evaluate the total situation, the offensive and defensive forces, the placement of the fort, the nature of its food and water supplies, and so on. All forts have some weakness. The key is to choose the right one."

Neeve surveyed the defenses, happy for their discourse to be on more comfortable ground. "Colania has turf walls that neither burn nor break, and I have never seen heavier gates on a Roman fort. It has plenty of water with a stream in back, and like Faustina, it probably has food enough for a long siege."

"Colania is a strong fort," Vectis agreed, "but sometimes the most glaring weakness can be internal."

"The soldiers defending the fort?"

"Sometimes, but in this case, the command structure."

"You mean Commodus."

"I mean Commodus."

As the huge gates closed, and the soldiers were taken to the fort's dining hall, Neeve asked quietly, "If Commodus is so incompetent, why would Rome appoint him as the commander?"

"Ah, Neeve," Vectis laughed. "I can tell you are not Roman. You think rationally, and that is not the way of Rome's noble politicians. They can best be described as harlots demanding a price. To get something, you pay something. You obtain positions of authority by enhancing the treasuries of senators and lesser officials, by stroking their egos, or benefiting them in other ways. Somehow the system works. As our politicians are quick to point out, Rome has fared well for nine hundred years."

"But in time of war—"

"Then it becomes a problem." He signaled his officers and together they followed the gate centurion up the main road past a collection of stone buildings and platforms loaded with supplies that appeared, at least to Neeve's untrained eye, neat and organized, not at all what Vectis had prepared her to expect from Colania. She saw no cluttered streets or walkways, no messy carts; no soldiers gambling or weapons heaped along the walls. Colania seemed the typical, organized Roman fort.

She noticed Vectis examining everything. "Better than you expected?" she asked.

He turned to her, his eyebrows raised, inquiring.

"The condition of the fort."

"Oh," he nodded, "much better."

"Then you are pleased."

"Very pleased." But he didn't look pleased.

Colania was impressive inside as well at out. Unlike most forts, the buildings lining the roadway were constructed of stone, with only the occasional wooden structure. When they rounded the last building and turned down the cross street, she saw Commander Commodus waiting in front of his two-story, stone office building. He was wearing sandals and a glistening white toga.

"Ah, Prefect Vectis," he called jovially. "Welcome! Welcome to Colania!"

Vectis moaned audibly. "A toga. A military commander in sandals and a toga."

Neeve found herself staring at the lightest skinned Roman she had ever seen. His ashen complexion reminded her of the rigid corpses lying on funeral pyres, and his hairless head, she guessed, would have reached no higher than the nape of her neck. Drawing closer, she found to her amazement that he had the smooth skin of a baby—no facial hair, not even eyebrows or eyelashes. On every finger was a pearl ring, except for his right index that bore a heavy signet ring embossed with a naked winged boy carrying a bow and arrow. Commodus smiled and, extending his arms, walked toward them. His white toga combined with his chalky skin made him look like a plucked chicken in Roman finery.

"Prefect, how good to see you," he said in the way one would greet an old friend.

"Commander Commodus," Vectis said curtly. "The northlands can be chilly for a toga, I would think." He didn't wait for a reply but brusquely introduced his officers and motioned carelessly in Neeve's direction. Again, she noticed how difficult it was for Vectis to conceal his feelings. Something was bothering him and it wasn't the toga.

Commodus seemed oblivious to his prefect's disapproval. He smiled at all the officers and reached up to kiss Neeve on the cheek, not an unusual gesture for a Roman to make during social introductions, but highly unusual in a military setting. Neeve wiped her face, trying to obliterate the smell of perfume left from Commodus's recently oiled head.

"Yes, indeed, Prefect," he said, "when I contemplated what to wear for your visit, I chose my best toga, little realizing how appropriate it would be. I am honored not only by your presence," and then fixing his eyes on Neeve, he added, "I am honored by the incarnation of the goddess Venus." He ran his eyes slowly over the entire length of Neeve's body before clearing his throat and saying, "You are quite right, Prefect, togas were not made for Britannia. Fortunately, I have two braziers heating the conference room upstairs. You and your officers will be more than comfortable there."

"My officers will be inspecting the garrison while we talk," Vectis said.

"I see," he said, his enthusiasm dampened for the first time. Then, recovering, "You will find a marked improvement in Colania's efficiency. I have assigned my best officer the task of implementing your First Centurion's orders."

"From the looks of it," Vectis said, "he has done a fine job."

Commodus beamed.

Vectis dismissed his officers and was about to send Neeve somewhere when Commodus intervened. With his eyes on Neeve, he said, "Prefect, I cannot allow this Gallic dove to flutter from my presence." He reached for her hand and patted it softly. "Tell him, my treasure, would you not rather be here with us than dining in some dingy kitchen with a collection of dreary officers? I can easily have our food brought to us—delightful victuals, the best in the northland."

"Well ...." Neeve glanced at Vectis, seeking approval. It was an opportunity to learn more about fort strategy, and besides, she thought, conversation with Commodus promised to be far more interesting.

"I have no objection," Vectis said.

"Splendid," Commodus said, blowing into his hands for warmth. "Let us leave this inclement weather to the Celts. I will have turbot soup brought to my office instantly, smoldering hot." He smiled. "After that we can discuss matters leisurely, over a table suitable for a queen of the Nile." He took Neeve by the arm and escorted her across the wooden platform toward the doorway of the central building.

The conversation did prove interesting, and informative. Even the meal was delightful, as Commodus had pledged. Yet Vectis was all business. He made his strategies clear to Commodus, and underscored his determination to maintain lines of communication among the five outposts and the Wall forts, but not once did he respond to Commodus's lighter comments, even when they were preposterous tributes to Neeve's resplendent loveliness, as he called it, a blessing from the gods.

At first Neeve wondered if Vectis's seriousness was a contrived part of his prefect role that he assumed when the need arose. She discarded the notion. She had often seen Vectis discussing issues of substance at Faustina—something deeper was vexing him. It had to do with the snatches of conversation she had overheard at Stragenia. Priscianus had warned Vectis about Commodus. But warned him about what? She thought about Vectis's odd comment that Commodus might be more than a buffoon.

"Well," Vectis said to Commodus, "I have nothing more, unless you—"

"Nothing, Prefect, except to entreat you to leave this goddess with me." His lips formed a leering smile. "Colania has great need of her services and I will personally see to it that she is bathed and oiled daily with—"

"You have neglected to ask me about your transfer request. Why is that?"

Commodus looked stunned, and not because Vectis had interrupted his ridiculous request. There was something else, something hidden.

"Well?" Vectis demanded.

"I ... I am here at your pleasure, Prefect," Commodus stammered. "If you wish to transfer me, I supposed you would inform me in good time."

"When we last talked you were eager for a transfer."

"I am here at your pleasure," he repeated.

"Yet you begged for a transfer."

Commodus sat blank-faced, as if he were trying to think of a response.

"I find it strange that you have complied with my conditions for the transfer—increasing efficiency at Colania—yet you seem unconcerned about the transfer."

"Ah, yes!" Commodus said, as though he had just thought up a reason for the complication. "When last you were here, Prefect, a shadow of sickness had eclipsed my life. I was unwell ... yes, quite unwell. That has lifted, you see."

"Have the Senate messages bolstered your health?"

Commodus's pallid complexion mutated to gray. He tried to articulate something but lost his voice. He blinked several times, rubbed his face with the longest fingers Neeve had ever seen, and then squeaked out the words, "I don't understand."

Vectis leaned toward Commodus. "I have little tolerance for political games. Now, tell me about these dispatches from Rome."

"Oh, of course, the dispatches," Commodus said with a defensive laugh. "I had forgotten them. They contained nothing significant, you understand ... simple inquiries about the state of affairs in Britannia."

"Send someone to fetch them."

"But I no longer have—"

"Where are they?"

"Destroyed. I ... they were unimportant so I discarded them."

Vectis leaned back on his couch, angry. "Who sent them?" he asked finally.

"Senator Alfenus Crescens."

The return trip to Faustina went quickly, with brief stops at each fort and a six-hour overnight at the third outpost, Alauna. They kept the conversation light, laughing over the lecherous looks she had received from Commodus. Only once did Vectis comment seriously on Commodus, saying that something didn't sit right, but that he had no idea what it was. As to Vectis's ill-timed declaration of love for her, thankfully, he avoided the subject.

31

The winter before the attack was brutally cold. Winds swept down from the northern sea, freezing lakes and rivers, and battering the island with hard, granular snow. Wolves prowled the village dumps and howled outside the night sheds where docile sheep hid. Everywhere in Caledonia, townspeople filled cracks around their windows and doors; they banked the outside walls with snow and replenished their rapidly diminishing woodpiles.

Neeve remained in Fort Faustina, and ventured out only to take a few mapping assignments along the arterial road. It was her concession to Vectis. He no longer wanted her to map the northern sectors, and she willingly complied, especially since she could easily send Taranis her information from the southern sectors. With the advent of winter winds and sudden snowstorms, Neeve had begun to use a village contact near the arterial road. The arrangement worked well but Neeve missed seeing her brothers.

On the few occasions that she did visit them, they were at home, as were most Caledonians, waiting for the spring thaw. With the Druid tribute and the purse from the Roman emissary, supplies were adequate. War parties mostly attacked weapon trains along the arterial route and occasional mile forts on the Wall. Neeve's continual flow of information had become vital. Her brothers were astonished at her ability to provide precise dates and times when the Roman carts would appear, and more than once Taranis called her "first" warrior of the Caledonians.

They were also interested in Jupiter. Apparently, he and his special unit had destroyed several building camps along the river, forcing a minor rebuilding effort in the cruel winter months. Neeve had heard nothing about his excursions and promised to find out what she could. Again, she was warned to take extreme care when dealing with the African centurion.

As the winter grew colder, Taranis and Eston were dismayed by the failure of Neeve's little rock bathhouse. The dugout designed to collect rain had frozen solid. Neeve could see their humiliation and assured them that she had plenty of access to the bathhouse at Faustina. Not to be outdone by the Romans, they ripped off the top of the boiler and filled it with snow. Then, lighting the fires, they stood back and cheered as, there in the dead of winter, the only Caledonian bathhouse started cooking.

During those winter months, Neeve grew comfortable at Faustina; she felt as if she belonged. She had become fond of many people, and found herself wishing that winter would last forever. But spring was coming, she knew, and with it the horrible war. How strange, she thought, that her interest in Vectis should grow, not diminish. He represented everything she hated. Rome was evil and corrupt, and survived by enslaving others, yet she longed to be with this Roman guardian. How utterly strange.

One afternoon when Neeve stopped by the central office, she found Vectis in a somber mood. He asked her to wait in his office while he talked with a courier who had arrived the day before. Neeve was concerned by his solemn manner. Until now he had always been happy to see her, and any change in his behavior stirred old fears. He might care for her deeply—maybe even love her as he had once said— but he was still a Roman officer, and that she must never forget.

She pushed his unusual behavior from her mind and got down to business. Watching from the window, she waited until Vectis had disappeared down the main street. Then she moved quickly to the back room. She opened the precious document that rested innocently on the third shelf, the same document that had almost caused her ruin. Before her lay the exact numbers and kinds of troops along the Wall. Vectis was meticulous with numbers and Neeve could see where he had made minor changes in the figures. Reproducing the data in her drawing had been painstaking, the effort taking three weeks to complete. She had told Vectis she wanted to draw a picture of fort life from the vantage of his office: the row of little shops—carpenters, ropemakers, potters—the huge gates and exercise square, the soldiers milling about. And every time he left her alone in the office, she would insert additional numbers and names in the hair of soldiers, along the cross-beams of the gates, in the tiny swirls of dust that followed a passing cart, and even in the image of the Roman god Victory that stood so arrogantly at the corner of the parade ground. She had learned from her earlier mistake.

In short order Neeve completed her task and returned the document to its shelf. She felt a surge of pride as she inspected the drawing. She had accomplished the impossible. With feathery touches of chalk to smudge the more dangerous areas, Neeve had managed to copy all three pages of the most important document in the entire fort. Now the Celtic tribes would know exactly what to expect from each garrison on the Wall.

Then came the guilt. Always the guilt. Vectis trusted her, trusted her completely. After their tour of the outposts, he had instructed everyone, including Julian and the centurion Jupiter, to knock before entering his office. Now she could sift through documents without fear of interruption. No doubt they thought Vectis was heading off an awkward situation, though in truth not once had he and Neeve taken to the couch. He seemed to want something more than just a physical relationship.

When Vectis returned, Neeve was sitting by a charcoal brazier, sipping a steaming cup of Celtic beer. Someone had bolted an iron tray on the brazier top and as winter approached, Vectis had begun heating kettles of beer. The day was unusually cold and there appeared to be no end of the snow that drifted from the skies. Neeve boldly showed him the completed drawing of fort life. He expressed mild interest, little more than what good breeding required. There was no doubt about it; darker matters occupied his mind.

Neeve poured herself another cup of beer in hopes the hot liquid would soothe her bundled nerves. It didn't help. She sat pensively as Vectis shuffled papers on his table. What could have brought on this change of behavior? He wasn't interested in her drawing, so it couldn't be that. Had he somehow discovered that she regularly inspected his documents? She twisted a handful of hair, disciplined herself, and plunged forward. "I sense something bothering you," she said.

He looked up. "It can wait."

"Is it serious?"

He straightened his ink box, then his papers for the third time.

She felt her heart rate increase.

"Yes, it's serious, Neeve," he said, rubbing the weariness from his eyes, "but I'm not sure this is the time—"

"I would rather hear it now than later," she said, swallowing.

"Don't be too sure."

Neeve tried to remain calm as he walked around the table and sat on the corner. He drummed his fingers on his leggings, then fixed his eyes on her. "What would you think of someone who never told you the truth?"

"I ... I would wonder why."

"Would you feel betrayed?"

Her heart pounded. "I would wonder about the reason. Sometimes people do things they regret, but they do them because they must ... because, well, they are trapped, like a bird in a cage." She looked away, unable to maintain eye contact.

"And what about love? Could a person love someone and be a liar?"

"Please, Vectis ...."

"I need to know what you think."

"Then I say, yes, it is possible to love someone and not tell the whole truth. Sometimes truth is a hard thing, and better left unspoken. Who can change the way the gods have ordered our lives? We might want to, but we cannot." The brazier seemed unbearably hot and Neeve shifted away.

"I'm glad you feel that way," he said, rising, "because I have not been telling you the truth."

Neeve eyed him, unsure where his conversation was leading. He picked up a dispatch from the table and said, "Yesterday a courier brought this ... it's from that senator I told you about, Senator Atilius Titianus."

"The one you do not like."

He moved to the bench across from her and in a voice thick with emotion he said, "My sister and father have both died."

"I am so sorry," she said, feeling an enormous sense of relief. They could as easily be discussing her role as a spy, she knew. "I am sure you want privacy," she said, rising, and collecting her drawing. He said nothing so she started for the door, then stopped. The monstrosity of her attitude suddenly hit her. Here was a man who obviously cared for her—maybe even loved her—who had protected her and had saved her own brother from certain death, and now when he tries to make a confession of sorts, though she had no idea what it was, she walks out. And worse, when he tells her that his sister and father have died, her only feeling is relief. Her selfishness had no limit.

"Vectis," she said, "I ... I am truly sorry about the news. I wish there was something ... would you like company for a while?" She didn't wait for an answer but moved beside him on the bench and grasped his hands. He seemed both embarrassed and appreciative of the gesture.

For several minutes they huddled together, saying nothing, listening to the hiss of the wind at the window slats. Finally, Vectis said in a quiet voice, "When we first met I told you how wonderful Britannia was, and you declared your love for Roman things. Both of us were less than truthful."

At times like this it was best to wait, so Neeve waited.

"I was not eager to come to Britannia," he said, "and especially to Caledonia. It seemed like the edge of the world. I confess that I am no better than Julian, because I too hate the rain and the cold and the snow."

"Since we are telling the truth," Neeve said, trying to lend him emotional support, "I have no liking for the cold either."

"But on our walks you said—"

"I know. Around Romans we all pretend to love the harsh winds and freezing rains, but inside we long for summer days. Not that we would want a whole year of summer days, but it would be nice to have fewer wet ones."

"You would like Rome. We have a cold season, but much shorter than here."

"Yet you came to Britannia."

"Loyalty is prized among Romans, so when they asked me to come, I said 'Hail Caesar' and pointed my horse north. And I have done my best to strengthen these outposts ... not that it'll do much good," he added darkly. He looked at her. "Then I met you. In this frozen wasteland—excuse me for saying that, but I am trying to be honest—I found you at last. And there is no place in the Empire I would rather be."

The sincerity of his words moved her.

"But I have something, not very flattering, that I must tell you—"

"Please," she touched his lips, "you need not—"

"I do," he persisted. "And you need to let me talk."

His voice carried a mild scolding that caused Neeve to sit back and listen. She was not sure her conscience could bear a confession from someone she had so shamelessly manipulated.

"When I read the news about my sister and father," he said, "I realized how fleeting relationships are, and how precious. I loved them dearly, and now they are ashes in decorated urns."

"I am so sorry, Vectis. It must have been a shock."

"It was," he said quietly, "but I learned something. There are other people in my life I never want to lose. My soul might be heavy in sorrow, but it's also alive in hope ... hope in a future that includes you."

Neeve caught her breath. She had often fantasized an exchange like this but it was just that, a fantasy. She knew she was falling in love with Vectis but continued on her destructive path. How foolish! He was Roman, and she a Caledonian spy. She had grown up in the shadow of the Wall and hated these people who had murdered her father, mother and baby sister. But during the long winter nights as she prepared for bed, she sometimes imagined being alone with Vectis, making love. The fantasy even burrowed into her dream world, and despite the cold, she would awaken at night drenched in sweat, her heart pounding, her lips speaking his name. Then she would chide herself for her foolishness and go back to sleep, but she knew she was falling in love with the Roman prefect. And now her feelings had become her enemy.

Neeve took a breath but remained silent.

He turned to her and said, "I cannot bear the thought of losing you."

Neeve had no idea what to say. She mumbled something in return. How stupid to encourage him! Their relationship couldn't possibly work. She needed to stay away from this man, not grow closer to him. Where was her judgment? How could she love someone who had the power of death over her?

He was reaching for her now, his fingers warm on hers, gently squeezing, enclosing her entire hand as if he were protecting her. In another circumstance the thought of a Roman protecting her would have made her wonder whether she had become irretrievably mad, but in her heart she knew that this Roman would never harm her. She felt safe with him.

His hand moved up her arm, caressing her lightly, sliding over her shoulder. She sighed inwardly, chastising herself for the trickle of desire that was growing inside, but making no effort to pull away. His lips brushed across her cheek, stopping at her ear, nibbling. She shuddered and moved closer. Yes, at another time, in another world, she could love this man. Really love him. But not now, not in their present circumstances. And yet, what she felt for him was more powerful than her will. More powerful than her loyalties to Caledonia, and yes, even more powerful than her need to please her brothers. What she felt was love—strong and pure, alive and right.

"It's been a hard day for you," she said, drawing back slightly, trying to gain control.

"It has," he agreed, "but I am so glad you're here with me."

Neeve met his eyes ... and saw the same love radiating out of him. How could they not come together? How could they deny what was beyond them both, beyond place and time? She wanted to close her eyes and shut out the world. Two lovers alone in a darkening room, thinking of nothing but themselves. Was that so wrong? Must she always deny her feelings because she had duties to perform? Neeve, the Caledonian spy. Was that all she was? Vectis's sister would spend eternity in a decorated urn, never to feel again, never to love or be loved. Neeve couldn't bear the thought of such emptiness and pushed it out of her mind. She refused that fate for herself, never to love or be loved, and with full knowledge of what she was doing, she leaned forward and buried her face in Vectis's tunic. His arms surrounded her as they had at Fort Alauna's bakery, and she could almost smell the fresh loaves of stone ground bread.

For the next few moments they were content to enjoy the warmth of each other's bodies, and the simmering anticipation that only lovers can know. She could feel the stir of his breath in her hair, the strength of his arms at her waist, and a trembling desire fluttering in her belly.

He shifted positions, one hand easing up her body, the other resting on the back of her neck, his fingers gently kneading, sifting her hair.

She pushed her head back into his hand, wanting more, wanting to feel every soothing movement of his fingers exploring her hair. A ripple of pleasure shook her body and she tilted her face upward, inviting him.

He bent forward and kissed her with a tenderness that belied his ragged breath and taut muscles. It was a gentle kiss and so brief that Neeve found herself exquisitely teased and wanting more. They kissed again. The light movements and the warmth of his breath made her lips unusually sensitive and she could feel even the tiniest tremor of his mouth. He sucked softly on her lower lip and ran the tip of his tongue from one corner to the other. Her breath was coming faster now and she wondered whether he could hear her heart pounding. Inside she felt an incredible ecstasy, and an intense desire to give herself totally to him. She kissed him deeply and pushed away the menacing thoughts beating on the gates of her mind. She refused to listen to the voices telling her to flee, telling her that this relationship would be trampled under the heel of marching armies.

She ran her hands across his back, pausing, feeling the bunching muscles of his shoulders under his tunic, and his hard chest pressing against hers. She clung to him, drinking in the sensation of his closeness.

His hand slid under her tunic, and she trembled at the touch of his fingers on her bare flesh. She raised her arms as he pulled the Roman garment over her head, exposing her breasts, her nipples taut and waiting. He bent his head and took one in his mouth, gently cupping the other with his hand. It was exactly as she had imagined, and a cry of pleasure escaped her lips. He teased her with his mouth, with the tip of his tongue, driving her wild. When she thought she could no longer stand the exquisite pleasure, she cried out, and he brought his mouth over hers, roughly, and she could feel a throbbing deep inside, and she knew she must have him now or die. With a passion as great as his, she crushed herself into him, wanting him, demanding him.

Gradually she lost all sense of being separate from him, and in total abandon, she moved and moaned and clutched her precious Vectis, until it seemed as if she were floating above the world. He had taken her into his arms, she realized, and now she was sinking into the soft pillows of the floral couch.

In urgency, they kicked off their boots, and with a passion that was almost comical, helped each other squirm out of their leather trousers and other garments until he stood over her, naked, staring at her nakedness.

"You are so beautiful," he gasped, and Neeve opened her arms to him, calling him home. He knelt next to her and nuzzled his face into her neck, kissing her softly.

She was beyond caring about the future, the past. She loved him with her entire being, and whispered her new mantra, "I love you, Vectis—My Heart, My Soul—I love you."

She lifted up and their lips touched, and then their cheeks as they held each other. She curled her fingers over his shoulders and felt the hard line of his body on hers. Oh, how good and right this feels, she thought. Somehow, everything would work out. It would! She would make it work. During the next minutes as they moved in rhythm together, she felt as if she were running through the woods, naked and free. Vectis was beside her, loving her, kissing her, and she laughed in the wind. There were no Celtic warriors in the hills and no Roman oppressors. They were alone, and very happy.

Afterward, they lay quietly on the couch with a soft linen blanket partially covering them. Vectis gazed at her.

"What?" she asked.

A smile crinkled the corners of his mouth. "Commodus was right," he said. "You are beautiful, like the goddess Venus."

Neeve flushed. She could imagine how many genuinely beautiful women there must be the streets of Rome. "What about my resplendent loveliness?" she asked, trying to cover her self-consciousness.

"I was about to mention that," he said, brushing a few stray hairs from her face.

She rubbed a foot back and forth against the corner of a pillow, further evidence of her self-consciousness, she realized.

He touched her hair lightly again. "So fine and clean," he mused, "as if you wash every strand separately."

"You know little about Celtic women," she said. "We scrub our hair every day, with strong Celtic soap."

"In Rome it has become the fashion for fullers to use your Celtic soap in cleaning garments, but I have never seen it used in the baths. Roman women spend so much time piling their hair and dressing it with pomatum ointment that I'm sure they would consider it a waste to scrub out the perfume."

"In Londinium I oiled and perfumed my hair."

"You?" He laughed.

"In ringlets. For a whole week."

"It must have been awful," he teased.

"It was. I hated it."

"So you scrubbed your hair with fuller's soap."

"Until my scalp burned from the lye."

Vectis smiled and ran his fingers the length of her hair. "I love it just the way it is."

"One day I might surprise you and put my hair up."

"I cannot imagine. My sweet Neeve, trying to please the Romans."

"Not the Romans. I would be trying to please you."

The comment touched him. "Everything about you pleases me," he said, drawing her closer. He kissed her warmly on the lips. "I never thought this day would come. For some reason I have sensed ...." He paused. "Well, it seems silly, but I imagined a barrier between us. I thought you were shutting me out, but now I know it was only me." His face tightened. "Neeve, earlier I said I needed to explain something to you not at all flattering."

She laughed. "You seem to have been distracted."

He chuckled and patted her leg. "Yes, that's true." Then he grew serious. "I really need to—"

"Vectis," Neeve said, "let us agree to let the past sleep. I too have things that wither in the light, but please, can we not forget the past and start new? Totally new. Unless you murder babies, I forgive you."

He smiled good-humoredly. "Even Romans don't murder babies, but there is something you should know." And then he told her the story of the little slave girl, the death of her father and the guilt he had for having caused her so much pain.

When he finished she sat in silence. "A sad story," she said finally.

"Sad, yes, but it has molded my thinking to this day. In my young mind I loved her, and when she betrayed me, it made me distrust outsiders, especially Celts."

"People like me."

"Especially like you. Can you understand that?"

"I can."

"So from the beginning I did not trust you or your brother, and I thought the worst when you tried to protect yourself by pretending to know Legate Julius Verus. I had you followed by scouts, and even searched your room—"

"Please, I understand.   I forgive you.   We can start new. Everything new."

"One more thing and I will have swept my conscience clean." His brow furrowed. "The slave girl ... my memory of her never dims. When I'm alone she calls to me. When I push her from my mind, she comes to me in dreams. I don't know why, but she is always there, reaching out from the stockade." He looked intently at her, as if he expected her to say something.

"Maybe she wants forgiveness," Neeve volunteered, "for deceiving you."

He shrugged and said, "The strangest part is that you look like her, particularly your eyes."

"I look like the slave girl?" The comparison disturbed Neeve. She looked like the girl who had deceived him. She laughed in disbelief. "You Romans always think Celts look alike. Many of us have yellow hair and blue eyes—"

"It's not just a similarity. Over the years I have seen many Celtic girls, and there was never one like her, or you. That's why I was so shocked to see you in my office, staring at me with those incredible eyes of yours. You even had water dripping from your hair, the way she did that day on the blocks."

"The slave girl had wet hair?" The coincidences troubled her.

"They dunked her in a tank to clean her."

Long moments passed before Neeve could speak. She suddenly felt chilled and pulled the linen blanket around her neck. Now she understood why he sometimes gazed at her strangely.   She straightened her back and said, "So I am like a nightmare you want to go away."

He pulled her close. "I never want you to leave. Not ever. I have waited my whole life for you, but now I'm afraid the truth will drive you away. I'm afraid you will think I merely want release from my past ... and in a way that's true. But, believe me, my past has nothing to do with my feelings for you." His eyes searched her face. "I love *you*, Neeve. I tell you about the slave girl only because I want no secrets between us, and because I want you to understand why I distrusted you."

"I understand."

"You do?"

She nodded.

"Good," he said, plainly relieved. He ran his fingers through his dark hair and looked at her earnestly. "I realize that a Roman and a Celt—"

Someone knocked at the door.

"Oh, not now," he lamented. He bounded off the couch and scooped up his tunic. Neeve bolted forward, suddenly realizing she was naked. She pulled on her clothes as quickly as she could. Vectis was across the room, straightening his belt and tunic before opening the door a crack. Neeve glimpsed Julian. She heard Vectis whisper urgently to his friend, then shush him when he chuckled.

"Sorry," Vectis said as he sat down beside her.

"That was Julian?" she asked, knowing it was.

"I sent him away."

"What was so humorous?"

"I don't know," he said, evading the question. "He finds humor in everything."

Neeve let it pass.

Vectis sat up straight, looking very solemn. "I know it might be difficult for a Roman and a Celt to ... what I mean is, I don't think there will be a problem with the two of us being together, because people are the same the world over. At least that's what I have found," he finished lamely.

She stared at him.

"This is not going well, is it?" he said, flustered. "What I'm trying to say is that, over time everything will work out for us."

"I am not sure what you mean," Neeve said. "You want to continue our relationship. Yes?"

"Yes, but ... marriage," he said with a slight tremor in his voice, "I'm talking about marriage."

"Marriage?" Her heart pounded in her throat.

"Yes, I'm asking you to marry me."

Neeve blinked. "You cannot be serious." Something in his eyes said he was. "Why would you want to marry me?"

"Why? Because I love you."

"A Celt? You want to marry a Celt?"

"I want to marry *you*."

"Well," Neeve laughed awkwardly, "I cannot marry *you*."

Shock registered on his face.

"You are a Roman," she said, as if that explained everything.

"I have been Roman this whole time we have known each other, and it hasn't hindered anything."

Neeve found herself staring at the charcoal embers glowing in the brazier. "I was not expecting this," she said, unable to pull her eyes from the crimson glow. "Romans usually take things. I thought you might have desires for me—as a bed partner or even a mistress—but never marriage. How would you ever explain a wife like me to your friends in Rome?"

"With pride."

His words barely registered. She was wondering how she would explain Vectis to her brothers, especially Taranis.

He continued. "I never wanted you simply to satisfy my needs— like a harlot from the camp followers. Don't you think I would have taken you before today, if that's all I wanted?"

She suddenly had no difficulty concentrating on his words. "You have always treated me with unusual respect," she said, "and I knew we had something special. But marriage ... it never occurred to me."

His face softened. "Do you love me enough to marry me? It would mean leaving Britannia and coming to Rome."

"I do love you and would follow you to India, if you asked. But I—" She broke off, unsure what to say. How could she allow him to enter a marriage built on lies? "I was married before," she said hastily. "I never told you that."

"It's all in your records—the bill of divorce, the witnesses, the date—everything."

She looked at him, pleading with her eyes for release. "You know nothing about me," she said, "absolutely nothing."

"I know I love you more than I have loved anyone in my whole life." He took her hand.

"No!" She pulled away. "This is all wrong, so terribly wrong."

"You said that before. It's *not* wrong. Our love is beautiful and good."

"That is not what I mean." She covered her face to escape. She needed time to think. Why had she allowed herself to get into this mess? Now she would have to concoct more lies to survive. No, she told herself, no more lies. But what else could she do? She could never tell him about her activities as a spy.

"Neeve, what is it? Did something happen in your marriage that—"

"No," she said, forcing a smile.

"Then what is it?"

Neeve sat rigidly, trying to think. She felt short of breath, and her mind raced everywhere without contributing a thing.

"I told you about the slave girl," he reminded her.

"You did, but this is different."

"Different! How is it different?"

"It just is," she said, rising.

"That's all you intend to say?" Frustration was creeping into his voice.

Neeve walked over to the window. The snow had stopped and the fort was blanketed with a layer of white. Gangs of men were shoveling the walkways and platforms, but she hardly noticed them. "I know I am being terribly unfair," she said into the window slats, "and if I could change things I would. You are the most wonderful man and I ... I am not worthy of your love."

She heard him shifting on the couch but he remained seated. When he finally spoke his voice was gentle, with no trace of the earlier annoyance. "I don't know what to say. I cannot believe there is some mysterious evil about you."

She turned to face him. "You can rest your mind. I was never a Druid priestess or anything like that. It is just that this is not a good time for us to marry. In a year or two I will tell you everything, and you can decide if you still want to marry me."

"We don't have a year or two."

"I am so sorry, Vectis."

He nodded.

In the stillness Neeve could hear the carts hauling the snow from the streets. Her shoulders suddenly felt chilled from the wind that moaned through the slats behind her. "This might be a good time for me to leave," she said.

Vectis crossed the room and put his arms around her. The fibers of his tunic were hot from the brazier, and she snuggled into him for warmth. "I don't care if you have a hundred secrets," he said resolutely, "I will not let you go. We will lock the past in a bottomless pit and together set out to create a beautiful future."

"You still want to marry me?"

"More than anything."

She pushed her face into his neck. "I do not deserve you," she whispered. A thousand thoughts flashed through her mind. What about her brothers, and Caledonia, and her mission at the post? She had completed her mission, she reasoned. All she had left was the troop deployment information, and she could deliver that to her brothers when the cold weather broke. And deception? She was not really deceiving Vectis, she told herself, because all this work had taken place before she declared her love for him. From now on, she would be completely loyal, and never again would she mislead him.

But what about her promise to tell him everything in two years? Surely he would expect an explanation. She groaned. She would have to tell one more lie. She would say she had returned only part of the emissary's coins, and had taken the rest to her brother, and that ever since, she had been guilt-ridden. But never would she reveal the truth—that she had been a Caledonian spy, and that time after time she had deceived him. The truth would remain buried in the secret chambers of her heart. Vectis might have the luxury of confessing his failings, but she did not.

His voice broke into her thoughts. "I know you don't deserve me, but does your silence mean yes?"

She smiled and struck him lightly on the chest. "I do not deserve you, but yes, my answer is yes."

"Your answer is yes?"

"My answer is yes."

His eyes shone. "My wife," he said slowly, mulling over the words.

Standing by the window, they held each other, and kissed again and again, drinking in the sensation of the wet warmth of their mouths.

Suddenly a horrible thought struck her; she had no dowry. All she owned was the tract of land on which her roundhouse sat, and she could hardly offer that. "Vectis," she said, "I know Roman men expect their brides to contribute a dowry, but I—"

"A dowry!" he said, pulling back. "If I wanted lands or bankers' notes, I would have chosen a skinny matron from Rome. Besides," he said with humor, "we have your growing account at the fort, don't we?"

"I had forgotten about that! One gold *aureus* and a silver *denarius*. Rather respectable, I would say."

"Ah, but maybe I'm marrying you for your money."

"At least I have you in the bargain."

"You will always have me," he said, and then he added, "I just pray that the fates never spirit you away."

"The fates would not be so cruel."

His face grew serious. "The way of the fates is hard. At the edges of my mind, I still have fears—"

"What sorts of fears?" Neeve asked, rubbing his arm lightly. It was an uncomfortable subject, but it would be worse not to ask.

"That is the odd thing," he replied, "I don't know. It's just a cold feeling, a premonition of ill tidings, I suppose." He snorted at his foolishness. "I'm sounding like a gloomy soothsayer. Soon I'll be proclaiming judgment day, when the heavens roll back like a scroll." He sat quietly for a moment. "Even so, I sense something." And then, staring at her, he asked, "Don't you feel it? Doesn't our love seem fragile, like a lamp in the night breeze?"

"Hold me," she said, "I need you close." A hollow feeling welled up inside and threatened to overwhelm her. Their love could not endure, and somehow both knew it. The night was coming when their fragile light would flicker and die.

Still clinging to him, she said, "Promise me, Vectis, that you will always love me."

"Without end," he said.

"That no matter what happens, you will judge me by the motives of my heart."

He was looking at her now. "Always," he said, but concern grew at the edges of his eyes.

She couldn't stop. "And even if the sky should crash down upon us like boulders, you will still hold me dear in your heart."

He took her by the shoulders and said, "I will *always* love you."

"And I vow on the brows of the ancient gods, that should the blackest darkness befall us, I will never cease loving you."

The two stood quietly, as if the slightest movement, the slightest sound, would tempt the gods to withdraw what small happiness they had seen fit to bestow. Neeve shared Vectis's fear. It seemed as if the forces of nature were arrayed against them.

"Declare me now," she said. "I want to be totally yours."

"Now?"

"If you are willing."

He patted her hands and moved toward the door. Opening it, he said to the orderly, "Get Julian. And find me a flute player."

Minutes later, Julian appeared at the door with Jupiter, their hair still damp from the baths where the orderly had found them. Behind them in the hallway stood a half-dozen officers, including the chief engineer and the officer in charge of fort defense. All had a hard look on their faces.

"I thought you might need them," Julian said crisply. "What's happened? Caledonians?"

"Worse," Vectis replied. "Marriage. I am declaring Neeve as my wife." And then looking past them, he shouted, "Let that flute player through!"

Everyone broke into laughter except Jupiter, who shifted his eyes to Neeve and did nothing to alter the brooding expression on his face. It unnerved her. She looked away and tried to laugh gaily, but a strangled sound escaped from her throat. For a time after her injury, he had seemed concerned about her well-being, sometimes stopping to talk, but she maintained her distance. Avoid the dark centurion, her brother had said, he is very dangerous.

When the officers had gathered around, and the flutist was playing softly in the corner, Vectis declared his love for Neeve and his intention to marry her. She had been to many Roman weddings and knew that men simply declared their intentions, rarely their love for the bride, and his declaration warmed her deeply.

"We really should have a sacrifice," Vectis said, "but with the Caledonians at the gate, and the priests ever sensitive to protect Rome's anointed ones—themselves—they have naturally followed the divine call south."

Amid the laughter, Julian spoke up. "We may all feel confident in assuming their blessings. This very day I will dispatch a rider to instruct the few priests left at Colania to perform a proper sacrifice. I am certain they will find good omens."

"Have you ever heard of a priest finding bad omens at a wedding?" the engineer asked to everyone's amusement.

The room hushed as Vectis took Neeve's hand and uttered the traditional words, "Will you be the mother of my family?"

"I will," Neeve replied.

With Julian prompting her, Neeve asked, "And will you be the father of my family?"

"I will," Vectis said. He then placed on the third finger of Neeve's left hand his mother's family ring.

Again, Neeve waited for the prompt, and repeated the ancient Roman formula, "Where you are Gaius, I am Gaia." With that, the room burst into shouts of congratulations. Several officers clapped Vectis on the back and kissed Neeve on the cheek, and the flutist played his merriest tune.

Julian beamed in Neeve's face and kissed her three times, once on the lips. "I have never seen Vectis so happy," he said. "You cannot know how much he loves you."

Officer Nepos sidled up to her and smothered her cheek with his lips. "This is the happiest day of my life," he gushed. "I know you both will have a long and prosperous life."

Then Jupiter stepped forward and kissed her. Neeve could feel the steel grip of his hands on her as he spoke. "In Africa we have a saying: 'New companions, new allegiances.'" The inky blackness of his eyes bored into her. "May fortune favor you," he said, before turning and leaving the room.

A chill swept over her. An odd thing for him to say. He couldn't have meant that a prefect's wife would have new obligations. His words were more ominous. She bit her lip. He knows! Why else would he say such a thing? He must know—or suspect—that she had been passing information to the Caledonians. She took a breath to calm herself and willed her mind to be reasonable. There was nothing to suspect. Nothing at all. If Jupiter knew anything he would have demanded her immediate execution. It was his way.

Vectis was staring at her from across the room. She smiled weakly, trying to pull herself out of the gloom that had so savagely possessed her. He bid the last officer goodbye and came to stand beside her. "You have just married the most important Roman in all of Caledonia," he said. "Why so sad?"

"Only in Caledonia?" she asked, speaking too loudly in her struggle to reach equilibrium. "I thought you were like those fat senators from Rome with their big villas and gold houses and heated pools."

"What do you know about fat senators?"

"I know that not one of them is like you." She gave him her warmest smile and the pleasure in his face melted her anguish. "I am so happy," she said, moving into his arms.

He stroked her hair lightly and slipped his fingers into the loose strands, caressing underneath, and sending a chill down her back. As she nuzzled her head against the warmth of his hand, she thought about the plaited hairstyle of Roman women. "I mean it," she said. "One day I will change my hair to look like a proper, submissive, Roman wife."

"I doubt you could ever be submissive," he said, his arms encircling her waist and drawing her securely to him.

"I will be whatever you wish," she said, "do whatever you wish." Her last words fell to a whisper. She wanted so much to make him feel the depth of love she had for him. From the beginning she had deceived him, used him, exploited his love. No lie was too insensitive as long as she got what she wanted. But that was behind her now. She would make up for it by being the most devoted, the most faithful, the most loving companion he could possibly imagine. Vectis was more than she had ever hoped for in a man and it wasn't fair that he should suffer for her mixed loyalties.

They kissed again. Long, warm, sweet kisses. She drew her head back and gazed into his dark eyes. "Oh, Vectis," she said, "how I love you. Take me to the couch again, I need you now." Somewhere deep in her mind she glimpsed the dark, glowering eyes of Jupiter, but he was far away.

32

In the dead of winter, madness stalks the people of the north. The days are short, brutal and cold, the nights dark and interminable. The inhabitants spend so many hours staring at the inner walls of their dwellings that a fever overtakes them, a kind of cabin fever that breeds strange and quarrelsome behavior.

Hardly before the spring crocuses had poked their heads through the melting snows, frenzied Caledonian warriors were roaming the hills, fighting among themselves and lashing out at Roman installations and depots on the supply routes. They seemed more interested in producing chaos than acquiring goods, and more than once Vectis had reports of Caledonians killing Roman soldiers but leaving the supplies untouched.

Having been warned by Priscianus of the deleterious effects that long winter months could have on outpost soldiers, Vectis had Jupiter create diversions to counteract the situation. Duties were rotated constantly, competitive games replaced drilling, soldier units were shifted from one outpost to another, and several hours were added to the bathhouse routine. Constant change was the key to Jupiter's plan, and while not entirely successful, in the end it produced healthy soldiers.

Change had also been beneficial for Vectis. Never had he known such joy and contentment. The days that followed his wedding were filled with love and laughter, and if in the coming months he died by the hands of the Caledonians, he judged his journey to Britannia province would have been worth it.

But spring was upon them, and his pre-winter dispatches to the Senate and the Imperial liaison had been greeted with silence. He had to assume that Rome was delaying its decision to send additional troops to Britannia.

Adding to his concern was a disturbing shift in Neeve's behavior. She hadn't left Faustina since their marriage, but she was determined to go on one last mapping assignment. For weeks she waited for a break in the unpredictable spring weather, and when it came, she insisted on leaving, and no amount of talking on Vectis's part could dissuade her.

At daybreak she sent an orderly to the stables to ready her horse. Vectis stood in the doorway of their reception room watching her fasten the bronze brooch of her winter riding cape. She had a determined look on her face.

"You know this is senseless," Vectis said.

"I had hoped you would understand."

"Well, I don't," he said, trying to make her feel uncomfortable.

"I shall be gone less than three days. It is not as if I have never mapped before."

He laughed in derision. "You were almost killed twice!"

She pulled the cape over her shoulders but didn't respond.

Vectis shook his head in disbelief. "Don't you care what I think?"

"Of course I do," she said, "I care a great deal."

"Then why would you continue mapping?"

She looked weary. "We discussed this last night."

"Your responses last night made no sense."

"I tried to explain—"

"That you want to run off mapping for no good reason," he said, finishing her sentence.

"Please, you are making this extremely difficult. The day we were married you agreed I could continue mapping."

"I know, but spring madness has possessed the Caledonians out there. There is no reason to risk your life."

"I need—"

"Need! What do you need? You don't need the money. Every time I offer to send something to your father you say it's unnecessary."

"It is not the money. It is just that—"

"Then what possible reason could you have for wanting to map?"

"I need time to—"

"A reason! Give me a reason!"

"If you would quit interrupting," she said, "I might be able to."

He gestured for her to speak.

"I have told you two or three times already," she said in an overly patient tone, "that I am not used to being cooped up in a fort all winter. I need to get away for a few days."

"Fine! Join a supply train and go south of the Wall. That way, at least, my soldiers can protect you."

"I would rather do a mapping assignment."

"Listen to me, Neeve—"

"No, you listen. We made an agreement that I could continue mapping after marriage. Are you forbidding me to go?"

Vectis felt trapped. "No," he said, "I am not forbidding you anything. I simply want you to consider the danger."

"I have considered it, and will be cautious. I promise."

Vectis muttered his disagreement.

"You act as if I know nothing about the hill country. When you came here, I was the one and only mapmaker, in case you have forgotten."

"You want to do maps? Do maps. Do all the maps you want." His voice was rising in spite of his determination to be calm. "I have no objection. But take escort soldiers with you. Is that too much to ask?"

"Everyone knows you cannot spare the soldiers."

"I have plenty of soldiers to escort my wife."

"I do not need them."

Vectis threw up his arms.

"I do not *want* them. I want to be alone."

"Maybe you haven't noticed," he flared, "but there are thousands of drunken Caledonians roaming the hills out there, and I can tell you, they are tired of being cooped up too. They would love to get their hands on a traitorous Celt who barters maps for Roman silver." He used the word "traitor" to anger her, but she didn't take the bait. She merely repeated her pledge to be careful.

"What is the matter with you? There is anarchy out there. The Caledonians themselves are having trouble gathering their warriors. They are killing each other. Next week a trio that has been rampaging through the middle sectors, raping and murdering, will be brought here for execution—and they are not the only ones out there. We constantly receive reports of women and children butchered in their roundhouses. This is not a good time for you to be mapping some hillside. You might never come back."

She moved toward the door.

He was desperate now. "I have given you my permission to go, and I'll stick to my word, but I am asking you to stay."

Something in her face indicated that she wanted to leave.

Vectis exploded. He had asked her politely—almost begged—and she turned her back on him. "You want to go?" he heard himself yelling, "then go!" He grabbed her by the arm, ripped open the door, and pushed her none too gently into the hallway. "Goodbye!" he shouted. "Hope you don't suffer long when they slit your throat to the spine." He slammed the door, spied the bust of Chiron grinning at him, and smashed his palm into it, toppling it to the floor. It rocked back and forth, face up, not even cracked. He kicked the god of wisdom behind a curtain out of sight; he was in no mood to be mocked.

For a full minute he stared at the dark wood grain of the closed door. He knew she was on the other side, but he said nothing. He was too exasperated to speak and down deep hoped she would come to her senses. Finally, he heard her say in a small voice, "I love you," and she left.

Vectis dragged himself to the nearest couch and flopped down. "Wonderful!" he said out loud. "The gods are smiling on me today."

He stared at the floor, thinking. What has happened to her? She suddenly feels this urgent need to go mapping. A few days, she says, and all my craziness will be gone. So might her head, he thought. He rubbed his face and eyes, and pushed back his hair.

As the minutes drifted by, his rage drained from him, and he felt ashamed. A deep sadness filled him as he recalled how happy they had been just yesterday and how roughly he had treated her today. He had a strange way of showing his love. How could he be so cruel? She wanted to feel useful, to take a simple mapping trip, to be alone in the open spaces. Did he not promise her she could? He told himself he merely wanted to protect her, but it was not the whole truth. He selfishly wanted to be with her every minute. Time was growing short. In a month or so, depending on the Caledonian threat, he would be forced to send her south for safety, and if Rome delayed too long in dispatching troops, none at the outposts would escape. The hard truth was that he and Neeve might have less than a month together.

"Maybe only days," he murmured, if the Caledonians stumble across her. He pushed himself off the couch and strode toward the door. He would catch her before she left the stables, apologize and give her his blessings. It was the right thing to do. No harm would likely come to her, but he should never allow her to leave like this.

Outside the stables, he saw Jupiter. The centurion was watching Neeve over the cut-away wall as she talked to a stable hand tending her horse.

"A mapping assignment?" Jupiter asked.

Vectis nodded.

"The Caledonians are eating each other out there."

"Spring frenzy."

Jupiter paused before speaking. "She refused an escort?"

Vectis eyed him. "Why do you ask?"

"Just curious."

"She refused," he said at length.

"Did you offer her Scythian riders—they wouldn't slow her any."

"I offered her everything. She wants to be alone for a while. Tired of being fort-bound, I guess."

"Can't fault her for that."

"No."

"But it is dangerous," Jupiter said. He took a breath and leaned toward his prefect. "Tomorrow I leave for my outpost visits. I could go alone and follow her. Two or three days more are of no consequence to me, but they could be to her." He spoke as a matter of fact, but his words were ominous.

"She must never know you're there."

"I'll conceal myself well."

"Thank you," Vectis said.

He nodded and left.

Seconds later Vectis approached Neeve. She had completed strapping her bows to the tall roan mount, and was about to leave.

He called to her. "I forgot to give you something."

She turned and without thinking, smiled.

She was truly pleased to see him, he thought. His heart ached. This was the Neeve he loved so dearly. "I forgot to give you my love," he said.

"I had it in here anyway," she replied, pointing to her bosom. She squeezed into his arms. "I am glad you came, though. I want to take every bit of your love with me I can."

"I am sorry," Vectis said, "so sorry."

"It is not you," she whispered, "my dear, dear Vectis, it is not you."

Her kiss was hot and moist, and then she said, "If you want me to stay, I shall. I will not complain."

"No, you go," he said. "Just be careful. Be ... very careful."

She kissed him again and together they walked to the gates.

That afternoon Neeve had the queerest feeling. As usual she had ridden to her designated sector, turned off the arterial road and checked for signs of a scout following her. There was nothing: no dust on the flats, no sudden flight of birds or animals, no unusual quiet in the forest. Nothing. But something wasn't right. She pushed from her mind the image of the crushed-faced emissary lying in wait for her. If anyone was out here, it would be a Roman scout.

She crossed a desolate moor and veered into a wooded area, knowing that anyone following would have to cross the moor quickly or risk losing her in the woods. She waited inside the tree line, thirty feet from her entrance point. Nobody crossed the moor. She wondered whether her pursuer might leave his horse behind and crawl through the grassy areas. She was becoming irrational now. How would he follow once she resumed riding on the other side of the woods? A cold thought fluttered through her mind. Maybe he intended to kill her in the woods. She dismissed the idea. Anyone wanting to kill her could have done so much earlier and with greater ease.

She inspected the moor, searching for the slightest stirring of the grasses, but there was nothing.

She decided to push her way through the thick woods, leading her horse as best she could along the animal trails. Every few feet she peered over her shoulder and often she stopped to listen. If he was there, he was very quiet.

Straight ahead, the woods thinned and dropped into a ravine. On the other side she spied an arrow-shaped slice where long ago mudslides had cleared the trees and rocks, leaving smooth, green grass. She led the roan down the grade as quickly as safety would allow. At the bottom, spring rains had pooled and the freezing waters numbed her feet. With some effort she navigated the opposite hillside until she reached the break. She glanced around. It was a good place to rest her horse and to heat a cup of root tea. She tied the roan to a slender oak in plain view of anyone approaching from the other side, and built a fire—large enough to be seen within the gorge. Then, bow in hand, she circled back down the hill.

At the point where the trail began its steep climb, and where she had a good view of the ravine, Neeve wriggled into a rock cleft, and waited. She doubted anyone had followed her this far, but now she would know.

A half-hour passed. An hour. She was being overly cautious, she knew, but the feeling that someone was out there nibbled at the edges of her mind. She turned to go, and then on a whim, or perhaps because of some deep-seated fear, she made one last survey of the darker sections of the woods. Her eyes stopped on the patches of spring runoff. She had examined every tree and rock along the ridge, but hardly paid attention to the flooded areas. Who would lie motionless in the icy waters all this time? Even the fabled Iceni trackers could not survive an hour in such bitter cold.

She raked her eyes across the darkened wetlands, looking for suspicious roots and broken trees. An Iceni, she guessed, would spare his body by keeping as dry as possible—draping himself over a log or scrunching under knots of brush-covered rock flats. About fifty feet out were a number of fallen trees, jagged at one end where they had been snapped by a sudden wind. On one she noticed a curious thickening, like a dark growth swelling the bark, and a face peering out at her. It couldn't be, she told herself, but the longer she looked, the more she saw the hunched body and shining eyes staring at her.

Neeve drew an arrow. Her good sense told her to leave, but she had to find out. She pulled the string back to the corner of her mouth and watched the arrow sail across the distance, splashing in front of the log. The swelling remained as still as if it were part of the wood. This is madness, a voice inside kept telling her. Suppose a scout really is hiding on the log and he rushes toward you. She loosed another arrow that overshot the log and smacked into the bark of a broken tree.

Suddenly, the stumps came alive, looking like stubby warriors marching toward her. None of it was real, she told herself, just the woods playing tricks. She swung her head around. In the shadows opposite her she saw something move, or someone. A shadowy figure seemed to grow, looking like the hideous, crouching beast in the Druid temple that Taranis had told her about, with human limbs protruding from its mouth.

Her imagination was galloping now. Every niche and hollow pulsed with life and she had the greatest urge to run. She closed her eyes and drew in a deep breath. It was a mistake. With her eyes closed she panicked, half expecting a hand to reach out and grab her. She whisked her bow over her shoulder, and wrested herself out of the lookout rock. Her heart pounded in her ears as she scrambled up the embankment, and her constant glances back only increased her anxiety and made her slip more than once. About halfway up she tried to master her fears by making one last, serious inspection of the lower area. What she saw made her legs grow watery. The swollen log was no longer swollen; from the higher vantage, it looked like an ordinary log.

Neeve snapped her knife out of its sheath and bolted up the incline. At the edge of the grassy patch, she broke into a sprint. Not even bothering to kick dirt on the still live coals, she yanked at the roan, whipping his haunches as he moved skittishly toward the top of the ravine. A branch swatted her cheek, burning her face. She jerked the hood of her cloak over her eyes, bent her head, and pulled her horse up the hill. Minutes later, on level ground, she flipped into the saddle and lashed the roan through the trees until she came to another section of rolling grasslands.

More than an hour of hard riding passed before Neeve felt comfortable, and even then she questioned every twitch of every bush and tree. She tried to use common sense. Had someone been stalking her? Ridiculous! Why would anyone take such trouble? She knew what had happened: the woods had spooked her. No tracker—not an Iceni, and certainly not a Roman scout—could have followed her today. In any case, someone following her into the woods would have been on foot and would have ended his pursuit once he reached the grasslands. No man could run as fast as a horse.

As night fell she built a fire, ate several biscuits and washed them down with hot beer. She glanced at the blackness around her and felt terribly exposed sitting by the fire. It was happening again; fear was swallowing her saner self. Not long ago she would have snuggled closer to the fire and enjoyed her solitude. But that was the problem— she didn't feel alone. Someone was after her. Someone like the emissary. He was out there now, and if he hadn't yet discovered her fire, he soon would. She debated whether to smother the flames with dirt and keep only the coals alive for warmth, but that would be foolish. Without the flames, the wolves would come.

The whole situation was senseless, she told herself. She had not one shred of evidence that anyone was out there. Even the swollen log came from her imagination. She might as well face it. Her experience with the emissary had taken its toll, and she was glad it was over.

Neeve's eyes swept the blackness again. It was a useless gesture that only increased her fear. Someone could be twenty feet away, maybe even close enough to touch her, and she would see only the night.

No one was there.

The wind moaned in the heather.

Or was it a human voice?

Fear owned her now.

It was time to go.

She would let her imaginary pursuer—for that is what he was— watch the firelight from his hiding place while she slipped into the night. By tomorrow she would be back at her roundhouse, and there she would deliver the troop deployment information to her brothers, and be done with it. After that she would be in Vectis's arms and they would forget they ever had a dispute. And never again would she insist on mapping.

Hastily, she pawed through her pile of firewood and pulled from it a straight branch and three heavy logs. She dumped the logs on the fire and banked the edges with rocks. They would burn for hours, and if there was a tracker, he would not think her so foolish as to try riding over night terrain, but would maintain his vigil so long as the fire lasted. She took the knife from her hip and hacked the branch clean, leaving a sturdy pole. Then with a length of twine from her saddle, she bound the knife to the end of the pole. Night riding was risky, but at least she had a weapon to discourage curious wolves.

By dawn Neeve had reached the edge of the valley that led to their family home. A morning fog had rolled across the land, making it impossible to see beyond a few yards, and forcing her to slow her pace. Looming ahead, she could see the soaring shafts of granite that marked the entrance to the ancient valley trail. The banks of mist were so thick by the entrance that it was difficult to see the rock.

Suddenly, one of the smaller shafts near the path moved.

Neeve yanked hard on the reins to turn her horse. Too late. The mist had taken form and was pounding down the trail toward her. She jammed her heels into the roan's side but a dark shape appeared in front of her and caught hold of the reins, wrenching them from her hands. She whipped her head around. Hot blood surged through her body. Two men!

The first man was beside her now and holding a battle-axe over his shoulder, poised to swing. "Climb down," he roared, "or I will take off your leg."

A shiver ran through Neeve as she thought of the axe splintering her thighbone. She swung her leg across the saddle and slid to the mud path.

The man dropped the axe and was on her the moment her feet touched the ground. He ripped the knife-pole off her horse and threw it down, then seized her by the hood and twisted her around until her head was pressed firmly into the saddle. He thrust his hands inside her cloak and ran them over her body, probing roughly in the most intimate places, but not in an intimate way. He wanted her weapons, and when he stepped back, her ankle knife lay on the ground. The second man scooped up the knife, then the pole as he loosened the twine at the end.

"A woman," her assailant said with surprise.

Neeve turned on him. "If you had let me speak," she said indignantly, "I could have told you I'm Taranis's sister."

He shoved his face closer, revealing the leathery skin of an older man. "Yes," he said, pushing back her hood, "I've seen you before. Why are you riding at night?"

"Someone is following me ... a Roman tracker, I think."

He shook his head. "Not anymore. You passed two other sentries back there."

A chill ran down Neeve's back. "How do you know they are still—?"

"Alive?" he said, finishing her question. His leathery skin cracked into a smile. "Oh, they are still alive. Like this boy," he said, motioning to his younger companion, "I trained them myself." The man stepped away from the horse and cupped his hands, making a peculiar whistling sound, like no bird Neeve had ever heard. Seconds later a similar sound came through the fog, and then another, then two short trills, one from each sentry. "Still there," he said, showing clear pride in his work. "Can't duplicate that sound easily, and can't know how many whistles to make at the end."

Neeve relaxed. She could see that the old man was a master at his craft. "I left a decoy fire," she said, "and set out in the dark. But I was still worried he might not be fooled. This tracker has great skill—like an Iceni." She chose not to mention that he might exist only in her imagination.

"You have nothing to fear from Romans here. If he is as good a tracker as you say, he would have known when he crossed into Caledonian territory, and a poor one would have been discovered long ago. This whole area has a dozen Caledonian camps, and hundreds of scouts combing the hills and woodlands. We continually signal to each other and keep fresh by working half shifts." He motioned to the younger man, who stepped forward and presented her with her knives.

"Want the pole?" the young man asked.

Neeve glanced at the pole and twine lying on the ground. "Just the knives," she said. She turned to the older man. "I must go. Are there other scouts in the valley that might stop me?"

"Commander Taranis has posted scouts everywhere," he replied. "But you won't find the commander in his roundhouse. He left several days ago to inspect the camps."

Neeve couldn't hide her disappointment. The drawing she carried was packed with Roman troop information that only she could interpret. She needed to see Taranis and time was slipping by. In three days she had promised to return to Faustina. How could she find Taranis, sketch her maps, and return in the allotted time?

"I know where the commander is," the scout said on seeing her disappointment. "At least, I know how to find out where he is. All information on his whereabouts is funneled to the scouting post at Lanaxi, a day's ride from here."

"Lanaxi," Neeve said, stunned. "That's a long way." She gritted her teeth. "Well, if that's where I have to go, I'd better not waste more time."

"I'll escort you."

"That won't be necessary. I am capable of finding Lanaxi by myself." She had no reason to distrust the sentry, but since her unfortunate encounter with the Roman emissary, she had become wary of all strange men.

The old man tilted his head. "I said you are safe from the Romans here, but there are many reckless warriors heading to their training camps and I cannot let you travel alone. The commander would never forgive me."

"You have a horse?" she asked haughtily, suggesting he was too lowly to own one.

"Beyond those shafts of rock," he said. "Even a poor scout would have heard him shudder moments ago."

Neeve thought she detected amusement in his eyes. She smiled in defeat. She liked him, and oddly, trusted him.

33

Neeve heard discouraging news at Lanaxi. Taranis was at a camp two days distant and on a straight line away from the sector she needed to map. It would be a week or more before she could return to Faustina. There was nothing she could do. She needed to see her brother and that was that.

Traveling with her leather-faced escort proved enjoyable, despite her concerns over the mounting delays. He had a story for every situation. When the conversation turned to the Druids, he told her about the time a priest was chanting off key, and Divicos threatened to roast him over the fire. Never sang off key again, he said. His numerous tales about his daughter were a transparent, but appreciated gesture to ease her mind about being alone at night with a strange man.

By mid-morning on the third day, they reached the blind canyon where the training camp was located. Tents of all sizes and colors were scattered everywhere, unlike the rows of box-like tents in Roman camps. Except for two guard posts, the entire grounds looked deserted. The warriors were scaling rocks behind the camp. She and her escort followed a guard to the central tent—a beautiful goatskin tarp, ten feet high at the midpoint. There she found Taranis talking with five other commanders.

"Neeve!" Taranis cried with delight. He embraced her, and still holding her with one arm, displayed her like a trophy, saying loudly, "Caledonia's *first* warrior has returned with more information on the Romans."

Neeve shot a startled glance at her brother. The commanders were aware of her activities at Faustina, but two guards stood at the entrance of the tent, as did her escort.

"There is nothing to fear," Taranis said. "I am happy to inform you that your spying days at Outpost Faustina are over, and you, my dear sister, can take a well-deserved rest. War is coming soon and Caledonian lands will once more belong to Caledonians. The gods are with us."

"The gods are with us," Neeve responded in a whisper that was lost in the deep voices of the other commanders. She stared at her brother. "You want me to stay?"

"Not here," Taranis said, smiling broadly. "Somewhere out of the fighting zones, like Celywic in the north. Remember Celywic? You liked that area when you were little."

Neeve nodded. "I remember," she said, thinking about her days alone by the Ordvgi River, waiting for her brothers to return from war with the Romans, and wondering how she could tell them their mother and little Nes had been captured. And then came the horrible news that they were sending her to live with Pablius and Matidia. But none of those experiences compared with what faced her now. How could she ever explain to Taranis she had married a Roman and intended to return to Faustina?

She willed the thoughts away and said, "I have important information."

Taranis waited.

"On troop deployment along the Wall," she continued, "the exact numbers and kinds of soldiers at each fort."

Taranis glanced at the other commanders, who were making noises somewhere between surprise and delight. He turned back to Neeve with concern on his face. "*All* the Wall forts? How could you remember ... you didn't steal a Roman document, did you? I warned you about that."

Neeve raised a hand to assure him. "I concealed the information in a drawing," she said. "Even the prefect complimented the picture. But I do need a scribe to record the data."

Taranis's face relaxed. "You have done your usual thorough job, Neeve, but you should not have taken such a risk." He squeezed her shoulder in a gesture of pride. "But you are here—I cannot deny that—and never again will you have to deal with the Romans. This I promise."

The Celts had not committed their tongue to writing, but lately Taranis used southern Celts with Roman writing skills to transmit his messages. While they waited for the scribe, Neeve retrieved the drawing from her saddlebag and showed Taranis and the commanders how she had inserted numbers and fort names into the drawing.

"Amazing," Taranis said, "truly amazing. Those Romans had no idea what they were letting into their precious fort the day they opened their gates to you."

Neeve smiled weakly as the commanders congratulated her. She couldn't help noticing the hate in Taranis's eyes when he spoke of the Romans—how could she tell him?

The prospect of learning the precise numbers of troops at the Wall forts excited the commanders, and they marveled at her ability to make sense of Roman writing. When the scribe entered the tent, they gathered around the drawing and stared at every squiggle she interpreted as a fort name or troop number. Writing was a mystery to them and she could only imagine what it must have looked like when she pointed to a wisp of dust and said, "Caracalla wall fort: one hundred sixty auxiliaries, twenty Scythians."

It took over an hour to record the information and by then she and Taranis were alone, except for the scribe. Fascination aside, duties needed doing, and one by one the commanders had left. At length, Taranis dismissed the scribe, instructing him to have four copies ready for the morning dispatch.

And then they were alone.

Neeve picked up her drawing of Outpost Faustina and thought about her life back there—of Vectis and Julian and Jupiter—so far away. She fiddled with the scroll, rolling and unrolling it. One edge was torn and she ran her finger along the tear, thinking how shredded her own life was becoming. She watched her brother instructing the cook he had summoned—the only one capable of making different foods taste different, he had said—and it didn't go beyond Neeve's notice that the meal Taranis had chosen was her favorite: boiled lamb with barley bread and goat cheese.

She sipped a cup of herb tea that warmed her to her toes. "This is good," she said, looking over the rim of her cup.

Taranis nodded. He dragged a heavy travel box near her, sat down, and gulped his tea. "You must feel relieved, getting away from that fort."

Neeve hugged her arms. She had to tell him. She had to tell him now. No, not now. Maybe after they ate. Yes, they would eat, and then she would tell him.

"Neeve?"

She looked up. He had been saying something but her mind was in a fog.

"Are you all right?" he asked. "Tired from your days of riding?"

"I suppose I am."

"Everything will change now. No more snooping around forts, or dangerous night rides, or attacks by filthy Romans. Caledonia will be free again." His eyes drifted away. "Think of it, Neeve. You, me, Eston—farming the land again. Of course, we'll have to find you a proper husband. Can't have all the village men tramping around the homestead trying to win your favor—they'll ruin the crops." He laughed, enjoying his own humor.

Neeve tried but couldn't summon a smile. She kept thinking about how to tell him.

"I thought you might threaten to find me a wife, but I see you're tired." He pushed off the box. "Rest. I shall be back tomorrow."

"You're leaving?"

"I keep to a schedule. That way every one can find me quickly. Tomorrow afternoon Eston and I will be back at this camp. In the meantime I must meet with Forgall to coordinate outpost strategy."

"But I need to talk to you."

He moved toward the flap on the tent door. "You rest. We can talk tomorrow."

"I will not be here tomorrow."

He stopped.

Neeve bit her lip. "It's hard to explain, but I have to return to the fort."

"What?"

"I do. I must go back."

"There is no need to go back. You have given us more than we ever expected, and now with the troop listings of each Wall fort ... there is no other pressing information."

"It's not about collecting information."

"What is it about, then?"

"Could you sit down?"

Taranis took two quick steps to the travel box, never once taking his eyes off her. A tightness at his mouth showed his anxiety. She had seen it before. "Well?" he said.

"I have involved myself in a bit of a complication."

He widened his eyes for her to continue.

"I need to return because I ... because I belong there now."

"What are you saying?"

Neeve took a breath. "I'm married to the prefect at Faustina."

His brow furrowed. "The prefect forced marriage on you?" A dark light crossed his face. "That Roman pig! You don't need to return because of—"

"He didn't force marriage on me. His name is Vectis Trebellius—"

"I know who he is. He banished me from the fort."

"I love him, Taranis, more than I ever thought it was possible to love someone."

A long time passed before her brother spoke. He just stared. "You don't love him," he said finally. "Fear does strange things to the mind, and you were under enormous pressure in that fort."

"It wasn't the pressure. I loved him then, and I love him now."

"You don't love him," Taranis said in raised voice.

"You don't understand—"

"Oh, I understand—"

"No, you don't," she said quietly.

"He is a Roman! That is all I need to know."

"Yes, he's a Roman, but he's not like other Romans."

Taranis snorted. "All Romans walk the same road. They dictate the actions of free people and kill anyone who stands in their way."

"He's not like that."

"He *is* like that!" Taranis said, slamming his fist into the wooden lid of the travel box. "He comes from the same people that killed your father and sold your mother and sister to the slave market. Have you forgotten that?"

"It was a long time ago."

"A long time ago? Your sister might still be alive. Have you thought of that? What do you suppose these precious Roman people of yours are doing to her right now? Beating her? Maybe raping her, over and over—"

"Stop! I don't want to hear—"

"No, you don't want to hear this, do you? That's what Rome is all about. Control. Control of land and minds and bodies. Control of everything! Crawl or die, they say. Worship the magnificent Emperor—and the master who owns you—and Rome will let you be a happy slave. You might even be allowed to farm your own land, as long as you pay their levies, and as long as they don't give your land to some traitor who has wheedled his way into their good graces."

"I'm not blind to the evils of Rome, but it's not Rome that I love. I love a man—just a man—no different from you."

"Oh, he's different all right. He comes to Caledonia from the end of the world, and here in our land he plants his standard and demands to be called master—"

Taranis turned to see two aides hesitating in the doorway. The food had arrived. They placed it on a low table and left. "Neeve," he said in a less strident tone, "be reasonable. At the festival of renewal Caledonian warriors will receive the Druid blessing, and by next month when the water channels are free of ice, we will attack. Every Caledonian tribe will rise up and throw off the yoke of Roman slavery. These puny forts cannot stand—we will assault each one with thousands of warriors and destroy them. You can't go back to Faustina. By summer there will be nothing left."

"I still need to return."

"To die in the fort? Because that will happen. Once this begins, I can't protect you there."

"Taranis, I might be able to do something at the fort—maybe persuade the prefect to leave Caledonia."

"You live among Romans, but how little you understand them. These people never leave territories they conquer. They fight. Only this time they will die."

In the back of Neeve's mind, she remembered hearing about the Romans leaving their eastern provinces because they cost too much to maintain. It could happen here, she thought, if she could persuade Vectis to withdraw.

Taranis stood. "I cannot delay any longer," he said. "All I ask is that you wait until Eston arrives tomorrow and the three of us will find a solution. Is that not reasonable?"

"Yes, it is, and I dearly would like to see Eston, but I cannot wait. Even if I leave this afternoon, I'll be overdue."

"Overdue! What evil wind has possessed your mind?" His face turned red and the veins popped out on his neck. "You prefer Romans to your own people? Is that it? Have you no shame? Running back to someone that would cheerfully nail any one of us in this camp to a tree." He ground his teeth.

"You are angry with someone you don't even know. If you could meet him—"

"I did meet him! And I was lucky to escape with my life."

"I meant talk to him," she said quietly.

"I will talk to him, all right, at the end of my sword."

"I love this man, Taranis, and you know that. How could you want to kill him?"

"Because I am Caledonian. And so are you, if you need reminding."

"I know who I am."

"Then remember that Caledonians are different. We have never been a slave people, and even when armies defeat us, we go on fighting. That is why we're free." He stabbed his index finger at her. "The Romans have hounded us for generations, and it's easy to become weary of the fight. They march across our lands, build forts and roads where they choose, and collect taxes on land they do not own." His face reddened again. "If you go back to that damned Roman, you are no better than the cowering Votadini you pretend to be. You betray—"

"Enough! I have heard enough!" Neeve felt her body shaking.

"Then *listen* to what I'm saying."

"What right have you to talk to me this way?"

"All I'm saying—"

"What right? I should like to know."

"Will you listen?"

"I am sick of listening!"

"I'm saying that every generation must stand against nations that would enslave them, and it's our turn now. If Father's generation had taken your attitude, do you doubt we would be Empire slaves right now? Of course we would, and you know it."

Neeve glared at him. "What do you think I've been doing these past months? Do you suppose it's been easy getting information out of Faustina? Or does my work not count as taking a stand against Rome?"

He looked embarrassed. "I never suggested your work was easy. You have done a magnificent job—"

"Yes, I have! And it's been very dangerous. I risked my life to bring that emissary's money to you, and now the troop deployment information. So don't tell me I haven't done my part."

"You have done your part ... and more. Father would have been proud. I'm sorry for saying otherwise." He rubbed his face as if in contrition and said gently, "I'm afraid for you if you return to Faustina. We need to talk more about this. Stay until Eston arrives tomorrow."

"Forgive me, Taranis, but I cannot."

"You can if you wish."

"No, I really—"

"I don't understand this," he said, suppressing his anger. "I am your brother. I would give my blood for you, but you will not grant me one day so we can talk?"

"I'm sorry."

"Then I will force you to stay—for your own good. I'll place guards on your tent and you *will* be here tomorrow."

"I am not a child! I'm your sister, but I will not be dictated to. You are acting just like a Roman."

The words seemed to slap him in the face. He ran his fingers through his long yellow hair and propped his head against the tent pole. After a silence, he closed his eyes and said, "How can I let you go. There's nothing but death waiting for you at that fort."

"Taranis," Neeve said softly, "the gods have smiled upon me thus far. I beg you, let us trust them a little longer. Give me the chance to save my beloved. You might not think so, but he is different, he really is."

"He is not different, but I will spare you any more debate on the matter." His shoulders slumped. "It's my fault. No one else is to blame. *I* sent you to Matidia and her Roman husband. *I* sent you to the Roman fort with all its dangers. I just didn't think of this one. It's my fault entirely." He gazed at her and half-smiled as he said, "My little Neeve. So grown up." Then, expelling some air, he said, "My scouts will take you to the Roman road when you are ready, if that is your wish."

"Thank you. I will need them to stay with me while I map a sector—that was my reason for leaving the fort."

He nodded.

"Also, I would like one to be the leather-faced scout that escorted me here."

"I shall give the orders. The gods go with you."

"And with you."

He kissed her on the top of her head, and left.

34

Vectis stared at the thick document on his table. Three times he had tried to read the report on Caledonian tribal movements, but it was no use—he couldn't concentrate. Neeve was in trouble. He could feel it. Eight days ago she had left for a simple mapping assignment. Eight days! Twice he sent out scouts to scour her assigned sector, but they had found nothing. She wasn't there, nor along the arterial road, nor in the surrounding sectors. His worst fears were clawing at his mind; Neeve was dead, and he would never see her again.

A knock at the door. It was his aide. "Prefect, you asked to be notified the moment the First Centurion arrived. He just entered the gates. Shall I send for him?"

Vectis sucked in a breath and said as calmly as he could, "Tell the centurion to report after he has eaten and cleaned the travel dust from himself." He turned and moved deliberately to the brazier where he poured a half-cup of Celtic beer. As he sipped the steaming brew he wished he could march out of his office, grab Jupiter by the throat, and demand to know what had become of Neeve. He had been following her and should know something. But of course he would wait; he was a Roman officer, and Romans of his stature were supposed to possess at least a modicum of self-restraint.

A deep growl sounded in the hallway outside his door. It was Jupiter presenting himself to the aide.

"Enter," Vectis called, showing no self-restraint whatever.

Jupiter pushed open the door and strode across the room. His face was drawn, his uniform unkempt.

"You need not have come immediately," Vectis said, motioning for his centurion to sit.

He remained standing. "How can I help you, Prefect?"

"You can tell me about Neeve," Vectis replied. He had learned long ago not to take offense at Jupiter's blunt ways.

"I take it she did not return."

"It's been eight days."

Jupiter seemed to be processing the information.

Impatient, Vectis asked, "How long did you watch her?"

"A day and part of a night."

"Had she completed her mapping assignment?"

"No. She passed through the assigned sector and continued west."

"West?" Vectis was confused. "Why would she ... did you follow her?"

"I did."

"And?"

"And I lost her."

"*You*? *You* lost her? How could you lose her?"

Jupiter shrugged. "I think she knew someone was following her. I took great care, but she seemed to know."

"Where did you see her last?"

"West of sector forty, riding west. I had been following her on foot and had to return for my horse. Then I searched the flats until I found her fire. When it died in the middle of the night, I approached her camp and found her gone."

"Did you track her at sunup?"

"For several hours, until it became too risky. Her trail led straight west from sector forty into that belt of Caledonian training camps. Even with a fog I dared not continue. Every few hundred yards I was encountering Caledonian scouts."

"Well, if they could detect you ...." Vectis stopped. The thought of Caledonian warriors finding Neeve with Roman mapping materials was too much for him. "What I don't understand is why she would continue west when she knows the westerly sectors are crawling with

Caledonians. Do you think she became frightened and lost her bearings?"

Jupiter's brooding expression irritated him. The least he could do was to look concerned. "I asked you a question," Vectis said coldly, "and I want an answer. Is Neeve lost, on her way here, or dead?"

"She is not dead. That much I know."

"Fine," Vectis said in a clipped voice, "then you don't think the Caledonians captured her." He took a breath before asking, "Could she have hidden and now be on her way to Faustina?"

Jupiter hesitated, as if he were deciding how to respond.

"Centurion," Vectis said formally, and angrily, "I am growing impatient." He had never known Jupiter to hesitate about anything and his behavior was frustrating.

"I do not believe the mapmaker will be returning to Faustina or any other Roman installation. She has completed her mission and is now back with her people."

"Her mission?"

"She was a Caledonian spy," Jupiter said flatly.

"A spy? That's not possible. I know this woman."

Jupiter's face was stone.

In the quiet Vectis could hear his father's warning: "Never underestimate the enemy, and never trust them. The Celts are born liars." But not Neeve. She was the little slave girl in his dreams come to life. She loved him. "What evidence do you have?" he demanded.

"While I was touring the outposts, a centurion told me about a man he met at Velunia on the Wall, who used to run messages for the horse tribe."

"The Epidii."

"The same. You saved him from certain death on your winter outpost tour—he was tied to a tree."

"I remember."

"The man claimed to have seen the mapmaker in the presence of the Caledonian commander, Taranis."

"In his presence? What does that mean? Riding with him? Living with him? In the same town? What?"

"He saw them in the same village—"

"That's his evidence?" Vectis didn't hide his scorn. "I imagine hundreds of other people were there too. It means nothing."

"They stayed in the same roundhouse."

"Who? Neeve and this Taranis barbarian? I don't believe it."

"The informant claims that early last summer Taranis was meeting with other Caledonian commanders in this village, and that the mapmaker and Taranis were lovers. For over a week they lived together in the same roundhouse."

"Lovers! That is ridiculous. In early summer she had barely arrived from Londinium. How is she supposed to have struck up a love arrangement with the great blood god himself in so short a time? The Caledonians are extremely suspicious of new faces. It's not possible."

"How do you know the mapmaker was in Londinium?"

Vectis paused. He didn't know, not really. He just had vague references from Neeve about things she had seen in the city. He glanced away, trying to bridle his frustrations. He thought he had settled these questions long ago, but apparently not, and Jupiter's continual use of the term mapmaker in place of Neeve's name grated on him. He kept his voice level when he asked, "If this informer is so talkative, why didn't he speak of this while I was with him?"

"He was afraid that his words wouldn't be translated properly. The mapmaker was your translator, was she not?"

"You know she was," Vectis snapped. "What else did this dog say?"

"Nothing more, except that he wanted silver for his information."

Vectis snorted. "Does that sound like his information is credible?"

"It lessens it, I would agree."

"Makes it useless, in my mind. I can tell you, the last person I would trust is this informant. He will say anything to get his hands on Roman coin."

"Odd that he picked the mapmaker to lie about."

"You have other evidence?" He was no longer trying to conceal his annoyance.

Jupiter pushed on. He seemed oblivious to Vectis's frame of mind. "Since we arrived the Caledonians have devastated our supply trains. Varying the times of shipments and using decoys did nothing to hinder their ability to intercept the carts. They seemed to know which trains carried supplies, and which did not. I told you before, and I will tell you now, someone with access to high-level information has been supplying the Caledonians with dates and times. That's how I operated with the Marauders in North Africa—I bribed the non-Roman workers in the forts for information."

"Yes, we have a spy somewhere, maybe more than one—I never denied that. But it has to be at another outpost, or at the Wall where the supplies originate. How could it be Neeve? She cannot read. And I know that for a fact."

"Do you?"

"Yes. Where would she learn? In Londinium where you say she never was? And if she was there, how would she so quickly link up with this Taranis?" Vectis shook his head. "It doesn't fit."

"Not if she came from Londinium in early summer. But suppose she arrived last year or even the year before?"

Vectis waved off the idea. "Are you forgetting that the Caledonians almost killed her when she mapped too close to their training camp? If Neeve was so friendly with this warlord, others would know of it and provide her protection."

"That baffles me too, unless it was a mistake. But what pieces we have fit. She's a non-Roman with access to a flood of information and she often travels outside the fort. We have someone who links her with Taranis, and now that war is approaching, she heads straight for the Caledonian camps we know Taranis controls."

"I don't believe any of it."

"She was riding west," he repeated, "into Caledonian territory."

"She must have been lost."

"She stayed the night in Taranis's roundhouse."

Vectis glared at his centurion, but even as his anger boiled, he knew the African was probably right. The man was far more skilled in the ways of spies than was he, and if anything, he was a shrewd judge of people. He remembered how much his father had wanted

Jupiter to accompany him to Britannia. For good reason, it was turning out. Even Neeve's folding doll with its deceased parents counted against her. How could he have been so unseeing? The darkness of defeat swallowed him. He placed a hand over his eyes and conceded, "She insisted on not having an escort."

"No escort and not even an attempt to map her sector."

She was rushing back to her blood-crazed lover, Vectis thought, and the reality of it tore a piece from his soul. He sank deeper in the darkness. He had no control. Somehow he managed to ask, "Your desire to follow her was not out of concern for her welfare, was it?"

"No."

Vectis found himself staring at the *corona muralis* medal on Jupiter's chest, as if solace could be found there. It was true; he knew it in his heart. She was just like the slave girl in the stockade. His father had warned him but he let his heart pull him along. He thought he was being careful, thought he had acted properly, but her sparkling eyes and sweet words had drawn him like a siren to the rocks. And now she was in Taranis's arms, laughing at how easily she had exploited his childish declarations of love. What a spectacle he had made of himself! He had even given her his mother's ring. Worst of all was the bleak thought that Neeve had only pretended to love him, and her heart belonged to someone else.

Jupiter cleared his throat.

Vectis glanced around and straightened his back. He had played the fool but he forced himself to act with dignity. "I want you to find Julian and have him examine the documents in my office thoroughly. We will assume that the Caledonians know their contents."

"A wise decision, commander."

Vectis shot a glance at Jupiter, trying to decide whether he was being mocked, realized he wasn't, and dismissed his centurion.

Jupiter stopped at the door. "She was a clever woman," he said. "I too misread the signs, and I had nothing at stake. There is no dishonor."

Vectis said nothing as Jupiter left, but he knew it was the first time since their arrival in Britannia that his centurion had stepped away from his role as a Roman officer and tried to speak to him personally. A small consolation for Vectis's foolishness.

On the tenth day after her departure from Faustina, Neeve arrived back at the fort. She was fortunate to return as soon as she had, given the difficulties of finding her brother and the probes by Roman scouts in her sector. None of this could she use as an explanation for her lateness, of course, and she was prepared with a story about Caledonian warriors passing through her area, delaying her mapping. Another lie that she hoped would be the last.

Neeve smiled at the guards in the outer gatehouse and passed through the turf walls, all the while suppressing the urge to shout, she was so excited about being back. Soon she would gaze into Vectis's black eyes and kiss him gently on the mouth. She would place her hand in his and feel his fingers close on hers, warming her, protecting her. How she missed the sound of his voice and the feel of his arms around her. War was coming but it could never touch their love. Theirs was a love like no other and as she rode up to the gate, she believed, they could prevent the awful clash of armies.

Neeve transferred her horse to one of the grooms waiting for travelers at the inner gatehouse, and then hurried down the main road toward Vectis's office. Soldiers marching in box formations filled the parade ground, and Neeve wondered what the occasion might be. She recognized the dark shape of Jupiter, prowling panther-like through the troops. He turned toward her. Even from across the square, Neeve felt his eyes burning into her, and she looked away. Then, glancing back, she saw to her deep dismay that the centurion had started across the parade ground after her. The last person Neeve wanted to see was Jupiter. Whatever his concern, it could wait. She quickened her pace toward the central building, whisked past the guards, and down the corridor toward the vestibule where Vectis's aide sat.

Safe at last, Neeve calmed herself and greeted the aide. He rose and started toward the office door, as if to knock. It opened suddenly, only a few inches, but it startled him as much as it did her. Neeve saw a hand gripping the edge of the door, and by the sound of the voice on the other side, she knew it was Julian finishing a conversation with Vectis.

A surge of joyous anticipation swept over her as she stepped sprightly toward the door. She grabbed Julian's wrist playfully and spoke sharply, "Open this door!"

Julian jerked the door open and instantly turned white, the way one would upon seeing a spirit. "Neeve," he sputtered. "You're back."

"Did you think I died?" she said with an abundance of cheer. And then, looking over his shoulder, she saw an equally pallid Vectis. "Oh," she said, growing serious, "you did think something happened to me. I am so sorry." She rushed to Vectis. "I am fine, just fine."

Clutching him to herself, she rubbed the palms of her hands over his back and sighed, "Oh, how I missed you, my love." She kissed him several times on the cheek, and then on the mouth.

Vectis remained dead still, as if the shock of seeing her had paralyzed him. Then he removed her arms. He looked into her eyes without saying a word.

"What is it?" she asked.

His vacant stare unnerved her as he pushed her away.

"Vectis," she said, "what has happened?"

His voice was distant and cold. "I have duties to perform." He turned to the aide gawking in the open door and said, "See that this woman remains here until I return." With that, he marched out the door.

"Vectis, wait!"

But he was already gone.

"Julian?"

Her eyes searched his, pleading for help, but he too turned and followed Vectis down the hall.

The aide closed the door firmly.

For a full minute Neeve stood like a discarded statue in the center of the office. She was in desperate trouble. She breathed carefully, as though the merest puff would bring someone through the door to point an accusing finger. Her eyes moved, from one stark piece of

Roman furniture to another. It looked alien ... hostile. She was trapped in a nightmare of her own making, only this nightmare was very, very real. And very dangerous.

Her heart pounded and she felt dizzy. They know! They had to know. And now ... and now what? She gripped the edge of the table and tried to think. What would they do? Banish her? Execute her? From her throat came a tiny sound of despair. Oh, she knew what they would do, all right. She had no doubt at all. Execution was part of Roman culture—especially when it came to spies.

Neeve steadied herself on the table before inching toward a narrow couch. She sat down gingerly, as if the heavy oak struts would collapse under her weight. Her hands trembled. She inspected them thoroughly, and then clasped them tight, squeezing out the fear. Terrible events were about to overtake her and she had to contain her growing distress. She felt so unprepared. In the early days at the fort, when she sensed danger at every turn, she might have handled it better, but not now. Her dreams of happiness had been dashed like pottery on a rock and her aspirations to loyalty now seemed almost silly. Imagine a Caledonian wanting to be loyal to a Roman. But she had tried, so very hard, and Vectis would never know.

Vectis—her own dear Vectis—had called her "this woman." He was no longer hers; she had lost him. His voice sounded like those of the callous Roman soldiers that swaggered about Londinium. They had no pity when Celts dropped to their knees, begging for mercy; they simply carried out orders. Duty and loyalty to the Emperor— that's all they cherished. But Vectis was not like other Romans; he was different. Wasn't he?

Trumpets snapped her to attention—outside she could hear the calls of centurions and the neighing of horses. She went to the window and opened the slats. Scores of fully armed soldiers stood motionless in rows across the parade ground, facing a wooden platform.

Vectis led a processional down the main road, riding on a coal black horse. Jupiter, Julian, and several other officers riding two abreast followed him. Behind the officers walked three men, bare from the waist up, hands bound behind them. One had a leather strap around his neck that fell in two strips at his knees. Two guards walked beside each prisoner.

A disturbing sensation, like the swelling of black waters, engulfed Neeve. She had witnessed this same event before. She moved closer to the window to see crowds of somber non-Roman workers lining the streets. They had been given permission to watch. The Romans liked spectacles.

Behind the prisoners came the standard-bearers of the auxiliary, and a long column of foot soldiers, marching uniformly, six across.

When the soldier column had formed two square detachments on either side of the platform, the guards dragged the prisoners forward. Vectis and his officers dismounted. Julian handed Vectis a long roll of parchment. He turned to the prisoners and read a declaration sentencing them to death for rape and murder. When he finished, the soldiers gave a loud shout, extending their right arms into the air. Vectis signaled the guards, who pulled two of the men onto the platform. The guard behind each man forced the head back while the front soldier raised his sword, and plunged down hard into the exposed chest. The roar from the ranks shook the window slats.

Neeve stared in horror. "No, please no," she whispered, "not Vectis." Her whispering turned to groans, and the pain came in waves, each crueler than the last. "Not Vectis," she kept saying to herself, "please, not Vectis." But it was Vectis whose unyielding form she saw by the platform. Now with a flick of the wrist, he directed the soldiers to remove the bodies. They threw them into a waiting cart.

Images from childhood swirled around her. For so long she had blocked out those numbing moments when she had watched her father die. It was a long time ago, she had told Taranis, but now those distant events were hurtling toward her like a boulder down a mountain, growing larger and more threatening every second. She stared out the window, a captive of her own sorrowful past.

Suddenly, the man with the straps dangling at his knees cursed loudly and kicked at the soldier holding him. He twisted and leapt sideways, thrashing and cursing like a man possessed by a demon. A soldier stepped from the ranks and smashed the butt of his sword into the prisoner's face, leaving him swaying at the corner of the wooden platform. Blood gushed down his cheekbone and onto his bare chest, and immediately four or five soldiers grabbed him by the arms and dragged him to the center of the platform. He sank to his knees, howling.

No, Neeve said to herself, this was not her father. This was a vicious killer—the worst of the three—whose evil had caught up with him. But as she pressed her face into the slats, all she could see was her father, and the Roman that had executed him. An acute sense of grief and loss gripped her, and she felt the ground give way, and her body fall into a dark, swirling pit.

She hardly noticed sliding down to the floor, or her back scraping on the rough logs of the wall. The pain felt good, almost cleansing. With her head tilted against the logs, she stared into space, not moving, not even blinking. Vectis was out there, she knew, with his hand raised, motioning to the executioners to tighten their leather straps. Soon the soldiers would cheer ... yes, she could hear their shouts of triumph vibrating in the slats above her. She knew the executioners had begun pulling on the strangle cord.

Her dear, sweet Vectis—a Roman, like every other Roman.

She couldn't breathe. Her lips trembled, then her hands, and then her entire body. She felt as if she were drowning and she pressed her face to the floor, gasping for air. All she could feel was the numbing cold from that day on the hillside and the wet clay on her face. She remembered throwing herself into Taranis's arms and sobbing uncontrollably, but from that day to this, she had never cried—not when she stood on the glowing coal, or when her brothers sent her to Matidia, not even when the Romans took away her mother and sister. She had bitten her lip until it bled—but she never shed a tear.

Now, as she lay on the floor of Vectis's office, she began to cry. Hot tears rolled out of her eyes and down the sides of her face to the floor. She had tried to hide from the world, but the world would not go away. Images of Empire soldiers dragging her brothers along the streets passed through her mind, and for a moment, she saw her sister cowering in the corner of a room as the crushed-faced emissary towered over her. Taranis was right. She had forgotten how truly evil Rome was. Her duty to her family and Caledonia must come first. To think differently was to dishonor those who had given their lives to free the north.

Neeve waited mutely as the seven officers seated themselves in a semi-circle around her: Julian, Jupiter, a recording officer, the chief engineer, the chief defense officer, Nepos the supply officer, and the prefect, Vectis. Two guards stood at the door.

Julian opened the examination with a pledge of loyalty to the Emperor and the standards of Rome. He then informed the recording officer that the prefect had exempted himself from the proceedings because of an abiding interest in the accused, but that he would remain as an observer.

Neeve tried to breathe normally. She licked her lips. She cleared her throat. She shifted on her bench, trying to find a comfortable position. Julian said something about Roman courts that she couldn't make out. All she thought about was the dismal way her love had ended with Vectis. Julian asked whether she understood the significance of some point in Roman law. She tugged at her hair. Yes, she nodded, she understood. Understood what? She didn't know.

Again, Neeve shifted on the bench and folded her hands in her lap. It was upsetting. She did not know what to do with her hands, and she couldn't stop fidgeting. Folded in her lap looked the most natural, she guessed, but now she was pulling on her trouser-legs as if she were extracting burrs from the day's ride.

Julian addressed her again: "State your name for the recording officer."

Neeve glanced around at the solemn company of officers. They had witnessed three executions, and were about to authorize a fourth. She was being tried as a spy, and the penalty was death. This was Roman law. Not even Vectis could change the law, and he had chosen to watch in silence. Her eyes stopped at her erstwhile protector. He was sitting rock still, staring straight ahead. It was as though he had never known her. She felt a twinge of self-pity. Yes, she had deceived and betrayed him, and he had every right to be hurt, but he knew what would happen to her now. At least he could have compassion.

"State your name for the recording officer," Julian repeated.

Oh, Vectis, she said inside, please look at me. Just once. Don't you understand? I had to do it. And then, as if he heard her pleas, his eyes shifted to hers. But they were empty eyes that swept on past.

She pulled off her Roman wedding ring and dropped it onto the low table in front of her. It rolled once, then lay dead. Vectis was a Roman; he would never understand. She still loved him, but everything was over. The joy, the sweetness of life—all had turned to ash and she no longer cared whether she lived or died. "My name is Neeve," she said, "Neeve mapmaker."

"Neeve," Julian continued, "you have been accused of sedition against Rome. Do you understand this charge?"

"Yes," she said.

"Spying for Caledonia, that's the accusation. You understand this?"

"Yes."

Julian opened a folder and detailed the evidence against her—her recent journey into Caledonian territory, the witness who identified her in the company of Taranis, and her access to information in Vectis's office that matched with the Caledonian attacks on supply trains.

"You admit to meeting with the rebel commander, Taranis?" Julian asked.

"Yes."

"And to an ability to read the Roman language?"

"Yes."

"So you read documents in the prefect's office and took the information to the Caledonians."

Neeve glanced at Vectis, who had now turned slightly toward her, evidently interested in her answer, but his face still expressionless. "Yes," she said, "I can read Roman script." No point in denying anything. Jupiter had followed her—she knew someone was there—and the tree wretch had placed her with Taranis. Even with her denials, they would condemn her to death. She had seen it before. If she had to die, she wanted them to know the truth. She was sick of lies.

"And the other mapmaker that was with you," Julian asked, "a Caledonian warrior?"

"Yes, but he was also my brother." She decided not to identify her brother as Taranis the commander. She could imagine that Vectis felt foolish enough without being told that the Caledonian in his fort was none other than Taranis himself.

Julian had completed his part of the proceedings; it was her time to speak.

"I have no defense," she said. "All that you say is true. But I am not from a tribe of sheep like the Votadini. I am Caledonian." She allowed her pride to show. "I didn't spy for profit like your tree wretch, but for the love of my homeland. Caledonians have always fought for freedom and I was proud to contribute in the great struggle. I am only sorry that ...." She broke off, unable to speak her mind.

"Continue." Julian's voice was gentle, not unkind in the least.

"I ... never expected to be torn in my loyalties," Neeve said. It was a weak response, not worth saying, but it was the best she could do. She wanted Vectis to know how sorry she was that her duty demanded such acts of betrayal, and that even though their love could never be, she still held him close to her heart. But she could say no more.

Still, Vectis's face showed no response—he was a proper Roman soldier.

Julian thanked her and asked whether she might have been forced into giving information to the Caledonians.

"She *is* a Caledonian," Jupiter said in disgust.

"Yes," Julian said, "but—"

"I was not forced," Neeve said. She knew Julian was trying to help, but it was too late for that.

Julian kneaded the back of his neck as one did when trying to relieve an irksome stiffness. Then he called for the verdict of the officers.

Jupiter spoke first, his cruel eyes locking onto hers. "This Caledonian has regularly supplied the enemy with information. She is therefore guilty of sedition, and must be executed. There is no other option."

The chief defense officer spoke next. He was ill at ease pronouncing judgment on his prefect's wife, but Jupiter's forthright declaration bolstered his courage. "I too find this woman guilty of sedition," he said in a shaky voice. "Execution is appropriate."

"Guilty of sedition," the chief engineer said quietly. "Execution."

"Guilty of sedition," the recording officer said. "Execution."

"Sedition," echoed Nepos, the supply officer. "Execution."

Neeve kept her eyes on the floor as her judges pronounced their verdicts. It seemed like a long time before Julian spoke, and when Neeve looked up, he was staring at her. In a steady voice he said, "I find this person guilty of gross misconduct and recommend she be sold into slavery."

"The charge is sedition," Jupiter said, "not misconduct. How do you rule?"

"Innocent of sedition," Julian replied, "guilty of misconduct."

Jupiter mumbled something. He was not pleased with Julian's recommendation of leniency. There would be no death sentence if the senior presiding officer voted otherwise, and once in the slave market, anyone could buy her, including Julian or Vectis. Neeve knew how difficult it must be for Julian to stand up to the centurion, especially when her guilt was obvious.

Jupiter rose, no doubt to intimidate the others. "This woman is a Caledonian warrior," he said, placing one large fist on the table, "and a spy. The Caledonians make no distinction between women and men, and neither should we. She has admitted her guilt, and the penalty for such crimes is death. Is the presiding officer prepared to defend himself in Rome when the record of our actions is read to the Imperial court?"

The defense officer spoke up: "Perhaps the prefect might rule—"

"The *prefect*," Jupiter said forcefully, "has exempted himself from the proceedings. He cannot rule. Five of the six officers examining this Caledonian have found her guilty of sedition. There is only one verdict we can reach."

"I agree," Vectis said quietly. He turned to Julian. "I appreciate your loyalty, but the prisoner is guilty of sedition and must be convicted of such. I cannot allow you to sacrifice yourself for her or me."

In the silence that followed, Nepos turned to Julian and said in a syrupy tone, "I think we all agree that the prisoner has placed Faustina in a vulnerable position. As much as I dislike having to pronounce judgment, I see no other option than to follow the prefect and first centurion in this matter."

Julian ignored the comment and studied Vectis for long moments before closing his folder. Finally, he turned to the recording officer and said, "You may record a unanimous judgment: sedition. Execution will take place at sunup tomorrow."

35

"What I want to know," boomed Atilius in his most solemn voice, "is what our Emperor intends to do about the uprising in Britannia." He swept his eyes across the other senators gathered in the Senate chamber. "Must we wait until Britannia's hordes soak the ground with the blood of our noble soldiers before we make a recommendation?"

"This is unseemly talk," an older senator said. "Do we even know that the tribes are preparing for war?"

"We have the reports from the governor, Julius Verus," one senator replied with irritation in his voice.

"Governors always exaggerate their danger," another said, equally irritated.

Senator Titus Severus rose to speak. "For ten years I have heard the same chorus from certain members of this august body." He motioned carelessly toward Atilius. "It is forever the same. Move German legionaries to Britannia or we will lose the whole island. My dear friends, if we listened to these bell-ringers every time a few warriors waved their swords on that miserable island, we would have no legions left in Germania."

Laughter rippled through the Senate.

"Faced with the choice," Severus continued, "I would sooner risk an uprising in Britannia than have the German hordes beating on the gates of Rome."

Loud affirmations greeted his comments.

Atilius rose. "Our troops are facing more than a few warriors in Britannia. My late wife's brother, Vectis Trebellius, reports that northern Britannia cannot stand without reinforcements. In the past Trebellius has acquitted himself with distinction in Egypt and North Africa, and I do not consider him a bell-ringer." Atilius seated himself with dignity, knowing his words would have the appropriate bite.

One of Atilius's supporters stood. "Have we forgotten that the father of Vectis Trebellius, First Centurion Gaius Trebellius, often warned the Senate against turning a deaf ear to the commanders in the field? Who here would call him a bell-ringer?"

The Senate exploded in a cacophony of voices, with Atilius's supporters getting the better of it.

"Old Trebellius predicted this disaster for Britannia," shouted one.

"Remember his dying words," cried another.

"He predicted his son would fall on Britannia's soil," someone else said.

A senior consul appealed for order but it was several minutes before he was able to bring peace to the assembly. Finally, with quiet restored, he motioned to Titus Severus.

"Senators of Rome," Severus said formally, and somewhat defensively, "I do not discount the danger in Britannia, and I have no objection to transferring some of our auxiliary cavalry from the German provinces as a precaution, but removal of whole legions would unnecessarily put the German frontier at risk."

Atilius rose heavily to his feet. It was the moment he had been waiting for. "I have long maintained that the Emperor's Wall is a monument to flawed policy. I say this respectfully. We would not be in this crisis, had we taken the whole island instead of wasting scarce resources building a second Wall."

The Senate murmured its approval.

"Yet I must confess," Atilius said in an earnest voice, "that my present judgment is colored because ... well, you all know ... I have a family member at risk in Britannia, at the most distant outpost." He paused, allowing the pain of his difficult position to sink in. Someone said a word of comfort and Atilius swallowed hard, blinking away a sudden glistening in his eyes. At times like this he almost felt the pain he was talking about, as if it were real. Atilius considered such genuine emotions a gift from the gods. At this very moment, three outpost commanders were prepared to abandon their posts, leaving Vectis stranded above the Wall. The boy would be left to die—on Atilius's instructions—but even so, Atilius could feel the proper emotion. An amazing gift! It should bother him, he knew, but Atilius felt no sorrow. Rome must come first. Even Vectis believed that. The boy's sacrifice was necessary to ensure a more sympathetic reception by the Roman people once Atilius seized power. For the good of Rome, Atilius was forced to act harshly to ensure a smooth transition of power.

The senator took a breath and spoke full-voiced, sounding like the statesman he was. "My first responsibility," he said, "must always be Rome regardless of how it affects my family." He inclined his head toward Titus Severus. "Senator Severus is wise in his judgments. The German frontier is indeed a dangerous place from which to draw troops, and now with Dacia on the brink of rebellion, we might need our German legions to march east. I, therefore, intend to say no more in this debate and bow to the will of the Senate."

During the next hour Atilius listened to the discussion boiling in the Senate. He had handled it just right, he thought. He had made it clear that the Emperor's failed policies were responsible for the current mess, and that the Dacian threat precluded sending more than a token number of reinforcements from the continent. He had argued passionately for the defense of Britannia, but in the end had been a statesman by allowing the Senate to sacrifice his family for the good of Rome.

Joy filled his soul when the Senate approved Severus's recommendation of sending limited reinforcements to Britannia. With so few soldiers being sent to the island, Antoninus' Wall was sure to collapse, and with it the season of Imperial incompetence.

The hours passed slowly for Neeve as she waited in the narrow chamber of the gatehouse. True to Roman form, the room was bare except for the necessities: a bench, a table with water, bread and hard cheese, a chamber pot, and of course a wall chain that secured her hands and feet, allowing her movement in only one end of the room.

She had hoped to speak to Vectis privately, and after the verdict requested an audience with him, but he turned away, uttering the single word: "Guards!" As she watched him leave, all hope vanished, and her mind turned numb. They took her from the office to the usual holding cell near the center of the fort, then toward evening brought her to the gatehouse. Maybe they intended to have a bigger parade beginning in the passageway between the turf walls. It didn't matter. She no longer cared. Let them do what they would.

An hour after sundown Neeve awakened to the lock clunking on the gatehouse door. She rubbed her face and straightened her back against the wall where she had been resting. She would never have believed it possible to fall asleep on this of all nights, but evidently she had been dozing.

The door opened.

Cold air crept into the narrow room, chilling her legs.

"Who's there?" she asked as the door closed.

No reply.

Neeve squinted into the gloom and saw a dark form slipping along the wall toward her. He dropped to his knees in front of her and grabbed at her legs. She jerked sideways, but the chain held her fast.

"Be still," he whispered as he gripped her ankles and pulled her legs apart as far as the chain would allow, about eight or ten inches.

It was Jupiter. He intended to rape her!

"What are you—"

"Silence!"

He fumbled with a key, trying to unlock the manacles on her ankles so he could open her legs.

"No!" she shouted, bracing her back against the wall and smashing both feet into his face. He was unprepared for such a hard thrust and fell backwards. Neeve kicked at him again but he spun sideways and twisted around on top of her, his face inches from hers. She jerked her body but couldn't move. Her hands were caught in his one enormous palm, and his other hand covered her mouth. She bit into his fingers as hard as she could.

"I am trying to save your life," he hissed in her ear.

She stopped biting.

"Now be quiet," he said, "and don't bite or kick me again."

"Why are you—"

His hand clamped over her mouth again. "Say *nothing*."

Neeve obeyed.

Within seconds he had the manacles off her hands and legs, and led her to the door. Outside, the camp was quiet. Clusters of torches flared in the breeze at every guard post, but no guards. Neeve ran her eyes along the road, but saw no one. They hurried toward the outer gatehouse, Jupiter towing her most of the way. At the outer post, Neeve discovered what had happened to the guards. She saw three men and the Centurion of the Guard bound hand and foot and facing the ground. Jupiter must have done the same thing at the inner gatehouse and guard posts. She wanted to ask whether he might have been recognized, but decided to keep quiet. She could feel the bruise on her cheek where his fingers had clamped over her mouth the last time she spoke. Neeve followed him through the portal in the huge gate, across a double plank that spanned the ditch, and onto the smooth grounds surrounding the fort.

"Listen carefully," Jupiter whispered. "Above us on the wall of that fort are guards whose job it is to watch these fields. On a dark night like tonight, they mostly listen for unusual sounds, so maintain absolute silence. The land is filled with traps and pits and hooks that will rip your stomach open. You *must* stay directly behind me until we reach the end of the protective belt. There we can talk, but not here. Is that understood?"

Neeve nodded.

"Take hold of my tunic," he said, stuffing the back hem into her hand, "and keep your mouth shut."

Not once as Jupiter picked his way across the field did Neeve feel the slightest temptation to talk. Several times the centurion took a wrong turn and had to backtrack, and once his searching foot caused the ground to give way before him, exposing the sharpened stakes mounted at the bottom of the pit.

They moved gingerly through rows of iron hooks and ankle-high slivers of metal, and stretches of straw-covered ground with yet more traps and pits. Neeve followed closely in Jupiter's steps. The smooth ground gave way to more rocky terrain and then fell gradually toward a field sprinkled with small trees. Still she followed.

Ahead she saw a horse tied to a tree. She tugged on the bottom of Jupiter's tunic that she still held in her hand. He kept walking.

"Jupiter," she whispered, and then loudly, "Jupiter!"

He stopped.

"We must have cleared the field by now."

"Long ago," he replied and continued toward the horse.

Neeve hurried after him. "It's a good thing you remembered that field plan," she said. "For a moment I thought you had forgotten."

"There is no plan," Jupiter said. "The idea is to use the walkways, not cross the protective belt. It can be hazardous at night."

"No plan?"

He ignored her. As they reached the horse he said, "I suggest you use the arterial road until dawn, then ride west into Caledonian territory."

"Why are you doing this?"

His eyes inspected the rolling fields around them. "You had better go."

"Today you wanted me executed. Now you risk your life to release me."

"Your knives," he said, handing them to her. "You will find a bow, arrows, some food and water on the horse."

"You will not tell me why?" She held his eyes.

"You ask too many questions. Accept the fates. It's easier." He pushed the reins toward her.

Neeve grabbed his hand. "At least tell me why you didn't want me sold into slavery. I might have escaped that way—with a lot less effort."

"Few slaves ever escape."

"But you didn't want me taken to the slave market ...."

He nodded. "I was concerned that the tribune or prefect might attempt to buy you, and that would have put them at great risk. The Imperial examiners are not fools."

"You wanted the record to state that the officers of Faustina acted properly. They condemned me for sedition, but I escaped."

Jupiter grunted.

"That's why Vectis asked for the death penalty ... because he knew Julian could be in serious trouble for disregarding his duty."

He motioned for her to mount the horse.

"Please, I ... I need to know something." Her voice trembled. "Did Vectis ask ... or maybe hint that you should free me?" She held her breath, afraid of the answer.

"He knows nothing."

"Nothing," Neeve repeated softly. She felt so abandoned. She had no right to expect his help after what she had done, but still it hurt. "Yet *you* risked your life for me."

"Not for you. For the prefect."

"I don't understand."

"You don't need to understand."

"But I do, I really do."

The centurion blew out in resignation. "When the prefect upheld the execution sentence, I knew he would come for you in the night. I could not allow that."

"Vectis would have rescued me?" The thought warmed her.

"He would have risked everything to save you. That's why he had you removed from the regular holding cell to the gatehouse. He also replaced the guards on the night watch with inexperienced ones."

"You wanted to protect him."

"I am better at this sort of thing. Disabling guards without being seen is a lifetime skill, not one to be learned in a night. The prefect was bound to incriminate himself. This way the blame can be attached to incompetent guards and stealthy Caledonian warriors, not the prefect. In fact, the prefect will have performed his duty to the letter—even insisting on death for his wife once he discovered her deception."

"A noble Roman trait."

He shrugged.

"Thank you for telling me this."

He nodded and helped her onto her horse.

She looked down at the dark centurion. "I know you hate me for what I've done."

"Hate?" He shook his head. "I don't hate you, Neeve mapmaker. I admire you. You conducted yourself well—even fooled me for a time."

"You would have gladly executed me."

"Not gladly."

"But you would have."

He patted her leg. "You are the enemy."

"Yes, I'm the enemy, but I don't want you or anyone else at the fort killed. And I still love Vectis. I never meant to ... what I mean is, once I committed myself to him, I tried to be loyal ...." She looked away. "You would never understand."

"I understand more than you think."

She explored his eyes. "Yes, I believe you do." The wind shook the leaves on the tree beside them. "Well," she said, forcing a smile, "it's less than an hour till the next watch."

He looked amused at her concern. "I'll be back in time. At dawn I will send out a party of soldiers to find you. If you head west at first light you should have no trouble."

"I owe you my life."

"Yes, you do." He slapped her horse on the rump.

THE DESPERATE HOURS

Two Months Later

36

Never had Atilius spent a more enjoyable morning.

Shortly after sunrise Balbinus arrived at his Roman villa with splendid news. Four of the nine Praetorian cohorts, and all three urban cohorts, would support the senator in his move against Emperor Antoninus. Atilius Titianus felt like a god about to ascend the clouds of heaven. He had to promise the cohort tribunes much, but now he had urban troops to control the streets, and four Praetorian detachments to march on the palace. With northern Britannia collapsing, and German and Dacian hordes restless, many were disillusioned with Emperor Antoninus' overly cautious approach. The accusations had started; the time was ripe. And surprise was on his side. It would not be long before he seized control of the Imperial throne.

All morning he waited for the courier. Rumors of a catastrophe at the Antonine barrier had been circulating for days, and it was no surprise to Atilius that Emperor Antoninus had done little to prevent it. At last report the ridiculous man had instructed Britannia's soldiers to hold their positions until reinforcements arrived. Reinforcements! How could he possibly think that a half legion from the Germanic frontier would make any difference? Rome would be well rid of Antoninus and his timid ways.

A servant entered the dining room where he and Balbinus were reclining, and informed him that a courier had arrived.

"The dispatch," Atilius said, holding out his hand.

"There is no dispatch, my lord," the servant replied.

"No dispatch?"

"The courier has a verbal message only."

"Indeed! Send him in."

He and Balbinus exchanged glances, but neither breathed a word lest an ill-spoken thought change the winds of history. When the servant had brought in the courier and retired to another room, Atilius said calmly, "You may proceed."

The courier spoke from a memorized text. "Governor Julius Verus reports that the entire Brigantes, Selgovae, and Caledonian tribes are in revolt. He cannot maintain the integrity of Antoninus' or Hadrian's Wall, and has given orders to dismantle a significant number of Britannia's forts. He will consolidate his legions and auxiliaries at strategic locations to preserve their fighting ability."

"Is that the full message?" Atilius asked, betraying nothing on his face.

"Yes, but the consuls have called for an immediate session of the Senate to discuss sending further reinforcements."

Atilius dismissed the courier and turned to Balbinus. "You will go personally to each of our loyal cohorts and instruct the tribunes to stand ready. Within three days I shall claim what is rightfully mine."

"May I be the first to worship you," Balbinus said, bowing low.

Atilius gazed upon his aide, so devoted, and so sensitive to the will of the fates. He sensed the aura of destiny that surrounded his master and could do no other than fall down and worship. Atilius knew how important he was to Balbinus, to the faithful cohorts willing to die for him, and to the senators and governors who saw his star rising on the horizon. Yes, so many needed him, but the one that needed him most was Rome herself. He would not let her down. Centuries from now, the song of Atilius would ring across the mountains and valleys of the world, and millions would praise his name.

It was his destiny.

The prisoner had escaped and Vectis was glad.

Neeve had used him, lied to him, betrayed him, and most painful of all, she had given herself to the bloody chieftain, Taranis. Yet somehow he still loved her. He had even kept the frayed, old, rollout doll she treasured. It made no sense. Nothing made sense when it came to Neeve.

He was hurt, even bitter, he had to admit. He cringed when he recalled her pretense at learning the language, and the ease with which he had fallen victim to her charms. She was nothing more than a skilled Caledonian spy sent to find the weak vessel, and he came running. He remembered how she had dropped her eyes in pretended shyness, and tried so hard to make herself understood. How absurd he must have looked coaxing the words out of her as she stumbled along, and then bragging about Rome while she shrieked: "I knew there be towers in Rome city!"

He had been manipulated like a stringed puppet, and yes, the humiliation of it all ran deep. His pride had taken a severe blow. Even so, no amount of shame could ever have induced him to take her life. The Neeve that entered the fort may have been a spy, but the one that left was his wife—and she loved him. He truly believed that. He could never do her harm.

When she returned from her excursion to the Caledonian camps, he knew the penalty would be death. He conducted himself properly by calling for a prompt trial and by withdrawing from the proceedings. He even demanded her execution at the trial. The record would show exemplary behavior on his part and no one would have suspected Faustina's prefect of planning her escape.

But someone else released her.

Someone with unusual skill.

Jupiter was indignant over the inability of the guards to prevent enemy warriors from entering the fort. For an hour he harangued the troops, but in the end granted mercy to the guilty. From time to time we all underestimate the enemy, he said. What matters is how we handle ourselves afterward. With that, he dismissed the soldiers, deducting only a month's pay from the guilty.

Vectis was shocked. He had never known Jupiter to be so lenient. The centurion explained his decision by saying that, as battle approached, he must strive to increase morale. Vectis accepted the explanation, but was sure no Caledonians had climbed the fort's walls that night. How would they have known their spy was in trouble scant hours after her return? And how could they have disabled so many guards without being seen? Only one man could accomplish such a feat, and he was not born in Britannia.

The weeks that followed were difficult. Rome gave strict orders for the outposts and Wall forts to maintain their positions in preparation for the coming of the southern legions. But the legions never came. Soon the campfires appeared in the hills, and loud shrieking and dancing. When the Caledonians cut communication lines between the outposts, everyone knew the siege was about to begin.

Vectis hoisted himself up the ladder that led to the south tower. He found Julian with his arms stretched across the corner beams, staring out over the protective zone to the arterial road beyond. Already shadows crept across the land. It would be dark soon.

"I don't expect they will return," Vectis said. He was speaking about a search detail sent out that morning to find the night patrol.

"No, they will not return," Julian said, eyes fixed on the distant road. "You were right. A search detail was a waste of good men."

Vectis rested his hand on his friend's shoulder. "You are not to blame," he said. "It was my decision."

Julian's face twisted in anguish. "I pushed you into it. I was the one who called it poor policy to leave men out there without knowing whether they were alive or dead."

"We made an effort. It failed, but at least the soldiers know we will not abandon them when times are grim."

"What do you intend to do about the search detail?"

"Nothing."

Julian nodded. Sending out more men would be foolish and everyone understood that now. "It looks so empty out there," he said, changing subjects. "Never thought I would miss seeing the smoke from the squatters' ovens. It won't be long now, I suppose."

Vectis gripped the wooden supports beside Julian. "The camp followers have a divine gift for disappearing before the flood."

Julian smiled. "There's something to be said for gathering one's tents while the cloth is still whole."

"And leave this magnificent fort in the hands of the Caledonians? I expect the promised legions are already trekking up the arterial road—led by Commodus himself in his finest toga."

They grinned at the thought, but in spite of Atilius Titianus's assurances that the Senate would send legions without delay, both had serious doubts that the reinforcements would make it in time. All outposts and garrisons along the Wall had been ordered to maintain battle readiness until the southern legions arrived. Sound policy if indeed the legions were marching north, but a disaster if they were delayed. At last report the Brigantes and Selgovae tribes had attacked Roman garrisons between the Walls, and some were pushing north toward Antoninus' Wall. With the Caledonian tribes on one side of the Wall and the Brigantes and Selgovae on the other, the Antonine forts would be isolated, and would not last long.

Where were the promised legions? Vectis wondered. He knew he must act, and soon. But how could he? His orders were to maintain the outposts until the legions arrived.

Julian read his thoughts. "You want to confront the Caledonians, don't you?"

"We have better equipment, better trained soldiers and, joined with the other outposts, a solid chance of defeating the Caledonian army in a set battle. It would take them months to regroup and by then the legions will have restored order."

"They have four or five times our number."

"The Celts fight for glory. We fight to win. Have you forgotten Suetonius Paullinus's battle against Boudicca's massive army?"

"I have not forgotten," Julian said. During Nero's reign, Boudicca's warriors overmatched Legions XIV and XX by ten to one, but at the end of the day, 80,000 Celts lay dead on the ground. The rest fled in terror. "Suetonius won a glorious victory," Julian agreed, "but that was a hundred years ago. The Celts know our methods of war now. Have you considered what we would do in the event of defeat?"

Vectis shrugged. "Retreat to the nearest outpost. But if we win, and I think we can, the pressure from the north will be reduced and the Wall soldiers can concentrate on the southern threat."

"*If* we win."

"I know it's a gamble," Vectis said, "but if we hide in our forts we will surely suffer defeat and create the same horror we are trying to avoid. Jupiter is convinced that the main Caledonian tribes are not pressuring the Wall, but have been assigned the task of destroying the outposts."

"In hopes of overwhelming us and sending us fleeing to the Wall."

"Exactly."

"And when the Wall defenders see panic-stricken stragglers clawing at their gates to get in—"

"They will think the wrath of the gods has befallen them. Panic breeds panic."

"We don't have much choice," Julian said.

"Then you agree we must attack."

"Yes, but what about your orders?"

"Orders? Maintaining the outposts at all cost is political fancy, not orders."

"You would disobey—"

"No, I will not disobey an order from Rome. I will follow standard procedure and leave a third of the men in the outposts to defend the walls, but if I could," he looked intently at Julian, "I would gather everyone at one outpost, then use it as a home base from which to launch our attack."

"That would certainly give us more men in the field," Julian said.

"Ah, yes, but Rome wants us to save *all* the outposts, which means we will probably lose them all."

"I believe your plan will work," Julian said firmly. "We will combine the available outpost soldiers, attack the Caledonians and defeat them, and we will not abandon a single outpost in doing it."

Vectis clapped Julian on the arm. He needed to hear an affirming word.

"When do you propose to leave the fort?" Julian asked.

"As soon as possible. Late tomorrow."

"Runners?"

Vectis nodded. "When darkness falls we will send them to the other outposts."

It had been a strange day for Taranis. That morning the gates of Fort Colania burst open, and out came the soldiers and mounted officers, pounding south toward the Antonine barrier like a herd of spooked animals. With less than a mile to the Wall, they made it safely, but it was a sloppy evacuation, unlike the usual Roman withdrawal. Any commander would have been ashamed of such an exhibition, but from Neeve's depiction of Commodus, the odd little man commanding the fort, shame would have been a minor concern. Self-preservation was paramount.

Then, as if afraid of being left behind, the next two outposts, Julianus and Alauna, dismantled and burnt the timber buildings in their forts, standard practice when evacuating a garrison. Romans left nothing to the enemy. By mid morning the two had joined and were marching south in their hollow square. Taranis sent Eston to flood the backside of their ranks with arrows to make them break and run. A quarter mile from the Wall, the whole square dissolved, and panicked soldiers fled to the safety of the Wall.

The fourth outpost, Stragenia, also burnt its timber and headed south. But oddly, when they reached Alauna and found it empty, they turned back, and headed north toward the most distant outpost, Faustina. Twelve miles from Faustina, Forgall intercepted them and destroyed most of their forces, but not without suffering severe losses himself. The soldiers at Stragenia fought stubbornly, and never once broke ranks. A small number even sliced through Forgall's army, and were now marching furiously toward Faustina. They would arrive before nightfall. No matter. Taranis knew that defeated soldiers would only create fear and panic in the distant fort.

Taranis could almost smell the terror oozing from the enemy's pores. No legions had arrived, as he had predicted, and the Wall soldiers sensed their isolation. With the Caledonians pressing down from the north, and the Brigantes-Selgovae tribes moving in the south, the will to fight would soon be gone.

"A great day for Caledonia," Cronn said, sweeping his eyes across the flats. "Only one outpost left."

"It will be a great day when the last Empire soldier leaves our soil," Taranis replied.

As they rode back to camp, Taranis tried to unravel the mystery of why the most distant outpost should be left to fend for itself. If the Romans had designated it as a bastion in the north, why would they not have supplemented it with soldiers from the other outposts? It made little sense. Alone they could not survive.

Vectis heard the cheers from the far end of the fort. A quarter hour after he and Julian climbed down from the tower, the sentries on the front wall began calling out in excited voices, "The legions are coming!" By the time Vectis arrived at the inner gatehouse, a considerable crowd of off-duty soldiers had gathered, and Jupiter dispersed them with a look.

"What is it?" Vectis asked.

"Soldiers," Jupiter said. "That's all we know."

"Legionaries?"

Jupiter shrugged. He turned his face upward and called to the sentry in the south tower, "Continuous report."

"Centurion," the sentry called back, "I see a squared unit of soldiers approaching on the arterial road."

"Size?"

"Centurion, too dark to tell."

"We will know soon enough," Jupiter said to Vectis.

Vectis glanced around. The off-duty soldiers had melted away, but those still working in the shops and hauling carts up and down the roads were straining to hear the conversation between Jupiter and the sentry. Vectis could hardly fault them. Legionaries meant life.

"Centurion," the lookout called down from his tower perch, "I have a square—looks like a century."

"Others?"

"Centurion, I see no other units."

"That takes care of our legion," Vectis said.

Jupiter agreed. "Must be outpost soldiers," he said.

"None is scheduled to arrive—"

"Centurion," the voice carried down, "the square is single line, maybe fifty soldiers."

"Outpost soldiers?"

"Yes, Centurion, auxiliary soldiers flying the vexillum of Stragenia."

"No other soldiers?"

"Centurion, I count forty to forty-five soldiers, half wounded."

Vectis felt a terrible weight in his chest. Why would Priscianus have sent a column of soldiers north? Something was desperately wrong at Stragenia.

He turned to Jupiter. "Isolate the incoming soldiers. The last thing we need is a rumor of disaster floating about. Bring the ranking officer to me and see that everyone in Faustina is kept informed of our situation. Within the hour, tell them, they will know everything there is to know."

The room was dead quiet as Vectis waited with his officers for Jupiter and the ranking Stragenia officer to appear. No one speculated on the meaning of Stragenia's soldiers racing north. With wounded in the group, everyone knew it was not good.

Jupiter entered the room and fixed his eyes on Vectis. "Prefect, we have a problem."

Vectis braced himself. "Is Stragenia under siege?"

"Stragenia is gone, Prefect. What remains of its soldiers entered our gates moments ago." Jupiter glanced toward the door. "Commander Priscianus will explain."

Vectis stared at the old, bushy-browed commander swaying in the entranceway. His right arm dangled at his side, his hand twitching. A surgeon stood behind him, supporting his weight.

"He insisted on walking," the surgeon said.

Priscianus pulled his arm from the surgeon's grasp, took a feeble step forward, and straightened his back. In a wavering voice he managed, "Prefect, you have been betrayed." That said, he wilted like a dandelion in a fire. They propped him up on a couch and gave him sips of hot Celtic beer. He would not live long.

"What can you tell us?" Vectis asked the fallen commander.

Priscianus coughed weakly and said, "The other outposts have abandoned Faustina. We are alone out here."

"How could they abandon their forts?" Vectis asked. "Our orders are to maintain these outposts."

Priscianus said nothing but the despair in his eyes spoke volumes.

Jupiter spoke. "Priscianus told me that the governor of the Britannia, Julius Verus countermanded those orders."

"Countermanded the orders?" Vectis was stunned. "Why was I not informed?"

"Priscianus received those orders only yesterday," Jupiter said. "He sent couriers on to you but the Caledonians must have intercepted them."

"What are the new orders?" Vectis asked.

"To dismantle the outposts," Priscianus replied. "And to consolidate ... troops at the central post of Alauna."

A sensible order, Vectis thought. "Why are the troops not there?"

"I don't know," Priscianus said. He was down to a whisper now. "We were nearing Alauna when ... scouts reported back ... the outpost had been abandoned."

"An attack?" Vectis asked.

He waved the suggestion away weakly with his hand. "An orderly retreat," he said.

"Did they burn their timber?"

"Piled and burned."

Vectis remained silent. He wondered whether any at Faustina could survive.

"... sent runners to ... next outpost," Priscianus said hoarsely, his mouth clamping shut, as if the act could prevent his spirit from escaping.

Vectis moved closer. "You sent runners to Julianus and found it also had burned its timber. Is that it?"

He managed a slight nod.

"What about Colania?" Jupiter asked. "You said it too had been abandoned. How do you know?"

"I know Commodus," Priscianus whispered, the death rattle in his throat. He closed his eyes and murmured, "I see ... snow on my bones."

The surgeon bent over him and listened to his chest. "He is gone."

"The fates have severed the thread of life," Nepos said from the side of the room.

"Had he a wife?" Vectis asked.

Jupiter answered, "A son only. He asked that his sword and armor be sent to him in Tarraco, Hispania."

Vectis instructed the surgeon to make a wax impression of Priscianus's features. If by some miracle the legions rescued Faustina, a plaster mold could be sent to the son.

Minutes later the little circle of officers gathered again to discuss the situation facing them. Their grim faces told the tale. Faustina was isolated. Vectis nodded to Jupiter.

"Yesterday the outposts received orders to consolidate at Alauna," the centurion began, summarizing. "Today the outposts have been dismantled. I see only one explanation. The three outposts have deliberately abandoned us."

"Comments?" Vectis glanced around the group.

Julian's expression was incredulous. "I find it hard to believe that even Commodus would disobey a direct order from the governor of Britannia."

"Unless he and the others are receiving orders from elsewhere," Jupiter said.

"Another set of orders instructing them to retreat to the Wall?" Julian shook his head. "Who would give such orders?"

Jupiter shrugged. "They are gone, that much is certain. I agree that no commander would abandon his post without authorization. But Rome is full of intrigue."

Vectis felt sick. Atilius! Atilius Titianus would give such orders. He remembered Sabina's words: "Atilius is a proud and ambitious man. Sometimes I think he wants to be Emperor." Atilius and not old Senator Alfenus Crescens sent the dispatches to Commodus. He probably promised Commodus and the others the Esquiline Hill to abandon their posts. Now he understood Commodus's sudden lack of interest in being transferred. Vectis thought about Kallias. He had a senatorial edict signed by Crescens. That too was Atilius; he probably used Kallias as a spy. And no doubt Atilius was the senator who released Kallias from the surgery in North Africa after the killing of Vinestalk Vatinius. Yes, it was clear why Atilius wanted Commodus and the others to abandon their outposts. And the reason shook him.

Jupiter was still talking. "The last true order came from Legate Julius Verus, who wanted us to gather at Alauna. That is what must be happening throughout the entire lowlands—forts consolidating to preserve their fighting ability until the legions arrive from the continent."

"There won't be any legions from the continent," Vectis said. He spoke rapidly to the aide at the door, ordering five separate couriers to deliver a message to the Emperor.

Julian asked, "Does this have something to do with your brother-in-law who promised us legions?"

Vectis nodded. "Atilius Titianus never wanted legions sent to Britannia. His plan is to embarrass the Emperor, and that will happen when Antoninus' Wall collapses. And to maintain the goodwill of the people, he used Commodus to make certain that his 'favorite' brother dies in northern Britannia."

"A risky wager," the chief engineer said. "What does he gain?"

"Maybe the Empire," Vectis replied.

Astonishment filled the engineer's face. "He is plotting against the Emperor?"

"I think so."

The defense officer said, "Commodus and the others have begged for reassignment since they've been out here. It looks like the senator paid them to abandon their outposts, expecting Stragenia and Faustina to be cut off and destroyed."

The engineer said, "So later Commodus could claim that Prefect Vectis ordered a retreat to the Wall."

Vectis raised his hand to conclude the conversation. "I need recommendations."

The defense officer spoke quietly: "If the centurion is correct that Legate Julius Verus wants to preserve the larger, more central forts in northern Britannia—and I think those were Verus's orders—then we might want to consider leaving for the Wall, and soon. The five outposts were supposed to gather at Alauna. We cannot do that now. We cannot stay here either because we need the other forts along the arterial road for support."

Nepos seized the moment and began speaking passionately, to the point of embarrassment. "No legions are coming!" he said. "We cannot stay. We must leave now." His eyes darted around the circle of men. "Don't you understand? We are forty-five miles north of the Antonine barrier. Forty-five miles! If we stay here we will die. The only option is to march south."

"Engineer," Vectis said, inviting his opinion.

The engineer leaned forward on his bench. "This is a strong fort, Prefect, but it cannot withstand a sustained attack."

Vectis turned to the defense officer. "How long?"

"Depends on how many we have to deal with," the officer said, pursing his lips.

"Count on ten thousand," Jupiter said.

He pursed his lips again. "They lack efficiency ... say a month to clear the protective zone, another to assemble their rams and siege towers, and to probe our defenses, and a week to overwhelm our walls. Sometime during the third month I would guess, maybe earlier if the bloody Taranis is all they say he is."

Vectis's face flushed at the mention of Taranis. Every officer in the room knew Neeve had shared his bed, and even now was ... no, he refused to believe it. She would never give her body to another, not as long as he was alive. He glanced around but saw no recognition of the embarrassing problem. They all seemed absorbed in the task at hand: survival. Vectis fixed his eyes on Jupiter. "What do we gain by staying?"

Jupiter answered, "With the Caledonians buzzing around us, we relieve pressure on the Wall for a month or two."

"Enough time for Verus's southern troops to arrive at the Antonine barrier?"

"No," Jupiter replied. "If reinforcing soldiers were only three months away, Julius Verus would not be consolidating forts."

"An excellent observation," Nepos said. "Maintaining this outpost for two or three months makes no sense at all. If we left now we could join with a southern fort and increase its capabilities—"

"What about our orders to maintain a presence above the Wall?" Julian asked.

"Officer Nepos here is of the opinion that we will sacrifice our lives for no good reason," Jupiter said.

Nepos nodded agreeably, oblivious to the contempt in the centurion's voice.

"And he might be right," Jupiter continued. "In three months the *presence* Verus wants above the Wall will be gone."

"Yes," Nepos said, "precisely my point."

"Then you think we should leave," Vectis said to Jupiter.

"We have little choice."

Vectis studied his officers. "The question is, can we still make it to the Wall? Priscianus's troops encountered thousands of Caledonians along the way."

"They operate under chieftains," Jupiter said, "so their vast numbers are not effective until they settle in a place and unify their command. We might be able to knife our way through and still preserve a sizable number of our troops."

"Three quarters? Two thirds?" Vectis asked.

"Half, if all goes well."

37

The soldiers at Faustina worked feverishly through the night, watering the mules and horses, packing carts, burying coins and altars, dismantling central buildings. Hope lightened every burden, quickened every step. They were heading south.

Vectis was on the broad way, organizing a line of carts with officer Nepos when Julian approached him. It was almost sunrise and Julian's armor glowed faintly in the predawn light. "I am misfortune's child," he began, "I bear ill tidings."

"Caledonians?"

"Arrived in the night." He looked wanly at Vectis. "Twice now we've made plans to leave Faustina. I think the fates have determined we belong here, and just when I was dreaming of North Africa."

"I am sorry, Julian. Let's go look."

"Wait!" Nepos cried, grasping Vectis's arm. "We must leave now! The Caledonians are still in disarray. We can fight our way through."

"Take your hand off me," Vectis said.

Nepos obeyed instantly. "Prefect," he said solicitously, "If we stay here, we will die. Every hour will bring more Caledonians until they will simply overwhelm us with their numbers. We will lose men, certainly, but everyone is willing to take that risk. I remind you that the officers will be at the center of the hollow square—"

Vectis leveled his eyes at Nepos. "One more word and I will have you flogged."

Nepos stood mute.

"If we do leave," Vectis said, "I can promise you this. You, Mamercus Nepos, will not be with the officers at the center of the square. You will be swinging a sword on the outside row with the valiant soldiers that fight and die."

Jupiter was already on the patrol track when the Caledonians arrived. In the gray light, they moved like shadows as they hauled weapons carts, siege towers, and wooden flats to defeat the fort's protective zone. They had gathered at the north and south extremities of the fort, leaving the center open.

Vectis motioned toward the northern forces. "They are flying the standing bear," he said. "That's Forgall. Who is at the south?"

"A collection of smaller tribes," Jupiter said. "I have not seen most of the banners before: the raven, the ribbon and star, the fox. But they have probably united under one chieftain for the duration of the siege—who, I don't know."

"The center is open," Julian said. "Are they inviting us to sally out?"

"They would like that," Jupiter replied, "catch us in a claw movement."

"Can we break through them, use another gate maybe?" Vectis asked.

Jupiter surveyed the Caledonians. "There are too many, Prefect."

"You once said that Rome had endless armies and endless resources."

Jupiter gave Vectis a partial smile. "I was wrong, then, wasn't I?"

"What is that?" Julian pointed to a cloud of dust moving along the river and away from the fort.

"Deserters," Jupiter said.

Officer Nepos and about thirty riders were trying to escape along the river. Suddenly, they veered west, then north. They were trapped. During the next minutes the three officers on the patrol track said nothing as the dust cloud churned with angry swirls, then drifted away.

Julian spoke, ignoring what the three had just witnessed: "What do we do now?"

Vectis grimaced. "We become the presence that Governor Verus wanted above the Wall." He turned to Jupiter. "Organize the men to defend Faustina. Tell them everything about our plight, that we are alone, that we are facing a large Caledonian army, that every day we keep the enemy here is a day lost to them in the south. But give them hope. Remind them of Legions XX and XIV, how on the southern end of this island they put to the sword 80,000 Celts in a single day. Tell them they are as well trained as any legion in the Imperial army, and then say that the legions are three months away."

As Vectis concluded his orders, he sensed the centurion's approval. No legions were coming; they would never leave this place. No one—not Jupiter, not Julian, not himself—would escape. But at least they would die with honor, unlike Nepos. Vectis fingered the soft pouch on his belt that held his family ring, and he wondered whether Neeve was among the Caledonians gathering on the other side of the protective zone.

The journey toward the last Roman outpost was unsettling for Neeve, to the point of pain. For two days she moved steadily north with Taranis and his warriors, and every few hours a rider appeared with reports of Romans being killed. Mostly the victims were stragglers from the defeated outpost, Stragenia, but sometimes they were non-Roman workers from the forts.

Neeve hated what the Romans had done to Caledonia as much as anyone, and she knew they would leave only if the cost in lives became intolerable. But she also knew that many Romans were good people obeying the orders of their Emperor. How could she justify killing every single one they found, and especially those who had merely worked in the forts? It bothered her that Taranis would issue such orders.

The problem bubbled to the surface when they arrived at the abandoned Stragenia. Sitting on their horses, she and Taranis watched as hundreds of warriors slipped over the walls and passed through the open gates of the outpost. Almost immediately, they heard whoops and cheers coming from the fort, as if the warriors were chasing wild boar.

"What are they doing in there?" Neeve asked.

"A hunt," Taranis replied. "With all the Romans hiding along the way, there were bound to be some in the fort. They left the gates open hoping we would think it was deserted." He smiled as if he found that amusing.

Neeve stared at her brother, horrified.

His smile faded.

Shrieks rose from the fort, piercing her like a dagger.

"Neeve," he said apologetically, "this is not a place for you. War can be—"

"I understand war. I understand that you need to kill the enemy, that you cannot allow them to escape to reinforce other garrisons. What I do not understand is why you would allow this ... this game!" She gestured toward the fort. "Listen to it!"

His eyes burned into her but he said nothing.

"If you insist on killing them," she said, "why not do it with some order?"

"Now, you listen to me," he said in a low, angry tone. "You know nothing about war or about handling men. We are not Roman lackeys that march in a line and obey the peeping of trumpets. We are free-blooded Caledonians who fight from the heart because we love this land. All we want is to tear the Roman yoke from our necks and breathe free again. This *game*, as you call it, is essential to building morale." He pointed to the huge body of Caledonians gathered around the fort. "Every one of those warriors would love to be inside. But just listening to the terror of Romans on the run fills them with the power of the gods. Can you not understand? Warriors need to feel power over the enemy. This *game* does that for them. At least it helps. If that seems cruel, then so be it."

Neeve persisted. "Why would you—"

Taranis snapped the reins, wheeling his horse around.

"Wait," she cried after him, "I'm not finished."

"Yes, you are," he said, and rode back to the men gathered round the fort.

By the end of the week the blood god had arrived.

Taranis's warriors filled the center between Forgall and the collection of lesser commanders. His red banner fluttered ominously in the wind, chilling the heart of every soldier in Faustina. Vectis suggested, and Jupiter agreed, that a troop assembly was imperative to maintain morale. Nothing like a talk from Jupiter to remind the soldiers of Roman duty.

During the following weeks, Vectis and Julian often found themselves on the patrol track, studying the Caledonians, and searching for weaknesses. With the arrival of Taranis, the enemy seemed to have had a burst of energy, eliminating most of the hooks and traps in the protective zone in half the expected time. Every day the Caledonian work groups drew closer to the fort, and every day larger numbers fell victim to Scythian arrows and Scorpion bolts. Finally, they switched to night details, a prudent move that forced Vectis to hold back the Scythians and missile crews unless they had a reasonable certainty of hitting the enemy. Faustina's armory was not overstocked with bolts or arrows. By the beginning of the third week, the zone was cleared.

With amazing speed the Caledonians assembled their siege machines and soon were testing the fort's defenses. Bands of warriors rolled out crude catapults and tried to destroy sections of the patrol track running atop the walls. Their real objective was to test the accuracy of scorpions and heavy catapults, but Scythian archers picked off the exposed Celts, making the heavy weapons unnecessary. Determined to see the defensive weapons in action, the Celts wheeled out thick log shields, threatening to set the gates afire. This time Vectis obliged the enemy. The catapults set in the center of the fort hurled huge boulders over the walls, pounding the shields to pieces.

Hours later Vectis and Julian were again on the patrol track when they heard iron wrecking bars tearing apart the corner towers. "What is going on?" Vectis demanded.

"I have no idea," Julian replied, looking from tower to tower where soldiers were dismantling the elevated corners.

"Find out!" Vectis said. "You should know these things."

Minutes later Julian returned with Jupiter.

"You asked to speak to me, Prefect," the centurion said.

Vectis turned. "Why are the carpenters dismantling the towers?"

"I instructed them to do so."

"You instructed them?"

"I did."

Vectis felt the irritation growing. "You have an explanation?"

"Our catapults work poorly over the corner towers," he said. "I think the Caledonians have discovered that."

"So you gave the order?"

"Yes."

"Do you think it possible, Centurion, that some day you might consult me before issuing such orders?"

With no particular emotion Jupiter replied, "I don't think so, Prefect. We have only a day or two left."

Vectis looked at him, stunned by his attempt at humor. The weeks of tension had contributed much to Vectis's foul mood, he knew, but for some reason he couldn't shake his anger. "Centurion," he said, "from now on—"

"Or at least for a few days," Julian added sardonically.

Vectis stared at Julian, who grinned. He suddenly realized the ridiculous nature of his request.

"My apologies, Prefect," Jupiter said.

"Yes ... well," Vectis felt his anger evaporate, "from now on I want to know when someone is about to tear down part of this outpost."

"One would expect the prefect to spend his last hours praising his centurion and tribune," Julian said, "rather than reprimanding them."

Vectis had the grace to be embarrassed. "Actually, I was thinking the same thing," he said.

"Romans!" came a harsh Caledonian voice from over the walls. The three turned their eyes to the edge of the former protective zone, where a huge warrior stood alone on a mound of grass, his long, red hair tied behind him, his arms folded to give the impression of strength.

Vectis called down to the centurion at the gate: "I want an interpreter up here immediately—one with a loud voice."

Seconds later the interpreter was on the track beside the three officers, confirming what they suspected. It was Forgall.

"Watch the sunset tonight," his voice rumbled, "because it will be your last. When darkness falls the most brutal warriors ever to strap on a sword will swarm over your walls like ants scrubbing for honey. And do you know what the honey is?" He laughed roughly. His finger jabbed toward them. "Your heads! Did you hear me, Romans? Tomorrow morning, not one of you will have a head."

"Is he out of Scorpion range?" Vectis asked.

"Not by much," Jupiter replied.

"Maybe we can draw him closer," Vectis said. He turned to the interpreter. "Tell him we cannot hear him."

As the interpreter called out to Forgall, Jupiter ordered the Scorpions on the front wall to site the target.

Forgall continued his speech, refusing to be lured closer. "The warriors are eager for darkness," he shouted. "Everyone wants to collect a Roman head. But there are so many of us, and so few of you. Maybe we can chop your heads in half!"

Jupiter glanced at Vectis. "He knows the range."

"Have them fire anyway," Vectis said.

Twelve Scorpion bolts ripped through the air, hurtling toward the Caledonian commander. Seconds later Forgall saw them, black against the sky, and immediately took some quick steps back toward his lines.

"Laugh!" Vectis shouted, and the soldiers along the wall laughed and hooted.

When the Scorpion bolts crashed into the ground short of where Forgall had been, Vectis called out in a loud voice, pausing only for his equally loud interpreter. "The coward Forgall flies the standing bear. Better if he used the running bear." He called for laughter again. "Is Forgall now the leader of the Caledonians? Where is

Taranis, the fearsome blood god? Hiding in his tent? Is he afraid of Forgall?"

"Romans!" Forgall shouted, trying to recover. "Tonight, you die!"

As quiet descended, Jupiter said to Vectis, "Sowing discord seldom works, but it was a valiant try."

"Will they come tonight?" Julian asked.

"Not likely," Jupiter said. "They want us to have a sleepless night."

"They still have not cleared the north side," Vectis said. "For some reason they have chosen to use corridors to move their warriors to the open areas."

"That is a mistake," Jupiter said.

"It is," Vectis agreed, "but what advantage do we have if we remain in the fort?"

"None."

"What do you recommend?"

"That we wait," Jupiter said. "There might come a time when we can catch them against the barrier."

Neeve hadn't talked to her brothers in weeks. It was just as well. Since their arrival at Faustina, a deep depression had engulfed her. She associated these surroundings with so much happiness, and she half expected Vectis to come riding across the grass, waving his hand and smiling. "A walk to the bend in the river?" he would ask, and she would take his arm and press close to him. But the days of innocence were gone. Now was the hour of sorrow, of Toutorix, of blood and vengeance.

Her brothers were avoiding her.

Ever since she complained about the killing of Romans at Stragenia, they had suddenly become occupied elsewhere. In truth, they were busy. They had spent long hours increasing the efficiency of the camp by organizing it into competing clusters. Those who cleared the largest area of the protective zone, or assembled the most joints on a siege machine, or brought back the superior game, would be publicly acknowledged at the close of the day. The method was effective, but often pitted one commander against another, bruising egos in the process. When lesser commanders outdid their superiors, Taranis and Eston found themselves busy smoothing the feathers of humiliated leaders.

Yes, her brothers were busy. They were eager to destroy the last Roman outpost in Caledonia, and it mattered little that Vectis was inside.

Neeve sat alone in her tent, rubbing her boots with bear grease to protect against the rain. It had poured all morning, torrents of water that beat on the roof of her tent, and cascaded down the sides. It reminded Neeve of her childhood, when she used to run barefoot through the streams of water that gushed down the old rutted roads near their farm. She remembered falling one time and being surprised at how warm the water was that washed over her legs and arms.

Today was cold and damp.

Outside the tent, she heard a familiar voice. Taranis entered. "I want you to leave," he said before the flap had even closed behind him.

Neeve continued rubbing her boot.

"Did you hear me?"

"Yes."

"Well?"

"I intend to stay."

"I want you to leave," he repeated, adding weakly, "Eston and I both agree."

"You told Eston about Stragenia?" she asked, looking up. Water was still dripping from the bottom of his knee-length coat, puddling around his boots.

"I told him you were upset."

"And now you think I will make a nuisance of myself. Is that it?" She stared at him.

"This is a difficult time for you. In a few months, when things change—"

"I am not leaving."

"Be sensible. By staying you are only asking for more pain."

Neeve inspected her other boot.

"Do you think I enjoy watching you suffer?" He wiped water from his neck. "I ache for you."

"Then do something, Taranis."

"You know I can't. We must destroy this fort."

"Must you kill every Roman in the fort?"

"I don't want to talk about that."

"I do," she persisted. "Do you have to kill everyone?"

"There's a cart waiting for you," he said, ignoring her question.

"I deserve an answer!" she shouted.

His eyes fixed on her. "I think most will die, yes."

"The other outposts retreated. Why can't you let these Romans leave?"

"Do you think they would leave the security of their fort with all of us out here?" He snorted to indicate how foolish he thought her request was. "No Roman commander trusts the word of a Caledonian. Besides, I cannot order the other tribes to stand down while the Roman forces vacate their fort and march south toward the Wall."

"If you gave the order—"

"It's not that easy," Taranis said with a distinct edge in his voice. "You saw Forgall yesterday—strutting around, calling out challenges to the Romans as if he were Bronix himself. Do you think I can simply order him and the others to do my bidding? They are commanders, as I am. Even now, Forgall refuses to clear his area of Roman hooks and traps. He insists that corridors are a better use of his time. If I can't convince him to remove simple barriers, I certainly can't order him to abandon the siege."

Neeve kept her eyes on him. "Are you not in charge?" she asked in a demanding voice, refusing to give an inch.

"Yes, but I can't call off a battle because my sister loves the enemy prefect."

"Why not?"

"Why do you think?" Taranis flared.

Neeve continued to stare.

"You know why not," he said, "because for two months a whole lot of Caledonians have risked their lives clearing barriers and filling trenches around the fort. If we don't attack now, they'll strengthen their forces and kill Celts later." He shook his head wearily. "Stay if you want, but you won't like what you see. I can do nothing to change the course of events. The gods have ordained an end to Roman tyranny and I am simply their instrument to bring it about. If I falter, or try to alter circumstances, someone else, like Forgall will complete the task."

With that he left.

38

The day of exultation had come.

Atilius inspected himself in the polished silver glass. Magnificent! Simply magnificent! Never before had he worn military garb, but a commander of a military operation must dress appropriately. He waved off his fluttering aides who preened and plucked at him; a military man had no need of such obsequious functionaries.

He stepped back to get the complete view. Such a pleasing sight! His scarlet tunic and silver breastplate bespoke the power of Rome's Praetorian Guard — the same Guard whose units were already moving against Antoninus in his palace on the Palatine Hill. He touched the short Spanish sword and wickedly sharp dagger that hung at his waist, so alien, and yet so in keeping with the mission the gods had foreordained.

"Senator," an aide called from the atrium door, "a carriage approaches, escorted by a large contingent of the Praetorian Guard."

"Is Balbinus with them?"

"He is," the aide replied.

"Then give thanks to the gods for their unfailing judgments. The hour of ascension has arrived." He signaled and a vial of narcissus perfume was poured over his head. Servants dabbed up the drippings of oil that trickled from his hair, and lightly powdered his neck. The senator closed his eyes and communed silently with the deified Emperors of years past that surrounded him like a cloud of spectators. He sensed Augustus and Vespasian, and especially Trajan, urging him on. It was time to bring order to the weakness and chaos that had stalled Rome for forty years. It was time to use the legions the way Trajan would have used them, to expand the borders of the Empire, and to fill her coffers with gold. But first—he savored the thought—first he would ride in triumph to the Palatine Hill. He wanted to look Emperor Antoninus in the eyes when the bumbling fool was taken bound to his carriage, for his last ride.

And then he would reorganize the government. He would replace the sluggish Imperial bureaucrats with dynamic officials who had a positive vision for the Empire. No longer would the caretaker mentality be tolerated. Emperor Atilius Titianus would be remembered as one who brooked no adversaries, who ruled with a rod of iron, who got things done.

Even the Senate would echo the mind of the Emperor. Those who persisted in willful disobedience would be purged. Atilius had no doubt that after a period of cleansing, the Senate would eagerly do his bidding. He had not forgotten those who mocked his military speeches—Atilius the Warrior, they had tittered—but now his time had come. Now they would pay.

How they would pay!

Especially Senator Titus Severus.

At sunrise the urban cohorts had placed Severus in custody, as well as a good many other senators who had foolishly cast their lots in with him. How he would enjoy watching Severus beg for his life, bubble out his appeals for mercy, and receive none. Atilius would call for the dagger of the lowest ranking soldier in the palace, usher Severus into a windowless room, and there have him end his contemptible life.

Rome was his now. The Praetorians controlled the palace and the Imperial agencies; the urban cohorts had sealed off the city, its roads and bridges, its waterways and stables—everything was under his control.

Atilius followed his entourage of servants to the courtyard where Balbinus's carriage was arriving. The clatter of the Praetorian horses' hooves was sweet music, conjuring visions of a conquering army on parade.

"Hail, exalted one," Balbinus cried with a rapturous look on his face.

Atilius fought for control. You are only mortal, he whispered to himself. Then, regaining his proper wits, he asked, "How fares the Empire?"

"The Empire rests in capable hands," his aide replied.

Atilius nodded with satisfaction, swept his eyes over the Praetorian escort, pausing to acknowledge the Centurion of the Guard, and then stepped into the open-topped carriage. "Let us leave these common lands," he said. "To the Palatine Hill!"

It had rained nearly the entire day. Somewhere behind the thick clouds the sun was disappearing, mottling the sky purple and black. Vectis ran his eyes along the patrol track filled with soldiers and Scythian archers. They had removed the corner towers, giving the fort a flat appearance.

"If they come tonight," Jupiter said, "they'll have trouble firing the gates."

"And the ground is too soft for siege machines."

"That leaves ropes and ladders—if they come tonight."

An hour before dawn they came, like a huge, swelling shadow darkening the land as it approached the fort. Vectis ordered the Scorpions and catapults to hurl their missiles toward the center of the approaching mass. Screams rose from the Caledonian hordes as the heavy rocks bounced and rolled across the ground, and Scorpion bolts whizzed through the night air, striking unfortunate warriors as they crawled toward the fort.

Caledonian horns sounded, discordant and mournful, and instantly thousands of warriors jumped to their feet and shouted. The sound was so loud and so shocking that many on the patrol track cried out in fear. Shrieking and howling, the crazed warriors raced toward the fort. They slammed their hooks into the soft, turf walls and scrambled up the sides like rabid animals after a wounded bird.

Above them on the patrol track, the Scythians released their arrows briskly, striping off wave after wave of the snarling creatures. Soldiers jammed their spear tips at adventuresome Caledonians who pulled themselves up the beams that supported the patrol track.

Still they kept coming.

They breached the southwest corner where the tower had been. Vectis saw his chief defense officer fall. He hollered at the soldiers to seal off the area, but his voice was lost in the clamor. Suddenly, the Caledonians were everywhere, crawling up the wooden structure and pouring over the walls. Below, Julian obeyed his orders and sent every man up the ladders to defend the walls. They had no reserve now—even the cooks and supply clerks were on top thrusting their swords.

Slowly they regained control of the patrol track, and then the turf edge. The sun rose, and with it came the horns sounding the retreat. But Faustina had lost over two thirds of its men.

A dozen Caledonian commanders gathered at Taranis's tent near the center of camp. Each brought with him his sub-commander and two warriors who had distinguished themselves in battle. The official purpose of the council was to share information gathered during battle and to plan the next assault. The real reason was to give commanders an opportunity to revel in their triumph and to extol the valor of their warriors.

"I swear on the brows of the gods," one of the younger commanders said, "that I saw the ground open up and Esus rising with a flaming sword."

"I felt his power," another cried.

Deep voices rumbled, "The gods are with us."

Commander Cronn paraded double the expected number, four warriors, before the council, detailing their extraordinary valor. His scarred face twisted in triumph as he shouted, "I think the Romans finally understand that this is Caledonian land." The men cheered and hooted.

As commander after commander rose to recount the bravery of his warriors, Eston slipped in beside Taranis. "A great day," he said.

"It is," Taranis agreed, clasping his brother's shoulder. He stepped back and ran his eyes over Eston's yellow tartan, stained from battle. "The Romans still have fight in them," he said. "Be vigilant out there."

"I'm always vigilant," Eston replied with a grin. Then he asked, "Any word from Neeve."

Taranis shrugged. "She still refuses to leave, and if I know her, she'll insist on finding the body of her Roman when this is over."

Eston groaned. "What can we do?"

Taranis shook his head. "There's nothing we can do. She is so stubborn."

"She loves him," Eston said. "As odd as it might sound, I think she truly loves this Roman."

Taranis considered that a moment before saying, "I fear for her, Eston. I see no way out, and I fear greatly for her."

Forgall had begun to speak in a booming voice when a messenger shouted, "The Druids have arrived!"

The tent burst into a cacophony of voices. Forgall left the front of the tent and bulled his way through the warriors, pausing only when he reached Taranis and Eston. "We have already received their blessing at the festival of renewal," he spat. "Why are they here?"

"Divicos wants to bestow on us a *double* blessing," Eston said wryly.

The redheaded warrior snorted. "Divicos! He has come to grab credit for our victory."

Taranis stepped in front of Forgall. "Whatever the reason," he said, "we must respect the high priest. And *you*, Forgall, must control your tongue. There are common warriors in this tent."

The big man clamped his mouth shut and stormed past Taranis.

"Something is happening," a sentry shouted from the patrol track.

Vectis scrambled up the ladder and gazed over the wall. A peculiar green mist had spread across the edge of the protective zone. Suddenly, dark hooded Druids appeared, as if from out of the ground. Their unearthly chanting sounded like a dirge he once heard coming from an Egyptian crypt, mourning the death of a child.

"Druids," a deep voice murmured beside him. It was Jupiter.

Vectis squinted into the mist. "The fates may be shifting our way," he said finally. "If we kill those Druids, the warriors might take it as an omen and leave."

Jupiter glanced at Vectis and then turned back to the Druids. "You're grasping at air, Prefect. Killing Druids will not stop the Caledonians."

"Maybe not," Vectis replied, "but Celtic warriors believe the Druids have special powers that thwart the enemy."

"True, but I told you long ago that ambushes and tricks fool children and dogs, not determined warriors."

"Our soldiers are spent," Vectis said. "We've nothing left but ambushes and tricks."

"Can't argue with that." He swept his eyes over the growing mist. "We would have to destroy most of their magicians to have any effect."

"And if we took out their high priest?"

"That might do it," Jupiter said, nodding. "Killing the high priest could shake the foundations of their belief."

Vectis turned back to the Druids, who had begun chanting and whirling in a circle. Round and round they went until the dark form of a railed cart appeared in the haze. It was the oddest thing Vectis had ever witnessed. He was certain no cart had been there moments earlier, but then the mist seemed to thicken and take the form of a cart.

"Thirty-seven of my unit survived the attack," Jupiter volunteered. "If we charged through the fog they've created, we might be on them before they knew it."

The green mist boiling around the magicians had now drifted across the entire zone, and even toward the fort. It was as if Hades had opened and vented its foul air, so sickening was the stench; it smelled like rotting flesh. Through the haze Vectis could still see the stooped figure of their high priest, a man advanced in years, clutching the cart railings to stand.

"These mists won't last long," Jupiter said.

"How soon can you ready your unit?"

"They're ready now, awaiting your orders."

Vectis paused. "This is a death mission," he said. "You must know that."

"I know it's a death mission to remain in this outpost and wait, you were right about that. It may be that Fortune will favor the desperate."

"To increase Fortune's favor," Vectis said, "I will march a column of soldiers out the north gate as if to assault the rear of Forgall's army." He held up his hand to prevent Jupiter from objecting. "With those barriers still intact, they'll find it difficult to bear down on me. They might even hesitate to attack you, if they think the main body of Faustina's soldiers is about to sweep around their northern flank."

Jupiter called down the orders and looked back at Vectis. He placed a hand on Vectis's shoulder and said, "You take risks, but always for the right reasons. I'm proud to have served under your command. May the fates spare you."

Vectis glanced at the familiar *corona muralis* on Jupiter's chest, and then into the once-forbidden eyes. "I pray the same for you," he said, holding his centurion's eyes, "but my prayers will go unheeded unless you move with purpose. Your mission is to destroy the Druids, and nothing else."

"I understand," Jupiter said, and climbed down the ladder.

The warriors stood at a discreet distance, feeding on the power that radiated from their holy priests. The noxious green fog that had escaped from the bowels of the earth when the magicians appeared, now drifted among them, burning their eyes.

Taranis had to give the priests their due. They possessed an uncanny ability to raise the spirits of warriors. From everywhere he could hear voices calling out praise to the ancient ones. "The gods are with us," some were shouting. "The Druids have claimed the ground," others cried. In the distance he could hear the magicians hurling invectives at the evil ones and shrieking, "Let them burn in pain." And as if the fog had brought with it the armies of Toutorix, the pounding of hooves grew louder and louder.

Accompanied by two officers, Vectis led a column of soldiers out the north gate. Along the wall he had stationed six Scorpion teams, a precaution in the event of a hasty retreat, though he doubted the machines would help much. Julian and the chief engineer he had left behind, Julian to maximize the fort's defenses and the engineer to command the catapults.

At the same moment Vectis had made a great show of exiting the fort, Jupiter slipped out the opposite gate and headed for the Druids. Standing on a slight rise, Vectis could see through the haze Jupiter's soldiers bearing down on the dark-robed Druids, driving their spears into them as they thundered by. The terrified magicians scattered, trying to escape the needle-topped Roman spears. Only the aged high priest remained defiant in the face of death. Grasping the cart, he screeched and hissed, and twisted his body like a serpent. From his mouth came hideous laughter and eerie voices. When any soldier approached him, he pointed his bony fingers at his tormentor, and called down curses from the gods. Fire exploded from his fingertips and foul smoke swirled around him. No soldier wanted to strike a priest with such power.

Suddenly, the unmistakable form of Jupiter swept through the haze toward the old priest. With one swipe of his sword he lifted the magician off his feet, tumbling him over the rails and down into the drifting mist.

"Prefect," an officer called, "the enemy is moving against us—on both flanks."

"Sound the retreat," Vectis said, "forward march, shields on backs." He had already observed Forgall's disorganized warriors trying to react, but with the hooked barriers impeding their progress, only the outer ranks had mobility. But Taranis's warriors concerned him. Jupiter had taken them by surprise, as had the column of soldiers that marched out the north gate. Their indecision had cost them the lives of more than a few priests, but now they were streaming across the protective zone, trying to intercept Jupiter and his unit.

"Move!" Vectis said audibly, as if his voice could help Jupiter and his men, who had spun their horses around and were lashing them toward the fort. Vectis himself had shifted his troops into double-quick time, the quickest pace soldiers could move while still maintaining battle readiness.

He glanced over at Jupiter's riders, who were trying to maintain speed through the pitted surface where the rows of defensive hooks had been ripped out. Across from them on harder ground, a knot of Caledonian horsemen was swiftly approaching, cutting them off on the angle. Jupiter and his unit would not make it.

Abruptly, Jupiter swung around and charged straight for the Caledonians. With a sword in one hand and a dagger in the other, he crashed into them, arms flailing, like the frenzied barbarian Vectis always suspected he was. A half-dozen Caledonians dropped from their mounts, or lay slumped over, but more were coming. One, a lanky Caledonian with a yellow tartan, leapt from his horse and slammed his knife into the centurion's chest. As the two men struggled and fell to the ground, Vectis could see Jupiter still thrusting with his dagger. Then they were all around him, like dogs on a sheep.

Vectis's jaw clenched as he forced his eyes away. Jupiter's sacrifice had given his unit the precious seconds they needed to reach the north gate. Julian waved them in; they would be needed on the walls.

But Vectis was in his own death struggle now. His troops were still a hundred feet from the north gate when Forgall's hordes swung around the barriers and threatened to swallow them. "Scorpions," Vectis shouted, and the order was passed across the hollow square to the soldiers assigned the task of manning the weapons. Six bolts of iron shot through the air and crashed into the oncoming hordes, creating holes, briefly, but hardly slowing the mass of leaderless warriors.

"Ratchet up, flat trajectory," called the officer in charge of the Scorpions. Time for one last volley before the Caledonians overwhelmed them.

Then the huge stones from the catapults came heaving over the walls. Nothing scattered barbarians like giant rocks falling from the sky. As the soldiers neared the gates, the square funneled into a single six-man column that marched smartly into the fort, gates slamming behind. Outside, the Scorpions hissed a second time, and the crews left their machines and dashed for the portal entrance.

The attack was brief and ragged. Some of the Caledonian warriors had ladders and ropes, but most clawed their way, like crabs, up the turf walls. Enraged by the death of their priests, they threw their bodies at the soldiers defending the patrol track, and even breached several positions before their commanders sounded a retreat.

Vectis surveyed the wounded and dying along the wooden track. The soldiers had fought well—a credit to Jupiter—but too few remained to defend the walls. Killing the priests had been a last, desperate attempt to stave off the inevitable. But nothing would stop the Caledonians. They would regroup and attack, and this time Faustina would fall.

39

Senator Atilius Titianus waved to the urban soldiers posted at every intersection. Never had he seen Rome's streets so empty. A sense of power heated his blood as he surveyed the Imperial city from the open-topped carriage, and listened to the clopping of the Praetorian horses that surrounded him.

He suddenly felt the full weight of the responsibility he was about to assume. The Empire depended on him now, from Britannia's Walls to the Euphrates. The outposts were gone, he guessed, and no doubt the Walls were being overwhelmed at this very moment. But that would soon change. After a season of punishment, every barbarian on that cursed island would gladly bend his knee to him. For a fleeting moment he wondered whether he really could conquer the lands that had eluded other Emperors, whether he could bring about the prosperity he so often talked about. But it was a fleeting thought. The fates had always been kind to him.

The senator's eyes rested on Balbinus, his faithful aide for so many years. He was smiling, eager with anticipation. For over twenty years Balbinus had served him, and served him well, and Atilius determined in his mind that such devotion would be justly rewarded. His slovenly appearance fit poorly with the sleek new image of efficiency he desired to bring to government, but Atilius would send him somewhere, perhaps to tend his lands in the provinces.

"I want you to know," he said, "I will always have a place for you."

Balbinus's eyes shone. "Your generosity is boundless, my lord."

"Of course, I will require other advisors in my new capacity."

"Of course."

"And there will be pressure from many quarters to appoint those who have supported me ... and so forth, you understand."

"I am satisfied being your personal secretary," Balbinus said. "I seek no higher office."

"Yes ... well, we might have to make some changes," Atilius said, "but we need not discuss that now." He smiled. "Let us enjoy the day. It is like no other."

"Indeed, Senator, like no other."

Ahead Atilius could see the Palatine Hill where his new life would begin. "The Praetorians have matters well in hand," he said, surveying the sea of scarlet stationed at every entrance to the palace.

"They encountered no resistance. Several of the palace cohorts even joined with our strike force."

No resistance! Atilius licked his lips. Given the choice between a bumbling caretaker and exciting new leadership, the Praetorians raced to his support.

"Where is Antoninus?" Atilius asked darkly.

"The Praetorians have taken the Emperor—the former Emperor," Balbinus corrected himself, "to the receiving hall to await you there."

"And Senator Severus?"

"I instructed the guards to bring him also."

"Before this day is over, I want every senator—every single one, mind you—who supported Severus or the Emperor to be brought to me. I want to pronounce judgment personally."

"It will be done, lord."

Atilius noticed that Balbinus was uncertain how to address him— as Senator, or lord, or Emperor.

The carriage stopped.

He turned to Balbinus and said, "When I place my foot on the first marble stair, I no longer will be Senator, but Emperor. You may address me as such."

Balbinus bowed as a Praetorian opened the carriage door for the new Emperor.

The receiving hall was empty except for the Praetorians stationed at each door. From an adjoining room came Titus Fulvus Antoninus the Pius, fifteenth Emperor since Julius Caesar abolished the Republic. He entered the domed hall in what appeared to be a stupor, with his head tilted downward and his walk heavy. When he reached the Imperial couch, he plucked at his toga nervously, straightened his posture, and sat down. His furrowed brow betrayed his anguish.

Senator Atilius Titianus strode the length of the hall, savoring every step. He imagined how Augustus Caesar must have felt when he tore the crown from Marc Antony. Now two hundred years later, a new Augustus had arisen, at whose feet all men would tremble. Behind him came Balbinus and the Praetorian bodyguard. Atilius kept his eyes on Antoninus, relishing every second of his misery. How still he was, playing the Emperor one last time. Atilius was tempted to cry out in a loud voice, "Remove yourself from the Imperial couch," but that would breach his moral code. He was a gracious man and would allow Antoninus to depart in dignity. If the foolish man wanted to hear his sentence pronounced while he sat in majesty, let it be.

"So you have come," the Emperor said, "and dressed in military red. I never thought you would take the route of your father."

"And that is your problem, Antoninus. You cannot anticipate the fates."

"I suppose not. I knew you had ambition but—"

"*Ambition*," Atilius sneered, "has nothing to do with it. "What I do, I do for Rome!"

"Ah, yes, Rome." He rose. "And now what is to be done with me?"

"You will join your fathers," Atilius said. "After an appropriate period I might even have the Senate deify you."

Antoninus laughed hoarsely. "That is certainly novel. First you drain my veins, then you deify me."

"You have, in some respects, been a good Emperor. I have never denied that."

"And what is to be done with my heir, Marcus Aurelius?"

"He will join you."

"And Titus Severus, and my supporters in the Senate?"

"They will all join you," Atilius said, irritated. "And I tire of your questions."

"I simply want to know—"

"Enough!" Atilius screamed, his neck burning with his rage. "Who are you to question me?" Then, turning to Balbinus he said, "Have the Praetorians bind this man in my presence. His carriage awaits."

Balbinus stepped forward and dropped to his knees before Antoninus.

"What are you doing, you imbecile?" Atilius shouted.

"He is paying homage to his Emperor," Antoninus said. "Rise, Gaius Balbinus, you have rendered a great service to the Imperial realm."

A jolt shot through Atilius's body. He whipped his head around. Senator Titus Severus was entering the hall from the adjoining room.

"Your aide," Antoninus said, "came to Senator Severus with information so ... so utterly evil, that I refused to pronounce judgment on you until I heard it for myself."

"Praetorians!" Atilius called, desperate, daring to hope that he might have control.

"These are not your Praetorians," the Emperor said quietly.

Atilius's heart pounded in his chest as the Praetorians seized him. He tried to focus on what was happening around him, but he could not. He had lost! Everything—gone! The Emperor was dividing his properties now—a quarter to Balbinus, a quarter to Severus, and the rest to the state.

"Atilius Titianus," the Emperor said, "you are guilty of treason and will be banished to the island of Psara in the Aegean Sea."

"I am not afraid of death," Atilius said, trying to remain stouthearted.

"But I am," the Emperor said. "I would like others who follow me to be slow to malice and quick to mercy." He turned and walked silently from the hall.

"Antoninus the Pius!" Balbinus cried. "May the gods bless your name forever."

As the Praetorians took Atilius by the arm, he glared at his former aide and wailed bitterly, "How could you do this to me?"

Balbinus shrugged.   "One of my informants intercepted a dispatch from Vectis Trebellius warning the Emperor of your treachery." He dropped his voice. "I couldn't risk that another had gotten through." He smiled. "A prudent man never chains himself to the destiny of another. He must study the currents."

The last words Atilius heard as he left the hall were those of Titus Severus. "It's a small island," he clucked, "but I hear they grow fine asparagus."

Eston was dead.

Neeve stared at the cold, unmoving form that lay on a pinewood bench under the canopy of the central tent. How unlike himself he looked, his body flat and toneless, his skin gray. He had the shriveled look of death. Branches of green holly decorated his upper body, contrasting sharply with the snowy funeral cloth that encased him. She felt a rising desperation as she gazed at his lovely face, his alert eyes, now forever closed. "Oh, Eston," she murmured, and a cold wind rippled the narrow canopy, chilling her to the bone.

"Neeve?" It was Taranis. "The warriors will take him now."

"No, please," she said, "not yet."

"The pyre is ready," he said, slipping his hand over her shoulder. "Some of Eston's warriors have been with him for ten years. This is important to them." He led her back into the tent and had her sit on a cot.

For nearly an hour she remained there, unmoving. In her mind she could see Eston laughing and chasing after her, the way he had when he was a boy. Moments before, it seemed, his body had been full of life, and now he was gone. Death was all around her, but she'd thought only the Romans were at risk, not her brothers.

"Taranis," she said, "pledge to me that you will not die."

He nodded silently.

"I want to hear you say it."

He sighed.

"Pledge," she said, grasping his hand.

He placed his rough fingers over hers. "Before the gods, as they give me strength, I will not die," he said. "This I pledge."

She leaned into him, trying to draw from his strength. In the stillness she thought about Vectis and wondered what she could do. This very moment, he was alive, but soon .... She pulled back and looked at her brother. "I have lost Eston and cannot bear to lose another," she said. "You know what I'm asking. If I ever needed you, it's now. You cannot allow Vectis to die."

He listened, but said nothing.

She closed her eyes.

"I will use the Druids," he said finally. "In their present state, they can demand nothing. I will say the gods want to spew the Romans out of Caledonia, as one would spew out filthy water. Living messengers of defeat, that is what they want."

"Oh, Taranis," Neeve said, her eyes filling with tears. She grasped hold of him and buried her face in his shoulder.

Even from a distance, Vectis knew it was Neeve riding toward the fort; he knew the long, graceful lines of her body, the flaxen hair flowing in the wind. Two imposing warriors wearing long coats and leather trousers flanked her, and one carried the red banner of Taranis.

"Hard orders," Vectis called. "Archers sheath your arrows."

The order was repeated down the walkway. The last thing Vectis wanted was for some zealot to shoot Neeve out of her saddle.

Julian motioned toward the red banner. "Must be the blood god himself."

"He might wish he had never come," Vectis said, his eyes narrowing. "Get one of those Scythians over here."

The riders stopped fifty feet from the fort and the one with the banner called out something in his native tongue. "Romans," Neeve translated, "Taranis, glorious leader of the Caledonian nation, has granted you mercy. You will surrender the contents of your fort, surrender your standard, and leave immediately."

A murmur of relief rose from the soldiers on the walkway. Julian silenced them.

Vectis stared at Neeve. Her eyes, like crystals, shone up at him, but with a touch of sadness. Julian said something about Jupiter's attack on the Druids, how it had broken the Caledonian spirit. Vectis knew better. It was Neeve. Somehow she had convinced Taranis to allow them passage. A dark thought flitted at the edge of his mind — she had given herself to him again. He shifted his eyes to the arrogant looking warrior holding the flag, a huge, rigid-faced commander with a scar running along his right cheek. Exactly as Vectis imagined Taranis would look. He couldn't tear his eyes from him. Taranis! Not fifty feet distant. The Scythian could take him in an instant.

No! He disciplined his mind. What she had done with him, she had done. At the trial she had talked about torn loyalties. How did he know what forces were buffeting her? He would not allow personal feelings to jeopardize his men's lives. They depended on him. If there was hope from any quarter, he would seize it.

"Are you Taranis?" Vectis asked.

"The great Taranis does not talk with defeated Romans," came the answer. "My name is Cronn."

"We cannot surrender our standard," Julian said quietly to Vectis, stating the obvious.

Vectis called down to the warrior, "Tell Taranis we accept his offer. We surrender the contents of this outpost and will leave within the hour."

Neeve called back, "Taranis also requires the Roman standard."

Vectis knew he could not surrender the fort's vexillum to the Caledonians. "Roman soldiers must take their standards with them," he said as convincingly as possible.

Cronn seemed to understand even without a translation, and he was not impressed. He began shouting and pointing at the soldiers along the wall. "You will surrender your standard," Neeve translated simultaneously, "or you will all die." Then she added in a voice meant only for Vectis, "It is a small thing to ask, the standard."

When Vectis repeated that he could not surrender the standard, she grew pale. She shifted in her saddle and bit her lip, as if she were wrestling for a solution. "You must understand," she said finally, "the commanders all agree that you will surrender your standard." She paused. "Taranis *needs* that standard."

The message was clear. To convince the other commanders to allow safe passage, the barbarian chieftain had promised to humiliate the enemy, and his method was to demand surrender of everything in Faustina, including its standard. They were at an impasse.

"The armor," Neeve cried out. "Maybe the prefect can offer the great Taranis his armor."

"Yes," Julian shouted back, lying, "It is a great humiliation for a Roman commander to surrender his armor to the enemy."

Vectis waited as Neeve translated. The two warriors talked briefly, unsure how to respond. Finally, Neeve shouted, "He will accept. I will see to it."

"Can we trust her?" Julian asked.

"I was wondering the same thing," Vectis admitted.

"Our options are rather limited," Julian said with a lop-sided grin.

"They are, but we must leave with dignity." He turned back to Neeve. "Roman soldiers are forbidden to surrender their forts to the enemy. After we close the gates, will Taranis agree to wait until we have gone before taking possession?"

Without consulting the two warriors, Neeve replied, "My brother has limited patience, but he will agree."

The words shot through Vectis. Her *brother*. She called Taranis her brother! He rolled his head back and stared at the open sky, and a deep anguish possessed him.

"Did you hear what she said?" Julian asked. "Could Taranis have been that mapmaker we banished from Faustina?"

Vectis was too numb to speak. Torn loyalties, she had said. How wrong he had been about her, how utterly and wretchedly wrong. Her words came flooding back to him. Promise me you will always love me, she had begged, that you will judge me by the motives of my heart. He closed his fingers around the ring-pouch on his belt, and gazed into the eyes of his beautiful Neeve.

The Caledonian commanders sat rigidly on their horses. The straight, parade-like line they had formed contrasted acutely with the profusion of colors, and the shapes and sizes of their armor. Behind each commander stood a warrior bearing the banner of each tribe, and beyond them at a distance were the hordes of Caledonians. Vectis recognized Taranis instantly. He was the mapmaker, Neeve's brother.

Vectis nudged his horse toward the commanders and stopped before Taranis. There was nothing in his eyes, no hatred, no triumph, nothing. Vectis unstrapped his breastplate and removed his helmet. He handed them to a warrior who carried each piece separately to Taranis. The blood god took them and held them over his head as the Caledonians shrieked and howled. Then he threw them in the dirt. The roar was deafening.

In the clamor, Vectis surveyed Julian and the troops. They looked dirty and unkempt, with armor stained and tunics ripped, but for the most part they sat erect, eyes fixed ahead, as if under inspection by Caesar himself. They were to show no emotion, not to even glance at a single Caledonian. Even in defeat Roman soldiers had the power to disgrace their enemies. The Caledonians would get nothing they had demanded—not the vexillum from Faustina, not even its contents. The outpost was already burning. With ropes and torches and barrels of pitch, the engineer had arranged destruction of the workshops, granaries, carts, weapons and catapults. Already ropes had burned through, and torches were dropping on pitch-smeared surfaces. The Caledonians would get nothing.

Taranis moved closer to him. He drew his knife, a heavy blade, honed to a fine edge. He leaned over in his saddle and took hold of Vectis's belt. With a snap of his wrist, he sliced through the leather and threw that prize to the ground.

The humiliation was complete. As Vectis turned to leave, the big, red-haired commander named Forgall asserted his authority by looping his spittle at him. It missed.

At the far end of the line sat Neeve, her hands resting between the horns on her saddle, silently watching the proceedings. Her eyes moved to his, staring at him the way she had that first day. He stopped in front of her. Something was different ... her hair, tied up like that of a submissive Roman wife.

He opened the flap of his saddlebag and drew out the folding doll. Reaching across, he placed it in her hands, and for one exquisite instant, felt the cool touch of her fingers.

The small column of soldiers disappeared rapidly down the Roman road, some riding horses, some marching, and not a few wounded strapped in tarps along the sides of mules.

Neeve unrolled the doll. Inside she found the pouch, and her gold wedding ring. She slipped it on her finger and stared wistfully after Vectis, wondering how she would ever find him.

Not long after, with Taranis standing beside her, they heard the news. The Romans had set a delayed fire, and most of the weapons and granaries were lost. Taranis glanced at Neeve, and then back at the dark line of Romans almost out of sight on the horizon.

"This Roman of yours," he said, "he would make a good Caledonian commander."

Neeve was about to comment when the chanting began, low, undulating moans at first, and then shrieks and curses. On a small rise in the land, a gaggle of surviving Druids had gathered in a circle, and they were growing more hysterical by the moment.

"What are they doing?" Neeve asked, repulsed by the knot of Druids circling and chanting, and poking at something with sticks.

"I think they have found a Roman who is not quite dead."

"Why are they so frenzied?"

Taranis shrugged. "An important Roman, maybe."

Instantly, Neeve knew which Roman they had found. She burst across the soft earth, mangled by the Caledonian clearing teams, and slammed her palms into the back of the first Druid she encountered. He was lighter than she had expected, and flew through the air, crashing into several other Druids who hit the ground in a tangle of robes.

"Get away from him, you vultures!" she shrieked, picking up one of their gnarled walking sticks and swinging it like a cudgel. They scattered before her rage and melted away.

Neeve dropped on her knees beside Jupiter. His eyes were barely open, but his lips were curled in an undeniable smile.

"Mapmaker," he croaked.

"I'm here," she said.

"Even the Druids fear you."

She smiled slightly. "They know my brother is Taranis."

"Ah," he said, "your brother."

"Vectis has gone," she said, "with all the soldiers."

"Good."

He lay there for a moment, his breathing rough and irregular. "They will send him to Rome," he said suddenly.

"Rome?"

"Not hard to find. All roads, they say ...." His voice trailed off.

His eyes were closed now and Neeve felt a strange sadness. Jupiter had killed her brother, but to him Eston was just another Caledonian. She could not hate him for that. Besides, she owed him her life.

His final words rasped at her. "My head ... don't let them take my head ... those Druids."

Neeve grasped his hand. "They shall not touch you. I will see to it."

She was certain the centurion had smiled at the end.

Ragged patches of fire leapt high into the night air as the huge logs roared and crackled over Jupiter. She'd had them construct the pyre on top of the turf wall, and as a concession to the Druids, she had his body covered in pitch to symbolize his evil. The centurion, she knew, would not have cared.

Somewhere over the horizon, Vectis moved steadily southward. Jupiter said he would be sent to Rome. She wondered what the Imperial city would be like.

ABOUT THE AUTHOR

William V. Crockett is a writer, scholar, and professor in New York. A graduate of University of Winnipeg, Princeton Theological Seminary, and University of Glasgow (Ph.D.), he has lectured and written extensively on theological issues. With his expertise in classical antiquity, Crockett is making his mark as a novelist. His two novels, *Worlds Apart* and *A Celt in Rome* are set in the second century Roman Empire. He lives with his wife, Karen, in rustic Sussex County, New Jersey, where he is hard at work on a modern thriller, *The Apocalypse Gene,* set at Yale University.

17418959R00307

Made in the USA
Lexington, KY
14 September 2012